FOR THE CROWN OF NADIA

DARYL OMAR

Novel Eden

FOR THE CROWN OF NADIA

COPYRIGHT

Novel Eden

ISBN: 978-1-7361425-2-3

Ordering Information:

Quantity sales. Special discounts are available on quantity purchases by corporations, associations, and others. For details, contact the publisher at the address above.

Orders by U.S. trade bookstores and wholesalers.

Please contact the author, Daryl Omar through email offredfc@gmail.com

Please leave a review on goodreads!

Printed in the United States of America

CONTENTS

LETTER TO READERS

Dear Reader,

Thank you for your purchase and interest in my story. It was taken over five years to create this piece. If I am generous perhaps seven or eight years to have even put it on paper.

I dedicate this story to the late-great Ron Williams and Desmond Manu. Two young men taken in their prime. Two men who exemplified what being a good human was all about. Generous, loving, misunderstood, and hardworking. I dedicate this book to you brothers, to the families you left behind and to all the other young men like you taken in their prime. Blessing to the family of Phillip Hamrick as well.

I thank of course Amanda, Audrey, Omar Sr., Brandon, Skylar and Shayla. To Mike, Josh, Jon, John, Eric, Steve, Chris, Scott, Blake, Chardonnay and the fresh white kid who always dressed nice. To anyone who feels I forgot about them, I apologize. Thank you for giving me the confidence and support systems to even write. And I thank all you readers who purchase this book. Please leave a review and feel free to contact me. Shout out to Ms. Gordon, Ms. Bartholomew, Mrs. Reyes, Mrs. Spriggs, Mrs. Cohen, Mrs. Sackett, and Mrs. Grandma Norris for recognizing my talent and never allowing me to perform below my worth or ability.

Prepare for an absolutely wild ride,

Daryl Omar Shabazz

CHAPTER 1

Just Friends

Halle Gregor

The front door opened while I was still in the shower. Morgan was home. I timed it perfectly. Today was his "day off". He didn't have to spend all morning and afternoon in the office pushing papers. He was just getting back from Nadia from spending the whole night there fixing up his rental properties. He always comes home exhausted and weary. I made it a special effort to beat him home after my classes and get a few things ready.

"Hey, Morgan, are you hungry? I was thinking about ordering something." I asked as I left the bathroom wrapped up in only my towel.

He didn't look up, standing at the kitchen counter flipping through the mail. "Naw, I'm not trying to spend money right now, but thanks Halle." he nods.

"I'll pay, I wanted to feed you." I lean over his side as he separated all the junk mail.

"Ha, what are you talking about? You don't cook Halle."

"Well, you work yourself ragged and going without food. It doesn't make any sense to me."

"I have to. There's a lot to get done." he says reflexively in defense.

"No, no, I really admire it. I've never met someone who works so hard." wrap my arms around him, hugging him from behind.

"Oh, thanks Halle, ha." His smile is so warm and god, he's so handsome.

"So, it's my treat! What would you like?"

"Eh... I don't know. I don't really want to spend your money like that. Oh, there's a coupon here for pizza, how about that?"

I turned him around, taking the mail from his hands. "Morgan, I am Halle Victoriana Gregor. Money is a nonfactor. Whatever you want, say it and it's yours. Today is your day off right? I want to make it your day. To treat you like a King."

He looked me over, "Halle, you don't have to do any of that. I'll be cool." he gives a slight chuckle, "Nat would kill us if she found us like this so maybe you should bugger off."

"Relax. Let me take care of you. I bought a body relaxing bubble bath for you. I'll run you a bath and rub your shoulders for you while we wait for the food to get here then we can eat together, watch a movie and smoke. You'll love it. I have it all planned out and even rented a movie." I take his hand leading him to the couch where a few menus sat, all specially picked by myself.

"You Nakan girls never accept no for an answer, do you?" he chuckles sitting down on the couch. He lets out a groan, stretching out his body then plopping out on the couch. "Halle, you really don't-" he sighs as I begin taking off his work boots.

"I'm a Gregor. I always get what I want. I'm telling you, this is what I want to do Morgan. So, if you want me to be happy then let me." I toss his boots aside then reach for his belt.

He grabs my hand, "I'm Natalie's boyfriend."

"Oh, has she forgotten that?" I sneer pushing his hand aside then moving to begin taking off his shirt, "You can't wash with your clothes on."

He was silent, letting out a sigh. Their relationship was one of his least favorite topics to talk about though it was all they fought about. In their case, talking, whenever he got home.

"Not sure what to say..." he lets out a contemplative sigh.

I climb onto the couch next to him, kissing his cheek and nuzzling his neck. "I'll be a good girl for you, Morgan. I'll even give you back to Natalie when she's around. But when we're together, I'll take care of you, kay?"

"Not okay, I really don't think I can fly with that, blue bird." he rubbed my cheek, "Sorry, that just doesn't seem kosher."

"If you readily accepted, you wouldn't be the man I thought you were, Morgan." I kissed him softly. He didn't reject me. Though, he didn't really kiss me back either.

I moved to kiss him again. I wanted to feel his lips again. It might be my last time before his conscience got the best of him and he walked off to their room. I raise his chin, and kiss him. His strong arms wrap around me pulling me into his lap. We kiss. His lips tangle with mine as he gropes and squeezes me. My towel falls into our laps. I couldn't help but let out soft moans, feeling his warmth and his strength being in his arms. The smell of his musk was intoxicating. The sweat and toil from a long day's hustle.

I wanted him down to his boxers. I wanted him to fill every inch and crevice of my mouth with that cock Nat raved about. Damn your honor Morgan. Just be mine.

"Halle... enough of this before Natalie finds out. She will never forgive us." He barks like a drill sergeant tossing me aside like I weighed little more than a feather.

"Just a bit more, just a little more, baby." I jump on his back steering him back to the couch but he pulls away tossing me back down.

"Yo... this just can't be me anymore. Ha, maybe before when I only had a business or was at The Academy. But now, I just don't think about it the same. I'm not that much older but- I just don't have it in me to hurt Natalie like that."

"Baby, Natalie will NOT find out. You're a man. You need a real woman as you build yourself and your empire. Don't worry. We don't need to have sex. Okay? Not that we even could. My dad is saving my virginity for marriage."

"Really?" he was considering it.

I smile kissing him once more. "Well, maybe a bit of head... or a lot of head if you let me... but no sex. I mean- if you wanted we could knock from the back. But not pussy, I'm saving myself for marriage."

"It's difficult to believe Halle Gregor is a virgin."

"My dad is very protective of me. Plus, I just haven't met any guy who I want to give it to. I love to party, and the attention comes. I'm not quite a fan of the men there. I could take most their girlfriends if I wanted... and do. But, if I was going to consider a man worth my first time, it would be you, Morgan."

"I'm honored, but you're backtracking pretty fast." he laughs.

"I am not!" I stomp my foot, "I am not going to let you inside me, Morgan Ellys. I am not easy, now apologize!"

He raised a brow to me, "Better watch your tone, girl. I'm not apologizing for shit. Take offense to nothing if you want."

"Men do not speak to me that way, Morgan Ellys."

"Shame, you're a spoiled brat. It would do you some good to have someone talk to you like that."

"I'm not spoiled..." I suck my teeth.

"Halle, you're the most spoiled brat I've ever met." he pats my butt, squeezing it and pulling me back to him. He lifted me by my butt and put me on my back. I tear down the collar of his shirt, grabbing his neck to kiss him. "You're not going to be putting your insecurities on me Halle."

"What do you want for dinner?" was all I could say behind blushing and giggling like a schoolgirl.

"Is that your way of admitting you're wrong because you won't admit how spoiled you are?"

"Shut up..." I held him close, "I can definitely be picky, so be happy you meet my standards, Ellys."

"Ha, picky is very accurate. You referred to this place as a closet when I moved in."

"I said it's the size of *MY* closet." I correct him.

"Yeah, I guess that makes a world's difference." he found himself so funny.

"Is that really what you think of me, Morgan?" I pushed him away before he could kiss me again. "Do you think I'm just some spoiled brat?"

"Truth be told, I don't really know you too well." he sat up on the couch, holding my towel for me. He seemed unmoved by my nudity. The women he's probably seen naked. I wonder if I was his first fling outside his relationship with Nat. I doubted it with his ease and confidence. Seemed too natural for him, maybe he didn't cheat on Nat but before Nat he was probably swimming in women.

"Would you like to change that?" I asked.

He let out a sigh. He shook his head, "I'm not with that anymore, like at all. I had my fun, played my games. I have to get more serious about this life shit. I barely have time for Natalie. You want me to try to fit you into all that chaos? No thank you."

"You already take life too seriously, Morgan. I just want to hang out with you more, just the two of us. Go to a movie, do lunch, or even hanging out here, today, like this?" I bluffed.

"I'll think it over in the shower." he let out a yawn as he stood up. "Look, despite all the shit in our relationship. I love Natalie. She's been here for me, and truth be told, my life isn't making all that much sense right now. I'm not going to screw that up for sex."

"I don't want you to leave Nat only for sex, Morgan. I'm only suggesting that you and me hangout more often. I don't need to be sexual with you to like you. I already like you." I rub his cheek, "Do you understand me?"

"Halle... relax, I wasn't expecting any of this. I just wanted to make a sandwich, smoke a bowl, watch some mindless TV and take a nap before work. I appreciate your plans and ideas but maybe you should find your own boyfriend?" he groans brushing me off.

"You're so simple to please, Morgan." I took his hands in mine, "Go shower. I'll call the deli. Turkey's your favorite right?"

"Turkey, Roast Beef and Provolone." he kisses my knuckles then leaves me to go to the bathroom.

At least he couldn't keep his hands off of me. Dad will be happy with my progress.

CHAPTER 2

We Suppose To Be In Love

Morgan Ellys

I saw the darkest side of my soul. It isn't that I never hit or laid hands on Natalie or any woman for that instance. I have even killed women in combat. I've committed many horrific crimes against women and humanity. It's never been because they're women, gender doesn't mean anything to me but I suppose what people find most horrific. A lack of emotion and a knack for violence didn't make me a good mate. Women fell in love but I don't quite understand what love is. I value respect. I only value respect.

Since I was a child I never allowed a man to disrespect me and breathe. Women raised a grey area in my life... I don't remember my mother. Women drive me to a point of irrationality and insanity then blame me for outrage they incite. They'll lie to your face, say whatever comes to mind, or will argue to oblivion without any evidence just their blind emotionality and anecdotes. I warned every woman I've been with not to bring me to those deep waters of torrential feelings. I had so much I kept inside my entire persona has become a dam against my extreme feelings. I only get along with the ones who listen. There are those who won't stop until they get a rise out of you, whatever emotion it was they needed to see the depth of it. You had to cry, you had to scream, and you had to die laughing. They didn't want emotion or a relationship, they wanted a show.

I know why Natalie hates me. It doesn't take a rocket scientist. Her lust for revenge against Halle and against me for every minor infraction against her ego was my creation. A sick part of my psyche welcomes conflict, to break the social contract and break out into a fist fight till your knuckles bleed. Natalie only cares about her perspective. It's never worth a real conversation. There is no world outside of hers.

We manifest our reality ourselves. I've done my best to convert my darkness to good use. Natalie will demand, bark, scream, or cry out as if her soul was attempting to escape her flesh. We struggled with conversations over God. She only worshipped money and herself.

I'll be her boogeyman. I'll be her monster because the greatest fear of a devil is an Archangel. The thoughts, emotions, and fears of sheeps and savages won't deter me from my purpose. Rakil has shown me something beyond this, so that is what I will pursue.

Man or Woman, Saint or Sinner. None of this holds to me any longer. I will fight everyone if I must. No one will disrespect me and no one will stand in the way of my kingdom. I accept my guilt. I will stand by my beliefs and convictions. I am not entirely sure what Natalie's perspective to me is as she grips to this toxic relationship. I don't really care, honestly. Every day of our miserable relationship is the same. We're both so stubborn. She's haughty and prideful. I am like an immovable stone with a horrific rage. I must see all sides become forming a thought. This is critical to an assassin's survival. She only listens to herself or her yes men. We're different entirely and highly combustible.

It was the ninth month, mid November about eight months after I resurrected. I had nothing, and had no say. I had left the liberty of death and was forced into Naka to apprentice under the Devil, Colin Mayer Gregor.

I had met Natalie and Halle a few years earlier. Halle I had known of my entire life in some capacity though we never formally met. I know of the Holy Father Mordin Wolfe but I never knew he had children or was allowed to copulate. I never knew Natalie existed. Thus, I had to hide my entire relationship with Natalie since being in Naka. Not only because of her father but because of how toxic everyday became.

She had zero respect for Halle and despised me, yet held both our relationships in high esteem. As if we were lucky for her existence. She would spit upon my views as if I wasn't speaking and fight me over everything! Not, strongly held an opinion, FOUGHT!! I remember November clearly.

I had gotten home around 22:00 from a weekend The Patriarch, Colin Gregor. I never had energy but never slept either. I don't get tired. Every time I closed my eyes I felt death welcoming me back lovingly, to wake up from the cruel reality back in the ethereal heavens. The relationship proved no solace either. I needed my own space and neither used it much, preferring their own rooms. I got back from my trip early and I had a tremor of a migraine from all the lessons from the conference. Struggling to embrace truths and views I hated but had to accept as reality.

It was a conference assembling the top 2%, no one knew of the meeting. The workers were paid extra for their secrecy. Old wrinkled men in their fifties and seventies speaking on how to control the world populations. The believed they spoke as fathers, with paternal ideals of guiding the world. In truth it was all about protecting their estates, assets, and employees, especially controlling their managers. Everyone kept speaking about "The Day" and it was fast approaching and they had to prepare.

I was the only outsider around. There were investments meetings, political presentations, decisions upon the next world leaders, and discussions about economics as most people spoke about sports or themselves. I was forced to accept the distance between what made folk not rich, but wealthy. Most would never be able to reach over the wall. Nor would these men allow them to come close to exceeding their expectations which were so dismally low. These men had 70% of the world's wealth. The workers there were servicing their oppressors with smile because it was the first day they had ever made $14 an hour. After the weekend it went back down to $7 an hour. To feel rich for a day I suppose. I sought wealth, so I endured their lectures.

I hated life itself when I walked into the door. Feeling as if I had to make a drastic decision between good and evil I was too young to understand. I don't want wealth nor world domination like these men. Or is that how the lust for power begins. I didn't want to talk to or see anyone. I took a shower then sat on the balcony still soaking wet drenching my sweatpants and t-shirts. I looked as if I just got out the ocean, I felt as though I was still drowning.

Halle was the first to come see me. We had begun flirting back and forth. She came on pretty strong at first but it was much needed. I told her it was reckless considering Natalie would try to stab me in my sleep if she found out. She's tried for less.

"Hey, you're out here all alone." Halle noted as she opened the glass sliding door.

"Yup..." I mutter unable to look away from the expanse of the Western ocean on the coast of La Vida, Naka.

"Do you want to smoke with me?" Halle asked, "It's our usual time. You've been out here for hours... are you okay?"

"Nope..." I say solemnly.

"Alright then I guess I'll leave you alone." Halle relented back inside the villa.

It wasn't long before I could hear Natalie and Halle squabbling. I couldn't make out their words nor did I try to. My full attention upon coping with all I heard over the weekend.

My blood-boiled, I feel like a powerless child. I wanted to stop their plan but there was so answer to it. Their logic wasn't only flawless. They only functioned with rationality unable to even perceive emotions around them. As if they had no emotions themselves outside of vice. It was the normal people living in irrationality, unable to separate their perspective from the eminent domain pushing them out their homes into shanty towns, or raising housing prices until the whole building or neighborhood was purchased. They complained endless but had no idea it was all planned.

I had no idea I was supposed to fit into all of this. The only reason I was invited was as Colin's Ward and being a young multi-millionaire I raised a fascination for them. I had managed something they thought impossible for humanity. Earning a million dollars in Nadia which they thought was ransacked and dilapidated. I don't know why those men were so willing to share their perspective and wisdom to me personally, pulling me aside to espouse their knowledge and theories. I had an endless amount of questions without the words to ask them. I began to understand the grand intellect it took to ask quality questions. I needed clarity on only one I would ask both Ray and Colin.

Why does the world operate as it does and when did this system of grand disparity begin?

"Excuse me, Excuse me Captain Pompous! You just waltz in the apartment without saying Hi to anyone? You don't see me standing here trying to talk to you for the past five minutes!?" Natalie's tanned olive skin had goose bumps for the cool winter air coming in, dressed in boy shorts and a halter top. "You can either talk to me or pack your shit. I'm not playing the quiet game all night with you again."

Natalie was the Queen of Veiled threats and empty gestures. She wasn't used to people calling her bluff or standing alone. When our stubbornness met it was a head on collision. It began to set a precedent for how extreme the fights got. Saying and doing whatever to get the other person to back down was purposeless when both people were unrelenting forces. I was seeking solitude and she was a combustible force seeking my attention by any means necessary.

"Gaia to Morgan, you selfish prick. You better get some sense and speak to me!" Natalie began flicking my ear.

I turned to look at her, brought back from my thoughts and vibration, beginning to lose the questions in my head. I closed my eyes and began rubbing the bridge of my nose wondering what I would have done if this was a grown man heckling me. I would probably grab him by the throat and toss him off the balcony, hoping for his own sake he made it to the pool below. I felt an even more desperate need for silence and solitude. Packing up didn't sound too bad. Right now I want to leave Naka for good.

I stood up trying to maneuver past her but she thought it was cute standing in the way. I was too angry to enjoy her beauty. My eyes were beginning to turn. My energy began to flare up. I had a legendarily explosive temper acting out quickly and harshly.

"Please move before things get ugly Natalie. I'm not in the mood. I'm just going to pack up and leave since that's all you tell me anymore." I wasn't polite beyond the courtesy.

"I don't want you to leave. I want you to listen to me Morgan! Especially if your selfish ass is gonna ignore me! You can talk to Halle, and spend time with all those people over the weekend but you don't have time for your own girlfriend!? Fine then, you don't like me it's obvious so leave." Natalie began seething with anger.

I took a long look at her already knowing where I would take things if pushed, "You don't know what you're talking about at all, Natalie. I do love you. Tread carefully. Stop saying things you'll regret and don't mean-

"Or else what, you're not going to do shit you coward!" she shouted in my face.

It struck a nerve vibrating through my very being. I had two days around the root of all evil and chaos in the world. Organized evil and chaos veiled by wealth and group grope. I may have been killed in the process or been on a manhunt but I could have killed every last one of those men. Was that not what I sought as a resolution to all this madness? Did I lose my opportunity to solve the world's ills the only way I knew how? Was it my own cowardice?

It was rare I wanted to cry. The coldness began mixing with the blood-boiling anger as a hurricane began shaping in my heart.

"You don't have shit to say? Jah'Enshishi, how did I get stuck with someone so pathetic? So lazy and weak! You don't do anything but run around all day. Sad about this or that but never satisfied. Now, you won't even talk to me!? I may have helped you if you weren't such a wimp!" Natalie kept pushing me with a smug grin.

"Move, I'll leave and you'll never hear from me again." My eyes were fully red, boring a hole through her soul.

I spent most days bouncing between La Vida, Baja, Hez, and The Gregor Estates in Naka. Not to mention running my businesses back in Nadia. I had explained this to her every day of the week. The debutant heiress didn't care, listen, or support anything I did. A chick who wanted to do nothing but go to school or to parties nothing else existed in her world.

I swallowed my words, glaring at Natalie until her beauty was no longer appealing. My emotions no longer mattered. My emotions didn't care whether she was a man or woman, where she was from or of ramifications. I was ready to break something and needed to leave immediately before it was her. If I had more ability to focus I might have been able to simply blink away. Maybe I needed to jump off the balcony and hope I made it to the pool below.

"If you want to keep your pretty little teeth, I suggest you get the fuck out my face, Natalie!" I said holding my anger back the best I could.

She began laughing, "Who the fuck to do you think you are?"

"I know I am a decorated veteran with over three hundred confirmed kills. Wolf First-Class and Captain of the Regulator Regime, I fought for your damn country! All you ever do is treat me like some dog or worn-out shoe. Get the hell out my way before you learn what all that really means, Natalie. I don't want to hurt you." I warn again.

"Morgan, you aren't shit to me. This huffing and puffing doesn't mean shit to me. You're not gonna do shit. And you won't be shit without me." Natalie took a step back as I approached her.

"Care to test your theory?" I asked staring her in the eyes with my ruby red ones.

Natalie cowered down wanting to speak but was too afraid with me directly in her face. I shoved her aside with a single hand. I stormed inside beginning to fit as much as I could back into the suitcase I had unpacked only a few hours ago.

Natalie found a burst of confidence with my back turned, slamming her fist against my back with all her force, "Who the fuck do you think you are putting your hands on me?"

"That's it." I spun around, snatching her by the throat, squeezing her hyoid to stop her speech entirely ripping her off the ground. I stared at her feeling absolutely nothing left. "I could snap your neck like a fucking twig. Leave me alone and let me leave."

"Kill me, kill me then you fucking animal. I don't care anymore! If you don't love me, I don't give a shit anymore kill me then!" she cried struggling to pry my hand loose.

I sighed as she tried in vain like all the men two to three her size when I was half the age and size I am now. The memory didn't resonate with the moment. I did love Natalie... I tossed her aside on the floor then returned to packing my bags. She ran back up to me trying to pull my bags from my hands crying for me not to leave.

"I have no idea what you want! You are not going to talk to me anyway then act like you give a damn about me Natalie!" I screamed.

"All I wanted you to do was talk to me you bastard! Look at what you did to me! You can't just have a conversation with me? You don't give a fuck about me!" Natalie broke down crying hysterically.

I was mortified, looking around in confusion as I tried to make sense of how she says she felt.

"I don't want to talk at all Natalie. You're utterly disrespectful. You come here screaming and shouting at me like I'm your child not your man. I'm leaving!" I throw my hands up in the air.

"You are not! I forbid it! I am showing you the same respect you show me. You are not fucking leaving me, Morgan!" Natalie rumbled in a demonically deep voice akin to Enshishi's itself.

I stood there astonished trying to figure this girl out. I felt she only wanted to keep me around to be the one to leave before I left her. She wanted me to be her miniscule perspective of me, a man she barely knew at all these years. To be wholly dependent and lost without her but I was everything before I had even met her. Things between us had completely eroded. Everything I confided in her she used to rip me apart on a daily basis, digging deep into my insecurities and sheltered thoughts. She didn't care or know what she was unlocking. She acted as if seeing me in a blind rage was all she needed to get through her night. She used my own mind and emotions as weapons against me on a daily basis. Yet, she managed to become the victim. I don't need victimhood I needed solitude. It hurt deepest because at my core I still loved her and wanted her more than anything. Her beauty is unmatched and the sex unrivaled.

Natalie is outright aggressive then feigns victimhood and innocence as if she doesn't know why you're retaliating. The relationship had been dying long before this day, if it ever truly existed before the exchange of fluids. I worried too much for someone who would easily turn against me at any minor infraction. So much left unhealed and unsaid.

I learned to leave when someone doesn't want the best for me, only herself.

Our relationship was always like this, it took today to fully understand, to truly see how tumultuous it became. The same dance of hatred, anger and disrespect. We used to have sex to make up, rough, debauch inside every hole she possessed. After long there was no sex, we weren't even sleeping together unless exhausted from fighting. I wouldn't even speak to Natalie or avoid going home to La Vida all together.

After we fought I took another shower. Natalie locked herself in her bedroom. It became my practice to take a shower or bath whenever I was stressed. The steaming waters became my only true friend in the house with motives or agendas. My worries, my fears, and my doubts being washed down the drain leaving me clean. I lathered up a few times too many, trying to wash away the night, trying to wash away my childhood.

I was trying to cleanse myself of forbidden knowledge and demons of rage controlling my mind. Trying to rid myself of the conclusions others have reached of humanity and existence. I wanted to be washed clean as a baby. To be completely free of my life, my consciousness, and my path yet, when I stepped out the shower those crimson eyes stared back at me through the fog of the mirror. Reminding me of everything I and my people had been through.

Colin noted the darkness presiding over me as if his own darkness recognized my corrupted spirit. He lied to me and said the darkness was my power. The darkness only made me feel weak. Even the night sky has the moon for light does it not? He and Natalie wanted my soul to be in their hands. For me to consumed in darkness and misery. I deserve far more than Nakans will ever consider offering me. A Nakan only cares about what you can offer or do for them, even their own children. One evil resolved into the next. All sins bind and hold to our soul self.

I knew this because the virtues I learned in Nadia taught me. Dying in Nadia made me come back feeling pure and free. Being in Naka feels as though I walked under a waterfall of filth, I have no interest in losing my soul. I withdrew from the world, unable to trust because no one understood. Her I am, a man living their dreams. Attempting to tell them their life is for null, and the path is narrow. Yet, these people struggling in misery believed they knew more.

They built icebergs to sink ships of those growing tremendously. I sold my ship and invested in my own island. I'm counting down the days until I would never have to deal with this continent again. I had enough to retire early and live a simply life free from everyone. Or spend a few more decades building.

My soul didn't need materials or consumption. My soul needed healing, understanding, and growth. My meditations reminded me I cannot heal in the very system that attempted to broke me. Soon, I would be free. No more military life, no more money haunting me, and no more women draining me of my life force. Free of people, judgment, hatred, and distractions.

Solitude became my only method to heal from a lifetime of damage. Aloneness and silence became its own Nirvana. Being around people was hell, those who lied and said they loved me. In truth hatred ruled their souls.

Peace came in solitude and meditation brought clarity. Yet, none of these people could understand. They followed a pathway straight to misery and hell, one I spent my entire childhood upon. They refused to listen to anyone even themselves, trembling before the truth of the world outside of Naka. Praying to Enshishi the world outside Naka is worse than Naka, never praying to improve themselves or their home.

I have no more energy to educate the world. I have no interest in leading or controlling people. I enjoy the new life I'm creating. Soon I will be free of Natalie, and all she represents. This also meant being free of Leslie, I could never return to The Regime after what I did. All the destruction I presided over within and leaving.

In 22 years now what is my life's worth? When no one believes you possess the wisdom or knowledge you do based solely on origin of birth and age. Yet, I must sit and watch as they fumble upon simple problems and dark decisions to destruction out of ignorance and pride. I know pain and misery, I didn't find until I found Rakil, and then he helped me find myself. Solitude brought me wisdom. And wisdom told me to leave the world to its ways. I did not need to be of it. There's nothing left in Naka, no one wants to be saved. Their only salvation was in the very things destroying them money, sex, false knowledge, and idolatry of those undeserving of worship.

We chose pride over character in Naka. This is a mistake I will never make again. I can only ensure this by taking the oath with my own inner-kingdom and soul. I need to detach from this world.

"Sweet fruits of solitude find me long after the torment of life. Lift my woes and worries to the Heavenly Father and Heavenly Mother. Soothe my aching soul and mind. Heavenly Brother, Ada, still my heart so I may embrace these people as you do."

This is the prayer I began reciting in distress. Whisper, plead, cry, or meditate upon. God hears all and he doesn't need to hear too much. We fooled ourselves to believe God is gone or does not exist. To believe money or sex can replace The Heavenly Mother we live on. We only fool ourselves, allowing the world to fall to corruption as we worked to an early grave.

There's more to life, yet little to life at all. Simplicity will rule my soul and guide my mind. I leave complexity to the philistines and predators.

Rakil, free me from this life and world of sin. Help me find my peace. To help others find this peace, to live in your name, to cultivate the Mother, Gaia, and to live in the image of your son. Help me to grow closer to you. Save me from this darkness.

CHAPTER 3

Time & Space, A Life After Death

Rose Paz Andale

He sat with his back facing the door, staring out the wall-length windows overlooking the lake. It was a dream for most people. Sitting above the clouds, dressed in a navy blue bespoke suits and custom cobbled shoes. For Morgan Ellys the comforts of society were of heavy acceptance. The ex-soldier had grown used to the cots and floor mats, the discipline and order of military life. To play civilian was one thing in itself, but to play millionaire was a whole new headache.

He sat with his back facing the door. A book underneath his hand, legs crossed in lotus position. He claimed it helped him think better. His spine fully aligned like an antenna connecting him to God.

He sat with his back facing the door, in his small office overlooking the city skyline. Legs crossed over the other in lotus position.

The door knocked twice. His ears perked up, his eyes glued to the book but no longer reading it. Training was hard to shake, that and PTSD. Maybe he shouldn't sit with his back toward the door. But you'll never fully adjust to society if you don't embrace these meaningless tests.

Every nerve in his body jerked. His chestnut skinned cheeks jerked back tight into a strained smile.

"You will not conquer me today, old friend. Not today." he repeated the mantra he often said to little avail as the seeming bloodlust roared at the gates of his self-control.

His body wanted to move. It wanted to take to the shadows where it felt safest. It wanted to reach to his waist and grab one of the daggers that bought him the millionaire lifestyle. But neither of those were acceptable answers. There were no shadows. No daggers but the far more disturbing reality... nothing to hide from.

He could sit like this for days on end without eating or seeming to sleep. I wondered if he was even human anymore, after all he's been through in this life. His ex-girlfriend was happy to offer me the job as his housekeeper. To make sure he was okay as his mind slowly deteriorated from isolation.

I watched him from the doorway leaving him quickly. He owned the home but was rarely ever home. I felt bad for taking her money but she seemed to think it was important someone be here to watch his home. He does come back, make a mess of my work then leave off for days or weeks on end without any notice.

I wonder if he'll ever notice me.

CHAPTER 4

A Father and Daddy's Girl

Halle Gregor

Halle sat at the dinner table of the illustrious Gregor Manor. She stole awake a few hours earlier than her sleep regiment. A princess needed her beauty rest. She sat at the table fiddling with colored pencils, her tongue hung out of her mouth as she drew away with complete focus.

"Is someone in here?" An authoritative voice snapped the air.

The Patriarch Colin Gregor awoke for his fencing practice. The man was as feared a businessman as he was a swordsman. He was retired but, "liked to keep his edge sharp." Fencing was his new fascination after spending a lifetime mastering the sword-fighting styles across Gaia.

Colin approached the dining room, "Halle, what are you doing awake? Dr. Richards said clearly, 9 hrs of sleep a day. Were you out partying again, are you just getting in?" Richards was her personal physician. The middle-aged woman made over $200k annually just to attend solely to Halle when needed. "You know, your beauty is of high importance to me, sweetie."

She always had difficulty speaking to her father. His eyes made it feel like whatever you said was a lie. She didn't make a habit to stray too far from the truth.

"I was just working on some designs, daddy."

"You were?" The Patriarch prowled closer, peering over her shoulder, "Why are those women so long?"

"That's just how you design, dad. Most of your models will be that shape."

"I'm putting money into this garbage?"

"No... I- I meant my models. It's for an assignment. My professor is having us design for a fashion show. The winner gets their designs in La Vida's Fashion Week."

"Oh, fine." He nods, "When did you pick up this hobby?"

Halle began putting away her sketches, "I majored in it for two years now, dad. I own a boutique... I'm twenty now not twelve. I have businesses not hobbies."

"Ha, did I really let you waste two years of your life to study drawing and dresses?" Colin seemed to believe it to be the funniest thing he's ever heard, "You always seem to catch me with a glass of whiskey in my hand when you want something." he pats her shoulder, "This is good stuff... you consider opening a business?"

"Do you really think they're good, dad?" she smiles ear to ear with pride.

Colin shrugged, "I could probably find you a teacher."

"I study this already dad... I'm the best in my major. I'm graduating a year early!"

"Oh...?" he rubbed his neck chuckling, "Ha, then maybe you need to study again dear."

Halle stood to leave.

"Hold on, hold on now, it was just a joke. I'm sure your drawings were nice. Come here a sec." he brushes her curly locks out of her face. "That's my beautiful princess." he kisses her cheek.

"Thanks daddy." Halle holds his hand to her cheek. "You can be really mean."

"I'm a man sweetie, sometimes I don't know what I say." he kisses her on the lips and pats her butt, "So, are there any new men in your life, Halle?"

"Dad!" she groans, "I don't want to talk about this with you."

"Come on sweetie, I want to know who's after my fortune."

She wondered whether he spoke of her or his wealth.

"No one particularly, when men hear my name they run the other way, they want nothing to do with me."

"That's because if they don't run fast enough, I'll catch them." Colin grinned proud of his violent streak.

"I think I met someone who isn't afraid of you." Halle smiles, "Natalie's new boyfriend will be moving to Naka to stay with us. He already picked up a third of the year's rent to cut costs. He's really sweet. The hardest worker I know. We met him a couple years ago. He disappeared but Nat called me up saying he would be crashing with us."

"He's living there with you?" My father said in contempt, "I don't like this at all."

Halle smiles, "Well, I do. He's really nice. He and Nat don't really get to see each other anymore now that she's interning for you. She's really excited he's moving from Nadia to be with her."

"What's his name?" my father rubbed his chin, "One of my business partners have been telling me there's some young upstart in Nadia. Is this boy staying with you, a Morgan Ellys?"

"Yes! That's him!" Halle was overjoyed, "I can't wait for you two to meet!"

A grin came over Colin's face, "I know him quite well actually. It sounds like he needs a real woman in his life, pumpkin." He rubs Halle's chin, "This is your purpose. This man has a lot of promise... Go after him, Halle. When you two get close, I'll make him your husband."

"No way... I already tried. He's loyal to Natalie. I rather let them be in love."

"She's a Wolfe. She isn't a real woman like you, Halle. She will never treat him right. Besides, we can't let someone of such promise end up marrying the Wolfe family, now can we? I have been watching this boy closely over the years. He will be my heir. You don't want to be undutiful now would you Halle?"

"No, sir I wouldn't. He's going to be my husband?"

"I will it to be so, so be a good girl and show daddy what he's taught you had been for good use. Bring this Morgan Ellys home for the family." He kissed her cheek, "Good talk, Halle. Keep up the drawing."

"I'll make you proud!" Halle calls after her father as he leaves to get to his fencing session.

CHAPTER 5

Descendants of Gods among Men

Morgan Ellys

Colin called me up early in the day with laughter in his voice and a scheme.

He had begun teaching me the business side of life. He made me vice president of his company, strangely enough as his daughter was finding her way between me and Natalie. She called to be a buffer, said she was keeping me from leaving Natalie. I hoped in a way Halle wanted me for herself. She tried to act tough and say she was only in it for the sex. But that wasn't the mindset of a Gregor. Gregors are winners and champions. Set to their purpose and their way of doing things. Coy may have worked on everyone else Halle met, but she cared for me.

The moment I arrived at the Gregor Estate, I was greeted by a young woman named Ananda. She gave her introduction then brought me up to the cigar room where I and Colin discussed our affairs after some golf or boating.

Ananda informed me to take a seat. The young lady rolled me a blunt the size of a Cohiba. Poured me a rock glass of Don Perignon, then got on her knees proceeding to give me the best head I've gotten in my life.

When my nut came, she swallowed without missing a beat. Right after she eagerly pulled out a condom. That's when I stopped her. I needn't explain. She gave a wink then got right back to work, teasing and sucking on my cock. Taking her hits off the blunt and sipping from the glass.

When Colin finally came to us, she was in my lap. My balls were drained and we were laughing about some dumb shit. We didn't even notice him come in. No idea how long he was there watching as my eyes had been closed from the high and liquor sedating my system.

"Hey there, how did you enjoy, Ananda?"

Ananda kissed me on the cheek, "Will you need anything else, Master Ellys?"

"I'm fine, thank you, dear."

"Hurry on now," Colin sits in his arm chair, "She's one of the best girls. Damn near as good as her mother." Colin licked his lips. His appetite was incorrigible compared to mine.

"Sir, did you say her mother?"

"Don't worry, on that boy. My staff has been loyal to the Gregor Family for generations. That's how you keep good service. Take care of your workers, and they'll take great care of you. Take care of their families and well, you see how enthusiastic that girl was to serve. It's hard breeding good slaves. It takes a very firm hand to train a good slave like my Ananda."

I could only nod. I had long quit playing the game of morality and better judgment. Colin had a different way of viewing the world. One I can't quite understand. The man was born wealthy, not rich but *wealthy*. His view is debatable but his vision for his family is undisputedly admirable. We never began this relationship because we agreed. He wants to see his family reach new heights. I want my legacy to want for nothing. What better partnership?

"I've been hearing some disturbing things from my daughter, son. Halle seems to believe you want to call off the wedding."

"I never claimed to love this arrangement you've found me in. To my understanding this was business."

He grins, "Ha, that's my boy. Yes, yes it is." Colin had a self-assuring laugh, deep and hearty. "I wish Halle had such a sense of duty. Instead the girl prattles on about feelings and love."

"She does?" I asked in awe.

He nods, "It's intolerable. She *was* a strong advocate of the idea of marriage. Now, it's how the feelings will be unreciprocated and she doesn't think you'll be happy. I keep trying to tell her how big your smile will be once my fortune is signed over to you." he shook his head, "You and the Young Wolfe definitely stirred something up, but you choose wisely. I'm just glad I got you on my team before Mordin laid eyes on you. Those Wolves are maniacs. He would have killed you on the spot." I found it best to let Colin talk himself to whatever point he wished to make. You would get few words in edgewise. "The Wolfe has quite a mischievous streak, huh? I never imagined her disobeying her father. I tried to tell Morgan he was too easy on her. But I guess you knocking her head against the headboards was enough to keep her loyal, huh boy?" he begins laughing.

"Natalie is a good woman. She's been a great help to me in the office."

Colin enjoyed his laughter for one. His smile faded when I didn't join in. The dull silence set us at odds. I took breath regretting the past half hour of my life.

"I think love is nice for the first couple months. Natalie would have been far more valuable as a good daughter! What good is a woman with no family name to protect her? Without her father's protection she's another lost lamb in the world at prey for Wolves. I love the irony. Ha, part of me almost wishes you went through with it to see how Mordin handled such a thing. I welcome you into my home and offer you the greatest delicacy I possess. Natalie hasn't even brought you in front of her parents. Such a shame Morgan, is she embarrassed of you?"

"Watch yourself, Colin. I care for that woman regardless of your understanding or your grudge with her family."

"Ha, I hate Wolfes. Old blood feud with those smug bastards, they have refused any Gregor from marrying their family centuries ago. Their people used to paint themselves in the blood of my fallen ancestor after eating them. This was a thousand years ago, but the fuckers walk around with the same pride and bravado as if they got done picking off Gregors last week."

"How do you know of that, sir?"

"Ha, boy I know everything! True history is passed down father to son. The mind, the mouth, the soul… they never forget. We talked, we spoke. My grandfathers, great grandfathers were all historians, men who studied finances, politics, and war from the beginning of time. History existed son. It's only muddled by the poor and migrants who leave their home and their name behind. But the old families stayed as units. We stayed whole and choose who we wanted to make history with, wisely. A name is power. The Gregor name is the ultimate power."

"Wow… I barely even know my grandparents."

Colin smiled as if there was a secret he wanted to share, "Would you like to meet my forefathers?"

"Uh, sure where are we going?" He doesn't exactly accept no for an answer, so I learned to to monitor his requests.

"Follow me." Colin stands all grins. "This is great! I thought I would have to wait until your wedding day to show you this Morgan."

I sobered up quickly. Colin wasn't the idle type. A man didn't make a fortune stay fortunate being idle.

We walked through the castle for five minutes of his clapping and excitement. Then outside, skipping over Lady Gregor's garden, the highlight of the outdoors with the heirlooms and wild community, it was wild but kept, as if no one touched the garden, it cared for itself. We walked further for a mile or so.

We exchanged few words. Colin held his grin, smiling ear to ear. Mostly repeating, "I can't wait for you to see this!" and me replying, "I hope this is worth it."

Colin took me into a dense jungle off the Gregor Estate. The Gregors lived in the same manor for a thousand years. Since they built their first settlement and turned it into what it is today.

We walked until we reached a small shack in the middle of the jungle.

"Here we are." his smiled widened, if that was possible.

"Oh? This isn't what I expected... you keep your father in here?"

Colin's smile faded immediately, "Are you some fucking idiot?" he shook his head pushing the door open to the shack where there were only stairs descending into darkness. "Hand me that torch, boy."

There was a torch with a gilded handle, the torch looked as if it had never been lit before... yet existed for centuries.

Colin waved his hand over the torch and it blossomed into orange and violet flames. The staircase filled with light revealing intricate symbols and designs along the stairs as we descended. The stairs went down narrow and straight for a couple of stories underground until we reached a long hall.

"Be careful, dust. No one is allowed down here but Gregor men." He patted my back leading me along the sole pathway surrounded on both sides with liquid magma, and on the outside of that seemed to be a stream pouring in from a nearby river.

There were figures in the darkness, towering over both of us, nearly scraping the ceiling nearly fifty feet high.

"These are the Gregor Patriarchs before me. Dating back to when those sick albinos changed their calendar."

They stood aligned on both sides. Statues carved out of stone, clay, and marble. Some stood encased in gold. Many made entirely of Obsidian, volcanic rock.

"Every Gregor man since the beginning of our remarkable family is in this ancient mausoleum." Colin beamed with pride, "One day... these doors will be opened once more to non-gregors to create one more statue before their lives are sacrificed to Enshishi. My statue of course! A terracotta statue, so that it may strengthen through the test of time as our family name. Then... decades will pass and... your statue will be built, Morgan. By then, you will be a man. A true Gregor Patriarch, you're statue will be made of granite and gold." He wraps an arm over my shoulder. "What do you think, boy?"

"I- I can't process this...."

"You don't have to, it's your presence. You are here. Clear your head. You can still hear their voices granting us wisdom and encouragement."

Colin closed his eyes and took in a deep breath. "I used to come here all the time as a young man, around your age. Ask these brave Gods for their wisdom and words. Convene with my fathers."

I stood in awe... before me were forty statues scraping the ceiling of an underground tunnel. Each was a real man. Each man lived a life and had a story of conquest or amelioration. Each of these men was the blood of Colin, who stood with his arm wrapped around me as if he was finally passing down the torch.

"One day boy, you will marry my little girl and make me the happiest man in Gaia. To finally have an heir worthy of catapulting the Gregor name to Godhood. I thank Warren every day for having found you and brought you to me."

There stood, in the shadows all the way down the line. A statue stared down upon me with a punishing presence as if staring at the sun. The Lord Commissioner, Patriarch Maurice Gregor. Colin's father, he attempted to bring peace to Gaia by restricting The Regulator Regime from world domination. He is the man Colin killed in order to become The Patriarch of The Gregor Family.

"Breathe it all in boy. The future is bright for us Gregor, Volcanus!" He raises a fist then looks to me to join in.

I merely nodded, "Seems amazing, Colin." I pulled from under his arm, pacing down the grand hall until I could look Maurice in the eye. There were rubies lodged into his eye sockets. The only one of the sort in the whole hall, I felt like I was staring at my own face. "You loved your father?"

"I was a dutiful son. I waited patiently."

"Is Halle a dutiful daughter?"

He smirks, "Far more dutiful than I had ever been. I thank Enshishi for blessing me. God is good, isn't he? But you know all about that now?"

"I don't quite understand."

Colin shrugged, "She's not important, boy. But this, this moment is. Take it all in. Breathe in this fresh Gregor air. You are bound now my boy, you are destined to go down in Gregor history!"

"I am honored."

"You're goddamn right, you're honored." Colin smiled bright, "Boy. There are only two things that matter in life. That's love and power. If you can balance the two, you are a King. You can have both if you know your means. But we're men. When we find boundaries we push through them. We know no means. It's the flaw of man. So, that creates two different men, those who avoid the inevitable boundaries and those who push through anything before them. We are the men who push through whatever attempts to bind us! Through any boundary before us, all things yield before us, we yield to nothing. We are the fire and the future of humanity. We are Gods, boy! VOLCANUS!" he holds out his arms filled with the glory of the catacombs.

Colin seemed to stare at me and see all the things he wanted in his heir. The more I got to know this man, the more I understood the two of us couldn't have been any more different. But these were old men, though not so old to have grown addled. He was far too old to be anything but lost in their ways. Silence was my best policy to deal with Colin.

CHAPTER 6

A Love Affair

Halle Gregor

I was dressed in a beautiful citrine sundress, holding hands with Morgan as he waltzed me down the streets of downtown Nadine in Nadia. He says everyone in the area had enough wealth not to be concerned with cameras and paparazzi. We blended in better than we could have anywhere else. He wore a plain pair of jeans, and a t-shirt holding my hand, and a bottle of wine in the other as we sought somewhere to sit down and celebrate his new house.

So, marriage didn't work out immediately as I wanted but he said recent events made him reconsider settling down. He called me around five in the afternoon saying a friend of his was leaving to Esha and he wanted to see me. I drove right over. Three hours later we were in Nadine riding around looking at houses until he pointed out one he had been speaking about for awhile, a few years or so but the former owners wouldn't budge on the price.

A beautiful lakehouse built by hand over fifty years ago. He says he was waiting to see if the price switched. I urged him to buy the house outright and get some property under his belt. Worst comes to worst, he could fix the place up and flip it for a higher price. He grinned and told me he already bought it. He wanted to know my opinion.

There was a strange element of romance to it all. Though, he repeatedly said, “I only need a friend with me.” I knew he was the man I would be married too. For him to consider me his friend flattered me to no end. Morgan had no friends... His birthday recently passed and he’s notorious for going on a tirade or disappearing, yet here I was right by his side.

We found a small park with a pond filled with geese. He sat down straight in the dirt. I stared at him as if he was crazy but he didn’t budge, making me sit in the dirt and goose poops in my beautiful dress. Only for him would I get a dress dirty.

We spoke until the sunset, until the bottle of wine was finished and we were both stupid drunk. Laughing and walking through Nadine buying appetizers and street food from every place with a nice name and a bar. We laughed and walked around until my feet hurt in my sandals. Until Morgan was drunk, slurring, with a permanent grin on his face. I almost didn’t want him to stop drinking knowing when he was sober it would all fade.

When we got tired he lifted me up, and we disappeared into the fabric of space time, reappearing in our apartment back in La Vida. About a 7hr flight away in a blink of an eye. He let me down, claiming he needed to get some air leaving me to go onto the balcony.

This felt like a usual thing now. My toes curling in the carpet, bent over some piece of furniture as he buries his manhood inside me. I never expected things to lead here. I can have my fair share of unrest. Not much, but enough to feel unease. I was walking naked through our apartment with his seed still dripping between my legs. How long until he was mine? All mine? Asking for a threesome on his birthday turned to all this? I was under the impression it would be one, maybe twice for confirmation... then it became three times because it was so good. Four times because, why not we could keep going. He's been inside me nearly every day since she upped and left. So, when will he be mine?

"Babe, are you thirsty?" I call, fondling my breast as the draft hardens my nipples. "You have coke, ginger ale, and some iced tea." Damn, draft.

There's always a window to be found open here. He was always too hot, I was always too cold.

He enters dressed in his birthday suit finest, his half-erection swung boldly from between his legs. He was six feet of under-appreciated love. He wasn't carved from stone but it was clear he was made of fine marble. His maple-brown sugar skin was almost as sweet as the branch hanging from his waist.

He clutches my butt roughly. We kiss as his erection begins pressing against my belly. He bit my neck, easing inside my wetness.

"Ada, I just wanted to know if you were thirsty..." I moan as my eyes roll behind my head. Feeling him stretch my already tender vagina, it didn't stop me from wrapping my arms and legs around him.

We kiss softly. He kisses down my neck to my shoulder, slowly stirring inside of me.

"I'm a little thirsty." He says as I unfurl on the granite island countertop. He clutches the curve of my hips, easing himself into my guts. He didn't understand how long he was... How it felt to have him pressing in my diaphragm. I lost the feeling in my toes as my ability to speak was reduced down into moans with my tongue flopping from my mouth.

He's ravenous. This is the third time since we got home only a couple hours ago. At the door, in the shower, and now here on the table when will all this be mine?

"Do you want to go to my room?" I ask, noticing the front door gave a clear view of our act. "Be a bit more discrete..." I continue as he withdraws so I can finally speak. As soon as he slides back in I lose my ability to talk. I loved it. My legs tingle. I could feel a fire building in my belly as its warmth fills my limbs. He strains to suck my nipples.

He looks over his shoulder and scoffs, "she isn't coming home..." He mutters. He pulled out of me, my senses rushed back far too quickly. I sit up a bit dizzy. He crosses to the cabinets and grabs two glasses.

"Did I say something wrong?" I ask feeling exposed. His sudden coldness sent chills down my spine. His glance made me feel bare in my nudity as he stared at my very soul behind those eyes.

He hands me a glass of wine. I accept it graciously. It was time to be the side bitch. I drink to avoid sighing, hopping off the counter.

"I'm sorry..." He mutters taking small sips from his glass. He just wanted to be drunk but didn't want to drink. "Are you trying to smoke?"

I smile, walking over to him. I ease him back inside my wetness. Our hips grind against each other as he uses his free hand to fondle my breasts.

"Of course I do baby, you know they call me the Witch Doctor right? Because I have the best weed, and this pussy leaves you under my spell." Though he didn't seem to get my sense of humor, I look to see him biting his lip as I lean back to kiss him. "But you have to fuck me like you did the first time." The benefits of being a side chick, you never have to deal with the bullshit.

I've become the one thing he looks forward to. I can do no wrong. But with guilt and regret being one bad night away, I couldn't let this dick slip out of me, metaphorically and presently. As he thrusts his hips into my backside, I can feel a pool inside me. My juices were being mixed up with his precum, my lubricant of choice. I didn't want to stop being impaled, impaling myself to wistfully pull apart, savoring every inch of him before having it all over again.

I nearly choke on my moans as he begins slamming into me and holding me against him. He digs his nails into my hips, to dig deeper. I grind my hips against him beginning to lose my ability to speak, "god dammit, baby... Fuck- fuck me- "I stammer as I begin laughing. Tears fill my eyes as I laugh. His deep thrusts felt as if they were pressing against my actual voice box. I wanted to scream. I wanted to scream as loudly as possible. I wanted to belt out to the sky but it was stuck just like my orgasm. He was slamming against the floodgates of euphoria. Every thrust brings down the dam. Small screams escaped my throat. "You're so close baby, you're so fucking close!" I began cheering as my hips began moving all their own, trying to guide him.

As I moved back, I didn't feel him. Did he pull o- SCHWACK!

"YES OH MY FUCKING GOD YES!" I rejoice, screaming and shouting. His hips came late and the floodgates broke down. I was laughing and crying. My body felt weightless. My skin was on fire and my breath expelled a bit of smoke.

"Baby..." I groan trying to control my convulsions.

"I'm going to cum..." He grunts.

"Mhm..." I couldn't let him pull out, I needed him inside me. "Go for it baby," I purr automatically as he begins panting. I could feel him throbbing and growing inside of me. I belt out, "Come on, baby please! Make it wet so I can slide all over that dick." It was slow at first then a waterfall. Mine came in waves but his was a crash. I felt breathless as he filled me with his seed. We melted onto the floor I did all I possibly could to keep him inside me as we slipped over. Our hips moved from our heavy panting, milking out the last pulls of our mutual orgasms.

"I love you..." He whispers.

I try to respond but my voice hasn't come back yet. I feel the coldness return.

"No, I'm sorry I shouldn't have said it..." Wait, no. God, why can't I speak!? "I guess I should go." He begins pulling out of me. Wait, baby... Not yet. Dammit, speak! But I was far too lost in ecstasy to find my voice.

I lay on my back. I could still feel him inside even though he was halfway to the bedroom. I was just getting to my stomach by the time he came out in sweatpants and a T-shirt. I can see the blunt dangling from his mouth, sparking it as he passes the threshold. Why the sudden change? Christ... I just wanted to lie on the floor and gush.

He's so damn insecure.

I pull myself up, my legs shaking underneath me as I move to the bathroom down the hall. I was walking on clouds trying not to slip through. The toilet was a much relieved help. I sit, catching my breath and letting my heartbeat come back. Did he say "I love you?" Holy fuck and I didn't say anything. Ha, that's why he's so upset? I let out a sigh as my bladder finally released from all the pressure.

I look at myself in the mirror. "He said he loves you, Halle..." I giggle, my cheeks flush red, "he said he loves you!" I fall into a fit of laughter as tears roll down my eyes. It's about damn time! I smile brightly rushing into the bedroom to grab my grinder.

Morgan kept a small shrine in his bedroom where the preparation for all our vices goes down. The centerpiece was a vase filled to the brim with his beer caps. I don't know how he drinks the shit. Beer tastes gross! Give me a glass of wine, good jazz, and a joint anyday over beers, blunts and bbqs his motto for life. But that's why I loved Morgan... That's why I'm so- so washed up and captivated with all this. I know it's wrong. I know it's not fair to either of us. But, he deserves better than Natalie, much better than being hidden. I've waited and I've been supportive but dammit, dammit I deserve him too!

I pluck a few choice nugs from my dugout to fill my strawberry red bowl. I step out on the balcony to find Morgan sitting now with his cup of wine. I didn't even hear him come back inside...

"You were in rare form, Mr. Ellys" I sat in the vacant lawn chair, staring out into the La Vida skyline giving way to the dark black sands and ocean. "How the hell did you two afford this place before I moved in?"

"Construction, I make more than I need, so... I guess I splurge where I can. I've paid the rent off for a year after a big project for your dad. Natalie stays more than I do. My second job arises every now and then so I dip out to Nadia. It was nice to have a reliable house. I haven't had a real place to stay other than the villas in Erdu. I have a few properties but other people live in them now." He extends his lighter to me. "Here."

"Thanks baby," I give him a wink, loving the breeze against my skin. I inhale letting the smoke burn the back of my throat. I inhale deeply then exhale blowing the stream into his face. "Are you mad at me?" I finally ask not wanting this night to fall into awkward silence and talks of the future. I just wanted to enjoy him and this moment. He's always fretting, always so anxious... Just shut up and love me.

I extend the bowl to him. He cracks a slight smile, noticing it's still rolling. It was a mean thing to do. But it was ruder to leave the bowl rolling. He clears the bowl, releasing it with a sigh.

"I'm not..." He shakes his head, "no, I'm not angry with you. It's just... The last time Nat and I had sex was so long ago. I just get a bit worrisome at times it won't work out."

My lips fall into a bow as I notice the redness in his eyes. He'd been crying out here?

"Do you usually smoke this much?"

"She says as she takes another hit..." He rolls his eyes.

"I'm smoking marijuana this is all natural, grown in my own garden, harvested by my own hands, sweetie." I preach.

"You're so full of shit... I know your dealer!" he laughs having given me the supply

I break out laughing, "well, someone grew it..." I roll my eyes, "you're missing the point."

"Oh, I'm sorry did you make one?"

"Asshole..." I kick him softly.

He lets out a chuckle as he takes the bowl.

"Whatever. Can you answer my question, are you mad at me?" I am more concerned with all the deflection. "What happened with you and Nat?"

"That was not your original question."

"I'm adding more now."

"You can't add more!" He sniggers, taking another hit. Blowing O's out his mouth.

"Oh, someone's been practicing I see?" I set my legs on his lap. "What happened?"

"You don't have to ask about this."

"I know... I'm doing it anyway. I want to know Morgan. So, stop beating around the bush and just tell me."

"The hell didn't you say anything? Just something even if it was disgust. Just something to let me know what you felt in return? I mean, that was so embarrassing. I gave up everything to marry you. I at least want to know you like me."

"Well, if someone wasn't so damn restless maybe I would have been more in control of my faculties."

"What..?" He raises a brow, "what does that mean? Are you already high?"

"What? No! Shut up!" I laugh, "I'm saying if you didn't fuck me so good then I could have responded. I don't even think I was of this world when you said it. I felt like my body was on the astral plane. Of course I love you Morgan. I'm marrying you."

"It was honestly that good, huh?" He rubs his chin. His blushing was adorable as his dimples poke out. "Well... I didn't know. I'm sorry for rushing off like that."

"Morgan, I've stood by you all this time. If I didn't feel the same I wouldn't be here. You do understand that right?"

"Yeah, it's just... Sometimes I need to hear it or feel it. It's hard for me to just go off of word alone with people. I- maybe I'm dumb but it's hard to just, know that."

"You have to seriously stop doing that. Don't tell me you love me then do all this second guessing." I crossed my arms.

"What? I'm not doing anything."

"Yes, you are. Stop, projecting your bullshit on me! I am not Natalie. I didn't do this to you. I'm not going to pay for her crap. I shouldn't have to be superwoman just because she tried to break you in two."

"I wasn't projecting on you..."

"Yes, you were! What's with this teary-eyed crap about all this?" I sigh, trying not to let this ruin my high, "I have no track record. I've done nothing to you, nor is there nothing I haven't done for you! I don't deserve that."

"Why does it always have to be about you?"

"Always? What do you mean always...?"

He paused catching himself. He looked away pretending to look out over the Caritas River. He looked wounded. It's rare I saw Morgan's scars but this. He was a broken man... She didn't try to break him. She dug underneath the muscle to his heart and actually managed to pull it off.

"Baby... What happened with Natalie?" I asked concerned with what she had done this whole time they dated.

He rubs his neck, staring up to the sky. "I never realized how unhealthy our relationship had become. How truly bad it was all this time. There are some nights I want to cry but I just can't. There are other nights where I'm just so angry. But I have no idea why... Am I angry at her, myself or the situation? I have no idea but I feel it, and I feel it so strongly." He begins choking back tears. "I was good to her... But dammit I could have been better. I know I could. But I was too damn good to her. But I still couldn't make Natalie love me...well to show it. I don't know if she loved me at all." He takes a long drag from his cigarette, "Sorry. I don't want to go on about this..."

"That's fine, with me." I agree with a bright smile.

"But it shouldn't be..." He groans, "I'm so tired of feeling this way over Natalie. She isn't even in my life anymore and sometimes she's all I think about."

"She feels the same-"

He scoffed, cutting me off, he didn't believe me. I didn't care to explain.

"So, what are you going to cry about it?" I challenge him.

He looks down at the ground then his eyes trail off elsewhere.

"I'm sorry... I didn't mean it that way. I just- no, no I'm going to say it. You keep doing this. We fuck, we smoke, you cry about Natalie. I'm tired of it! You're not going to say you love me then keep doing the same thing. So, if you're just gonna cry about it then I'm going to go inside and let you hug it out by yourself. If you want to begin moving forward then, then kiss me." I poke his chest.

"What?"

"If you're in love with me and you mean it. Then kiss me."

"That's not going to prove anything."

"Fine then, if you love me tell me what happened that makes you so insecure about sex?"

"Jah'Enshishi, why are you so blunt?"

"Shut up, you like it." I give him a wink. "If you would just be forward instead of being so cryptic I wouldn't have to be."

"I know you're trying to help, Halle. I really do... but-

I nearly pounced on him, kissing him as deeply as I could. He held me, burying his neck into the nape of my neck. "I wish I could be stronger for you."

"You don't have to be Morgan. I'll be strong for both of us."

"I truly do love you. I wish I could be more descriptive with fluffy language, because you deserve that shit. You deserve to be serenaded. You deserve love. You deserve so much I feel I could never give you."

"You already have Morgan. Damn, ha. You're amazing. I wouldn't put myself in this situation if you weren't. You're a good man, Morgan. The world may never truly appreciate how wonderful you are. You don't have to talk about Natalie, I rather we didn't even mention her name. If you want to check into therapy or see a counselor, I'll stand by you. But if you love me... let's love each other, live for me."

He cracks a smile, the first genuine smile I've seen in awhile. He leans back, "Are you high, yet?"

"Nope..."

"Want me to roll another blunt?"

"Yes, please!" I cheer, clapping my hands as he stands to head back inside. His butt was so nice and taut. "Babe, get me some more wine too!" I shout after him, already sipping on his glass.

He had woken up this morning with some major headache. He was claiming to be Ada or some creature from the other realm. I didn't understand what he was babbling about. Now, he seemed to be fine. He'll be heading off back to his world in Nadia. I'll be staying back in Naka with my father until the wedding arrangements could be formed. All I need to do is enjoy my night. Hopefully my good spirits will wear off on his eteranl melancholy.

CHAPTER 7

Drinking With the Devil

Morgan Ellys

I was done with my apprenticeship soon to be leaving La Vida, Naka attempting to rebuild my life and make a name for myself in a new continent. It didn't occur to me in the first few years that I had even died. Not until the visions and night terrors... Perhaps I always knew and repressed it. Three years later, this was the beginning of the downswing and I called up my current mentor to lift my spirits.

The man set to be my ward called me up before I could hit my apartment. Insisting I spent my birthday with him. He was excited to hear I was alive, though I'm not sure who told him. I don't quite know who knows I'm alive other than Rumya and a handful of Nadians. I didn't go out much since awakening in Graham in that basement. I made my way a few thousand miles West in Naka after my ordeal in Nadia.

I knew the location in Naka well enough. I had at been in the old capital Jardin a few times in my early training. It's where I met Carmen Cruz and Natalie Wolfe. Colin loved this Gentleman's Club in Jardin east of the city of La Vida. A small little town bred for big spenders and those who wanted their money. The former citizens only lived to serve the wealthy that used to the town to relieve themselves of sin and return to their lives of smiles and sanitation.

I sat alone at the bar, sipping a rock glass of Scotch.

When I had my first drink of whiskey at 16, Colin said, "Drink up boy, the burn will put hair on your balls." Over the years each sip lost its heat. Now, every bottle might as well be water. Maybe Ada could turn whiskey to wine. Maybe I'll get some satiety then.

I didn't see any other way out the trap. It didn't seem to matter who you were, didn't really matter if you were a dentist or just the garbage man. The whole world just flipped. Families dissolved. You could spend four years in school getting a degree to what end? Then have the levy of indentured servitude over your head for the rest of your life.

After leaving the Regulators, every sign pulled me back to business with Warren or Gregor. I take Warren up and continue patrolling the Void, and assassinating marks, this path nearly destroyed my home, even if I was never born there. I take Gregor up and could make billions through blood, sweat, and nepotism.

I didn't want a million dollars. I needed it. To just- escape all this shit. Everyone fell in the hole. I saw families up and leave the homes their families built because taxes skyrocketed. Their homes sold to people who couldn't afford them. Houses foreclosed for miles. Then the banks took everything. The families three times displaced before the banks sold the houses to another unwitting lot wanting their slice of "the good life". Millions homeless with more houses empty than ever before. So many starving while so much went to waste.

I didn't understand back then. Now, it had a sick justification I hated myself for having. Hell... I'm a man grown and I still don't get it. Capitalism never made sense to me. Open borders for corruption. What the people needed was never available. Instead they're constantly being sold some plastic crap. It was killing Gaia. These parasites would do anything to sell opportunity and convenience.

I left the devil of death, for the devil of debt & finance only to find out they are the same devil and had made it nowhere.

Few eating the most from everyone's plate then feeding them damn scraps of their own plates. The recession was painful. The backs of the original Nakans broke heaving up the exorbitant nation's rising elitists. Where there was once warmth around the fire in the days of the Dragon, so many were still left in the cold. And those backs never healed under the Gregor Family. But the Gregors keep on building regardless, building a generational wealth upon the backs of those who wanted so desperately to be rich. Instead of uprising against The Gregor Family the people of Naka worship Colin Gregor as Enshishi. Even his enemies see him as a Guardian for him simply not ending their lives.

I could go on and on breathing the bible of debt and capitalism. But what a hypocrite I would be. I'm nearly a multibillionaire. I should be happy. I should be overjoyed but in the pit of my stomach. I think being broke was better. Before the women, the accolades, and the opulence I buried myself in, in order to find peace within myself. No peace felt better than watching the last Regulator fall a few years ago.

"How are you doing, ole boy?" My father-in-law sat down next to me at the rather vacant country club bar. He wore a blue sports coat and beige pants. Dressed down for the evening I see. It was a wonder there was ever enough fabric to fit his 13 ft frame. Warren and Colin brimmed with Guardian Energy. Both were giants among most men. "You look like shit." He chuckles waving over the bartender, a girl with tan skin and auburn hair.

I grunt not bothering to respond. My usual tone whenever I was addressed with something or anything these days.

"In my own name!" his favorite phrase, damnation and blasphemy to the Father, "We're here to celebrate your night and you look like a damn corpse, boy."

"This doesn't feel like anything. Just the same incentives you've been giving me just more drugs and women." I yawned. "Perhaps that was what was ragging me dry."

Trying to keep up with the devil himself in the world of vice and naughty deeds was a dead's man journey alone. I had more living to do than trying to impress Colin in his own game. I was brought back from the dead to endure an entire life of this?

"What?" Colin rubs the bridge of his nose with frustration, "the hell is this supposed to feel like, son? The night hasn't even begun!" he slams his hand on the bar. "This is a goddamn emergency. I need two jack and cokes, a rum and tonic, and two shots of your finest Scotch, now! And some coke if you're hiding it up your snatch tonight." he shouts at the bartender.

The bartender begins. "Sir, I'm dealing with another-

"Who do you think is gonna have the fatter tab at the end of the night? Me or that needle dicked faggot?" he stared the other patron in the eyes daring him to say something. "Get that sweet ass over here and serve me! In my name, I demand it!"

"That's- that's fine Tiffany, go ahead. I can wait." the renowned owner of the steel mills cowered before Colin. "Jah'Enshishi, all praise is his I swear!" he raises a shaking glass. "Please, let me buy you a drink."

"I don't need your fucking pleading, Davison. Just sit the hell down and mind your fucking manners you're being loud." Colin curses at the man then turns his attention to Tiffany. His demeanor switched up. He extended his hand, "How are you doing there, beautiful? Do you dance as well or do they keep you behind the bar?"

"Just a bartender, Mr. Gregor." she had a polite smile, but an underlying settlement of irritation and fear. She concealed it well. Almost as if she was used to the feeling but never quite over it. Especially not with the Patriarch staring you down ready to take whatever he wanted.

Tiffany reminded me of one my Kandakes when they're hit on at the bar. I switched to a bartending staff of young handsome men, saved on the harassment. I lost a few thousand a month in tips, but I had extra security when needed, something I thought far more valuable. However, after a few months the handsome men bring in more females, who strangely loved seeing other women naked, and the female clientele brought in more men. My club, Rumya dubbed The Crown. Her management accounted for a few millions but it was my work in bridging Naka and Nadia bringing me billions.

I should make a visit and check on Rumya before I go home. It's been long since she's shared my bed. I'll need her after all this.

"How about you have a couple drinks with my son-in-law and me, huh?" Colin winked, rubbing her chin gently. His hand the size of her head damn near.

She looked to me. I offered her little in the way of neither support nor interest. All I needed to do was keep Colin's dick out of her. I found that being my usual job when young ladies came around us. Colin was incorrigible. However, the more he drunk the more needed to make a point of his power. Usually taking it out on young girls, at times I felt compelled to come solely to protect his victims from him. Luckily he mostly drank in his own castle these days. Oddly, the town wasn't too far from his property.

"I- I'm not allowed." Tiffany lied.

"I'll buy the place and have your boss stripped to his jockeys so you can ramrod him all ya want. How about that? You can have Davison as your footstool for the night if I so bid it. Whatever you want, what's going to put a smile on your beautiful face?"

"Ramrod?" she asked confused.

Colin leaned over and whispered it in her ear. Tiffany covered her mouth and shook her head in disgust.

"If you don't like the sound of that, I can ramrod you a bit later instead, how about it, sweetie?"

She looked to me once more with pleading eyes under her cool. As if she knew I knew I could stop it if I chose.

"Um, Mr. Ellys, can I help you with anything else?" Tiffany came over to me.

"You're focusing on me." Colin snaps his fingers at her. "What, you like him more than me? Well there you fucking go then. Suck his dick then. It's a celebration all the same. Well, that's appropriate I suppose she's more your age. Come around this bar and pleasure my friend now."

"Come on now, Colin. Let the girl do her damn job. Not tonight alright?" I groaned already not in the mood.

"Not tonight? Every night! What is wrong with you, boy?" Colin lost the little interest he had and turned back to me. "Hurry up with those damn drinks would you? You're taking forever." He barks over the bar as if he wasn't just trying to seduce her.

Tiffany left us relieved, pouring the drinks with lightning speed and going back to the Steel Tycoon, Davison at the end of the bar.

"We toast to wealth, health and good pussy, salud!" Colin cheers, holding up the Scotch.

I toss my shot back like it was water and chase it with the jack and coke with the same blasé boredom.

"That was a double shot of Howard Hursh's best goddamn Scotch. I've set men on fire with that proof. And you just drank it like tap water. What the hell is going on here Morgan?" Colin sat lowering his voice.

"I already told you."

"Are you sick or something?" his form of sympathy.

I never trusted Colin as a man, but I did trust him as family and a mentor. I know he had no idea what I felt. But he knew what it was like to bear my burden. Though, he shouldered it with an arrogance and belligerence I found admirable and spent so much of my life trying to emulate but couldn't. Colin's ferocious tenacity and Warren's cold-edged patience were my building blocks. It left me with nothing but confusion, pain, and death. I was neither of those men. I never will be. Those they have both been me before and were further on this path than I had ever been. So, I watched and listened... waiting to make my own trail.

"I thought once I broke the millions mark I was supposed to be happy. I dropped my whole life for this... For one billion dollars and it feels like it did when I was fucking dead. I just feel like I've wasted my time searching for more absence."

"As profound as you think you sound. It's only a billion. A billion is the new 6 figures." Colin shrugs, "like a bachelor's degree being the new diploma. You're just getting started Morgan. The good feelings don't come from money. It comes from having enough wealth to last yourself and your generations. What you're looking for comes with power, glory, and respect. That's just the market we're in right now. It's for the illustrious and the influential only. You don't want all these vagrants and pests, with their hands on your wealth, these beggars and their failed causes. I'm trying to get you into the select group before the doors close completely. Pretty soon you will only be wealthy if born into it. The doors are about to close for the majority of people. I have a plan to secure your family for generations."

"I have to do more of this shit?" I growl, "I thought it was just a billion Colin... This business shit isn't my steez man. I'm not trying to be trapped in a suit for the next 3 to 5 years."

Colin grins slapping my shoulders, "you may not have to, boy. Put a damn smile on and take some pride in your goddamn accomplishment." He pats my back. "I have a grand plan. I've been working up with Warren these past few years."

I muster up a smile taking in a bit of his warmth. Colin always had this aura of confidence and charismata. He's the type of man who says he'll make it to the moon and then spend the rest of his life jogging the distance on a treadmill then say 'Look I fucking made it!'

He always found a way to applaud himself for something. And since we've been mentor and protégé, I suppose he found ways to applaud me as well as of late. Warren withheld affection. He's just that type of man, wounded and his heart was cartelized from the pain of eternal war. Colin's love for himself was contagious and washed over to those immediately around him before the fires evaporated what washed over from his cup.

"I guess you're right." I smile sipping the rum and tonic, not my favorite but nor was sobriety as of late.

"You guess? I don't need a guess. You're goddamn right, I'm right." Colin slaps my back with a bellowing laugh.

"Ha. I suppose so."

Colin growled. "Get this man, another shot. Maybe then he'll find his damn smile and wits." Colin bangs on the bar once more. "You're really starting to kill my mood, son."

"I wasn't aware that was possible, sir." I push the rum forward as the liquor starts to take effect.

He grinned, "Ha, as if I would let some runt ruin my damn night. Not once, not ever, not now, not tomorrow. Get your shit together." He grips my shoulders and shakes me. "I have great news for you!"

"The marriage...?" I ask, knowing Colin and Warren always had preferred interest in who I would marry. "Who was your proposal your daughter or Leslie?"

He froze and stared at me. "I will slap that shit out of you, you pussy eating runt. I wanted to say it!" he threw a small tantrum slapping his full glass clear across the room. "You do not interrupt a man's damn speech!"

Colin fumed slamming his fist straight through the bar counter.

I chuckle, "Halle told me earlier today. Plus it was pretty obvious more so after you called me your son."

Colin rubs my shoulders with an uncomfortably tight grip. "Boy, if I wanted to kill you. I would have killed you ten times over, ten years ago, with ten goddamn bullets if I pleased. But I didn't. So, here you are, alive. Well, healthy, and a billionaire all by your hand and my design! Smile before I take it all back." He sighed but it wasn't long before his smile returned, "You're going to be my son-in-law and preside over the greatest wealth on Gaia. How about it boy? Be my ward, learn from me. And when I die on my 60th Birthday as all the greatest Gregor Men, you will be my heir."

"You say it as if I have a choice." I discretely wave down Tiffany for a refill. She quickly serves us another round then retreats.

"You're goddamn right you don't!" Colin laughs, "Tiffany bring that sweet, tender ass over here and get us two more shots, hell four more. I'll celebrate for this fucker."

I took the shot from the bartender and held it up, "Salud."

"Sal- motherfucking- lud." Colin toasts with me, and throws his shot back. "Holy shit!" he spits out a breath of fire, coughing.

He had a fit of laughter, calling over another round of shots to keep himself going. I swore the man was 75% 100 proof vodka rather than water.

I drank my whiskey and wiped my mouth. "I think I'm going to call it a night. I have to be at the construction site in the morning. And I want to stop by the Crown, and check on my girls tonight."

"I'll be damned if you leave me alone. This is our night as father and son. We're going out!"

"You aren't my father yet, Colin... You can hold ten guns to my head. This isn't ten years ago. This is today." I had been out of the mood for the past hours. He was standing between me and keeping my girls safe from men like him.

"Warren isn't here to protect you, boy." Colin's favorite threat, "I suggest you sit down. I can be rather violent when I don't get my way. Been that way since I was a boy and it isn't changing soon. Your birthday is my birthday, you better celebrate."

"Nor is he here to protect you." We make eye contact and he relents, "Good night, Patriarch Gregor. I'll see you at the shotgun wedding. I'll be moving out of Naka within the week." I throw him deuces and sulk off.

"Smile dammit! You're going to become a Gregor!" he shouts after me.

"I'm too drunk and miserable to smile." I wave letting out a sigh, trying to find a good place to blink.

I passed by familiar faces, but none I called friend. They smiled and raised their drinks to me. 'I remember you from such gala...' or 'I was reading in the paper, congrats on your new club, good luck kid.'

They hadn't an idea who I was only that I had a billion dollars but what else mattered to these people? Despite how they viewed the world, they saw me as one of their own. I was the man who killed fifty of their best hired guns and protectors. I was the man who gave up his life to end their sycophantic tyranny. All they had for me was smiles, cheers, and good fortune. Malzov Tal, this world made no sense.

I promised I didn't share the same connection. I felt more at ease with my men from the worksite, building up in Exigo back in Nadia or in the Clementine Forest territory, on the borderlands of Naka and Nadia. I don't know. Those men knew me. These men barely knew themselves. They knew spreadsheets and value. They knew how to sit on their asses and look important. But when their toilets clogged they picked up the phone before a plunger.

They have no issue watching people starve and suffer in the name of wealth. The more I progress in this life. The more I inherently see the flaws and sin. But this is the only way. How do I save this city and keep my soul intact? When the only way to do anything is money?

Is that what I must sacrifice for my dreams to come to fruition?

The only hand extended is Colin's... Perhaps it's time I take it instead of being so defiant. I'm not even sure why I feel this way. I'm having fun aren't I? I'm enjoying myself. There are beautiful women about. But-something deep inside me said there was more to life. This all seems inevitable and with Colin's wealth. The things I could accomplish are boundless. But the same feeling assured me, I could do what I needed without any of the wealth.

In a battle I can win, in a war that I know, with blood, fists and swords. The wealthy are cowards. They hire others to do their work. I'll take my fortune as I know how. I didn't have the stomach to allow another to die for me. Nor the vanity to allow others to work while I was idly by watching and cracking the whip taking all the credit. I trusted my employees, all of them. And they all trusted me.

Looking back... those moments with Colin, listening to his outbursts, watching how he carries himself. He was still a child, in that huge body. He believed himself Gilgamesh, behaved much like him too. But Gilgamesh was redeemed in the end. He didn't die a monster or a tyrant... I'm not sure Colin will meet the same fate. He just wanted to spend his money, drink himself, ingest anything in front of him, and fuck any woman that moved. He wanted all the benefits of being a King without the work or being a role-model. And with 40 years of his partying... he wants me to take his life and assume the businesses he failed to manage or operate.

Looking back... I was far too trusting. I was sitting in the presence of the devil himself waiting for him to become Sovereign. He saw me as his sovereign, I was the one he chose to cleanup his mess. And everyone will say, 'Look at what his father-in-law taught him and left him' instead of saying "Look at the brilliance and acumen of Morgan Ellys."

I couldn't see in my youth. Blinded, trying to impress everyone but myself. I wanted to please all factors against my own inclinations of right and wrong. The lives I took and the women I hurt. And I'm to marry a girl as sweet and innocent as Halle Gregor?

Those moments... that year began my descent into this deep depression. I used to blame him, I used to blame myself. But the only thing I truly held in disgust all these years was becoming another Ray Warren or Colin Gregor. I want to be my own man... I want to do things my own way, with the people I love and cherish. Not out of mutual dependency and my hubris. No... In Nadia we will be as one until we unite as Ecru once more.

They will rue the day they stood against Nadia. No. We will not befriend. We will not war. We will prosper. Remove all shackles of dependency and prosper while they scurry for new backs to carry the burden of their endless greed. And if they wish to stand against Nadia then they will break under their conditions of war. We fight for liberation. They fight for greed. I fight by my men and their men are hired mercenaries with no loyalty.

With Colin's wealth what should take generations will take years. I wouldn't have to worry about fixing homes or the area. I could fix my people and give them the careers of fixing their own communities, the only job that mattered in Nadia.

But with my own works and status, I could do more. It'll be harder work but I will save Nadia.

I was once willing to sell my soul to preserve the lives of my people. Before I knew the value of human life, before I knew the value of my own life... before I came to love Halle or Natalie. I will gladly die once more for its freedom. To live in the glory of refusing the devil and overcoming regardless of what he threw at me. This seems far more of my path.

I'm unsure of who will fight alongside me. I had few allies. I had few associates I kept contact with over these years. I will simply have to finesse this on my own. Hold faith in my women to stand by me in my strength and weakness. And create a pathway for Nadia to prosper and grow into its former glory. This is my charge. I must still find some solution for the wedding. Could I still possibly wed Halle without being bonded to Colin's whims?

I remember spending the rest of the evening those years ago with Rumya. Right before leaving for my last mission, she was such a sweet girl yet I resist any time with her over these years. Praying she had found freedom from waiting for me return. Rubbing my back and telling me we'll stack paper until we could buy all the territory we needed in Nadia. She was my Kandake, my warrior queen. I wonder what she would say if she saw me now, ha.

A few days ago I was my worst when I showed up a mummy on her doorstep. Now I'm in Jardin with The Patriarch Colin Gregor. Giving up the dreams of wealth and grandeur, giving up the hookers and strippers, freebies and accolades to go straight and run a city.

Though, I don't think Halle or Natalie would allow room for a third woman in my life. They had their hands full enough trying to get rid of each other. I'll let them focus on such things. I'll concern myself with Nadia. This is a King's duty, no?

If they had worked as friends I wonder what good we could have brought unifying their families' blood feud. Instead the eternal war continues. Warren told me the eternal war wasn't fought on the battlefield. It's fought every day and makes the battlefield inevitable. If you could win the eternal war you could have peace yet no man has solved it yet.

CHAPTER 8

Old Soul

Morgan Ellys

Somedays I wish I could smile with the genuine happiness I see in other people. They laugh joke and go about life as though there's no hardship or problems. Their undeserved bliss is enviable. When they meet issues, their initial instinct is to complain, to balk, or to just ignore them. I wish I surrendered so easily, instead I toil on or drive my mind rampant with worries as to what's wrong. It's driven me insane. Even being left alone with my own idleness, my brain never stops... things to be done, worries and frets, I used to not get sleep.

Insomnia it's called.

My mind would just be left on.

Will... Peace of mind... Everyone else seems to have it.

They prattle on and on about what celebrity wears what, what's happening in Esha or Erdu, or just binge on television. Those things never interested me, at least not enough to be my sole source of entertainment or all I had to offer to a conversation.

Since I was a boy, I felt off. As if I was seeing something no one else could. Or-

"Mr. Ellys, your accountant is here. Would you like for me to send her in?" Teddy spoke through the intercom across the room on my desk.

I poke open an eye from my lounge couch and let out a labored groan. My back cracked as I stood up. My neck throbbed. I limped over to my desk, my hips far too tight. I didn't take my pain pills. I hate pills... Cavemen just fought through it. Crushed up a poultice then sang prayers to their maker, and a bit of wishful thinking. I'll live. I plop in my office chair, happy to be off my feet again.

"Mr. Ellys, are you alright?"

"Yes, I'm here Terrance."

"Terry, sir..." We've talked about it time after time. My memory has been slipping from me these days. "Should I send Ms. Wolfe back?"

"Yes, Terrance, I mean Terry... apologies for the formality good sir."

The line went quiet giving me a moment's reprise. I took a moment to breathe counting "1-2-3-4-5-6-7-8-9-10..." deep breaths to center myself.

The door pushed open and a woman already rather tall, now wearing heels. Her legs were so shapely and slender but her pumps and stocking made her irresistible. She wore a bespoke pinstripe dress suit, sewn by a friend of her family. This one cut off mid-thigh, enough to have my man's attention. She flashed me a bright smile, the best orthodontic work money could afford.

"Hey, how are you babe?" She said in her smoky voice once the door was closed.

"Natalie." I responded with a curt acknowledgement.

She was thrown off by my distance. She raised a brow and laughed it off uneasily, taking a seat across from mine, the other chair given to her purse.

"You okay? You look terrible." she crosses those long legs over the other and smiles. "I missed you, babe. I wanted to check up on you for lunch."

"I haven't been sleeping and-

"Is your back still bothering you?"

"Yeah..." I sighed, "I have to tell you something grim."

"Did you take your medication?" she took my silence as her answer. Natalie frowned, "I assumed. Your voicemail was rather sullen. I wish you weren't so cryptic."

"I'm just not sure how to tell you. I wanted it to be face to face."

"Just tell me..." she sighs, "You're just making me nervous, ha. Come on, I'm tough."

I rub my temples, "I've been promised to another woman recently... to Halle." I let out a sigh. "Colin wants us together. There was little I could do, less I could say."

The color flushed out Natalie's face and she covered her mouth. She opened her mouth but only managed to stammer as anger flashed through her veins turning her olive-skin red.

"How...? Why would you... when?" she frowned trying not to break into tears.

"Take a breath."

She never listened, "when did all this happen?"

"Well, I suppose in Colin's mind it's been happening for sometime. But, we went to the bar over the weekend, and he told me he planned on wedding me to Halle."

"That's one thing about you cheating but- marriage? Marriage, Morgan? We never even spoke about it, now- We have years together, what did I do to push you to marry her?"

I thump my temple repeatedly, the constant pressing releasing pressure, "It's- the situation isn't like that. Neither of us proposed. I've been promised. It's to the same. The marriage is being arranged."

Natalie only took a moment to put the fragmented story together, "how did her father find out?"

I shrug, "he walked in on us. But- it seemed too convenient. He didn't ask. There was no real discussion. He told me I was marrying his daughter."

Natalie's tears rolled down her face, "why didn't you two say something?"

"Halle wasn't there. It-

I take a breath, "You can't refuse a Gregor, Natalie. Especially, when I'm staring The Patriarch of the Gregor family in the face, he could have shot me."

"This doesn't make sense! You two are moving straight to marriage?"

"I took her virginity... in your little threesome plan. It was to be promised to her betrothed. Now, it's me."

"You were Halle's first?" she said out of disbelief rather than a genuine question.

"He walked right in on us..." I lean back, "she had been probing me and probing me. I kept trying to tell you but you brushed it off, as you do everything I say. She said it would just be sex then- Colin Gregor himself stepped right in with a bold grin and a silver and gold Beretta pointed at my skull. He said I betrayed him. I was supposed to be his Ward and I was fucking his daughter." Then he congratulated me on it repeatedly for weeks, telling me I was lucky and would be happy.

"Why were you even doing it there? This doesn't feel right Morgan. Why would Halle even put you in that situation? Halle isn't that dumb. She knew-

Natalie stopped, "She would have known Morgan, Halle would have known!"

I shrug, "I just thought you should know."

"Do you love her?"

I sighed.

"Morgan!"

"I find it hard to resist the feelings I have for her... She's beautiful, we have chemistry, and our connection seems like it's from so past life. I'm not sure if we're in love but- I'm fine with this decision. I'm fine leaving this life for her to be happy."

"You bastard, how dare you?"

"Natalie... I've been trying to tell you. You kept brushing it off!"

"This is my fault, now? You couldn't keep your dick out of that maniac's daughter and it's my fault?"

"That's not what I'm saying!"

"Then what are you saying?"

I sigh... you can tell a woman a thousand times. They never listened. "It doesn't matter." I take a moment to look over at my girlfriend before my demise. "I'm not sure there's anything we can do- I just- I didn't want you to hear it from anyone else. I haven't even gotten my own mind wrapped around it. It's only been a few days I've known. I just- I thought telling you was the decent thing to do."

Natalie covers her eyes, "I- I can't believe she would do this to me. I can't believe she would just take you like this. It's not right!"

I nod unsure of what I could possibly add, better off letting her grieve.

"Do you love me, Morgan?"

"I did... once. I tried, and you made it very difficult to want to be with you. Maybe it was me, maybe it was you. I don't care to know anymore. I'm sure it'll bother me. But, I'll figure it out on my own as I do the rest of my issues. Good luck, Natalie."

She smiled for a brief moment before her tears returned. She let out a sigh. Her mascara had run down her cheeks.

"I can't just take this, Morgan. We can't! We're in love. We have to do something."

I shift uneasily, unsure of how to tell her. I settled on "No..."

"What?"

"I loved you, Natalie. But no."

"You want her?" Natalie was flabbergasted.

"I'm not saying that- I – Colin held a gun to my head but when he lowered it, he extended a hand. We ate steaks. We spoke. I haven't even met your parents... in five years. I loved you but- our relationship, that isn't something I'm going back to you hiding me, ducking, and being confided. When does that end?"

"Babe, my parents aren't very open to the idea..."

"I'm good enough for Colin Gregor but not for your family?"

She was speechless.

Nor did I expect a response.

"I thought I had time." Natalie's tears dried, she said it quietly and thoughtfully. "I thought you were here to stay..."

"Time is finite Natalie..." I take a sigh, "I just wanted to tell you, as your boyfriend, as your lover, and as a man, it seemed like the only decent thing to do. To tell you straight up so you didn't hear it from anyone else. I love you, Natalie. But I'm not going to be with someone ashamed of me. Not when another woman is attempting to make me a King."

"I'm not ashamed of you baby, I love you and you love me." She manages to sob from behind her hands and tears. She reaches for my hands and I let her go.

"Nat... you know where I came from. I can't go back. I can't live that way again because of you."

"You're an asshole! Why are you being such an asshole!? You're supposed to love me!" her tears turn straight to boiling fumes. She snatches up her things and storms off. "This isn't over Morgan, I'll be back!"

I didn't expect her to understand. I just wanted her to know. There's no going back to that. There's no going back to any of it. I can be a Gregor...

CHAPTER 9

Lunch with Friends

Natalie Wolfe

Halle sat across from me applying her makeup as if it was no big deal. The rock sat on her finger shining in the sun.

"He's taking me to the movies tomorrow! It's not a grand opening or anything but it's sweet."

"I really don't want to hear about it, Halle."

"Are you still upset?"

"It's been a month!"

She lets out an exasperated sigh, "a whole 30 days."

"I'm having lunch with you, Halle. I should be strangling you."

"Why are you mad at me? I didn't even do anything. I just woke up and daddy let me know I'm marrying Morgan!"

"Fuck you, you don't have to sound so excited."

"What? Ha, why... He's incredible."

"I know he's my boyfriend."

"Not anymore..."

"Excuse me?"

"I'm engaged to him!"

"Halle. You're not even going to try to help me?"

"Ha, Nat, this situation is so much more complicated than you think it is. I don't have any control. It's all Dad and Morgan."

"What the hell was that asshole thinking?"

Halle shrugs, "I let the men speak."

"That's so weird... You go home and play princess."

"I don't play princess. I am a princess."

"An heiress..."

"It's basically the same thing as a princess." She shrugs, "I did hear Daddy say once Morgan takes over. We'll have a real kingdom."

"What?"

Halle shrugs, "girl... I'm just happy I got married to Morgan and not one of my dad's partners or one of their sons. All praises to my father, Enshishi!"

"Halle, I don't get how you can be so happy with yourself. Do you not even feel a little remorse?"

"I feel like... A little bit. If it was anyone else we would be stomping that bitch's face in, burning her fake ass Prada and Gucci handbags and make their daddy's bankrupt. You know I got you. It's me!" Halle smiles brightly, "he's so damn handsome and smooth-

"You got him from me!"

"I know. God, I can't wait until we move back in together."

"You two still haven't?"

Halle shakes her head. "My dad's been keeping me here until marriage." Halle smiled, "But we fool around. Babe teleports and shit, so he'll blink over to see while everyone is asleep but he says it's dangerous if my father caught us."

"I guess if I was going to lose my virginity it would be Morgan. Oh wait. I did. Help me get my man back Halle!" I groan.

Halle groans, "Just be happy for me. We can share, Nat. I want to get married to Morgan. You don't! I never said you had to leave. You kicked us out."

"I'm pretty sure he doesn't want to get married either if your dad is involved."

"But he is getting married! And I'm excited for my wedding! You, as my friend should too. Will you be one my bridesmaids? I already asked Carmen to be my Maid-of-Honor."

"No I won't. I'm not going to your damn wedding."

"Uhhh...you're my best friend. If you're not on my side then who will be? Come on Natalie, you did nothing but complain your entire relationship with him. Let us be happy."

"Halle..." Natalie rubs her temples. "I cannot begin to articulate how self-centered you're being. You're marrying my boyfriend!"

"You break up with him every other night for no good reason! I'm marrying Morgan Ellys. Halle Ellys! That sounds so good together. Oh, what if I hyphenate it? Halle Victoriana Gregor-Ellys! I love this! We're going to be so happy together!"

"Halle!"

"My happiness is making it very hard to want to be sad with you... Why don't you try being happy for me. It'll feel better!" She smiles brightly as blissful as could be.

"Halle I could kick your ass. All happy and shit, who the hell do you think you are?"

"Well, I know I am Halle Victoriana Gregor." She grins ear to ear. "Don't forget, hyphen Ellys!"

"How could you be so happy to be married?"

"I'm marrying one of my best friends. I'm getting married to Morgan! I get to be his right hand forever. The sex with someone you love has been so bomb this year."

"He doesn't love you."

"Well, not yet but we're definitely compatible, the sex is great and he genuinely cares about me. I don't know he isn't like anyone here in Naka. He's not in it for the money or power. It's his duty. I respect it. I'm not sure how to describe our feelings. When I think love, I think cupcakes or vacations. I feel- at peace with him, safe and genuinely cared for by him. It's not like sunshine and rainbows. It's more like the warmth you feel from the sun."

"You get married because you love someone."

"You get married to make your family stronger. At least that's what daddy says. If a marriage makes you weaker it's a waste and it'll only end in ruin. Why get married or bump skins with someone who will end your bloodline in a couple generations? I'm going to make Morgan beautiful babies."

"Your father doesn't care if the two people aren't even happy together? That sounds like Colin, anything for making him more money."

"We discussed disrespecting my dad, Nat... it's about power. With Morgan leading our family, father believes we could create a new history. We could finally take control of Gaia instead of being restricted to Naka. With Morgan we can gain control over Erdu and Nadia as well."

"I'm fuming. You're rubbing your marriage in my face. I already lost my best friend I don't want to lose you too."

"I'm not your best friend?"

"Morgan was my best friend. At least he was once." I sigh.

"That's so sweet." Halle coos, "but since I wasn't your best friend I guess I really don't have to care after all."

"Halle..."

"I'm serious Natalie. I'm not interested in helping you two at all. We can be friends! Now, Morgan is off limits. I tried helping you two. You did everything possible to self-sabotage your relationship."

"I shared him with you."

"Yeah... look how that ended up. You were caught slipping. He definitely didn't think you were friends. He said he thinks you hate him."

"He hates me! And he won't admit it. He won't just say it. He hates me..." Natalie paused and places her head in my hands. "He won't even speak to me. He pretends I don't exist and he seriously just... kills you."

Halle shrugged. "I have no idea what you're talking about."

"You'll find out eventually. He isn't what I thought he was. I don't know what I think anymore but I know I want him back." I decided firmly.

"I haven't started thinking about it. Waitress! Waitress! Hey, I'm ready to order!" Halle begins to wave down the server at the service station who comes over with a smile and her damn camera for a selfie with us.

"Are you really not even listening to me?" Natalie rolled her eyes. "I can't believe you."

I put on my best smile momentarily for the picture then go back to chastising Halle.

"Oh my god, oh my god, shut the fuck up. I swear to my father if you keep going I'm gonna smack you. How long have I listened to you, Natalie? For yeeaars I have given you advice and respected you and Morgan. I even kept your secret. Can't you stop being so selfish and be happy for me? I'm getting married to the man I love regardless of who he is to you or how he feels about me. If we're friends, you should be happy for me."

"You said it yourself. You're not my friend. So I don't have to give a fuck about your feelings. Enjoy your meal, you stupid bitch." I stand up and begin storming off.

"Natalie, wait!"

"What Halle!" I shout turning around.

"You should still RSVP for when you get over it. You don't want to miss it. My wedding is going to be amazing guest list closes at the end of the month. So you have at least a couple weeks to cool off."

CHAPTER 10

Sunset

Carmen Cruz

Morgan's birthday was yesterday, he's usually a brooding mess of indecision around this time. I usually avoid him whenever it comes around until a few days after. He told me once, his birthday only reminded him of how alone he was, and all he lost.

I guess I don't fucking exist, selfish insensitive asshole.

I tried spending it with him once but we ended up fighting the whole time. I never made that mistake again!

We shared one thing in common. We grew up in The Academy far from our parents. Morgan never knew his parents or his homeland of Nadia. He came to The Academy at I was orphaned... for undisclosed reasons to the public. I met him through Patriarch Colin Gregor.

When we were girls the Patriarch told the three of us, Me, Natalie and Halle, that Morgan Ellys will be Enshishi. Setting a competition amongst us over who would be his Queen. We organized to work together but the will to compete was always our biggest problem. The rivalry, fake friendship was always so petty. He was the only thing we agreed on and loved.

I was his lover for many years in our childhood. We had arguments and fights. I was the only one to ever be with him until I graduated from The Academy as Colin's star pupil. Sadly, I'm a bit older than him, leaving him for all types of chicks trying to replace me.

I was too concerned with public appearances to speak to him in the open. Afraid of what people would think about us. Natalie, terrified of her parents and how they would skin them both alive and have a new kid or adopt to replace her. Halle, simply never got a chance, too young and she was being kept for marriage.

Whoever married Enshishi would be the most powerful force on the planet. We loved him dearly, but neither of us was brave enough to truly... date him. Always rendezvous and hidden, even amongst each other we kept our secrets, outright lying to each other about being with him. Such a damn shame, I always had inklings of suspicion they were hiding something from me. Over the years our relationship has become so strained.

Morgan's birthday left him vulnerable, weak, and depressed. Most importantly it left my precious vicar lonely. These are all unbefitting of the next Enshishi. He would need a woman by his side who can understand what he's going through. Not one of these thots who just want to talk about his feelings. He needs someone who knows how to love him the way only he can be loved. The Lion will gladly be consumed by the Wolf, all the Dread Wolf must do is eat, and The Lion must lead. I wonder how hungry Morgan's been. Someone must fuel his fire and his ambition, to give him the hunger and power befitting a man of his stature.

I gave my beloved a ring on his cellphone, wanting to wish him a happy belated. Hopefully meet up after a few years of being on his bad side.

"What's the word, bird?" he greets me with a surprising joy.

"Happy belated birthday, baby, are you doing anything tonight?" I matched his energy.

"Eh... not really, a good friend just left to head home to Esha. That took out my plans for the night. I was hoping to be with them tonight." he sighed with a clear sign of sadness and disappointment. "How about you, what do you have planned?"

"With them...What happened to wanting to be alone on your birthday?" I scoff, "Why didn't you call me?"

"Well... I didn't call them either, she was my neighbor. I chilled, she chilled with me. Her mother is sick so she left for Esha." I could imagine that stupid matter-of-factly smile on his face. "What's up with you?"

"I'm in the Zilaypenah area filming my show... I was hoping you would want to meet up for some loving and dinner." I giggled hoping to warm his heart.

"No, I don't want to go on your show. You know what happened last time. I think I might just go downtown and take myself to dinner. A good friend told me to date myself. Spend some time getting to know myself."

"That is the dumbest thing I ever heard. Morgan... you know yourself. You're Captain Ellys, Lord Luno, and Vicar of Enshishi. Come on, baby. I didn't get to spend your birthday with you. I want to see you."

He sighed, "Carmen, that's not who I am... that's all you wanted me to be. I'm done with the Regulators and I'm done with Colin Gregor."

I had to take a moment to gather myself and make sense of what he was saying to me. Did this woman turn him? Where has he been these past years to make him say something so blasphemous!? Colin isn't going to want to hear any of this and Enshishi will be even more upset Morgan is turning to the enemy's side.

"How could you say any of this, Morgan... where have you been?"

"Dead for two years then in Naka most of this year, I've been- look, I'm not interested in more female issues."

"I wasn't aware I was an issue, baby." I say innocently, "Where are you going to eat? We can double masturdate. I need to get to know myself better as well, and would love to get to know this new you. Then maybe, hook up after with both our discovered selves. It'll be a nice foursome you, yourself with me and I."

He chuckled, "I don't know Carmen. I was going to walk around town. Stop wherever I felt like eating."

"Those are hard details to follow, Morgan. Are you ducking me?" I asked irritated, "Baby, you're not being fair."

"How long do you celebrate your birthday?"

"All month..."

"And what do you do?"

"I have an extravaganza! I go to all my favorite bars and clubs, I limit my recordings, and I take a vacation to the beaches in Maya and Naka. And enjoy my adoring friends and fans sending me gifts across the world." I clap hoping he was going to finally take some of my advice and listen to me.

"Well, I'm having an introvaganza. I'm going to be alone. Do what I enjoy most. Head to the mountains build my cabin and homestead. I don't have friends. I don't have fans. I don't enjoy bars and clubs. And I'm going to find out what the hell is inside of me." He sighed, "I'm not interested in what you want from me, Carmen. I need more than drugs, sex and money."

"You can't do that! I want to be with you! What if you have a mission or something?"

"I don't do work in the Regulators anymore, didn't you hear me? I've been dead for two years. I resigned." he sighs, "I guess you haven't heard any of the news."

"Haven't heard!? I know everything, Morgan! How dare you!" I snap at him, "You're being a selfish jerk right now, you know that?"

"Hmm... then what am I? Why bother with me?" Morgan asks chuckling, "Since you apparently know so much, enlighten me."

"You are Luno... you are to be Enshishi when you kill Colin and become the Lord Commissioner of the Regulator Regime. You are going to be the strongest man on Gaia and, as we discussed, I am to be your wife! You will be the strongest man on the planet, and I'll be your handler to make sure the sheeple and lemmings follow you."

"I slayed the Dread Wolf, I have no interest being associated with Colin or the Gregor Family. And as I said, I am no longer affiliated with the Regulator Regime. I'm sorry to inform you, Carmen. I know you had a high stake in my success but- it's of no interest to me. I've been under the radar for awhile. I rather enjoy infamy and peace."

"Infamy... Morgan, you're supposed to be my saving grace! Who the hell is going to protect me now!? Morgan! Answer me Morgan!"

"Well, I'm sorry to disappoint you. Death wasn't too kind upon me. It's changed my allegiances and my mind on many things. I'm afraid I'm not the man you wished for me to be."

He hung up the line.

I was fuming, terrified, trying to catch my breath and gather my thoughts. He was off the grid. My Vicar was going off the fucking grid! What, what am I going to do?

I called Morgan back but it went straight to voicemail.

I dialed a new number in my phone, tapping my foot aggravated. Being kept out the loop was one thing, but he threw me off completely with this madness. He wasn't only giving up everything I worked so hard for but he was trying to leave the world!? I had to get answer fast. I hated being out of the loop.

"Hey, girl what's up?" Natalie picked up.

"Hey... I wanted to ask you for a favor. It's Morgan's belated birthday. Can we go visit him?"

Natalie groaned, "I don't want to talk to you about Morgan. Ask Halle."

"What the fuck- I thought you couldn't wait to get close to him?" there was something fishy going on, something very strange I needed to get to the bottom to. "Natalie, what happened with you two?"

"Carmen, why are you calling me, for what?" she asked even more irritated.

"You better watch who the hell you're talking to Wolfe!" I snarl sharply, her senior and before them both in line for Morgan's affection. "I'm not having a good day. I wanted to go for a date with baby boy but he's talking about going off the grid. He's saying he isn't Luno and doesn't want to be known as Enshishi. What the hell is happening?"

"Well, I hear him and his girlfriend had issues. Maybe he's just showing how weak he is... running away like he always does." Natalie mutters under her breath, "So, what if he's not the Guardian of Fire, I can do much better job than he ever could!"

"Morgan does not run. Morgan doesn't fear anything." I say in retaliation, "What happened with you two?"

"Nothing, Carmen, damn why are you being so nosy? Call Halle with this bullshit." she was starting to get rude.

"I don't forget transgressions easily. I'm a Nadian not an Eshan. I know you know what's going on Natalie."

"I have no idea what you're talking about. Nor, do I care to know. I'm busy. Please call someone else." she fumbled over herself.

I hung up on her, growing absolutely furious with all this nonsense.

I called Morgan again but got no answer.

Why was no one thinking about me!? How could no one consider telling me what was going on? She told me to ask Halle but there was no way the airhead heiress had any idea what was going on with Morgan.

Hmm... it's not too far to get downtown from here- but did he mean downtown Nadine or downtown Exigo... or downtown La Vida? I knew he could find me in an instant if he wanted but I can't just pop holes in reality and jump around wherever the hell I wanted.

"AHHHHHHHHHH WHERE ARE YOU, DAMMIT!!" I scream to the heavens.

CHAPTER 11

After The News Hits

Morgan Ellys

Natalie showed up at my downtown office right as my day concluded dressed like I've never seen. Usually she comes to see me in her business attire or dressed for the gym. Rarely did she ever come in a cocktail dress flattering to her long chocolate legs.

"Hey baby!" She greets me with the first bit of excitement in likely half a year before all this relationship crap really hit the fan. "I got us lunch. It's waiting back home."

"Uh... We don't live together anymore Nat."

"I just wanted to invite you over. I cooked."

"You cooked?" I chuckled rubbing the back of my neck, "what is all this?"

"You were right." She drapes her arms around my neck, "I've been neglecting my strong, industrious, and handsome man. And I'm sorry. I want to make it all about you today baby."

"I’m at work Natalie. I can't be playing makeup with you."

"You at least admit there's making up to be done?" She sneered as if she caught me in some trap.

I let out an arduous sigh, "your guilt isn't my problem, Nat."

"It isn't guilt, Morgan. I'm being serious. I want to be a better woman for you."

"Don't you think it's a tad bit late for that? Considering you know... I'm getting married?"

"But you aren't married yet." She moved to kiss me but only got my cheek. "Babe, give me one kiss."

"It wouldn't just be a kiss. They say kissing makes babies." He wagged his finger at me.

What did she think? I would be happy to see her, let along play along with this facade.

"Morgan. I made oxtails. Can you please come over? It's lunch not dinner."

I was defeated as soon as she said oxtails. A man can't resist his favorite meal. Besides they're expensive. I couldn't waste the meat. She knew my weaknesses. Damn.

"Alright... I'll come by. I'll give Halle a call and let her know what's up."

"I rather you didn't." Natalie sighed, "I'm trying to win you back, Morgan... Can we not involve her? As you can imagine this isn't exactly kosher."

"Natalie how can you expect me to do this with you?"

"You said yourself. It's stupid to leave someone because you love them... It's just as dumb to marry someone you don't love. You left me because you didn't think I loved you. Let me show you I do. I at least deserve a shot Morgan. I have the oxtails on the stove. I didn't expect so much resistance."

I rubbed my temples, she knew my favorite food?

"Baby, not like that. I just- baby please let me be your woman. Like you wanted, like we both wanted."

"I want Lunch. That's all. I don't know what else you had planned." I pick up my phone and begin texting Halle.

"What are you doing?"

"I'm texting Halle..."

"Why?"

"I'm sorry. Are we going to have an issue with me respecting my fiancée? If so then I don't need to be doing this with you."

Natalie bit her lip, "Halle is a Gregor, Morgan... Can we work on us in private?"

"I'm just telling her we're going to lunch for closure."

"This isn't closure."

"Maybe not for you but this is it for me. It has bad news written all over it. I have to focus on my business, Natalie."

Natalie tried to kiss me again, her lips brush against mine. "Just kiss me, baby, give me one kiss for the road."

"Nata-

She pulled herself in closer and smacked one right on my lips. We kissed. I missed her taste... Our lips fit together so well, sucking and biting on the other's bottom lip. I pull away and she tries to move back in.

"No."

"Morgan..."

"I'm still in my office, dammit. Can you try not to ruin my life while trying to ruin my marriage? Speaking of Gregors, if Colin finds out about any of this... This situation isn't as simple as you make it, Natalie."

"You don't think I know that? You don't think a Wolfe knows what Gregors do? I'm not worried about them. I'm worried about me and you."

"That's very Gregor of you."

"It's very... I want you back. I want you back Morgan!"

"Yeah, I heard you the first few times. Let's hurry up. Get some privacy."

"Oh privacy, one last toss around before you become a married man?" Natalie straightens up my tie.

"Who says toss around?"

"Can we just go? I'm hungry and horny..." Natalie kisses me once more before we leave the office.

CHAPTER 12

So, I made it?

Morgan Ellys

It's been seven years since I left The Academy, a matter of weeks after celebrating my 24th birthday.

There are women breaking off their engagements to sit with me. There are lawyers and council members sitting down to ask me my opinions on the world and their business. It all seems so bizarre. It's been a few years since I nestled into my position in society but it still feels foreign, perhaps it always will.

No one ever told me this is what it meant to be wealthy. With contracts, agreements, and handshakes I am bound to so many things. What time does one have left? This person wants to discuss a business deal. These people wish to sit for a meeting. I wasn't built for this lifestyle but it loved me.

I am a warrior.

I spent a life upon the proving ground of men and I was victorious. I sharpened my wits, braved the human condition. Life has gotten so dreary.

I am a millionaire, but only in name? What sense does any of that make? My house is far too expensive and the women in my life eat the other half. I am supposed to be happy but I only feel this pitless hunger feeling as if I need more. But I know I don't. I know for a fact I do not.

I have lived an entire life surviving with far less than any can imagine. The grass is never greener, they say. No, this grass is live and thriving, I feel as if only I think it's bad. Am I jaded?

I sleep in a 10,000 thread count bed on the nights I do sleep. 5 nights out of 7 I'm up... planning, thinking, and trying to make sense of this world. Then around people, I have little more than blank expressions and prerecorded messages. I feel like Nietzsche, but my stomach doesn't bleed every ten seconds. How did he manage to stay so damn spritely with ulcers? If he can manage, I suppose so can I.

I was only a soldier... people have normal lives after the war. They go back and have families and friends. I grew up on a military base, went to school in their academy... to my knowledge I have no family left.

The news says I'm the most eligible bachelor in Erdu. If that's true, why am I so discontent and alone? This has been the sum estimation of my life. People fall in love with finished products and don't appreciate the pressure it took to craft diamonds. We are all coal in the beginning. Instead of emulating strength, we emulate the imitations of it. I am strong. My life has proved that as fact.

They whisper that I was supposed to be some King, the lost forgotten prince coming to reclaim his throne. The closer my birthday got... I felt like a pauper. All the riches and women in the world but it felt so damn empty.

You spend a life with sycophants and that's all you begin to see in others. Everyone wants to live vicariously through you. Most people offer nothing more than expectations and obligations. I will invest my money. The riches felt meaningless to me because it seems so endless. You don't get to this point until your time is of value to you. There must be something better in the works. If not you become doomed to this shit. Blaming externalities for why this dead end job is only paying end's meet. I allowed other men to be my masters... no more. Time is the only currency we have, and nothing else seems of value to me anymore.

These people make me sick. They want what they don't need. And sacrifice need for want. But seeing it amongst people so wealthy... they honestly cannot see what they have.

They seemed addicted, no different than heroin junkies fueled by their next sale, but always lusting for one sale more. Not junkies, I meant heroin dealers. What is a junkie but someone's child becoming a victim to a society of escapism? This Nakan lust for more and more, for what your neighbor has and what you could never have then feeling shamed for not having it. I seem to get on very little, so my wealth grows due to lack of use. There are men earning more than me who end their year poor. Only to make the wealth back and repeat it again!

I acknowledge my fortune, my station, and can't ignore the thousands who would literally kill to have my spot. There are poor kids, starving and veterans on the streets, and famine. I donate... I volunteer but in truth, it all seems for null. Everyone else throws their money at problems. I don't see them there building these roads, houses, and businesses. They hire a manager who hires others then fire these people at will. In Nadia, we are using our own hands, our own life savings, and our own life energy to rebuild Nadia.

One day I died, died for years. I should have died many times over in my career. Yet all the same, my accomplishments are not enough. Who will be at my funeral? Who will read my obituary...? No kids to leave all this to and no woman who I can fully trust. I don't wish to spend forever with these people or in this world. All I have are my wealth and my thoughts at this point. So many faces I've left behind, some dead... some by my hand. Some moved but most I had to shrug off like ill-fitting jackets. Who do I share these thoughts with?

I was always focused as a boy, with that I had few friends. I was always driven. With that I had many enemies. My time with the Regulators allowed me open autonomy, funds, and resources to carry out the expanding government's whims. I also adopted their enemies as my enemies. Hmm... the things I've done in the name of "Peace and Order" have become paradoxical. Duty was all I knew.

Perhaps that's my issue. Mid twenties with more accolades than I have had real relationships, more sex than I knew people. I spent a lifetime defending the ignorant innocents for their own safety against horrors they claim do not exist.

There's more to life. I assumed it was wealth. That's all anyone ever spoke about when I played civilian. God have I only been playing a civilian? Is that how much of my humanity I've lost over these years?

I live alone in a lake house now. A lake I never quite swim in. I pay extra to keep the lake maintained and running but nothing truly keeping me bound to it. I enjoy my days off when I get to watch the kids splashing about. Having the fun I had long forgotten. I call them kids but in truth they are only two or four years my junior. Though, my house is paid for and they play school. Their grand issues in life are their report cards or some other over-privileged bullshit. Not the concerns of others or the betterment of the world. That is the burden of men. It is why most men choose to stay children.

Today is a rare day off. About once a month I have a day where there are no engagements, no work to be done at home, and no thoughts lingering in the back of my mind. My bullshit meter has prevented me from going into the office of late. My father-in-law to be has pushed me to my wit's end. But today I am free from all this! The house to myself, I can finally train, meditate, make sense of all this at least for a few days to simply have my mind and be at peace.

My training taught me to sense presence in absence by reading energy signatures.

There is someone inside my home.

I attempt to shake the feeling but find myself standing behind my desk, silencing my mind to better feel the energy in my two story house. My mind has gotten the best of me as if late. I feel as though I'm being watched or followed. My ex called it stress... Training doesn't just disappear, it's conditioned. She never quite understood or perhaps she did and she's best as my fiancée.

My body lagged. My muscles felt sore and heavy. I can't fight like this but I could defend my home. It'll have to be quick whatever I choose to do. I snuck in an extra training session last night to take advantage of my day off. It can quickly become my demise with the delayed-onset muscle soreness.

I snuck out my home office and crept through the house as a shadow. Even out of the military and playing civilian stealth was ingrained. Even with the lactic acid weighing me down, my movements were hushed.

The second floor is clear. An assassin on the first floor seemed peculiar. There are enough windows on the upper level to choose from but I'll bite. My time has come, so be it.

My descent was clumsy and forced. My hamstring buckled with each step. I was a duck. I could have been shot dead had my intruder been waiting.

I looked around the living room... It was awry. My scan was only quick enough to realize many of my things were missing and out of place. Straightened up, polished, and neat as opposed to the disorderly mess I had left them.

It took only a moment for my gears to flip. The sound of footsteps made my consciousness recede losing all mental limitations. My body lost all sense of weight and pain, giving way only to my instincts and training. I burst into the kitchen. My hands found a knife upon the kitchen island, my formerly freehand, by only a few seconds, had my intruder's throat squeezed in my fist.

"Who sent you?" I snarled ready to drive the knife through the young woman's neck. I've stood with women smaller and deadlier. Sex mattered little when it came to fighting. Only force of will.

"What the fuck is going on! Who are you? Don't kill me! I swear to Baat! Please, Jah'Ada save me!" she called upon the Gods, flailing and crying like a civilian.

"My apologies..." I relent, pulling the young woman to her feet. "I believed you were an assassin, forgive me. I didn't know I wasn't alone in my own home."

"So, you leap on me? What if you cut me?"

"The intent was to kill you. Be glad you weren't registered as a threat."

"I wasn't- You're going to kill me!?"

"I repeat my question. Who sent you?"

"I- I'm Rose- Rose Andale, we've met before! You offered to help me, at the convention, you don't remember?" she puts up her hands.

Empty, half the size of my own fists meant she would not punch me, it did not explain why my senses said she was dangerous.

"I meet many people Ms. Andale. It's a pleasure to meet you again." I extend a hand.

"Dios mios, pendejo, you nearly knock me unconscious and now you want to shake hands?"

"That was an honest mistake." I let out a sigh.

"No. No it is not! Bumping into someone is an honest mistake. You catching me in the shower would be a welcomed mistake. But you tried to kill me-

"I do not try to kill. Had I wanted you dead you would be dead."

"People actually say that shit? That was terrifying coming from you." Ms. Andale was frantic, walking about holding her chest. The poor girl looked like one of the children playing by the lake. "Why would you do that?"

"I thought there was an intruder." I walk to the stainless steel fridge and pour her a glass of water from the iodized filter. I took few chances with my water supply. "Good?"

"No!"

"Shouldn't you go back to your friends, then?" I let out another sigh, rubbing my temples. Dealing with a child was not one of my intentions for this morning.

"Those people out there aren't my friends. I work for you, you asshole."

"You claim you work for me?" I set the glass down, "Hmm... curious."

"You cannot honestly be this oblivious? I was told the owner was never home. Not some deranged lunatic going about killing people!"

"Let's not get out of hand. I don't just go around killing whoever only the bad guys."

"You're twisted."

"No, I'm retired." I stretch out growing bored, "find yourself a uniform, your current dress is entirely too inappropriate."

"They're leggings. Are you going to kill me for that now?"

"You have quite the mouth for a maid."

"Housekeeper slash administrative assistant is what my resume says..." She corrects. "The job description had no dress code." She paused looking me over, "Though, aside from the murder attempt. I can't really say I'm complaining to be standing with thee Morgan Ellys. Who knew you were handsome and psychotic."

“Many dead men...” I rubbed my neck growing uncomfortable and unprepared for this interaction. "How do you even know me?"

"Duuuuh, you did a Carmen Cruz interview and legit walked off camera mid interview. That's pretty ballsy." She seemed impressed, leaning forward and all. "Why did you do it?"

"Those types of people don't care about truth. They want falsehoods and scandals for tabloids. That was a lifetime ago."

"It was only a few years ago...”

I rubbed my chin trying to recall the interview more clearly but nothing came to mind. I made a habit of walking off from public engagements. I only did radio interviews and a few brief convention speeches.

"People still talk about that you know?"

"I don't keep up with what people talk about. You just recognize me from that. I don't quite remember The Karma Show."

"Her name is Carmen, the voice of the beautiful people? How do you fuck up her name, it's so easy."

I shrug looking around the kitchen, "So, what do I pay you for exactly, housekeeper?"

"I cook, clean, and watch the house. I don’t believe my checks come directly from you but definitely from your circle."

"So, someone from my circle hired a maid..."

“Fine, call it what you want, as long as your letter of recommendation says Administrative Assistant."

"Letter of- I didn't even know you were in my employ. I won't lie for you."

"But you would kill me?"

"That was forever ago!"

"Baaah, I'm so tired of you." she throws her hands in the air, "you seemed so normal and handsome on tv. Now... you're weird, psychotic... and still- I'll be honest, you're still rather attractive. I totally get why girls date crazy guys now."

"I- Okay, whatever enough of your teenage gibberish-

"I'll have you know I am 20, sir! Thank you! I'm a student at the Nadian Institute of Technology. I'm not some little kid."

"You're so emotional..."

"I AM NOT EMOTIONAL TAKE THAT BACK RIGHT NOW!"

I raise my hands in defense, "Alright, alright just calm down."

"Hmph..." she crosses her arms over her rather full chest, "I would be fine if you didn't get me so riled up! Jumping on top of me like that then being so oblivious to me coming onto you. With your weak ass apology..." she bit her lip.

I drop my head into my hand, "Ms. Andale you're embarrassing yourself."

"I am- I'm embarrassing myself? Are you serious!? You try to kill me, get me hot and bothered. Don't remember me or how we met. No, sir, you're an asshole. Now, take me to your bedroom and make it up to me with some rough sex." she grabs my hand and begins walking for the door.

"I think you need to find a new place to work." I take my hand back with a chuckle.

"That's funny, bro?" she crosses her hands over her chest again, my attention couldn't be drawn away.

I can snap a man's neck without flinching. Speak to a CEO or Village Chieftain without having to stutter. But this young woman made me take pause. I have never quite met a woman so fierce and mouthy. Maybe I should take her up on her offer, enjoy having this new maid walking about this house. At least someone gets some use out of the home.

"I don't meet many women, so... bold and outspoken." I do my best to mend things. "I just don't take such interest in my employees or comrades anymore. Sorry."

Her heart looked like it sunk in her chest. I prepared myself for the worst.

"Not even just a bit of groping? I mean- You're young, rich and handsome with a beautiful, firecracker as a maid. You're not even trying to feel a girl up? What's the point then?"

"A clean home I believe. I don't recall hiring a maid but if I did it would be someone older, with a mold, and preferably a hunchback who kept to herself. Not someone so young and attractive."

Rose stood at around five foot five with peanut butter skin. Her body was supple and voluptuous. She was firm as if she works out or used to once. The type of body I would have spent money on in my youth. Her hazel eyes never moved off of me. Her leggings were nearly stretched see through.

This creature was working in my home. She was off limits and under my roof due to sexual harassment laws. I'm glad I've been able to avoid her thus far. She was in trouble. My fiancee will be furious.

"You're only a few years older than me!"

"In age, I've lost many years of my life training and travelling."

"It's because I'm a maid..."

"You're my maid, yes!"

"And if I quit?"

"Then you would be horny, unemployed and no longer my issue." I can't fire her without lawful cause. That was a lawsuit. Being unable to take my eyes off her chest and butt isn't probable cause for termination. I must be an adult. Be professional.

"But you do like what you see?"

"It doesn't matter. You're my employee." I shrug.

Her jaw dropped, "Quit playing, there's no way you're this much of a stone wall."

"I don't play, sadly. I'll be in my study."

"The booty will be here when you come back down. I see you eye-balling pretending you don't like me."

"Actually, you can leave my meals outside the door. It's best we do not get involved."

"Your ex-girlfriend told me to make sure you eat and went outside today."

Am I some damn plant? Make sure I get sunlight and water? Does Natalie believe I'm some damn dog? So, Natalie hired Rose... Without my directive, why would she hire someone so young? She must be trying to ruin my wedding with Halle. Unless, could Rumya have hired Rose?

"We'll need to discuss other means of employment for you. I'm soon to be engaged and I cannot lose my future because of some hot young maid."

"You're getting married? I didn't hear about that from anyone."

"How would you have?" I asked, suspicious.

"Hey, I'm Rose Andale, huge fan of your work. Nice to meet you." she gives a sweet smile.

I scratch the back of my neck, "Look, my ex likes to play games. I don't know why she hired you. I'm sorry you got in the middle of all this drama."

"You and Rumya hired me. You said you had an opening and would help me with school. Your place is only like a ten minute walk from the university. And the only place available in my price range."

"You pay rent here?"

"No... I live for free. My price range, duh. I'm supposed to clean your house and pay you rent, vato loco?" Rose looks at me as if I was crazy.

"Rose- I don't recall this meeting we had discussing any of this even if I did faintly remember you. I'm sure I would remember a woman as naturally beautiful as you." I gulped knowing my only weakness in this world sat between her legs.

"We met about a year ago. We met at a conference. You walked out of there as well. We spoke briefly. But you said you felt like you didn't belong as though you were needed elsewhere. You were still rebuilding Nadia, you don't remember?" she claps her hands together and bows her head, "I'm sorry if I was too forward! I didn't know you were taken. It's not every day your hero just pounces on you."

"And now I'm your hero?" I let out a sigh.

She smiled brightly, "No, you have been my hero! I owe you so much I could never repay. All that you've done for Nadia, you protected all of us from the dogs. You saved our lives when you came to Nadia. I fell in love with you, truly and honestly. Then you disappeared. I didn't know your name all that time but then I saw you on the Cruz interview and I just knew you were the same man. Then the conference confirmed it with my own eyes, you were real. You are the man who saved Nadia from the Hounds."

I covered my mouth and back away. There weren't many days in my life I attempted to repress. I have done terrible things to people who have deserved it. But the day I turned my back on The Regulation Regime was first and foremost on the list. Few people knew. Those men are all dead and buried. Their families believed they died honorably.

I told myself I performed my duty. I was an agent of the growing world government. I was trained for the protection of Erdu, and all of Gaia, correct? I was supposed to protect citizens, was I a hero...? No. What I did was not heroic. It was a massacre.

It came back, the little girl and her mother, defenseless aside from their prayers to Ada for salvation.

I murdered over fifty men, how could I be her hero?

Had I fallen sooner or failed, she would speak a different tone. She was of age and body. They would have- I rather not think of what they would have done to her and her mother.

My face turned solemn as I looked at the knife on the ground.

"Morgan... please, I just want to-

"Don't touch me. Don't follow me. Perform your duties. Stay out of my sight." I warn as I turn about-face.

"But- why?"

"I don't want to remember, Nadia. Too many men died that day."

"Yes, yes they did. You saved us from those men! You saved the whole city! Thanks to you, they never came back! The Hounds left us alone for years now!"

"Ms. Andale, I did it for my conscience. You and your mother, the other Nadian girls would have been raped or tortured. I'm not sure if I'm a hero, I do know I won't be anybody's monster."

"I know what would have happened. And that's not the least of it. You can be stubborn all you want. You're my hero." she stares me in my eyes.

"Do- Not- Call- Me- That."

"Jah'Ada, why are you so difficult?"

"I took the lives of 50 military Rottweilers. I exhausted everything and died that day. There's still nights I don't sleep because of that. I'm glad you're well. But- you'll need to find a new hero and in time, a new place to work. I'm afraid this arrangement won't work out."

She simply rolled her eyes, "you're my hero and I'm not quitting. Don't give me that. You were rebuilding Nadia after!"

"I tried. I tried and I failed. As I've done with other things. The only thing I did was kill my brothers... and the news reported it was the citizens. I live with the truth."

"You and all of Nadia." she rolls her eyes muttering under her breath.

I was right to fear the intruder. If word gets out I would be having guests far more lethal than my new maid. The other Wolves would be after me.

"Can you defend yourself, Ms. Andale?"

"I love how you say my name..." she swoons, "Everyone gets it wrong. You say it so perfectly. Like I was made for your tongue, I mean like you were made to say my name like... you're at it."

"Enough drivel! There is no way out of all the people that day you could possibly remember me."

"I was looking right at you as you came out of a grown man's ribcage. The parts I could catch anyway. There was no way I could forget what you looked like, I fell in love with you... What!? Okay, calm down like I low-key fell in love. High key, it was a crush because i'm totally not a crazy stalker. You were just dead in my basement for a couple years. Like- I'm not even sweating you like that anymore."

"I don't believe you. I think you're fucking with my addled mind." I sigh.

She blushed grinning ear to ear, "Well, I'm definitely still sweating you but I promise I'm not a ***crazy*** stalker."

She was still so much a child. She says she owed me her life yet a voice in my head told me to eliminate the loose end, wishing I didn't relent or ask who she was just moving the blade across her throat. Just drive the knife down and toss the body in the lake. My every instinct told me to kill this woman but she looked so innocent.

"You cannot tell anyone."

"No one? Is this a secret? Why is it a big deal, you did a good thing! Plus I may have told my best friend in the whole world but she is almost about thousands of other people who saw you that day. Or replayed on the news or internet, you were pretty huge until the video got banned."

"The funny thing about good and evil is the relativity depending on whose side we're on." I rubbed my chin thinking if it was even possible someone could have recorded that day. "I kept this a secret for so long."

"So, saving the lives of millions for 50 is evil?"

"I turned my back on The Regulation Regime that day. I was a Captain, Ms. Andale... I put everything in my life aside for the sake of your city. All the work I had done under my title, my allegiance. I took the lives of 50 Rottweiler... people's sons and years of training wasted. The Regime's finest men gone at my hand, that's a war crime. If word got loose there would be 5 Wolves on my property ready to kill both of us without hesitation. I am one. I know one other who may not kill me depending on how she took our last phone call. The other three I had never met. Maybe 8 out of the 10 Wolves on my door, do you know how to defend yourself. I asked for a reason, it wasn't a threat. Unless you find that second part as threatening as I do."

"I can fight. Like, I can defend myself but not against the shit you did... You killed armored soldiers barehanded in a hoodie. You're telling me the Regime has more soldiers like you?" her eyes sharpened, "I didn't know there could be more."

I grimaced, "there aren't many... but there were enough of us created to keep world peace. Most of us were kept separated. For situations exactly like this one I find myself in."

"I- but- how are you alive if it's so wrong?" she asks, "Why would God save you if you weren't in his divine plan?"

"That's classified, Rose. I did much in my life that I'm not proud of but only in reflection. It can't change my decisions or actions. I'm happy you're well. I'm happy for your city. I just wish to live my life. I'm not a hero."

"You are mine."

"You stupid little girl, don't you hear me?"

"I hear that you're angry about saving people, maybe you are a monster." she rolls her eyes, "you're a delusional asshole."

"Yes... far better you keep that in mind than your illusion. I've done much I'm not proud of for The Regulators." I bow my head. "Nadia was my way to take it back. I found no absolution in my death or their deaths, only more darkness."

"Well... Maybe you were meant to help and protect Nadia. Not kill for it. Now you have me." Rose offers me her hand.

"Yes, another life to protect when the inevitable comes knocking." I sigh wishing I had my freedom to protect myself without having to worry about the death another bystander.

I excused myself, sipping my tea as I left for my sanctum in the basement.

HEROES, GODS, AND MEN

CHAPTER 13

Rose Paz Andale

The awkward moment when you meet your childhood hero and he turns out to be an asshole. A handsome asshole.

Hmm... I had no idea he was a Dog all this time. I thought he was one of the Masked Vigilantes hiding underground in Nadia. Popping up all over since the first Hound wave a few years ago that took all the men and guns away before he came.

About a decade ago the greatest man who ever lived was assassinated. The last protector of Nadia, Obatta Sameera. Without him Nadia was in a fray. Fingers were pointed all over for who was responsible to take the helm. This Regulation Regime from the east came and decided for us. People were being put down like dogs... bodies were leaving the city, arrests, and forced recruitments. In a matter of months most of the men were gone. Children, women, and old folks were all that were left. Those men who were left had gone into hiding after Sameera, we believe and hope they are these vigilantes fighting off the crime but those are likely just the kids who grew up during the decade who couldn't stand it. I ran with a band of Masks for a bit, fighting the power and new government.

When the Dogs showed up media coverage absolutely halted. No one knew. Hounds preached peace and order but they didn't give a fuck about either. Not until the smoke clears and they move on to the next territory.

I was thirteen when the tanks and vans pulled up for processing or whatever they call abducting people and whatever else the Dogs felt like.

As their line formed all those willing to fight in Nadia were losing heart. We had no real weapons to combat the tanks, shotguns or assault rifles facing across from us.

A single man walked out from the crowd. All he wore were a pair of old sweatpants and a hoodie. On his back were two of those swords in old Naka, Katanas I believe. He had no fear in his body. He walked up boldly and unafraid. He told the Dogs, "I protect these people, turn around this city is under Wolf jurisdiction." They called him a liar. Laughed in his face. Talked about how Wolves were myths. They sent forth their men and it began.

I was terrified. They got their hands on me and my mother, tearing at our clothes and pulling us toward an alley. The things they said, I had never heard before. My stomach churned but my mother told me not to cry or scream. What they were going to do...Then silence. I looked up to find two hands coated in crimson red, tore through my attackers ribcage. He flung the body listlessly toward the carnage behind him. Piles of dead bodies still in their armor, killed in a similar or more brutal fashion. I had no care. I was safe.

I made eye contact with Morgan. His eyes were a brick red color. Not His usual dark browns. His swords were gone. Just him and his bare hands. I had never even seen anything of this nature, not even in movies. I was filled with a deep joy I never knew again. He gave me a nod, wished us to be well then he was shot twice by shotgun slugs. He looked more irritated than pained. He turned and disappeared from before us. Then reappearing out of thin air before the gun men and tearing the rest of the Dogs down. Leaving a sea of crimson red oozing liquid dripping down the street from the next couple days.

When it was all over. Morgan was on his feet looking around. His eyes lost the reddish coloring, returning to the brown eyes I saw this morning. He screamed, he shouted. Then he fell to his knees. Then... he died. Before all of our eyes. He seemed like a different thing entirely back then. Not even fully human. Now, he seems like a normal guy, well Morgan Ellys, but a man. Not all the things we came up with as kids. A spirit, a defender, a demon of Sameera's wrath was Cameron's guess. It was his son... after all those years.

We hid his body in my basement, my friends and I. We had to save him. My mother was a vet. We patched him up as best we could. Those injuries were grievous. We cleaned the wounds, stitched him back up. Bandaged him as though we as a mummy and kept him on life support the best we could with the saline solution and liquid food from my mother's clinic. The cost of keeping him alive outweighed any sign of his return. My grandmother visited and I pleaded with her. She kissed my forehead and went into the basement for an hour. The power went out and the water stopped working for a week. She returned and said he was alive. He was alive and I would be his Queen.

The masks took up the resistance under their motto, "Dogs bleed too." For the sea of crimson left in the streets on Moss Road. I'm not sure Morgan even knows what he started in Nadia. Those men were agents of the devil himself, Colin Gregor. They had no good in their hearts. He's a hero... he saved our city. How could he possibly feel differently?

I guess dogs only know duty...

For these five years I thought he was moving with the vigilantes. I could have sworn to Jah'Ada and Jah'Anki he was Crimson himself. But no... my savoir, my beloved, is a misanthropic hermit. Alone by his lake. Guilty by his own good deeds. Such a shame.

The city needed him. But he doesn't even have himself anymore. Nor did he fully have his mind. He could spend days on end without human contact. Nor, did he seemed to longing or bothered by it.

I can't judge... he seems to be lost in that head of his. He looks like he loses himself up there often. I wish I could reach out to him in a greater way. But when I see him I'm either too frustrated with him, or too horny to consider being friends. Either maid or lover was all I could think of, it's all he saw me as apparently. A place to put his cock, or a woman to keep his house. That's how he saw me.

"Ms. Andale, can you put some tea to boil. Bring it down to the basement when it's ready." my phone flashed his text message.

Ugh, you could just call or say it yourself? Since my first day really sitting with him, I've been angry. And sad. We could have made love all over his house. Thanked him properly and laid in his arms for the evening after I made him whatever he wanted for dinner. I mean- If he wanted to ease his wounded spirit. But he just hides away in his study or his basement. He gets no calls, he has no visitors. I'm not sure he even realizes he's depressed. He told me he was basically waiting to die.

Not a hero, just not a monster. He needs better company. How could someone fill his head with such nonsense!? Good thing he has me now! I'll turn his spirits around.

I set the kettle on the stove and sat on the island flipping through my emails. He comes downstairs in his sweats. Probably from his study.

"Hey, Morg, what do you want for dinner?"

"Morg?" he raised a brow, "Can't say i've been called that before, Roe."

"A sense of humor."

"Have to laugh every once in a while."

"How often is that?"

"As often as it takes not to cry. How is the tea coming along?" he changes the subject immediately, to my irritation.

"Just waiting on the kettle."

He steps up to the kettle and places a hand against it. It begins whistling immediately to his touch.

"What the hell... I just put it on!"

"Trade secret." he winks, taking out two mugs from the cabinet, "join me for a cup?"

"Yes, please. I pulled up some chai tea." He grabbed the green tea, "Or not." I roll my eyes.

"I'm going to meditate. I don't want anything on my stomach unclear."

"It's tea, bro."

He chuckles, "it's- ha, yes I suppose it is, that's the sensible way to look at it. Chai usually comes with cream. It's unsettling to my stomach. I want my body to be purely parasympathetic when I meditate."

"Digestion IS parasympathetic." I roll my eyes.

He raised a brow, "Uh, yes, that's correct. Impressive, Rose. What's your major?" he actually smiled, a slight one but I'll take it over the brooding.

"I study business management and diplomacy." I say with pride, "Did you attend university?"

He looked up with a momentary eyebrow raise of impression. He smirked, "Bright future for you. I did construction after I awoke in Nadia, and throughout my time in the Regs. My father-in-law taught me real estate and finance. I enjoy working with my hands not pens and words. A few investments, bought a couple businesses with the profit, and good management." He shrugged, blaise as could be, "I didn't see a need for a degree. Life is about personal capability, whether or not it's acknowledged. I never took to plaintive validation. Results are the only thing I rely on."

"Plaintive validation?"

"People are either going to tell you what makes you feel better, or what makes them feel better. I only respond to honesty or results. I don't need the medals, accolades, or compliments. I rate myself."

"Pretty rigid."

He nods, pouring the tea, "If you don't use your own standards you're left to rely on others and most people's standards are unreliable. They barely have a standard for themselves, let alone them judging you."

"Gee thanks."

"I don't know you, Ms. Andale. You've kept this place in order without directive and stay in good shape. You'll be well off with a bit more regiment and discipline."

"I've been using the gym, downstairs. I swim in the lake too! I want to be able to go across and back by the summer."

"Have you now?" His eyes seemed to glisten though his face didn't have much of a change in expression. He let out a sigh, "I used to do a few laps like that when I first bought this place. About 10 or so a day."

"But- Dude, the lake is like a mile wide."

He nods, “My body had been badly injured so I had to take things easy back then, I did a lot of training in the lake for rehab.”

I swooned inside my head.

"Why did you stop?" I was curious, graciously accepting his tea.

He sighed, "My body's been slowing down.” he took a pause. “Like I said, my training took years off my life. Being dead for two years doesn't quite add to that condition. My body has been shutting down on me. If it isn’t the Wolves, I think it’ll be done for me soon regardless. I felt like I needed to rest in case I needed to really go all out soon.”

"You say that... but you didn't like... die, right? Just a coma? Did you truly die? Then you *were* resurrected." She said certain.

He shrugs, "I was out of commission and unconscious for two years. No control of my faculties. On a cold table. I awoke and my body was freezing cold. Numb and paralyzed. I'm not sure what you would call that. Coma, requires some brain function, no?”

"Have you considered just taking a vacation? You died, then got up and started making a million dollars and construction? Swimming for 20 miles a day. Maybe you do just need rest."

"Hmm... “ He sips his tea as though the idea never occurred to him before the conversation. “As I see it, I wasn't' supposed to survive my Wolf initiation. I certainly wasn't meant to survive Nadia. Plenty of missions I skinned by on my wits or sheer muscle-memory. The way I see it, I've been on borrowed time. At this point, I'm waiting for the end. Might as well get what I can out of this body until I fall for good."

"That's depressing as fuck. Real winners take a break."

"I’m retired.”

"I don't think you know what a break is... and if you’re retired you certainly don’t know what that means.”

He rubbed the back of his neck with a deep laugh, "I can't disagree with that. I work pretty hard."

"You don't come home and you don't sleep. All you do is work."

"Jah'Baat... you sound like Halle." he spits out under his breath before sipping his tea.

"Halle... as in Halle Gregor? You know the Heiress of Naka?"

He nods, "The Patriarch has wished for us to wed for sometime. She is the woman I mentioned."

"That's the man who approved the attack on Nadia!" I seethed.

Morgan sat down his mug, "you asked how I was alive and why more Wolves haven't come. That is why I am to wed Halle. That's the agreement I made with the Patriarch. To continue on the Gregor Legacy."

I covered my mouth, "he knows?"

Morgan sighs, "Ms. Andale-

"He's the reason you feel guilty!"

"With reason, I-

"You saved lives he wanted to kill! He's been telling the whole world it was Nadia's fault since you died! My mother says Colin Gregor is the devil. His father wanted to save Nadia. The Gregors are supposed to be some sovereigns! He killed his dad then turned his back on Nadia by sending his Dogs! How could you be friends with him?"

"He is NOT my friend." Morgan snaps. "He knew my mentor. He had an odd interest in me since I was a boy. He's the only reason there aren't Wolves hunting me."

"He's the devil! If you marry his daughter then you're turning your back on Nadia. That makes you no better. And everything you did would be for nothing! Meditate on that buddy."

He was quiet for a moment, sipping his tea. He let out a sigh, "Rose, this world is filled with horrors you couldn't imagine. It needs order. That day in Nadia should have never happened but much worse has happened and has been planned. I have seen it and stood against it. But-

"But nothing! Nadia can govern itself! We don't need The Regime. Gregor did nothing but arrest our men and leave us for rape and death by his Dogs!"

"I'm not discussing it with you further. We've already said too much. You don't know enough to see things clearly."

"Going to kill me? Shut me up and make daddy happy?"

"Watch your mouth, little girl." His voice turned cold.

"Go for it, Morgan. Finish what daddy dearest started!"

"I have a father and it is not Colin Gregor!" he roars, "Now shut your insolent mouth before I rip your damn tongue out!" flickers of red appeared in his brown iris.

I stood paralyzed. My mug fell from my hand shattering on the ground but I couldn't move. It didn't stop him from continuing.

"You know nothing of what you're speaking about. Gerald Knox wanted the mafia to run Nadia, it would not be stood for! Bryon Qatar and Obatta Sameera wanted revolution and expansion. It would have been a war with an army Nadia does not have! I made a tactical decision for peace. 50 men died to save far more than just Nadia. It was for global stability!"

"Bryon Qatar wanted peace." was all I could muster.

"The Qatars wanted revolution!"

"Maybe, but Bryon wanted peace and freedom."

"Freedom is bought with coins or blood, and Nadia is poor and disorganized! Sameera wanted to tear down the walls and start another Ecru Revolution. He believed himself the incarnate of Foremica! He would have ended up having Nadia lost entirely, absorbed into the other four nations disappeared from history just like Foremica."

"Foremica?" He actually knew about the Father of Ecru?

"Oh, a name you didn't hear of? You were oh so knowledgeable a moment ago."

I gritted my teeth, "No..." he thinks I'm stupid it's better that way for now.

"7th century warlord. Tried to take over the world. Believed himself the descendant of Rakil himself. No man is a God, Rose. Nadia had to be dealt with. These lunatics act and work, claiming it's under god's will to kill, pillage and destroy. They must be stopped. He warred and warred. All the territories he got on his global killing spree. The citizens fought behind him reclaiming all the territory until is old age."

"Like The Regime does today? You drank the kool-aid, Morgan."

"I drink tea, Rose. And I'm no longer affiliated with The Regime, I am retired from all military duties effective on the exact day you speak about. Now, carry on with your duties. We have nothing left to discuss." he was a jarhead lunatic, but the drill sergeant bit was sexy.

"I'm done for the day. It's past 17:00 soldier boy." I roll my eyes.

"Then excuse me as I leave you to your duties Ms. Andale." he nods and relieves himself, taking his mug with him to his sanctuary in the basement.

Likely the only house on the lake with a lower level. I hadn't considered where he had been this past month. Man has his own sanctuary but denies he is a guardian.

How droll. I used to think, "This poor man..." but no, he's an agent of the government. I can't bear too much sympathy. At least, he was, he says he's retired. Makes sense why he's alone, trying to kill intruders. He's scared or far too cautious. If he thought Nadia wasn't worth saving then why would he save us? Why would he live here if he didn't feel tied to the land? He's rich, he could hiding anywhere in the world... why here?

CHAPTER 14

Who Are You?

Morgan Ellys

You died for Nadia... You laid on an operating table in a vet office for two years for those people. You would turn your back and will wed into the family that forced that to be a reality? For nothing more than perpetuating petulant greed and ignorance? There was nothing but women and children... their men are probably still rotting away in Nakan cells. You would so easily do this to preserve a life you obviously no longer care for?

I sat cross-legged in my sanctum. Breathing deeply. Returning myself to center.

Have you no control? To fight the girl... allowing a stranger to shake you? To make you question your morality... So frightful of Wolves and boogeymen you would allow yourself to assault a child?

Breathe... get your wits about you, old man!

You're angry because she's right!

She's an honest girl. You need that right now. In the world of sycophants, surrounded. Ready to have given in. She will keep you honest. Just breathe. Just wait and live. Stick to your convictions.

Return... If Nadia needs you-

You know it does!

No- it doesn't need me.

It needed Bryon Qatar. Now, he's gone thanks to me. I am his replacement, that is all.

She's right... what happened in Nadia was wrong. That's why you fought. You died for those citizens. What do you stand for now!? Today, what do you stand for!? Not yesterday, not when you were a child.

I can't fight another war. My body is worn, it's rigid, my training hasn't been the same.

Rest...

I haven't rested in years. I thought death was rest. I thought retirement from the military was rest. But rigamortis has shaken me still. Made me stiff. The stress of living amongst sycophants has made me cloudy, and erratic. I rely on my instincts and past training.

I don't know what is what anymore...

I can't continue making excuses. I can't continue living this life of absence and mediocrity. Nadia became my charge when I drew my blade against my own. I-I must find some end. What do you conclude? Has death turned you coward, Morgan Ellys?

I stood, picking up my teacup and looking around my home gym. Rest... Death... Rigidity. I'm only in my twenties. Shake off the dust off. We have a long road ahead of us.

My ears perked up to the sound of the door creaking open at the top of the stairs.

"Hey, Morg, can I come down?" Rose took a few steps down the stairs, "Are you still brooding in the dark?"

"Standing in the dark, now." I reply.

She began walking down in barefeet, "I wanted to say I was out of line. I-

"You were right, Rose." I relented in admitting before she could begin.

"You son of a bitch, I worked hard on my apology!" she snapped.

I chuckled, "I'm happy for whoever hired you. We'll see where things go."

"Don't tease me, Morgan."

"Do I seem like a man who would joke about matters like this? I haven't been to Nadia in all these years. To be called a hero. Thank you."

Rose blushed, "shut up... you know you're great."

"No... No I don't. I'm a monster, honestly and truly. But I make the most of it."

"Morgan, how can you feel that way about yourself?"

"Because I have the evidence and memories to prove it. Trust me."

"You may be a bad ass mother fucker, but you're not a monster."

I smile, "thank you, Rose. Your humor is welcomed. Welcome to my staff." I pat her shoulder.

"Did you just maid-zone, me?"

"Ha, Rose. One step at a time."

"How many steps until your bed?"

"Is that all you're concerned with Rose?" I let out a sigh. "I need an ally."

"Okay. I can do that!" Rose cheers up.

"Uh... that was easy."

"I don't want you thinking I'm just some ditzy kid swooning over a childhood crush... I'll help however I can, Morgan. I promise."

"I want to help Nadia. I'm responsible. I'm not sure how but- you're right. I must fix what I've created. I left the city defenseless and broken."

"Will you still marry, Halle?" Rose held my chin.

I chuckle, "Rose-

"She's the daughter of the Devil."

I sterned up, realizing she wasn't merely swooning or attempting to divide me from my spouse. "As I said. One step at a time. You study diplomacy, sudden changes cause wars and distension. I'll see if I can negotiate. I'll have to teach you how to protect yourself and the house."

"You're gonna make me a bad ass?"

"I'm going to teach you to defend yourself, Rose."

"But against guys like you?"

"That'll take far more time than we have. There aren't many like me. I will worry about them. I will teach you to defend my house and Nadia if it so comes to that."

"I'll be like your side-chick! Sidekick... I said sidekick." she stammered.

I shake my head, "You're going to be trouble."

"I'm a great student. You can teach me quick."

I nod, "Let me see your guard then."

She stands, holding up her fists. Too low. I tapped her elbow and she raised it immediately. Her feet were spread too far. I kicked them closer gently. She was firm and strong. A good base for training.

"Good, good, not half bad, Rose."

"I'm pretty strong too."

"Yeah? Let's see what you got?"

I raise my hands for her to try out a few jabs. Before hands are up she throws a right jab as if shot from a bullet. It cracks against my chin, an instant KO. The kid's got promise.

CHAPTER 15

That Was My Best Shot

Rose Andale

Morgan sat up like a corpse risen from the dead a few seconds later. I suppose he's used to that by now. I had my hands over my mouth speechless as he stood with a smile on his face. I knew I was fired.

"You're going to be a good student, kid. What a punch! I knew Dogs who couldn't hit me that hard. Fast too. You've had some training for sure."

"You're a lunatic, you're acting like I never hit you at all." I shake my head, throwing my hands up in the air.

He let out a bellowing laugh. "I've never been hit that hard before in the face. I had to think about it."

"Really? So, think I could be a bad ass?" I rub my knuckles, "If I could get a KO on you, right?"

"Absolutely! I'll need a sparring partner." he grins poking my ribs, and cornering me.

"Hey, hey, I just got a lucky punch!" I welcomed him.

"Then let's train for you to get a few more lucky punches." he gives a wink, "I might just enjoy your stay, yet."

"Might? I'm amazing company..." I mutter slapping his shoulder.

He nodded, "I have to go, now. Much work to be done." He pats my butt, "It feels good to have some purpose and duty, again."

"I'm happy I could help you see the light. You're a good man with a bad past." I hug his arm.

"I've been thinking about it more of late. I've been stagnant, paralyzed for a long time. It'll be a process until I'm at 100%."

"So, I didn't do anything?" I ask confused.

"Ha, thank you, Rose. I do appreciate your honesty. Don't change."

"My honesty?"

"You're bold, outspoken and deeply passionate. You'll make a fine leader one day."

I nearly melted from joy.

I followed behind Morgan as he went upstairs, I felt like a lovestruck puppy chasing after the new pitbull on the block.

He turned quickly on his heels walking up the stairs and I nearly crashed into him. As I fell back, his hand jetted out and grabbed me. Gently pulling me back, with such strength and speed. He believes himself paralyzed?

"A warning, Halle does visit often. I need you to be on your best behavior. I do not want any conflict between the two of you. She's my fiancee, don't make me choose. She'll win every time."

"How did you end up engaged to Halle Gregor?"

"I- Well, I guess it was inevitable. We always knew each other. I liked the idea of marrying an old friend. I used to date her friend. Halle and I were- intimate during that relationship. And then... Colin Gregor got his wish."

"Why does he want you?"

He let out a sigh, "In truth I hadn't the slightest idea, outside of mutual respect of ability and seeking an heir. I could never rationalize Colin's voracity for me in his corner. He believes himself one of my great mentors these past years of my life. I trained and learned from the Commissioner most my life though. I was never allowed around Colin when I was a kid in the military. It wasn't until I was 11..."

"Wow... you're like King Dog."

"I wasn't a dog at all. I was a Wolf." I correct her sharply. "I've been an operative since I was a boy. I spent my entire life in the Regulator Academy in Erdu."

"I thought you had to be 18 to enlist in the military?"

"Like I already told you, I wasn't a soldier, I was a Wolf... I had little choice in my placement nor my existence. I was a child... following whatever adults told him."

"What's the difference between wolves and dogs?"

"It took 50 of their best in full riot gear, Rottweilers, to bring me down empty handed. Wolves are a whole different level. Gregor and Warren are far beyond that."

"But how strong could they possibly be? They are humans, right?"

Morgan grimaced before repeating, "There are horrors and mysteries in this world the governments wish to keep concealed. That's why we have Wolves, Rose. To keep the darkness out of the light."

"So... if you didn't grow a conscience that day. It would have been 50 of them and you? Does the government need to be that strong?"

He had no answer. Just excused himself.

CHAPTER 16

There Is No Finish Line

Rose Paz Andale

I missed my boss' birthday. What do you get the man who wants for nothing? Morgan can be so difficult. I imagine he will respond the same to tube socks as he would a vacation, a slight smile and a polite thank you before ignoring the gift. Not that I could afford a vacation or he would even take one. I was hoping offering him sex would suffice but he was even less interested in me than taking a vacation.

I swear lately he has been working himself into a rage, the past couple days he has been so irritable. The wedding is stressing him out I imagine. When he is not working, he's drinking himself into a stupor to sleep. When he isn't drinking he's looking for more work to do. It seemed wrong to watch a good man try so hard to kill himself. I'm his maid, is it my place to say anything to him?

My phone rang with a text from him, "Rose, can you come to the living room for a minute?"

I was told after five o' clock, I was off the clock aside from making him dinner. I typically leave the food inside of a container in the fridge. Tonight he ate with me, in silence then he began drinking some Whiskey. I left him expecting to take a nap and finish my homework. I wonder what he could possibly want.

I roll out of bed, pulling on the pair of shorts at the foot of my bed rushing out to see him.

"Sir, can I help you?" I ask rubbing the sleep out my eyes trying to seem attentive.

"Uh... Is this usually how you dress when you think I'm not home?"

"I'm sorry sir. I wanted to get here quickly. I seriously put on the first thing I found without thinking."

He bit his lip not responding at first. He shook his head trying to adjust himself slumped on the couch, setting the giant book he was reading on the table. The book was so heavy it shook the entire wooden table.

"My, my you've never paid me this much mind before?" I blush realizing he was legitimately checking me out like a human and not a subordinate.

"Apologies, I meant no disrespect. I thought I saw everything the first time we met but seems there was more I desired. It's the drink." He slapped his forehead beginning to rub his temples.

"When I thought I caught your eye you pull on your serious face again. What can I do for you, sir?" I tease him leaning over him to clean up his cup, giving him a better view of my blessing.

"Wow, I was going to ask if you can get me another drink but suddenly I think I've had enough." His eyes linger on me, following me until I standup, "My apologies, Rose."

I bite my lip, "I really don't mind. I'm happy you're seeing me as more than your maid. Ha, it's been a bit awkward since I started living here. You literally didn't even know I existed." I bounce from one foot to the other feeling my juices rushing between my legs with how he gazed at my body.

"Has it?" his hands run up my leg, feeling my butt as if he was making sure it was real.

"I was hoping we would have more of a working relationship. Even just brief interactions, it's hard to know whether or not you're even home."

He nods, "I never had a maid before. I didn't expect one so attractive."

"Well, I'm not sure what you expected. The job pays great and then there's room and board. It's hard for a student to pass up. I have a couple years left in University. I could stay until I finished my Master's and Doctoral program if you wanted."

"You seriously enjoy it?" He nods again beginning to crack his neck from lying across that stiff couch.

"Uhh..." I giggle, sitting next to him beginning to rub his neck and upper back.

"I look that bad of shape, huh?" he chuckles feeling his joints pop and crack to my touch.

"Ha, not really it's honestly quite the opposite. I'm embarrassed to say. The work is easy, you're rarely here. I'm mostly cleaning after myself. I don't know why she thought you needed me. Working for someone as young and handsome as you is its own benefit as well. Times like this I think you might like me."

"Things build up over time. A shirt on the floors becomes a pile of laundry. A dish in the sink becomes dishes. After having a brief chat with Rumya, this was strongly urged."

"Oh, so you did speak to her?"

"She spoke highly of you Rose."

"Oh wow, really? I was really surprised you even knew my name to ask her about me." I giggle moving my hands to his lower back.

"Ha, is that so? Wow, you know your outfit is a bit distracting." His eyes were on me, no apology and this time there was no effort made to look away.

"You're easy on the eyes as well." I crawl into his lap getting better access to his neck and back smothering him in my b-cups, "So, this our first night hanging out together."

"I suppose it's a long time coming." He squeezes my butt making me moan to his touch.

I kissed his forehead then his cheek. Is that his dick? I'm feeling his girth pushing into my yoni through his slacks and my shorts. I started moaning feeling out of control over myself, as he was able to make me cum without fully penetrating me, "How are you inside me with our clothes on?"

"Oh shit, I'm too drunk. I didn't know you could feel me." He stammers trying to justify pushing me off him.

"I was not complaining." I let out one last moan rubbing my clitoris still feeling him, "Your dick is huge, Morgan."

"Trying to take advantage of your drunken ole boss, huh?" he starts to chuckle, "Sorry for throwing you."

"I'm glad this is so funny to you. Are you going to finish what you started?" I began shimmying out of my shorts.

"That's a loaded question." He rubbed his temples.

"I wasn't trying to make things awkward but there's no way I can go back to bed like this Morgan."

"I've never had a woman say such a thing. Are you serious?"

"I don't care how you finish me up but you better finish what you started."

I grab his chin, planting a kiss on his lips. He grabs a handful of my butt. Our tongues swim in the other's mouth. I let him go hoping he would pull me back but instead he walks away. Cursing under his breath asking himself, "how could I do this to myself again?"

I held my lips, still feeling them tingle from his kiss. I wanted him even more than I knew was possible to crave a man. I followed him into the kitchen where he was brewing some coffee.

"Are you alright, Morgan?"

"I'm damned if I do and damned if I don't... I lose everything if I sleep with you but this wedding will drain me of my very soul if I follow through." He shook his head.

"If that's the case why did you leave your girlfriend? Why get married if you feel this way?"

"Rose, please take a seat. I want to explain this once to you and never again. I'm in this wedding because I cheated on my girlfriend with Halle Gregor. I love Halle but this isn't in any of our control. This wedding and stress is all her father's doing. The Patriarch wants me as his son, so when he dies I become his sole heir and takeover Gaia in his family's name."

"Oh, wow that's heavy. Holy shit... and you still chose to get married?"

"I didn't have a choice in the matter. I love Halle too much to see her lose her inheritance, abused by Colin's greed for power. I'm not sure I can save her without marrying her Rose."

"Does anyone else know?"

"Halle knows, she isn't dumb... she's just happy it's me and not someone else."

"Why would he give his wealth and power to you instead of his daughter?"

"He hasn't done anything to prepare Halle for leadership. He wants a man to take control not his daughter. Would you trust your life's work and family fortune to someone who does nothing with money but spend it."

"What else can you do with money?" I ask confused.

He rubs the bridge of his nose feeling irritated with me, as if I proved his point.

"Relax, Morgan. I'll fix you a big cup of coffee and get you a couple aspirin."

"Thank you Rose." He sits at the island.

"So, that's why you're so stressed and drinking. Seems like you're worried about losing a woman you love and losing more money than a man could ever need. If you weren't doing this to appease the devil I might feel bad."

"I feel too far gone to care about the devil. I already murdered so many people and broke Natalie's heart. I wanted to have them both. I thought it was possible to love both. I hoped it could bring peace to their families but-

"I would have let you have both if it avoided all this drama and pain. Doesn't your ex-girlfriend, this Natalie girl, understand you have no choice in the matter?"

"I didn't tell her I had no choice. I tried to spare her feelings by telling I made a decision. Hoping she would be angry with me and leave things alone. She saw through it. Would you want to lose your man to your rival and watch her hand him a fortune? Natalie didn't love me but she didn't want to lose me. Our relationship was dying regardless."

"Personally, I want you in any capacity I can have you. I think if she's trying to ruin your wedding she's being unfair and selfish. Especially if she knows, you're in some deal with the devil. I imagine she could be a bit more understanding to help you get out of it."

"You never dated me. You have to take me in whatever capacity you can get me. She was supposed to be my girlfriend..."

"I guess I can't relate." I grin pouring his coffee then fetching the cream and sugar, "You deserved both or else you wouldn't have been in the situation."

"I can't believe what you're saying. You're saying you would be my mistress and play your position if you were in the scenario?"

"Are you kidding me? I would give you everything I could, everything your wife couldn't and wouldn't do, I would because you deserve it." I grinded against the bulge growing between his legs, "I would make sure you never needed or wanted for another woman. I would make sure my King is always satisfied."

"Now, I'm your King?" Morgan smirked raising a brow.

"You're my Young King." I blushed at hearing how I sounded aloud as I stirred in the sugar and cream.

"You understand I'm getting married right? You will never be my wife." Morgan hesitates.

"I'm not offended by the truth Morgan. I'm your house-keeper. I don't need to marry you as long as you let me finish out my degree in your service. I am not here to ruin your marriage. I'm flattered you're trying to jump my bones. I just want to see you happy. Honest."

Morgan takes long gulps of his coffee as I continue grinding and winding my hips on his lap. I guide his freehand across my body and down my flat stomach until he begins playing with my yoni.

"Open your eyes. I want to make sure you're thinking about me." I whisper barely loud enough in his ear.

"Damn girl..."

I lean back trying to kiss him again but I meet his coffee cup instead.

"Where do you expect this to lead, Rose?"

"Ha, well I was hoping it would lead to the bedroom. I would settle for here in the kitchen or on the staircase trying to get up there. We don't have to move fast. I don't ever want you to regret being with me." I held his tie pulling him in to kiss me.

"Can you please let me go Rose?" he asks politely.

"I'm sorry... am I fired?"

"I'm fine Rose, you didn't do anything. I'm not sure if this is what I want. I have enough regrets on my mind to add more."

"We can slow down, Morgan. We can stay like this alright?" I cuddle up with him, kissing his neck, "I'll be good, promise."

"Please Rose, let me go. I need some air." He whispers in my ear, kissing my cheek then scratching my scalp.

"Are you mad at me?" I made no effort to hide my disappointment stomping away, beginning to clean his cup.

"What? No, I'm not mad at you. Why would I be?"

"Do you want the truth? I've been honest so far, it's because I want more than a professional relationship with you."

Morgan rubs his temples, "I will never understand what you girls see in me."

"Well, your huge dick definitely helps make up for you being emotionally oblivious."

He shook his head hiding his smile under his hand.

"Can I watch a movie with you in your room? I give really good massages as well as you now know."

He rubbed his aching neck thinking it over in his mind.

"Come on, it'll be super platonic. I can rub you down. Maybe order some late night delivery on me. No sex, touching all over your muscles will be enough for me."

"Well, why not? I've never been offered such a thing from anyone before man or woman. Let's give it a shot."

"Great, go to your room and strip. Put on a towel and I'll be right there to rub you down."

"What are you doing?"

"I'm going to order pizza, grab my oils and change into something cuter that won't have you trying to dick me down. Relax, I'll be right there."

I sat on Morgan's back. My lips couldn't help but rest in a soft smile no matter how hard I was trying to be serious. I rubbed his thick densely muscled back, kneading him with my soft hands as he snored under my weight. I fought with myself over doing a good job to keep my cover or enjoying the opportunity to explore this man's beautiful body.

Each time I hit a sweet spot he let out a moan prompting me to grin with pride cheering inside my head and say, "Damn, right you like that!"

I inched down to sit on his legs to get a better angle, feeling on his taut butt as I admire his chocolate skin. I trailed up the wings of his back up to his shoulders nearly losing my head wondering how such a man could be real, be here with me right now. I used my muscles from doing Pilates, swimming in the lake and fiddling around with his weight room in the basement. It paid dividends as I pressed out the knots in his back nearly melting from hearing him moan to my touch.

I flipped my curls out of my face, my smile widening as I found the sweet spot where his back bundled in his rhomboids. I didn't warn him as I rolled out his middle back with my elbows, pressing my weight as he let out a scream, groaning and clenching the bed as I pressed out where he held everyone's baggage. My panties were drenched as he fell into ragged breathing. I slowed down glad I could really enjoy my job even without having him break my back in tonight.

I licked my lips with pleasure, feeling his powerful body shiver anticipating my touch. I stood up, motioning for him to roll over. He hesitated but relented as I began working my hands into his neck. He willingly moved over to his back so I could rub his clavicle. I nearly flooded on the floor seeing the bulge pressed against his towel. I bit my tongue wondering how he would taste pressed against my tonsils, if I could fit him in my mouth at all.

Morgan sat up as I straddled his waist pressing all my weight against his bulge. We stared into each other's brown eyes, it felt like electricity filled the room as his erection lifted me for a moment until I pushed my shorts aside letting my panties be our condom as his bulge pressed into my yoni. I parted my lips, leaning into kiss him as sparks ran through my spine he turned his head last minute trying to get up.

"I really have to use the bathroom for a second." He tries avoiding eye contact.

"Oh?" His bulge was pulsating inside of me, I knew in a few seconds he could probably press against my cervix, "I'm not going to tell anyone Morgan, I promise."

"There is going to be nothing to tell. What happened to platonic?"

"Look me in the eyes and tell me you don't want my tight pussy choking that anaconda you're hiding. Let me finish your massage. I'll give you the royal treatment then you can decide if you want to tip me with a happy ending." I relaxed guiding him inside me, rolling my hips as I maneuvered my panties aside.

"Are you on the pill?"

I bit my lip, awkwardly nodding as ran my hands up his stomach to his barrel chest, up to his traps. I moved my hands in waves, moving his blood quicker to get the nutrients sent to each part of his body much faster. His muscles bulged with blood and he let out a cough feeling his head probably get lighter.

"Are you water bending my blood?" his eyes feel from my eyes to my shoulders eventually closing as I went back to simply rubbing his stomach.

How could he feel me blood bending? "Did I hurt you?"

"No, I've been caught by a coven of witches before and one was a blood-bender. I could never forget the feeling as having someone try to take control over my plasma again. You were quite gentle but whatever you were doing was not subtle at all. Are you trying to kill me?"

"Are you alright? My grandmother taught me a healing technique. I was moving the blood much quicker to accelerate cell healing and your stamina would increase tremendously permanently. It'll clear out your lungs as well and I was preforming a dialysis on your kidneys after drinking."

"Don't I need a physician before you experiment on me?"

"I'm not experimenting, I know exactly what I'm doing. It won't hurt it. It's one of my many talents Morgan. I am a trained healer from the High Priestess of Qatar herself, Lady Marsha Qatar." I vouch holding my hand to her heart.

His eyes tightened at me not in disbelief but suspicion. He glared at me from his back studying my expression as if comparing it to the last times I told him the truth. I was so close to having sex with me and having his baby inside of me. If he got me pregnant, I wouldn't have to care about who he marries or who fights over him. I would be in his life forever. I only needed to get his dicks inside me. And I would need him to put up a performance. Who am I kidding his eyes scrutinized me. He likely played my story repeatedly in his head. I felt like such a stupid fool for allowing myself to get so close and fail over something so grandiose. Why would I blood-bend when he doesn't even think I can defend myself!?

"Morgan... relax, please relax I would never stab you in the back. I was not doing it to hurt you or control your body. I swear, I'm a water-bender I meant no harm. I promise. Just- please let's not end the night lying to ourselves or fighting this feeling anymore. I'm willing to say I want you. If I go back to being only your maid tomorrow so be it but I want you. I can't contain myself anymore."

"We're done here Rose. You don't have to go back to your room but you need to get out of here. I'll pretend you didn't what you did and leave your heart in your chest without ripping it out like my instincts are telling me."

"You would kill me?"

"My instincts have been telling me to kill you since I found you in my kitchen." He says without lying.

"I would never hurt you, Morgan." I gulped unsure I could take him on in a fair fight or at all. Especially half-naked knowing what he could do to a grown man wearing armor, dozens of men wearing armor. I raised my hands in the air getting off his waist.

"I can't promise the same thing Rose. So, let's forget about anything that happened tonight. You will go back to being my maid tomorrow and that's all you will ever be to me. There are no feelings here. You are a sexy woman. Of course, I would have sex with you. I try not to think with my cock anymore. I'm not a child anymore and I'm getting married. Thank you for helping me put my priorities in order. Now, please leave me alone with any fantasies of ever being with me."

I held my heart feeling it crack, wanting to cry right there but I managed to run back to my room before burying my face in my pillow crying in the darkness. Glad he at least didn't fire me. I was so close to having his baby.

CHAPTER 17

Who Is The Guest?

Halle Gregor

Today is another beautiful Nadian day! The sun is shining, everyone is outside playing in the fresh air. Such a wonderful day to be a Nakan!

I had the top down in my BMW convertible, speeding on the highway with my braids flowing in the air. A smile plastered on my face. Excitement bubbling out of me with laughter every few moments as I sang along to 5th Harmony's "Work From Home".

"You don't have to go to work, work, work, work. Let my body do the work, work, work, work. We can work from home!"

Going to see my handsome husband. He sounded so groggy on the phone last night so I flew me and cute little car out to visit him. His voice was in unusually high spirits despite the drawl in his tone. My father complained Morgan hadn't been going to work for over a month like he fell off the planet. When I called, he said he planned on being alone all day in his stuffy basement meditating. I was not going to allow him to waste his time off depressed and brooding about old war stories.

I bought tickets to a movie and made reservations for dinner downtown Nadine that we could walk to from his lakehouse. He refused to visit me in the city. Said it wasn't his scene. So, I was stuck traveling to him in Nadine far outside of the city life. I don't think he even leaves his house anymore. I worry about him... but he says he's fine, so... I have to respect him to handle his own life as I enjoyed mine.

It's been tough trying to stay engaged to Morgan. He has an issue with nearly everything I do. And we seem like polar opposites. My father say we're both fighters, we make it through. Besides, the most eligible bachelor on Gaia, deserves to be married to its most beautiful woman! I can't wait until we can go out as a married couple. No longer hiding for politics and peace treaties or worried about my friends.

My father didn't know how our allies would react to me wedding Morgan. Natalie seemed pretty pissed off. My father thinks he planned everything between me and Morgan. I was relieved when he gave me his blessing to go all out with Morgan. My plans for my dream wedding were near completed and they had little choice but to both deal with it and whatever rivalry they have going on for me. We're Gregors, It's better to act then have to apologize than to get nothing done at all.

I pulled up to the beautiful lakehouse he relocated to after Natalie kicked us out the apartment. A necessary upgrade. A good place to raise a few of our kids but we'll definitely need to sell this place and move into daddy's manor as soon as possible! I would be home sick after a few years on our own. We could even keep the lakehouse for his office or a vacation home. You needed room to stretch your arms walking around your home. You can walk from one room and already be at the back of Morgan's house, it was peculiar. I was used to having to drive to my frontgate not poke my head out the door and there ya go.

Use your money, baby. It's yours! Ha. He claims a billion still isn't enough money to be fruggle. Or he tries to tell me he must be smart in how he spends his money. He's just cheap sometimes. Never wants to buy me things or take me out. It would be very tough being with Morgan if I didn't have my own money. He made me open a business because he didn't want give me money. Being married to him will make everything worth it, daddy says.

I parked along the semi-circle driveway in front of the door and took a few steps to the door. I kneeled down grabbing the spare key from underneath a fake rock. Usually knocking or calling his phone was useless. It was so hard knowing whether or not he was home with how modestly he lived. And I had no interest in waiting outside for half an hour while he meditated or did the mountain of busy work on his desk.

I pushed open the front door, all smiles until I saw the half-naked woman laying across his couch.

"Who the fuck are you?" I raise up my customized Stunnah shades, and balled up my fist.

"I'm Rose, who the hell are you?" she cursed, stretching out on the couch like a stray cat. “I live here.”

"Halle Victorianna Gregor, what the hell do you mean you live here, bitch?" I marched up to her ready to break her neck.

“Oh shit...” she crushes under her breath,

“You really need to get out of my fiance’s home before you get hurt.”

“Is that a threat or a promise Princess.”

“I don’t have a nail appointment for another couple days. You’re gonna wish you waited to piss me off.” I was happy I decided to wear flats and stud earrings today.

“We can talk this out... I was only taking a nap. I didn’t think anyone else was home!”

“Half-naked in your little booty shorts and bra like you own this fucking house?” I was bewildered, punching her in the gut by surprise. I drove my knee into the side then tossed her inside the side of the couch. I looked around the room wondering where Morgan had been.

Morgan often said I had my father’s temper. Sometimes he laughed it off. Sometimes we fought about it for an hour until I admitted he was right. I was Daddy’s Little Girl after all. I wasn't going to ever admit defeat without a fight.

Rose tried to get to her feet. I hopped across the coffee table cutting her off. We wrestle, she was strong but still wasn’t shit. I kicked her in her hip with my shin like Morgan showed me. He said the hip was a center of movement, a kick there would knock even him off balance. I grabbed her by her hair and under her arm, wailing on her for the disrespect while beginning to choke her out for the nudity. I was going to put her to sleep just because I can. She needed to learn her place.

You come to visit your fiance and there's a half-naked bitch in her panties and tanktop walking around, saying she lives in the place! What the hell is this?

She lifted me up slamming me to the ground. We wrestled. Punching and clawing for each other.

“Get off of me!” she screams as loud as she possibly can kicking me away. "Is everyone in this family, a homicidal maniac!"

"It's a prerequisite to being in the Gregor Family." I retorted wiping my hair out my face then kicking her in the chest sending her to her back to mount her again, "I refuse to believe Morgan allows this!"

"Morgan loooooves it." She groans trying to keep me away with her feet, managing to nearly kick me in my teeth.

"Watch your mouth!" I run after her and she scampers around the couch like a coward. “Fight me!”

"Watch yourself Rich girl, you got as good as you gave. Let’s talk it out! You just started hitting me. I didn’t even get a chance to talk!"

I cut my eyes at her. She's lucky this is such a good day. I won't allow her to ruin it for us. I knew about Morgan’s past. I know how we met. I wasn’t going to be caught dead as hypocrite. If he wanted an open relationship then fine but she is going to know who she’s serving.

Otherwise, I would make her clean her blood from the carpet. No one disrespects a Gregor and simply walks away. And you absolutely DO NOT walk around their husband's house naked with an attitude. My grandmother would have burned her alive but that was a different age as my dad puts it.

I knew Morgan was unhappy with our arrangement but another woman already? I promised him I would improve! I only needed some patience and time.

"Did you realize, I'm the maid?" she asked with sass.

I parted my lips then laughed hysterically, "you're just the maid?"

"Just the maid?" she sucked her teeth, “Yeah... I’ll be humble since it seems hard for you.”

"Oh my! This is hilarious. I thought you were competition! My apologies, sincerely. Morgan is going to be so angry with me for beating up his help. I am so sorry for hitting you." I couldn't control my relief.

"He'll probably fire me for messing up that pretty face of yours."

"I don't think you can lose your job for flailing on your back like a dying fish? Yes, he'll be so upset with you for not defending yourself better."

"Morgan loves me on my back." She tries to get my goat.

I smile, "I bet he loves your insolent attitude too. Morgan can be fucking you silly. I don't care you're not engaged to him. I AM!" she sings holding out her ring and dancing away from me.

"In fact, he thinks I'm outspoken and bold."

"Funny, he thinks that I'm meek. I suppose sometimes my Lord Husband is wrong though. Why the hell don't you have clothes on? We're going to get to the bottom of this indolence or start a round two. Maids most certainly have dresscodes, 24 hours a day, 365 days a year. Is this your uniform?"

"You're his fiancee..." I shrug.

"Jumping to the husband thing pretty soon though!" She said with such cockiness and satisfaction. "So, you're the reason he's so dead on the inside. I knew it had to be his terrible girlfriend."

"That's far enough! Don't lose your life over a man you know nothing about, maid. Morgan has his own demon and personality. Someone needs to smile when all he does is frown."

"You sound like a toothpaste commercial."

A growl rumbles in my throat.

She just laughs, "Can't face the truth?"

"There was another woman before me. From what he says a whole slew. A few murdered bodies. And some wars he fought. He had a rough life. Look at all those factors if you want someone to place blame upon. But no... that's good ole Morgan. He's always been like that. Still, he keeps fighting."

"He's not like that with me but good thing I'm not competition, though." She smiles smugly.

I never believed I could be so incensed by a maid. The idea she is living with my man while I am all the way in Naka pisses me off to no end. I could never get Morgan alone or get close to him. Sneaking around and hiding. She gets to live with my man?

In that instant my consciousness peeled away as I jumped out my chair, leaping onto the couch she was on. She barely moved in time.

"Come back here so I can hit you!" I shout chasing Rose through the house.

She laughed, hopping over the furniture and running toward the kitchen. Probably to get a knife. I swear I hope she gets a damn knife!

"What is all this?" Morgan comes from his basement sanctuary. He looks us both over before that usual look of disappointment crossed his eyes, "Rose, what did I tell you about your dress code?"

"We agreed during work hours only. It's long after five o' clock! I just woke up from a nap and she waltzed in and pounced on me! I had no idea you were even home! I was taking a nap, Morgan, this isn't my fault!" Rose whined.

"Go, change now." he says plainly as if this was an everyday occurrence.

His voice never raised no matter how angry he seemed. His base tone was threat enough. His eyes could put you into submission.

Rose poked out her lips and stomped away.

He turned to me and raised a brow, "You attacked her?"

"You're fucking kidding me right? I would never have my maids dressed like that! We're getting married soon and you're in here banging your maid but can't even keep her in uniform? That's basically like hiring some chick to just live with you and clean your crap. If that's all you wanted then no matter you and Natalie didn't work out. She is in violation for me to walking in here with her dressed like that! I want her penalized Morgan!" I demanded loud enough for her to hear me.

"To be honest with you. I barely even know this girl. She made a good point about comfort and me not being around. It made sense. I wasn't about to deal with it. I'm not having sex with her at all. I know how it looks Halle but I'm not playing you." He puts his hands up in the air.

Morgan wasn't as accustomed to the lifestyles of the rich and famous. He probably just saw her as some woman who cleans and cooks. He didn't understand the status difference. It was just like Morgan to let his lessers run around like they were his equals or lived here! She was employed and that's all that keeps her here. When her employment ends poof. This place better be absolutely spotless if she thinks she is staying here.

"She kinda lives here even when she's off the clock, Halle. It's a bit difficult to set a dress code in her free time. Not to mention I wasn't even aware. I haven't seen her all day, I swear to you!"

"What!? You won't even let me move in!"

"Your father makes too many demands. He wants my loyalty and my soul. It's too much. If we were getting married, the two of us I would have no issue. I feel like I'm marrying your father instead of you."

"Sooner we get married the sooner you won't have to hide you're sleeping with your maid." I tease him.

"I swear, I am finding out about her working here the same time you're finding out. I would never set myself up for failure by bringing a woman in my home. I'm trying to put the pieces of her story together. She cooks, cleans, stays out of my bedroom. She says she is a student going to the local university. I guess I do want to give her a shot. I honestly have not been considering sex with her and I don't want it. I feel I am close to something in my training."

"What? How could you not? She is very beautiful. Many girls carry weight poorly but it suited her frame and curves. Morgan, are you feeling okay? Usually you would be all over a girl like her, what's wrong? I already told you, I don't mind sharing you."

"Halle, we have discussed this I'm honestly trying to be a better man." he rubs his temples. "Besides, all you will do is in Nadine is go downtown to spend money. You have multiple businesses to manage and your classes. You can't drop your whole life for a wedding or me.

Well, I at least I don't want you to feel you're choosing between your life and your freedom like I do. Enjoy your life for a while Halle you're young. If you open a new shop here then that'll definitely give you a reason to move in. Might solve your other issue too if you let someone manage the other shop."

"And I thought I understood you until I saw her in her panties. If you weren't my fiance instead of fighting her I would have kept her for myself. If you don't want her then I'll keep her."

"Are you hearing yourself right now Halle?"

"Better her than Natalie. I'm supposed to be your wife! How would we survive until death do us apart if I don't support you in your decisions? If you're trying to have sex with your maid I rather you talk to me first."

"I am not trying to have sex with her Halle!"

"She's very clearly trying to have sex with you if she's lying around half-naked for you to find her."

"They're shorts and she's still off the clock. I-I- I didn't even know she was wearing them. I hear you Halle. I understand you. But listen to me, I had no idea about any of this, please understand me."

"So, you weren't looking at her? From the way you're talking you obviously find her attractive." I cut my eyes at seeing if he was really so naïve.

"Halle, I don't understand where all this is coming from. I wasn't even aware of how she was dressed until I came up."

"I'm your wife, Morgan."

"Your father and I are still in negotiations. Nothing is final, yet. I'm not trying to imply anything, Halle." He takes a deep sigh.

It hurt to hear but hurt more to see how the situation was killing him, "Is that what you've told her too?"

"As I'm trying to say. I haven't told her much of anything but the truth. We have an arranged marriage by rites of your father, The Patriarch."

"We have a goddamn relationship you should be respecting, Morgan! We had something before my father ever got involved." I rebuttal.

"I didn't invite him into our relationship either, you did." He retorts.

"He just showed up in our relationship, alright? He's my dad what am I supposed to do Morgan?" I conceded tired of the same old tired argument. This is all he and Natalie fought over were marriage rites and the insane dowry.

He rubs his temples.

"Just say that you hate being with me, Morgan."

"Jah'Rakil..." he mutters, "Halle, I do not hate you or being with you. You know how deeply I feel for you for what we've been through. I am here, and I've been working on us but-

"Don't say it again, Morgan..."

"You have glaring issues, Halle." he finishes, as I say it. He sighs covering his face, "Jah'Rakil, I was not prepared for this today. Halle, I didn't even know you were coming today."

"Do you even care how much that hurts to hear? You have her in your home and that's what you say? How are we to ever get married on this route, Morgan? Our communications need a lot of work. We're supposed to love each other, want to be with each other. You don't even care about getting married." With every bit I was bursting at the seams, steam pouring out my ears as I fought my anger and tears on how terrible the marriage was working out already. He didn't even want to share a maid with me.

His silence was worse than the truth.

"Are you falling for her?" he asked me.

I broke my anger for a moment with intrigue breaking a smile for him, "I might be in love!"

"Halle, I have far larger concerns on my mind than which one of you have feelings reciprocated. I'm not focused on love or marriage right now, you're right. I still love you and want to see you happy. You know that but-

"We've spoke about it repeatedly. Yes, yes, I knoooow business, business, business. Alone, alone, alone and blah blah blah." I was tired of hearing it repeatedly.

“It’s more than business this time, Halle. Nadia has come up. I need to do more than reconstruction and real estate. I really need to step into leadership here.”

"You're letting Natalie affect us!? She hurt you, now you just want to be alone and miserable. That is not fair! Sorry... I misheard you. You usually say Ecru when you refer to here.” I motion all around me in the new continent.

He bowed his head. I think he even frowned, "I do apologize.” He sat at the kitchen island, “Natalie is not a factor in my life anymore. I apologize for what she’s left in my head and how that affects you. But I said Nadia, not Natalie.”

"Baby..." I sigh, hugging him and kissing his cheek, "Baby, if I just got to spend more time with you then I could show you, I'm not this horrible person you think I am. And I can show you how much you mean to me. We need a normal living situation together even if you don’t want to get married. You are not going to keep this chick in your house if I’m not enjoying it as well. Alright?”

“I don’t think you’re a horrible person. I think you're over privileged and entitled. You don't know the harshness of reality."

"And she gets it?"

He sighed, "I'm not sure. I wasn’t even thinking about Rose but she is from Nadia."

"Kept a prize, huh?" I smile.

His eyes flashed red at me in an "I’m not some serial killer, I don’t keep trophies I’m above that. I’m Nadia I-"

"No, absolutely not Morgan. Don't ever raise your voice at me to defend her again. That is the ultimate insult. I'm at least your damn fiancee, don't come at my neck over some fucking maid."

He focused his tone to be more constructive, "My fathers were from Nadia. She is not some pet, Halle. She's a person, they are people. She is a reminder of what I did... of what I preserved. It’s like the memories all came back at once then she showed up.” He ripped at his small afro having another war memory. He’s been so in his memories this past year. He was always talking about The Academy.

"Nadia, needed to be subdued, baby." I rubbed his back, "are you okay?"

He grimaced, out of disgust more times than not. If not disgust then pity. I wasn't quite sure which, nor did I care, it was all the same after a while anyway.

"That is not what happened in Nadia." He shook his head.

"Oh, great. What did I do now? How am I stupid this time, Morgan?" I groan.

"Halle-" he takes a breath before continuing and his eyes lose their reddish tint. "Halle, you've barely even stepped out La Vida. I'm not saying you're stupid. But you won't understand Nadia when your father told you some stories about a land he's never even bothered stepping foot in only in conquering. Just sends his fucking troops to sin for him."

I rolled my eyes unable to respond because I had no idea what he was even referring to anymore. He claimed to respect my father but had so much hatred and animosity whenever he brought him up.

I don't know when he got like this. Seems he's mad at everyone today. He was stewing in war memories again. He used to be The Regulation Regime's golden boy. My father says he loved Morgan as a son. He said he practically raised him in the academy. My father said men with good hearts were always haunted by the past. Morgan could have been a General had he returned from his mission in Nadia. If he was still faithfully doing Enshishi's work. Instead he wanted to return to civilian life and refuses to explain why he would give so much up.

Even still my father offers him our family's Wealth as a dowry. He refuses! I defended him. Natalie looked at him different. I had to hear her mouth for months about how he was being a coward, and how she didn't understand how he could give up such a powerful position in the Regime. She was not happy about our marriage one bit. They were even angrier I refused to force him back into The Regime. I refused to even bring up military life to him. It only ever stresses him out or makes him impossible to be around.

I can't truly complain. He claims inexperience with civilian life but he's managed to make a billion dollars within a few years of it while others stay poor for lifetimes. He maneuvered just fine and was loved by many when he was still out and about. I don't know why he can't just be happy. Morgan is wealthy with a beautiful wife-to-be. And workers who love him. I will never understand why this man can't just be happy! Now, Nadia is his new reason for depression.

Instead he fights me... fights daddy. He's stuck in the war. Everyone is just trying to move on right now. Everyone wants to heal. Dad and Nat are the only people I know willing to fight a war over their pride and traditions. I don't want Morgan dragged into such a mess.

"Morgan. You do understand that I'm on your side, right? I love you."

He sighs, "For now you do, yes."

"Why must you be so distant? All you ever do is push me away. I've been trying to stand right here by your side. All I ever wanted was for you feel for me as I do for you. I love you, Morgan. Sometimes I don't feel the same."

"You don't think I know what love is, that's what you're trying to say?" He shook his head, "Halle, I'm not being distant we just aren't close. I don't feel close to anyone anymore. I don't try to pretend anymore. We're getting married. I don't have to pretend to agree with your beliefs or like your dad. But- You just- I'm not sure we can ever get where you want to be at a personal level. You're looking at the bulk of my life without you in it now. I guess there is more to learn about me but it's nothing you want to hear and nothing I want to remember."

"We could be, though. You fight me every step and push me away. I understand you are fighting your past and memories. I am not asking you to sit around ruminating about who you use to be Morgan. I am asking you to join me in living for the future of you who can become and everything you can do for people."

"You want to share a house and have a relationship, but we don't even share reality." He chuckles, "I suppose right now we don't. I never seen it your way."

"So what if I don't understand everything you've gone through. Couples at least try, Morgan. Damn. If we're going to get married regardless, try being happy with me. Try making me your wife instead of chasing after the Roses of the world! Why do I always have to share you with some other bitch? I want some alone time with you. I guess I do want Rose gone. I came here because I wanted to be alone with you."

"Halle, we are to be awed by the will of your father for the sake of continuing the reign of the Gregors."

"Yes, yay Team Us!"

He shook his head in object disgust, "I have no interest to be a Gregor. Nor do I believe myself capable, nor willing, of ever living out your father's dreams. I want you to carry my last name. Not to be castrated with yours for your father's sick control."

"Where is this coming from? You and my father are friends. At least you two could be if you put your prides aside to get on the same page. My father has a great deal of love and respect for you. I don't know why you can't reciprocate."

He just stared at me. "You're so naive. You believe everything Colin tells you? Colin doesn't love me. He doesn't respect me. He has the satisfaction of seeing all his experimenting, tinkering, and fucking up my life came to fruition. I am the monster he created all these years! I thought I could save you from your father. So I loved you. I thought maybe you would understand and see things my way then we could live free. Instead, slowly you try to get me to see things his way. I cannot give up all the progress I made and everything I've done to get away from your father and the military. I have nothing against you Halle. I at least wanted to propose to you myself. Not being told and demanded to marry you!"

"I'm naive for observing reality, Morgan? Come on don't just sling insults at me to please your new bitch. I'm not about that at all! I am my father's daughter. I am not my father!" I was honestly starting to understand him.

Morgan used to stand for something, and hold himself to a standard. As of late, he's done nothing but feel sorry for himself. If he's so upset and sad, be happy! He's not the type of person who can be happy if he feels controlled. It's probably why the military had to make him a Wolf. To stop him from turning against The Regime. Send him the other direction toward their enemies so he never turns around to see what they're fighting for in the long run. I guess he saw through the whole war for peace bullshit.

"For believing your perspective to be reality." he spoke in code.

There was always some point I missed. Some deep moral failing on my part. Always some reason we can't just be happy. Why he was better than me and right about everything. I'm getting exhausted with Morgan always telling me what I'm doing wrong. I have no idea how to fix this situation on my own.

"Fine, Morgan if this is how you feel we'll call off the wedding."

"Your father won't allow it." Morgan sighed, "I've tried to renegotiate his whims multiple times. Even operating as head of his company to inherit things through merit. He wants that and more, he's incorrigible."

My heart broke. I found it hard to even breathe, "You already tried breaking off our wedding?"

"Halle, I don't mean it like that. It isn't about getting married to you. I want to cut off all the strings he has attached so I'm not some puppet."

"Is that how you see me?" I began rubbing my eyes feeling completely thrown off by even seeing this maid.

"Hmm..." He raises his brow as if I didn't just say that.

"When did you ask him to end our wedding? You're so fucking insensitive Morgan, I wasn't even being fucking serious about calling it off! I want you to love me, like you love all these fucking hoes! Why can't I get that fucking attention? Who is this chick, Morgan? I'm not even allowed to move-in with my man. But here she is? How old is she even?"

"She's 20..."

I stare at him as if he lost his fucking mind. I smack him in the back of his head, "Who the fuck do you think I am, you son of a bitch? You have some younger bitch in here too?" I shout at him. I swat him with my purse.

He lets out a sigh, it didn't even faze him. Nothing ever does... I was going nowhere, neither was he until this was fixed. We were bonded to this union. So, this is how he feels? Hitting him didn't even feel good. Not as good as hitting, Rose... at this point I'm fighting myself as he's pinned against whatever drama is in his own life.

"I attempted to renegotiate terms in our cigar room meetings. Your father is stubborn, and reckless." Morgan pulls me in close. He holds my head and kisses my forehead. "Halle, I don't know how you think I feel about you. But I want to be with you. More, than any other woman at least. I just don't think you understand where I'm coming from. I haven't run a nation or a company before. He wants the world, Halle. I can't do that... I don't believe in that. He just wants to see his views come to fruition regardless of who's in his way. Even if there's a hundred more Nadias. I used to not care about what your father and the regime wanted. I thought I could join or sit by. I was wrong. What the Regulators are fighting for right now, I don't believe in. And- After, Nadia I really couldn't fight for your father again."

"Morgan I understand all that. Can we figure things out with this maid?"

"Jah'Rakil, Halle it's like you're not even listening to me. This isn't about you or Rose, it's about...It's about absolution. For everything I've done... for who I was. I'm concerned with the future of Nadia and the world."

"Absolution?"

"To be absolved."

"I'm not stupid, Morgan I know what absolution means!"

Was I offended too easily? My will broke to quit over a possible tryst? My family is depending on me to wed Morgan. If not Morgan then who would I wed? I don't believe there's another man alive my father trusts as much as Morgan. I know there aren't many men I could love as much as I do, Morgan. But... I'm naive. He goes on rambling about insanities and these conspiracies. Everything my father tells me to just ignore or are rubbish stories. The idea of Morgan honestly believing these things was terrifying. Especially if this is all he's been focusing on for the past month.

"Morgan, are you having sex with your maid, yes or no?"

"She's my employee, Halle." That's how his mind worked, that was the man I was dealing with and all the rationale he needed. "Look, Halle. Those years ago... when I disappeared. Your father gave me orders to destabilize Nadia. I fulfilled them. I did it. I got rid of Bryon Qatar. It wasn't the army that came. I was sick to my stomach. I called back to base, let them know it was complete then a week later, the fucking Rottweilers were there for roundups. And- and- I just can't just fucking live with that shit anymore, man. Qatar gave me this old book. He asked me... 'how could a man kill you for freeing your people. I fight for freedom... I fight for the people.' As a Wolf that is what they told me I do. I thought I was a superhero, I thought I was good... but I wasn't, I was an evil fucking dude. I did sick fucking things for the Regulators, but then your father calls everything I feel teenage rebellion. As if my my impulse to kill was natural. He wasn't even moved by it. It was another sick test for him, another fucking example of him seeing what I would do.

But it wasn't like that, anymore. When I saw those troops coming. I was a kid again after my father died. After that earthquake destroyed our homes. Seeing myself before I even left Nadia. It was like trying to save myself. My first days of training, when things seemed peculiar. I was staring at a new level of this shit. And... I couldn't stand by the Regulators. I even smirked when they arrived. I thought it was my rescue brigade looking for me. They didn't even know who I was. They didn't even know Wolves existed. Those were men I saw around the yard, at mess... they were brothers of the force, man. But I was nobody to them... They cared nothing for life, they had no respect for life. They were prepared to kill and rape women and children. They didn't even see them as people. It wasn't hard to make the decision, I didn't have time I went with my gut. But... I kept telling them to resist, to cease, to end it and leave... but they kept fighting. They kept corralling. And no one could fight back. Too scared... too weak... already dead. I don't remember any of it. Just flashes when I came back to consciousness and the pain and sight was too horrid and I lost self again. But it was different. It was always crisp before. But it was dirty, it was violent, with energy that didn't even feel my own at times. As if something was working through me. It kept saying to trust him. That he was me. And we are one. And he would protect me. Then... I died."

"Praise, Jah'Ada!" Rose cheers from the staircase.

"Rose!" he barks, his eyes once more flash the same reddish color. "Down here now!"

Rose ran down wearing a pair of leggings, "I'm sorry... I- I wasn't listening long. I didn't want to interrupt. Are these more appropriate?"

"Enough! Have you heard? Both of you? I am not concerned with this love nonsense right now. Nadia is in turmoil. That is my focus. You can help me if you wish or you can find yourself out until things are brought to order."

You couldn't even tell Morgan to eat or sleep. How did my father ever imagine telling this man who he would marry. He's so drawn to duty... I've never met a man like him. I loved him now more than I ever did before. I'm not sure I could love a man who would blindly follow my father anyway. It wouldn't be the Gregor way to expect Morgan to comply. Eventually these two had to settle things to the death for my hand in marriage.

"So, this is what's been bothering you for so long? I didn't know. I assumed it was me. I didn't know of Nadia. I had no idea you were ever involved." I raised my hands conceding my anger.

"No. No one knows the truth of Nadia. Therein lies the problem. It was destroyed and everyone profits off its demise. And not a single one knows what has happened. This I cannot stand for, this I cannot abide by."

With that Morgan turned about face and left us standing there. There was no more to be said. No more I had to say at all I was smitten.

I look at Rose. She rolled her eyes and looked away from me.

"I don't know why you're here, maid-

"My name is Rose Paz Andale, thank you very much, Halle Victoriana Gregor." she huffs and walks over to the fridge. "Oh, great the one day he chooses to eat and he ate my food! Jah'Rakil, Morgan I wanted my oxtails!" she groans shouting after him. "I'll just have to order something I guess." she carries on as if I'm not even there.

I let out a sigh, "As I said, I don't know why you're here. But if you are my love's ally then I will tolerate you. Besides I love oxtails. I'll pay but you need to order me extra oxtails. They always want to be greedy with them." I extend my hand. "I don't believe Morgan will be joining me for the movie or dinner. Do you want to join tonight, to give him some space? He usually works best alone."

"Ha, is that some sort of joke. I'm not going anywhere with you. I don't need your fucking handouts. I'm not some broke bitch because I'm a maid, I needed a job and this gig pays pretty good."

"Listen, I used to be young and foolish too. I am telling you, we let bygones be bygones. Besides if you're going to be living under this roof, you better learn some respect."

"I respect Morgan." Rose says innocently, "I like Mr. Ellys a lot."

He wasn't even in the room anymore. Who is she? She didn't need to kiss ass. Or is he actually different around other people?

"Morgan isn't going to kill you in your sleep at three in the morning, remember that." I said shrugging. "But I'll choke a bitch out, as you know." I tilt my head, clapping my hands, "ha! Beat that ass."

Rose quieted down. The girl wasn't a fighter. I was rowdy and willing, day and night.

"Look, I'm prepared on getting drunk tonight get over this latest Morgan drama. I am not leaving you home alone with him. You are coming with me."

She looked quiet, sweet and innocent. Even more reason to vet her. A strange woman pops out of nowhere. Maybe it is best I get some time with her. Besides... I rather not leave her alone with Morgan. Not until I know why she's here and what they've done together. She's too much his type.

"Change your clothes. The reservation's for 21:00, I was going to take a walk downtown Nadine because it was a nice day but... I don't want to anymore. I'll drive us. Look, I'm trying to get over today. No more fighting. It's time to party, alright? It's my girl Kole's new restaurant. It should be lit."

"Dinner and a movie with an heiress? I guess I'll bite." Rose smiles, "What should I wear?"

"I'll help you!" I clap my hands always willing to help the less fortunate. "If we can't find anything maybe we have enough time to go shopping first."

So, this is the world of Morgan Ellys. Beautiful women and battles. More money than he needs. He wonders why he's not happy. I suppose with the weight of the past on his mind it makes sense. As long as it isn't about me. And this chick isn't fucking my man. I'm good. It wouldn't be long before he beat his demons like he beat the military's.

CHAPTER 18

The Future Guardians

Halle Victorianna Gregor

"I want to begin this by saying from this moment until the conclusion of this lesson. I am not your lover, nor your employer. I am your Sensei. My word is law. Absorb what I say. I am not a good teacher."

Ooooh, my baby looked so good serious. Not his usual serious. But his drill instructor bit is my favorite in bed.

"Yes baby!" I wave, biting my lip. I can't believe I get to marry him. This took a lot of patience and endurance. But finally, I'm Queen Ellys.

"What did I just say?" He scolded me with those eyes.

"You said you are not our lover, nor employer but our Sensei." Rose bowed at her hip.

"Prrt you don't stop being my man because you want to work out." I roll my eyes stretching out.

She kept looking at me as if she wanted to hit me. Morgan wouldn't let her hit me, right?

"Okay, I want to begin by seeing what you already know. I'm judging by technique, energy emergence, and survival. This is a warm-up I always use on recruits to gauge their skills."

"Survival?"

Morgan tapped his lips figuring a way to explain. He did it often when we fought. "Well... After a certain point you're fighting people just as good as you. In my case, a lot of guys who were better, older, bigger, or smarter. I can't count the times nothing more than pure animalistic instinct bought my life from the reaper. Or when I've had to use the 'Crimson Glare' against my will. I call it *losing self*. It's like separating myself from the beast... But I lose self and I survive."

"Alright, alright don't get too in your feelings. The last thing I want is another war story." I yawn.

Rose sucked her teeth at me, "I thought it was interesting, Sensei."

"I can kiss ass too. You look good in your sweats babe. I wonder who bought you them! Oh right, ha me. I have good taste don't I?" I applaud myself.

"Did you just compliment yourself?" Rose shook her head. "I'm sorry you've had to deal with this for so long."

"Excuse me, I definitely complimented him too... I think. Pretty sure telling someone their clothes are nice is still a compliment."

"Enough of this bickering. No more of it. Control it. Focus it. And use it for strength when you need it. Now, isn't the time to be a woman. You are a warrior. Now, fight."

Rose held up her guard circling me.

"What's up, you're gonna hit me?" I laugh rolling my neck.

"I'm gonna knock you out." She grinned.

"Ha, I bet you can't even fight." I scoffed rolling my eyes. "You probably hit like a child."

Morgan rubbed his chin, "Actually, she hits like a freight train..."

Rose smiled, "I used to be a mask... They called me Mariposa."

Morgan didn't seem shocked. He also didn't seem pleased. But if I was going to be fighting some street thug then I wish I would have been warned!

I inhaled a deep breath. She strafed to my left her arm swinging hard into my neck. Her forearm swatting me to my knees. She moved so quick I didn't even get to land a hit!

Rose stood above me with a nod, walking over me like I was the street rat. Oh hell no!

"Halle, you telegraphed your move." Morgan barks at me.

"Don't fucking yell at me! I don't even know what that means." I shout at him.

"It means you're a shallow, transparent, vapid bitch." Rose kicks me in my ribs and drops me to the ground, rolling over on myself. She looked to Morgan immediately who was unmoved. Rose smiled. Mounting me. Not even giving me a chance to breathe, so rude!

I grab her arms as we wrestle, elbowing and kicking at each other. She broke free of my grip and grabbed my neck and my head tossing my head against the ground, then slamming her knee into my gut.

"Enough. Reset." Morgan walks over to us. "I said reset, Rose! Off of her, now." Rose's temper faded and she hurried off of me. She began running off, "not so fast."

"What? Am I in trouble?"

"Help your opponent to their feet." Morgan gestures his head. "It's important to always remain respect, even with your enemies it prevents you from getting too cocky or underestimating your opponent."

Rose looks confused but listened to Morgan as if his words were law. She held her hand out to me.

"I don't need her help. I'm about to kick your ass." I swat her hand away, getting back to my knees. "Owwie ow ow... God my sides. Why did you let her do that!"

"You were preparing to use pyrokinesis. Considering your lack of skills focusing your power. You could've killed her. I was prepared to intervene." He looked at Rose, "though that shouldn't be a problem for you huh, vigilante?"

"So, you'll help her and not me." I roll my eyes already over this.

He just stared at me, "Reset, let's go! On my mark. Prepare from collar tie."

Oh, I know this one! Morgan showed me.

Rose sets up with me brimming in overconfidence. I didn't know what she was smiling about. You don't hit a Gregor like that and live.

"On my mark. Begin." Morgan barks.

I drove my knee straight through her sternum. Her body tried to heave but I held her in the crutch, or whatever Morgan called it. She was pressing her weight down to muscle me to the ground. She probably thought because I was petite I was weak. I held her up with my strength, slamming my knees into her until she fell. I tossed her aside. Leaving her on the ground with her new confidence level.

"Reset." He barked.

I was prepared to walk away but wasn't going to hear his mouth about respect and shit. I extended a hand looking away from her waiting for her to grab it.

Rose looked up at him aghast, "you gotta chill homie, I need to catch my breath."

"Would a real opponent let up, vigilante? Would a rapist? I said reset. I am judging you on survival. You're hurt. Are you going to cry it better, or are you going to win despite it?" There was no arguing with Morgan.

As she prepared to speak she second guessed it. Taking my hand and just stood up. She took deep breaths and put back up her guard. Learning the real side of Morgan. He was ruthless-aggression incarnate. I guess he was too calm to appear as such but he said there was something inside him he needed to control.

"Let's see what you got street rat." I flex.

"I AM NOT a street rat, rich bitch." she curses.

"Set, half guard. No striking. No hair pulling. No speaking. I'm tired of both your mouths. Rose on bottom, Halle on top."

Rose frowned, looking at Morgan sideways. She never saw this side of him. She didn't know it got worst. I remember when I loved him before I knew. Made it hard to keep loving him... But I managed. Turns you on once you realize he won't do anything to you. Makes me feel safe to know he had a switch.

"Is there a problem, Rose? Did I hurt your feelings?" He stepped up to her looking down at her. “This is a fight-

"You're acting like a fucking dick head. I get two girls fighting over you makes your dick hard. If you ever talk to me like that I'll knock your ass out again."

Nope, she had it all wrong. I sat back and smiled loving seeing her chastised for once.

He stepped up to her and stared down at her. He didn't need his glare, his energy was scary enough. "Madam, this is not a good time to take that tone. If you're going to be insubordinate. Go inside, pack your bags and go back to wherever the fuck you came from. No one asked for your presence and you're a liar. You're a fucking maid. Be happy this isn't how I choose to talk to you on a daily basis, now set!" He ends it slapping her butt. "Do something about it." He did it again.

"I'm not going anywhere, Morgan." She shoved him away.

"Fighting spirit, glad Nadia taught you something." He japed.

"Okay, that's enough." I step up. "You two are not gonna be doing that in front of me. Whatever the hell it is you got going on. If you have an issue with Rose, I'll take care of her. She's right. You're not that man anymore. I don't want to see that side of you... Ever again."

He claimed it pained him. He was more the merrier, gardening and landscaping type than the destruction of humanity type. He said there was an old Bushido saying, "better to be a warrior in a garden when war came, than a gardener in a war."

He nodded backing down. I'm glad my words still mean anything to him. My dad taught me early, a man wasn't afraid to put a woman in line. My mother never liked to be disciplined so she ran away. My father says she's just a coward. I don't think Rose learned that.

"Rose, I will knock your teeth out your mouth if you ever threaten me again. Is that better for you?" He looked at me.

Rose shoved me away, "you're so cold blooded, huh!?" She shoves him again. "You're a fucking bastard right? You'll hit a woman?"

He grabbed her by the throat, and kicked her feet from under her. He held her down like that. Her body imprinted into the ground.

"I have nearly been killed by many women. Leslie Steele, the current Lieutenant Elite for the Regulator Regime was my sparring partner in the Wolves, and since we were children. I have trained many pups and dogs alike, male and female. If you think that wet little box between your legs means you're incapable of violence, there's a whole other breed of women you've yet to see not afraid to fight. You two will take me on. Set. I won't use my glare."

I wonder what made him so high-strung? He hasn't been this brutal in a while.

CHAPTER 19

Two on One

Rose Paz Andale

I was wondering where the ground went. And my back started hurting milliseconds after I kissed standing goodbye.

Morgan paced away from me, shaking his head continuing on, "If you think this world honestly cares that you're a woman. You're out your mind. There are so many dangers. You must defend yourself! And you two both must get out your feelings. This is impersonal. This is instruction. You two are partners. Help each other get stronger. You two can try to take me on. First to land a clean hit wins the exercise. It's nearly time for my meditation."

He cracked his neck and didn't even raise his guard.

I didn't hesitate but Halle pounced on him tearing him off of me before I could get up regardless. "I told you no, Morgan!"

He snatched Halle off his back like taped paper and tossed her on top of me.

He let out a sigh. "There's going to be so much to teach you two. Rookies..."

"Rookie?" Halle cursed getting off of me.

"Stop disrespecting me, Morgan!" I snapped.

I got to my feet and took after Morgan. He sighed. I punched furiously but he was ducking and dodging effortlessly. He held up his guard as I hit him full force. The veins popped in my shoulder. I only managed to push his planted feet back in the dirt a few inches back even as I drove my full strength into the punch.

I saw Halle blur taking his side. As she began to swing he hesitated. His eyes growing Crimson for a split second before he closes them shut, staying true to his word and rules. He bypassed my guard, gripping me by my collar before tossing me right into her like a bat.

He hops back. "Alright... That was close. Good Halle. I was expecting you to flank me, instead you took my side. Close."

"How did you move so quick?" Halle asked.

"Obviously you haven't been listening to my military record." He monotoned.

We both looked at him with shivers. His speed was superman human. It felt like I was moving in hours and he moved in millisecond's.

His intense stare even without the red eyes was terrifying. It made me rethink my strategy and who I was dealing with. My images of the poor innocent man were fading away. Replaced with the reality of this being one of the strongest forces on the planet. His only measure was if we could land a hit on him. To him we were less than rookies, we were just civilians.

He asked if I knew how to fight. Hand to hand wasn't my specialty but my mother and grandmother taught something far more useful since I was able.

"Halle you know pyrokinesis right?"

Halle smiled.

She helped me to my feet. "We're gonna show this dick, what we got. Cool? Time to step it up a notch."

"Age before beauty." I grinned.

Halle's smile faded and she let my hand go, letting me fall back down. Morgan was behind her.

"You're a team-player." I strain, getting up on my own.

She spun around exhaling a breath of fire at Morgan without hesitation.

"Whoa!" He dropped down and somersaulted backwards into the air, shielding himself with only his arms crossed.

He pushed off his back foot to reset himself only to catch himself falling into Halle's next trick. Halle spit at him in succession, missing every shot as if she wasn't bothering to aim. The look in his eyes, he noticed she had no control. He sprung once more getting closer to her. I didn't move in time to stop him from shutting her mouth shut. He held her mouth as she squirmed and screamed, swallowing the fireball in her mouth.

I raised my hands, and wept the water from the lake dragging it laboriously through the air and knocking the pillar into Morgan as he caught his landing. He caught me out the corner out the corner of his eye. He evaded the first swing by releasing Halle and jumping aside. As soon as he landed on his foot, the pillar of water pendulum was already crashing into him knocking him straight to the ground.

He picked himself up. Brushing the water out his afro and smirking. "That was nice, you two."

"Ha, nice Rose I wasn't expecting that." Halle gave a thumbs up.

"Well, water is a bit harder to control than spitting up fireballs." I panted, falling to my knees to catch my breath.

Halle looked at me and snorted out smoke. "You're treading on a thin line."

"I'm watching me out perform you." I shrugged. "And I'm the only one who's hit him. And got him off you. I believe you mean, 'Thank You'."

Halle smiled and turned, "I can do more than fireballs."

"Halle..." Morgan warns. "Control your frustration."

"You can take it, baby." She inhaled deeply as the temperature began to rise tremendously her skin radiating orange.

"We haven't practiced this!" Morgan shouts.

Halle squats down inhaling, and then exhales spitting out a lava plume. It rains down magma. Morgan disappeared before us. I watched in awe as the searing magma spewed from her gullet entrapping me without an inch to move in either direction. I accepted my fate until

I felt a hand on my shoulder tearing me out of reality. He drops me a second later, staring down from the roof. I look around frantically wondering how we got from point A to point B.

"She just wanted to show off. She never listens." he shook his head, irritated as all hell. “It's gonna be the death of us one day.”

I can show off too. I held my hands up spotting a rain cloud overhead. I wring my hands squeezing the cloud dry as it downpours atop of Halle and her fireworks.

Morgan looked at me out the side of his eye. He said nothing just nodded.

"Baby?" I ask rubbing his shoulder.

"You lied to me... You're not a maid. You're not innocent. You're not some student. What are you doing here?" his voice was cold. He refused to ask in front of Halle.

This wasn't how I wanted to tell him. It was what it seemed.

"I am, I am..." I say in defense. "But- Baby, the only thing I haven’t told you is that, I was a mask, and maybe, that Baat is my grandmother.” I poke my index fingers together, “I promise. I am a student, I am your maid and-

"You're Halle's family?" his look went from anger to confusion quickly. “This makes no sense to me.”

"Ew, no. She is bastard seed. My grandmother was raped and held hostage... Halle I guess is my aunt or something if you had to be literal. I consider her nothing. Nor do the rest of the Qatars. She chose to be a Gregor, she’s Colin’s daughter my Grandmother was used.”

"If you wish for me to be honest with you, Baat. I'm going to need to know what's going on." he bypassed me entirely staring right into my eyes with those brick-red forces of nature. “What is going on here?”

I felt the world peel away around me as if I was falling asleep. My grandma often told me to simply remain calm when she had to take control. My eyes sparkled like crystalline sapphires as I held his hands dropping to my knees.

"I love you, I've found you, and I'm here to serve you as your Queen as I was meant to!” Baat grabs his collar, “Please, understand! Colin wishes for Enshishi to claim your soul as he did with Maurice Gregor. Maurice was claimed as ward under Mandel Gregor. A family of half Guardian bastards. Rejecting the very seed and duty bestowed to them. If you wed Halle he'll claim you. He wants your firstborn child. He wants you to expand the Gregor territory to claim the world. I cannot allow this. This is beyond Colin... The Guardian of Fire has been corrupted for centuries, now. And no one knows, they believe him sovereign. He believes himself Rakil's opposition, Rakil's equal. I am your ally, Morgan. Ada I live for you!" she pleads for him to understand.

He nods and walks off. Unimpressed and unmoved. We told him nothing he didn't already know... we should have just been forthright. Though, we didn't know who we were dealing with either.

"I have an issue with stripping free-will away from others. I suggest amending your method of communication." He let out a sigh.

My grandmother was shocked, we both froze. Bowing our head.

"I will do my best. This is what the two of us have found best. This is the bond between a vicar and a Guardian. I- I'm not sure there's much I can do from such a distance. My true form is in Grand Baa'th, my body is in Maya."

"Do better." He mutters. "Or be honest."

"I feel you don't understand."

"No, I don't. And I don't care to." Morgan growled, "The Dread Wolf attempted the same bond with me. He claimed it wasn't an issue. I felt tainted and dirty every time. Do better!"

"You must care! It'll stop you from communicating with Ada when you need him. Your mind must be open to Rakil and his son."

He only nodded.

"Do better." He repeats. "Ada needn't rely so heavily for me to push his agenda. Do better. She is a girl not your puppet."

"She is my granddaughter. Not your tool."

He jerked his lip spinning around, "I wish nothing for the girl but her happiness and safety! I have my own issues. You have placed your pawn here to manipulate me and ruin my marriage! I asked for none of the feelings I have for her! You've betrayed my trust!"

"Morgan it's okay. Honestly. This is how me and grandma communicate. It's fine. I accept this." I attempt to plea. To get him to understand it was far more natural than he could see from his position.

"You don't have to. Your mind doesn't need to be open for her to filter through and pop in when she wishes."

"I call upon Baat's help and grace, Morgan. She doesn't control me. I love her. She is my grandmother and my patron. She helps me as a Guardian should."

"Perhaps my ignorance on this matter is a boundary. But that's only cleared when you're speaking freely on the matter." He sneak disses. "You were not straight with me, nor was she. I don't want to be bothered with this right now."

'He doesn't understand. He's too stubborn in his own way.' Baat sighs. 'Ada was always so distant from me. He never understood my methods.'

Her methods? Now I was reconsidering Morgan's words. Morgan was a guardian as well. I suppose as was Halle. Neither of them went through this, did they?

'Grandma... Do you truly end up with Ada?'

'I have never been far from his side, nor his bed. We find each other in every life. Our love is inevitable. Though, I will admit not always permanent... Ada has a habit of dying or disappearing. I have a habit of interrupting his rules as I please, creating my own. There have been inceptions of me to stay by his side, but most times- we don't understand each other, we only love and love fiercely.'

I hold out my hand, "Morgan help me, you got me up here."

"No, you put yourself here." He jerks away from me. "Ask Baat to help you if you are truly her ally and not her pawn." he hopped off the roof and rolled to his feet. A two story fall shaking it off as if it was any given Tuesday. He didn't need his power to be strong. He walked off from both of us, leaving Halle as she tried to hug him.

"He doesn't trust me Grandma..." I felt near tears.

'No... he trusts you. It's me he doesn't trust.'

CHAPTER 20

Meditations & Revelations

Morgan Ellys

The greatest trick the devil ever played was convincing men they were lesser than their Masters. As if it is somehow a lacking upon the slaves, rather than the circumstance of servitude to justify their station. Those who hold the chains bleed. Those who hold power, live and die. We are all mortal. Why the helplessness? They sell their lives and souls. They do so vehemently and eagerly.

They subjugate themselves with such conviction. Believing one day their meager suffering will bear fruits. Fruits when they've never cultivated the soil of their own existence. When the harvest comes they realize their lives are barren. It's always externalities. Always outside, it's never within self they find prosperity.

No... it isn't their servitude that leaves them enslaved. The sad truth of the world is many rather be slaves to their neurosis and vanity. Serving their Masters proudly than to pay the cost of liberty. They accept the plaintive validations of their worth to be presented outside the means to free themselves. Remaining in doleful comfort of subjugation.

I can't blame them. I bought my freedom in blood. I bought my freedom on the back of the very system I now wish to fight. There was a large amount of sweat equity.

But if you cannot release your shackles... you can still release your mind. Have your mind to yourself. Most won't even do that! Trapped in self, and trapped in the system. Too afraid to fight or too ignorant to release. There is a battle. I weep for the latter. Enraged by the former.

When does your condition reach an end in which you can finally have enough? Too many wish to remain meek. Therefore I must be the Lion amongst Lambs. I must fight the battles of all those who cannot fight. The proud roaring voice of all those who have been silenced.

All that matters is that I see my end. I can see the problem and I wish to solve it.

But how? I know the immensity of my enemy. I know the depth of this issue. How far their tendrils reach. I stand alone against a franchise. Against a hulking breathing incarnation of power, corruption and greed. And most days... it seems as though I'm the only one who realizes this war.

"Morgan, are you meditating?" Rose calls down. "I wanted to ask you something." She says as she gently walks down the stairs.

I leave my lotus position and stare up at the ceiling in the dimly lit sanctuary.

"No fighting in this room." I caution.

"I don't want to fight. You have enough on your plate." She sits next to me and begins rubbing my temples. "Back then... what made you fight for Nadia?"

Hmm... and here she comes with this.

I shifted uneasily, getting her hands off of me. I closed my eyes and took a deep breath.

"So..." she asks, "Are you not sure?"

"I know but I don't think I could explain if I wanted."

"So, you don't want to?"

I shook my head, "No, Rose. I simply did what was necessary. The Regulators couldn't have Nadia."

"Why? What's so special about Nadia?" she asked.

"Today? I suppose not much at all. The world has watched as Ecru's been reduced to nothing. Geopolitical power shifts, people break off their treaties." I let out a sigh, "A bunch of myths and notions of the end. Nadia was rumored to be the birthplace of the first man, Ada. Thousands of years ago most these territories around the center of the world were known as Ecru. Now, you have Maya, Naka, Erdu, and Esha but Ecru has been torn down to just Nadia over the past few centuries. I was curious as to why in the Academy. Did my own research after and during my time at the Academy."

"Did you ever find out why?" She asks cross-legged and listening intently.

I sat up, "It's rumored the vicar of Ada and his bloodline were killed in the 2nd Age. But- I'm not really religious. I'm not sure I believe in all that. Sameera believed himself to be the restart of this bloodline. Many others have claimed the same. There is only Rakil. No man is a god."

"Jah'Ada..." she awes, "So, that's where this is all from? I never really learned about all the history and lineages. My grandmother and mother taught me a lot, but the history of Ecru was never of concern, mostly healing techniques."

"I simply had access most wouldn't realize was accessible and have seen more than others could believe. I don't believe men are gods... but the power of Enshishi and Anki I have seen. Part of me feels as though I've heard their voices speaking in my skull, maybe that's schizophrenia. But it must have been my conscience." I confess and rationalize.

"What if the voice of God and conscience are one in the same?" she asks insightfully stumping me.

"I- huh... what if? There are a thousand of those questions. Many what ifs." I respond but washed over her words in my mind as if I had found the key to eternity.

"You wouldn't have gotten this far if not by the grace of Baat or the strength of Anki."

"You believe in both?" I was quite surprised, "Most barely believe in One. It's rare you meet people with the original teachings."

"In Nadia we are raised to observe the five." Rose grinned.

"You know of Ada, then?" I rub my chin. I realize her favorite expression was more than just a curse. "He is your favorite?"

Rose beams, "Weeell... people did believe Bryon Qatar was a prophet. But he never claimed to be Ada... he actually said he would bring the First Man." She smiles. "How strange right after Bryon disappears, you're around to defend us from evil."

"Do not look at me that way, Rose!" I could feel her gaze.

Rose laughs, "You went through unholy conditions, walked with demons, and still fought for what was righteous and just! You're indestructible. If I was going to vote for a contender-

"That's blasphemous, stop speaking." I grit my teeth refusing to hear the rumors chasing me my whole life.

Rose shrugs, "Is that why you don't believe men are gods? You don't wish to be one?"

"No. Men are messiahs, prophets, but this talk of vicars and gods, no. I refuse to believe that, Rose."

"I kind of agree. There's talk of people manipulating elements and creating fireballs and rainstorms. That's bullshit, too right? This talk of Metahumans?" she asked as if she already had her answer, "You know the truth Morgan. Is it true they're here among us already?"

I let out a sigh, "Classified information..."

"Holy fuck, really it's true?" she claps, "Are you a meta too?"

"Hmmm... It is. As can I. Though, my pathway to elicit my abilities was far more strenuous than most."

"Why? How do you do it?" Rose thumbed my hip, "Do you think anyone can?"

"Rigid training, meditation, convening with your spirit and element. It must be within you. Cultivate chakra and take on all that is. Find the element you convene with and live through it."

"You make it sound simple. My Grandmother was quite skilled with water. I suppose I should follow in her footsteps."

"Many things are simple until it comes to doing the task asked."

"So,full of witticisms. What is your element you're living through then?"

I nod, "I believe you saw it within Nadia."

"But there was no fire or water. You just poofed."

“Well... I know a bit of Earth because Warren was my mentor, and he attempted me on that pathway as a kid. But my training switched to controlling the Ether once Colin had input. He knew something about me, me and Ray didn’t.”

“Maybe he just wanted his enemy, close?” she asked unmoved.

“Why would I be his enemy? I barely knew the man outside of being my father-in-law, we seemed like allies to some extent.” he paused as if something in his memory strained him. “Damn... you’re right.”

“Well, there seems to be a grand amount of knowledge of who you are, they’ve kept from you. Much more that you know and refuse to accept.” Rose tapped her lip, “How can we get back your memories?”

"There are many secrets the government seeks to guard us from. Though to conserve their powerhold or to protect citizens. I have yet to figure out. I stopped trying to make sense of all this after Nadia. I try to see good and bad, but with so many suffering I can't be idle. Eventually a true man must act regardless, according to what is right in his mind."

"What do you plan to do?"

"I believe for me to find absolution, I must return to Nadia to do what is demanded. The people need a leader."

"You would want to be its leader?"

"I'm quite honestly not even sure if I could be an effective leader. I was autonomous. I reported only to the Commissioner." I scratched my scalp, “want isn’t entirely the right word.”

"Dude... Wolves can't be real. That is way too much leeway. You were a child, only reporting to the Commissioner, with Gregor’s eyes on you?"

"Many things go bump in the night. We fight them. Well- fought. Anyway, political leaders are usual targets for quick drops. We thought nothing of humanity beyond volatile and fragile. I signed up to protect, not to dismantle. Well, I was a prisoner turned assassin. I was told I was protecting. After Nadia I knew it was a lie."

"At least you're fighting for the good guys, now!" Rose claps, "So, I came to ask about Wolves and Hounds. But also... you need to eat.

We're about to leave and you still haven't eaten enough yet. Also, fuck you for eating my oxtails."

"I eat at 15:00, a large meal, and another at 22:00."

"Hmm... you're never home or locked in your office. I don't believe you eat. Definitely not a good meal."

"I- I nourish myself." I rub my neck as Rose cut her eyes at me, "Look, you're not my mother. I don't need a keeper."

"The hell you don't need a keeper! You don't eat! And by the way, buddy, meditation is NOT sleep."

"I'm trained to-

"I don't give a damn what you *were* trained for or in. The war is over soldier. Time to eat and sleep. Time to recover and rehab. If you won't come then I'm making you dinner before we leave." Rose grabs my ear beginning to tug me.

"Rose, I-

"I'm not going to hear it. You've been in the house all day. You haven't gone outside. no one but Halle has visited. Now, you want to argue about eating and sleeping, with me. Nope! Nopity nope nope! This is not the war anymore. You're no longer a Wolf. It's time to take care of yourself. Be human for awhile."

The greatest trick the devil ever told...

"You've seen me slaughter men. Yet you speak to me as if I'm some child. You don't fear me?" I swat her hand away.

"Please, you wouldn't hit me. You said you only fight bad guys. You're too calm to be violent. You didn't kill out of cold blood... you saved us from the Regulators. Bryon Qatar said he would bring the messiah and Jah'Ada, you came! You came and literally messiah'd all over 50 men in bodysuits with guns, and you were bare-handed. Then died, and here you are. How could I fear you for defending me?"

I stood against Regulators, as if that fits into Qatar's prophecy. I believed Qatar thought himself the messiah. But no. He believed it to be me. All he told me that night. Of the fifth Guardian. He believes me of all men to be Ada? He truly was a lunatic.

"Rose, right place, right time."

"To take down 50 men? 50 Rottweilers. To die and be reborn? You made me believe, Morgan. You're incredible. In Baat's name you may not be Ada, but you are truly incredible."

I don't recall myself ever slowing down to realize even less to remember.

"Are you blushing?" she grins.

"I-I've never really heard this before." I admit.

"What?"

"I thought I should have been stronger... To hold some conviction. But I'm lost, Rose. I don't know if I did the right thing. I was raised in the Academy and abandoned it all. I don't know what I believe to be true anymore. Nothing more than the boogeyman and the power of Gods."

"Morgan, you were a child. You made the best decision a boy could."

"I was no innocent bystander. I was a weapon of war, Rose. Trained to carry out orders. Then I became an autonomous weapon of mass destruction known as a Wolf."

"Morgan, stop and smell the funeral flowers. You were 18 and decided to turn against everything you knew. I get you're confused but for your own sake, can you acknowledge the pressure all this puts on a child? It was wrong what happened to you especially since you were brainwashed."

"Do not say that..."

"What do you call indoctrinating children? Torturing them. And having them blindly follow orders?" Rose stared me in the eyes, daring me, "Are you going to hit me, Morgan? If not I suggest you listen."

"I will admit. I don't acknowledge the affect my training took but you must acknowledge I cannot unsee what I've saw, and I have done what I have done, regardless of it being right or wrong."

"You have a future. Don't give me that bullshit. If you really don't see an issue with what happened to you. Then please, stay away from my home. We do not need another Colin Gregor."

"Colin was not my sensei. The commissioner was." I snarl at her.

"Then why does Colin want you, Morgan?"

"I don't usually think on my Wolf days, Rose." I rub my temples but she relieves me of that quickly. I didn't stop her, her hands were softer and she was far more gentle than I was being upon myself... Hmmph... seems like I should note that. I let out a sigh taking a stroll, "When I was ten, my squadron was taken to the woods. We were strung from our ankles. Our bodies dangled. Our arms tied behind our backs. Colin was a sergeant. He watched, he proctored. I watched children die next to me. After days... most recruits were happy just for it to all be done. I refused to let Colin get to me. I refused to be his student. I don't know his obsession but it's been present my whole life since I was ten. When I was finally untied, I used my eyes for the first time. To wipe that fucking smirk off his face. I went into a blind rage, my vision turned blood red and I decked him in the face with all the life force I had left."

"If you hate Colin then why marry Halle?"

"I knew Halle outside of Colin. She stood by me when the world abandoned me and I abandoned it. She's all I've had for a time. Leaving that won't come easy."

"Is that enough to marry the daughter of the devil?"

"Rose, I'm done prying into your life and you are done prying into mine."

"But you don't ask about my- oh..." she frowned, "I understand, I guess. Am I making you uncomfortable?"

"You pop in my house. Make me relive my worst memories, accuse me of being a messiah, and now you're trying to ruin my marriage! You're not making me uncomfortable. You're beginning to overstay your welcome. I'm quite capable of making my mind up on my own, Rose."

Rose leans forward, nuzzling my neck and kisses my cheek, "I want you to realize the world has been waiting for you, while those two men have kept you from us. We've needed you while you have been lost in doubt. If you realize that... I'll drop the subject."

"Rose... please back up."

She kisses my cheek once more, her soft lips pressed for longer this time before she pulled away.

"I'm going to make you dinner, now."

"I am not a god, Rose."

"No... but maybe you're great all your own. If Warren and Gregor have taken this life long interest-

"Those two-

"Are they human, Morgan? Answer me that in your own words. Are those two men, human?"

"I-" she had caught me. I was a boy when I saw Colin and Ray fight for the first time. I was asked to flee. In my youth I thought myself capable of standing with them. But the power that radiated off those men was not of Gaia. I doubt it was even of this realm. Both were expert swordsmen and metahumans, but there was more to it. Both grew well over ten foot tall, and weighed as much as baby cows. "I don't believe Rakil is a comprehensible force or image. We might be something but we are not him. I was to wed Halle to not find out, for the betterment of the world it is best we do not know. The wedding is on as it stands."

"You're scared of them?"

"I learned from Ray Bradley Warren before he was Commissioner. Then I was a boy and he was a shrewd Captain. He took the helm after the untimely death of Maurice Gregor. Control spread like wildfire. He had a magnetic appeal about him. Nadia was not the first or only. Order was being spread throughout Erdu and Naka. Before The Regime, lands governed themselves. This grew from a precinct of volunteers to what it is today. Fear is a minimum. Others like them exist, two to my knowledge at the same scale if the myths are correct.. Those who can stand against entire armies if they so chose. Instead they lurk behind their own armies. Fear? No... Object horror rests in my chest for whatever in the world Colin and Ray are. If Colin sneezes an entire city could be ablaze... I have trained with Warren and he's created tremors accidentally. They're imbued with something greater than Gaia, and are both old men in a field most men die young. Yes, I'm scared."

"If no man is God, then maybe you should call upon the father?"

I frowned, "Rose, Jah'Rakil doesn't want to hear from me."

"Would it hurt to try?"

"Rose, can you start dinner, something filling."

"Morgan, please pray. For me?"

I said nothing. There didn't seem to be much to say. My tongue was stuck in my throat and did not move.

"Can I pray for you?"

"I- uh- okay...?" I wasn't aware you could pray for other people.

Rose got on her knees and clapped her hands together. "Bow, your head, Morgan." I followed her instructions. "Father, Jah'Rakil, creator of all. Morgan is a man with a good heart. Please, allow him to see his own loving nature. Redeem this man. Stand with him and find him happiness. He tries as he can to do well, but in his mind he does not know what that is. Allow Morgan to see pass his mind and see with his heart. Set him upon the path you destined for him. In your name, father Rakil. Amen."

"You ask the father to save me, but not Nadia?"

Rose hugs me. The young girl has such a warmth to her. Her heart pounded against mine. "No man should ever feel as you do. Messiah or not. I don't care. I wish to see you happy. To find some solace."

"I need absolution to find solace..."

"Then find yourself. Look around you Morgan. You bask in blessings of the Father but cannot see all you have! Money, women, power. God has already forgiven you or you would be dead. You must forgive yourself, now. Forgive yourself and begin recovering."

"I have many things, Rose. I can acknowledge that. I am not blind. But things are all externalities, all vanity. Houses and women... these are not what make a man a man. It's his works. And I feel barren."

Rose rolls her eyes, "Morgan, you're only like 25. You have your entire life to find absolution or whatever you want to justify your depressive, masochistic, and antisocial bullshit."

"Bullshit..." I shake my head repeating her words, "It's only bullshit when it's inside your head. I have true sin, Rose."

"Morgan, do you think you're the only person with sin?" Rose sighs, "Don't lose your present being consumed by the past or wrapped in the future. Do you want to know what my Abuela says about mistakes and sin?"

I raised a brow waiting for her to continue on.

"Man can fix mistakes with virtue and good deed, but only God can fix sin." she wrapped her arms around me and kissed my cheek. "You're a man with a good heart. Rakil, Baat, they see your heart. I'm not even sure they care about your actions and mistakes as much as they care how you fix them."

"He's the Father..." I sigh, "My sins are a weight, Rose. But I know my charge for absolution. I was told and I took up said charge. I try to focus but-

"Did Rakil tell you himself?" she interjects.

"It's about perspective as well, Rose. I can see the issues, and the problems." I rub my temples, "I don't wait. If there's a problem. I fix it.It's how I am."

"Then it's time to look in the mirror and begin working, Morgan."

"So, it's me?"

"You're trying to fix an entire city, and turn against everyone to do it. People love you and your heart... but if you can't be humble and admit this task is too much for you. If you can't see your own good heart and convictions. You're going to fail. And you'll take a lot down with you. I'm not saying you can't do it. But not like this, not as you are, not with all the shit you're dealing with. Focus on Morgan, pray more."

"I meditate."

"That's great for when you're strong. But prayer is for the meek. It's humility. To fall before Rakil and ask for his guidance and blessings. How do you hope to help the helpless if you can't recognize your own helplessness?"

I leaned back. Outwitted by a girl who popped into life out of nowhere. There was an energy about her familiar yet foreign.

"My training taught me finality. You'll die regardless. Die with purpose. Die with dignity. Die for the Pack. The only thing I ever knew even before the Regulators... lost, death, absence, neglect. Being with Natalie was so easy because that's all I knew. Daunting misery and abuse but- there's more to life. I'm still so immersed in darkness... I never realized I've never seen the light."

"Sometimes we are the light in the darkness. Darkness is all some see. That's why they love you in Nadia. You're their light."

"Hope.. the only currency I have."

"Hope and Faith is all you need sometimes, baby." she kissed my cheek once more. "I can't wait to see you back at 100%."

"I've never considered.. I never took time to recover from Nadia."

"Well, now you have plenty of time, babe. Enjoy it."

"Okay, not a problem. I guess." I rub my chin, "So... how do you relax?"

"Ha, excuse me Mr. Parasympathetic?" she chuckles.

"I'm serious. I- I admit that I don't do it or take time for it. But- How?"

"Well, you can start by eating some food, understand?"

"My body is slowing down, my mind is foggy, and feels so distant. How could I possibly manage Nadia like this? But there's so much work that must be done."

"You can do it tomorrow, Morgan. Just sit down, better yet come out with us tonight."

"That's procrastination. It keeps people stagnant."

"And spreading yourself too thin doesn't? Being exhausted all the time and barely moving? Having a beautiful wife and maid, you're not fucking?"

"It goes against my training, Rose."

"Didn't you turn against all that?"

"I turned against those attacking, Nadia. Not my training."

"What good has your training done in real life?"

I let out a groan falling to my back and staring up at the ceiling, "Why must you be so honest, Rose?"

"You love me for it, don't you?" she grins ear to ear. She crawls over to me. Her lips bypass my cheek and she kisses me on the lips. She licked her lips, "You know... Halle is upstairs, she thinks I'm in the shower. I can show you how to relax if you really want baby."

"Stop, Rose."

"Come on... just entertain it. See how it feels." her hands ran up my thigh. "God, you're swelling right now."

"Stop!" I sit up.

Rose smiles innocently, "We're human, right?"

"She's in the house, Rose."

"So, do we start when she leaves?" she teased me, kissing my neck, "I've waited years to be this close to you. Don't let a girl down, baby." she whispers in my ear.

I reach out to grab her butt, "you're going to teach me how to relax, huh?" I squeeze it harder, "So, soft and firm."

"Supple." she moves to kiss me but I pull away.

"I suppose that's how I must be. More supple."

"Be whatever you want. Just don't let me go." She swoons in my ear, "enjoy it baby, I'm yours."

"Rose, I'm-

"Engaged, yes... but for one day be a millionaire and take advantage of your position, please."

I stand and shake my head. "You should get ready. If we're going to go out." I couldn't blatantly disrespect Halle in our own home.

Rose extends her hand and I help her to her feet, "Will you truly come?"

I shrug, "I highly doubt you and Halle would have let me stay home anyway..."

I took another long look at Rose's voluptuous body. I was a boy last time I felt this horny with a woman. This want and hunger to have her near. Whether sex or just being against her. She plucked something in my mind that kept me captivated. My options have always been so limited with my work and my "masochistic antisocial bullshit". A young woman, so beautiful is in my home, she's in love with me. A young woman so brilliant and insightful. So tender.

I pulled Rose closer and she surrendered to me. The feeling was intoxicating. I slapped it, squeezed it. I wanted her on a level deeper than carnality. Her energy was so familiar yet foreign. I kissed her, lifting her by her butt until her legs wrapped around my waist and her arms wrapped around my neck.

"Who are you, Rose?"

"Jah'Baat, Rose Paz Andale. I'm all yours, Morgan." she held my chin pulling down to kiss her. I held her body close as she moaned softly to my touch and kiss. I had forgotten this feeling. This desire to simply hold another person. "I love you, Morgan."

"Alright... that was... that was way too much, Rose." I pull away, "Halle, can not find out."

"Do we have to pretend it didn't happen?"

"I- I- we should both start getting ready to go, Rose."

She grins, "just a little more. I like how you play with my butt, baby."

No man is a god. I'm only human. But- wrong is wrong.

"Get ready to go, Rose." I repeat giving her a nod before leaving her in the basement.

Was this what a man in my position was allotted? It seemed expected. Even Halle was angry but- not surprised. I mean... Am I just weak? Or is this truly what my life has become? Am I just for this?

I need to worry less. Relax old man. Breathe. You're going out with two beautiful women tonight. Get ready for tonight.

"Will you tell me more about your version of history on the way over to the restaurant?" Halle asked as she got in the driver's seat.

CHAPTER 21

Our Path Commands All

Morgan Ellys

"Come on, girls. I thought you were both ready!" I shout from downstairs, Halle's car keys in my hands. "This is not an hour long affair. Put on some clothes and lets go." I was the last to get ready and the first done.

"We're going in public, caveman. I need to look appropriate." Halle is the first to retort, popping her face down the steps, still half-dressed in my bathrobe. At least her hair was done. I liked her like this with her curls bouncing in her face, rather than the styles she usually comes up with.

I could hear Rose's snickering upstairs. At least they were getting along.

I let out a laborious sigh and sat on the couch, grabbing a book I've been scouring for a few years but never brought myself to finish. A book given to me by Bryon Qatar the night I was sent to neutralize him. I was sent to kill a man instead of fear he gave me a gift. Peculiar at best.

"How do I look?" Rose bounced before me in a yellow sundress, flowing around her as she did a quick spin.

"You look great, Rose." I give an approving nod barely looking up, far more absorbed in the tome.

"I suppose I couldn't expect more excitement." she curled her lips, containing her palpable disappointment with my response.

I had been doing this enough to know I needn't care. I preferred my women naked otherwise wear what you want. I couldn't really care at all for the cloth before we reach that point.

"Maybe... we should keep our distance for a bit?" I suggest.

She blinked at me as if what I said wasn't in common tongue and sat next to me.

"What are you reading?" Rose gets up underneath me placing her hand on my knee, "I've seen this one sitting around. You actually read this brick?"

I begin to warn, "Rose-

"Kings of Gaia? This book is old as dirt man and it's huge, what is this?" she continues ignoring me, "What, don't look at me like that. Answer my question."

"History book of all the Kings of Gaia since the 2nd Age. I was given this by Bryon Qatar."

"He gave you a book?" Rose asked perplexed.

I nod, "It's how I've learned what I have about Ecru. At least this perspective. It was written by a Ecru born historian in the former territories of the reformed Ecru. He was Eshan by modern standards, Ecruen by his own."

"How did he consider himself Eshan and Ecruen if the region between Esha and Ecru no longer exists?"

"Hmm... it's a very old book, Rose. It might have been written before or shortly after the creation of The Void. There are a few villages in the mountain vallies beneath Exigo who speak of it. I've even been to the border regions along the Balkans where they defended Maya from the void. Some people live there, it's remote and their families have fought the void for generations. Untouched by the Regime and unknown by Nadians. He's from there, it's still Ecru to those people, and they still keep ancient customs." I explain having done my research into the man, "Aalem Ibn Sufari. Aalem was the title of the master monks of the ancient Erdun Monastery. Obviously he was very well-educated for his time. The library in ancient Erdu is incredible."

"Handsome and smart." Rose grins leaning to kiss me until she hears Halle coming down the steps, "You lucked out."

Lucked out of another fight between these two.

"How do I look, baby?" Halle stepped down the steps in one of her designs. A short cutting number, Gregor Sun-Orange Citrine fabric, mid-thigh showing off her slender honey legs, in a pair of amazon sandals. She had such an immaculate talent with needle and thread. Wish she did more with it for Nadia. "I look amazing, don't I?"

"Yes looks fine." I look up with a nod, "Now, are we ready?"

Halle immediately pouted as the temperature in the room began to rise as Halle glared at me. She crossed her arms stomping her foot down before exclaiming.

"I'm going to keep changing until I get an appropriate response." Halle begins marching for the steps.

"No, you are not, it's almost 21:00, we're heading out!" I stand dropping the book down on the solid oak table.

"What's that?" Halle asks picking up the book and skimming through it. "Naka is in here, aaayyyyee!" she cheers. "Oh, that's my name! Victoriana Gregor."

"She was the first Queen of the Gregor Family." I note, "Gregors have some strange customs."

"Hm?" Halle looked up, "Like what? Why strange?"

"Well, major reason why I won't marry you without you taking on my name. You must kill the current Patriarch. First and foremost with Gregor descent. Victorianna came to power after strangling her father in his sleep, quite proud of the act as well. Her rule was short, she was married and her husband took the role of Patriarch."

"Bullshit... why couldn't she be Matriarch?" Halle sucked her teeth.

I shrug, "She was Matriarch. Naka is a warring nation. People thought a woman at the helm would bring that to an end. And it did. I imagine the rest of the world would be quite happy with that repeating. But Gregors are all about the family traditions, usually."

"We are very proud people. Wait a minute. This makes us seem like assholes. Murdering and pillaging? That's not true. We spread Order and Peace, my dad said. Enslavement of Ecruen in 1600... What is Ecru?"

Rose laughs under her breath, "I can't believe I get to see this front row. I have never seen a Nakan read anything not approved by their Compulsory Board. Halle Gregor's first time reading a piece of heresy. Go easy on her."

"Shut up, Rose! I read a lot of books, I'm in college duh." Halle snaps.

"Halle, genuinely I am not trying to insult you this time. You go to a Nakan College and Nakans usually don't like outside perspectives." Rose tries to explain.

"Morgan, do you agree with this book? It's filled with lies of my family!" Halle tosses the book back on the coffee table and crosses her arms.

"I have a Nakan Heritage and History class Halle. It's made before the Compulsory Board. Nakans were taught agreement and disagreement rather than comprehension in through higher education. Things were based on validity and soundness less than affect or themes or how they affect people. Get straight to the point. Does it make sense, can you use it, and is it true? Summarized with, do you agree? Otherwords, does this promote Naka or not? If not, Nakans have no use for it."

The table shook under the weight of the book. I was silent but her eyes and heart demanded an answer. Answers I wasn't prepared to offer.

"I thought they taught this to children in school." I rubbed the bridge of my nose unsure how to respond.

"I suppose they left out he gorey details for the sake of citizenship. Rakil bless Naka, right?" Rose giggles.

I let out a sigh, "The Gregors are not Sovereigns. Even Enshishi is no sovereign. In the original tale of the Guardians, Enshishi warred against every Guardian, killing them in their own homeland on Gaia seeking to see who was strongest. He murdered Anki and Baat. Before he could reach Anka, Ada stood before him and stopped him. I can't agree or disagree with the book. Sometimes things are just true."

"That's a lie. Ada killed them all! Enshishi saved us from Ada!" Halle says frantically, "Ada tried to kill us all, and he took the life of Enshishi out of jealousy and rage. Ada is- Ada is bad!"

Rose laughed hysterically, "And I thought you were drinking the kool-aid, Morgan. She drunk the whole pitcher!" she falls over herself, "That is so bastardized I have no idea. Enshishi is the Guardian of Fire, power and destruction. What part of that is heroic?"

"It's what I was taught." Halle pouts looking to me for refuge. "In school they taught us Enshishi is the one true God, and the Guardians are his servants. Ada is the usurper who tried to overthrow Enshishi from his rightful throne."

I pull Halle close and kiss her forehead. "We all learn the stories of our people, the way our people wish to tell us. Sometimes we wish to be honest, often times however, truth is spun to fit our desires and keep order."

"Do you think I'm a monster like these people? Is that why you hate me? Is this book why you won't marry me, Morgan?" Halle looks up to me so child-like for the twenty-two year old girl, soon to be twenty-three.

"I don't hate you, Halle-

"He hates your father and family." Rose said before I could.

I was drawn between truth and comfort. I had to tread carefully.

"Shut your mouth..." Halle warns beginning to heat up.

"Both of you hush!" I bark. My head was already throbbing just anticipating the rest of the evening with these two. "Alright, I'll teach you some of what I studied. Enshishi was no hero of history but he is an incarnation of The Guardian of Fire nonetheless. He is fire itself then the Gregors transferred their power directly through murdering the former Guardian and allowing the spirit to use their vessel. You then become a Vicar. It must be controlled and harnessed properly. Great things have been done by Gregors and their many cousin lineages. Maurice Gregor was said to be one of the four greatest men to ever live. With the other leaders of the world who wanted peace and an end to the bloodshed. Ecru was the only nation ever at peace for longer than a century. Erdu has been warring for a thousand years straight with or without The Regime. Maya has been at war with Naka since its existence. Esha and Naka have constant civil wars. Ecru... had Ada. Each Guardian is not meant to save the world. They only need to manage the conflicts in their own region. So, Enshishi is the perfect Guardian for a place like Naka. No man is God though. No man is greater than tomorrow."

"Then your dad killed his father to become Enshishi. It ruined everything. I think you might be cool as hell Halle. You're a chill chick and very beautiful. I definitely only hate your dad." Rose put her hands up in defense.

Halle was quiet. It was the first time I've seen her distraught. She was biting her thumb near bloody. She looked at me to say something but I bowed my head. I had nothing to offer her in way of words of reprieve. I merely sat with the truth ready to offer it whenever she needed. I didn't want to be the one to tell her. I had always believed she's been well-educated in these matters and chose her ways as a Gregor. I didn't know she was being indoctrinated like the rest of the nation. I suppose Colin wanted one person on Gaia to love him as he fantasized his daughter. Only she held the truth of what her father had done or hadn't.

"Not every man is a hero of history..." I swallowed, "I didn't prepare for telling my wife-to-be her father was a homicidal maniac. I thought someone taught you these things already Halle. All I can say is no man is greater than tomorrow."

I said Warren's favorite phrase. Suddenly realizing the desperation in the words there might be some justice on this planet for a man like Colin to be stopped. For one day, as the good men die in their beds that the bad die with their eyes wide open. Only I could probably deal with Colin, as a friend or an enemy. To kill him... to kill Halle's father regardless of how I felt about him seemed to be overstepping my boundaries.

"We can't all be Morgan Ellys." Rose smiles proudly, "I think you should marry Halle and I'll have one of your kids. We can be a real family."

"You are one of the most disrespectful and unprofessional maids I have ever met in my life. How did you even get a job in this field?"

Halle's eyes tightened as she observed Rose. "I hope you don't think either of us is fooled by whatever stalker shit you're pulling here. I'll find the truth about you Rose Paz Andale and when I do there will be hell to pay for how you're trying to humiliate me. I'll ride the wave and enjoy the experience hoping you're cool. When I find the truth about you that's when we'll see who's laughing you arrogant bitch."

"Your father killed my grandfather in front of my grandmother then raped and kidnapped her, that's how you were born. I wouldn't be surprised if your father had something to with killing Morgan's parents too. The only reason you even exist is from your father raping my grandmother." Rose crosses her hands over her chest, "I'll leave you alone Princess, history will deal with the Gregors. Ada will find himself to Colin's end one way or another."

"My Mother was a Nakan Traitor and she abandoned me and my father while I was a girl. So, if you're from her family then it explains a lot about why you're so sketchy." Halle stretches out to her feet letting out a yawn. Smiling brighter than sunshine as if none of it fazed her, "So, what else of my people? What else of the Gregors and Naka have I been lied to about? What else is a lie?"

"Your father is a murderer and he raped your mother to have you. It says a lot about why you act like a mindless spoiled bastard."

"I heard you the first time." Halle punches Rose. Then follows up with a lightening fast right jab square in the face then throws her to the floor.

I intervene before Halle pounced on her. I looked at Rose with disdain and she immediately lost her smugness.

"I- I lost control of my vessel. I apologize to both you sincerely. I really need this job. I really need this job. I'm sorry." Rose holds her hands up from her back, pleading with Halle.

"Apology accepted. See you in training in the morning. I'll wait until then to take my anger out on you. What you said makes some sense." Halle kissed my cheek, letting me know she's alright.

"Take a seat next to me, please. I don't want you to take anything I have to say the wrong way." I patted next to me on the couch. She doesn't make noise just sulks over. Her natural glimmer was dim. I take her head between my hands and kiss her forehead. "Your father is not a good man, no. You are not your father. My issues lie within Colin and Colin alone. I do not hate you. I love you Halle Gregor. You're a very powerful light in the darkness of this world."

"You hate my family, why? Everyone hates my family. Why?" Halle throws her hands up as if she had no idea.

I sigh, "Gregors don't care for anyone other than themselves. Other lives, other people's cultures, other people's beliefs... they have no respect for anyone or anything but Gregors. Even amongst their own they take advantage and abuse them, there can be no hope for others. The Gregors are not good people." I turn pages into the book finding a good page, one that brought things back to the beginning, "The power of Fire was harnessed after Gaia and the oceans. Enshishi was the third Guardian, he was created out of Ada's anger and rage. Through history there have been those who have conquered the flames. The other families of Naka before The Gregors. Before the Gregors, the power was vested inside another family in Naka, the Ancient Dragon Family of Murashima, who harnessed Ryu. Like Maurice Gregor, they wished for peace, their family created a way to tame the spirit of the fire just as man has conquered fire to raise civilization. Fire is not in itself evil but the power it presents is too tempting. Enshishi represents when might is far too corruptible of the mortal moral fiber. He promises many things but only satisfies himself at the end. It takes a strong man or a pure heart to quench the eternal flame of life. A Guardian of Fire is necessary in the world. Your father is just... he's just fucking evil, Halle."

"We were not the original Guardians of The Fire?"

"No, unfortunately not but your ancestor Mandel Gregor held the torch for quite a longtime. He was said to have harnessed the spirit of Ryu after combat with the former Guardian of Fire."

"Then

"Halle... If you wish to know more then you should do research there are plenty of resources around. I suggest you read for yourself or ask your father and mother. I am not an expert. I only know as much as

I know. However, I can tell you the Gregors were not the original nor were they ever meant to carry the eternal flame."

"But I know nothing on this, Morgan! It isn't only my father. This information isn't available in our schools at all. He tells me I am an heiress and who is meant to wed but- I was not aware of this at all! We're not even taught this in school." Halle says panicked, short of breath as her understanding of life fleeted.

"Your father believes he is Rakil's Gift to humanity. I was hoping you would figure out on your own it wasn't true." I scoff.

"The entire nation thinks my father is god. When was I supposed to make that spiritual breakthrough?" Halle shook her head then asks, "What is Rakil?"

"You don't know Rakil?" I ask concealing my disgust.

She nods in embarrassment.

"He is the creator... he is the father of all upon Gaia, he formed the Guardians. Rakil is God."

"Enshishi is god..." she recited under her breath more out of disbelief than correction.

"Who is Rakil? Baat... Anki... who are these people? What do their names mean?" she held her head as the pain made her crown chakra strain, she rubbed her temples as she continued reading faster than I could manage myself.

All she thought she knew was being challenged by facts.

"You know nothing of the Five Guardians or the Father? Not the Mother Gaia even?" I took a deep breath remembering my own ignorance once and how much destruction I was used for in my ignorance.

"I only know what my father teaches me anything else is lies or frivolous."

"What has your father taught you?" Rose asks showing the first sign of sympathy since they met.

"To be a dutiful daughter and a good wife but Morgan won't marry me so what good is all that?"

"Well, sex doesn't make a relationship for me. No offense but if I was still controlled by my dick I could have sex with anyone and be happy.

I need an actual connection and to be able to have a real conversation with you. I feel like we do things to hide we have nothing in common and never actually talk to one another. I definitely feel a deep connection to you Halle. You're also honestly the most beautiful woman I have witnessed in all my life.

A cord was plucked deep inside me. My heart ached. For a brief moment nothing but rage flashed over my body, though it subsided into grief and pity for this poor girl. I have held her to such a standard as the Heiress but she is no more than a child. Mislead and used as we all were. I believed Halle abnormal but she was the standard. No one in Naka was educated about the world outside of Naka.

"Halle, read more. Educate yourself. Allow your mind to be your own." I suggest unable to say anything else.

"You can teach me, Morgan. I would listen to you. I love you." she rests her head on my chest.

"Halle, you must think for yourself." I shake my head, "You are becoming a Queen of Naka regardless of me and you must have your own mind. I cannot control your life Halle. You're going to have to lead a nation. Are you seriously telling me you don't know about it?"

"You are my husband. You have my permission to think for me. This is confusing to me. I don't know what the truth is about this, you tell me."

"Is this all your father's teachings?" I asked quieting down, a strained shock rested on my face of how vastly different his advice had been for us.

She nods. "He says a good wife concedes only to her husband instead of accepting the world and fighting her man. This is why he couldn't bear my mother. That a woman's mind all her own is a dangerous thing. She should only live to serve her father and husband then build her own. A woman isn't meant to serve the world."

"Many believe such a thing but they reach that end of their own volition. Learn for yourself Halle. I cannot judge what is just or not. I am one man of no importance. I would wish for you to think for yourself." I rub her cheek, the poor girl. It's a sin to lie to children.

"Do you think I'm stupid?" Halle asks me, looking me straight in the eyes.

"You are not the brightest but it doesn't seem like anyone tried to educate you. I don't think you're dumb, maybe naïve because you're young. I feel someone tried very hard to limit your growth as they did mine. So, I'll give you the same suggestion I was given. If you read more and listen to others who disagree with you then you'll likely learn more and be able to make your own mind. You definitely have a lot working against you, but I can see now it's your father's doing, not your own. He was trying to create something with you but it wasn't a Queen."

"Can I borrow this book? I'm curious about the history of Naka." Halle asks me.

"There are many books out there outside of the Compulsory Board. Maybe you should start with another? I need the knowledge in this book very deeply, but... I have faced such resistance in picking it up and sitting with it. Feel free to skim through it whenever you're here." I scan my library for something more palatable.

"What book should I read, baby?" She kisses my cheek with a smile, "this is exciting! I thought I knew all that I needed to know. There is a whole world out there!" she skims the pages, "Anka... Anki... are these not one in the same?"

"Guardians of Air and of Earth. Anki of the first realm, Gaia but now only holds domain over Erdu. Anka, was the last Guardian, of the fourth, Esha. Alright, Halle. The world began with only Gaia and Rakil. The Father and the Mother. Together they begot, Ada, the first man. Ada's first brother, is the Guardian of the Mother, Anki. After Anki, is Ada's sister, Baat, the Guardian of the essence of Life, Water. Then, Enshishi was born... When Enshishi was born, he declared himself King, above all else, King and God of this world. He killed Anki and Baat, and then came to Esha to claim it for his kingdom because he had burned so much of his own, and the others. Rakil refused and warned Ada of the destruction and death of his siblings. He said it was because-Because he only worked and never showed his emotion basically." I froze in remembrance, "Ada approached him and fought for his siblings and killed Enshishi, the enemy of all, the brother of none. Enshishi has twisted the history. Made Ada seem as the grandest evil, because it is the only power that could hold him. There are stories of an Ancient Ada named Onyx who conflicted with his place as Ada, torn between the shadow and the light."

"What happened to him?" Rose asked.

"He created the New Ecru after warring against his father to end the spread of Ecru. He went on to bring about peace to Gaia after taking over the Ecruen Basin. The other territories readily turned to his way out of love and respect. He spent the rest of his days in Oblivion, a boundary between the heavens and Gaia until his death then people says there was no Ada for 1000 years afterward. His daughter became the newest Guardian of Gaia."

"That sounds awesome... Ada seems like a good guy." Halle rubbed her chin, "Things are so backwards in Naka."

"Well, Ada was the son of Rakil and Gaia. He was- well, I suppose he is more Rakil than Gaia while the Guardians are more Gaia than Rakil. The story says Ada was born of Gaia in the image of Rakil. The Guardians were born of Ada and Gaia."

"Why?"

"I only have my personal theories." I shrug.

"Tell me, you know so much already! Tell me the story my beloved!" Halle cheers me on.

"We must go, Halle. We are running out of time. We'll be late." I decline regardless, unsure of the facts, only having my theories from my meditations.

Halle pouts, "I want to learn more about this book!"

"Do not whine at me." I rub my temples, "You are a woman grown, not some child."

"Tell me, baby..." Halle kissed me on the cheek disarming me completely.

I chuckled, "Ha... okay, I'll tell you... I believe Rakil created the Guardians because he understood the world would keep growing beyond his original creation. He must have, he's omniscient... life exists elsewhere in this world. He must have the recipe or something. So, when he created Gaia, he created Guardians to do just that. Protect us, and guide us, sometimes from a distance, sometimes far more hands on, sometimes from ourselves as history tells. Their primary goal is to do his works on Gaia, and watch over his creations on Gaia. When Guardians have failed to do that, these God Kings, they are overthrown by the forces of Rakil himself or by the people they failed to protect. I believe Guardians also used to be stronger. Humanity in itself, in my studies, used to live longer, have more abilities like Guardians. There were also much less people than today, living closer to the center near Ecru. The wars and kingdoms in the book show how lands have divided and split themselves. It also speaks of migrations of many Eshans into Naka, Nakans moving to Erdu and how Erdu has been at war since the death of Ada. Well, not explicitly but if you follow the political shifts in correlation with the territory gained you can see everything working from the center of Ecru outward, going to the far corners. The furthest from Ecru, the worst it gets and the more people work against their true self. In short, I was able to track human history back to Ada. Though, this is just a theory."

Halle smiles, "I love this side of you, Morgan." she rubs my chest, "You will be such an amazing husband and a great leader. I love you."

"I love you too, Halle." I reaffirm her kissing her on the lips.

"Do you truly?" Halle asks pulling me closer for another kiss.

"Hey, guys, it's like 21:30, shouldn't we get going?" Rose reenters the room holding our coats. "We're going to downtown Nadine, right?"

I stood and extended my hand to Halle. I kissed her forehead once more. "I cherish you, Halle Victorianna. You will bloom and grow into a wonderful woman. You only need to push yourself. Embrace the challenges of the world. And love all those regardless of their background. You'll find yourself. You are not bounded by the sins of your family unless you choose to honor them as your own."

"Do I not know myself?" Halle asks.

"One, who knows nothing, cannot know self. And one, who does not know self, knows nothing. We are always constantly discovering who we are as I'm learning. It's best to keep an open-mind even in our image of self. We cannot be omniscient, we're not Rakil." I offer my best response.

I could see Rose out the corner of my eyes. Envy was not present but there was a longing I could sense. She focused not on me instead on Halle with a smile on her face.

"I'll meet you two by the car." Rose says leaving our coats on the arm of the couch before taking her leave of us.

"Have you two had sex?" Halle asks me, taking my hands in her, "I won't be angry... but how she looks at you. I do not trust Rose to respect our marriage arrangement. I- maybe I have what I have coming. But, I love you Morgan. I want to see us work."

"She has- expressed interest, expresses interest far too often. I wasn't aware she worked here. She told me Natalie hired her, said my girlfriend hired her..." I rub my neck, confused of how Rose got here.

Halle rolled her eyes pushing away from me, "Why the fuck would Natalie do that? Why is she such a sore loser!? She's always trying to fuck shit up for us. If it's not enough that you never stop thinking about her, now this shit?"

"I am leaving Natalie in the past. I do not think about her all the time. I am focused on you Halle. I have already discussed with Rose she'll need to find new employment soon. She's been working for a month or so she said. Once I return to my work schedule it won't matter. I might keep her if you two can work things out. She says she needs the opportunity. If you two get along tonight, I can consider it. If not then I'll have to fire her outright."

Halle rolled her eyes, "I never feel as if you are truly mine, Morgan. Your heart and mind are always elsewhere."

"My mind is focused on absolution, Nadia, and Rakil's path for me. Little else matters right now." I assure Halle.

"So, you're not having sex with Rose?" she stares at me intently.

"Halle I have never had sex with Rose. Now, let's go. We will be late."

"Do you hate my family, Morgan?" Halle asks me again.

"Halle... I don't even know your whole family. Only you and your father, enough of the questions please. Let's enjoy our night." I was shocked I was the one saying it.

I cracked a smile.

"Wow. Whoa, usually I have to tell you that!" she picks up our coats and kisses my cheek. "Come on! It's such a beautiful restaurant you'll love it."

I only nodded, turning off the lights in the house. Halle looked at me longing for the response but in my heart I didn't know anymore. There was so much for her to learn. Time was of the essence. And I had a city to save from her father. Do I love her? Should her father's transgressions even fall upon the shoulders of such an innocent creature? There stood the woman I've shared so much of my life with... but in truth those memories were fleeting and falsified. What in truth do we share anymore?

I woke up this morning prepared to meditate then rest and spend my day in solitude. Now, these two women have shown me I must leave my home and do more. I suppose our path in life truly does conquer all.

I must accept who I am... in the least accept I have a purpose greater than what I have done. If Colin Gregor could see such potential in me then it's true I've been blind to myself. Halle has stood by me for so long. But it was Rose who removed this fog, and opened the doors of my own kingdom to me. Halle hasn't an idea what's even going on in the world outside of Naka. Rose has been directly affected by it. Halle was far from dumb... she had a blissful way about going through life. I can't blame someone for being manipulated by tradition.

It is a man's duty to take on a wife. If he can care for more than one... is this my charge, Rakil?

No more of this. No more neurosis. Let us enjoy our evening. Let us enjoy each other's company and if only for this evening, and only this evening. Let us be happy with what we have.

CHAPTER 22

Don't call it Coincidence

Natalie Wolfe

I first met Morgan in the Academy 8 years ago. He was a different man then if you could call him a man at all. He never quite said what he did... I never had to question since he never paid for anything. I can't say I was never curious. We left each other, he would disappear and return. Kiss me on the forehead then tell me not to worry about it then be gone before his lips finished pressing my lips. The more I saw of Morgan the less I wished to know. He would lock himself away for days at a time. Even when he was home he was mentally gone. You could sit with him and he wouldn't even know you were there or just be off in thought. He was always waiting to be called away somewhere but never wanting to spend time with me.

He was such a sweet loving man, leaving him seemed wrong at first... I stress at first.

We met one summer on the beaches of La Vida District, my hometown. I was sipping a mango colada, eating the remains of the fresh juicy mangoes pulled right from the trees outside our condominium on the beach by a few of the cute bartenders who worked in the lobby of our apartment.

Now technically, Halle saw Morgan first that day but I knew him longer plus we work together. They knew each other for sometime but when I saw him I knew I needed him. He seemed like a nightmare disguised as a dream, I felt I finally found someone who understood my torment trying so hard to help people when all you wanted was to be left alone.

We worked together in the logistics department of GregorCore for a couple years, making love and making money since we first met. I was an intern and he was the big bad VP of the board under Colin Gregor himself. I had my share of time with him alone usually ending up partnered on projects.

There sat the most beautiful chocolate god I had ever seen. Alone, reading a book on military strategy. He wore a white linen suit and sandals, a pair of shades on his face like a modern messiah. His body was leaned and toned. Halle claimed to know him from The Academy in Erdu. He had to be mine. The moment I saw him talking to Halle, his smile and laughter, I wanted him.

Halle tried to tell me she had some feelings but he wasn't really the romantic type. She told me he was some military golden boy, he seemed too young to have ever stepped foot in the military, maybe he worked on computers or something. She ran inside the apartment for a moment to use the bathroom. When she came back I was lying next to him plotting to get my spine rearranged. Talking and laughing it up before we exchanged numbers. At first I was pretty content letting it go, but I didn't want someone else to have him.

That's the last time I saw Morgan really happy. We exchanged numbers, enjoyed our time then he disappeared for two years claiming to have died. Nothing he ever said made sense. He came to Vida to mentor under Colin. Since he'd been back, he said nothing other than he had died and went to bed for two days straight at a time. He just kept saying "This can't be real...", "How Did I get here?" he was speaking gibberish or reciting conspiracies. Or he was dead silent, staring out on the balcony for hours with his eyes that weird red color that sent terror down my spine. He was irritable to say the least. Snapping at me, going crazy yelling at me to respect him, we fought relentlessly. He'll leave then come back like nothing happened. It was like every day was on reset.

It drove me mad. It drove me to other men... it drove him to Halle.

I came out one day and they sat by the beach. Laughing and shooting the shit. From there... they were so buddy, buddy. Our relationship was even secret from Halle until we started making love more regularly. I began to feel like the hole he fucked, sex to ease the agony of being so wounded then he returns to his laughter and happiness with Halle. Or the other women he doesn't know I scrolled through his phone to find.

His birthday came and I thought maybe I could spice things up. Show him how much I could love him better. That I could nip things in the bud and share as Halle wanted. It backfired, oh boy, did it blow up in my face. They went from being buddy to disrespecting me outright in my own home. All those two needed was an excuse and permission. That's if they weren't already going at it like rabbits behind my back.

I've never hurt so much. I had never cried over another person, especially not some man before then. I had never been cheated on, even in a sport.

I wanted her out. I wanted her gone. But all I got was "You're the one who brought her here!" or "She makes me happy." How does it feel to know you put your love in the arms of another woman? He carries her over the threshold and leaves you in the rain.

If it wasn't for Halle occupying all his free time then maybe we would have worked things out. He suddenly started spending all his time in Nadia or at work plotting this grand escape from Naka. Then came home and wanted to sleep alone, if he didn't sleep at his office or Nadia, if he ever slept at all because of his nightmares. The times I've caught him and Halle on the couch because she claimed to be checking on him after one of our fights drove me insane. I wanted to check on him and it was my job but she claimed to be helping me.

I lost my bestfriend and my love in one swoop. How the hell is helping someone marrying their boyfriend right from underneath them?

I sat on the outside staring in the entire time as they laughed, and grew merry. All while I sat around waiting for him to come back to me, to come home.

It was like having a knife in my heart every day. I felt so... inadequate to Halle Gregor forever. Inadequate to the Airhead Heiress voted the most beautiful woman in Naka. The pain was crippling. I couldn't talk to him without crying or yelling after a while I admit. Then I refused to cry in front of him, I refused to show weakness. So, instead we fought mercilessly with me spending my night crying because of the fight then hearing Halle's giggling in the other room with I suffered. I yelled. I wanted her gone. Thinking if somehow she left I would magically have a better relationship. That Morgan would go back to loving me, if he ever did...

Half our relationship, I waited for him to love me. The other half I watched him love another woman. It was crippling.

Now, they're still together. She swoons about marriage. Her father rubs the arrangement in my face everyday telling I would be lucky to find someone like Morgan. I most feared how my father will suffer once Morgan is at the helm of GregorCore. He lived like a vagrant but whatever military strategy he studied worked wonders for his business acumen. He seemed to be Enshishi's hand-selected heir and vicar.

I consider myself over the situation. Dating some melancholy, self-deprecating military jerk was never how I imagined my life going. A brief intermission in my regularly scheduled life... it felt more of a drama than comedy without my boyfriend and best friend. I pray to Enshishi they suffer their own fate and face karma for all the pain they caused me.

I have to say. It was quite the thrill. Every night a laundry list repeated over and over again about what was wrong with the world, with people, and my favorite topic, me. How long can one tolerate that depressing garbage? I loved Morgan the best I could manage. I had my own life and my own issues. A budding career as a tax accountant, I would soon be taking the bar exam to become a tax lawyer.

When I agreed I thought I was dating, "The Man"! No, just another all-talk loser with a handful of ideas and dreams, with no idea of how to live them.

Leaving me for Halle? It disturbs me to my core.

It's that, which I cannot forgive. That I will not get over until they both understand exactly how they've made me feel.

I remember the last day so well, standing at the stove making Morgan breakfast after they both threatened to leave. I thought I would surprise him. I was supposed to be out of town that weekend but got back early. As tired as I was I wanted to treat my man. He seemed so distracted and distraught about Nadia that week. But Halle came out bubbly, laughing, wearing one of Morgan's shirts. She froze when she saw me and the laughter stopped. Morgan came in after her. I stood by the stove shaking with anger, choking back tears. Only able to look down as my tears fell into the eggs, I knew it was over.

I tried to play house. I tried to make things work but I just felt disgusted with myself having to share my man with a Gregor.

The pain didn't come from the sex. It wasn't as if Halle could have sex with him with these crazy fucking Gregor rules she so faithfully follows without question. It's despite them having sex they were still so fucking close! He used me like his cum dump and treated her like his best friend. All I wanted was to grow old and wealthy with him like my parents did. He wanted happiness... bullshit.

No... How he would smile and nestle up with her. How happy they looked until I came along. I was eventually just waiting for him to leave me. Meanwhile I was trying to summon up the courage to leave him. Over a year had passed, I should have asked for the strength by Enshishi to kill them both in their sleep. He said he hated me because I never spent my time and energy making the relationship work. How dare he say I didn't try when he's marrying my best friend!

I was young. I was cowardly. I was naive.

I hope they both rot in hell. I hope Colin joins them. He smiles and flaunts their marriage in my face every day in the office. I should have quit there... but my father wanted peace in Naka. My family never knew about Morgan and me. No one could have known about Morgan and me.

Maybe, now I can breathe and truly just get past this shit.

But I know. I know I should have killed them both instead of crying in those damn eggs.

I should be over this now. I should have this past me but every time I see his face or hear her name. There's an insatiable anger, pain and yearning no man and nothing can sate but this stupid idiot.

I was invited to an event by my friend, Kole. She opened a new restaurant in the rural area of Ecru. As Morgan forced me to call it during our relationship since I apparently had no respect for Nadia. Nadine was apparently apart of some ancient Ecruen super power. Whatever, it was Naka now, and that's all I cared about.

"Hey, girl!" Carmen waves from the other side of the restaurant as I arrived.

It was a beautiful Nakan evening. And my best friend was sitting, legs crossed in amazon sandals and an emerald green shawl. Carmen and Halle believed themselves some fashion trendsetters. Most of Naka agreed. Carmen called herself The Voice of the Beautiful People.

"I ordered for you." she informs me matter-of-factly.

"You know I hate when you do that?" I sat.

Carmen rolled her eyes, "What's up your ass?"

Do I tell her my ex-lover is marrying Halle? It had scandal written all over it. Carmen hunted those down for a living. The Voice of the Beautiful People, the Queen of Drama.

"Love problems? Go ahead, let your heart sing, girl."

"You know I'm not dumb enough for that around you, Carmen. I know you far too well."

"Psh... you think you know me." She smiles teasing me, pouring me a glass from the pitcher of sangria on the table. "So, did you know Halle was getting married?"

"Uh... yeah, I did."

"I've been watching them for the past half hour with such contempt. He's too handsome for her. I want a good story on this as soon as possible but he's been gone for two years, no word, no trace and no one is talking about him."

"What? They're here?" I ducked my head down behind my menu and began scanning the room.

She nods to a table in the corner. There they were. To rub it in they had another woman with them shoving it down my throat of how quickly they moved on. Eating, laughing, and having all the happiness in the world. I should go up and tell that girl all about those two backstabbing bastards then we'll see if she wanted to eat with them.

Oh, Enshishi, you tempt me!

"What do you know about them?" Carmen teases, "I've never seen you so upset!" she licked her lips.

"I don't know anything." I mutter turning around and polishing off my drink, pouring another.

"No one really knows much about him. Word is he just disappeared as a kid."

"What do you mean by disappear?" I asked, "Morgan never spoke of his childhood with me and I assumed he was always too angry to discuss it."

Carmen shrugs, "I don't know. The asshole walked off my show before I could get anything out of him. That was a few years ago about Nadia. People have been telling me they've seen Halle with this guy. Leaving your apartment and at parties with you... kind of like that girl over there. Do you know her?"

"Morgan does not party! And no I've never met her before." I said at disbelief knowing Carmen had some card up her sleeve, some information she was withholding from me as it's been since we were girls.

"So, you do know of him?" she grinned, "Spill! Tell me everything!"

"You tricked me..." I needed to remember who I was sitting with before I ended up on the front page of her e-Mag or on her show.

"Girl, you played yourself drinking like that. You people always slip up." She was so proud, "but no, tricks up my sleeve. Cross my heart hope to die."

I wave her away wishing I never trusted any of these Gregors or whatever the hell you call Carmen.

"Come on Natalie, seriously you can talk to me. What's wrong Ms. Wolfe?"

I let out a sigh and tossed the wedding invitation in my purse on the table.

"Praise Enshishi, they look so beautiful together. Did you RSVP yet?"

"It was supposed to be me Carmen."

"I thought you didn't know anything?" Carmen rolls her eyes.

"Well, around you I feel like I need to be discrete. He was my boyfriend and now he's engaged to this bitch."

"Are you sure he knew you were dating?" Carmen looks over to their table to see him and Halle kissing. "I've never seen two people look so in love."

"Yes he fucking knew we were dating, are you serious right now? It's complicated. I really don't feel like discussing details."

"My lips are sealed Ms. Wolfe, you look so distraught. I'm here whenever you want to talk. I'm going to enjoy this soft-core porn. Do you think they're sharing him? Halle never struck me as the sharing type."

"I am distraught. I'm absolutely flippant, I'm livid. I want to ruin their night I swear to Enshishi I want to fuck this up." I looked over the invitation I was staring at Halle's sneering, spoiled bitch face when I should be having an amazing dinner with my best friend, "He was my boyfriend, I introduced him to Colin Gregor through this skank. He and Colin became best of freaking friends, now he wants to become a Gregor. That's basically everything to this point. If it wasn't enough I have to compete with Halle. Now, there's already another chick? Like is it really hard for a guy to keep his dick in his pants?"

"Why does it have to be a competition?"

"Are you serious? Like, are you actually kidding me right now? You know my parents and you know her father. It has always been a competition. Colin has been mentoring and grooming this guy for the past year and a half... he's good at what he does and if he leads the Gregor Family then... we might lose the competition."

"I mean... do your parents dislike him?"

"Honestly, they don't even know about him. I have literally never brought him up to them. I'm terrified of what they'll say." I bury my face in my arms. "My parents are very selective of whom I date and quite honestly, they've wanted to arrange a marriage for me. Morgan and I had to be a secret. If my parents didn't like him they might have never spoken to me again."

"If you like him why wouldn't your parents?"

"My parents are very strong believers in family. He's evidently from poor stock. They want me to marry country club guy or a son of their friends but... Morgan and I were in love?"

"Were in love?"

"Well, we used to be madly in love. I was madly in love anyway. I never met a man who knew me so well or who I got along with better. We wanted the same things from life. We worked together for Colin. We made love whenever we were alone since the first day meeting him in the office."

"If any of what you're saying is the truth then why aren't the two of you getting married regardless?"

"Colin's little dream world bullshit. He took him from me! Would you turn up an invitation to be a Gregor? I don't know many people who would."

"You seem to have come to grips with it, why the anger?"

"I'm livid... but... Morgan already told me. I hate seeing him angry so I learned to bite my tongue when he's involved. I'm not angry at Morgan. I'm pissed off at Halle and Colin! Colin will not stop talking about it in the office! He even calls Morgan his freaking son, taking him around everywhere. It's all Colin. Morgan wants a new daddy."

Carmen nodded coolly, "I'm awfully sorry... have you spoken to him since?"

"No, I would burst into tears if I had to face him. If I got to close to her then I would attack her on the spot. No one even knows I loved Morgan. I don't even know if he loved me. How would it look if I just flipped out?"

“I still think you should at least talk to him. Love is stronger than money. Maybe tell your parents as well, if Morgan is good enough for Colin then why not them?”

I tapped my chin believing she did have some sort of point, even if she did sound crazy. Maybe if I get Morgan alone and remind him what he’s missing out on being with Halle. But if I sleep with him again and tell my parents they might disown me for lying this entire time and Morgan marries that skank anyway. The risk is too great.

“Well, then I guess you made up your mind. You’ll allow fear to keep you from a man you love. I don’t know what you even really can do, Ms. Wolfe. If you’re too scared to love him, I can’t say it’s a wonder he moved on to someone who loves him... very publically. Isn’t Halle a virgin? They look like they’re up to something scandalous. Look at the way the third wheel is looking at them. She really wants to hop in there. I don’t blame her it looks fun. They look beautiful as a couple.”

“I never saw it your way.” I sigh wiping away a tear unable to handle seeing him happy with Halle after being miserable with me.

“I suggest if you love him, let him know at least. And if you want him in your life then tell your parents before the wedding. I’m going to try to figure out what’s going on with them when they leave. This dude has been a virtual ghost. The only information I could find was his balance sheets and tax reports. And that he owns a few clubs in New Haven and Nadia. His tracks are covered, it’s like he’s hiding or doesn’t want to be bothered. I never imagined a young rich recluse type.”

"He owns what?" I nearly fainted.

"He's balling, girl. He owns a few small farms in Nadia and nearly 100 acres of land in Erdu. He was the dude trying to rebuild Nadia then again he just... disappeared again. They say he’s a reclusive, eccentric billionaire, and I dubbed him most eligible bachelor in Nadia when he was on my show. I did a little of my own research, a few years back. Halle introduced us. Well, maybe it was Colin but I barely remember it was long time ago. I only know he’s a very high-ranking Regulator.” Carmen looked away from me sipping her sangria looking at her new favorite show.

A smirk crossed her lips and she let out a sigh. When you realize everything someone's been trying to tell you were truth and you refused to see it. He told me and thought he was lying to me. Then he asked me if I don't trust him, how things could ever work out? I thought he was trying to manipulate me or scare me. No... he was being real. The one honest man in Naka and I called him a liar.

"What the fuck, that cannot be the same Morgan. Morgan is a loser! No, no... he's supposed to be mean, all talk no action, he's supposed to be the bad guy here! Not me! There is no way that guy has a billion dollars. I worked with him and- He- He made the deal without me. He asked me to invest a few million dollars, I laughed at it. I thought he was just trying to get laid!" I felt like my head was about to explode.

She shrugs, "Everyone I've spoken to claims he's a cool guy. I think he's a ghost and an asshole... but cool. At Speeches, conferences people love him. Then poof he's gone for two years without a trace."

Absolutely, not! This is impossible! I paid for everything! He has clubs? He was rebuilding Nadia? Where is all this coming from? Why didn't he tell me!? Why didn't I listen to him? When I leave a man he was supposed broke and broken. Halle must have paid for that and put it in his name! Yes, yes. Of course he would only marry her for money. That's the only way. Nightclubs...? He doesn't even drink. There he was sipping wine and shooting the shit with her.

I- I can't believe this. Did I leave too soon? Did I even have any idea who he was this whole time?

I rubbed my temples, "How much does he have?"

"Excuse me?" Carmen sips her sangria.

"How much money does he have?" My head was spinning. It couldn't have been enough to bother myself over.

"He grosses 3.5 Billion and growing, his portfolio is amazing."

I nearly drain my glass trying to contain myself.

"I took a few notes from his speeches, too. Good lectures. I got to know him a little bit. Yeah know after he spoke at some convention a couple years ago or whatever. That's how I got the interview. I don't really know him. Then he walked off the face of the planet. After some convention in Nadia and walked off my show! Aside from the dough, I can't get anything on him. I guess now I can ask you!"

Providence. Providence! Blessed be the name of Enshishi!

"His name is Morgan Ellys, he works with me at Colin's firm. At least he used to. He hasn't shown up in a few weeks. He's a depressed military loser."

"So, Colin does know him?" Carmen sighs, "I thought maybe Halle was creeping around without daddy dearest knowing. This was Enshshi's doing then maybe we should stay out of it. It doesn't seem wise to make an enemy out of Colin right now."

"Well maybe, we need a new Enshishi. Morgan is just like Colin, a holy, self-righteous dick and apparently a hypocrite as well. If he became Enshishi then we're stuck in the same place."

"Excuse me, how do you know him though? This is the exact opposite of all I've heard from other people and this sounds very personally opinionated. Do you actually think he's dangerous if he marries Halle?" Carmen leans in.

Her sincerity flees for a split second in snake-like smirk before returning to an expression of genuine, nearly convincing sincerity.

If I tell her the truth, I'm taking myself down too. No, no, Carmen hates Halle. She would love a chance to grill her. And damn does Halle deserve it! They both do. All the secrets he kept! If could tell Carmen my side about him and the cheating maybe she'll help me? They're both done.

"Well... Morgan and I had a *tryst.* Halle stole him from me. Well, more like they- Well, You know what my parents would do if they found out, I was dating." I made sure we were on the same page. "And Colin didn't know, but after he found out, he wanted them married immediately!"

"So, she was sneaking around getting dick! I knew she wasn't so pure. Acting like the sun shines out her twat."

"I'll tell you everything you need to know. I want Halle on your show. I want you to destroy Halle. Keep me out of it."

"Your secrets are safe with me, girl." Carmen pulled her hand across her lips.

"They better be, Carmen. They better be. Or my phone is going to be ringing up some people to make sure the same happens to you. I'll end your show with a call if you let this get back to me."

We watched them the whole dinner. The WHOLE dinner, not even a glance in our direction. Not even an acknowledgement. Morgan hasn't spoken to me since we broke up. Not interested in being friends. And now he has two women under his arms. I hope these rumors destroy you, Morgan. I hope Carmen ruins your life. You two will know exactly how I felt! And hopefully, worst.

CHAPTER 23

Thanks for the Memories Even Though They Were All Bad

Morgan Ellys

"I don't think I've ever eaten that good at a restaurant before. You two got one of everything on the menu. I'm going to pass out from this food coma. Morgan, hold me." Rose trust falls backwards.

I quickly duck, lifting her up. To be honest I wasn't quite paying attention until her body dropped so suddenly.

"What is wrong with you, girl?" I remark, shoving her back on her way.

Rose giggles, "Can you believe he thinks his body slowed down, holy crap he's like a cat or something."

Halle giggles along with her. Glad they're getting along, one less stressor for tonight. I can probably trust them at home alone tonight. Something called me back to Exigo on the other side of Nadia. Being so closes to it... I never moved to Esha because I couldn't live so close without seeing The Garden of Eden. It was difficult living in Nadia without venturing to see the ancient temples in its heart, with the concrete monstrosity hiding it all.

I didn't move too far from Exigo. People believe Nadia to have always been concrete and structure but only a few decades ago the lake I'm on was once rural Nadia. Only a couple hours' drive from the city ruins. I walked from Exigo to Nadine once in a comatose after finding myself in a vet's basement. Dragging my body along the highway like a man possessed. The first day I sat at the park staring into the sun, my body worn subconsciously demanding rest. I took in the energy from the sun and pushed along my way. I couldn't process what I saw. And it was all I saw for months. If I didn't have night terrors, it didn't leave my brain. I felt like I couldn't be around anyone. I had two years to spend with Colin Gregor, after being dead for two. I never showed up when I was alive again it's the only thing I remembered I needed to do.

I thought spending time with my girlfriend would have been for the best. Cool the mind and ease the spirits as I rebuilt but there was no solace. I felt I was better running to the forests in Erdu to live out my days. Life hasn't made sense since Nadia. I wish I could have stayed with Rumya but being so close to the city made my mind frenzy.

I was walking in my thoughts, hand stuffed in my pockets ignoring their petulant conversation best I could until I hear Halle screaming.

"Is that Carmen Cruz, hey girl!" Halle waves frantically, she had a few drinks too many.

My stomach churned. The hairs on my neck stood up. I only ever felt that from around the wall of an unsuspected enemy holding something lethal. The last time I felt this way death stood moments away, it was a split second difference between my escape.

I looked up and around the parking lot. My spine rattled, sending a blood curdling familiar fear and energy. There's no way she is here... no Karma can't be coming to collect her pound of flesh. It was danger I knew that. My breathing rushed but I couldn't figure out the cause. It was the energy of another Wolf. There was no bloodlust maybe I can handle this peacefully for once, whoever makes eye contact first would be the winner.

I saw the devil in a green dress wearing amazon sandals designed by Halle. She seemed familiar but nothing of note since she's been out of training, to my knowledge at least. Carmen was my mentor when I was young. We were the two last Wolf agents initiated. After us, the recruitment program was shutdown. The Wolves were still used for the bidding of The Commissioner. Why are Natalie and Carmen in Nadia? What is Enshishi playing at sending his pawns twenty minutes from my home?

"Carmen Cruz! Holy shit, Morgan that's the girl we were talking about." Rose whisper shouts in my ear tugging my arm trying to pull me along, "We should go like now! They've been watching us the entire night!"

Huh... I didn't even feel her energy in the restaurant. This was her attack... It's Carmen not Karma. I gritted my teeth the fleeted memories drifted in my head, stuffing down any emotions or memories deep inside my gut. All the places I could have put my dick in my youth. I chose the Queen of Deceit, the succubus. Leaving the Rumya saved me from her before I left for Naka before my death... I was a different man then her career was just budding. We had hopes to be a power couple. Then I dated her two best friends. I haven't seen her in three years. I was hoping it would be longer.

"Halle, let's go, hurry up." I gesture with my head as Rose and I begin walking.

"Wait, I need to say hi." Halle holds her hands up waiting toward the green-eyed woman.

"No, let's go, now. She is not a good person." I jerk with my neck walking ahead.

"Hold on, Morgie I'll be right there, god. You're not my fucking father." Halle rolls her eyes now going in defiance.

"Rose, go to the car." I let out a sigh.

Rose nods and rushes on ahead, but making sure to keep an eye to enjoy the show.

Carmen wore the grin of medusa, her strong citrine eyes to match her dress, wearing her hair dyed jet black and straighten down to her chest. Her smile was a weapon, curdling my stomach slowing my reaction. It looked just like Colin before initiation. The joy in violence, torture and torment as much it destroyed us, she loved what grew from the ashes. I felt I remained destroyed.

"Halle, let's go, now." I reach her arm in time and try to pull her to the car.

"You're not my dad, Morgan. In Enshishi's name, back off! She's my friend, maybe you should find some." Halle drunkenly tears her arm from me and continues slurring and stammering, laughing at her own jokes, as Carmen just nods with that plastic smile having Halle under her spell.

I let out a labored sigh. Carmen has many things but she had no friends. That's something we kept in common.

Behind her came the devil in a red dress.

"Natalie! Hey! It's been forever." Halle's inebriated waving felt humiliating, "Both my girls are here! What's up bitches?"

Natalie looked at us with a smug grin rolling her eyes. I'm sure Halle missed the flash of disgust before she smiled as wide as Carmen. My heart took a cool pause like a sniper before the pull of the trigger. I registered the situation as a top priority threat. All it took was a cellphone camera to ruin my wedding before we even had it. They were conspiring for our heads. Why were they both here? I guess the joke's on me.

"It sure has, Halle. You look like you had a good ole time." Natalie waved, "I'm in a hurry. I'll see you later. Hey, Morgan what are you getting in?"

I gave a curt nod and turned my attention back to Halle. Gently grabbing her hand trying guider her away from the darkness. She was in the jaw of a wolf and she acts as if she has no idea. The girl was being so oblivious, still all smiles and slurs. She looked a mess and saw these women as her 'friends', friends like hers were why I kept to myself my whole life.

"Have you met, Morgan? His husband-to-be, have you RSVP'd for my wedding yet?" she points to me.

"I believe we know each other quite well. How've you been baby boy?" Carmen licked her lips not taking her attention off Halle quite yet, "It's nice to see you again Captain Ellys far from Erdu aren't we? This is your introverganza right?"

She was covering herself as well. Neither of them knew. I had ammunition in this war of words and emotions. I wasn't willing to use it on women I loved. Even knowing in a heartbeat, they wouldn't hesitate to do the same against me. I had another way.

Another curt nod, "Sup?" I reply.

Carmen seemed disturbed by my unfamiliarity.

"You, know we had many callers after your disappearance for all these years. I was curious where you went. I guess you can say my feelings were hurt." She flashed irritation but her sycophantic smile permanently affixed. "Word's getting out about the happy couple. I would love to have you on the show to spill the deets on the wedding, Halle. Or, maybe you could talk to Natalie in private, Morgan?" she laid her ultimatum in smiles and hugs, stroking Halle's head like a nursing mother.

Halle stopped and looked at me, finally realizing what was going on as Carmen refused to let her head go.

"What the hell are you doing? Let go of me Carmen!" Halle worked her way to my side. Questions were all over her face as she took in their betrayal.

Bless her heart God.

"And who is this little plump dumpling, Morgan?" Carmen's grin finally broken as Halle came back to her senses.

"Excuse me? Morgan and I are just friends... I don't know what you're talking about." Rose throws deuces and walks away from the situation.

"How, friendly are you?" Carmen pulled out a microphone hiding inside her purse. "Because my research says you too are a bit more than friends. And the world knows my word is better than gold."

I reached for my waist but found no kunai, nothing to stab that witch through her throat. No, that isn't how these people handle things.

No, they were cowards and gossips. They had no words for your face, nothing but smiles to your faith and fangs behind your back. Their cruelty was behind closed doors and in whispers, as if their discretion made them sovereigns rather than vile. Sycophants and jackals filled Naka. They washed themselves in dress and feast to ignore poverty but never solve it. They only acknowledged you based off your balance sheet. Even amongst their own, even in their own families they will stand upon your back to hold themselves higher. There were no friends in Naka, only conveniences. These are the people I spent a lifetime serving as death, expanding their way of life and grasp of the planet. I felt sick to my stomach even more than seeing these two conspire against my fiancee.

I pulled Halle behind me. Word of this escaping could ruin Halle's reputation. She was many things... especially better than their vendetta. Moreover, no one was going to disrespect my wife!

"Your show is a sham." I spat to gain her attention.

"Excuse you my show is world fam-

My pupils dilated by me forcing them. The pain hurt deeper than seven hells but after so many times the pain is expected. I can focus my intensity by the pain rather than fear its affects. I know how much I can take. In addition, I knew whoever the finishing blow was set, anyone on the other side stood no chance in hell afterward,.

Carmen's citrine eyes fell back into their naturally green color in response breaking eye contact with me, cursing as she tried to fight my mental suggestion dominating her will. It was too late. I already sent my intention to her mind, a little girl tired of playing at war.

"You're done here! You're done!" she made her threat, making the mistake of meeting my eyes once more. I felt a fool for assuming she was a greater threat if a single glance could have sent her away all these years. She was weaker than I thought, or perhaps I was stronger. The words and information she had, no, she may not be able to kill me but she was a threat again once she got back to her studio. Could I kill Carmen right now in cold blood?

Carmen's eyes glistened in reflection of my Crimson Glare. Carmen drops the recorder and stomps on it. She stomps until the pieces were barely visible.

"I'll talk to you all later. I have to feed my cat." She says in a dream-like state.

With that the pain subsided and I allowed my eyes to turn back to normal. She'll be like that until her objective is complete. Feeding the cat, I know she does not own.

I hated doing that... I hated it more because Colin taught me.

The King's Eyes were because I was of Old Ecru, a bloodline dating far before the renaming to Nadia. There aren't many of us of pure blood left. I understood why the world feared us. Colin told me there were things my eyes could do that made Rakil cringe. I could barely stomach it but regardless, I used my tools of the trade as any assassin would. God have mercy on me for my past.

"What did you just do to her!" Natalie screams, "What was that!?"

"Go home Natalie..." I warn.

I felt myself restrained in doing the same to her... I couldn't. She was only angry. She was rightfully angry.

"Carmen? Carmen? Carmen you don't have a cat!" Natalie calls after Carmen.

Carmen walked off none the wiser. She was gone and the recording destroyed. We'll have to deal with their plans on a later date. She won't remember seeing us, but she'll remember whatever their damn scheme was before seeing me once her and Natalie reconnected. I want her gone, not infantile. To stay off their show and keep my wedding out their tabloids.

Warren told me, "You have to judge by your own pain to gauge the damage you do to others. There are those of us who feel nothing when destroying the lives of others. Those men were all tyrants."

Perhaps I should have put Carmen out her misery. That woman was no good, born evil and loved it. She and Natalie were both advocates of Enshishi. They never knew any other life than serving this world domination plot.

Halle looked at me in shock but followed me regardless as I began walking to catch up with Rose.

"What did you do to her you monster!?" Natalie shouts after me chasing after us.

"You walked out on us remember?" Halle shouts.

"Sorry for getting sick of being cheated on/" Natalie sucks her teeth, "You're still playing the victim, Halle?"

"Natalie, you invited her into the relationship!" I repeated for likely the 100,000th time since meeting this girl.

"Not for you two to fall in love! She was supposed to be your fuck puppet, not me! I was supposed to be getting married to you not her! Me! It's supposed to be me!"

My lip twitched. I opened my mouth to speak but nothing I haven't said before was to be said. I had spent too much time dwelling on all the things I could have fixed with Natalie. Nadia needed me. I needed my mind focused. I don't need this shit right now. I was soon to be married this chapter with Natalie needs to end.

Halle was right... I once tried to deny my past with Natalie for affecting us but she was right. This has gone on long enough. Now, there was a new woman, amazing and all the things Rakil can deliver upon a man. Yet, my heart still rested in the hands of this succubus. I needed to take my life back from Enshishi fully.

Halle blushed, beginning to apologize for not listening. She grabbed my arm walking in dead silence, her alternative to remorse.

"I loved you, Morgan. Does it bother you she only did this to make her daddy happy? You left the one who loved you for daddy's little fuck doll! You cheated on the woman who loved you!" Natalie didn't have sadness, she only had anger.

"I did not do this for my father. I did it for my goddamn self! I love Morgan too. You were just the worst at it." Halle replied.

"Me? All I got was Mr. Stone and solemn, he was a miserable wreck!" she keeps at it.

"And none of that has changed. So please let us go. You obviously don't like or love me or anything. Let it go. We did nothing but fight and fuck. It's toxic. Even I was so bad and I was a monster then for your own sake don't let me put you through it again. Find someone else Natalie, let this go!" I sigh.

Halle frowns whispering to me repeatedly, "I'm sorry Morgan. I didn't know she was here. Let's go."

"You do not walk away from me! You do not turn your back on me!"

"Don't let her get to you young Ada." a disembodied voice said in my ear as clear as day.

"That's right, run back to daddy, Morgan. Run back to Colin! He makes all your decisions for you anyway, right?" Natalie shouted her favorite line as loudly as possible.

My lip twitched.

I was losing the battle with my self-control, I'm not sure she wanted my attention as much as she believed.

I squeezed Halle's hand to the point she stared at me refusing to express the pain in me crushing her hand. I stopped out of mercy. I needed to be an adult. Bottling in emotions would kill me and put everything at risk. I need to deal with all this, and deal with this shit now!

Natalie had never quite known the man she was dealing with. She was reckless, over-privileged and prideful at that. One of the elitist types who think studying and typing about all day consisted of a hard day's work, than an arduous mental exercise of boredom. There was place for both. But this girl-

"Take Rose home Halle. I think I'm going to have to hide a body tonight." I kiss her on the forehead.

"ABSOLUTELY NOT!" Halle drags me along, "You will ruin the peace treaty."

"I am not Gregor nor Wolfe. I can do what I want."

"You can't just kill your issues Morgan." Halle whispers to me.

"I'll only do what's necessary." I assure her, kissing her and letting her go after Rose to the movie they had planned. I could always catch up. "Enjoy yourselves. I'll see you at home."

Natalie fought with emotions and words. It didn't matter what I did. It stung and melted deeply into my spirit. They attack me from the inside to allow me to kill myself. It wasn't just out of anger. No, they were calculated. She wanted to be under my skin, to live there then tell me to get over it.

It was just us outside the restaurant.

"I have no words left for you, only actions. I've said what I had to say." I was cold and distant.

"Those sorry ass emails and letters you sent me?" she scoffed, "You're better than apologies and sad ass letters."

I felt a switch hit in my brain I often questioned my emotion. I felt confident in this conclusion.

"What are you planning, Natalie? You and Cruz, what are you planning?"

"An interview you can't run from. One Halle can't just be a loveable ditz through. I told her everything I needed to about us."

" You told her everything? You told her we just got done having sex in your apartment just the other week? You're so full of shit. Why are you making this worse than it needs to be? Why do you constantly make this harder than it has to be Nat?"

Natalie smiled, "Baby... come home." she caught me off guard batting her eyelashes. "I miss you. This is between Halle and me... I want you back. I'll call everything off. All you need to do is come home."

Anger surged over me. Deeply wanting us to be a possibility, replaced quickly with the nights I wished Natalie would call me. Wishing we could discuss things instead of the senseless arguments and fights. Figure things out. But- It just wasn't possible. We talked far too much and we both knew life was about action.

There are certain people you inevitability meet who only bring the worst out of you, every dark rudimentary flaw crippling your psyche. I am best when left alone... but being with Natalie was absence in presence. Even with her in bed next to me, I felt nothing. Speaking to her was only echoes. As if all I ever done or said disappeared into some void of her utter apathy. She twists the truth like a knife in my back. She's playing victim, convincing me to believing myself a monster...

Halle believes me the only man she will ever love.

Rose calls me Messiah.

Only Natalie who has scorned me, calls me monster. The only woman I have to ask to treat me properly and instead has destroyed my perspective of self. Who left me in the hall of my thoughts night after not without so much as leaving on the light.

I call her Jezebel... I call her Lilith. She calls me Luno or Enshishi. A match made in hell.

There is no question of where my loyalties lie... Natalie will always be a reminder of the boy I once was an infantile sack who solved all his problems with killing. Kill... that's him speaking. That's the boy speaking to you.

You cannot kill all your issues Morgan.

You cannot kill yourself...

You cannot spend your days waiting to die.

You can only live to die another day. Only live to fight one more battle, to live for the pack and to die with dignity. This I still believe.

So, what is this here? Standing with this woman, I once called lover. This woman I once clung to as if life herself. I lived on her every word, desperately seeking her approval... reminding myself of all my flaws and imperfections but never helping to fix them. Why do I still want her touch and her kiss? Why does my heart call me so deeply to love the woman who has hurt me?

"Baby... I'm sorry that I got angry. I wanted to be friends. I told you that. But- You wouldn't call, you wouldn't even look at me. Do you know how that hurts? You wouldn't even tell me you were planning to marry her not just dating her Morgan. You would marry her, so that we could never have a second chance!" She took me to the waters I had no experience in, with words flowing off her tongue like machinegun fire. A conversation I never imagined happening. Being unprepared was no different from being unarmed.

Natalie's body was slender and tight. She stopped speaking as I gripped her plump ass in my hands, her lips fit with mine perfectly. She had me back in her arms as if we had never let go. Her dress lifted for me and her panties fell to her ankles. She moaned in my ear, guiding me to her wet heat. It wouldn't be a reunion without one for the road.

The town was dead outside the downtown lights. Quiet aside from Natalie and me, trying to forget the pain we have caused each other by drowning it out with sex, our narcotic to sate our addiction to pain. It was no different from any night of our relationship. We broke up because we hated each other. She believes it's because of another woman. No, it's because we lost ourselves in the other's world forgetting our own. None of that matters this deep inside her guts. Her nails dig in my back, as she told me everything and anything to get my nut, having her orgasms, shaking freely and wildly. She threw her head back with a loud grunt working our hips together.

This moment seemed as though I was suffering in the rumination of this relationship. In a single instant, it was empty as I let my go inside her. The whole time together reduced to fucking and fighting. Meaningless once all the energy was gone. Only to recover and fight again but never to solve the problem.

"I can't believe you... I spoke of marriage with you, and you only ever entertained the thought." I grunted, her flaming hot walls of sweet hell wrapped around my dick.

The animal inside of me howled, the dread wolf that lived in my desire all these years, howling with excitement. I went back for seconds enjoying Natalie as long as I could before our passion gave way to exhaustion.

"Morgan, I wanted to marry you... you were unstable. You physically abused me then you act like I'm crazy." she began moaning in my ear, fucking with my memory and my emotions.

I held Natalie's hip down, finding no difficulty penetrating her other than her tightness. She moaned as if she was just as surprised. She tried to gain some control but with a slap on her ass or pinch of her nipples she eagerly surrendered, satisfied after all this time we still ended up as two animals lost in carnality. She lifted my chin and kissed me wildly, our bodies slamming into each other. As she moaned, her walls tightened around me with every stroke, swearing she was cumming. I found no pleasure. I couldn't trust this woman anymore... and hadn't any idea who she, or who I was anymore. I was fucking a stranger and she was being mauled the man she met years ago she called a monster. What the hell are we doing?

"Life isn't some damn game that you can play when you wish then pack it up when you wish." I was cold and distant, fucking out anger and latent aggression.

Natalie bit my ear, "I know, baby. I know... but you're my love, my bestfriend. I'm just glad you're back."

She was so confident it made me sick. She viewed me as weak. That I was truly so fickle to forgive and forget? I refused Rose to end up back inside of Natalie.

"You left Natalie." I muttered finally remembering things properly.

"I was hurt! I was angry!" she held to me, emotionally retarded too lost in pleasure to realize my tone of voice.

"So was I! Do you think you hurt alone in this world? Do you think simply because your feelings get hurt or you feel trifled on, you can just act and react however you please without any sense of care for the other person?"

Natalie looked up in agitation, "You're ruining my orgasm." she averted eye conact as I glared at her still buried deep inside of her guts.

Natalie groaned as I pulled out of her. We began to get our clothes on together.

"Why can't anything ever just be simple with you? You're getting pussy, just shut up and we'll deal with this whenever." she begins with the same routine of running around the conflict.

"Yes, we'll keep having sex despite all our issues like last time. You don't even like me Natalie. Why did we do this at all? This was a mistake. We can't see each other again Nat." I shook my head sitting on the bench, pulling a blunt tube from my pocket and lighting it.

"You are a murderer don't give me that. This is the best place for you to be. You left me to move to rundown ole Nadia? Are you kidding me?

Let me know when you're coming back to the apartment. We can chill by the beach again like old times. I still have your bags..."

"I killed so that people like you could sleep at night. But you know what? I regret that. I regret the work I put into a relationship with you, The Regulators, and to Colin. I hate myself for it. I died in Nadia. Did you know that? I lost my very life and the first thing I did was come back to you, Natalie. I could have stayed in Nadia. You abandoned me, you laugh at my dream of rebuilding my homeland. I spent all this time lost and in my fucking feelings over you! And you don't even think I love you!? You are out of your fucking mind if you think in your wildest fucking dreams I would ever crawl back into a relationship with you after all this! It's not about what you did to me. I do remember everything I did to you. I remember everything I did period. I can't allow you to return to that Nat. Move forward with your life."

She stared at me unmoved, "You don't get to decide that for me Morgan. You are mine."

No matter what I said, she never listened. That's what angered me so much. I could talk and she would tune me out as if it was fine. It was blatant and utter disrespect. Was this was the woman I missed? There was no way I could be so stupid any longer.

I was angry enough to rip her head off her shoulders but it would only prove her point. I had a perfect view into her soft brown eyes. It was useless. She wasn't even worth the anger or violence anymore. This was over. It was long over.

I took a deep breath, putting away my mental rifle. I already got my mark on Carmen.

"I do love you, baby. I swear. I knew our love had an expiration date but now we started fresh." Natalie tried rubbing my crotch, incorrigible and unaware.

"An experiation date you didn't plan on informing me on. You should have led with that Nat. If all you wanted was some dick I would have never caught feelings for you." I was disgusted with myself.

"Well. You would have just got upset and left me. I do love you Morgan. You just make me a little crazy." She was finally honest.

"Better us just break up for good, finally, face to face, because we eventually just have to, right? Just let good ole fate, take care of things, right? This is a horrible way to spend our life fighting one another. We don't need to spend our lives abusing each other." I extended my hand to Natalie wanting to let it go.

"Well yeah! See, you get it. Let's just enjoy ourselves a little more before you go." Natalie giggles pushing my hand away then spreading her legs once more for me. "Morgan... Ha, part of it is you. Look at how you're reacting. Like I don't I have my needs as well."

"You were too much of a coward to love someone fairly so you just stayed for the dick and life advice until they realized they should move forward? I fell in love with you. I could have gotten sex anywhere. I could have left Naka all together if I knew how you really felt the whole time. I could have been happy alone. I HAD A GOD GIVEN RESPONSIBILITY! I came back to you, a fucking atheist harlot who cares nothing about my soul."

"Yes because I was your obligation, your sense of duty. I want to be more than someone's burden Morgan. Other men don't find it hard loving me like you refused to. I'm not their obligation or an option. I am their priority and main objective soldier boy."

"Other men? Ha, you mean those guys who blow through their paycheck on you even though you're a damn heiress?" I shook my head snickering.

"At least they spend their money on me. Lo and behold Morgan, the self-made billionaire but your girlfriend paid for everything."

"So, my inability to do makes it okay? All the things you could have done but refused to!? I'll cut you a freaking check if it's about the money Natalie. I used to want you back. Now, let me know what I need to do to end this shit. You think I built my empire using Halle's money?"

"Don't fucking insult me, New Money. I am saying you do not love me. Those men love me. You wanted me. You had to have me. You were obsessed with me and made me your little sex slave."

"What the fuck are you talking about?"

"I was scared of you Morgan. For god's sake, we were children but you were an absolute monster, a murderer. I don't blame you for being whatever you are but God. I was a virgin when we met. Then you turned me into this, what did you call me some atheist harlot? I revered you like a God Morgan. I let you use me however, you wanted. I am what you made me."

"That's one thing if you wanted things to work longterm but you didn't. You knew what the issues were between us. You refused to tell me your side of things. You refused to be honest. No... There's no sympathy for you and I don't need your empathy. You were too lazy to act upon any of this reverance you apparently had. And too afraid to love someone as much as you claimed. I put my heart on my sleeve and went after you."

"And you remain abusive and demoralizing." she rolls her eyes, "same ole Morgan. You haven't changed at all."

I almost let that defeat me. I had conquered the Dread Wolf but not myself. The beast's howling in my ear stopped, he was panicked. There would be no release for him.

"Great thing we aren't together then." I smiled ear to ear finally letting my heart free.

"Morgan I want to be friends!" Natalie grabbed my hand, "You can still visit the apartment. Halle invited me to be in the wedding. We can make things work."

"For what? You're not the resistance. So you're not the hold on this closure and opening a new chapter." I let myself breathe beginnging to understand what I never could.

"No, so there's more to our life than this but there's no more us? Can't there be more to our lives than fighting and pretending we don't know each other?" Natalie squeezed my hand.

"I don't know who you are, Natalie. Not anymore, Deuces." I begin to walk away throwing a peace sign.

"I'm not going anywhere." Natalie grabs my arm digging her nails into my flesh.

"Get off, Natalie!"

"Why do you feel so comfortable talking to me that way? Just tossing me out your life like it's nothing. Like I'm some used tissue!" Natalie cries out.

"I lost people I actually loved and who cared about me without any say. You think I'm afraid of losing someone who was too scared of what her friends would think to even take our relationship seriously? You make endless excuses for why you couldn't love me. Your weak ass just needed a survivor's complex to get you through life. But sadly that only works outside the face of the truth. So be it. I'll be your bad guy. Leave me and mine alone. Leave it all alone. Leave. Don't come back. Don't think about me. There's no room for you in my life. Take this moment and keep it as my gift to you, the monster of your delusion."

"Ha, Morgan like you weren't an asshole? Like you weren't abusive and suicidal! I saved you. I brought you back! You owe me everything you have!" Natalie tried dragging me back.

"Yeah but despite all that I gave everything I had in our relationship. You always held back. Well I hope the new guy is worth more because you're not coming back in my life." I had lost all my emotion regarding this, my mind cleared back to rationality as I snatched my arm away.

"Morgan... We need to bury the hatchet to be at peace and at amends." Natalie pleaded, "We can still work. You're worth being with me now!"

"There is no amends, Natalie. You were a cunt. I was an asshole. I don't need friends who bring out my worst. You don't inspire me. You don't make me feel good about myself. You make me feel like a monster, and when that isn't enough, you make me feel like nothing."

"And you make me feel like a helpless child." She was clawing but found no surface, the only wounds were bruises of past mistakes, long healed and no scabs remained.

"Guess I'm a monster." I mutter, "So be it, I am a monster. At least I tried. I'm the lunatic. I'm the danger. I'm the schizoprehenic psycho and paranoid freakshow. At least I tried loving and never stopped. You never even bothered to try."

"Don't put words in my mouth, Morgan."

"I put no words in your mouth. Life is about actions and you had many. Goodbye, Natalie. I have no interest in solving this anymore. I was at least at peace before tonight. I found a place to be at. I don't need you ruining my life."

"Okay... okay I can accept that, but can you finish me up?" She stared at me with a slight fringe of a smile on her lips.

I fought the urge so deeply. Women bring something out in you, beyond sparring, beyond the emotional jabs and fights. There is a chord they pull onto so deeply that I don't quite understand. They poke, they jab, they get all their satisfaction out of this emotional distress. I only feel satisfied after my fist has met my problem. There is much work for diplomacy... but I wanted to tear her neck off her shoulders. She represented everything at this moment I was at war against and it stood right before me.

She wanted me to hit her. Since I wouldn't, she wanted sex. I won't give her the satisfaction again. She would run right back to her friend Carmen and let her know about the psychopath ex-reg who laid hands on her. She would laugh with that to the bank after suing me. That's how these people fought. These were the people living off the backs of my Nadia... These people wanted Qatar dead.

I turned around and stuffed my hands into my pocket. I pulled off the monkey tie. The noose wrapped around my throat. Never again in my life will I wear a tie to show that I am of worth. I tossed off the jacket, hopefully some homeless man will find warmth. I know these people won't touch it. The moment it hits the ground it becomes trash.

"I hated my time in La Vida."

"Where are you going!? Morgan!?" Natalie raved. "DON'T FUCKING WALK AWAY FROM ME!" she roared behind me, "COME BACK HERE NOW!"

She didn't want me to leave, didn't want me to stay. Some women just want to see you under their thumb, or see you miserable. I just wanted my freedom from Enshishi.

So, I walked...

Until her screaming was inaudible, Until La Vida was long behind me, Until I cleared the stretch of the Lake, and further beyond that.

Until my shoes grew uncomfortable and I kicked them, off with my socks, holding them in my hands to walk baerfoot.

I walked until I was in Nadia, standing where I stood years ago when I was on the cusp of manhood where I cut my own stomach open to atone for killing my fellow Regulators.

Rose asked me why I was so down... Why the good in my heart isn't enough. I knew who I was before I saved Nadia. I was not this Ada, I was Luno... The Dread Wolf, what they called "The Lord of Darkness". I clung to Warren's guidance and directives as law to prevent falling down such a path of darkness. My mentor saved my life and kept me redeemable. I was a child, under the influence and constant assail of Colin Gregor's wishes for me. My own sick carnal desires and actions caused this hell.

I'm not delusional enough to believe my sorrows and heart are enough to undo a lifetime within the Regime. No, I was not a Hound. No, I did not work within the precincts or citizen reprehension. Wolves focused on higher concerns. When a group gathers to destabilize governments, you call a Wolf. When creatures cross over from other realms that could cause nationwide ego death, you call a Wolf. When a freedom fighter wishes to resist the spread of government, you need a Wolf. We're conditioned to be egoless disciples of Enshishi and fulfill his wishes and I was their Alpha.

Rose believes it's enough to simply feel remorse. Turn to Baat she'll say.

No girl, Ada is my absolution!

My soul can't rest until I undo my works! A life spent as a weapon of the government. And dutiful, unquestioning activity. She believed me a victim. I don't believe in victimhood. My teacher was Lord Commissioner Ray Bradley Warren, the Steel Warden of Erdu. Since a child, I admired his sense of rule and Order. He was the light where Gregor always seemed to be... as Rose would say, "the devil". Being just, patient and when it's time to act... we rip apart our enemies. Ray will speak first then act.

Colin is all action and no remorse, no second-guessing, no sense of guilt, anything to build the Gregor name. There's an admirability to that. There's joy to that. But more than anything else it's a detriment.

Warren always understood the good of all. Colin plays the system for his own ends. I fear I've had too much Enshishi in me to even return to Warren. I don't think I could truly look him in the eyes Duty was always first to Warren.

Would Warren understand my actions? Could he forgive me?

It has been a lifetime since we said our goodbyes... I was still a boy then. Colin found out of my crimes when I was a man.

I was walking through the lower east of Nadia, a district called Exigo. I used this place often when I was scouting on Qatar back then. He believed himself a man of the people.

"Yo, kid!"

I heard my attention called.

"My name is Morgan. I never took kindly to being called kid."

An older man approached and extended a hand to me, "thank you."

"Thank you?"

He shook my forearm fiercely. "Bless you. Ada, bless you!"

"I only did what was right."

"Son... you did what no one else would, what none of us could! If this city was swallowed by the Dogs..." he shook his head, perishing the thought. "I have lived here for 70 years. Thank you."

I nodded, "What do you want for this city?"

"I want the Nadia I was raised in before the Dogs and Jackals. Back when the Lions actually protected us!"

"Who are the lions?"

"The son is not the father. Maurice Gregor, Enshishi blessed is his name. But the child... the child is not the father. He leaves us to die."

"How would Nadia react if a new ruler was to step in?"

"Please do, brother! Please do!"

I nod, "All things in time, all things moment by moment."

"You saved us once... we've waited for your return and here you stand. Ada, I see it in your eyes. Ada... bless you as you bless us."

"No man is a God, old timer."

"No man is an island, young man. But gods do walk amongst us... they always have." he had a glimmer in his eyes, "You know this better than anyone, don't you?"

"Thank you for your kind words." I move to leave but he refuses to let me go, "sir, I am not the man to hold on to. I am no savior. I heard what Qatar promised but I-

"You let him go! You let him escape. He believed in you, as we believe in you. Do you not see this within yourself?" Rose warned me this wasn't a secret within Nadia.

"I'm afraid not... I- I am no sovereign. I am sorry, sir. But I am not the one you seek-

"Then why are you here?" he asked with his one good eye, the other had a huge purple cataract.

"I refuse to let the Gregors or Regulators take Nadia. If I can continue to resist their spread, I shall. This is where I find my absolution." I confided in him.

"Why boy? Why? So, many leave, so many have fallen. I watched you fall. Yet here you stand anew. If you are not him then who are you? What else has your life pointed you toward?"

"I am not, Jah'Ada. But I refuse to see this city fall to ruin. I wish to help, truly I do. But- I just could not be Ada."

"So, even if you are not our Guardian... you will accept his responsibility?" He smiles brightly with his toothless smile. "You resist your calling. Your eyes have seen all. All you must do is look through them."

"Look, yes I am. Yes I have." I let out a sigh. "I will do all I possibly can for this city. I will continue to protect it."

"Because you are its Guardian! You are its Guardian. You're called for this! It's in your blood!"

"I never knew my family. My earliest memories are of the Academy."

"You were taken, boy, your father was killed. Now, they want your birthright!"

"Who are you, old man?"

"You may call me Razikiel. Just an old man who's seen the best and worst years of Ecru, I love dearly. I raised my kids here."

"I've heard you old man. Razikiel. I have heard your words." I lost my words as my eyes met his.

"Do not hear me. Believe me. I have seen the works of your father. Your works will be greater!"

"If you knew my father, what is his name?"

"Your father was the Rebel King without a crown. You were the son before the fall! Do you not know, boy?"

"I was a Wolf... this is all I know before my death." tear filled my eyes, "Who was he?"

"Ask your Masters, they will tell you the truth. They wish you servant because you are the true King. The only King of Gaia, son of Obatta Sameera."

The Rebel King without a Crown was my father this entire time.

It's time to change that, father. Your memory won't be lost to these sycophantic monsters.

CHAPTER 24

The Return of the King

Morgan Ellys

I walked through the streets of Exigo with my hands in the pockets of my slacks. My head low as I walked through the valley where the river Tigress spilled into a massive lake. One of the two water masses in the land-locked region of Nadia. It was a miracle. This is where the who's who of those who sold their souls lived. Those unaffected by the Hound occupation to the east, living their lives as usual. Just as deluded as the rest of the world as to what happened in their own home. These people couldn't wait for Nadia to be absorbed into Naka.

Rose and Halle didn't need to know I was here but there were matters out of my control that needed attending. Men I needed to speak to face to face before I put my true campaign at risk. I've never had people fighting for me before, perhaps only those who worked underneath me or for a mission but never those who in reality commit their life to my cause. Only those bonded to me for their survival or personal gain.

I understand you, Razikiel to give these people honorable lives. Those who support us are investing something far more valuable than gold or wealth. Their faith in our success is something money cannot buy. It is something I seem to have more here in Nadia than Colin has anywhere in this world.

These people do not know me. But I know them. I see in their eyes they are waiting for me to reveal myself as I truly am. As if I'm to promise them the future and lead them in the streets with festivals and parades.

This sadly wasn't how I believed life worked. I am an assassin... this does not change because I am Ada. I am not a leader. I am efficient and focused. Something I believe far more important than a figurehead or manager.

I have no interest in men and women following me to their deaths. Living and breathing on my every word and pause. No, live well and free within yourselves. Be happy as you are. You don't need to be like me.

I arrived at the Knox Family Compound. The stroll was much appreciated. I had words with Don Knox. It wasn't a mystery as to where the drugs in Nadia had come from or the corruption. The men of this city are in chains and you will poison their women? Those eating off the works and love of my people were at an end. Not to mention these assholes attacked my club without any true recompense. The exploitation and abuse were at their end. It's time for Nadia to stand and stand firm.

This is something I could never understand about humanity. We see others struggling so we increase their struggle? We are all facing and working toward the same ends. In the success of our brothers we find our own success. Even I, a Wolf can understand this. But here was a Family that built itself upon the underbelly of the city.

Here in the Red Light District crime was law. There was only one justice, The Knox Family. I spent most my days in Erdu... there are stories and tales of Knoxes who were great men. But just as the Gregors in my mind. I care very little for how nice one is, or how well they smile or shake my hand. I will judge you upon your merits and your work. You are destroying my people and preventing them from being whole within their life and time on this earth. You will face judgment either by God or your peers.

The Knoxes had a beautiful riverfront compound stretching the whole block. Wrapping around and the Lake and holding a barricade for what traveled within the Tyre Lake and Tigress River. This was unacceptable. My people starve and the Jackals swell themselves on the lake?

"Who are you?" A large bald-headed man asked me, dressed in a navy blue suit. "What are you doing out here?"

"I'm just admiring the architecture while I'm going for a walk."

"People don't walk around here, punk. Who are you?" He asks poking me in the chest.

"I am the man looking to speak with Don Knox." I replied with a smirk. "Can you take me to him?"

"The Don is busy, punk. Fuck off!" It was usual grunt talk, unable to think for himself or be respectful.

I slammed my palm to his chin with full brunt force, slapping his brain against his skull then smacking his face. It looked as if I barely moved had there been cameras. Too quick and forceful to cause a fuss was the usual mission, now it was a habit. He slumped down to the ground like a lifeless rung. I stepped over him to pry open the electric gate then casually walking up the esplanade to the front door. I stepped in front of the huge yew wood door. I knocked twice waiting about until the door pushed open. A young woman met me.

"Um, hello, sir..." she curtsies, "who might you be?"

I covered a single eye allowing the open eye to turn deep crimson.

"It's a pleasure sure. What can I do for you?" She reintroduced herself. "I am Valarie."

"Be a good girl and take me to your boss."

"I will take you to Don Vincent immediately." she curtsies once more and begins walking in a trance.

"Thank you, ma'am." I bow my head allowing my eyes to return to their original brown hue.

I followed an enjoyable distance behind her buxom frame as she tours me through the ancient house.

"Our home was originally built with marble and wood. It's always been curious to me how robber barons would sit so comfortably while the world suffered. She opens a door to a man seated behind the table.

"Thank you dearest." I leave her to return to her duties.

She looked at me as if she had just opened her eyes. She felt my intent and backed away. She didn't look long enough to see my face. She simply fell over herself backing up.

I pushed the door open to the study on the second floor of the compound. "Are you Vincent Cree?" I approached his desk.

"I'm not the fucking Pope." He scoffed. "The hell do you want? Who let you in here? Is this a free for all? Anyone can just step into the Don's office. I have an empire to run kid. Hurry on. I have a secretary for that. Where the hell is my daughter?"

I tore a hole through the room reappearing before the Don with my blade at his throat. He looked up aghast. I looked down upon the man seventy pounds lighter than me and a decade short of proper training. He reached to his hip for the Glock. I kick him straight in his chest knocking him out his chair straight to the ground. I grabbed him by his throat lifting him up and flinging him against the wall across the room.

"What the fuck..." the Don winces as he begins to pick himself up.

I kick him straight in his ribs. He falls back down. I kick him once more. I grab him by his throat again to drag him to his chair. Sitting him back down to look at me, brushing the dust off his shoulder and smoothing out his clothes.

"Now, that we've nipped your indolence in the bud. One more time, are you Vincent Cree?"

"Yes... yes I am, who the fuck do you think you are boy?" He stammered.

"I am Ada. I am the son of Obatta Sameera. I am Morgan." I paced the area behind his desk and the wall of bookshelves behind him. "You are going to release this embargo. I'm going to buy two of these buildings from you. The fields near the mouth of the river are mine. On both sides, do you understand?"

"How much are you giving me for the buildings?"

"Your life, I will take the buildings a sign of your fealty. You will send the contract to my office by this weekend. My lawyers will discuss it with your lawyers. If you step out of line, I will kill you without repercussion." I cut my eyes at him.

"Ha, fuck you. If you were gonna kill me you would have." He chuckles, "start talking cash, kid."

"I'm a very patient man, Cree. This is mercy. Yes, I could kill you if I truly wanted. I trust this is evident. The truth is that I could kill every man in this compound by lifting my hands. Then who will police the streets for me?" I turned his chair around, stepping on his crotch as I lean in to stare him in the eyes. "I have a vested interest in the prosperity of Nadia. You help me. Our partnership will be profitable for both of us. My deal is that simple. Refuse it if you want. I'm prepared to wipe you off this planet. Nadia is changing. Anyway standing against those winds of change is bonded to death."

"My life is worth a deal with the devil then you could pony something up kid."

I spit in disgust. "You're already doing the devil's work in assisting Enshishi in poisoning and killing your own people. You have a new King now if you wish to stay in Nadia. I can make your compound my new base of operations without you here or you can continue to work but for the Son of Sameera."

"I need cash, kid. That's how shit works."

I cut my eyes at him. "You are wearing my patience Vincent. You seem to believe I'm giving you an option. Repent and join my cause or I will fucking kill you."

I needn't raise my voice. I didn't need to change my tone. My intent was in my eyes. I needn't use my eyes. You could stare into them and see every man I've killed and exactly how they died.

"You can fight me. You can shoot me. But the end will be exactly the same. I will conquer you and anyone who stands against me, it's my nature. I will drag you to the center of Nadia like a wounded dog and put you down in front of all these citizens who seem to fear you. I am not a very nice man when angered Cree."

"You're not joking. You're the real deal, huh?" He held up his hands. "I don't have a choice..."

I nodded crossing the room to the door. "Expect my men within the week. Stay indoors. Plan my works. I will approve all you can and cannot do. We are going to change this city."

"Thank you for your mercy... Thank you Ada." He bowed keeping his hands extended where I could see them.

"If I have to come back to see you, if I ever need to speak to you again then I will be here to kill you. I do not micromanage. Do my works or I will kill you, it's very simple. You have worn out your stay on this planet Vincent."

"I-I-

"This was your one and only warning. I am the King. You can serve me. Or you stay out of my fucking way."

I stared at him.

He nodded. "I understand. I will- I will change, Ada."

"I pray that can save you, Vincent."

I tore into a hole in air before Vincent. The world opened up to me. And I stepped through. It closed behind me. Leaving no trace of my presence, only three people knew. And only one knows who I am. Perfect.

Who was next?

I stepped out in Exigo before the gym. I walked up looking around the harbor area on the other River of Nadia. Seems Vincent holds tide over one. This boy seems to be protecting the other.

"The Son has returned!" The old man's voice called out. He hobbles to me all smiles and wheezing laughter. "You have come back!"

He hugs and squeezes me tight.

"You were right old, man." I return the embrace.

"We are always right. We've seen this all before."

I nodded. "I need to speak with Mark."

"I'm afraid Markus isn't with us... he's disappeared. The Wolf Pact is without a leader."

"Then who can I talk to?"

"I am here with Mr. Murashima."

"Lead the way, Razikiel." Divine providence was always a beautiful thing.

He pats my back then begins tugging me along through a low hanging door on one of the warehouses. A man trained with little kids. Going through Tai Chi formations as the kids followed along in sync.

There was an elderly man from old Naka encircled by dozens of kids no older than ten or twelve. He led the formations and the children did their best to follow his lead.

"You must be at peace with your energy. No elevation. No release. Cultivate and hold it within you. This is the way to vitality." He seemed quite frail but held a menacing presence deep within him that seemed all too familiar yet different. "Even when you feel the anger or the stress of life press against you, resist. We are stronger than the tide. We are stronger than the pressures of life. We are the essence of life itself."

I sat down in my lotus and closed my eyes taking in his mantras.

"You will face insurmountable forces in life. They stand to nothing against the human spirit. Nothing against the power of life, these enemies use and conquer death. We represent all that is life and liberated. It is your energy that will lead the next generation. You must be in control of self to conquer the enemies that conquer death."

The mantra stopped. And there was the sound of all the children and running about and laughing as they headed out to play on the equipment or spar. I opened my eyes to find Murashima walking to me.

"Lord Ada." He bows. He didn't need an introduction. "It is kind of you to join us."

"You are my elder, sir. Please stand." I remained in my lotus, seated beneath him on the floor. "I enjoyed the demonstration."

"I am glad. I simply try to teach what has helped me. What brings you to us today, young Ada?"

"I wished to speak with Mark about the future of Nadia. But now, I have come to listen on the past of this city. What's happened?"

He nodded. "We will go for a walk. Come back tonight. I close this gym at midnight when many of the young men are done with training and go on to put on their masks. There are a few I wish for you to meet."

"I thought the men were arrested?"

"Yes... but they left sons. These sons have grown. Lost and confused. They follow false guidance. I thank Rakil for Markus. He is a good-hearted man. I pray he is well. But he is also but a boy. I have many people looking for him. I fear he was captured..."

"Captured?"

"There are those of us who see the suffering of others and try to ease it. There are others who see suffering and only wish to capitalize upon it."

"Hmm... I suppose I can meet up with my girlfriend, after all."

"We must cherish the women of our life Ada. Cherish them so they may help us grow stronger. The feminine nurtures the masculine, only if the masculine leads the feminine."

I was silent. I have left my women unguarded in the heart of the city, to Colin, to these streets and now possibly to Cree. I believe in some ways they must fend for themselves but they are not as I am. They do not have the same strength or focus. They are not built and have no mind for the true dangers of this world.

"I will return tonight, sir."

"I hope you are ready for a walk."

"Indeed. There is another matter I must ask while I have your attention... Are you Saito Murashima?"

The old man smiled, "Bless you, child." he begins to chuckle, "He is my father. He is in the mountains with my son and his disciples. He is not much for civilization."

"He's a wise man."

"I trust you speak because of the Guardian of Fire?"

"Enshishi, yes... but you call him Ryu, why?"

"This is a topic better saved out of the ears of children, don't you agree?" he patted my arm, "My grandfather is in the mountains of Tartarus."

"Nothing lives in Tartarus."

"My grandfather hoped to change that. I visit every so often. He would be honored to see you, though Ada. It would bring him delight to see the first son is someone so strong and respectful."

"I am honored by your words."

Halle letting me off long enough to come to Ecru was one thing. If I went off to Tartarus in search of Saito and Bryon, she would leave me. I had enough to do what I needed. Too much information leads to neurosis. My woman needed me at home, assisting her in saving this city and making Colin Gregor one less item for her to worry about.

"Can you at least tell me how to defeat Colin Gregor?"

"To defeat a man is easy. You need to worry about his spirit. If you kill him then his spirit will possess your soul, Enshishi. If you leave him, he will kill everything until you kill him. I fear he is an unmovable object in your pathway."

"You know?"

"This is the eternal fire... it cannot die, you either contain it, learn to use it, or you try your best to sate it. I believe there have been many men and many forces who Enshishi claimed. My family originated in the Edo District of Naka. We had a patron from a thousand years ago when Ecru still existed. Hiro the First Dragon, he conquered the spirit of Enshishi after seeing how darkness had consumed the Ada of that generation. He turned the Lion into the Dragon our people cherish today."

"Ada can also be tempted by darkness?"

Takio Murashima nodded, "The vicar can be tempted to good or evil, and in this the Guardian becomes corrupted. Every Guardian has itself, its shadow side and a fully realized self. For Enshishi, the Lion and Dragon sit on opposite ends of the Sun. To claim the world or to sit upon its wealth, to save Gaia or to save humanity, it's a very difficult decision I imagine. The redeemed allow the next Enshishi be born pure as a Phoenix. Hiro is said to have gone through all these steps. People rumor we have discovered the secret to eternal life in Edo and Kisaka."

"There is no killing Colin... he must be redeemed?"

"That would be foresight, that would be wisdom and mercy uncommon in a man so young.From what I know about Gregors, it's too little too late."

"I don't intend on allowing Colin to walk around whole. I will tear pieces from him. But I will leave enough for the next generation to be spared another tyrant. We need all that."

Warren had a point... Order was needed but not his form of enforcement. No, the world needed tranquility. Conflict was inevitable. Violence was necessary. But peace and compassion must be our guiding forces. I will attempt reason with Colin. I will need to pray to Rakil I keep myself from killing him.

CHAPTER 25

When Hell Freezes Over

Natalie Wolfe

I was sitting in Carmen's two-story penthouse living room in Graham with her head in my lap. I needed Carmen back to 100% if she was going to host her show. Morgan wasn't going to be out fucking the world and be rewarded for his bullshit. All the things I've paid for. All the time spent arguing with this asshole.

I don't care about Morgan's marriage or his money. Neither of those things can sate my retribution. I will have my own millions once my career takes off. And there was no possible way we could work. He chose a child's response. Ignoring me? As if I didn't exist or occupy that position in his life? That scorns me! How can you just cut someone out of your life like that? Especially after cheating on them!

"Can you tell me one more time what happened?" Carmen said she had a minor concussion and her memory had been hazy. "I remember looking at him and then BLANK!" she claps her hands.

"He did something to you. His eyes would turn colors when he was angry. Weird things happen when he looks you right in the eyes. You just walked off like nothing happened at all. He could end an entire night of fighting with a glance. He had a power over me."

"What the fuck is this guy? Sounds like some mind freak stuff." Carmen sat up, "I knew Morgan early in his career, I'll be honest. I never knew this side of him. No one thought he had kinetic abilities. Now he's a freaking weapon."

I wasn't aware they knew each other at all outside of a few meetings. Carmen seemed to think I knew more about Morgan than she apparently did. Some ammunition she could use on her show.

"I met him in the academy. I always figured he was just some psychopath they hired for interrogations." I rolled my eyes.

"Yeah? That's all you really that's think he was to you? Some psychopath? Look, I have a damn concussion or something getting involved with you. Morgan, is something else entirely... but he isn't a psychopath. If we're going to break him, we must be honest." Carmen held an ice pack to her head and shook her head. "What was he to you?"

"No... I-

"Look, I'm not trying to hear it. My head is killing me. The last thing I care about is you crying or some shit. So, let's just breathe. And give me the facts." Carmen rolled the bridge of her nose.

I could always count on Carmen to keep me in check and out my feelings. A woman needs a friend to keep her from being emotional.

I bit my lip, "He was charming... then he went away. He came back like he never left. Found out he was fucking my friend who he swore he wasn't fucking!"

"You're bringing this petty ass drama to my show? I got a concussion just because you're mad he was fucking Halle!?"

"What?"

"Natalie... come on. I hear a few girls have been with him while you were dating. That's what those dudes are like. Think the world revolves around them and all women do is suck their dick and stroke their ego. I'm sorry no one put you up on game, but you don't need to put up with that shit with men. Make them serve you."

I smiled, "I never knew that was even option... My father would kill me!"

"They do all this for us, girl. Men would kill their best friend just to say he fucked his wife. They're depraved. That's why I don't keep one.

I'm not bringing this shit on my show. We'll get you something better. We'll get your brains fucked out. And you'll be good as new."

"I have someone in mind..."

"Who?"

I grin. "I could sleep with Colin... get back at both of them!"

"Do it! That will be so scandalous! Halle would never forgive you." Carmen gushed, "Ha, I thought I was evil. You have great hope as an advocate of Enshishi."

"Colin would never stop calling me. He'll know I do it better!" I grin. He was an misogynist assholes, but he was also handsome and powerful. I'm not sure how I could ever justify it to my father, maybe it's time the Gregors and Wolfe aligned to take over the world?

"Better than who? He's never been married... ? Who are you talking about?" Carmen caught the whiff of a scandal. She tapped her lips trying to put pieces together.

"Carmen, cut it out. No one is supposed to know."

"Wait, you meant better than Halle? At what? Sex? Ha, Morgan or Colin?" she did this for a living. "That's where our story is."

"Carmen... can you just-

"You said you wanted these two buried, did you not? I need something juicy to hold over her. Get out your fucking feelings and lets destroy our enemies!"

"Yeah... but not that. I have integrity." I looked away.

The Wolfe family never worked in mud-slinging. We had enemies but because our enemies hated and envied us. As my father explains, our family were the followers of the Phoenix, Rakiham. The rebirth when the eternal flame went out. Our ancestors were in a cave for 7 days, and 8 nights with little more than a flame for our warmth, sustenance and protection. Before the 3rd Age, we knew nothing but suffering and plight. Killed by all, and used as slaves. Until eventually we stood up and fought back for ourselves! My father would never approve of this course of action... I needed to maintain my family honor.

"Integrity? Girl... this man fucked your best friend and treated you like garbage. He was abusive and controlling. Why don't you let the guilt go and let those lips loose!" Carmen shot up and rubbed my shoulders. "Looks like you need to loosen up more than me. Come on now. Lay it on me girl. I'm all ears. Supporting you all the way."

"Well... Halle and Colin... are more than daughter and father."

"I knew she liked her dad too much! That's why this bitch walks around like the sun shines out her ass." She bursts into laughter. "Oh my god, this is great. I don't even need to bring her on the show. I'm tweeting this immediately! I knew those Gregors were crazy, I never knew the rumors of how fucked up they were with true."

"No! Wait! Carmen!"

"And sent!" she showed me her screen, 'Halle is daddy's little girl.' Posted right up online.

She was brilliant. Suspicion would do the rest. She didn't need to invite Halle. Halle would have to explain herself now. The world will hear all about the butt slut and the rabid dog she's dating. After Carmen spreads the word half the world would let their imagination run wild over one tiny little blip. It wasn't as satisfying but it felt so devious.

"You hated Colin too right? Let's get both these fuckers. Get a sextape going." Carmen was big on ruining other people's lives. She had few friends or allies because no one trusts her. "Why are you looking at me, like that? You want everyone to know right?"

"Excuse me? Absolutely not, Carmen. My life isn't for your ratings. Halle or Morgan. I'm not trying to piss off Enshishi."

She rolled her eyes. "Whatever girl, you came to me for help. You better be ready to play. Halle's gonna wonder who told me. You better be ready to come on the show too."

"Absolutely not! I am not getting involved. I told you. You keep me out of this! I have a peace treaty to maintain."

She shrugs, "the world will wonder... you know how Halle plays. She doesn't hold punches. And she doesn't play fair. She fucked your boyfriend to prove she was better than you. You know that was the only reason."

"She isn't better than me, and Halle knows that. Morgan likes shallow girls. She's perfect for him."

That's how she must feel. You know that's how she is! Jah'Enshishi. What do I do?

I knew Carmen was playing me. But she had a point... no one could protect me but me. Last time I relied on someone he was emotionally unstable and unreliable. I needed to make sure my bases were covered. I was already too far along as it went, I was the only story she had. Carmen spoke of Halle, but she was a savage she looked at me ready to drop anything she could use.

I pulled out my phone and quickly typed up, "Halle loves psychopaths."

I showed Carmen the phone and she smiled with pride, "Vaaaguue... we're gonna start a trend. I have an idea. Hashtag Hallefessions."

"Make HalleFessions its own page... make it anonymous." I add.

My phone pulsed twice quickly.

Favorited by Victoriana. Flashed on my notifications. With a picture of Halle with her braids out in a wild mane. Her curly hair was down to her middle back.

"Who the hell is-" I dropped my phone. "That quickly?" I wasn't ready for this at all.

"Well... you did kind of put yourself in there girl. But don't worry. I gotchu. We'll both be on the show. We'll get Hallefessions going over some wine and ice cream. Go back to your hotel. Take a shower. Cool off and come back after I've called up some dick for later."

"What happened to ice cream and the page?"

"Need a well balanced diet of protein girl. Can't fill up on wine and ice cream alone. Your mama should have taught you better. Now, run along I have to get things ready."

"Alright, girl. I'll be right back."

What moments are you going to remember when this story hits the fan Morgan? How badly you've scorned me? Or continue rattling on about how I wouldn't sit idly by as you went on with your brooding? You were nobody when we met, Morgan Ellys. Nobody.

I left Carmen's apartment with the return of long lost energy and pep.

My phone buzzed twice.

"What's good?" Victorianna, location Nadine. Reply. I hesitated walking to my car. I tucked my phone away.

What the hell is Halle doing in Nadine? She's supposed to be in La Vida or the Gregor Manor. She's supposed to be in Naka, why on Gaia is she in Nadine?

She would just have to deal with me when we get on the show. I have nothing to say to Halle or Morgan for that matter.

I slipped into my car. I started up my Pearl White Sonata and let her purr as we backed out of the car complex.

My car began beeping then stopped. I rose a brow. Did Carmen forget something?

"Text message, from, Haley Gregar, 'You Home?' Twenty minutes ago." My car informs me. "In-coming caller, Haley Gregar." The car begins vibrating around me as I drive down the road.

"Decline call." I say growing irritated.

What the hell does she want? If she has anything to say to me, she can say it for the cameras.

The ringing subsides.

Finally... silence. Alone with my thoughts. Free from all this. Now, we wait.

The Car sang in windchimes signifying"Voicemail from, Haley Gregar."

"Eh.. ?"

"Hey, Nat it's Halle. What's good, girl? I'm in town. If you need to let some steam off you could bring it up with me woman to woman. Not this Carmen shit."

I didn't need this right now. She could wait.

I turned my head to see Halle's orange BMW cruising alongside me. She holds up her phone then drops it. She follows my car for the next half hour even with me taking side roads. Once I got to my hotel they would keep her out. There was security.

I parked my car and got out quickly. Setting a pace to get out as quickly as possible. Before...

"Natalie. Are you going to act like you don't see me?" Halle says in my ear right on my heels.

"You think you can just harass me like this?" I turn around. "I will not be accosted!"

"Bitch, save it. What's good? All that shit up on the web. What do you and Carmen have to say? Say that shit now."

"You can share your side of the story on the show." I nod, beginning to take my leave.

"The show? You did fucking tell Carmen!? The whole world is going to find out!"

I shrugged, "You and Morgan should've thought of that."

"Natalie we were children then! We have bigger concerns now. How could you?"

"Like your wedding? Right? Or fucking your dad."

Halle looked at me bewildered, "you did not tell, Carmen I was raped by my dad!" Her voice small and weak, a low grumbling in her pathetic throat.

I smiled having Halle Gregor completely at bay. Like things were supposed to be to begin with. Maybe there was some use to all this... Morgan was soon to be a wealthy man. If I could remind Halle of her place perhaps we can just work this all out.

"I did and I can control Carmen. She won't tell, if you cancel the wedding." I sneer.

"Done."

"Just like that?" I laughed a bit uneasily by her lack of hesitation.

"Just like that." Halle nods.

"Now, come upstairs... we can talk." And we're going to make a little video.

Perhaps I could get a video of Halle for Carmen... reinforce my case and really remind Halle who's game she's playing. I won't even need the show now. This worked out far better than I intended. My father would be proud. Blackmail was always sweeter than conflict. She came right to me, Enshishi has blessed me. Now, she'll be eating out the palm of my hand. And she'll be eating me out. Halle Gregor will serve the Wolfe Family like she was meant to all along.

My grandfather used to tell me stories of how the Gregors killed and ate us... other humans. You look at the Gregors they all walk with their heads so far up their ass. Morgan fits rights in.

"I'm sorry it ended up like this, Halle. You know how Carmen gets. You get to talking and she just eggs you on. After a while I didn't even know what I was saying, I just needed to talk to a friend, ya know?"

Halle was quiet walking behind me. Meek and timid like a kitten.

"I was all tears... I couldn't believe the things that I said. Honestly, I didn't even tell her, she just figured it out herself." That last one wasn't even a lie.

"Yeah..." she says simply with a sigh. "Let's hurry this up."

I smiled, "quick to come up to my room, huh? I wonder what you have planned for me. I can't wait for my apology."

"Your apology?"

"If you don't want Carmen dropping the bomb, then you have a bit of apologizing to do." I kissed Halle's cheek. She pulled away but I grabbed her chin forcibly kissing her on the lips this time. "I missed you, Halle."

"What the hell, Natalie. Stop..." she blushed. Backing away from me.

We got alone in the elevator. I wagged her over. Sliding my hands down her pants and squeezing her butt.

"So, soft. I can't wait to spank you...make you crawl around the floor and beg like a good bitch. I can't wait to try my new toy out. My Halle Gregor life-sized doll. To use as I please for these next few hours, right?" to take this video over to Carmen's.

I bit her neck as I kneaded her tiny butt. The elevator stopped and she shoved me away.

"What the fuck, Halle! I should tell Carmen right now!"

"Relax... relax..." she held up her hands returning to me as an older woman entered the elevator.

I sucked my teeth as Grandma pressed the floor right after mine. Wouldn't be able to get my fill before getting off the elevator. I stood patiently. Watching Halle. We made eye contact every so often. Each time I whispered the punishment in her ear.

Spanking.

Eating me.

Sucking my strap.

And bending over for me while I ravage her from behind. I'll take her virginity if Colin and Morgan already hadn't. It wouldn't count. At least that's what I'll tell her. Halle would be so easy to convince. Look, at her. She can barely wait to be punished. She's so antsy. Switching foot to foot. She keeps looking at me like she can't wait to get her hands on me.

Say what you might about Morgan... the sex is incredible. If he has money and power then maybe now he might be good enough for me. We'll at least have our fun with Halle until I move on from the both of them this time.

The elevator shaft opened. I patted Halle's butt barely able to wait myself as I soaked between my legs. Her mouth was fantastic. The days of her and Morgan feasting upon me were much missed and long awaited.

I pushed Halle against the wall. Grabbing a handful of her hair and biting her ear. "I can't wait to make you lick this pussy up. I'm soaking right now." She squirms. I jerk by her ponytail and she lets out an almost instinctive moan. The whore. I jerk it once again and her body surrenders with laughter.

"I really can't wait to show you all that Morgan's taught me." Halle giggled so innocent and naïve like a dim lamb.

"Me neither." I cup her breast with my free hand, moving under her shirt and squeezing her nipples.

I would have very well took her in the hall if I had a cock to fuck her with. Instead I forced her alone down the hall. Tugging on the ponytail like my personal bitch leash. When we got to the door, I shoved her along inside.

She stumbled in and began taking off her black hoodie. She had on sweatpants and a pair of trainers.

"Get naked... go to my room."

"I came here to talk..."

"Talk after your mouth is full." I push her along. She pushes me off and turns to me as if she was gonna hit me. "Halle. I said go in the room!"

Her fist slammed against my jaw as I moved to grab her. She grabbed me by my hair and drove her knee into my side. I dropped to my knees in excruciating pain. "What the hell!"

She rushed to close the door, locking and latching it.

"I couldn't wait to get you out from the public. You think we're cool Nat? You think you can disrespect me however you want without consequences? Why did you tell my shit to Carmen?" She asked. Her knee rammed into my ribs again. "Was that your business to say?"

"What the hell Halle! What the hell is wrong with you!" I cried out trying to crawl away from her with all my strength.

I wished I hadn't asked. Her knee drove into me again, knocking the wind out of me and cracking a rib. I'm going to sue her for everything she's worth.

I broke out laughing, "I can't wait to take pictures of my face and send them to my lawyer!"

Halle smiled right back at me. "You were angry so you went and ran to tell everyone. You haven't learn your lesson. You keep snitching. You just needed your little time in the sun, huh? Just had to get involved while we're figuring out shit out and he's trying to rebuild a city. You're a selfish cunt. Carmen isn't your friend. She'll use you and stab you in the back. Now I'm going to kill you!"

"Not as long as I'm holding the blade. I'm already preparing for Carmen. If I go down we all go down!" I spit my blood in Halle's face.

"No, Natalie. I'm not going on Carmen's show. I'm not dealing with this little girl bullshit. I came to you once woman to woman, to let you know I loved Morgan. Now, I have to deal with you as a Queen. Stay out my business or you will see Morgan." Her tone was different than I've ever heard before. She's never raised a hand to me before in my life.

"I'll still forgive you, Halle... just relax. And say you're sorry. For all this." I began to pick myself back up. My jaw felt as if it fell off. So painful it was numb, my face was beginning to swell.

"No one is apologizing at all. What did Morgan say? An apology is useless without actions behind it. I wanted to get you alone Natalie. This is how I deal with my issues Natalie." Halle grabbed my throat digging her nails into my trachea. "Morgan was going to fall in love with me regardless. But I'm glad I fucked your boyfriend. You miserable cunt!"

She dropped beneath me and lifted me over her shoulder tossing me as if I was weightless slamming me on the ground. My face bounced off the wooden floor. I felt every bone in my nose snap after impact. I gasped for air but before I could breathe my face slammed against the floor again cracking my front teeth. "That one was for disrespecting my family!"

"Halle... please... stop." I pleaded as tears swelled my eyes and blood filled my nostrils, I began choking on my blood trying to crawl away from this maniac.

"Get a nose job, bitch. Keep my name out your mouth. We're not fucking kids anymore. I will kill you for this bitch!" She grabs my hair then face slams against the floor once more with more force than before. Blood and teeth filled my mouth as I was left lying there.

"I should kill you for how you touched me. Are you out of your goddamn, mind? I am Queen Halle Victoriana Gregor-Sameera! You do not want to see me again, Natalie! You nor Carmen! I'm not playing games with you little bitches anymore! Do you understand me?" She dug her heel into my neck.

I began to cry. How could things have turned so quickly? I could barely even move to defend myself. I had her outsmarted. I sullied her name. I recruited Carmen... and she just walked in here and-

"Oooawwwwwwrfgh!!" I let out a howling cry as her foot pressed down on the back of my head driving my face into the ground again.

"I asked you a question." Halle barked, lifting me off the ground.

"I understand, I understand I'm not stupid like you! I get it! I get it!" I shout.

"Shut up... You're going to stop calling me stupid!" Halle says trying to cover my mouth.

I bite her hand, shouting for bloody murder and help. It only took seconds for my voice to be drowned out by Trap music from the radio. I shouted but only heard the bass, drawls, mumbles, and shouts.

“BUCK BUCK BUCK BUCK BUCK GET EM! HOMIES GOING IN.” was blaring on repeat, drawled by some lean head. Halle kicked me, and kicked me... and kicked me. I felt my ribs break. I felt my spirit break. I felt so much pain the tears eventually stopped all their own. My shouting and screams of pain soon after. Turning into muttered grunts and groans. When one foot got tired she switched to the other, kicking me like I was a dog against the couch. I barely made it into my home before this.

She stopped, stepping over me and turned off the music. She sat on my couch and crossed her legs over the other.

"Sit down when you're ready to talk." She gently scrolled through her phone taking a few pictures of me.

I laid on the floor, unable to move with no strength. Unsure what bones were working and what didn't. My eyes were swollen shut. I couldn't even cry. I believed I could just sit there and play dead, but she just sat watching me with deathly focus. And my phone blew up with her Twitter feed rebuttals. I couldn't even defend myself. Not with my own hands. Now not even on social media.

We sat in silence. I laid... rather. I groaned in noncompliance. Crawling as best I could the seat next to her.

I laid tired and broken on the arm on the couch.

"You know, I wanted to be your friend for a long time, Natalie... but it's like you don't want friends. It's like you never loved us. You only think about yourself. This won't stand in the new world Morgan is creating." Halle finally broke the silence.

"What the fuck are you talking about?" I spit, "Morgan is a worthless jerk..."

Halle smiled. "If I was here for him I would of kicked you in your teeth for that. But I'm here for myself. If you plan on going on with this then Morgan WILL be visiting you and Carmen, because he is past the point of noncompliance from past hoes. If you come between the reconstruction of Nadia. I don't think it'll be this friendly next time. I would never be able to forgive you if you came between him and his goals. Stay out of the spotlight, stay off of TV, and stay out of Morgan's way!"

"Friendly? You fucking psychopaths... you two deserve each other!" I was ready to die, ready for my family to war against hers for centuries more.

"If I was psychotic believe me I would let myself kill you like I wanted to kicking your ass. But I'm letting cooler heads prevail and leaving you with a warning. You keep disrespecting me, I'll be back. You come at my man's neck again, I'll be back. You go in that show and spout your mouth, Morgan or Rose will be here. This is isn't high school anymore Natalie."

"No, no it isn't you Gregor bitch. I'll sue you for everything you're worth! I'll take all your family's wealth for this!"

"Sadly, Morgan's doing that. You'll have to speak with him about that." She shrugged. "Morgan broke off our wedding arrangements yesterday."

"I don't believe you... you're lying. He wouldn't do that." I let her right into my home, there never was a wedding, I fell into her trap.

Halle shrugged, "probably for the best. He would scold me day and night for this." She stretched out, "but aren't you lucky he's such a monster. It was me Nat. All me. Since the beginning. I was better than you. I wanted Morgan and I took him. Now, he's to be King. And you're still sitting here as if the world revolves around you. If you died tonight I would be the last one anyone suspects. The peace treaty will remain. And Morgan will be King. Are you ready to die?"

"I'm telling... Colin..." I barely managed to breathe. "He'll put an end to this. I bet he doesn't even know the wedding is off."

"You just don't quit." she kicks the chair from underneath me and my face smacks against the floor. She jerks my head up, "This doesn't end in compromise. This doesn't end with us as friends. It doesn't end well for you at all Natalie. You crossed a line along time ago and out of love for Morgan I left you alone. I won't let Morgan have it on his conscious. Quit all this or I'm tossing you out the window."

I was silent. I wanted revenge. But I wasn't interested in losing my life for it... I never imagined Halle would hit me. Morgan has proven he would. But Halle had never raised a hand to me, before.

I was bloody, broken, exhausted and terrified. I already would have to recover for weeks or months. I had no idea if death would be worst or better than the pain I felt.

“I will protect you.” A voice said in my ear.

“What?” I muttered weakly.

“Bitch, I said it in clear *Jugali*!” I understand our language. She flipped. Gregors were always so unstable.

In an instant I was laying on the ground holding my ribs. I looked up to the woman I used to call my best friend. She pressed her heel into the back of my neck once more trying to snap my neck.

"I need your confirmation of concession right now, or I'm going to have to do something I don't want to do to keep you from getting ahead of yourself." Halle demanded I admit defeat.

"All this over Morgan?" I cried.

"I could ask you the same thing. But as I said. I didn't come here for Morgan. I came for me and my family. No more fake friends. No more of this catty shit. See me face to face or keep my name out your mouth. I am Queen. Bow down or I'll end you." Halle stomped down on my neck with all her strength.

"I- I-I- ooooowwwwarrgh." I squirmed and cried. I refuse to plead for my life, I rather her kill me and go straight to hell. She dropped by my side and wrapped her arms around my neck beginning to choke the life from out of me. I dug my nails into her arm, using all my remaining strength but all I felt was the excruciating pain as she seemingly tried to rip my head off my shoulders.

"Don't break my neck Halle. Please. Please don't!" I cried in object horror, “Please don't break my neck more!”

"Keep my name out your mouth. Pay your respects to your Queen!" She twisted harder. I could hear the vertebrae popping as she torqued my spine. "Do we have an understanding!?"

"I quit. I'm sorry! I understand. You are my Queen! You are my Queen!" I break down, begging her to stop.

She lets me go and picks herself back up. "What's my name?"

"Queen, Queen Halle Gregor!" I pleaded.

Halle stepped off me, "come at my neck again if you want to." She left me there bloody and crying. Her footsteps left my apartment. The door slammed the music blasted.

I rolled to my back, reaching overhead for my cellphone. I took a few pictures of my face and sent them to my father. I fell back in defeat. At least if nothing more came of this. The Gregor Family would fall to the Wolfes. She should have killed me. I made the mistake of leaving my enemies alive and look at me. I tried to handle this like a bratty bitch. Like a Carmen Cruz. I was not a media star or a fighter. I needed my own way to get revenge. I was going to ruin her family.

If Halle was a Queen, I was a damn Empress. This won't be forgotten, Halle Gregor. Not so long as the two of us live on the same planet. I vow to get my revenge!

This is passed Morgan. I will see the end of your family Gregor cunt... I am going to end your entire bloodline.

I had no energy left. I had no strength to move. I feared closing my eyes but the pain was unbearable. I only need a few minutes of sleep. Just a bit. Someone will come for me. I won't die on this floor like a dog. I refuse.

Enshishi spoke to me... he won't let me die on this floor but it came at a great cost. My soul was all I had left to barter. Revenge must be worth it. It has to be worth it.

CHAPTER 26

Location of Self: Inner Kingdom

Morgan Leonticus Sameera

It's strange how we can talk about such finalities of life, when others die for these matters. We reach some level of jaded malcontent and we believe the world becomes blithesome and dull. As if there is some new title or science that will translate and manifest into some brand new idea of how to live life.

We change the rules in life and wonder why we become dissatisfied or insatiable. We constantly believe there is more than believe ourselves right in this idea of more. But there is little more complexity to life then one day we die and must do what we must to be joyful until its end. All life is meaningful. One can be fine where they are. But this does not mean to say there is not better in this world. One who always believes he is right becomes a tyrant. We must be open but reject those who speak only from perspective and limited perspectives at that. From a knowledge they believe is greater than others or unique.

I understand there is more to life. But I also understand I could stay exactly where I am and be happy. Maybe do it differently. But I am living my life as I live my life. And I plan to live this way. But when that understanding leads to trampling upon the lives of others or could lead others astray. It becomes paramount that I speak up. I understand someone's working understanding. If they live in good health and success... But if they said this to someone it will be perceived differently. If they said these things to someone where they wished to be or perhaps affected deeply by what they said. They would seem absolutely ludicrous.

There are many people struggling in life. But we attempt to compare groups disadvantaged by inability, and by exclusivity.

This cannot stand. It does not stand. And demons and vanity make us believe otherwise.

Nothing is true. Everything is permitted. I understand this better. But... this is out of necessity for those of us who do God's work to truly do it.

One must adapt the world to their perspective. Literally changing the way the world works in order to be in their perspective. And there are those with little effect. Because in order to manipulate the world one must understand how it currently works...

There are those who attempt to live a life of great worth within this idea. But have lost their very minds in the process. Believing them Gods because they have learned how life works. It is a human's duty to understand this truth! We teach our own and leave others to suffer as the world passes them by. Generations lost blaming their inability to understand this crucial law instead of merely teaching them then allowing them to fend for themselves.

As if by solely understanding this law that binds one is guaranteed success. We all rise and fall by our own merit.

No, our lives are not the same. Yes, we all define success in different ways. But there is a way for everyone to be happy. Violence is mandatory but we must save this for the unjust and criminals not praise them! Not use this as first resource: peace... tranquility... nourishment... growth... for every person to have their pursuit of a fulfilled existence. This is what will be the way. Contribute to this when your time comes and you will be rewarded greatly, to the best of your ability or to the fulfillment of your path in Rakil. One may be completely neutral to the idea of God and unwittingly do his works, due to good nature or standards of living. And others can speak the holy name and do holy atrocities beyond belief. Who goes to hell? The unwittingly devote or the mindlessly blasphemous?

What can decide this end? Only God and Only reality, this is God. Reality is it in itself we brand it differently and we try to manipulate it for our survival. But reality does not stop being reality because you're in the extreme cold or the jungle. We are all just beings attempting to live our life and feed our own. But there are of those of us who only extend their good-nature to self, this is evil. And there are those of us who boldly and chronically envision every individual on this planet as our own flesh and blood. This is good. There is no manipulation of philosophical argument. This is the imperative that Rakil himself has set. We are all bounded to it no matter how we delude ourselves or our followers.

I sit in my sanctum. Free from the stress and judgments of the above world. It seemed no matter what was done. There was always some-one set to be upset and discontent. When are the few times do these discontents have any real suggestions or ideas? No real progress is ever made. I am left to deal with nothing more than discontent. Reality has become a popularity contest. I have watched unfit leaders ascend to greater power to have it crumble atop of them. I have seen men of great merit stuck and stifled.

Reality has become Enshishi's playground built upon trickery and distrust. I know little anymore of what is real or genuine. Constantly evaluating my ability, driving myself insane as if there's more I could do or have done. I have conquered Enshishi and I am confronted of my eyesight. A monster is dead, and I should consider my health?

I'm not sure we truly understand what is real or meaningful any-more. Everyone is so ego driven they refuse to see rights or wrongs within themselves. We try to create these unique lives built upon self-proclaimed faucets and identities, all to escape our true selves.

I find myself categorized not understood. I find myself being talked over by confused masses. And I face a loss for other's egos and failures of self. Their lack of acknowledgment of their personal lacking and failures make me the monster!? To be blamed for life conditions and choices made by these forces, when they cannot reflect upon themselves or their identity to see wrong. No, evil and wrong only exists outside themselves. This is what I find myself surrounded by ego.

Even with Enshishi dead his advocates are plenty, chasing personal gain. None of them wish to save this world from evil. They want it more comfortable for their vice and lifestyle. Am I not different?

I have been charged with protecting these people. But how do I do such a thing when I meet someone and can immediately identify a list of characteristics and their personal ideology that keeps them right where they are.

I believed we were the savages of men. But I'm beginning to view humanity as the issue in itself. The world has been propelled past human consumption by human inventions and conveniences. We have made living a life uninteresting. We no longer wish to live, to love or act or hurt. We are immersed in our egos and selves.

I do not believe I can save this world. I do not agree many of these people are worth saving, they're not in truth my issue or concern. They are evil.

But are they evil simply because they have seen nothing but evil as glory? They admire, love and honor Enshishi in every breath and image. Yet, scream for my grace and creations.

How do I save a world so evil and vile? So, many lives lost to suffer. And billions with power to change the suffering and condition of others, can only hopelessly complain about their own life instead if trying to make the life of another more bearable. They live in this world for themselves. They are not my allies, not my children, not my fault. They have chosen their world, for Enshishi, for death, for corruption. I am here to purify this world.

To save the world as I have saved myself. To purge the evil and show the beauty of simplicities. I am not meant to save the world. I am only able to help and assist those who wish to save themselves. I will welcome those who want to build a greater world. I will allow those who only have interest and care for themselves to eat shit. We are one in this world.

If one is discontent without suggestions and methods of change. They are a blight rather than a concern. They are an irritation only reminding me more and more of this world and its flaws.

There only rests hope in creating a new. There is nothing more in this lost creation. To this miserable condition that exists in the tide of Enshishi and Anki's profane war against Rakil's children. So, this is what I guard. Life, Hope, and Truth.

CHAPTER 27

Regrets and Growth

Halle Gregor

God what did I do? What did I do?

I try picking up Natalie's head but it slumped right back to the ground. Her lights were out. But she was breathing. For better or worst.

I- I heard my father's voice telling me to defend what was mine. Well, not my father but- this Enshishi. I didn't realize how real this was. It was as if he was over my shoulder watching us fighting and arguing. Since children. I guess this is the only way it would have ended. If it wasn't me, it would have been Rose. If neither of us, then Carmen would be taking us to dry on her stupid fucking show.

I drag Nat's body through her apartment to her bedroom. I toss her on the bed. Do I call an ambulance for her? I can't. The sooner people find out the sooner the truce is broken. My father will snatch me back to Naka for war crimes and court. No, I couldn't, I couldn't do it. If it wasn't me it would have been someone. Natalie had it coming. It was us or her and Carmen. I made the right decision but-

Why are the consequences so much more apparent after the fact? I could have cursed her out and made her cry. But this- I damn near broke her in half and twice of that. I completely lost control and now she's going to try to ruin my family.

The first thing I wanted to do was run to Morgan. But he wouldn't choose sides, even when we broke up his heart was with Natalie. I need to go... Why the hell did I come to Naka? Nothing more than the sake of getting drunk and calling Morgan an asshole. I might as well finish what I've started and go after Carmen while I'm here. End this whole show nonsense.

I turn the music off and begin straightening everything up. Having a military boyfriend meant knowing how to clean or get berated for why there's dust on the feather duster. Natalie's place was spotless outside the damages. Morgan could have fixed the damage if he was here. Probably wouldn't.

He didn't like Natalie. He wouldn't want this for her at all. I- I didn't want this for my friend. But she made me.

What the hell was going through her head to make her disrespect me like that! We have never had that kind of relationship without Morgan. And he was the sole reason. Oh my god, oh my god, what do I do?

I picked up my phone. My speed dial was Morgan, Daddy, and my favorite store. I dropped my phone and began sobbing harder than before.

I can't tell Morgan anything yet. I can't call my Dad...

Damn, I can't believe where I've put myself. My anger and frustration getting the best of me, always, always, always. I punch the ground leaving a sizeable hole through the floor.

"Holy crap, I got stronger..." I looked at Natalie. If I did that to the floor, "please don't be dead!"

She coughs, "fuck you..." Then passes out once more.

"I'm glad you're well..." I rub her forehead and a tear fell down my cheek. "Things won't be the same again will they?"

"No, I'm going to... I'm going to ruin your family." Natalie strains.

"Good luck, my family is already destroyed. I have nothing left." I stand looking down at Natalie.

'Kill her beloved. End this before it spreads. End this before she runs off and tries to find reinforcements!'

"You're not my love, you're nothing!"

'Use your wits girl! This isn't trivial. She is our enemy, kill her now!'
"NO! I'VE DONE ENOUGH!"
'You will never assume my mantle like this. You will never harness my power! I am your last hope for greatness Halle. I am your salvation and greatness!' Enshishi snarled in my mind.
"You're evil... You're corrupted. I hate you! I hate you! I hate you!"
'You will never be my replacement like this!'
"GOOD! I HATE YOU! I HOPE YOU DIE! I HOPE MORGAN KILLS YOU! I HOPE THIS ENDS WITH YOU AND YOU NEVER COME BACK! I WISH I WAS NEVER YOUR DAUGHTER! I HATE YOU, I HATE YOU, I HATE YOU!" I Scream gripping my hair, bumping into the walls and furniture.
I grab the couch and whip it across the room.
"Get out of my head, get out of my head, get out, get out, get out..." I fall to my knees crying. "Please, mommy, please, please, Baat, mom, whoever, please... Get him out of me."
I felt a coolness around me and my tears stopped. The anger inside me began to fade, my hatred began to fade. I sobbed on my knees. "Mother, please... Release this demon, get Enshishi out of me. Please mommy."
'He is a part of you sweetheart... You must learn to control your thinking, your power. You must use it for good, in Ada's name and in the greater good. It's within you, honey. You're a sweet kind soul, born at the wrong time to the wrong people... I wish I had been by you. I wish I stood by you sooner. Come home, Halle. Your time in Naka is done.'
I held my stomach. My stomach was freezing cold but my sternum burned out. I began dry heaving.
I ran to the bathroom, nearly knocking the door off the hinges. Falling before the toilet bowl. I vomited. My throat burned as it never have before, as liquid magma began gagging up like bile inside me. I dry heaved, each heave choking me and burning me. I grabbed my throat, digging my nails into my neck.
'YOU TRAITOROUS WITCH!' Enshishi roared.
Please, please... I just want this to be over.
'You must warn Ada.' Baat warns. 'This boy must know what to expect.'

I can't speak, I can't talk how do I contact her...?

'You must think Halle... With your heart or your head. You must begin thinking you dense girl! Release the tension girl! Use your brain and stop relying on your father, you clumsiness and your temper!'

'I'm... I'm so pathetic...' I heave, my throat releases ejecting all the magmic bile within me out onto the ground. 'That's the key, insulting myself, great.'

'It's using your brain. Your energy must move upward. You need to release your father's corruption. You cannot rid yourself of Enshishi but- Ada, where are you? I wish I protected my daughter from that monster, where was I?'

'How are you even speaking to me. I don't understand any of this.'

'You called upon me... I am within you as well. You are my daughter.' it felt as if pain was in her voice when she said it. 'We- he was correct, I sought another advocate never believing we would face this day.'

'You sound so regretful.'

I vomited onto the floor, and toilet, melting through the porcelain until there was no sense even coming to the bathroom. I clutched my stomach, pressing against my sternum burning and pushing with my force. Lava projectile vomits from my mouth. Over the ground, the walls, and remnants of the toilet.

I picked myself up and leaned against the wall.

'Hurry, this is quite the scene get somewhere safe and call Ada. He must know what's happened. He must know more is to come to keep him from Nadia.'

'What? What's coming?'

'You shouldn't have come here... You should have came home as you said, you would. So rebellious- you are my daughter.' she sounded as though she was laughing but there was truly no sound. Just vibrations and waves. This is something different.

'Can I contact Morgan like this?'

'Ahhhyeesh...' she gripes, 'Had you two grown closer or understood each other more perhaps. Much time was wasted in his attempting to explain things to you, let along to this point. Had you not been my daughter, with so much of my essence. You might have been lost to me as well. Perhaps, that was Colin's attempt. You lived on an island of illusion.'

'You call Morgan, Ada but call father by name.'

'He is no true Guardian. Look at yourself. Look at what he's done to you. What has he defended or protected!? He has stolen the power- from his father and his father's before. Maurice was the only one of them made Guardian by natural birth. Whose father tried to kill him, for the first in Gregor history! But Colin- he couldn't wait to be Enshishi... Would you like to hear how you were born?'

'I love stories about me.'

'This isn't a love story. I was married, I had children and a family. Colin- while leading his tirade against Sameera and my family, the Qatar's while we were restoring Rakil's Kingdom and Ecru. While arranging the deal to return Grand Ba'ath to Ecru, Colin made his move. Maurice was willing, and even more, wanted to give Tartarus in a sentimental agreement. Before the ink could dry. He was dead. He was replaced and Colin tore the deal apart right in front of Obatta and I. Those two were instant enemies. Tartarus wasn't necessary. But his eyes turned on me. He broke into my house, he killed my dearest husband, Bryon the 1st, and he raped me until sunrise. I cried and screamed, muffled under a pillow until Colin was finished as if I was some slut! As if I was nothing more than some worthless slice of meat. One of the whores he had about him. It wasn't until the next morning I could even look away from Bryon's face. He made me stare into my love's eye the entire time. I am so sorry, Halle- after you were born. I tried, I tried. But I lost my mind. You refused to come with me when I attempted to rescue you. And I hated and feared your father. I wish I could have been your mother but-

"Don't apologize... That's not your fault. My father is a monster and Morgan will deliver us his corpse."

"I don't care to see him again. Colin has been dead for some time. He was too weak to be a Guardian. He wished to be historic as a Gregor. To reenact every element of that damn lie they've been preaching to the people. While we aim to rebuild and better the world. Colin's only intentions were control and destruction. To exploit the fullest power of Enshishi. To be Enshishi's puppet.'

'I won't be anyone's puppet... Not anymore. Can you help me get to Maya?'

'You have my permission, but you've also been spoiled. Find your way here and I will teach you all you should have learned.'

'Not all you know?'

'Dearest, I've been trained to be a Queen since I was born. My life was education and development of my abilities. I'm sad to say, had I never been raped you wouldn't be here. But- I knew you were of purpose. I refused an abortion because you deserved life. I hope you choose to do something great with the gift you have.'

'Oh your mercy upon your unwanted baby! My own mother doesn't want me.”

'For being alive, Halle. Life is the gift. This is the only truth to the world there is. I don't mean to be insult you. Frankly, I wish we had gotten closer and you would have came when you were ten when I came to steal you away. But you refused vehemently. And I had little time to spend in Naka let along the Gregor Manor. That night ended poorly. We fought like fiends over your freedom. Colin was nearly to bursting out his skin with Enshishi's aura. There was only so much I could have done without losing my consciousness to Baat. Your father is a danger.'

"So, is Morgan Sameera. He and Rose will handle this." I sniffled, digging my nails into my knees, “Mother, Morgan will stop all this!”

'Your faith in him is strong.'

"There's no one else on the planet I have more faith in to do right." I rubbed my throat. It'll be sore but, I'll recover. "Mom... Will Morgan ever marry me... Are you set on Rose?"

'They are in love, but Ada's responsibility is to Gaia and Ecru. I- I honestly don't believe you will be best. My granddaughter was trained as I was to be His Queen.'

"I'll have to prove you both wrong then..."

'Don't let anyone limit you, baby. Not even me. You have impressed me so much already. I only know how to elicit what you already have. You

will become a greater woman with discipline and guidance.'
"Thank you, mother... Let me get out of here before I get arrested."
'Yes, Yes... Good hurry off now. Return to Nadine, gather your things and get some rest. Leave in the morning. I will not corrupt your mind like Enshishi. I trusted you enough to make your own decisions so far. I will continue to trust in your sense. You will see the truth.'
"Will Morgan be there?"
'I haven't been in contact with him... Rose has been on her own, beginning her plans for the city. She's just as stubborn as you. I'm so proud of my child and grandchild.'
Hmm... even my own mother think they make a good couple. I guess these are the standards I must meet. Rose is pushing her plans. I have no choice, I must come to Maya. I can't fall further behind, I've already missed out on the childhood training."
I was already riding the elevator down to the front desk.
"Um, excuse me... I want to report a noise complaint on the sixth floor. I had to leave my room because it's so loud! Someone needs to figure out what happened up there immediately!" I approach the concierge.
"Thank, thank you I will have someone respond to it immediately thank you!" he graciously greets me, "And how are you enjoying your stay at our hotel?"
"Oh, I have had better experiences but there's a special charm to this hotel. If you want to keep your hotel I suggest you call an ambulance. It sounded very violent in the room, I'm scared witless over the whole ordeal."
"Thank you so much!" He says picking up the phone and dialing 777.
I was free. Speed walking I hopped into my car, flipping it on and pulling out from the parking garage. I kicked it in gear, and ripped toward the turnpike East to Nadine. There might be time for me to learn under my mother. For now I'm headed back to Morgan's...

I could still be a High Priestess if I applied myself from this day forward, Work hard toward fulfilling myself. My father was a liar, a rapist, and murderer! And I almost forced Morgan to follow in his steps... But I thought he and Morgan were twins. I was a fool to ever compare the two.

Now, Morgan is my salvation. I wonder how my father's cabinet is going to take his death. I hope it implodes and all we've harmed has gone free. I needed to get back to Naka regardless of how I felt about my dad. I need to lay low for a month or so before Natalie wakes up and tries to break the peace treaty. At least if he finds about this while I'm in Naka then Nadia won't be affected. We can handle everything in Naka!

I'll stop by Morgan's then head back to Naka until everything with Natalie blows over.

CHAPTER 28

Amenity

Rose Paz Andale

Halle said her goodbyes in the morning. A week of training under Morgan was brutal but quite informative. He was a class all his own in combat and proved so. Everyday Halle and I attempted to best him. We grew closer but as we grew stronger, as did he taking on Baat and a potential vicar for Enshishi with ease. Halle departed back for Naka. I would have to say, I would miss her a bit. However, this only meant I had Morgan to myself!

Morgan had left me to run some errands around Nadia, he said he had to visit his old businesses and inform them of his recovery, and his necessity. I delighted to see him with such new found energy. He had never truly forgiven me after our training sessions but seemed content to know Halle and I knew much more than we put on. His response to the betrayal was to simply not address it. He hadn't enough information to form an accusation. And I wasn't going to ruin his trust more by giving him reasons to question me. I still played dumb.

I had to work on repairing his trust if I would ever have a chance on him. He wasn't the type you could impress by being good at your job. He expected a good job to be done. He expected efficient autonomy. He essentially expected me to work as he did. No one directing him or commanding him. He knew what needed to get done and figured out how to complete his task. It was intimidating truly. I seriously could have used Halle's help, she knows him better than I do. I am living with a complete stranger afterall, no matter how much I stalked him.

Cleaning a house was easy but he ran a business. How would I catch his eye?

I had no intentions of simply remaining a maid. It would defeat the purpose of me being here. Him being engaged, let alone engaged to Halle Gregor was an unexpected conflict, especially without rings. His prudish temperament created another barrier. Though, if he was a normal man I wouldn't have been so willing to follow through with my Grandmother's task.

Morgan was downtown Nadia, and only Rakil knew when he would return. I was glad, it gave me time to speak with my Grandmother freely without worry of him walking in on me.

I sat in one of the guest rooms that I made my own. A few of my belongings around the room. My clothes hanging in the closet. I was hoping to have worn a few of my dresses for him by now. If he freaked out about my shorts then he would go berserk if he ever saw me around the house in one of my backless Karen Lawrence dresses, squeezing my booty in a headlock. He would love it.

I bit my lip staring at my closet. Him and Halle were recovering. I was happy for them both. I didn't have an issue sharing, my grandmother told me to expect a man like Morgan to have multiple wives, I should only focus on Nadia. But I wasn't even in the mix yet!

It's not as though I can simply walk up to Morgan and say, "Hey, I need you to dick me down until I'm pregnant to save the world from The Devil, cool?" We technically tried it. And he wasn't too fond of learning my intentions.

"Holy Mother, Baat... I call upon you to answer my prayers. I need your guidance." I kneeled over my bed with my hands clasped. "I do not know what to do about my beloved. He believes I am only trying to use him, and our love is not real. He does not trust me, and a wall has come between us. His heart belongs to another woman but I sense there is more than enough room for me in his life. Our goals align so well. All I wish is to take away his pain, and help bring his vision to reality. I want to want what you want for me, Baat. If this is not my place then please-

"Hush up now girl, enough of the doubts. What you believe is what will become, remember this always, understood?" I heard my grandmother's voice as what I could only describe as an invisible layer of clothing wrapped around me. Cool and wet. "He strains for you because his heart is so divided. His mind strained. And his soul bruised. Your beloved no longer knows right from wrong, instead of forming a decision he has become stagnant and melancholy. This is where you have found him, so he has remained. All you must do is navigate his ship."

"But what can I do about it?"

"Do you want the moral answer or what I would do?"

I bit my lip unsure how to answer.

"I want to save Nadia, I want what's best for Morgan, and-" I took a long pause, "I want to be able to live with myself afterward."

"You must show him you are the better option. Appeal to him as a woman, as a lover, as a friend, and as a partner but most importantly hold yourself as a Queen to remind him he is a King. This will not be easy and it will not happen all at once. Both you and his fiancee have my essence, but you were my selection, Rose."

"That sounds so hard."

"Then just seduce him. Get the baby and let the chips fall where they might. If he wants to care for the baby then hope he isn't a psychopath or something. This was originally your idea. I suggested you come to Maya and train."

"He is the Vicar though... he is the actual Ada."

"I know but... it's like you found your little crush but you aren't in love."

"I am definitely in love."

"You should still trying seducing him. Strategically he is far more subsectible on his back than when he is studying you so closely. If thinks

you are a plain ole student looking for shelter. Play your role and simply let him get what he needs from you. As we get what we need from him. If you too work out then wonderful, you were right. If not then there's always room for you and your son here in Maya."

"How! I have tried seducing him..."

"You tried throwing yourself at his feet like some horny maid looking for an easy paycheck. If he grows angry with his wife one day he may ravage you and toss you aside. But this is beneath the both of you, he knows this but you do not. You use your flesh so carelessly. Withhold then give like the ocean. When you pull away, withdraw completely into your work, classes, and focus entirely then when you are with him shower him entirely. Be like the ocean, he is away so pull away and focus on your goal. Bring your manifestation to reality."

"I don't know if I even want that! But- I want him. I don't know how to get him. He had a whole wife? Not to mention this other girl Rumya keeps texting and calling him late at night. What did I get myself into Baat?"

"Rose, you already have him. You are my vicar, you are more than capable of being with Morgan. You must begin thinking as a woman and not a child. A child chases a man. A woman knows her relationship is mutual whatever her relationship with that man might be a friend or a lover. He must be coming after you as you come for him. You lead him to you, you must be open but off limits. You must be sensitive yet strong. He must be able to have you but only when you allow him, and when you allow him shower him like fresh rain after a deathly drought."

I understood but with Morgan... how could such a thing be possible?

"I sincerely doubt he's ever had to work hard for a woman, Rose. If you lead him on even a short chase he'll respect the effort. Seduce him but make the ultimate decision his alone. And you must be clear in your intention! This is no different than controlling the waters, envision your goal, be clear in your intention, and then manifest your purpose into fruition. He'll gladly come to you. If you cannot live a lie then don't. I wish I had started by living the truth."

"I- I can do this. I can do this."

"I know you can baby girl, think elegance rather than sexy. You're already beautiful as a daughter of Baat, but it is your refinery, your maturity, your mind these are what will seize Morgan's heart."

"No, witchcraft, right?" I asked wanting honesty.

"He wants to want you Rose. You can see it in his eyes. He yearns for conversation with you more than what it is you are craving. If he simply needed a hole to put his cock, he would easily find one apparently." I felt the aura lifting, "You already have won a place within his home, win his heart and mind. Win his loyalty."

"I will. Thank you, Grandmother."

I didn't sit up quite yet. I took in a deep breath daring to do something crazy. Something I haven't done since I was a girl.

"Jah'Ada... please make your son open to me. I wish to ease his suffering and set his mind correct. He is stubborn, well... he is defensive. I mean him no harm. Help me find a way into his heart tonight. Please, in the least help me find a way into his heart. Amun."

I stood up, stretching out and going to my closet. I closed my eyes and reached inside, "Guardians of Gaia, guide my hand so I may find something appealing to my beloved."

I pull out a purple teddy with golden bows. I bit my lip having forgotten I even packed this at all. I looked around my room knowing I was alone but hoping to have caught the energy of what had guided me. I snickered, laying it across my bed. I was within my right to dress how I pleased after hours. Even more so if Morgan couldn't have me or wasn't even home. He would simply have to enjoy the view from a distance as I enjoyed myself alone this evening.

My plan was formulating little by little, I needed a place where I could spend the evening whether or not he came back home tonight. I suppose the most important part is enjoying myself. Though if he wanted to join, he very easily could.

I wanted a night to relieve myself of all the stress I've been taking on myself.

Morgan's issues were his own, and he wasn't likely to even appreciate me burdening myself by taking them as my own. Or even considering him lesser for facing the issues he has stacked against him. I needed to assure him, he was more than capable to manage his own life. I needn't worry about him loving me or his victory in Nadia, both were assured. I could never fake such overwhelming confidence within myself but Rakil created us to be together! He would be mine within time.

I peeled off my sweatpants and t-shirt. I shimmied out of my panties. Looking myself over in the mirror. I wasn't as petite as Halle, but Morgan appreciated my body nonetheless. I pinched my stomach, refusing the urge to curse myself. It's not about any of this tonight. I turned to my side cupping my full breast, admiring my voluptuous figure. My fingers slid between my legs, playing with my puffy folds and then letting myself smile.

"She could never pleasure him like I could. She could literally, never pleasure him as I could." I smiled wide. "I think I deserve a nice, long, hot bubble bath!"

I clap my hands together. I grabbed my bathrobe walking into my private bathroom. There was barely any room at all for my big ass to sit comfortably in this tub. I wonder if I should use Morgan's, anything better than me skinny dipping in the lake.

I peeked my head out of my bedroom door. I was definitely home alone. I took a deep breath taking my first barenaked step into the hallway. I held my head up, taking my time enjoying the draft against my body. My nipples hardened with my boldness, promenading to his room, my booty jiggling with every step. If he had walked in at that moment he would never be able to resist me.

I pushed open his bedroom door, immediately sniffing a familiar scent. I looked around in utter disbelief. The pungent odor. I halted my strolling flicking on his light to find his armoire cracked ajar. I pushed it open, grinning ear to ear as the smell became unbearable. I pushed aside his suits finding bricks of marijuana. My eyes bulged nearly out of my head. I closed the armoire and opened it once more expecting them to all be gone.

Unbelievable! All the things I imagined Morgan could have been, a smoker was not one of them. Let along anything of this nature! I picked up the only open plastic wrapped brick holding it to my chest, kissing it and hugging it. All I had in my bedroom was a 8th I had to go all the way back to Graham to pick up on the bus. A whole day long affair when he had the whole vault right here down the hallway! How many times have I dusted this damn thing?

I only took enough to last me the rest of the week… I would ask him later but knowing Morgan, I would be waiting for my first gray hairs before he would ever offer smoking with me.

My wonders didn't cease when I found a box on his dresser. My vibes told me there was something I could use to smoke with. With my hands filled with nugs like a trip to Wonka's Weed factory. I opened the little cigar box to find cigarillos laid out magnificently. Even the tobacco leaves had their own special scent. Not the cheap rollos from the corner chicken spots. No, these were real natural leaves something… something a millionaire would smoke. The package said Erdu where they have plantations of natural tobacco. Okaaaay, Morgan I see you baby!

I didn't want to tamper with his stash more than I needed. So, many I'll just take one… oh, holy Rakil there's a whole other layer underneath, he's not going to miss a few of these. I needed at least one or two for tonight. Then maybe one more for Cameron and Jazz to try out when I invite them to my new mansion.

If the weed stash wasn't enough. I spotted a picture on his night-stand. He was a child, probably ten or twelve. All smiles with a large man the size of a tree, and two other children each holding thumbs up in one hand and a fish in the other. The large man held a small trout, mushing up Morgan's braids. Morgan used both his hands to hold a fish nearly his size, a wide grin across his face. The two kids were on either side of him.

I lifted the photo and looked on the back.

'Nearly loss Uncle Ray, today. He made it up to us by extending our camping trip and took us fishing and kayaking! Caught a 30 lb largemouth bass my first time fishing with my barehands! Hinata was pissed he had to use a rod. Guess he wasn't quick enough in water lol.' written in sloppy handwriting. 'Me, Uncle Ray, Leslie, and Hinata.' in neater handwriting as if written recently then even smaller written, 'last time seeing Hinata before the *change*'.

I set down the photo, relieved to know he's had at least one happy memory within his past. Better than what I imagined he had went through probably fighting dogs and bears in Erdu...

I set my findings on his nightstand pushing open the master bathroom. The walls were painted a charcoal grey with a surprising life to them. The right side of the room was lined with granite countertops, and his and hers sinks! A built in wall mirror. Once I flicked on the light, smooth jazz played to drown out the dehumidifier. I walked deeper into the bathroom, looking for where he bathed. There was no shower curtain. Instead I found two faucets protruding out of the far corner of the room. I was confused for a few moments before I looked up to find a rainshower overhead. I was in heaven.

"This is how he's living... I really need to play my cards right or else I could end up rooming with Cameron again."

I wish I cleaned his bedroom more often but always felt uncomfortable walking in here. Not to mention the door was locked half the damn time. Bless my current adventurous mood. I turned the faucets to the perfect temperature. Steam began to quickly fill the bathroom turning it into a sauna. The wonders never cease!

I quickly ran out back into his bedroom, sitting on his bed to split open a cigarillo and beginning to roll a little something to smoke before my shower.

I suppose, I don't truly believe Morgan would be angry per se. He might make his bedroom off-limits again. I sincerely doubted finding me naked in his bathroom would make him all too angry. His first response would likely be to join me as if he walked into a dream.

I lit my blunt, quickly finding relief a few puffs later. I broke into a fit of coughs having never in my wildest dreams imagining finding something so potent! After three more puffs I was content. Setting my treat to the side. All giggles as I left to the ardent waters washing over me, I could easily make my own jacuzzi in a bathroom like this without making a big mess.

I closed my eyes, drifting away, feeling myself melting away with the waters. I crossed my legs, the thoughts of Morgan finding me bare in his shower turned me on to no end. Not a curtain or even a wall to separate us. I only found a bar of soap. Oh, he's one of those... Let, me stop because this strawberry pomegranate soap smelled absolutely delicious. I trailed the soap across my body, lathering myself up to no end. The scents of the kush and the soap made my heart soar. Once I reached my legs, my images of Morgan joining me lit my brain ablaze. I leaned against the wall, twirling my clit in circles with my middlefinger, suckling my breasts wishing both were him.

Cameron could attest better than anyone, another man had never put me in such a frenzy. Though, she hated Morgan since they met at the conference. He didn't leave the best impression. She is used to men swooning over her. I never got the same attention. She said I intimidated men. Apparently being big and intelligent was a turnoff to the big-spenders who wanted a girl to laugh at all their jokes and suck their dick on command. I didn't mind being submissive to Morgan, he was far more dominate I wasn't left much of a choice. His seriousness, his focus, and his sense of duty... even if for the wrongside of history. Not to mention the overwhelming generosity and understanding he's shown. There were so many layers to him. He was- perfect. The imperfection he had were fading away with his awareness of them and bothered him as much as they bothered the world.

I began reaching my complex. My face pressed against the wall, my eyes closed shut as I rubbed my clitoris biting my freehand. Moaning his name under my breath.

"Rose, are you home?"

"Yes! Yes! Yes!" I finally reached my tipping point, gripping the wall for balance, my leg shaking with images of him slapping against my backside.

"Rose?" his bedroom door opened.

I swear if he walks in here I'm going to lose my mind. It felt like I could hear him calling for me. I bit my lip as my fantasy was coming to fruition. I turned over my shoulder unable to stop my hand from moving. Giving him a full view as he stepped into the bathroom.

"Um... wow." he rubbed his neck standing frozen in the doorway.

"Can you wash my back?" I asked innocently biting my finger, "There was something wrong with my shower. So, I came in here."

"Something wrong with your weed too?" he asked ice-cold with a pissed look on his face, if he was nervous he didn't show it for the life of him leaving the bathroom door open as he walked back into his bedroom.

I licked my lips, walking in after him. I felt the layer of clothing wrapping around me. Keeping me warm as my nipples hardened and uplifting me. I stood before him stark naked as if I was dressed head to toe in silks and gold.

"Rose... I-" He began as I ran my hand up his chest, moving to help him with his coat. He was wearing a long-sleeve thermal I pressed him to wear to fight off the cold.

"You feeling okay?" I asked

He looked onto his armoire and dresser. "I see you found my stash."

"Is something wrong?" I asked lifting one of my chest to my mouth, my body still on fire. I pinched my nipples as if my caramel areloas matched its flavor. For all he knew it did. "Why are you looking at me like that is there something wrong?"

He rubbed the bulge in his pants, biting his lip. He only chuckled when I asked him shaking his head as if he was speechless.

"What's wrong, Morgan?" My second hand went between my legs, going back to work swirling my juices.

He raised his brow, "dress code went out the window, huh?"

"It is long after five, and I didn't even know you were coming home." I rolled my eyes, "Ooo... Ooo... Ooo..." I moaned finding myself reaching another climax.

Morgan's jaw dropped, "God bless..." began unzipping his jeans, "come here."

"For what?" I asked.

His face strained. I wanted him to tell me how much he wanted me, tell me what he wanted, to come after it.

"Listen, I'm gonna finish up my shower then get out your hair, okay?" I tasted my two fingers licking myself clean. "Do you need anything before I go?"

He reached in his pants taking out one of the most beautiful dicks I've seen. Nearly a foot from top to bottom with room to grow, thick like a soda can, with a head I wanted to suck like a lollipop. The weed made me so sensitive I could smell its saltiness from where I stood. More reason for him to shower with me. My head was going light, feeling myself lose control.

"My, my how unprofessional." I bit my lip knowing in a few seconds he would be in my mouth.

"Can you roll me a blunt?" He asked.

My mind couldn't register what was asked for a second. Once I understood I was pissed off. He thought he was slick. I didn't care, this was the reason I wanted him so damn bad. We were both going to work for it. I at least had two O's already, as far as I'm concerned I had the upperhand.

I walk away for a moment, coming back with the pre-rolled blunt I only took a few hits off of. I held it to my lips reaching for a lighter.

He smiled, "You're the resourceful type huh?" tossing me the lighter from the nightstand.

"Ask nicely, I might let you smoke with me." I smile taking a deep inhale.

"Might let me smoke my own stash?" I suppose I took that one a bit far, ha. "You scared of it?"

"Ha, a little... I mean damn. I already was feeling you. I didn't know your cock was perfect too. But I'll pass. I just wanted to chill tonight. I really didn't expect you to come home. I was really just taking a shower." I tease.

He cut his eyes at me, "So, you did all this to not have sex?"

"As I said, I wasn't aware you were coming home, Morgan." And you best believe I'm going to walking around this place in my teddy until you scoop me up, and are 100% honest with your intentions for me. "I suppose you've seen all of me, now we can have a real conversation some time." I give him a wink. "I'll left the shower on for you so you can take a cold one."

He only chuckled, "I think I'll be fine. I've gone long enough without sex. I'll manage." He stretches out his hand for the blunt.

"Ha, that's why you've been such a tight ass this whole time? Probably why you've been so depressed to. You need to be pounding a booty that can handle all that dick."

"And that's you?"

"Well... I probably could. But you're so big. You would probably have to get me really wet first." I watched intently for his response to my bold, "You'll have to eat my pussy first, eat me until I cum all over your face," he looked on as I pinched my nipples, I watched him stroke himself erect, "Then you'll have to go, really, really slow and spread out my tight little pussy."

"I can't take anymore of this if it doesn't have resolution. I've had a long day get moving or bend your ass over." He barked with irritation.

I bumped him with my shoulder before crawling onto the bed. I arched my back looking behind me to see him licking his lips. I roll my eyes shaking my booty in front of his face hoping he was hungry. I felt a cloth wrap around me. He fondled my breast as he dried my skin with a towel. I reached for his head, pulling him down, our tongues wrapped around the other. He pulled away from me. I feared it was a change of heart, but my back needed to dry. He spun me around by my hand. I smiled showing off my frame before wrapping my arms around his neck.

"I'm a little hungry..." he said, playing with my wetness, "Do you know what I can eat?"

"How about we order pizza?" I bit my lip teasing him.

The flesh was willing, but the invisible cloak prevented me from moving forward.

He rose his brow, “Pizza actually does sound great. You can get me a meatball pie with two orders of large wings. Get yourself whatever you wish.”

“Well, I never thought we would reach this point… well, I expected things to be different. I didn’t realize you were married. I mean at first, I didn’t care because fuck the Gregors. But… Halle is pretty cool you know? She’s really laid back once she gets her head out her ass.”

“We’re all products of our parents.” he sat on the bed.

“You can still play with my pussy… it feels really good. Massage class?”

“A lot of experience.” he sighed laying flat on his back, “People always want me for the physical, I suppose it’s all I expect after awhile.”

“I want your child but because I know you’ll be a good father. I would like my son to grow up like you. You remind me so much of my grandpa. Bryon Saleem and Obatta were very good friends of my Grandpa. As was my grandmother but she and Obatta were- they used to date before she married my Grandpa.”

“How’d that work out?”

“Well… the Qatars are pretty damn powerful.” I laugh, “I’m off the branch of the tree. My mother didn’t want to be involved in the politics. Her and her mother never got along, never quite saw the world the same. She married my father who grew up in Graham.”

“Your mother is a Warden isn’t she?” He knew more than I thought.

“Well… my mother had many siblings. My grandmother didn’t exactly believe in being controlled. She isn’t like… Baat, Baat, she’s kind of- well, corrupted in a way but I’m supposed to purify our generational curses.”

Morgan sighs, “So, that’s how you were wrapped up in all this?”

“Well, there are three forms of every Guardian. The base form, the shadow form, and the enlightened form. After she was raped she went crazy. The prophecy was coming true, she mentally died and didn’t feel safe anywhere. She went literally crazy. After she got back from Naka, she made really weird laws and rules. Then she disappeared until she was comfortable admitting to all our people she isn’t truly Baat anymore and has lost herself. Maya is far more understanding and forgiving. So, instead of hating her, we hate the cause of this war and conflict. The Nakans and Colin, specifically. Halle was the last child my grandmother had, she was around 40. So, my mother was one of many children. My uncle Bryon was her warden. I am her Vicar."

Morgan's lip twitched at the mention of my uncle's name. I knew I shouldn't have said anything but I really could not take his dick again so soon.

"What's wrong?" I lay in bed next to him, cuddling up to him and rubbing his chest. "Your energy dropped. What did I say?"

"I'm going to kill Colin Gregor. I feel as if I have to. All the men I killed where innocent was subjective at best. This man is guilty beyond belief. He has to be killed."

"Baby... You can't. You specifically cannot." I let out a sigh, "I can try to explain myself but honestly, my Grandmother can tell you everything if you allow me to channel her."

"While you're naked, and soaking wet between your legs?" he reached between my legs, pinching my clitoris sending small shockwaves through my body.

"Ooo, ooo, that is such an abuse of your powers." I blushed holding his hand. "Baby, she's already here. She looks out for me. This is what a Guardian does but especially for their Vicar. She has told me her greatest interest before she dies is ensuring you don't fall into the hands of Enshishi. She says... love is in mangoes and honey. Whatever that means."

If his energy took a plummet before. His poker face didn't switched but his vibes went through the roof.

"Morgan... Ada would be with you too if you weren't so anti-religion."

"I am not Anti-religion, I- I-I was in the hands of Enshishi my whole life Rose... at times I feel little different than Halle. I feel her pain in mis-education. Maya is a free nation, living for the growth and amelioration of itself and its citizens. Naka was built to fail, Colin told me himself. All he wants is the wealth of the world, he attempted to do the same to Erdu. He absorbed the Regime through its debt and his 'philanthropy'.

I know enough to get by but- I never believed once in my entire life I could ever be a Vicar or Guardian or whatever you wish to label it. I truly never knew. I can get by as a civilian, maybe an ascended soul. But as the King of Kings?"

"You're more than capable... can I please show you?"

"I- if you're fine with what your grandmother does. I can only promise to keep an open mind not abide by it."

I sit up, "Take off your clothes."

"What!?" he asks, "Rose, what is going on here."

"Just trust me, you'll love it. She misses Ada. She's going to help you connect with him." I straddle his lap pushing him to his back, "At least take off your shirt."

"I- fine, whatever. I won't let the Guardians call me coward." he sits up and pulls off his thermal, then shimmies out of his jeans. "These too?"

I nod with a smrik. He didn't have to, but I wanted his meat pressed against me.

I admit rubbing his beautiful cock through his briefs. "You can leave them on, but we want them off."

He pins me to my back. My cheeks flush red as I feel his throbbing head pressing inside of me. I lose my breath as he begins to enter me. I fall asleep and my eyes turn crystalline. I felt more liquids rushing to my vagina coddling his cock deeper inside me. He smirked proceeding inside my womb. His length nestling deep in my guts for a few strokes. Baat purred rubbing his chin, wrapping my legs around him. A large shockwave of energy filled the room as Morgan's eyes turned violet purple.

"Baat."

"Ada... it's been so long." she moans, "Let us enjoy our new mortal selves."

"Enough, Baat!" Ada's tenor voice had forbidding in his tone. No wonder he chose Morgan. There was barely a difference in their tone.

"It's a bit of fun, Ada. Don't be so dull." I rolled over given him the option to reenter me from behind.

"There are many other ways to have fun, many I do not approve of and have turned blind eye to. If you wish to enjoy ourselves, I will partake for Morgan's sake. His mind so stressful, I'm surprised he can function."

"That is functioning? Brooding, toiling, and worrying himself in circles? I could have been fooled. I want his cock Ada."

"Haven't you had enough?"

"He is enough..." Baat purr shivering as Morgan's length pulled out of me. "I feel like you pulled out my spine." I laid motionless. "I could never get you to lie with me."

"You are my sister."

"We aren't even physical beings! That is quite a mortal concept to maintain for so many millinea!" Baat snaps, "So be it. Women are not here for sexual desire and pleasure. Not even for men such as these? I have given the daughters of Rakil, the ability to heal with their sex."

"It is their love that is healing, such as your granddaughter here. She was a good selection. He however is still bonded to another woman if not more. You do not mind?"

"No, I do not mind. Ada deserves all women."

"So, is your law?"

"So, is my word..."

"As Baat or as Stheno?"

She hissed pulling away from him, kicking and swinging.

"HOW DARE YOU!? HOW DARE YOU!?" her screech was deafening. "I attempt to redeem your damn mortal and this is how you treat me! No fun for me? You insult me, and now this! I have loved you for an eternity and not once have you returned affection. HOW DARE YOU!?"

Ada sighed, sitting on the edge of the bed as if he and Morgan had never switched, "You are what you are despite what happened, I do apologize. But I cannot call you Baat."

"I haven't lost myself yet... I have not." Baat mourns, "I am slipping... I am losing form by the day. But I have not quit! And I have not lost myself. I will not allow such a monster to be born upon this Earth. I did not fail you, Ada. I was raped! My husband killed before me."

Ada bowed his head, "I should have protected you..."

"No... that's what he wants for you to doubt yourself! There was nothing you could have done!"

"You know how this ends."

"It does not have too!" Baat pleads, "He cannot be the one to kill Colin. His soul will be consumed!"

"What?" Ada didn't even seem to know. He wouldn't commit demo-cide so he likely wouldn't what happens if you try to kill a Guardian.

"This is what happened to Maurice Sameera! He fought the beast sealed within Mendel Gregor as his ward and Enshishi consumed his soul! Maurice spent his entire life learning from the first keepers of the fire, only for Enshishi to betray him. Now, we have to deal with one of his son's,Colin. A greedy, cowardly, and destructive man-child at the helm of the world."

"The boy can contain Enshishi, he will do good works because it is in his nature. He calls for me as much as he calls for the fire as he calls for the Earth. I have put him in the hands of the Guardians. And he learned from the Guardians his whole life. He will fulfill the will of Rakil no matter what." Ada was confident in Morgan, I wish Morgan could have the same confidence within himself. "So, it has been true Morgan Leonticus Sameera he was so named. Of his own, of the flames, of his father from the grounds of Erdu. He will be the greatest man to live, and the King of Kings. All options are open to him, he must decide his pathway."

"Ada..."

"I do not remain of this world. I belong in the ethereal."

"And look how this turns out, Ada! You leave us and we fail you! We need your guidance. The world has forgotten your teachings and call you heretic. You have not been in this realm for 1,000 years! And sporadic before then. You are not Rakil, your method is not working, we need you here!"

"I- I wasn't aware it had been so long. I was merely fighting an spiritual war the entire time in the spiritual realm. Not toiling with humans."

"Merely what? Fighting demons for them to spawn upon Gaia? Undoing principalities for them to form within Gaian politics and rulers. This is our battlefield given by Rakil. Allow the Archangels and Pure spirits to wage war within the heavens and ether. We need YOU here on Gaia. No more flames and more delegation. You and your mortal must align, and you two must be the ones. We need you to advance, you aren't so pure either, Ada. You can grow as well."

"You speak blasphemy but truth at once, how?"

"There is none above you?"

"There is only Rakil!"

"There is Nadir..." Baat corrects, "All praises to the Father who has given us life, and the Mother who nurtures us. But there is Nadir, and you have lived in defiance of this for five ages. There 7th Age approaches. You once spoke to me of transcendence. This perhaps all that has resisted me falling into Stheno is the hope of becoming greater than myself. You were the one who told me there is more to life, there is a greater self within us all even Guardians. This mortal can achieve where you and all others have failed. He is certainly devoid of Ego, his might set for duty."

"His actions need remain pure!" Ada reenforced.

"He penetrated me! I simply- I am weak to you and your advances."

"I- I can't disagree. The boy has had Luno within him."

"Because you failed Onyx! You failed to guide the one man who could have ended this all. You kept him from the world and sent him to Oblivion to fail!"

"I did not believe he would fail!"

"Nor did you know he would succeed!" Baat shouts, "You had no idea, but within his age, within his mind, Onyx men Sah'ra could have been the greatest King, alive to this day if you had stood behind him! Had you revealed yourself. But the Hawk watches, the hawk strikes when opportune, but the HAWK CANNOT LEAD!"

"I- I accept my failures."

"Damn, your acceptance. Fix your failures!" tears begin falling down my eyes, "This girl is yet innocent, and now she is no longer. She is now his responsibility. Assist him in caring for her and my daughter!"

"You should care for your daughter.

"If I take her Colin will eventually come for her... I- I am scared, Ada. He has legal custody over my daughter within those damn Nakan courts. We have no Mayan laws for such a thing. Without you by my side I am scared. Without you on this plane, I am scared. I move in shadows, I make dark deals, I do all but show my face I might as well be dead. He took all from me, and raped me while I could do is scream and await death. But he refused to kill me. And I could not kill myself. Enshishi only laughed. In my spirit and then in my flesh." Baat breaks down completely, the water in the bathroom goes out of control, beginning to drip onto the carpet of the bedroom. "YOU WERE SUPPOSED TO BE MINE! BUT YOU KEPT OBATTA FROM ME!"

"I- we cannot lie together."

"Ada... it has been 5 ages, and you act as if we were just born! Open your eyes. These are mortals. The only way they can ensure longevity is through procreation and protection of their kin! They do not live forever. They die. WE DO NOT! We bounce around body to body fulfilling our purpose. But these mortals are fragile. You abandon yours, you leave yours, you watch them die. You must walk by their side Ada!"

"He does not call upon me..."

"YOU DO NOT REVEAL YOURSELF! He was but a child and you allowed him to be consumed by the Dread Wolf. Where were you? What held higher importance! If this is the one you selected why put him through such strain?"

"My abilities do not work as yours... he must be open to me. He must allow me into him! I cannot simply seize control. He agreed to your little experiment this is not normal for us."

"Now you have a bridge. You are welcome!" the cloak faded and I was bare naked.

I looked on to Morgan sitting, staring at his shoes. He looked over to me with deep purple eyes.

"You... girl. What is your name?"

I froze matching his gaze feeling myself filled with joy and delight. I never believed within my lifetime I would ever witness The God's Eye. Even within myself I believed Morgan may only be a conduit or a Warden. But no, my beloved, my savior was truly him. And Baat says he only gets better.

"Rose Paz Andale-Sameera, I am to be Morgan Leonticus Sameera's wife... so was told to me by Baat."

"I wish you luck... there is much competition for his mortal heart."

"I hold his immortal soul, do I not?"

"You... if you abide by his word, if you shield him, if you promise not to betray him, even still I cannot choose you will have his firstborn. You may lay with him under my veil. I see the Muses singing through you girl. You could be the greatest form of Baat, yet."

"I- thank you Ada. I thank you."

"Now, put some damn clothes on..."

"Yes, absolutely sir! I will quickly!"

"First... roll this poor mortal one of those sticks. He will have a headache when he awakes. These eyes were opened too soon for his body to contain. He must rest. It truly has been a long day."

Morgan's eyes faded back to brown and he fell to the ground.

He braced himself on his forearm but didn't move. He was awake. He was quiet. He was like a panther calculating his next move. He licked his lips and sat on his haunches, staring up to the ceiling. He didn't look at me, we didn't make eye contact at all. I don't believe he has any idea where he was or what just happened. I couldn't imagine what the God's Eye revealed to him.

I did my best job rolling him a blunt with my hands still clamy from receiving Baat's presence.

"Baby, here's your medicine when you're ready for it." I rub his shoulders.

"Baat... the water... get the water." he strained, still crossed between and Morgan.

They... they were communing. And I helped him! I helped him!

I wanted Morgan back inside of me. I understood what Baat meant by removing my spine. I never felt so powerful, so capable, and protected. No matter what happened, I will keep my promise to Ada. I refuse to leave Morgan's side.

I run into the bathroom to turn off the shower. There was water all over the floor from my breakdown. I'm not going to be able mop all this up. If Morgan can use the ether to play with my clitoris. I could use my powers to in the least to clean this water, right?

I opened the bathroom window to give the water an exit. I stuck out my hands and grounded myself. Moving my hands to flow like ebbing waves, flowing back collecting the water to the center of the room in a ball. The ball grew and grew as I drew in the flood. I wish I knew how to lift heavier masses of matter. It seemed impractical weight-lifting could help me move water but it would help to get stronger. I strained picking up the ball of water, stretching out my arms turning it into a column. I was careful, guiding the column out the window then clapping my hands together smashing the column into rainfall.

I wiped the sweat off my brow flinging all the gathering sweat out the window as well to smell fresh then walked back into his bedroom, finding Morgan on the bed now.

"Rose... I'm sorry for calling you a stupid little girl. It seems I was the fool all this time."

"Yes you were... but I still love you."

His lip twitched uneasily, "I need to eat something. All my energy has left me." I was shocked but refused to comment. "Thank you for the blunt, would you join me after you order the pizza?"

"You remembered?"

"I am shocked, but I love pizza..."

"I would have never guessed." I smile, "I need to put clothes on."

He only nodded, unsure what to say.

"This is real...? This is all real?" he asked rubbing his head, picking up the blunt and holding it to his lips, "I can't believe it's gotten this far before I realized who I was." he lit the blunt and shook his head, "There's plenty to go around. I think I'm going to relax tonight. Watch a movie, and make sense of all this. Will you join me?"

"Absolutely, my beloved!" I clap my hands rushing out his room to get dressed.

My teddy was gone, replaced with a pair of violet pajamas pants and an orange tank top. I didn't question the works of my grandmother. I only followed her lead. Eventually I would be old enough to lead myself until then I needed to rely on her and Morgan.

CHAPTER 29

What It Seems?

Halle Victoriana Gregor

I left a note apologizing to Morgan for leaving so quickly, explaining I needed a few weeks of my time. The days were going by too quickly for him and he felt as if he was losing himself. I couldn't understand why his answer was pushing me away instead of having talked to me about all this upfront! The closer the wedding approaches, Morgan is trying to find some way out of it all to continue doing his merrily Morgan thing. Sadly, with this Rose character.

I had few options since Natalie wouldn't return any of my calls. And there were no other friends I could vent about Morgan and marriage. I found myself on the road right back to Naka.

My father didn't notice my presence my first night coming into the manor. I was a bit happy about it. I wasn't quite ready to see him after all Morgan talked about. All Rose verified. After all I read in Morgan's book... I knew my father my entire life to be loving, caring, maybe a bit demanding but there wasn't a way we were monsters!

"Halle, are you reading a book, sweetheart?" My father joined me in the kitchen holding a mug in his hands. He sipped his coffee taking the seat across from me. He wore a bathrobe threaded along his lapel with gold. The slippers I bought him for Patriarchival, the biannual festival to commemorate my father. He glanced up from his paper with a shock,

"Think Fast and Slow... is this for school? I didn't know The Academy was in session..."

"No, Morgan gave it to me. I've been reading a bit at his place." I smile proudly, "I'm devouring this book."

"That's a pretty big book, Halle." My dad comments rubbing his chin. "Is this an interest to you, or are you doing it for Morgan?"

"I'm already halfway done! It's really interesting. So many scenarios where just a few moments of thinking differently than usual-

"He gave you a book but what about the arrangement?" All he ever wanted to speak about with me was Morgan.

"Well... I guess we had a good time. He wants time to think about recent news, I guess I do too. Okay, so like I was saying by just a shift in your pattern of thought you would have-

"A good time? You two have been having far too many good times. Did he agree or not? Time is of the essence. I wanted this wedding years ago. He's stalling at this point."

"Daddy, I'm trying to tell you about the book! Can we talk about something other than Morgan? Damn!" I snap at him.

He sighs, "Fine, go on." He sits down and opens his newspaper, "Continue, i'm listening."

"Well, If you just change your pattern of thinking, even a small change in thought cadence, you can open your mind to whole new possibilities, or build a dependence on instincts. It gives many scenarios where people rely on archetypes, stereotypes, or poor thinking habits. I think this is what Morgan has been trying to get across to me."

He nodded and hummed an "mhm" every once in awhile. We spent most our mornings like this when we did see each other. Things seemed different though. Morgan, even if he doesn't agree with me at least gives eye contact. Or a rebuttal.

"Isn't that interesting, dad?" I ask, testing him. "About the purple dinosaur scenario?"

"Yes, dear. Quite, quite. Dinosaurs were my favorite part."

"I didn't even finish my sentence..." I said in disgust.

"Yes, and then what?"

I stared at him in shock, "Dad are you kidding me!?" I stand up, "you're not even listening to me!"

He lets out a long sigh, "settle down... it isn't as if you're saying anything of worth." he stretches out, "I've missed you, Halle dearest. If Morgan can't appreciate you, I surely can." he says setting down his paper.

I sit down and roll my eyes, "whatever."

"Thatta girl. Tough as her old man." he smiles with false pride.

How many mornings have been like this before I noticed?

Now to think of it. My father never wants to speak about anything other than Morgan or the marriage. Even when I was young he would ask me if I knew Morgan. When Natalie was dating him it seemed fated to be. This man was finally in my life and I knew of him from a distance for so long. There were always other men but... Morgan was the only man I could ever imagining spending my life with. At least he used to be. For all of their differences. Morgan and my father were so alike.

I was tired to hell with both of them!

Always busy! Always only concerned with their work! Never giving a damn about anyone else's feelings but their own! But since they don't have feelings, it's a losing battle every time. They were selfish, brutes at best. I was better off reading in my mother's garden or heading downtown La Vida. I could enjoy a cafe while I read instead of being blatantly disrespected by men who are supposed to love me!

"I'm going to get ready to go."

"Excuse me? Ha, why sweetie. Don't tell me you've gone and got soft on me." My father begins laughing. He grabs my arm and jerks me closer. "Come on, what's wrong, Halle dearest?"

"I didn't get soft. You're ignoring me." I pout, jerking my arm back.

"I heard you, you were talking about that book or whatever. Ha, I didn't even know you could read that well, babe. I'm impressed." My father smiles, "Good for you."

"Of course I can read. Are you kidding me? You didn't think I can read?"

"Read well, sweetie. Read well." He repeats as if that justifies what he said. "Probably be best if you didn't, there's a lot of falsehoods in books."

"You are joking... Well, for the record. Morgan doesn't want to marry me because he hates you and doesn't think I'm fit to be a Queen. I'm starting to agree with him. So, there's your mission report Sergeant." I stand up closing my book.

My father leans back in his seat, "Ha, that boy doesn't hate me! I practically raised him." He grins ear to ear, "He's like my own blood. He loves me. He has to." My father laughs as if he said some joke I wasn't aware of.

"No... No, he really doesn't. He actually hates you. And I can see why, you're such a dick, dad. I don't know why I haven't seen it earlier, but he's right about you."

He laughs, "Whoooa, what the mouth on you, babe." he gives me a wink, "How has that mouth been, love?" he leans in.

I roll my eyes. "I'm Morgan's woman, now. We're waiting until our marriage."

"Ha, no, no you aren't. Actually, until you get married you're mine." he mocks me, chuckling. "I'm happy you're home, dear. It was quite lonely without you."

Why don't I feel the same?

"College made you all independent, sweetheart? The education that I paid for? Calling home every other goddamn week for more money. I don't have to listen to a damn word you say while I'm paying for things." He pats my butt. "Come here, sweetie, love daddy. Stop being so mean."

"That's fine, Morgan will actually listens to what I say instead of disrespecting me to my face!"

"Ha, if you think he hates me, look how he obviously feels about you? All this time and he still won't marry you? I should kill him for using my baby girl. Would that make you happy?" He tries to slap my butt again.

I grab his hand, forcing it back in his lap as he laughs the whole time. It was one big joke to him. "He isn't using me!" No... you are, your own daughter.

"Does he love you?"

I gritted my teeth, "we're working on us!" I say defensively.

"Ha! That's what your mother wanted. To 'work on us', to 'find herself'. Then she takes a throne opposing our empire! Traitors, every last one of them. You can't trust anything that isn't blood, Halle. It's us sweetie, against the world. The whole world wishes to see the Gregors end, we can't allow that. They need Masters, a proud leader. Your mother could never grasp that."

With reason, "But she's my blood... She's my mother."

"So, half of you is a traitor." he breaks out laughing, so satisfied with himself.

"I'm not hungry anymore." I begin marching off.

"Go think about this sweetheart. Fast or slow, I don't really care!" He calls out after me.

He thinks himself so clever. For as much as they were alike. Morgan and Father were so vastly differently. Morgan was honest but he wasn't so... cruel. My father always japes and jabs. He wants to laugh things off as if words don't hurt. Then goes on some rant about, 'that's just how men are!'

I miss being with Natalie and Morgan. Being back home after the years all on your own was so surreal. I guess I romanticised being at home. Maids and Butlers were always busy, bowing and curtseying. I could barely walk outside here in La Vida without someone in my face or acting as if they know me. Back in Nadine with Morgan we can just walk around because no one really cares. Here, there's no rest! In Nadia, we could walk and how the people would flock around Morgan and I. Morgan had no appreciation for it. My father expected grown men to break their will to bow to him. Morgan would never ask for that...

I just want to get married, move out of here and be with my beloved. Rose seems nice enough. Three of us could figure something out. It would be better than being Heiress Gregor for another year. Than being in this house alone with my father for another week. I'm not sure I can continue being his dutiful daughter.

At least Morgan cared to see me grow. My father didn't even think I could read...

The walk back to my room took about five minutes to my wing of the Manor. I took a few spare moments to pause at my mother's Garden. There were a few servants there in prayer. They all quieted down when I came. It brought pain to my heart they would react such a way toward me. I left without wishing to bother them.

They had been suffering for so long and I was blind to their plight. Not just another empress who wanted mercy and comfortable shackles for her subjects. What has this life turned me and Morgan into? He has potential to be one of the sweetest men alive, but believes death and coercion were the base presets of our reality, ever awaiting being used. His heart so guarded from trust. And I have been literally oblivious these years! Living in a delusion of everyone's affections but in truth, I was being used. Both serving my father faithfully. Neither of us with a damn thing to show for it but further expectation of subjugation to him.

A few handmaids came and left my room. If they spoke or greeted me, I hadn't an idea. I sat staring out of my bedroom window tower allowing me to see clear across our property. We owned a plantation... All these years, playing around the Manor, the bows and curtsies were expected, and this is my first time seeing my family's legacy. Morgan called me naïve and I responded with anger. He knew the whole time didn't he?

"Lady Gregor, you look so sad, what's wrong?" My oldest childhood friend and my handmaiden, Ananda asks. She placed a hand on my shoulder. "I have come with some refreshments, I was told you didn't eat."

I heard her but couldn't pull myself back to her. I felt if I opened my mouth the only thing that awaited were tears and sobbing. I needed to be strong. At least until I found a way out of here. I understand, now my love. This life isn't so clear... is this how you see things? Is this how you've seen me? The Slave Master's daughter? That's not what I want for us. That's not what I want for myself. I love these people, I care for them. They've all helped raise me and care for me. I don't want to be responsible for any of this! I don't want to be attached or have my name on any of this!

Ananda poured me a cup of tea made of the nettles from my mother's garden. Though, my mother was gone her garden was still a highlight many of our staff flocked to. Especially after she left. I was never quite allowed to hang around there but always enjoyed the nettles and hibiscus. They prayed continuously there to Rakil and Baat. My father couldn't stop them so he did what he always did. He told me they were heretics and I was forbidden.

"Lady Gregor, can you hear me?"

"Sorry, Ananda, I was lost in thought. Thank you for the tea." I nodded. "You may leave me."

Is this how Morgan felt? Put upon this pedestal you're not even sure you want to live up to because of everything that's demanded of you? I'm the daughter of two gods... well, a god and a sea witch. My father the God, Enshishi and my mother the temptress, Baat. What does that make me then? A goddamn hurricane... I was a mess, no wonder Morgan was at such distance.

"What were you thinking about, Lady Gregor?" Ananda asked pointing to the seat across from me."Your beloved?"

"Just contemplating my life, dearest. Yes, please where are my manners, it's been so long, sit with me. It's been far too long and I can use the company."

Ananda looked fearful. I took a moment to swallow her impatient expression. She was such a sweet girl when we were children. We used to talk about everything together. I even took her to a few parties with me back in high school. But she seems so different coming back. She lost her glimmer while I was gone. She had such a sweet smile but barely opens her mouth. The poor thing was skinnier than I imagined she ever could be. She had full rose cheeks even just a few years ago. Now, sunken. Her eyes jumping uneasily about the room, looking everywhere but in my eyes. The contacts were rather unsettling, almost looked real. I was horrified... this is what my oldest friend has become.

Ananda looked around and shook her head. She had never been so formal nor frantic. The girl I knew had a sharp wit and mind of her own.

"I- I'm your handmaiden, it is inappropriate." she quickly refuted, holding the chair but pausing before sitting.

"Nonsense, Ananda. You are my friend and my family. Please sit with me. I wish to catch up." I needed to find myself quickly before I lost Ananda to our conditioning. I couldn't allow my drama to make me lose more friends.

"Is that an order?" she frowns unable to refuse me. Though now I questioned whether out of love or service.

"Must it be for you to simply have a cup of tea with me?"

"Lady Gregor... I- I am your handmaid, not your friend. We both know this. Please, don't fool me any further."

"Ananda, I- where is this coming from?"

Ananda closed the door after making sure no one was outside of it. "Where is your father?"

"My father? He's.. he's in the dining room, why do you ask?"

"May I speak freely?" Ananda's head was bowed staring between her legs. "You, you have been gone and there is much you must hear, but I- I shouldn't tell you... but- but you neeed-

"Absolutely, I've been waiting for you to. You can tell me whatever you need to Ananda. Your secrets are safe with me. If needed- we can tell Morgan."

Ananda sighs sitting with me. She leans forward to speak. I notice the full breasts in front of me, far larger than she could have possibly grown into. I covered my mouth at the scarring and handprints. Her contacts more like a cat's than the girl I once knew. What was left of her.

"Your father has become cruel."

"My father always been a handful. His temper-

"He's been using me as his own personal... plaything! I've been unable to tell anyone."

"I- I'm not sure how to respond. My father- You were as my sister, Ananda, it was only right for you to take my place once I left for university." I tried to reason.

Ananda covered her mouth, "Mistress, he did the same to you?"

"Well... If you're speaking of pleasing my father and being a dutiful daughter, then yes I have. He grooms me to be a good wife, it's his duty. As it was mine."

"He has taken my maidenhood! He forces me to pleasure him whenever he gets an urge, or to satisfy his whims no matter how humiliating! He beats me when I refuse. He doesn't hit me, he beats me then keeps me from my family until I recover. Threatening if I return." Ananda began to weep, "how can a man be so cruel? I cannot even look my own parents in the eyes. I haven't eaten a meal with them since I've gotten these. Every time they see me they wonder what is wrong. As if simply by looking at me they can see my plight. But if I tell anyone your father says- " she begins crying. "He would kill me, he would kill them, and just take another in my place until you returned."

"Ananda... it is an honor to be chosen by a Gregor." I was so shocked I could only repeat what I had been told so many times. I felt as she did once. I was rewarded though... taken shopping after my father relieved himself. "Especially a Patriarch... Do as my father bids. It isn't so bad. It's a daughter's duty."

"No, Halle. My father would never touch me as your father does! He would never even dream of it!" she begins to sob uncontrollably, snot falling from her mouth. She covered her face to hide her shame. "Every day is torment, every day is pain. I'm terrified... I think of jumping off the balcony-

"But... how can a father's love be wrong?" I asked her just as my father had asked me so many times.

She weeps while I served so faithfully. I couldn't understand but my friend needed me to. She needed my sympathy, my love. But to offer her either. Morgan would never lie to me. Morgan of all people wouldn't.

"Mistress, please, please do not tell anyone! He said he would kill me." Ananda grabs me in a frenzy. "I'm sorry, I have lost my place. I should have said nothing. Perhaps it's what you say. It's me, it's me. I swear. It's just me. Do not say anything, please."

I only nod. I've never seen such horror, aside from Morgan's sporadic night terrors. I didn't make such a comparison often. She nearly knocks over the table, clinging to me, weeping and sobbing in my lap as I try to make sense of it all. She grips the fabric of my dress, thanking me endlessly for my mercy. This woman was as my sister once. Now, in truth. I didn't care for our method of kinship.

"Thank you, Madam. Thank you!" she kissed my feet, "you were always my savior. You always protected me." she continued crying.

This isn't protection. I'm scared right along with you. How can I protect any of these people just as terrified as they are. If I'm scared and I'm his daughter...? How much have I turned a blind-eye to in the pursuit of dresses and parties. I wanted to cry but the feeling of Morgan's presence kept my lip to a quiver as I tried to process her pain and my own.

"Ananda.. What my father did... it was wrong?" I asked in all seriousness.

She looked at me. Her eyes dried as she cupped my hands. "It was horrid, Halle! It was terrible. I have never felt so used. So disposable. I felt as if I was just some piece of meat." she cried to me. "And he would kill me if I said anything."

"When... when my mother passed away, he said he was grooming me to be Queen... to be her replacement."

"Mistress, Lady Qatar fled Naka when you were ten and I was but 8."

"I- I only did what I believed to be my duty." I've been being lied to since I was only ten? By the man who was supposed to love, and protect me. Instead, he turned his only daughter into his sex slave. Nothing in this world had value or meaning to my father unless it was his. "I'm, I'm so sorry my sister."

Ananda embraced me. Smothering me in her silicon chest. She squeezed me and weeped. I could only sit in silence, holding onto her as I processed all that she said. My childhood unravelled before my eyes as all those moments and nights of servicing my father passed before my eyes. No matter how much it hurt. Or how uncomfortable, he would just ask me to perform my duty and I would. After awhile it wasn't so revolting or demeaning. It was the only quality time we truly had together. So, I clung to those moments and wanted to give the same to Morgan.

Morgan often called me naive. I never realized how much I've clung to my naivete to get through life. Reciting my father's words as if repeating verses from a hymnal. Living off my family legacy as if they were my own laurels. I can understand you clearer now, Morgan. I need you here. I need you with me right now.

I squeezed Ananda as we were both fell in sobs.

My father ensured I took the utmost pride in his teachings and in being a Gregor. While Morgan rejects it as if it's acid. My father recounts the glories of war and his service. I must pry for Morgan to mention anything at all. These were not the same men. Morgan is a quiet, humble, and kind man who won my heart. I no longer know what I believe my father to be. None of the ideas are kind or of this world. Everything in that old book, my family, my history, how could we be such tyrants? How could we have lived on this planet believing all these people to be beneath us, simply for not having our last name?

My Lord Father had a veil over my eyes for so long. Showering me with gifts and gold after having his way with me. Breeding me to be Queen, or whatever he wishes to call it... when Morgan refuses to even consider me worthy of being wife. I wished to be blind for so long. To be in distress and pain silently. I never knew where the feeling came from. I thought Morgan made me feel a victim and abused, I suppose he only revealed reality to me. I wonder if he knew the extent? No, my father would be dead if Morgan knew what he did to me.

We both froze at the heavy footsteps leading up the stairs. Ananda looked at me in horror as the lumbering steps meant one thing.

"Hurry, begin packing our bags. Quickly, much is still packed, find yourself dresses. We are not staying here." I whisper to her, "I will keep him from you, perform your duty. I will take all the bags you cannot carry. Pack, get in my car, and wait for me." I kiss Ananda's forehead.

She looks up to me in fear, she looks at me then to the door. She was paralyzed tears in her eyes, "He heard us." she began falling apart again.

"Ananda, I will not let any harm on Gaia befall you again. Nor will Morgan. Do as I ask, please. We will be out of here."

Ananda nodded.

My father stepped into the room. Having to duck down under the 7ft high doorway. Standing back to his 13ft height. A permanent grin on his face. It was rare I didn't see my father smile. If not it was usually replaced with anger. Morgan always seemed so calm, never showing how he felt though he felt so deeply... For so long I saw no difference between my father and Morgan. In this moment I never knew how or why. I may feel nervous or stupid around Morgan. I felt fear up to my throat as my father towered over me.

"There's my beautiful daughter!" He was wearing a sepia suit with a firm bulge in his pants. "Oh, you've run into your little friend." he said with pause.

He assesses the situation as if he sensed our unease.

In my youth I would run to him. All hugs and kisses before catering to what was in his pants. He would send me shopping afterward. New dresses no longer seemed of interest. He never had to hurt me, I never refused him anything. I'm not quite sure what disobedience would even look like. But all who defied the Gregors were punished. I didn't need to know, Ananda found out. All I ever wanted was to make my father was happy. All I ever wanted was to please Morgan as I pleased my father. Morgan would never ask me for such.

"Ananda come join us for a moment."

Jah'Ada, please... give me your courage.

"She can't. Ananda is busy packing my bags." I push my father back as playfully as I could without puking. I tickled him until he held both my hands.

"I don't care, move the lead out your ass, girl!" he flashed with anger.

Ananda was frozen with fear.

"Father, Ananda is quite busy. Please let her work." I pushed him along, hugging him tightly, "I missed you!"

He took the distraction and lifted me high, spinning me around, "As I have you! My you've grown. I hope Morgan enjoys the gift I have bestowed him. If not... I would gladly take it back."

His gaze was on me. The hunger I once wished Morgan had. The attention and longing to be with me only a father could give. Morgan would never provide me with the same. I felt myself returning to my father as a child all over again.

"Dad... please put me down. I don't quite feel well. Ananda and I were catching up, can you excuse us? I'm sure you and I will talk soon."

My father lowered me but didn't release me, "What's wrong, do you not miss me?"

"Obviously not nearly as much as you did." How could a father have such lust for his daughter? "I feel ill is all. I think I'm going to spend the week with Morgan. He's offered for me to share his vacation with him. I wish to bring Ananda along to train his new maid. We'll be there."

"Morgan didn't submit anything for vacation... he just hasn't been showing up to the office. I assumed he was working from home. Vacation then, yes, yes, that explains it. I thought perhaps he-

"Quit?"

My father's lips flinched from his smile as the uncertainty crossed his lips. My father was an avid chess player. He would lose his Queen and give up his bishops. If he lost Morgan he lost everything. He was elderly, and no Gregor man has lived over 66, my father's 60th year of birth was approaching. Though, he was as strong as he was regardless, and just seemed to be getting bigger rather than older.

"No, no, I will send one of my older maids, train her properly. Ananda has been... catering other duties lately." He replied with a brush of his hand, "Morgan has a favorite, she'll keep him good company and take care of you. Who is this new maid, I heard nothing of this?"

"Natalie hired her... I know little of her either." I sucked my teeth. "Bitch is always in my business."

"Ananda... she would not be good for Morgan. They don't need to meet. You will go alone, learn more about this maid. I will question Natalie, heavily, find some answers. I'll find another selection."

I couldn't let him on that I knew. With all I've heard as of late... I needed to hear it out of his mouth. Maybe it'll all make more sense if he just explained it.

"Well, I have missed my Nandi dearly. She seems so sickly and skinny. I figure a week with good friends in Nadine would lift her spirits. Morgan, has been wanting to have a barbeque. It'll be good for Nandi to have a more intimate setting. Maybe Morgan would-

"You cannot both leave, I refuse it." My dad says as if that was all. "I said I will find another. They cannot meet."

"Why?" I held my frustration better than I ever could with my fiance. "Have you too bonded in my absence? It will only be for a week. I'm sure you can go on without us."

His smile quivered for a moment. My father wasn't used to being challenged. You could feel the room's temperature switch as his blood boiled under his thin smile.

"You've just returned. I have... well, fatherly needs that must be attended to. I have waited long enough for you. If I cannot have what I wish, I will settle."

He said it...

"I've been rather curious how many other daughters attend to such needs." I cut my eyes, "As I meet more people off our grounds. Our life seems a bit startling father. The things I've heard of our family name and history. Have you lied to me?"

"We have discussed this, Halle! Those daughters are not the daughters of a Gregor! You are acting Queen regent, it is your responsibility to attend the King. That is final! No more of this talk. No more of this reading! Go to Morgan's and keep your mouth shut! Be a good, dutiful wife, do as he says and don't upset him further and ruin this! You've already done enough."

"I'm not the one he's upset with father... It isn't me. It isn't because I'm stupid, he doesn't like my upbringing. It's you." I stare him in the eyes. "I'm the Queen regent already? Since when was this? Why have you not told me! I am a Queen already, and you have prepared me for nothing!"

His smiled faded as he stared at me, "Yes... you are Queen." He said as if it pained him. He inhaled deep and shook his head. "With your mother's absence and your coming of age... you-you have been for sometime, since you were a girl. It was best for all we waited."

"Then should my duties not extend to rule, at least learning to assume your throne? Not just sucking and fucking your perverted dick!" I cry at him.

I had only been told of my father's temper.

His hand lashed out slapping me clear across the face sending me across the room and into the wall. My body slammed against the bed. I picked myself up and spit out blood. Trying my best not to cry as much as I wanted. Little of it from physical pain, mostly from the betrayal.

He rubbed his wrist, "I have told you about your tone. I suppose your distance has made you unruly. More reason why you need to be home. To learn your place. Neither of you are leaving here until the wedding. I will make this a goddamn traditional Gregor house as I wished!"

"If I am to rule-

He smacked me once more, this strike was followed by his laughter.

"I wouldn't let you rule a game of checkers. You're only use is getting Morgan to me. Morgan shall take over my kingdom, he is to be my heir. Your duty is to serve Enshishi. You will serve me or you will serve him! That is your only purpose, nothing more!" he growled as I had never heard.

"Enshishi..." Ananda fell to her knees, "Lady Halle... that is not your father, be careful."

"Morgan-" I bit my tongue. I needn't risk him hitting me again. If Morgan knew of his intentions... if my father knew what Morgan had planned. "Morgan will hear of this..." I snarled in the base of my throat.

It was nothing I had ever seen before. Regret... or fear. My father let out a huff and stood down. The beast Enshishi took pause.

"Is that a threat, young one?" he feigned pacing a short distance.

"It is a promise, father. Strike me or Ananda again and I will tell Morgan! Simply because we haven't agreed to marry, means little for our love. He despises you! All he needs is a reason. It's worst enough he'll wish to inquire of my bruises."

"Shit..." my father cursed, "The boy wouldn't understand. You will hold your tongue, insolent girl! He is not yet Gregor, he will not understand our customs." Customs he seemed to make up at will. "Get yourself up Halle, I barely put force behind those blows. You're fine, you're stronger than that. You're of my flesh and spirit."

"What you have raised me for?" I remain on the ground, holding my eyes, allowing a slight tear to fall from my eyes.

His smile faded all together. He glared at me in a way I didn't think possible. He wanted to hit me but I was protected by Morgan... even in his absence his shroud was over me.

"My husband wishes to know what you raised me for father. He believes me unfit to rule by his side. He believes me insufficient to be Queen. Now, I see it's all your fault! You kept me like some caged bird!"

Enshishi rolled his Sun-Orange eyes, "I raised you for exactly what you're good at. Something your mother couldn't understand and refused to abide by. Being a proper Gregor woman, not the half Mayan whore you obviously are. First your mother, now you. None of you women understand your place."

I backed up for my own good. The topic of my mother rarely raised without either of our tempers going awry.

"Lady Gregor, your bags are ready. Let us go." Ananda intercedes grabbing my arm, "We must go, your father has left us and we must go as well."

"You can flee if you wish, but your maid stays." Enshishi warns. The smile was off of my father's face as it rested sternly. "If you are to run and report what you have heard, that is fine. I have told you the truth. Morgan must decide for himself. We will speak on it in the morning over some golf or boating. With women far more understanding of their duties. On then you coward, run along and hide under your new father."

"You will not put another hand on her, I'm taking Ananda with me." I quickly got to my feet, standing in front of Ananda. "We're both done being your whores!"

"You mouthy little bitch! I told you I would cut your throat out!" My father roared, flipping the tea table over and out the window. The nail was in the coffin. He believed me ignorant to my sister's plight. "This is what makes you defy me? The words of some Eshan whore!? Over the word of your father, The Patriarch Colin Gregor, the True King of Gaia, The God Enshishi!?" He huff and puffs as smoke floods from his mouth, filling the room.

"I am leaving... I am taking Ananda." I back Ananda up in case he moves to swing again.

My father's anger subsided in an instant as if none of this happened. His grin returns and he tucks his hands in his pocket. "If not her, I will simply take another... perhaps her mother, and have her father hung for treason against their god."

Ananda squeezed my arm tight. "I must stay, I cannot allow another to endure his cruelty!"

"Cruelty? Such cruelty when you have moaned like a delightful slut as of late. You resist and fight as if I am monster. As if you hadn't enjoyed my teachings. Feign as some victim, young whore. Only we know what you have done for me. You as well, daughter. You both act as if you have acted unwittingly, as if your age is some excuse for my desire? You are whores both of you, whether I wait for you to be of age or in youth. Your friend Natalie is no different."

Ananda tears returned and she fell to her knees invalid, sobbing uncontrollably. A horrid sound as I had never heard from a human before.

"Father... what happened to you?" I couldn't believe the things he told me.

"I have not changed." Perhaps that was the point. Perhaps that was the issue and I just refused to see it. My father wished to resurrect something my grandfather sought to end. My grandfather wanted peace. My father wanted domain over everything, control over all but his own house was in disarray. I had no father, I only had Enshishi.

"Morgan is not like you... he will never fulfill your corruption." It felt as we weren't leaving. The 10ft tall remnants of my father blocked the exit and Ananda was barely able to stand.

"Morgan and I have far more in common than even you and I, that is for sure." Enshishi's laughter was guttural and cocky, it was familiar in brief moments of my father's love. "His work has already been done. And my work has been far done. All he must do is sit upon the throne. He will never be the same, the boy is worst than I."

"You do not know him... You've never bothered to know either of us." he crossed the line speaking of Morgan as such.

"No my dear, it is you who does not know the monster your savior is."

The words were choked in my throat, but once they came out it felt so proud.

"My Lord Husband, is Ada, the Guardian of Nadia and he will see your end!"

My father laughed, "Do you think he does not already agree? Your Lord husband? He will not marry you because he knows I raised such a willing whore. Perhaps your friend Natalie would be of more use to me in fetching him. At least she is a defiant whore. You believe you have found some refuge under Morgan. He is a boy. He is a Wolf. He is a God... you will never reach him and he will never save you in time. His soul is already corrupted."

I've never hit my father before. I had never felt the raw anger as I had felt. Not even my own wound hurt as much as his blasphemy. I bolt as quickly as I could. My father folded as I punched him straight in his balls. He dropped screaming, cursing, and enraged.

"You sucker punching whore! No honor! No respect! You little dumb bitch, I should have-

"You will not disrespect me again!" I find my voice. Breathing so hard, it was a strain to even care for the oxygen at all. "I am Heiress of the Gregor family. I will take my throne! You will not stop me!" I roared.

"You better run. Run and hide under Morgan before I wring your neck! Because no woman will ever speak to me as such. Do not lose yourself in this broken society for the feeble and weak. You are nothing before me, as mortal nor God."

"I will take my time... " but a bit of haste has never hurt anyone.

Ananda's panic didn't stop her from grabbing as many bags as she could and bolting for the door as quickly as she could. I gathered as much as my hands could hold as we began running from my bedroom.

"What did you do!" Ananda cried a good two yards ahead of me the whole way.

"I am to be Queen. I cannot continue to allow myself to be disrespected! Now, run and start the car. I will hold my father off." I turned on my heels, and taking a deep breath. "I need you with me... mother, Morgan... please, watch over me." I prayed under my breath, hopefully not in vain.

Ananda smiled, "I am so glad you're back Mistress Halle."

"As am I..." My father's voice was a low rumbling growl. "You're in dire need of discipline. I see Morgan has let you run amuck."

"My Lord Husband allows me to become my own woman. Not his fuck pet or underling."

"Those are all one in the same." Enshishi scoffed.

"I can't wait for you to die." I cursed.

"So, there might be some Gregor in you after all. Good to see your mother didn't make two children from that goddamn Erdun bastard."

Morgan told me not to let my anger get the best of me. You get too angry to a point you cannot think. I wish my body remembered.

I took a running start, dragging my Heather Hatton Steel luggage case. It was $1500 with premium Ercu mountain steel. I swung my bag at my father. His arm jutted out as if he was waiting for my approach. He grabbed my neck, boiling hot claws dug into my throat as he ripped me off my feet. I shrieked in pain as the heat felt as though it was going to rip through my flesh.

He stared at me with flaming orange eyes, "I had always questioned who sired you... you and your mother always had such trouble simply staying home and serving your Lord Gregor."

I strained, "So, you're as bad a father as you have been a lover?" I dig deep, prying into my father's hands with my manicured nails. Happy to have gladly went natural all these years than settling for acrylics.

My father's eyes peeled open as I was flung down the hallway listlessly. He always loved to show off how strong he is. I bounced off the hardwood floors, slamming into the wall.

"I'm not even trying..." he boasts, "You couldn't possibly be my child and be so weak. It'll be fine to kill you and your maid. I will have to explain for absence, but we'll gladly find another bride more willing to comply."

"Good, I have yet to get started either."

"Do you honestly believe I would let my cum dump, kill me? No, you will be disci-

His eyes bulged. He had no idea how fast I had gotten. The early morning training with Morgan and Rose. Gratitude for Rose waking me up and dragging me alongside her and my beloved.

My father blocked the first punch with a chuckle but had no answer for the luggage crate swinging like an anchor. My metal crate hits him square in the jaw knocking him off his base.

"You bitch..." he curses slamming into the wall and knocking down paintings older than the manor.

"I am a Lioness, not a dog! You will not command me!" I felt something boil down beneath me. A faint voice from my memory screamed at him.

He chuckled, "Lions breathe fire my dear, their eyes don't swell with tears like a fish."

"My Lord Husband has taught me much about that as well." I planted my feet, inhale, focus on your target, hands on chest for focus, chi, chi, chi....

"He did what?" My father had not yet recovered.

I took in a larger inhale. All my anger and rage bubbled in my solar plexus. I let out the decade of torment. Filling the hallway with flames and smoke. The sparks burned my nose. But not as I had blown out the windows and melted the hallway asunder. I didn't care to stay to survey the damage. The voice told me to flee. Run, and tell Morgan of all that had happened here and he will handle it.

I quickly fled the corridor before the smoke could clear. I ran out the house ignoring all the curtsies and bows between me and the front door. I slid into the passenger's seat of my BMW. Ananda pulled off before I could close the door fully. It mattered little we were on our way.

"You're alive!" Ananda cheered, "I saw the fire, I'm so happy you escaped."

"That was me." I held my stomach, burping up smoke. "I think my father is afraid of Morgan." The indigestion was soooo painful, like a fire was in my belly.

"He speaks often of your Lord Husband with such pride."

"He isn't my Lord Husband yet... but I'll need him to be if I want my birthright. How did I not realize the monster my father was all this time?"

"Because he was your father, Halle. You loved him... and love is blinding."

I let out a burp of smoke. Holding my stomach as my temperature refused to cool even with the convertible top dropped. Making our great get away toward Nadine. Hopefully Morgan would take us in. Hopefully I find the words to tell him all that's happened. If not, I'm sure my mother will help me.

CHAPTER 30

Civility Builds Bridges

Rose Andale

The one time this man has a visitor and I'm trying to take a nap and they're knocking on the door like they lost their damn mind!

I was sprawled across Morgan's bed, smoking from an old pipe drowning out the world with Miles Davis.

I take my sweet time getting into something Morgan would deem appropriate. The past week was great with Halle going back to school. She and he have been... odd. They didn't have the same passion as new couples but an understanding and love of a 50 year old couple. He's even seemed happier with her around. Waking up with the sun and groggily working out with us. The excitement with him training us was completely unexpected!

He was one hell of a drill instructor. I'm just happy I got to punch Halle in the face for a week... she got a few good hits in as well. So much to fighting I never really knew. Morgan says he might need to promote me to guard his house and find a new maid. I was happy he wanted to keep me around with his wife about. Seemed you got to call yourself that if you so much as made it to Halle's spot. Few people Morgan seemed to care for otherwise. Their wedding was scheduled for the next year. It was as good as done. I guess she had no spot, she was his fiancée.

Babe... just make me your wife and let's take back Nadia, with the two of us it could be so easy but with Halle he could probably conquer the world.

After last night how could you possibly deny my place here by your side? I know my grandmother isn't all she was meant to be but this is why I am here! NOT HER!

I finished all my work for the day. I still had a pile of school work and a few plans I wanted to get ready for when Morgan got home tonight. He left out once more saying he needed some air. Though, he would probably be in Nadia all night again, organizing and scouting as he put it when I asked why going out for air took ten hours at a time. He didn't want to move into Exigo and Zilaypenah too quickly and didn't want to alert too many citizens of his presence. But my snapchat was brimming with pictures of him being caught around the city. People were excited for the return of their messiah. Glad Morgan was finally accepting his destiny.

And the knocking continues... now they're ringing the doorbell like a maniac. Ada, make them leave me alone!

I run down the stairs wearing yoga pants and a long sleeve shirt I hadn't worn for years with Graham High School across my chest representing the good ole days with Grandma before the military came to our doorstep. With a bottle of water I was ready to turn into a shiv in case one of Morgan's old wolf friends were looking for him.

"Halle?" I peek out the hole.

No fucking way, she just left only a week ago! You're already back, what do you want girl? Leave us alone, it's my turn!

I tear open the door ready to recite everything Morgan had got done telling her only five or so days ago. But...Actually... she looks like she's in pretty rough shape. I found Halle shivering on the porch in her a singed nightgown. Her feet were caked with dirt and blood. She was sweating through the thin silk. Panting, her makeup ran.

The other woman with her looked like a Wes Craven damsel. She was studying me through thin slits for pupils and purple eyes. She was giving me the creeps with her ribs showing through her faded housekeeping dress. A pixie hair cut with purple hair and pale skin with two large breasts that didn't reflect her sullen malnourished cheeks.

I open the door and she runs in with zero concern for the door hitting me in the face. Thanks Halle, I knew helping you would suck.

"Where is Morgan?" Halle looks around frantically, "I need to talk with him immediately."

"Hello, nice to meet you." Her friend bows her head.

I cut my eyes looking at all the luggage in their hands.

"You know damn well, Morgan didn't want you- He isn't here anyway. He left for Exigo for the second time tonight. He won't be back until late, if he even comes back at all tonight. What happened?" I bite my tongue doing my best to be polite.

"Oh god, no... Ananda lock the door. Rose I need you." Halle grabs my shoulders, she was burning up as if running a fever but her hands felt freezing cold.

"No... I'm going back to bed. I'm off the clock and you're not my boss. We went over this Holly. I'm going to nap. It's been a very long night. You can do whatever you need to do and talk to your hubby when he gets back. I'm staying out of your business."

"My father might be after us!" she squeezes me until it hurts.

I gulped. I might be able to take on some military brass but Enshishi himself on such short notice? I had no way of contacting Morgan. I covered my mouth brushing her cheeks and looking her over.

"What happened to your face, Halle?" I rubbed her chin feeling my maternal instincts kicking in. She is still Morgan's love, even if I didn't like her I owed it to him. "What is all this about your father?"

She looked down at the floor, "I want my husband..." she falls to her knees and begins sobbing. "I have been such the fool. Such the naive fool! My father calls himself, God. How could I have been so dumb to believe a word he said? He's a monster. That goddamn book was right."

"Whoa, that's heavy and beyond my imagination." I say playing the fool, trying my best to be empathic to her pain as if it was my own.

If seeing Halle first learning her family history firsthand wasn't something, hearing the heiress herself damn her father was remarkable. I had to be dreaming.

"I- uh... alright, sit down Halle. I'll make some tea or something. I really don't think your father would come around here. Maybe we could go to my place deeper in Nadia? To see if we could find Morgan?" I suggest rubbing my neck, feeling like the cunt of the year. "Maybe you should go take a shower? I'll let you know when Morgan is home."

"Thank you, Rose." Halle tries to hold it together but collapses onto to the ground crying, refusing to move or unable.

I imagined princess in a lot of ways but crying? She's spoiled but I've seen her take a punch and nearly drown, afterward she just cursed me out after escaping.

"What happened, Halle?" I ask having to dead-lift her up the stairs.

She would barely even hold herself up, moving her legs enough not to trip over the steps.

"I just want Morgan..." she repeats between tears and complete silence.

"I- I understand but- you said your father might be coming? You're crying. I- I really have no idea what's going on here."

"Please, make the tea. I'll attend to Lady Gregor." the other woman relieves me of my duty. "I'm not sure we can talk about it just yet. First, we need protection from Lord Gregor."

"Protection...? I get to beat up your dad!?" I giggle trying to break the tension.

"My dad is very strong Rose... I need Morgan. He's supposed to have been some child soldier. I think Morgan's even stronger than my dad." Halle rolls her eyes, "If I couldn't beat him, you wouldn't stand a chance."

"Wait, you fought your dad? He did this to you?" I felt something deep inside me, an anger that didn't seem to belong to me. "Colin hit you!?"

Halle nodded as tears filled her eyes, "My father... he's a monster."

She didn't deserve that. Colin barely cared for his own child and Morgan still believed he could negotiate peace with him? Seeing Halle I knew things could only get worse before they got better.

I hate to say it... but Halle is stronger than me. I guess being the direct daughter of a Patriarch and High Priestess will do that. The daughter of The Water and The Fire Guardian, if Colin left her like this... Maybe I won't be beating Colin up. I could at least enjoy watching Morgan rip him to shreds after he caught word.

"Um, do you smoke by any chance? I'm really not in the mood for tea and I really need to calm my nerves." I was running out of ideas of how to comfort her but definitely knew what would relieve my stress. The night kept compiling. "I have a bowl packed and a blunt rolled for when Morgan got back, but I guess we can share."

Halle hesitated, "Where did you get it from? Morgan doesn't like people going through his things! We're going to talk about this once he gets here."

"Who do you think hooked me up with the good, good? He gave me an ounce to keep me out his stash. It'll make you feel better. There's little we can do until Morgan comes back but relax, breathe, and figure out how to tell him what happened with you. And... who are you?"

Her friend looked at me with cat eyes, they dilated wide then constricted to slim lines as she studied my face before speaking. God, please keep me still. What else was I bound to see tonight? A walking succubus, I thought these were only in movies. But if we're the future Guardians I suspect more horrors wait.

"Uh... why are you staring at me like that?"

"This is my childhood friend, Ananda. She was- well, more of the same happened to her that happened to me. Even worse so I imagine. She's a good woman, the most delightful and innocent thing... until my father got his hands on her. My father must pay for all he's done, all he's planning to do." Halle hugs her friend who has barely spoken since arriving.

I can't believe these are the words of Halle Gregor.

I raise my fist in the air. "Now, let's move this to Morgan's room. So, you can shower and we can relieve some stress. And watch his big screen TV he didn't bother turning on. We can make it our fort until he gets back."

I barely caught him before he left. He was just about to 'blink' as he calls it when I walked back in to get more bud. I felt like he had more than enough for me to experiment. I had never seen so much before in one place, it seemed impossible not to see how high I could possibly get tonight before turning in for the night. He would survive, and it was marijuana of all things. He must be growing it somewhere. Let me find out there's another room in that basement of his housing the holy treasure trove of Mary Jane.

"Lock all the doors and windows. Please do not answer the door for anyone else. Turn off all the lights. I can light a candle in his room. I won't feel safe until comes home. Make sure you lock the back patio door as well!"

I swallowed fearful of any possibility Colin would actually show up directly at Morgan's house. What did Halle believe was coming? Regardless, I rushed out to lock all the doors and close the blinds on the first floor. Shutting off the lights before sneaking into the kitchen to get some snacks. I set the security alarm and made my way to Fort Sameera where Ananda and Halle were showering together. I decided to join them in the shower rather than smoking alone.

We washed each other squeaky clean. Admiring each other's bodies and differences until the shower felt suffocating. Afterward, we enjoyed ice cream, pie, and a passed around a few blunts while watching "Pitch Perfect" and "Bridesmaids" before falling asleep all snuggled in his bed.

I stretched out in the middle of my sleep to find Halle up alone, watching SpongeBob and facing a blunt.

"Morgan still isn't home?"

"He's never home." Halle muttered, exhaling then extending the blunt to me, "You tapped out?"

"Never that..." I gladly accept, closing my eyes and enjoying the smoke filling my lungs before letting out the cloud.

"He tried to rape me this morning... my father. He's been molesting me my whole life. I can't believe I didn't know any better." Halle wiped her eyes, holding back her tears.

"What? I'm so sorry Halle, I had no idea!" my eye shot open as I began unbearably coughing.

"Me neither. I just wanted to be a good daughter. I wanted to make him happy. I told my dad I wanted to call off the wedding because Morgan hates me. And my father attacked me." Halle shook her head.

"I sincerely doubt Morgan hates you. He's madly in love with you. I think you're the only thing that makes him happy." I console her with the truth.

"Yeah, I guess so... I wanted someone else to know." Halle threw her head back revealing a second blunt on top of the several ones we had smoked during the movies.

She earned it after the day... after the life she must have had. I hope Morgan is on his way soon. I don't know how he'll feel about having to kill Colin Gregor sooner than he expected.

CHAPTER 31

The Dark Night of the Soul

Morgan Ellys

Obatta Sameera was supposed to be some dead rebel king. This man wasn't supposed to be my father... I almost hate to say things were easier as a Wolf. Tell you what to think, do, act, and be reprimanded otherwise. On my own I'm constantly questioning. My conviction was lost. I don't truly know what to believe anymore.

I spent the day in Nadia. I spoke to few people. A couple wanted to take pictures with me. Many in passing, thanking me. It was hard to keep a low profile when everyone knew your face. I was trying to find a new base of operations closer in the city. Trying to see what I possibly had the power to do in my limited capacity and current ability. Sparring with Halle and Rose gave me a workout but if either of those two could keep up with me I was truly below standard. I am in decent shape coming off the couch so to speak. But I was not where I was even in my early teens.

The city might be saved... but these people. Their spirits were broken. So desperate for leadership and sovereignty. But lacking any sense of will or self-determination. I spared them death and enslavement but in truth what remained after the absence of Sameera and Qatar was fear. People afraid to sleep. Afraid to fight. Afraid to speak up. Afraid to even look one another in the eyes. The city was deteriorated and barely making by. Depleted and reduced to these acres of urban waste and strife. They built these lives upon concrete. Nothing could grow. How could they eat?

The rest of these regions are presided over with goals and dreams of prosperity. Turning over into a greater technological age.

My people simply wanted to eat... to feed themselves. They wanted their men home and their families united.

I returned home with a heavy heart. I don't believe I had cried before or often in my life. Many nights with Natalie that brought me past emotional exhaustion. But to see such despair in the eyes of my own...

I opened my front door to find luggage at the doorstep. One with a giant dent in the metal like it was ran over by a truck. Name Brand and embroidered. Halle left this morning and came back ready to move in. I don't believe we said our goodbyes with the same mentality when I dropped her off at the airport this morning.

"Rose, Halle, downstairs at once!" I shout out.

I take a seat on the couch beginning to take off my shoes. I wasn't prepared for this. Ada... what you've shown me and the trip to the city. I do not have the energy to deal with these two, right now. Is there not enough going on without having to constantly worry about what they're doing right or wrong?

Physical exhaustion, I could endure. Mental exhaustion I could meditate or sleep off. But emotionally... I wasn't aware I had emotions let alone being pushed to such a limit.

I take a deep breath trying to find my center. As I had the entire walk fighting bouts of anger, sadness, and utter helplessness. But ever more proud to have spared Qatar's life. In the least these people's lives were in my hands, not their blood. There was still a situation worth saving and preserving. I suppose I am blessed for this.

"Baby!" Halle came downstairs first smelling like a Reggae Festival. "What's up!"

"You smoked my weed?" I rubbed my temples, "how did you even-

She grins wide then kisses me deeply, "I missed you, baby. Rose said I needed to chill out after today, so we cracked into your stash." Halle sat in my lap laying across me.

"Rose...? You and Rose, together?" I chortle, "I'm missing something here."

"I never knew you were a stoner! Holy crap, Morgan. You have a forest in your closet." Rose grins seating on the arm of the couch, "Damn, Morgan with the purple candy kush stash!"

"He grows it!" Halle says proudly.

"WHERE!?" Rose exclaims. "You're so full of surprises."

"My baby's amazing." Halle kisses my cheek sloppily. "I love you. I'm so glad you're finally home."

"When did you two become friends?" I chuckle taken off guard. Always happy to see these two aligned rather than at odds. In truth, despite my feelings they would make good friends.

Rose looked at Halle and quieted down.

"Hello, Lord Ellys." A third woman approached, skinnier even than Halle with cat-like eyes.

Her eyes... I've read of them before.

"Who is this?" I met a tribe in Esha all with the same eyes, the crescent awakening. Only monks had such the honor. "How did you awaken your eyes?"

"This is my best friend, Ananda. I needed to get her out of her living situation. I was hoping we could stay with you for awhile."

"Halle, you left and now you come back with a friend? How long was I out?" I rubbed my temples.

"Baby, we need to talk." Halle sloppily kisses my cheek, "Like, ahora... right Rose?"

"Yep... but maybe not now." Rose watched us.

I let out a sigh rubbing my temples. "Halle, it's been a very long day. Can we wait to discuss this?"

Halle looked at Ananda then back to me, "Baby... I lived a bad life. And- and- I thought it was fine. But... I was just naive. I didn't want to see. As if I was living in a bubble. And whenever someone tried to pull me out. I fought them or ran to my father. But, you can see through me and it hurts. You'll be angry if I told you."

I stared at Halle in shock. All I've been trying to get her to see for years.

What the fuck is wrong?

"Tell me what Halle?" I asked calmly cutting my eyes prepared for the worst.

"My father..."

Rose sat up, "Come on Ananda. We should let them talk."

"Stay." I command, "Everyone sit. Tell me what Halle, what about Colin?"

"My father... he wanted me to be a dutiful daughter. Obedient, docile. And- he wanted me to be his sex slave."

"I'm going to kill him." I say flatly. The only emotion that mattered was before me. Blind rage, "It's settled Rose, tell Baat I apologize."

"Ananda and I cannot go back to Naka."

"That's fine." I pat her leg. "I need to be alone. Unpack your bags there is a spare room where your friend can sleep." I say automated as I got out of my seat.

There was no meditation for this. There was no answer. No justification. There could only be action from this point forward.

"Morgan..." Rose grabbed my arm.

"Please, don't touch me... It wouldn't be safe. I'll be outside for a moment. Stay here. I rather you not see this girls. Find something to eat." I peeled her hand off of me.

Rose looked at Halle, "Halle, you should go upstairs and get the room ready for him."

"Baby, thank you." Halle calls after me as I leave them all crossing straight through the kitchen wall. "Morgan?" Their gratitude ceased giving way to worry and fear.

I ignore the door, fazing through it. My eyes burned a crimson red. The world faded away before me as the it becomes blurs of energy and time passing before me.

I let out a primal scream. Jumping to attack the nearest tree. Punching and driving my fist through its trunk. I snatched off what I could, going back in with another guttural utterance as I tear the oak tree from its roots throwing it into the lake. The tree crashed against the surface of the water creating waves. I pounced atop it from a thirty foot distance fueled completely by rage. Diving underwater with the fifty foot tree. Driving it deeper and deeper toward the bottom of the lake with each punch, kick, and force blast. I grabbed it by its base, swinging it wildly. At the bottom of the lake.

I will kill him.

I will kill him.

I WILL KILL HIM!

I am going to fucking destroy him!

All the pain. All the suffering. All the deaths...

Now Halle?

MY HALLE!?

MY HALLE!?

HE'S ALREADY DEAD!

I'LL KILL HIM!

"MORGAN! MORGAN CALM DOWN!" Halle calls out. Her voice cut straight through the water into my ear as if even the water was no separation. There was only ether and eternity. Of rage anger and the precipice of revenge.

My ears were so sensitive, even at the bottom of the lake it was clear.

I didn't have enough room to let myself go wild... There were houses around. Power wires and people. I was no Colin... I can't let my anger just consume me. Not here at least. As much as I wanted to I would tear down the whole city if I allowed myself to get out of hand.

I swim back to the surface. I fall over onto my knees, coughing and hacking up water.

"Baby!" Halle runs to me, Rose not far behind. "Baby, I-

I hold out my hand. "Stop... It's still not safe." I gripped the grass beneath me and it turned dead to my touch. "Please, back up... I was only like this once before. I need you all to go inside and get the hell away from me. As I asked! Learn how to fucking listen!" I punch the ground leaving a crater listlessly.

But of course they didn't listen. Too high or too wrapped in their emotions. They stayed.

"Morgan... we're not afraid of you." Rose says first, "but... don't touch me, because that was highkey fucking scary."

"There's a man speaking to me... " I growl. "In my head and I don't know the voice."

"Morgan, it has to be Ada. Listen to him!" Rose pleads.

'Breathe, young warrior. Peace is still an option.'

"Colin has to die!" I roar, "He has to die!"

Must you consume yourself to kill him? Colin is not our enemy... he harnesses our enemy. He wants you angry to continue your rage against flesh and carnality. You are more than this. He will allow you to consume yourself then absorb you when the time presents itself.

"What the hell are you talking about?" my stomach churns and my head burns. My forehead felt like it was in hyperdrive.

Look around you... You must learn to love. Your enemy has taught you hate. Baat wishes to teach you love. Listen to her.

"Morgan, just come inside we can smoke. We can talk and I have a lot I want to show you." Rose says reaching for me but flinching.

She was scared of me...

My lips jerked staring at Rose with Crimson colored eyes. She had two energies moving inside her. One orange another a deep royal purple, the divine rested inside this girl. Baat...? I have been so blind.

'Listen to her. You can see with your own eyes. You are amongst the divine. You are amongst your own, Young Ada. You must learn from them if you wish to win this battle. It is not one that can be fought. I have tried many times.'

I closed my eyes. My energy leaving me as I fell into a fit of tears. Falling over myself in anger, frustration. A war that I cannot fight... What type of war was this? Colin was man as I... Colin was Guardian as I.

And if you fight him, Young Ada. You will both die. This world needs you alive and well, more than it needs Colin dead.

"You lie... Colin's death will bring about peace."

"Morgan, who are you talking to? Who are you screaming at? Please speak to us." Halle clutches her chest.

'You're scaring them... is this what you want?'

They should be fearful! This world is reaching its end! Our enemies move against us! They plan our death and our demise. Men like Colin cannot be allowed to live! I will find them. I will purge this world of evil!

'Then what does that make you? You kill another to become righteous? You will use all the tools of your enemy to defeat your enemy? It simply makes the cycle endless. You will burn in hell as all the rest. You will condemn your soul to a fate worst than the death you coware before, out of what? Hatred, Ignorance? Is this not what you hope to fight? There is nothing to be gained in Colin's death. Not yet. Listen to those who love you.'

The voice in my head screamed at me. Commanding my ease. My energy faded, I fell to the ground barely able to hold myself up. I had only felt such exhaustion in Nadia.

"Ada...?" I ask.

'We stand together, Morgan. This is our war together! We may need to fight... but at this moment. Patience. This is what we stand for, my brother. Patience, Compassion, and Empathy. This is what you emit to these women. This is what they each see in you but you fail to see in yourself. You have been chosen by the father to do my work... to fulfill where I have failed so many times.'

"If I do not put an end to Colin..."

'Colin is a shell. A husk being used by Enshishi. He is nothing more than a puppet. Enshishi cannot be killed, nor can I. This is folly. But Enshishi's heir sits next to you. When she breeds he will take her child's body. Or if you fall to Colin in battle, he will take yours. This is what Enshishi wants. This is what he has guided you for. He hopes to bring you to this end. To consume you in your fear, anger, and blindness. You will allow this to happen? Your love sits next to you. Baat's heir sits next you. You have the future of this world in your bedroom. You will sacrifice living by example for the sake of past transgressions and rage?'

"I... I understand." My heart strained in reluctance, "Let us go inside..."

I stood up, wiping away my tears. And letting out sigh.

"Morgan Ellys, ladies and gentlemen." Rose claps, "That was fucking terrifying and he's over it like it never happened. I need a drink... I need a blunt... I need a nap. This shit is getting crazy." She stands and is the first to walk inside.

"Come, Lord Ellys, let me help you up." Ananda gets under me. The first to touch me. She avoids my arms, lifting me by my chest. "Is there anything I can cook for you?"

"I need a moment, my lady. Please wait.Let me rest." I hadn't yet caught my breath.

"Morgan... was that for me?" Halle asked.

"It was for the world, Halle... it was for all that I allowed to happen while I wallowed in self-pity and regret." What was I saying? "Yes, most of it was for you."

"I love you, Morgan. You are the greatest thing to happen to me." she covers her mouth.

I let out a chuckle. I fell from exhaustion laying on my back staring up at the sky.

Halle laid with me. Resting her head on my chest.

"I will lay with you until you are ready to go, my love." she was so warm. Her energy cool, quite similar to Rose's but with the deep eternal flame.

"Thank you, Halle."

"I love you, Morgan."

"I love you too,Halle."

Ananda stands, "I think I will leave you two alone and prepare something to eat. Will we be staying outside?"

"It's a beautiful night... we can enjoy the backyard tonight. A bit of music, some smoking and drinking. Grill something nice. We'll enjoy ourselves in the face of evil. This is the will of Rakil."

"Rakil Bless you, Morgan." Ananda curtsies then goes inside after Rose.

Yes, he has hasn't he? A house full of beautiful young women. The blessings of the divine. A wonderful house. And a purpose in my life... In truth I can be happy. Perhaps... perhaps I was all that was stopping myself. Is it true, I am my greatest limitation?

Unable to see the beauty of the Father Rakil in my inner and personal turmoil. This cannot stop us no. In the face of turmoil, in hardship, in struggle, we must smile. We must be happy, be loving, and be thankful for all we do have. This is the will of Rakil. This is how we in truth defeat Enshishi. This is how we contain the might of Enshishi to Tartarus and brimstone.

Who speaks...? Who thinks...? Ada...? Morgan...? It does not matter. For this moment forward, we are one. Do we realize who we are? If not, who we choose to be? We are the child of Rakil, born in his image, born in the grace of Baat, born in the strength of Anki, born in the tenacity of Enshishi, the wisdom of Anka, and the undying love and compassion of Ada. This is who we must choose to be if we ever hope to win this eternal, unholy war of evil.

I was no longer alone in this world. I may not have a family but these women sought my protection from the evils of this world. I was their King and they my Queens.

"Morgan, when you see the stars... what do you see?"

"The expansiveness of Rakil's might and his love... this is such a beautiful night."

Halle smiles, "It is."

Halle clung to me, kissing my cheek. Pointing out the different constellations her wet nurse taught her. Usually I would condemn her for such privilege but in retrospect we all had our own pains and worries. Who was I to continue judging her?

Rose returned not long later with a bottle of wine and an amount of weed we would need to discuss. Those took months to cultivate and harvest.

'Baat never quite had a mind for maintenance and sustainability.'

"The party has returned!" Rose cheers sitting with us taking my other side. "This blunt is for you el capitan. Fat enough to take away seven years of stress and bad girlfriends."

"Excuse me?" Halle pouts.

Rose laughs, "A toast!" she raises the bottle popping the cork. She takes the first swig of the bottle then passes it to Halle. "To Team Morgan."

Halle smiles, "Team Morgan!" she takes a large gulp, showing off the many years of partying before handing me the bottle.

"Team Ada, to the future of Nadia and peace across Gaia." I drink, the wine dribbles down my chin. Wine had never tasted sweeter.

Ananda comes out with sandwiches, "there wasn't much in your fridge."

"He doesn't eat..." Rose rolls her eyes.

"Oh no,no,no, that needs to change immediately." Ananda sets the tray down, "Turkey was all you had. Eat, Lord Ellys!" she nudges one toward me.

"Drink." I trade her the bottle, we toast. I bite the sandwich and she drinks the wine before coughing. "Ha, not your cup of tea?"

"No, but she was toking on the blunt like there was no tomorrow." Rose laughs.

"Shush..." Ananda blushes, "But when are we lighting those...?" she inquires.

"Lighter?" Rose asks, plucking one of the many in her mouth.

Those wraps cost me a hefty sum...

Halle snaps her fingers creating a spark, "I've been practicing, Morgan."

Rose roll her eyes, "So, have I." with a wave of her finger the wine danced out of the bottle hovering in the air before me, "Take a drink, my love."

I waited for Halle's outburst but she smiled, holding up one of the cigarillos and lighting it with just a snap of her hands. She extends it to my lips.

"Welcome home, girls." I give them a wink, opening my mouth for the wine to pour in. I take my blunt and stand walking to the edge of the lake. "For so long... I wondered what this felt like. Joy. Home. Love. I'm thankful for you women, gratitude."

"We're thankful for you, Lord Ellys." Ananda took a long drag, she looked like she needed it more than anyone.

The horrors this woman must have seen to open those eyes. They came with a sacrifice, or a great investment. I'll inquire at a better time.

It was a night filled with jokes and laughter. As our small family bonded together. No more strife, or tension. No more fighting or anger. Just love... Compassion, Patience, and Empathy.

This was how I commemorated my awakening. For so long believing myself dead. The living were far from done with me. These women wouldn't let me die.

"Finally, a night Morgan didn't hide away in his basement!" Rose does one final cheer.

"Oh... you got jokes now?" I shouldn't have been surprised.

"No, homie, I have truth." she rebuttals.

"We still have training in the morning." I confirm.

"Noooo... stop playing Morgan. My body hurts." Rose yawns, "I'm tired too, baby. None of that. Stooop!"

"You're showing progress. We can't stop now. With Halle here we have to prepare for Colin's arrival, if he's to come."

"Baby, my father is terrified of you. He isn't coming here." Halle had a wicked smile on her face, "When I mentioned your name he nearly crumbled."

"The devil should fear Ada." Rose chimes.

Halle only smirked, "He is pretty shitty."

"The devil, we speak of Lord Gregor?" Ananda asks, "Fitting... that man deserves all he gets."

"Did he hurt you as well, Ananda?"

Ananda frowned reaching for the blunt, "He robbed me of my maidenhood. He threatened to kill me. I just happy to be with you in this eden, Morgan."

"We are happy to have you, Ananda. You are free to stay as long as you wish."

"Wait... but where are they going to sleep?" Rose asks.

"I plan on sleeping with Halle." Ananda says

"I plan on sleeping with Morgan." Halle comments.

"I am not getting left out the harem..." Rose mutters, "I actually live here."

"I- I'm not quite sure what to say." I bow my head, taking a long draw and leaning my head back. "You ladies can have the bed, I might just stay under the stars tonight."

"I plan on sleeping with you." Halle repeats clapping her hands. "Let's make s'mores!"

"I plan on sleeping with Halle." Ananda took a polite toke, then a much longer one when eyes were averted.

"I- Do you have a tent or something? There are bugs out here..." Rose mutters, "Maybe I'll take a pass on the harem tonight. I'll get with you guys, next time. I have a bed."

"On second thought... a bed does sound rather nice. Perhaps I will leave you two outside as well." Ananda bows her head, poking her fingers together, "I mean... If that is allowed, Lord Ellys?"

I nod, "That's fine. We built a bathroom in the guestroom as well. You should like the arrangement."

She looked to Halle."He is nothing like your father."

Halle smiles with pride. "I have such a good eye..." She pinches my cheek and I jerk away. "Come on, let me pinch your cheeks!" she falls over me laughing, tickling me and mounting me. She begins kissing me intensely as if she forgot or didn't care about Rose or Ananda. "I'm always, so horny after I smoke... let's consummate our marriage, tonight." Halle bites my ear.

"Halle... we aren't married yet. Nadia- Still- Nadia needs me." I say between our kisses.

"Sometimes the best deal is no deal." Rose urges crawling toward me. She seemed to take some pleasure in seeing me and Halle. "You cannot have him to yourself, Halle."

Halle raises a brow and scoffs, “I took on the Patriarch of the Gregor family and escaped alive today. I deserve some alone time with my man. Regardless of the agreement.”

“I kick your ass in training all the time, Halle...” Rose smiles proudly.

“That’s because you’re mean, hateful and jealous.” Halle grinds her hips on top of mine, “Let’s go upstairs, Morgan. It’s getting cold and I don’t want bugs crawling on me anymore.”

“Great, I’m ready to smoke more!” Rose cheers.

“Jah’Anki, Rose haven’t you smoked enough?” I chuckle as Halle helps me to my feet.

“What? What? But... there’s so much! Tonight’s a celebration or whatever, right? Lets party! Put on some music, on the sound system you never listen to. Drink some wine.. Some more smoking. Maybe a little bit of sex and sucking?”

Ananda covers her mouth, laughing politely, “You are quite the lucky man.”

I laugh shaking my head, “Today has been a long day, maybe we should sleep?”

“What!? What? Morgan wants to sleep and eat? And he smokes weed? What is this world coming to? We truly are seeing a new tide in humanity. This is incredible.” Rose laughs, “I’m all for it.”

“Because you know I will pleasure him better.” Halle grins, “You can sleep in your bed tonight. I’m going to attend to the King.”

“No fair, you have back up.” Rose looks over to Ananda, “I am not being left out of this. I’ve waited far too long.”

“I think I will sit this out... I’m not quite in a mood for sex. But Morgan, you do need to eat more! I will make you more food.” Ananda claps her hands, “enjoy yourselves.” Ananda departs leaving us to return to the kitchen.

Rose and Halle stared at each other both with a slight smile, then they look at me.

“Let’s go, Mister. You’re going to enjoy yourself tonight.” Halle grabs me by the arm tugging me along.

“I’m rolling another blunt.”

"No, you are not Rose. It takes too much. It's a waste. I have a bong you can use." I let out a sigh.

"Stoner of the year... The secret life of Jah'Ada, a harem of beautiful woman and a weed stash."

"I did not ask for this." I hold up my hands.

"You definitely worked hard for the weed stash, though." Rose remarks.

"Oh, shut up Morgan. You love the attention." Halle rolls her eyes.

"I do not!" I say defensively being tugged along by these two beautiful creatures.

CHAPTER 32

CHAPTER 33

Divine Intervention

Morgan Ellys

When did my house turn into a harem? Being led up the steps behind Halle's slender waist and round hips, joined on my side with Rose's kisses and nuzzling, a handful of the butt i've admired for a couple weeks week. Half a month ago these girls were enemies, now they walked about as family. Rubbing my chest and and singing my praises. It felt genuine. It felt good.

All the walking back and forth, and my breakdown has left my body worn. It mattered little as Halle and Rose laid me on my back and took to removing my clothes.

Halle laid by my side, taking Rose's place kissing me and holding my cheek as Rose straddled my waist, rubbing my chest and shoulders. Halle excused herself, taking to lighting candles. Rose pulled off her shirt. Her breasts weren't heaving, but supple mouthfuls so I took to them as such. Sitting up as she held her breasts for me, moaning in my ear. Rose wrapped her arms around my neck, brushing her naturally curly hair out of her face. I bit into her neck she let out a light scream digging her nails into my back.

Halle sat on the edge of the bed, putting on a show as she stripped out of her clothing, tossing it all aside. She laid on her back on the edge of the bed, running her hands down her slim frame and stopping at her sweetness, rubbing in circles, you could hear how she stirred. Her body shivered, rising and falling as she watched us.

"Hungry, baby? Go eat." Rose bites my ear she lets me go, standing and crossing to where she had a little set up for rolling.

I move between Halle's leg, setting on my knees before her and pulling her hips off the bed in a single jerk. She bites her lip, as our eyes make contact, holding our gaze as my tongue swirls inside her. Suckling her clit, and slurping on her juices as they swell in her peach. Halle's moans turn into a fit of screams, her back arches and falls as she grips the bed sheets. My tongue moving faster with her spasms, until I left shivers running through her body. She finally fell on the bed, heaving and looking at the ceiling.

She parted her wet lips with two fingers, wagging me closer. "Come on baby, we don't need to worry about my father anymore. You'll handle it all."

I smiled, and kissed her forehead but shook my head.

Halle rolled her eyes, rushing me back on the bed, pushing me to sit. I sat against the headboard. The Heiress of Naka rested her head on my lap. She made it look angelic. She moaned as she ran her tongue up and down my long shaft, then popping my head out her mouth. Saliva dripped from her tongue. She took her time not bothering to rush... It was her cock why would she rush?

Rose returned biting her index finger as she looked on. She sat alongside me, sticking the cigarillo in my mouth and lighting it for me.

Her nipples hardened in the cold air of the night. She looked so perfectly slender, beautiful, with golden skin. But what lied behind all that? If anything of substance lied beneath it I didn't know anymore. I put a hand on Halle's waist pulling her closer suckling her breast.

My hand moved down her waist, cupping her butt. My dick hardened and she quieted down shying away from my size. Halle bit her lip looking away from me. I rubbed her nipple between my freehand and penetrated her with my fingers. She let out a soft moan and clung to me.

"I want you inside me... even if it's my asshole." She says muffled in my chest as she reaches for my manhood. "Why do you hate me? Why do I still love you...?"

"Why do you think I hate you, baby?" I ask as her legs spread for me, allowing me fully between her legs. There was nothing quite like a woman truly spreading her legs for me. The intimacy, she was inviting me to enter her very body and soul, to share nirvana with her for those moments.

"Because, you're always disappointed... you're always mad at me." Halle whines, her legs tighten up refusing me entry to heaven. "You don't seem to like anything about me."

"Then for God's sake do something about it! Improve. Read more. Meditate. Earn something with your human existence. You're a powerful young woman and instead you rather do the average and bare minimum. You're a woman now, Halle. You're a Queen now. If you want the world to receive you, you must concern yourself with more than your looks and name. There is more to respect than politeness."

We stared in each other's eyes. I saw my future in her beautiful brown eyes. She's the first woman to look at me with genuine love, to care for me or let me be free. I wasn't her possession or her obsession. She didn't need to say she loved me. I look into her eyes. They told me everything I could ever hope to hear in pure silence. I love her too. I would have never left Natalie if Halle didn't already have my heart. I was frozen as her innocent gaze broke contact looking at Rose then back to me.

Halle bit her lip reaching for my manhood, her eyes rolling to back of her head as she rubbed my mushroom tip inside her sweet wetness. "Why do you make me so horny?" she shudders as my head slips inside her. "Even now... I just want to be close with you. Even when you're angry with me I want you."

I eased deeper inside her tempting fate until we both knew we needed to stop due to her family's laws.

"If your dick wasn't so big, we could probably get away with it. You're going to split my little pussy in half" Halle tensed up around me, squeezing me deeper inside her. She relaxed letting me out of her once she’s had all she could handle. “I want you so bad, Morgan, you and no one else inside me… why can’t you just love me?”

“Halle, I love you more than I like sight. I love you with all my heart but… I cannot be the son-in-law of Colin Gregor.”

“Then just be the husband of Halle Victoriana.” She wagged me forward.

I felt incensed, I left her legs on my shoulders, entering deeply inside a tightness I was familiar with but gave so easily to me.

“Ada…” I moaned as my length pushed deep, south of her chastity taking the back road. I grab her waist, holding her down and kissing her forehead as I took the backstreet.

“I love you, Morgan. Don’t you know how dearly I love you?” Halle reached for my face as her eyes closed enjoying the familiar pace.

I grabbed her slim waist as I slammed into her butt. Halle groaned beginning to push me away taking all she could handle. My dick was still hard as a rock. My eyes drifted over to Rose, her eyes locked on me and my length as she waited patiently.

Rose sat on my mind… as I moved inside the most beautiful woman on Gaia. Was my heart so faithless? Or… did my heart simply not live here in my chest? Was I lost to nothing more than my violent instincts and lustful passion after all these years of war, death, and pain… seeking any joy and pleasure in this cruel world.

"It's my turn." Rose nudged.

Halle looked up, stroking me, "Take your clothes, off we want to see your ass." She grins ear to ear, sinisterly.

Rose made quick work of her sweatpants and panties tossing them aside. She didn't share Halle's pace. Moving quickly out of fear one of us would change our minds.

My length disappeared down Rose's throat, she greedily gags and moans, her drool dripping down my balls. I moaned fiercely. She came up a brief moment for air. Wiping off her mouth then returning to work. She stroked me furiously, my seed drips in her mouth, saliva dribbling down her cheeks.

"Not fair... you're using aquakinesis!" Halle exclaims.

Rose rolled her eyes, sucking my head like a straw. She pulled Halle closer and they kissed, sharing it between them as they both licked along my length.

"Holy..." I exhaust, watching them fondle and enjoy the other's body. I had sworn these women would have tried ripping out each other's eyes not long ago. Now, they were acting as lovers. I pulled Rose's hips back. She kissed and bit Halle's lips. Their wetness rubbed along each other as I slide my length between them.

Halle screamed, Rose cursed. I put out the blunt, wanting both my hands gripping Rose's god given assets. My dick swelled between them as their saliva kept me lubricated, stroking against both their tongues.

I lifted Halle with one arm, pushing Rose on her back before dropping Halle on top. As both began to protest as I eased between their vulvas.

"Morgan that feels incredible, you're a fucking genius." Rose shudders in moans. Halle moves her hips back against mine. Rose's coolness and Halle's warmth swarmed my dick. "Baby, can have sex please." she exhales.

"How, about we just enjoy the foreplay?" I suggest with a chuckle letting them both up, slapping Rose's ass as she rolled on her stomach.

Rose hums, her body arches down shaking her fine assets in the air rhythmically for my enjoyment. She pokes her butt in the air. I moved between her cheeks, burying my head in. Sloppily sucking and lapping at her pussy tasting our pineapples and strawberries. Halle's hands reached up, pulling Rose's butt apart for me. Her nails dug deep in her flesh making Rose scream out.

It was too much for me to resist. Even I was only a man. I needed to put my dick inside one of them...

Rose was bouncing on my face. Seeing how she moved so easily on my tongue, I lusted to find out how it would be on my dick. Halle would flip shit. I could not suffer now to wait until marriage. I was lost. I feel as if an average man would have tried fucking both aimlessly and have spilled his nut by now exhausted. I wanted more of both these women.

Perhaps now just wasn't the time.
"I need you to suck my dick like that again, Rose. I'm going to bust."
"You can cum inside me, baby. You like this ass don't you? You can hit it from the back." Rose offered.
"Morgan is mine." Halle sat up.

"Halle, he's hard as a rock. Are you going to deal with his blue balls?" Rose rolled her eyes.
"Let's just smoke first." I chuckle sitting back on the bed.
They eyed each other. They mouthed something I didn't quite understand then both left me on the bed alone.
I shrugged it off. My dick felt incredible, soaked in their juices swollen and relieved. I lay down and relit the blunt, closing my eyes and taking a few long draws.
Music began playing. I poked open an eye as 'Oui' by Jeremiah played.

Halle' sat watching helplessly as if she wasn't present with us anymore. She stared out blankly as if asleep with her eyes wide open.
"In Rakil's name... what have you done to her, Rose?" I forced myself to ask.
"I have reasoned with her to some extent but she was unwilling to comply." Rose looks up innocently, "She will return as herself in a short time. I promise. She'll believe it was all a dream and your happy marriage can continue. You have used the same trick in your lesser form. You taught me, well, Ada."
"No... no, you didn't use it on Halle." I wrestled free from her soft words and grasp.
"She is the daughter of the devil, still you defend her?" Rose rolls her eyes.
"She cannot help who she was born to Rose. Return her at once!" I demand.
"After... if I awake her now then you will not like the consequences." Rose insisted.
"If she agreed then what is your fear?" I ask.
"I wish to be alone with you. My mortal form can spend time with you,

my spiritual form cannot. This is how we must be together, my love. Will you refuse me again?" Rose petitions.

"I must... this is immoral. If you wish to have my child this was not the way. I cannot forgive such an atrocity. The only other one I know who uses her Guardian abilities against others is Carmen."

"I didn't do it to accept you. I did win the little game we played but... I wanted you to myself for a moment. Morgan, please don't be mad at me. I didn't charm her, she's just...hypnotized."

"You will earn my forgiveness in helping me raise Nadia as I have said. This is not how I want this Rose. I wish to bear children with my wife not a stranger or spy."

"You may take *wives*, Ada. We both wish to be with you." Rose tries to convince me.

"Then discuss it with Halle with her right mind. Without you influencing her thoughts or hypnotizing anyone." I relent unwilling to repeat my same mistakes twice.

"May I finish?" Rose rolled her eyes stroking my length before her face.

"Continue..." I permit.

My will was only but so strong with my dick between a pair of wet lips.

Rose smiles, "You truly are a good man... I shouldn't have been so hasty to have my way. Ada, I have failed you again... patience is not my strong suit."

Rose's head returned to expertly bobbing along my cock. A load of her saliva ran down her cheeks. She opened her mouth letting it drip down my length then trapped my dick tightly with her tongue or dispelled with her energy.

"I apologize, Ada. I love you, true."

"Many women have said they love me as well. Only if it's what they meant, instead of the true."

Rose frowned. "You know time is of the essence... Do not abandon our union chasing after your virtue and duty. It has gotten you killed before. A thousand years we have been without you and Enshishi conquered it. We cannot go another one thousand with you or your child as Enshishi."

There is no avoiding it. If I have learned anything it's that we don't have time to wait. Have to get it right the first time. If I am going to love these women, I must wed both... a union of Nadia and Naka would be far better than war. All sides can be at peace, and we could truly and honestly bring along a new tide. The three of us can lead the new age. If only we can convince Halle.

Hmm... It makes me wonder, how long has Baat been controlling Rose or Enshishi controlling Halle for that matter. I need to be weary. I'm not playing this game at the same level anymore.

I squeezed Rose's butt, kissing her deeply, our tongues danced with one another before she released for a moment. Rose kissed my neck. Rose kissed my chest. She kissed down my stomach. Her mouth wrapped around the head of my manhood her butt boldly in the air driving me wild. Her mouth was so warm and wet as if she was using her aqua kinesis. She moaned and slurped, holding onto my butt to keep me down her throat. She moved her head slowly allowing me to plow her throat.

She stared up to me, stroking me faster, "Are you going to cum for me, baby?"

"If you think head is going to sate my hunger then you have greatly underestimated my appetite for lust." I chuckled shaking my head.

Rose was quiet for a moment, taking me back into her mouth as she thought of her response. Rose took me out for a brief moment to readjust her position, allowing me to sit on the bed as she got on her knees. I leaned my head back. The long day began to melt away as Rose's head bobbed up and down. My dick swelled in Rose's mouth as she tried to ease more of me down her throat.

"Damn, baby... your dick is ridiculous. So, this is what Ada is packing?" Rose rubbed her jaw, coming up for air.

"I said the same." Halle raised her hand before it fell back down in exhaustion.

"You probably tear her apart." Rose bit her lips looking at me, "she's so small... you probably get so deep inside her, you just can't help but explode inside her." she stroked me, pushing her chest together.

"What the fuck, Rose...?" I moaned listening to her talk dirty.

She only smiled, using both her hands to stroke me. Her mouth wrapped around my head as she made love to me with her mouth.

I leaned my head back, thinking of the late nights sneaking around with Halle. How good it felt being inside her tightness. She could take a beating. Halle says I was the first person who's been inside her... Rose seemed far more experienced than that.

"Come on... inside me." she shimmied out of her shorts, bending over my desk. "Hurry I can't wait anymore"

This is how it started last time. Natalie was lost to me the moment I entered Halle. Would I lose Halle in this moment of lust with Rose? I can't keep making the same mistakes.

"I'm so wet...." she played with herself and I could hear her fingers swirled inside her for me to see, "just stroke that dick for me baby, I'll take care of myself."

That I could abide by. I eased my dick on her soft butt she grinding against me. Bent over my bed, showing me all I could have if I left Halle in that instant. It could feel truly amazing...

I could no longer resist sliding myself into her, deep enough for my cock to replace her spine. Rose held onto a silent scream as her back arched, her foot kicked the desk tapping out as her body fell flat on the desk. She choked on her scream as I grabbed her hair into a ponytail jerking her head up as I slammed into her as I wanted since the moment we first met.

"I just came from you putting it in... This is fate, baby. This pussy was made for you, don't you feel it?" Rose managed as she threw her ass back against my waist meeting my full force with her on.

Her walls squeezed around me like a glove a size too small. Slowly regaining her composure, and slowly winding her hips against mine. It felt wrong all those times with Halle. I was felt guilty, the sneaking, my bond and attachment. But Rose felt... it was a home I long awaited to be in. She felt custom-made for me, every inch of her body seemed design specifically to my lusts and fantasies.

I gripped Rose's hips, giving her all my frustration, all my fears into deep, strong thrusts. She kicked and held back screams, pushing her butt against me so I could feel every inch of my new paradise. She accepted all I had to offer even after her knees buckled I continued pleasuring her with my lifelong pains.

"Call me by my name, Ada... call me by my name." I pleaded.

"Ada... " left her lips, "Yes Ada."

Her hips moved faster, finding a better angle to give back shots. She gripped the sheets to match my thrusts.

"Say it again, baby. Who's blessing you with this dick?"

"Ada!" she screamed and my consciousness left me, my body moved as if mechanical.

I was back at Nadia. The brief moment of eye contact, clarity as I emerged from the man's chest, staring the young girl into the face. I was her hero, her reprieve from her assailant and saving her mother. I'm her hero...?

"Cum for me, baby... deep. Fill me up, Ada. Let's have a baby together." Rose cries for me.

I wanted to cum badly, I felt my nut on the edge of my dick but I couldn't find the release.

I smiled, the feeling was heavenly. Beyond sexual as our souls resonated with one another. I let out a deep laugh. My hands run along her body, gripping her neck and pulling her up. Rose leaned back, gripping my neck, grinding against me as we steal kisses and hold each other for support.

My seed spilled inside her, easing inside her womb. She stops for a moment and looks at Halle then looks back at me. She smiles unable to speak. We laugh holding each other, enjoying each other's energy.

"You're a good man, baby. Don't let this sway you. You and I are meant to be. Rakil has brought us together, Morgan. I am yours, baby. Whenever you want me, I'll be good. I'll let you work things out... but I'm yours, baby. Forever and always even beyond flesh and beyond life."

"I love you too..." the words came so easily to this stranger. It wasn't a thought or hesitation. I bent Rose over as excitement consumed me. Our skins slapped against one another as Halle her hands over her own mouth in horror.

"Young Ada... I must confide some truth into your vessel. May you remove yourself?" The voice in my head beckoned as Rose lay next to me passed out and Halle refused to look in my direction.

"I need a second Halle. I'm going to use the bathroom." I try to be polite as I lift Rose's arm off of me and try sliding past Halle's body.

"Me too." She wiped her eyes.

"Are you okay?"

"I guess I got what I deserved right? First we did it to Natalie. Now, you and Rose... I need some time as well." Halle got up leaving before me.

Before I could respond the voice in my head continued, "Before my first death, Baat was... she was regrettably raped and killed due to my inaction and ignorance of Enshishi's presence. He killed my sister and brother then set out to overtake Anka. I- I refused to kill Enshishi... I'm remised to say.'

"And you wish for me to let this bastard live!? Hasn't he done the exact same thing in this generation? To Saleem? To Lady Qatar?"

"When a Guardian dies, it is resurrected or the spirit overtakes the vessel responsible. Enshishi wants you to attempt to kill him so he can seize your soul. This or for you to allow him to reincarnate within your first born. I believe this is Baat's true intention."

"YES BUT I WOULD BE RAISING HIM! NOT LETTING HIM WAGE WAR AND DESTROY LIVES! TO SUBJECT KIDS TO SLAVERY! I will be his father if I wed Halle, which you pull me from for a life of loneliness and meditation before Rose popped up. Now you suddenly trust her?"

"I attempted to pull you from nothing but your flesh and instincts! You are not an animal. You are a child of Rakil above almighty. You need your energy. I understand this is war. This is not the first age. Many people will die. It is inevitable. But combat must be in the souls, not the flesh. Do you understand me, boy?"

"I- I reluctantly do. Any war has causalities but his I join The Gregors we can avoid war entirely! Though, I question. If not Colin, then why did you tell me to kill those men a few years ago? Why are you so selective of death?"

"Eventually I had to kill Enshishi. He destroyed everything, thousands of years of my work gone in moments. He was enemy to all, brother to none. Shakes your hand then stabs you in the back. Those men were not your brothers. They only came to destroy with no love or ambition for anything better. They were slaves... mentally and emotionally beyond repair. The only higher power they held was this man you call the devil. I needed you to be able to set them free. I expected you to view their armor, the insignias to realize they came from The West not The East. Instead, you killed yourself."

"Then why allow Colin to live? He is enemy of all, brother to no one, no?"

"He believes he has you. The spirit of the man is evil. I am unsure if Colin himself is of any true danger. He has become Enshishi's puppet."

"He raped Halle, his own daughter! The only reason I haven't put on my Trench Coat and grabbed my Fangs is because you tell me to resist... What about morality to your woman? What about defending our people? When do we quell all patience and take action, Ada?

"We are Ada. And since this is your body, I am Ada. If these God-Kings and Satanists continue manipulating the people of this realm, we will not commit war. You will kill them. And when you are done, perhaps I will leave this realm and allow Ether Guardian to unite with your soul. This war demands regret. I understand that now, it took a thousand years of observing to understand. The only thing separating you and Colin is remorse for your actions. I regret to tell you, killing him is not something you may regret but without the proper vessel, we face worst. If he dies naturally, the spirit of Enshishi must return to the Spirit Realm. Look at what Baat has done to these women... at least this is sex. The things I can teach you are horrific and powerful beyond belief.

But Enshishi? He has led men to slavery, to die in wars for greed and destruction. He teaches them they have the moral high ground. But there is no moral high ground in life. Especially not leading genocides and wars! You are not Baat or Enshishi, we are the Ether itself. Besides, Colin is the father of your fiancée. I doubt a woman with her fighting spirit would forgive your deeds with your maid as well as killing her father."

"You are right..."

"Perhaps in method but our goals are different. Though, I do see why Enshishi calls to you so your power of will is incredible even without our full connection, you are likely more powerful than him the strongest force on the planet. He fears you. Colin's soul can be purified if you do marry his daughter and inherit is foreign."

"Or perhaps... Halle can inherit Enshishi? Her power is nearly insurmountable when she gets some momentum going. She seems to have fought him once."

"We only now live in an age where people no longer believe in redemption. Enshishi is like a wild forest fire. Sometimes this destruction leads to new growth... sometimes if controlled it provides light and warmth. Majority of the time, it destroys everything including in its path. Whatever remains is changed entirely by the fire."

"I'm not sure that's a fate I wish for Halle after all. Ultimately, it seems her birthright regardless. Better her than some random person. Then at least I could continue to train her and help her control her power properly."

"My father, Rakil once told me, Enshishi is born of the rage I refused to face and my regrets. If this is where your rage and control is centered...? I see value in his works but his method, the ambitions of those fulfilling them is true evil. If you are intent to raise the child, then perhaps a reasonable negotiation or arrangement can be made. It seems he has selected you for a reason beyond being my vicar. This Colin sees a kinship in you, Morgan."

"I lived this long without a father. I will be fine without Colin as one."

"A boy can only see God through his father's eyes. Without a father... there is no God. Without a God, there is no boy. This is what has enslaved humanity. Without God, man worships the fatherless child, usually a tyrannical bastard."

"My true father is dead, Ada."

"You have more than Obatta, though he was a wise and charismatic man. He is not you. You have more than Colin, though he is a warlord and wealthy man. He is not you. You have a third mentor who favors you dearly and has protected you from Enshishi. Anki would never follow me, he is our family. I am not sure Anki is still of this realm. And This Commissioner Warren, he is more than your mentor, young Ada. You once viewed him as family have you not?"

"I haven't spoken to Warren in years. He would kill me for what I have done."

"He is a man of honor and justice. I implore you to travel to Erdu and speak to him. You deserve the truth from his lips. Not delusions of your guilt, fear and ignorance."

"Do you believe he will not see justice in your works? You killed yourself because you fear what this Warren thinks of you. You fear you've disappointed him and it suppresses your power."

"I... I cannot simply speak to Warren."

"You must if you wish to see Enshishi under control. You are not strong enough as is to face Enshishi. You are too clouded without removing this blockage. You are melancholy and misanthropic in your regrets. This is not how you use my power. Once this weight is lifted I fear you may be uncontrollable. Speak with this Warren. If worst comes to worst, you know you have two enemies rather than one. I believe you can defeat Enshishi on your own but not as you are... not with this weight you are using to crush your ambition and joy."

"Thank you, Ada."

"Learn to thank Rakil, boy. I am only as my father has created."

Thank You, Rakil... thank you for everything.

CHAPTER 34

Dead ringer

Natalie Wolfe

We stopped being friends long before we stopped loving the same man. His heart was swayed by Halle Gregor. I failed to make sense which bothered me more, losing him or to who I lost him. Now, Halle Gregor needed to be roasted. He'll never forgive me, but he's already never speaking to me again.

"Heeeeellllloooo world!"

Carmen says from the couch next to me. Waving across the live crowd. The bright spotlights pointed straight at her. She loved it. She got to skip tanning today from how damn bright those lights were.

The audience erupts in applause and cheers. Screaming her name and thanking her for existing.

Carmen bowed, allowing them to feed her ego. She slurped it all until she was sated. She wore a small red strapless shirt, wrapping around her chest and cutting above her belly button. Her waist high jeans hugged her baby doll frame, giving her the appearance of hips. She wore flats but still stood 5'9.

"We have a special guest today, a great friend of mine in terrible condition. Please help us wheel out, Natalie Wolfe!"

I took a deep breath. One of the stage hands flipped the applause light on. Someone grabbed my wheelchair and began pushing me along.

The applause stopped and turned into gasps and whispers as they saw me appear in a full body cast. My face still disfigured from Halle's- I mean, Morgan's. Get it right in your head, and you won't mess it up out load.

"Damn girl, what happened!?" Carmen covered her mouth in shock, despite the hours of coaching and consulting.

"My ex happened!" I try not to sound rehearsed. "He- he broke into my apartment, angry I left him and did this to me!"

The crowd cried out their overwhelming support. One of their goddesses were attacked by a lowly peasant dressed in King's clothing.

"I can't believe this, who was he?"

"Captain Morgan Ellys... He abandoned me to be with the airhead Heiress."

"Halle Gregor is dating the same man who walked off my show, the only man to ever disrespect me by waltzing off!? This show is where people seek truth!" She was a genius all her own, not even following the script anymore. "Now, he's laid hands on one of my best friends... How did he do it?"

"He- he broke in through my balcony window. He wanted to bring me presents, but when I refused him he got so angry he threatened to throw me off the balcony. I ran inside to go to a neighbor for help, but he turned up the music so no one could hear me scream. Then tossed me around like a ragdoll. I've never felt so powerless."

"As you should against some savage Dog Captain! Could Nadia and Erdu be trying to start a war with Naka?"

I sobbed up for the cameras but no one could see my face beneath the bandages anyway. Carmen told me the tears would send ratings through the roof and put his head on a chopping block. I wanted Halle but for some reason Carmen kept pushing Morgan. I wouldn't have looked good saying Halle did this to me. And him hurting me because I've refused him would be classic. It'll ruin both of them.

“He couldn't get over me. Even with the Airhead Heiress he wanted me back. I- I'm so glad you all are here for me." I try to move my arm but only cry. The crowd cries with me. "I just hope whoever is with him is listening! Run for the hills. He's a monster."

"What about Halle in all this?" Carmen asks sharply.

"I'm not sure she knows. If she had any sense which I doubt she does in that thin skull, she would leave him. But he probably treats her same as her father, sexual, abusive and controlling!"

"Booooooo!" The crowd calls, "Booooooo!"

"He's Colin's lapdog, his personal little man servant!" I feed the crowd.

"How could you date such a beast?" The next question was not in our script, Carmen sneered across me.

"He told me if I left him, he would kill me! The last day we spoke, we tried intimacy and I ran off. He stood there knowing it was the last time we'd speak to each other. I was so relieved to be out of the relationship. Until he wouldn't even look me in the eyes for all he did to me. Hurt more than knowing he was gone. But, I guess it was unavoidable." the lies felt better than the truth, and the people ate it all up for mid-afternoon snacks.

"What will this do for the peace treaty between La Vida and The Gregor Manor?"

"Well, since Halle had nothing to do with it, I would hope the Gregors would have sense enough to break off the wedding. However, I would have to say this can cause war if they side with Morgan. He is dangerous and cannot be trusted."

I was publicizing my pain before even speaking with my father or advisors in retrospect.

"Hey, hey... No more war talks!" Carmen says sharply under her breath. Coughing and patting her chest. "Haha, surely The Patriarch and Holy Father will find some peace, right?" all smiles, all for the camera.

I don't know how she did it.

"Well... Hopefully, they'll find more than anger." She turned to me with her wide smile with smoking orange eyes. I piped down understanding why Morgan walked off. A number of the audience was directly affected, if not half, they should know but they all sat cheering as if they had lost their minds. "But... The Gregors are very attached to Morgan. They may have chosen sides already."

Carmen smiled wider, "No, it'll be fine. This is La Vida and it's always fine in La Vida!"
The crowd laughed brushing it off.
"Carmen... Truth is this will have consequences."
"Yes, truth... How did you end up with him to begin with?" She cut her eyes at me, "if he's such a monster, why date him? Unless you just have poor taste and bad, bad, bad judgment."
I swallowed, this was definitely off script. Her smile was wide but the intent was in those citrine eyes. We were on air... We weren't friends, I was a story. I have to get off stage... I'm so embarrassed. Out here not only lying but looking feeble and helpless. Being helpless...Too bad for her the story was mundane.
"We both worked for Colin. He- he wasn't a dog. Then he seemed normal a handsome guy, strong, intelligent. Anyone would have fallen in love with him..."
"Ha joined then left!? What a loser." Carmen mocks and the crowd joins in.
"He- he served since he was ten... He told me one night while we were fighting to explain why he was so violent and abusive. Makes more sense in retrospect, I was hardly listening over thinking of an exit or what to call him. He's had a rough life..."
"Defending him now? I have no way to know whether you're lying to me tsk tsk tsk tsk Nat. These people want the cold Carmen truth!"

They wanted a story to chew on until the next gossip girl lit their tongues ablaze.
"It excuses nothing he's done..." I bite my tongue, "But should show the barbarity of the Regulator Regime taking in children! They must be disbanded and the troops sent home. If we nip it in the bud with legislation then we can disband-
"Ha, Natalie those pills must be getting to you. This is not a political show. We love our troops!" Carmen salutes. "Disbanding the Regime is ludicrous. You are ludicrous. And I think you're a liar and these people will agree with me right!"

The crowd roared with support and build up.

"Morgan said the Regime were monsters..." Try speaking into my microphone unable to adjust it.

"We're going to listen to Mr. Ellys now? He's one of these ingrates in the world and he's the one who's done this and anyone with half a brain knows It's obvious he's dishonorable, a traitor, and a liar because last time I checked, kids weren't allowed in the Regime! And you dated him. It's so sad when these girls get Stockholm syndrome folks."

"I assure you, he's not a liar. I can't say much about the others things."

"Ha, if that's true think of the size and violence of such a ten year old to sneak into the army! Eeeek!" Carmen fans herself.

"I- I-I- I can't believe I let myself sink this low to dishonor him. I wanted Halle's head on a pike. Instead he'll never forgive me... Now, we'll truly never speak again and Halle is scotch free. This served no purpose. Maybe Halle put him on, she never minded sharing."

"Nor did you right?" Carmen looks right at me.

I had no response immediately. If I had my body I would be furious. Indisposed... I wish I picked another team. I could have just called him. Carmen grinned. An amulet of Enshishi hanging around her neck, she picked her team already. I thought I was aligned but not if this is what we do.

"How much did the Gregors pay you...?" I ask, hurt.

"Oh, please Colin owns a quarter of the network, you Wolves own the rest! Controlling and polluting our media. I'm happy to be one of the few honest journalists left." She flashed a smile for the camera "And we'll be back after this commercial break! Join us and we'll have the loveable, Jared Mitchell and his band, Somber Nights! Maybe if we cheer loud enough they'll perform for us!" she raises her hands, her eyes closed in ecstasy and her pussy wet her seat from the cheering like an addict getting their fix.

The crowd erupts as if i wasn't there anymore. In my wheelchair, body plastered head to toe in a shell. It's exactly how I felt as a shell of myself, so despicable and angry.

I just wanted them both to pay but only I suffered the humiliation.

I could have gone to my father to deal with Halle or to Morgan... He would have been angry with me about speaking to him but would have dealt with Halle himself. I trusted a devil's advocate, a handmaiden of Enshishi to the doom of all three of us in order to take Enshishi's throne for her own.

Carmen only smiled and laughed, sucking up the applause and cheers. She looked at me with gleaming orange eyes. She lets out a sigh, having her fix fulfilled.

"That was great. Thanks for coming, bud. You're a natural. I almost thought you would have hit me. Well, if you even could." She winks, grabbing my wheelchair and begins carting me off. "Sorry to cut you off, I couldn't have you ruining my plans for world domination. If there's going to be a war. I can't honestly let these people know about it. I could explain later. I think I'm going to keep you around Natalie. I could get an entire month of content from this story after all."

"Your plans...? You want Enshishi's throne?" I was betrayed. In the least outwitted.

"Your little boyfriend disrespected me, and now he wants to be a King? Why him? I heard about Nadia, as did Enshishi. We refuse to allow it."

"You did this to ruin him... Why?"

Carmen waves off the people around us, secluding ourselves under a poster with her face.

"If Nadia realizes it can run itself that it doesn't need Enshishi and Naka. Everything falls apart. Those citizens are liquid assets, if they keep spending, we stay rich, yaaaay. If they follow your little boyfriend they'll no longer value money. They'll no longer ignore the wars. They'll know our little game. Things change."

"They're people." I struggle to get someone's attention.

Carmen laughs, "yeah, maybe...but right now until I die, they're a paycheck feeding all of Naka. If he takes a seat of power, begins demanding things. He's the real deal. This all comes falling down and I refuse to give up what I have for that bastard. Or those fucking cretins in Nadia, you can stand with Enshishi or you're against us. Rather simple decision girl. You were a sacrificial lamb but we can repair. Halle is out she chose him and she's getting out of dodge so he can handle business. I tried to get on his team. No room. So, you're either going to join me or I suggest you move your ass to Nadia permanently."

"The Nadians live on sovereign ground, how is that even possible...?"

"It may be, maybe not." She laughs, "They don't know that... They know nothing. It's better that way. They want the life, girl! They want our lives and as long as they have that desire we can sell and tell them anything. Don't grow a conscience on me now. You're a part of this, your family created this Natalie. Come on girl, it's not that big of a deal. It's not like we're killing anyone. They do all the work themselves. Just have to keep them in check. Keep selling the dream. Take this bump for a few weeks then when Nadia no longer has a leader we can take it over together."

"I'll have to think about it."

"Oh...?" Carmen sighs pushing my wheelchair facing a corner. "You do that, and I'll make sure my people give you plenty of time and space to think this one over. I know you'll make the right decision."

"You're psychotic! Take me home!" I screamed unable to move staring directly at the dusty corner away from any and everybody.

"I'm devoted to my God!" She holds up her necklace sucking her teeth, "I thought I had a friend in you. I thought you would understand! I thought you were someone who finally understood how it felt to want this blessing as bad as I do. It's so rare he's pleased... I guess I was wrong, you're not my girl. Shame, we could have been sisters under Colin with Halle. Never want for anything. He told me himself. Enshishi spoke to me when you went on your Regime rant. If we get rid of Halle and her boyfriend, I can have her place. Play ball and we can still get in there! Wow, I really am a monster." She adjusted me so I could see the screen, "eh, you should at least enjoy the show, right? Every ounce of admiration helps me sleep at night. Attention is power, ya know? It keeps me nice and young to compete with you young broads coming up. Toodles, girl! Make the right decision... Or feel free to stay there for a few nights until the world makes more sense to you."

The vilest evil was her conviction with pure nonchalance. Carmen hummed to herself a somber night song playing in the background. I once believed my father and Colin little different as men. Until recently Morgan and Colin as no different... but they were not three men cut from the same cloth. He didn't deserve this, and I had no interest being Colin's new rape pet... I always tried to stop Halle from being one. I wanted to move in with her to keep her from her father. Our friendship was supposed to start a new generation of peace and an end to centuries of war. Why did I help Carmen?

I let her in my ear. I let Colin in my head from all the taunting. I ended up here turning against the only two who could help me. My father would never understand. I felt like a pawn in someone's game. Only a few blocks until the end of the board then I could become whatever I wanted.

"Aye, Wolfe sorry about the abusive boyfriend, lass I knew the man but never knew him like that. Rough spot, yeah?" The familiar and ever obnoxious half cockney, half Verdun tongue was over my shoulder combined with the sound crunching of chips, and the stench of weed. "Yeah, know lass once you're better we can do some healing back in the Town."

The Town was the nickname for the bustling village of Verdu, Esha where he claimed to be from as he claimed to be in his 30s.

"Jared... Help me." I demand.

"Help you? Are you in distress, lass. I thought you and Carmen were best mates. This is a queer place for you no? What's your matter?"

"This is! Get me out of here. Help me please, get me out of here!" I shake in my chair.

"Most lasses ask for a song or an autograph. The persnickety Natalie Wolfe wishes for salvation from Anka? That's crazy, ain't it?" he takes off his porkpie hat and scratches his head. "This is majorly peculiante."

"Jared... Please." I say sharply losing my patience, too prideful to beg.

"I have to get on stage before the Queen Bee asks for me, ya see, lassy?" I bet he's impressed with himself. "But it does suck seeing ya desperate. I could not make two ways off your story. You answer a question for me with the honest truth and I break you free. Did Morgan Ellys do this to you Natalie?"

"No... it was Halle Gregor."

"Yo, Jax help the lass here to our bus, she wants to kick it with the band after the show." He waves over a slim man standing by the concession with a handful of chocolate malt balls, in the other was a tuna fish sandwich.

"Whoa... A mannequin this is heavy." The skinny slack of man trails up in a deeper weed haze than Jared. As if he lived in weed smoke. I nearly suffocated as he approached. "Trippy, man ha does it talk?"

"Jared, you help me not him." I groaned. I at least knew Jared from school.

"Whoooa dude! This is awesome. I've never spoke to a mannequin. They usually just sit there, ha." The man, Jax poked my face with his sandwich, "Are you hungry mannequin, this concession food is alright I might just sit and eat here."

"Two minutes, warning two minutes." The stagehand shouts from their clipboard. He looked at all of us and frowned. "No one's supposed to be speaking to Ms. Wolfe or else you have to deal with Carmen."

Jared spots my nervousness. "We're old schoolmates, brotha. I was just telling her howdy hey, ya know? No harm in old friends passing in the breeze, naw?" He wraps an arm around the stage director beginning to lead him off, "Hey mate wouldn't mind leading me to a bottle I could loose the snake in before we get the party going? I drank a pint of Jack and Jim, need to piss like a rager."

"I'll be honored to find you one." The stagehand smiled as only a fan-boy could.

"My man!" Jared gives us a wink and takes him away.

"Two minutes man... That's... That's like two minutes." Jax rubs his arm and sighs

"Get me out of here, please! Let's leave now for the love of the actual God!"

"Alright, alright... I just don't like being high and late. People start making jokes about ya. There are so many false connotations."

"I don't care!"

"You're so mean..." Jax mutters beginning to push me along. "I'm doing this for my bromigo. Not you." He exhales, getting me out of concessions without a single eye bated.

"Thank you..." I say humbly, letting out a sigh. "I picked the wrong team. I can't believe I let it end like this."

"You play footie? Or like basketball or something? Your team did this?" He was obviously more interested in weed and food than the past half hour.

"My- my old friends did this. Both old friends but one just jumped off my list."

"Uh right on dude... I mean girl." He corrects coughing awkwardly "so, no footie? One of your friends beat you up this bad? That's not cool. My buddies would never hit me let alone put me in a body sleeve. Those aren't friends."

"Well, I wasn't much of a friend to end up here."

"Aw, migita at least you admit it."

"I am not Migita you idiot. I'm Natalie Wolfe, daughter of The Holy Father, Mordin Wolfe."

"Whooa, we hate that guy he's like ultra-evil. And Migita just means little friend."

"I just need help escaping before Carmen leaves me here to rot."

"Yeah me too, Jared said we were doing a friend a solid showing up. I think I'll just stay in the bus and to spark up another j." Jax yawns slapping his forehead, "no... He said we'll have to play. A band can't get far without a drummer to keep beat." He sighs, "eh, big effin d. We'll jam it out. One quick blaze then back to snapping the snares and tapping cymbals."

I wanted to sigh but was being rude enough. They were helping me after all, right? Be nice Natalie. Anger and revenge has pushed you far enough, Natalie.

"Alrighty migita, here you go back at the ole van."

"Don't leave me in this hippie rape van."

"Hey, hey don't insult Moon Buggie like that... This ole girl is a legend!"

He opens up the back and pushes me to the edge. "Now... How do I get you in here?"

"You don't have a ramp?"

"It's a legend... It's not Kit." Jax sighs, "man, I wish Timbre did this, he's wuge. Could just lift ya up... Uh, would it hurt if I just like... Put you in then put in your chair?"

"What!? Are you mad?"

"Maybe a bit frustrated from the conundrum and your attitude but I'm chill." Jax mutters beginning to tip my chair over.

"What, what, what, stop!"

"How do you propose we do this then princess? You wanted to get rescued right?"

"Not being thrown in some hippie stoner van!"

"Well, that's not much of an alternative suggestion... or even remotely helpful."

Jax dumps me over in the van, I laid on my face, on the plush pillows all over the floor. I took a deep breath, feeling fine. I was complaining a bit less as I hyperventilated the marijuana permanently fumigating this van. Thanks for the tacty décor Jared. My wheelchair is tossed in after me, the doors shut and Jax let's out a sigh.

"I wonder if there's anything left in here." He sits picking up a water pipe.

"Hello! I'm on the floor?"

"I didn't forget the past five seconds instantaneously, migita. I need a hit if I'm gonna keep dealing with you." Jax groans, shamelessly bubbling up and then exhaling the fumes. "Aw man, this stuff is great. Bless Anka for Mary Jane! Jared always comes through clutch."

"Can you please help me up now?"

"Yeah, sure man." He smiles helping me up to my chair. "Want a rip, miga?"

"I don't smoke."

"Kay..." He rolls his eyes taking another hit.

I feel the contact high. My instincts tell me to yell at him. But the feeling made me smile. Morgan got into smoking in the ending days, drinking as well. He was so stringent before. I thought he blamed me, but if we did this together. I probably could have tolerated how much of a tight ass he is all the time. He might have been able to tolerate how much of a cunt I can be. Halle could never do for him as I could... But I could never be with him. This will just have to fall out from here and let the pieces fall where they lie. I hope he knows I tried. Tried to love him... I watched as Carmen ruined him. I let myself be center stage. I'll have that psychopath coming after me.

"Can you not blow that in my face, you waistoid!?"

"I'm not blowing it in your face. Your face is in the atmosphere of the joy fumes."

I giggled, "Joy fumes..."

"Want a rip now? This is mother earth's love. The strain is called, 'Anka's Blessings.' it's amazing."

"I have no hands."

"Eh, I got you here. I guess I can hold this for you for point two five secs then run to play drums." He kneels before me and holds the water pipe to my face.

"Wipe it off first..."

He groans gripping the Phoenix pendant hanging from around his neck. "You're the worst man." He wipes it off with his shirt all pouts and mumbles. "Here ya go princess hopefully. This makes you normal people for the ride."

"Ha, I am normal people..."

"Yeah, yeah sure." Jax rubs his neck, "alright, migita. I'm off. We'll be back once we're done singing for the wicked witch of the west."

"Ha, that's one of my favorite movies! Oh, oh oh do you have it!?"

Jax rubs his temples and shrines his pendant with his fingers. "Rakiham, Anka... Help me with my patience and such. Like, dude, forreal. This is going to be a long day. Thanks brother and miga, much appreciated for all the clutches up til now. I know you'll pull me through. Amen."

"That was the weirdest prayer ever." I mock, giggling to myself.

"Yeah, well... When you don't worship one dick who thinks killing and enslaving is cool. Then they're less lenient on how you reach them...

And they'll actually respond to you. Instead of having your friends beat the crap outta you." Jax rubs pendant necklace as he exits the van.

To think the entire time I thought he was a stoner waistoid. I was an intolerable intolerant bitch in his mind. Crazy how that works with mutual dislike and such. Most people worship me. This stoner can't stand me and still helped me. Maybe I should meet more "normal people". I don't know anyone who would help those they liked let alone their enemies. All I did was insult them the whole time... I could be staring at a wall. Sober at that.

CHAPTER 35

Is This Love?

Halle Victorianna

Morgan was one of the few people I knew who could wake up every day before 6am without an alarm. Even if all he does is get up and meditate to return to bed. This past week he woke me and Rose up to begin training. Rose was so excited. They agreed to it before I was even thought of to join. Lucky me for the afterthought.

Rose found her way into our bedroom from cleaning floors. Negotiating for time with my husband. And calling him babe without his authority. What happened behind my back? I could never understand.

Morgan began shuffling. That meant it had to be at least 5:30. I was not ready to be awake. I don't think I managed to sleep until a few hours ago. Keeping an eye on Rose. Last night was weird. I remember sucking Morgan then just... phased out. I caught glimpses of those two but it's like I didn't even have control over myself.

They began speaking of Gods and Goddesses, I suppose they called them Guardians to resist blasphemy to the father, Rakil. Whatever kept my father off of me I was behind. If Morgan believed it, I would trust his guidance.

"Wake up, soldiers. It's time to train." Morgan shakes me up.

"I'm up, Morgan!" Rose smiled sitting up. She was still naked.

She hugged up on him, he played with her booty as they kissed right in front me as if I wasn't in the room. Wow... I get it now Nat. I didn't think I would care. I didn't think it would hurt me as much as it did. But it fucking hurt. Why'd he kiss her first?

"Babe... can you two chill on that? It was one night, back to normal now." I clap my hands.

Rose raises a brow, "um... this is ongoing." She makes a slight giggle. "And inevitable."

I don't remember grabbing her neck but it felt damn good. She clawed into my hands trying to pry them off.

"Enough!" Morgan barks.

You're going to have to peel me off this bitch before I kill her Morgan. I swear to Rakil I will kill her. I tried. I'm tired of her mouth, tired of this arrangement and tired of all of this talk of fate and inevitabilities.

Morgan's hand rested on top of mine. "Halle. Enough."

I looked at him, "Can you even love one woman Morgan?"

I let her go and stood up off the bed.

"I'm not sure if I can love any woman right now."

I rolled my eyes, "I'm not some bystander. I'm not some child. And I'm definitely not some hoe. I'm Halle Victoriana Gregor. I will not share my husband with a maid!"

"Administrative assistant..." Rose mutters to correct me. Rubbing her neck.

"Excuse me?" I roll my neck.

"Nothing Rosemary's baby. Jah'Ada, you two need to figure yourselves out!" Rose hops up, "I'll be downstairs. Waiting for a fair fight."

"I'll burn you alive!" I wail reaching for her hair.

Morgan grabs me by the waist and pulls me off the bed. "Enough, what has gotten into you?"

"Me! She speaks of inevitability and you laugh with her. You're supposed to love me Morgan." I punch him in the chest.

"I was supposed to marry you."

I stare at Morgan with the rage of Enshishi himself. With all the pain in my heart condensing on me. A tear rolled down my eyes and I bit my lip until I felt blood bursts onto my tongue.

"I can't do this anymore..." I shake my head.

"Halle?"

"I can't Morgan. I hope that you'll love me. That one day you will forget Natalie and we can be. But no. No, this, this bitch takes my place! You give her all the love and attention that should be mine. It's you! You're supposed to be my husband to be and you're falling in love with a maid!"

"I'm falling in love with Baat... it's- I don't fully understand it either Halle. I'm just going with this." he sighed, "It's over my head as well. We can discuss this. Don't be so hasty."

"Yes, yes because you don't want any of this!? Because you don't want love, right? You don't want to love me! I don't want to force you to be here Morgan! You don't have to be here. You don't have to feel forced to be with me! I wanted you to love me. You don't even want to be with me. I won't sit idly by and watch you fall for another woman while you do nothing but point out my faults."

Morgan nods.

He lets out a sigh. "Halle...I don't love Rose."

He said it as if it hurt him!

"And you don't love me! And you don't love yourself! You didn't love Natalie! It doesn't have to be that way."

"Then leave Halle." he says immediately angry.

"Fuck you! We're engaged."

"I don't know what to tell you Halle. I'm trying like you are! I'm trying to make this work. I give you refuge here. This just happened! I don't fucking know what's going on either!"

"I want a man to love me. I don't want to be his damn duty Morgan! You don't have to be with me if you don't love me."

"I do love you..."

I stare at him. "You don't know what that is."

"Stop telling me I don’t know what love is! You want me to say I love you, then you tell me I don’t know what it is. I don’t know what you want me to say then. No... I don't. But if I did understand it. I would love you, Halle."

"How? You think I'm an idiot. You fantasize about being with a maid!"

Morgan sighs, "Halle this is bigger than just us. The peace of regions rests on our shoulders. Our marriage can bring peace to Naka and Nadia. The two of us can be great. We can be king and queen."

"Of my family's wealth... I'm done waiting for you to love me. I'm done waiting for you to finally decide. I'm going to Maya."

"Halle. Done be so dramatic!"

"Dramatic!?"

"You two asked for this last night! You said you understood. This is how we met."

"And how did that turn out?"

"Neither of you are like Natalie."

"Lucky for you, right?" I roll my eyes, "I'm not going to watch you leave me, Morgan. I refuse."

"Your father-

"You're handling him, right? I'll be in Maya far from both of you assholes!" I begin pulling my clothes on, tears swell in my eyes, "I can't believe I've tried so hard to be with someone who doesn't love me. Who will never love me!"

"That isn't true. Stop lying to yourself to spite me."

"I shouldn't have to change for you to love me Morgan."

"It's not about change it's about maturity, this is a perfect example."

"I'll just be immature then Morgan. I'm not putting up with you cheating on me. Absolutely not! I am a Gregor. I will be respected!"

"Why must you be so prideful and stubborn?”

I smacked him as hard as I could. "Don't you dare."

His eyes looked at me flickering between red and brown. "I'll pretend you didn't do that."

"I'm leaving before you go crazy on me."

"Yes. That's for the best." His eyes finally settled brick red. It made my skin crawl. "Maybe this was a mistake from the beginning. A little spoiled girl who can't look beyond her own ego, even for the peace of Gaia. I did not ask for a threesome last night. I was not expecting it and now you're up and leaving?"

I shook my head, "No, no it wasn't. I loved you. I loved and I would have done anything you asked, Morgan. But you-" I wiped my eyes furiously.

He moved to hug me but I had to push him away. I felt my heart shattering was I felt his heart beating out his chest in panic. What am I doing? Why am I acting like this right now!?

I couldn't let him see me cry. "You're so set on being miserable I just can't anymore. Good luck with Nadia. I have my own life to deal with."

He bowed his head, "I'm sorry Halle."

I took a glance at the man I loved so dearly behind a curtain of tears. He was so numb to it all. How many times he's gone through the same. If I walked out right now what would he do other than continue on with his life and move forth with Rose. If I stayed how long until she replaced me just as I replaced Natalie? I doubted for sometime whether or not Morgan truly loved me. I guess now I had my answer. Standing here ready to leave and all he does it say 'I'm sorry'.

"I'm not coming back, Morgan."

"That's probably for the best. You deserve happiness." He stared at the ground with his lips tight trying not to even look at me.

"You deserve happiness."

"Then stay." He says holding my hands, "Do not leave me to face this world without you by my side, Halle. I have taken much for granted. But-

"Maybe in another lifetime, maybe when all this concludes but... I can't do this Morgan. I'm just not built for this right now."

"Will you leave today?"

"I... I have to prepare to go. I will leave as soon as I can once I schedule my plane. I'm glad I didn't get comfortable. I'll have to try to get my car there as well."

He nods. If he was hurt he didn't show it. "I must get to my training and plans for the day."

"I wouldn't want to keep you from your girlfriend. I hope this one works out for you."

"I think I'm going to take a break from romance and train alone for now on."

"You said that to Natalie before you started dating me."

"And look at that coming to fruition. I didn't ask for us to get married either, it was forced on me like your threesome. You make it seem like you want these things so badly. You have no idea what you want at all." He said irritated at my mocking him.

I know I did all I could with Morgan. I know we reached every end we could reach. Some people just aren't compatible. Sometimes the past is all we have together. I can't be with a man who doesn't respect me. And I wouldn't want Morgan to have to settle. We both deserve better. I just wish better wasn't Rose. I wish I could be better but I'm right now and my father made sure of it. If he can wait and if I can murder Rose then we could be together. I have to get stronger than her first.

How did I manage to date someone so rigid? I'm a burning flame. I need air and space. Morgan is so preoccupied playing Morgan he doesn't have time to be himself. My sweet warrior monk, he was a Wolf, I was an heiress. No wonder he and Natalie clung to each other so dearly. Maybe Morgan was never meant to become a Gregor... maybe I was meant to become a Sameera?

I felt like I was waiting my whole life to meet Morgan. I just had to have him. I was patient. I was respectful to their relationship. But men like Morgan... they never had one woman. You couldn't control him. Society wasn't built for him, it was built by him. He belonged in the 2nd Age conquering nations or in the 1st Age meditating under a tree.

He told me once, "Everyday now I seem to think about just running off into the forest and never coming back. Civilization makes no sense to me." I was cross-faded and agitated over him carrying me out the party. I wanted more shots and he was going on and on about decorum and safety. I never really listened to him until after the fact.

"Is there any hope we can amend this before you go?" he asks fatally.

I shake my head, "I want to be the Queen... not the side chick. I'm done with this role while you search for love. Be happy Morgan. You don't have to commit yourself to misery with me.You're free."

"I'm not miserable with you. I'm miserable despite you. Life- Halle you know my life."

"No... I don't." I shake my head, "I don't understand it. I've never been through it. And it doesn't continue to excuse your behavior. I can't keep doing this. It isn't fun anymore."

He scoffed at that. It wasn't what I meant but it just showed the worlds between us. He shook his head his sympathies withdrawing as he realized the same.

"So, it's truly over?" he asks rubbing his neck, "Just like that? You two led me up here to rip this from me! You believe I'm choosing a woman I sparsely know over the woman I gave up everything to be with Halle? I could have stayed with Natalie if I knew you were this fickle."

"I don't think we ever had a chance... We were fooling ourselves. You don't like me- don't reply to that, you might say you but you don't. I can't change for you, Morgan. I can't stop being myself just to appease you or my father. It isn't fair and it isn't what I want."

"This is about your inheritance? I don't care your father's money. I'm trying to postpone the wedding because I don't want to take over your father's footsteps. I want to be my own man and I want to bring you with me."

I let out a sigh squaring up with Morgan and staring him dead in the eyes, "I will talk to my mother and maybe I can rule Maya and Naka when she's taught me all she will. Maybe then you will actually love me like you think you do. You want me to prove myself right? I'll conquer whatever I have to prove it to you Morgan. Then when you see me as an equal you have my permission to marry me not my father's."

I pulled him in, kissing him deeply, shoving my tongue down his throat unsure if it would be last time I would be kissed for years or months. I held him as he stared at me in confusion.

"I need to do this so you all stop laughing at me. I have to undo whatever my father was trying to do to me. And you need to see me for who I really am Morgan. I'm not a good person. I destroyed your relationship on purpose. I love you but... maybe when I take over the western hemisphere you'll see me as you see yourself."

He shook his head, "Your mother doesn't intend on giving you Maya and I have no interest in seeing you as you see me. I love you already. I already love who you are Halle. I'm not asking you to-

He sighs rubbing the bridge of his nose whenever he was giving bad news. "Halle, I don't want you as a servant, I want you as my Queen. You're refusing me despite me telling you I love. I hope you'll remember that on the Cruz Show. I am trying to rebuild a nation, and I have stood by this relationship. You can leave if you want. I'm not going to keep sitting here arguing with you."

I roll my eyes, "You don't know my mother. I don't even know my mother. Don't fill my head with that to keep me here."

He shrugs, "I'm fine with saying goodbye. You're right. I just don't want you getting your hopes up. You aren't fit to be a Queen. Your mother and father both saw that."

"No one's even given me a chance, Morgan!" I scream.

"I have given you a plentitude! Yesterday was another, and I thought we were on the right path. We take our chances, Halle! We don't wait. They don't fall in our laps. We seize opportunity when it presents itself. The average person doesn't get to sit around never wanting for anything in the lap of luxury then just ascend up the hill. I believe in you but you need to really dig deep to overcome it. If you don't think I can help you then I will not stop from going to whoever can help. I love you enough to let you be free. I would cage you or try to possess you."

"The average person isn't the daughter of Enshishi and Baat." I wipe my eyes.

"Good, yes my point exactly! You are the daughter of Colin Gregor and Marsha Qatar. Both of which have actively sought out new heirs. I wish you the best, Halle to prove they had an amazing daughter. You didn't need to be dutiful and you didn't deserve to be left. Focus on living your life."

"Fuck all our haters!" I cheer looking for his support.

"So be it." his apathy cut like a knife. I never knew how difficult he would take leaving. He fought for so many other things. I guess this entire time I've been one of them. "Good luck, to you, Halle. I love you and I know you'll be successful."

Morgan covered his eyes, beginning to sob as he felt around blind as if he had lost his vision. He found the bed, sitting and his tears dried as he took a deep breath fighting his pain with machismo pride.

"You too..." I depart to join Rose.

I had no tears left to cry. I couldn't watch him cry. I never meant to hurt him. I never knew I was capable of hurting him. No more heartache to spare over Morgan. His life was going on without me regardless right? He never intended on marrying me. On being by my side unless forced or no other option appeared. What sort of life was that to be?

My father wanted me to ruin my best friend's relationship to give someone else my birthright. Morgan didn't want to be a Gregor. Oh my god, I'm such a fool.

He only wanted me.

CHAPTER 36

Karma Collects

Carmen Cruz

The dust has settled and both Halle and Natalie are out of my way.

Natalie carefully contained in a cocoon like she always wanted.

Natalie sickened me. She thinks she's the first heart he's broken? That's a part of the game... When you pick your one, you endure and outlast all others until you're the last two standing. Natalie liked to start shit but couldn't end it. Getting her ass kicked by Halle in her own hotel room, goddammit girl. Halle would probably be sucking her thumb babbling over her words as she's done the past 20 years. People still think the dumb shit is cute.

Two birds with one stone, until Natalie starting freaking out about Halle and not wanting everyone to know. I couldn't blame her, but I would never let the Airhead Heiress do that to me.

They yammer and both bicker about what is rightfully mine. Now, he's done with both. The wedding between Halle and Morgan is broken off. Natalie is telling people he assaulted her. It's time for the heroine to pick up her lowly prince and make it all better. Those two can be so childish. Here we could all be the advocates of the next true Enshishi, instead they want to act like little girls. I believe in destiny, and I know Morgan and us were destined! But everyone is fighting fate. So be it. I believe in destiny, but I know I rewrite my future. The Queen of the

Media Blitz, and Wife to Enshishi. The younger, dapper, more respectable, Morgan Ellys, my masterpiece. I was salutatorian next to Natalie, Colin's prodigy as he so claimed.

When Colin introduced us, there was an unusual tint in Morgan's eyes I felt a kinship with. We both had advanced training with Patriarch Sergeant Gregor and now, Lord Commissioner. Taking in two refugee kids and giving them purpose. We were both Nadians lost in Erdu.

No one needed to tempt me or exhort me, I already had plans for Mr. Ellys. He would start with a career in the military, as an operative and raise up to Lord Commissioner of the Regulator Regime, while I went away to school for Fashion Design and Journalism. I would graduate valedictorian of my Master's Program, and be married to a genius war hero. Once he killed Colin of course, I would be sitting pretty upon the Gregor wealth with the most eligible bachelor on Gaia. As I intended roadblock, after roadblock, disappointment after disappointment such was the cost of hope.

He doesn't like I sleep with other men.

I don't mind him being with other woman, so he'll get over it.

He doesn't like my profession. We can start a new career of ruling over Naka.

He doesn't like how I stir up gossip. Once we kill all our enemies who would I gossip about?

He says he doesn't trust me. And that's very reasonable.

I mean sheesh... sometimes just take things for the surface and enjoy the beauty you're with Morgan. I never claimed to be a good person. I claimed to love him... Well, I do... did... do... hmm... this competition is getting to my head. Turns this way when you're the only one still competing, the competition is entirely mental. I'm only competing with myself. The woman he knew me as, as his trainer. Someone had to keep him in line. If I guy can snap and blow up the planet in a tantrum then you need someone to keep him sated. Pussy, drugs or training until he puked and could barely move, anything to keep him from losing his mind in Erdu.

I should feel more comfortable. He was a good protégé... even managed to surpass me. Victory is afoot but I can't shake the feeling destiny had another hurdle for me to leap over. Why did Morgan and Halle implode so quickly? Those two should be perfect for each other.

Hmm... who was that girl they were with that day?

I know if my nosy ass went alone like I intended I could have been eating on Morgan's tab that night. He goes off and dies without even a visit? I know I was cruel but more disappointments and roadblocks to overcome with time.

Aligning with Natalie was like taking two steps back, I thought the goal was Enshishi not this prideful bull. I spent my whole night listening to Natalie give me the same ole drifts about their shitty relationship. She should have never even put herself in that situation. All smoke no fire as always. Halle was always the first in line to marry him. Why would Natalie screw up the whole plan?

Halle gets her foot in the door. I coach them through marriage then hey, she is our friend Natalie. And we hold down the throne sipping mango coladas on the beach while he goes off to some mountain to brood. These rich girls had such big egos. They never knew real mistreatment or sacrifice. They both jumped the gun now they're out the picture. Hopefully for good.

Am I missing something? I hate being left out the loop! What is it... what is it... Hmm... Natalie had him, and Halle moved in on them is Natalie's side of the story. She's delusional. Halle and Morgan were supposed to be arranged before Bryon was assassinated by Morgan. So, that's why you're switching sides Morgan. So, he finally found out he is Sameera's son. What the fuck did you get me into Natalie?

It's worse enough I had Bryon killed... now Morgan? How far was Natalie willing to take this fight with Halle?

Who was that girl from the restaurant that night? I have never her before, maybe in a history book of Maya. She looked like a Queen from 500 years ago but she looked like a little kid hanging out with those two. Hmm... no, no Marsha Qatar, she looks exactly like Halle's mother.

There is too much I don't know. It's embarrassing to have so many secrets in my own webbing! I'm supposed to know everything about Morgan and yet their relationships were a complete mystery. And they've moved forward in completely different directions. I don't even know where Halle and Morgan are right now and we are running a media blitz against them.

I need to talk to Morgan and get him to fill me in on everything. He's the only one who ever tells the truth. It's so rare to find an honest man in Naka. I have to be careful with him now. He wasn't a boy anymore, confused and horny. He was a man focused and driven. I'm so proud of my work. Years of conditioning and pruning creating my perfect man. I needed to pluck my fruit while it was ripe.

I had a lovely beach house in Esha and I know he's never been to Esha. I could take him out for a week or two and make up. A secret rendezvous to discuss terms and fixing this wedding fiasco.

I scrolled through my contact lists, scouring my computer, my phones, my old phones, and old notebooks from years ago looking for a number to call Morgan directly. He blocked my cellphone and disconnected his cellphone service. I knew I had another number for him somewhere.

After ole bitch ass walked off my show, I deleted EVERYTHING. I burned gifts, I called his voicemail crying and cursing him out. I made fake accounts to give his businesses bad reviews. I was pissed. Then years passed on, he moved on and I'm still pissed off. It's so pathetic. How'd I lose control over him?

I thought he was dead all this time. I went to his funeral. I held onto his urn for two years straight. I guess I overlooked the possibility of him faking his death. We talked about it all the time before he left for Nadia but he was strongly against the idea. He started about some Rumya, and how he's going to head off and build a cabin in Erdu to live in with his country bumpkin. I told him it was a horrible idea and I forbade him. He bought the property anyway but I never allowed him time to go when training. The last thing I wanted was for him to be out of reach for good... that was five years ago and he's blossomed without me.

And I never want another phone call telling me Morgan is dead, again. I'm dying before him... he'll be at my death bed and stroking my grey hair. He'll tell me to rest in power then conquest and build a new world in my name. I love him.

Leslie and I spoke only a few years ago saying he never returned from Nadia. I wonder if she got the news he's playing renegade hero there all these years. I wonder if he even really died or faked it to escape Warren's Wrath. Leslie took it harder than anyone else. They spent their entire childhood together for him to... disappear.

I felt hope was lost until I saw how good he was doing while Natalie was crying about how he treats people. It was the first time in nearly twenty years I ever seen him remotely happy. What the hell does she expect from a man like him, smiles and compliments?

I wanted to reach out again but nope. Halle already secured her spot. Enshishi whispered to me his intentions to have Morgan wed Halle and kill Gregor. The Eternal Flame needs to burn brighter and shine light upon the world. Even I hated Colin Gregor. I tolerated him for mutual ends but everyone knows he wasn't his father or his grandfather. He was a failure.

Now, Colin is dead. I knew Morgan had my answers.

Morgan also had some moral contention with the basics of our life. I'm not sure how else to put it I'm evil... I like opulence, I'm greedy, I'm selfish, I hate kids, I hate animals, sometimes I take baths in liquid gold or $100 dollar bills. I don't care. I'm doing me. I'll donate some money and make social appearances for the tax break then I'm done. I take pictures then go back to my personal extravagance.

I mean, I'm evil but that doesn't need to concern others. I'm evil but Colin... he needed to always have his way, even if it goes against Enshishi's wishes, even if he didn't know what he wanted. Colin somehow believed being a vessel made him God. No, sweetie... you're a container. The greatest embarrassment in Naka, killing his own father, brother and showing the true worth of the Gregor Family, something far from good and beyond evil. He almost makes me look like a saint when I think about it.

Morgan would speak out on how there were numerous coups to overthrow Colin. The greater interest was invested in containing the Eternal Flame in Colin until Morgan could receive him. But then Morgan changed on us and I've been handling everything. Natalie wanted to receive Enshishi but she couldn't even beat Halle in a fair fight. Halle... hmm.... She's nothing like her father.

My darling knight went rogue. When asked about how to get reach he speaks about socialism, globalism, and peace. My Crimson-Eyed Knight speaking of government conspiracies and the evils of the Regime like it was Sunday night football. I wasn't a stranger to the topics, but Morgan was supposed to be the voice of reason, he knew we would never do anything... unless forced to destabilize Gaia. Things are perfect! This is the most comfortable form of slavery we've ever found. Completely ergonomic, it's voluntary and we allow people to vote for their masters.

Morgan felt the people didn't need masters... well when people are making billions from being masters. It didn't matter whether or not it was necessary or helpful to humanity my sweet Knight. If it makes dollars then it makes sense. If it makes sense they'll well tell the people something to make their ends justify our means. Not good enough for Morgan.

To know and understand how savage and uncontrollable the riff raff can become and to still believe they deserved freedom. It was ballsy but if you can kill a single Rottweiler you had little competition on Gaia, to be able to take down fifty of them... I couldn't imagine how much differently his brain functions than the people he attempts to liberate. If only he knew that he was supposed to lead the extraction and purification Enshishi dreamed of over Nadia. The goal was leaving only the strong to rule upon the planet and the weak to death or slavery. Instead, he was fighting for the riff raff.

I had a cushy seat as an influencer, eating five-star meals, and sleeping in the most renowned apartment on Gaia with a beautiful property on the Baja River. People never liked me, I never liked them. I wanted my toys and theirs. They wanted to share, always worked out great for me.

My mother was a nervous wreck, terrified of my father. And once I got old enough my father thought I could replace my mother. The news reported my mother killed my father, and got sent to an insane asylum. Instead, I set them both free. One night my dad came to my room and I lodged a steak knife in his pee-hole. My mother saw us and had the final snap to make her lose her mind. She tried to confront us seeing her husband mounted on top of me with his pants down bleeding all over her daughter.

Until I kicked him off of me into a puddle of his blood. I had the courage to do what she never could. No matter what he said or did to her she never fought back. From then on I knew I was stronger than her, stronger than she could ever be. The lawyers said she went into shock after killing my father. I think it was the hours of berating, and shaming her as she cried on the floor. Dumb bitch wouldn't even call 777. Laying there crying over his body, helpless with no idea what to do without her abuser. I could never do it.

I told myself... but we all find a way back to Daddy don't we? Morgan looked nothing like my father, but reminded me of him. The strong, hard as nails, dark, professional, psychopath, the type of man to slap the shit out of you, then kiss you on the forehead. I know what I like, don't judge. Morgan had compassion to him, he cared for others. He didn't choose military life it was demanded of him.

I'm a hellfire ready to burn down anything in my way. If I am honest with myself, as I always am! He gives me some much needed boundaries, and the sex is rocking.

I've been in a room with five men each taking their turn, it was fun but what took five he can do alone for longer. I prefer his cock to all others. If it's love or his stroke, I didn't care. I knew I needed him with me for me to find joy. It bothers me to know he's loving and fucking these other women but never offered me the same courtesy! He could give his heart to them but always wanted to be guarded from me, why, a little torture and manipulation so I'm the bad girl?

Miss Lieutenant Leslie Steele had him to herself and her friends throughout the Academy.

"The Airhead Heiress" Halle Gregor was the last with him.

I'm curious when Natalie forced him to make her official.

I don't know why she put herself in that situation. I'm not sure why he would even deal with her like that. They're polar opposites. She's just a greedy so and so. Wants and wants but not to give. I used to admire such a quality in Natalie. Though, I could never relate, I get my blessings through gratitude and skill. I stay against adversity, wearing my two-faces, and getting better at my job. I am the truth of Gaia. Whatever I say becomes reality. Even if I outright lie, it's truth to these people. Natalie was crying in my arms, acting like I don't know she drove that man insane.

Halle had him on lock, and the dick was withdrawn from the field. I'm sure I'm not the only girl upset about their wedding arrangement. I'm sure I'm not the only one who knows it has nothing to do with me. If I want to be in Morgan's life I could be, and vice versa, we're adults. We can keep a secret or be outright with it and let people speculate. Tell them we're friends and keep letting him treat me like his secret slut behind closed doors. We've been doing it for years and people still don't know what I've taught that man. Well, I guess Halle and Natalie have gotten to sample my hard work and training.

Even as a friend Natalie didn't come out and say who she was with, because she knew damn well I liked him! Halle was an adult, and hand-delivered me an invitation saying she's sorry but to be happy for her and I am. Natalie thought this shit was all about her, I think she honestly believes they're getting married to spite her. Her vanity had its own class entirely.

I had to put that together quickly. As soon as I asked her if she knew about Morgan she lied to me. I never came to Natalie about it because I was waiting for her to be a woman about it. Then when she finally tells me, she wants to use my goddamn show to do what eating ice cream while sucking his dick could have fixed. She didn't want his friendship. Then she got her ass handed to her. I knew his weak link couldn't be my girl. I dropped her.

She came out her frame on everything I believed in, I couldn't believe the audacity of her. To come out in a full body cast saying she's my girl. I told her wear your heels, and an Ambra Austere dress. Get the cast put back on afterward.

Instead she wheels her ass into the studio smelling like hot ass and sausages, complaining about how hot it was and how the world needs to see what he did to her. She must have forgot Halle kicked her ass. I knew Morgan would forgive me. I was on the clock, doing my job.

At least that's my alibi. He'll never let Natalie get over this and I will help him get rid of the Wolfes as well. Saying they're going to cancel my show because I made their whittle Natalie cry.

Get out of my face with that bullshit. I have the highest rated show on METV. If you get rid of me, you might as well get rid of the whole damn network! I listened to their jargon and litigations. Patient, nodding, and smiling knowing damn well I was calling Morgan afterward to capitalize on the wounded ego of the Wolfe Family. When I discovered I didn't have his number. Bringing me back to this situation I realized asking him for help was from the depths of desperation. If not Morgan, I had to return to Colin.

I've looked through everything!

I wonder if he's online.

I search him on my computer, typing in Morgan Ellys, Morgan E., and just Morgan but nothing popped up. Then I searched Morgan Ellys on the Data-blurb.

Data-blurb is a special access only, application designed for dignitaries and the affluent to network with one another. You can only gain access through invitation and initiation. There's also information and those who know the people you want to get into contact with. If Data-blurb doesn't work, then I could use the white pages, or search the GregorCore staff directory... I'll find you Morgan, be sure of that baby. Just need to find where you're at.

Who have I been with all these years? Who was I waiting for? Because the man I loved is gone. Though, I suppose I shouldn't care given this asshole got engaged without telling me.

So, be it... I'll make sure he makes up for it all tonight.

I had to be patient with Morgan. Catch him when he needs a friend and he'll cling like a monkey to a tree. There's no getting rid of him, and he takes such good care of me. It's the only time he even really listens or opens up. Only when he's weak do I remember he's human, somewhere in between the guardianship.

After killing Colin Gregor and allegedly dealing with Natalie Wolfe, he'll definitely need a few allies to get him through the lump.

Found it! A few messages, and a couple favors. This woman claims she sold him his house a few years ago. Gave me a cellphone number, and a couple web searches I found an address. A satellite image search later and I had the house and lastly the local phonebook online listing all the landline numbers. Ha, I would have never considered opening up the yellow pages. Though, I would never have found this new name.

Morgan Leonticus Sameera, so he is royalty after all? This is going to be fun!

The phone rings a few times and then kicks to a chill lo-fi hip-hop beat. Okay, Morgan with the dope tone.

"Hello, this is-

"I know who you are, baby. Did you miss- Oh-

"-King Sameera, this is my voicemail, please leave your name, organization, and request as to how the king can aid you. Thank you, Rakil Bless the reconstruction of Nadia."

You're fucking kidding me. Did this asshole just swipe my call? Oh no, sweetheart. I've waited too long for this reunion. You need to pick up your phone.

I call back only the exact same thing to happen, a few more times until he cut his phone off. Shame, this only means I'll have to try the other numbers I have for you now.

I call his alleged office number, pretty sketch because I found it on the 110th page of a forum in passing.

This one rang twice before someone picked up.

"Hello, the Sameera Home, Ananda Sameera speaking."

"Can I talk to your daddy?" I ask the little girl on the line, her voice of gleeful mutters as if she didn't know what to say. "It's a very important call."

"Um... I am not his daughter."

"But do you call him, daddy right?" I confirmed.

She didn't have a response, "I- I have no need to answer that question!"

"That is always indicative of a yes, it's fine. I call him daddy too. Are you the maid then?" I inquire sizing up who all is around my man.

"Yes... Well, Who are you?" she asks suspiciously.

"Carmen Aleia Cruz, the World's true Queen, calling for my King. So, if you could hurry and get the grumpy goat I'll be grateful. Thank you very much, Lady Ananda."

"I don't think Morgan wants to speak to the likes of you." she scoffs, just as good as spitting in my face.

Oh, the maid has some attitude!

"He doesn't pay you to think." I smirk. GOT EM!

"Yes, yes actually he does. I am not a maid anymore! So, thank you for calling have a nice day."

"If you hang up on me, what do you think Morgan would say?"

She hesitated. She wouldn't know. I knew he wouldn't care, he might even be grateful but she wouldn't know.

"What you did was very mean!" she showed her true colors, weak... Ananda... that name sounds so familiar.

"I know, but all I did was my job, hosting my show. Natalie-

"You both did it! You conspired against the King, now you call yourself Queen? Morgan doesn't wish to speak to you. Do not call this home again!"

"Morgan told me to call. He wants to discuss my terms of surrendering before him and submitting myself to his will, we had a phone appointment."

Discussing my qualifications and allegiance on my back seemed a great way to spend the rest of the week. I'm sure he would appreciate it.

Halle can't have sex with him, and Natalie bounced. It's probably been a long time since he's let out a load.

"I... I don't know about this at all. He would have told me he's expecting a call. I think you're lying."

"How rude, I can't wait to tell him how you're accosting me. So, he doesn't tell you all his moves, huh? So, I guess you're only paid for your perspective and to polish his cock once in a while?"

"Excuse me!? How dare you, I'll have you know, he is a good man and he does abuse me like that!" Her voice squeaked.

"So, you have sex with daddy willingly?" I tease her.

"I am a grown woman and I do not have sex with Morgan!" Ananda went full out on me. "I do not appreciate the accusations of a gossip girl!"

"Damn, you're really interesting... I can't wait until we discuss business together. You would make an amazing assistant. Take no offense to what I said, I'm just petty." I blow a kiss, "I'm sure we'll get along great. I'm just testing you."

"I- never mind. I'm getting Morgan." She left the line unsure. She'll whisper what she wanted but she was fragile. Morgan will get on the phone for nothing else than to make sure I didn't touch his new toy. I guess he left this one in the box.

Strange, he usually had an issue keeping his dick away from any girl breathing around him. He once told me he couldn't control the hunger he had. I couldn't keep up with his sexual appetite. I had to force him to abstain or else even seeing me naked turned into a month of being dominated by him when we were alone. Without the sex he had good control over himself, focused on his little pet project in Nadia fixing a problem that took centuries to manifest.

So, we made perfect sense as a couple, at least as friends. If I was daring, a reward I would send him nudes all day. I would run home from work, and every element of our time consisted of sex then sleepovers, turned to weeks, turned to a few months. He was so hesitant, always saying he needed to head out. But once my pussy started bouncing on his dick he spoke a different tune and I felt possessed by his spirit.

I would buy him some outfits, and pack a few of his clothes away without him knowing. I bought him a dresser and cleared out so of my closet space and gave away from shoes. Next time he visited I let him know he could stay as long as he wanted.

We used to spend the summer together, just as the show was coming along. I thought it would be great to get him on the air, and present our relationship to the world. Instead, I don't know... maybe I shouldn't have charmed him but he kept refusing. I finally made eye contact with him and got him all the way to the studio under my influence. He kept refusing to obey but he followed nonetheless, I didn't have the control over him I thought I did. Or maybe he was just mentally stronger than me. And he came back to right at the start of the show. We argued for a few moments, then he looked at one the crowd with his gaze, and he walked off. The studio audience didn't even remember him being there, but there was a bit of buzz about the walk off and us rerecording the show.

I'm not salty about him leaving... but we never spoke again after that. If we wanted to retire from military life and find peace, I would have let him go. I hoped he was in some mountain finding enlightenment until he started dating my friends and didn't even tell me! No one told me! I was pissed!

I'm not sure if he remembers or cares. I do... sex wasn't the same. Enshishi's blessings and voice weren't the same. As much as I tried to dry out my want for Morgan through sex, attention, dating, partying, or even worshipping Enshishi. He remained on my mind. And I wanted him near me.

In the spirit of love and competition, I believe I'm due my position by his side once more. Third time's the charm. We were too young at first, he was with other women, now... we're both single and the timing is perfect!

CHAPTER 37

CHAPTER 38

Is This Faith?

Morgan Ellys

"Excuse me, King Sameera... my King are you awake?" I could hear and feel Ananda's presence quickly approaching.

She squeezed me tight, stronger than she's ever been. Her once bony arms now tone and dense tightly squeezed around my neck, kissing my cheek. She places her forehead to my forehead, kissing my nose as she pinches my cheek.

She began joining us for training ever since about three months ago her recovery took a major upswing. It came with some pushing. I kept pressing her to join and she kept giving excuses. Until, Ananda came to me saying she was tired of the nightly fits of vomiting and cold sweats. I pressed her to take control of herself. She cried for three days straight telling me how insensitive I was for saying such a thing. She avoided me, telling me I was horrid. Eventually she came around when I refused to respond to such a thing in my own home. One day she came crawling into bed with me and crying on my chest about how she's only ever heard such things from Colin. She wasn't used to someone being so ***mean*** to improve her.

I... I've been mindful of my tongue and sensitivity. I had to for her, she was so delicate, and her strength came in doses but none of it emotional or physical. I loved the way she curled up to me as if clinging to me to be strong.

She had become a good pupil, but none too strong. Her greatest attribute was her mind. Her greatest limitation was her mind has been used for nothing but sex and housework her entire life. Damn shame, a waste of her pure brilliance. She reads faster than I can speak. I felt bad for our first time meeting. I was surprised she hadn't brought it up to Halle.

"I'm awake..." I yawn wishing I had taken a real nap instead of forcing myself to listen to the audiobooks on my cellphone. "I was doing some studying, listening to an audiobook."

I unplugged my ears not having heard the last twenty minutes of Jim Rohn that began playing after I had fallen asleep. Hopefully my subconscious will hold on to it, the video is 3hrs long. I'm going to check it off my daily goal list anyway. Good thing she woke me up, I still had to meet up with Rumya. She must be sick of waiting on me.

Her energy lightened up, perhaps she was smiling. Ananda came around, sitting in my lap. She kissed my cheek and hugged my neck.

"What's this about?" I chuckle.

"My butt has never been so big in my life! Rakil, I've gotten so much bigger since I got here. I never ate like this at Colin's. All these Mayan dishes, Rose have me cooking are amazing. And with your training, my butt's gotten so big!" she cheers bouncing in my lap, "I'm so thankful you got me out of my shell, at least around you."

"They say big butts are connected to strong intellect." I add.

"Thank you for taking me in your home." She kisses my forehead.

"It's no problem... uh, was this all you wanted? I'm as tired as could be. I should probably shuffle to bed and relax. I think I will to head to bed for a bit."

"Well, I've wanted to say that for a while but you've been preoccupied. So, I waited." Ananda tapped her fingertips together, sitting on my knee like a kitten as I rubbed her neck. She worked so hard, if she wasn't cleaning or cooking, she was reading for hours on end.

“I don’t imagine you only came in to thank me?” I ask stretching out, letting her rest on my chest.

Ananda was hesitant, “You have a phone call from Carmen Cruz."

“You picked up the phone for her why?" I groan.

"She says it's urgent, she needed to speak with the King." Ananda leapt off my knee as I stood up, “Did I do badly?”

“Why couldn’t she just text or send an e-mail? Damn near thirty and she’s still impatient.” I rubbed the bridge of my nose.

"I didn't want to take the call but I also couldn't tell Rose. I thought it best to come straight to you. Maybe lighten your mood first?" She tried rubbing my shoulder but I slipped her grip, "it's the downstairs phone, do you need help walking?"

"No, I'll be fine Ananda." I rub my temples, “I’ll take this call in my office.”

My thoughts interrupted to speak to the devil in a green dress. Women hated to see a man think. Carmen always seemed to know when she was least wanted. I have a family now. This woman is still attempting to bore her way into my life. There was barely room when I was 15 there damn sure isn’t room now.

My people spent their lives working for the benevolence of monsters, to no avail. They worked for the support of the higher echelon, if only they knew how much they were despised.

After a certain income bracket they believed normal people were cockroaches. Instead of teaching an understanding of money, everyone above turned into vultures, wolves, jackals, and foxes waiting to feast upon the prey of financial pedestrians. The world was being dragged to hell by gelatinous greed demons possessed by the lust for power and money. I suppose it’s my duty to stop them.

Even in my richest days, what I most enjoyed were my labor and its fruits. Never so much the money, I usually donated or reinvested my wealth to give my employees better salaries or to improve my home. You can do such when you live in solitude, no one can tell you what to do with your time and energy.

I suppose in some ways I should thank Carmen. I would still be a military man, broke and ambitionless if impressing her wasn't so damn expensive. Even taking her on dates took up most my stipend once the month was over. If we were ever going to be able to work out I needed more money or more resources. I had to learn how to invest and make my money work for me just to date her.

I started my first business in a strip club, she hated me for it. I grabbed some shifts doing construction and landscaping in Nadia. She cheated on me out of resentment. Then once I owned my own crew she tried to snake back into my life. Whenever things were bad for me, Carmen was the cause or nowhere to be found. As soon as the smoke cleared, there she was waving my banner. I got exhausted with it all and broke up with her.

However, my first savings, investments, and night club were created for her amusement and approval. We both loved secrecy. If you owned the place, no one knew what happened behind closed doors or scheduled meetings. If you both keep a good rapport, they assume you're talking business. No one on Gaia ever knew Carmen and I was an item besides the Commissioner's niece, Leslie Steele due to my infidelity and indecision a decade ago. Even then, she didn't know the extent. Not to think Carmen was the first woman I truly loved. More so the first woman who I could say I understood.

Her having her own place worked out perfectly. Since, she's a few years older than me she began her career and life while I was still finishing in the Academy. She got tired of sneaking around The Academy, not to mention getting her out to Erdu was a pain within itself unless she was in town.

Rendezvous, after rendezvous... the sneaking got old. Worst considering I had a strip club filled with women who never got my attention. Leslie and Rumya both provided stable relationships. Something deep and self-destructive inside me wanted Carmen's love, thinking I could ever make her happy. I knew I was viewing the brutality of the past with rose-colored glasses.

I preferred going to her, a simple blink in the neighborhood after a mission then kicking it with her until I was called again back to Erdu for Regulator work. If I was free, I would just hang out at her apartment. Even that simplicity got old quick.

I never met a woman so angry for a man eating some damn sausage and eggs in the morning. Calling me all types of lazy and worthless, she had enough money alone to feed a small quota of children. What'd she spend it on? Dresses and shoes then she still wanted my fucking money. I couldn't even get some pancakes in the morning!

I should thank her for such as well. She ruined my interest in the spoiled rich type. In the least prepared me for it...

I made the same mistakes twice with Natalie and Halle. Simultaneously, in fact right now with Rose. I didn’t learn my lesson from those fiascos until recently. I might be their type but they certainly weren’t mind. Spoiled and never knew a full day’s work between the three of them.

Had I known the three of them were friends I would have stayed in Exigo with Rumya or The Academy with Leslie, instead I dove head first into the fruits of Enshishi. I probably would have lived a better life. In retrospect I should have known the trio was all together, but I didn't watch reality TV or the news. All distractions and deceitful. That’s all it was on TV and that’s it ever is in real life. I kept to myself even in my youth, few friends and fewer recreations.

My life was training, studying, sleeping, working, and women. Damn fucking shame. Hindsight is 20/20 they say.

I headed back to my office and sat on the edge of my desk picking up the landline to receive the call.

"Morgan Sameera speaking... Who is this?” I say assuming she found my office number somehow.

"Carmen Cruz, darling!” she embellished as she loved to do, “How are you?"

"What do you want Karma?" I mumbled squeezing the bridge of my nose fighting the migraine fast approaching.

"You know... I was pretty angry when I found out you were engaged to Halle. I was even angrier when I found out you slept with Natalie." She began as if there was more to the story.

"I dated Natalie for over a year. We didn't just sleep together. I thought we loved each other. Sorry your friends lied to you. I'm very busy Carmen. Can you please hurry this along? This may be news to you but its history to me."

"Oh, yes, yes you're so busy. You haven't been at work in months. You should probably be careful how you talk to me before all your enemies realize your address. They might want to visit you." she pressured me.

"So, you did have the gall to call to threaten me. Do you realize how quickly I could snap your neck?" I fired right back.

"You know me and my temper, daddy." She said innocently, "you know better than anyone. I miss that, don't you? Having someone who knows you, everything about you, like they know themselves and you should visit. I'm your Eve." She purred for me, every part of her cheetah nature. "I've had a dry spell lately, been thinking about you a lot more this past year. I wanted to give things a go again since we're both single. How about it? We put an end to this little spout we have going. Team us against Natalie. Let's do it."

She knew about my eyes but not my new wife? Carmen must have bluffed off of what Enshishi told her in his final moments. He probably had few people to continue his work. If she thinks I'm stepping back into Colin's demented plans she truly had no respect for my intelligence.

"I'm engaged." I begin laughing, "You called me for a booty call?"

"No, you're not! You and Halle broke up! You and Natalie broke up! Don't act like you're going to leave the one who put you on to begin with. You owe me a chance, Morgan." Carmen snaps at me feeling embarrassed. "It's not just sex, Morgan. It's an opportunity!"

"There's someone else." I repeat still chuckling.

"What's her name...?" Carmen asked with dangerous intrigue, I heard pages flipping in the background "Do I know her?"

She began clicking her tongue penetrating my life with the same comfort as our last meeting years ago. This was just another day of the week to her probably. This was the worst case scenario. If she called as an enemy, I had justification to hang up and let it go. Trifling with any woman's heart was treacherous, but Carmen was not one to toy with, I had to handle this delicately.

"You're playing a dangerous game, Carmen, you know this right?"

"Dangerous? You can't blink unless you know where I'm at, right? Should I tell you, daddy?" Carmen purred. "I invented this game, Morgan. Can you find me?"

I let out a sigh, "Carmen what do you want?"

"Ask nicely." she splashes water in the background.

"Where are you?" I rub the bridge of my nose growing tired of her games, "Be a professional if you want to parley."

"You don't sound like you want to see me, Morgan!" she snaps at me even more water splashing. "You could come see me, if you're nice. I'm getting nice and clean for you, even shaving between my legs in case you're feeling hungry."

"Carmen, where are you? I miss you, babe. It's been so long since I've had you to myself." I roll my eyes playing along with her little vanity project.

"I'm home... In my bathtub, playing with my clit as we talk, are you going to come over? There's room here for you once I spread my legs for you. Ooo oooo ooooooo ooooo!"

I covered the receiver looking around the room realizing I was in my office. This wasn't the same at all from when we were kids. A youthful lust riled inside me, my body remembering the deep pleasure as my mind and heart remembered the pain.

My heart raced as I swallowed, choking on a response.

There was laughter on the other side of the line.

"Are you done!?" I snap into the phone enraged, "You called to taunt me? Halle wanted to break your neck for that bullshit piece you did!"

"Like she broke Natalie's? I'm glad you brought it up because I couldn't." Her laughter petered out with a relaxed sigh. "You would never let that happen to me... You would have stopped her if you knew what she would have done to Natalie. I know you Morgan. You should come over. We can discuss my surrender."

"Probably once upon a time, after the damage you've caused I would say you're more than deserving of whatever Halle brings. You're her problem not mine. She created this mess and she has to deal with it."

"Is there no love for me left? What if I wanted to be back on your team?" Carmen whined, "That's not fair Morgan. You're being shady."

"Colin's death has made many people turn cloak. I'm not desperate for allies."

"What if I took it all back? I recant my story and turn the fault on Natalie?" she restates her plan.

"You love playing both sides against the middle." I rubbed my jaw, "you're not going to like my answer."

"I want you to say it to my face. You can take all your aggression out on me. You know you can. I'm tough. You can come over, I'll give you the handcuffs and blindfold. And you can tie me up. Show me how bad I've been. You can even record it all. I'm offering my love, my allegiance, and my many talents to you. No strings attached. You can even keep the tape as collateral or a reminder."

"You're full of shit. I've never spoken to someone more so than you. You sink pretty low now that your master disowned you." I said in object disgust, "You never had loyalty to anyone but yourself, Carmen. I know you a well."

"Turning to you is low? Here I was thinking I was jumping to the top of the food-chain coming to you, King Shit. I see your self-esteem hasn't gotten better." she went for an unexpected kidney shot.

She had a way of getting me where I least expected it.

"Things are back as they were before you fucked my friends. Mind you, it's not like you and I had a bad relationship. Of course, there's drama around us, but be honest. You loved me more than those two. And you still love me." Carmen giggled, "Remember the good times."

What the hell is she talking about?

"Yet they were both made official girlfriends while you fucked me on the low. None of you even telling me, you were a thing! I'm offering us a chance to make things are they were meant to be originally. You can leave those silly girls alone and focus on us."

I groan, "Carmen you're so despicable!"

Carmen hesitated.

"Well..." She giggled, "Way to just open the gates, Morgan. Or what did you want me to call you when you were tearing up my guts, Lord Luno?"

"You're an advocate of Enshishi... We both were then. I'm a different man now. I repented. I am Lord Ada now if you wanted to get it correct and King Sameera to be more specific." I explained.

"Am I not allowed to repent? I want to be spending this conversation bouncing on Ada's cock. That's what the people call you now, right, Ada? My, my, Morgan you've switched up on me." Carmen teased, "you can look at it as simply as this. I'm a woman, right? You're my alpha as expected my life and pussy are yours, you're my new alpha male. Same deal as the others in your harem right?"

She was mocking me.

"No, and I don't want it. I have my own life and my own women. Don't call this number again-

"You sure you want me as your enemy?" She clicked her tongue, "You're giving up a hot free agent over hurt boyish feelings and pride? That's not smart Morgan. Use that genius intellect. I'm offering myself on a silver platter and I am only offering this deal once."

I paused for a moment. How did she get my house phone number? Barely anyone knew this number. Not even Colin or Halle. She had connections I could utilize or sacrifice to my enemies.

"How did you get my number, Karma?" I played her game awhile longer.

"See how useful I can be, baby?" She finally got me where she had wanted me. "I can even find people living under rocks. You think it's an insult. But I love when you call me that. I'm not evil, I'm an opportunist. Give me opportunity and I run with it. I always impress you. You got the first phone call on my job applications. I'm a free agent now. I offered Bryon Qatar this same opportunity without sex, mind you. I was loyal to you, look where I got him."

"Nearly killed, you feed me Intel on him all the time. You either use people or you stab people in the back." I refute her self-glorification.

"Yes, guilty as charged!" She laughs hysterically over the phone. "You know me so well, baby. However, you can't name a single time I turned against you, can you? I've never told your secrets. I've never said what's been whispered in my ears while lying in your arms. I'm calling because I love you, baby."

"Do not get comfortable calling me that, Carmen."

"Do you prefer, Daddy? Ada? Abba? Papi?"

I hang up the phone enraged, nearly knocking it off my desk. I kept Halle and Rose off her neck, neither of them could understand why.

Nor could I anymore, I regret my decision immediately. To imagine another show with Carmen lambasting me across Gaia, the results were catastrophic. My reign as King would be contended by armies not activists. I was supposed to be a dead man or a kid killed after being abducted. Could I possibly comply with Carmen for the sake of global peace or was I only trying to save my own ass with greater sin.

I'm no longer playing the mental victim but killing Carmen seems like weakness. Am I unable to deal with my past and reconcile who I once was with who I am now? I didn't feel comfortable being painted as this saint, above all, holier than thou. I had no special credence or code to offer. I only had what was within me, my own wits and common sense. I believed this is what we all had, this and a higher connection to the ethereal, nature, and others.

I don't believe people should be left to their own devices. I tried such a life and barely progressed anywhere or in anyway. I had flaws, sin, failures, and mistakes. I've needed to change my entire life and frame of thinking around, twice now. Now, returning to Nadia I find myself in the same predicament. I understand better than anyone simply because

I am set or meant to do something, it doesn't mean I can just pick it up and complete my task. I must grow into my greatness.

The phone began ringing once more.

I took a deep breath, refusing to let my emotions, especially not emotions for Carmen get the best of me.

I was tempted not to pick up but it felt like cowardice.

Was this an emotion or a fact?

I picked up the phone, "Carmen."

"I'm so sorry, Morgan! I'm so sorry! Okay, okay? Is that what you want to hear? I got myself in too deep. I'm in way over my head, and I need you. Ada I need you to help me."

For whatever reason I could never refuse her, she was my sensei once after all. The same thing took over me when Rumya called me the same. I couldn't refuse summonses.

"What do you need, Carmen?" I asked dutifully.

"The show was meant to bring down Halle and the Gregors but... I was intimidated out of it. Enshishi played with my heart, and told me I should take it all out on you and Natalie. I'm sorry!" she cried.

"You think I'm not aware of what team you're on, or what drove you to such lunacy?" I had few others words, so I decided to let her talk herself silly.

Sometimes that was all the help one needed. Sometimes it was all one could offer.

"You're the only person who truly knows me who's left. I- I turned on all my friends. I wanted the fame so badly. It was so sweet. It was intoxicating. I needed the attention Morgan but you... You fill me up. You were my first and I never felt so complete. I know you can fill me. If I was your only woman, I could take back everything I said, call the show a fraud and go back to my life on your arm."

"No..." I said without hesitation.

"What! Morgan, I practiced that speech for days!" Carmen whined.

"You're not going to drain me of my energy, I have other women who fill me with life and I'm already working on a new wedding arrangement. Not to mention-

"I know I'm a succubus, you know I'm a succubus! Alright, alright! I get it! But I became like this and you can heal me!" she interjected, "If that's what you're worried about, I know a cure."

I cracked my neck, taken aback by this new brand of crazy and deception. She was attacking me from a whole new angle I never combatted or knew existed. My concern for my enemies...

This woman has turned my entire city against me, and now she pleads for my love, assistance, and refuge. I could easily hang up and walk away from all this without concern or weakness.

Though, what growth would there be in that? I have to deal with Nadia regardless. All Carmen did was give those in doubt more reasons to feel as though they would have regardless. If I don't help her I'm defeating myself before I even begin.

The world of the broken and insecure created by the superrich without the discipline to become wealthy without robbing the poor. The citizens of the world worshipped people like Carmen Cruz. She probably started believing as they did, she was some goddess. Truly believing the devil's lies and distractions, she was a pawn in truth. They were all pawns, worshipping their very lust and enslavement to wealth. Hmm... perhaps Carmen was more of a bishop.

The Carmen I knew constantly needed comfort, and security. She would hold me as if she couldn't imagine letting me go. She needed too much maintenance and time to function. There was little inside of her to make up for the lacking. By the time I left her, the whole show took off. Right after my 'interview' she soared. Her need for attention and affection never settled. I gave her something she needed far more, something she craved.

True understanding, she did not have to talk for me to understand how she felt... I guess I felt the same at my core. Two scared children trained to kill and nothing but. I can't recall a time we weren't protecting one another.

The accolades, my work ethic, and my commitment were all derived from the family I never had to please the people who would never accept me. If I could be redeemed there must be something salvageable about

Carmen. I just need to keep my dick out of her because that never ends well. She always felt the greatest and our bond made sex incorrigible, like hugging someone with your very soul until you have both become consumed with the other's very being. Fuck...

"Baby, please say something! Morgan!" Carmen cries, "I'm sorry for trying to manipulate you, I need you by me!"

"I can't be near you..." I shook my head.

"Why not, I need you to hold me right now."

"You know why Carmen! You don't know how to keep your hands or your mind-control to yourself. And my fiancée will flip out. My maid will hate me and it will ruin everything I'm building. This phone call was enough to infuriate me. I can't imagine what she'll want to have done to you. I am not going to visit you or see you. What do you want?"

"I need you to hold me... Tell me it'll be okay." Carmen began hyperventilating, "Please, Morgan. My anxiety, you know I have anxiety."

"I can't tell you that but I'll allow you to make things up to me. Tell the truth on your show." I offer.

"I'm not going to subjugate myself if I can't have you to myself! Fuck your bitch ass fiancée! You cheated on me, you cheated on Natalie, and you can cheat on that bitch too!" Carmen began popping off at her mouth.

I hang up the phone. I rub my temples. It takes only a few seconds before she calls me back.

"I'm sorry..." Carmen was sobbing, likely screaming in the inside. "You're abusive. You don't have to do this to me."

"I'm not being abusive, you can simply stop calling and leave my family alone. I don't want to be with you, Carmen." I yawn, "I broke up with you for this exact reason. You're too clingy. You're too grabby. You hold on to me, drain me of all my energy and then expect me to literally move mountains to prove myself to you. I can't live like that."

"I want to be on your team, Morgan. I want to be your ally!" Carmen pleads in tears.

"That's something I can allow." I stretched out, "But before I can consider that. You'll need to recant what you've said about me, Carmen.

At least what wasn't true? You don't need to clean my name but at least tell people the truth."

"But we didn't lie about you... We only insulted you." Carmen said, "Morgan, things can get much worst. I need your power and protection."

"Tell the truth, something to clear the air and allow them to hate me properly instead of for your so called 'insults'."

"You haven't changed." She giggled, "You don't like being liked, do you?"

"It's uncomfortable, but if my enemies knew what I did for a living or my focuses. They would cease to be my enemy. Many people watch your show. Use it to do some good so I can focus upon what's most important."

"You'll only make more enemies, Morgan. I'm not going to do that. We're doing my plan and taking down Natalie." Carmen tries to put bass in her voice, "Listen to me, if you don't take down Natalie she'll only keep doing this attack on you."

"I'll make the right enemies. I'll make the enemies I want to have rather than those who would be my Ally but are more concerned with your mudslinging. What does Natalie have to do with any of this?"

She paused for a moment as if she wanted to rant but her discipline told her to keep her secrets.

"For starters, my network is owned by the Wolfe family. They've been cracking down since me and Colin's... disagreement. I won't be able to work without a script or a guest. Would you come on the show?" Carmen asked in her baby voice.

"Absolutely not..." I grunted, "Hmm... But this is very interesting. We'll be in touch Carmen."

"Baby..."

"Don't call me that." I remind her, "We haven't dated since I died in Nadia. You have the nerve to turn against me then try to romance me? Do you think I'm an idiot?"

"I thought you were mine." She didn't understand. I don't think she ever would. She was patient if nothing else. Years later and I'm still shocked she sees me as her object of possession. "You're my love, Morgan. They all only liked you. I love you, Morgan."

"Carmen. I don't belong to anyone but to Rakil." I clarify my convictions.

"Rakil..." She sucked her teeth, "Yeah, whatever Morgan."

I laughed, "I'm not the same dude I used to be. I can't be anymore Carmen. Not even a little bit, understood?"

"Nope, I wouldn't know unless we at least had coffee together at my place. I haven't even seen you since we broke up. Like you just said, it's been years. No pictures, no contact, you don't update your social media. I miss you."

I sighed, "I'll need to pray on it."

"Morgan, when did you start praying!? You said praying was worthless!"

"I was dumb, blind, and arrogant back then. I've seen so much, Carmen. There's a whole other life. There's a greater life to live than ever been experienced in La Vida or under Colin."

"I- I would listen to you, Morgan... you know that don't you? I would listen to you if you had something to preach." she got serious which was rare.

Her attitudes were always devious and sarcastic.

"No, I didn't know that." I rubbed my neck feeling an added pressure, "I left you because you were draining me. I didn't imagine you actually felt anything for me."

"Within my own way, I'm not a nice person Morgan. I had a tough life too. I loved you with all I had. I still love you. I could only protect you."

She had no parents either. She was a child of The Academy as well. She moved to Naka as soon as she got the opportunity because it had been her dream. It changed her a bit but she was always this dramatic. She always wanted to live in the city. You could be anyone you wanted to there, she said often.

"You understand me, at least you used to." Carmen whined more.

"Many of us have hard lives. Some people stay really kind and loving despite it all. Some people turn to the devil because they feel they're entitled to more despite their poor decisions." I gritted my teeth tired of being manipulated, she was used to my anger, but she never saw the more calculating side of my personality, she's never known me to be in control of myself.

It sadly only showed me how bad for me she had always been, turning me to my wildest passions and emotions, good or bad.

"Ouch..." Carmen muttered, "I'm vulnerable, you don't have to insult me."

"You're welcome. We'll be in touch." I try signing off again.

"Can I see you, Morgan? I need to feel you inside me... I need you right now. I really do. I'm not being a succubus. I need the man I love inside me right now. I at least want to lay with you."

I groan, "I would need to pray and talk to my wife."

"They'll both say no... Rakil wouldn't trust me, nor would your wife."

"Then why should I?" I broke out laughing already knowing the answer.

She was quiet, "What do you want from me, Morgan?"

"Turn your heart to Rakil, stop worshipping Colin. Pray to not be a succubus but miracles are rare these days."

"I'll go to church." she says boldly.

"Pray... I have my issues with churches as well. Pray, Carmen. He'll find you."

"Who are you?" she asked frustrated.

"Morgan Leonticus Sameera. I don't believe we've met before."

"Let's change that... I like this side of you more." Carmen giggled playfully, "I want to speak to you soon about buying my network. It could help you infinitely. We can be lovers on the sneak tip, after we both pray. So, if I pray you'll have to do some molly with me. I want to help you. I'm sorry, Morgan. I truly am."

"You're not sorry you're afraid of being irrelevant." I sigh.

"Only to you, I did it all for your attention. I did it for you. But you stopped caring for me or paying me any mind. Enshishi told me, you and I could still be together." Carmen sounded panicked, "Baby I wanted to go public and make us the power couple. You walked off the show then went off and died. My plan was for us to make it all the way to the top and fix this broken world. Instead you dated Natalie and Halle. Enshishi wanted you to be mine!"

"What I helped destroy for being blasphemous, told you, a place remained in my heart for you?" I asked curiously, "Why trust him?"

"Was he wrong? He was still a Guardian. I did not speak to Colin. I spoke to the true Enshishi, the spirit himself this is why Colin and I split. He wasn't too happy when Enshishi began speaking to me without his permission." She purred knowing she made a good point.

I rubbed my temples unprepared for any part of this conversation. I ran many scenarios about me having to get involved in this situation. None of them were pretty. I had never considered actually having Carmen on my team. I doubt the others would ever even allow it.

"Daddy, I'm here waiting for you... It'll only take you a second to get here. I'm not dumb. No one would know but you know how we do things. You might have to stop by tomorrow too." Carmen had far more to lose than I already loss.

If she was seen with me her career would be over. I'm beginning to piece the puzzle together. I needn't worry about word getting out. But if I went there without speaking to Rose or Rumya they would kill me. I would lose everything and be stuck with Carmen, Luno and Enshishi seeking revenge and wrath. Adding two women I actually love as enemies to my throne for the sake of someone I've been trying to escape my entire life.

"I have to finish my book list before I make any visits to old friends." I rub my temples, my migraine had fully settled in.

"Your book list, you're passing me up for a book!?" she shouts, "I'm in distress, having a damn panic attack. Come make love to me, you asshole!"

"Or I could stay home and finish my book as I planned to before you interrupted me." I mutter.

"No, no, no... Fine, I'll wait, I can be patient. You just want me to be out the tub when you come. No fun." Carmen whines, "Fine, fine. You know I'm patient, daddy. I'll wait for you. I'll be home all day I'm taking a mini vacation for a few weeks. Give me a heads up so I can order us some dinner. Maybe get a couple plane tickets and rendezvous somewhere quiet?

"I don't plan on leaving my house." I yawned, I needed a nap.

"You never do..." Carmen giggles, "I say how mad I am at you. You tell me you're dating someone. You still end up inside me, Morgan."

"Thanks for reminding me... I think I'll stay home." I chuckle.

"But my legs will be closed." she added, "We'll talk about the network and stopping Natalie. No sex."

"Are you sure that's possible? I have never been in the same room with you, without you wanting sex. Maybe not since I was fourteen."

"Until you spread my legs they're closed. You know I can't say no to you, daddy." her voice rattled down my spine as she moaned.

"Stop..." my dick hardened in my pants.

Even dating Natalie and Halle, Carmen was always around. They called her friend but none of them knew of our relationship. Even less about how each other acted when they weren't around. She played those two like fools and now made a national spectacle of both. I couldn't believe my cock is honestly thinking about fucking this woman. Can a man's penis truly be so stupid?

"I'm only being honest, Morgan. It's the truth. Remember when we would be left alone? You act as if your cock wasn't down my throat. We could never get enough of each other. I think it was even better taboo. Knowing I couldn't have you. You knowing I was awful for you. We would fuck like animals. I should have known you and Natalie were dating but I guess I believed we were the secret, seems it was all a game to you after all."

My irritation grew with my stabbing pain.

"Today maybe... But you'll think about it. And eventually we have to talk about what we'll do about the Wolfe family. I'm not an enemy you want to have, and I have given you my terms as an ally. I'm organizing a deal for you to pay a percentage of the network. I'll use my earnings to buy another portion. Together we can have a majority say in what goes on the air."

"I could start my own network." I suggest.

She sucked her teeth "Do you know how long it would take before you're begging for notoriety, celebrities, or attention to keep it alive? A week! Everyone watches METV already, it'll be easier to buy in and rebrand than to create a brand new network out of stubbornness. You are affiliated Morgan. You can easily dispel your enemies and come back to us. At least make your old friends, I can help with that." she had it all planned it out.

"I couldn't do that." I shook my head.

"Nadia means this much to you?" Carmen sounded more genuine than conniving, a hard thing for her to fake. She let out a sigh as if relenting, "Honestly, does being Ada mean this much to you, Morgan?"

"More than you'll ever understand." I confided in the only person who could ever appreciate it, "This is what I was born and spent an entire lifetime fighting against. Nadia means everything to me, Carmen. Please do not get in the way of this, bow out gracefully. We can talk when the smoke clears."

"I'm not a monster, Morgan... Well, I'm not as much of a monster as you make me out to be. If I was your wife, I would help you rebuild Nadia. How's that, you and I together?"

"Carmen, I'm not interested." I groan.

"Ha, you know it all ends with you and me, baby. When war breaks out, they'll call us to fix it. It was always meant to be the two of us."

"You're lying." I snarl, "Those are Enshishi's lies, I am not his pawn anymore!"

"Ha, I thought I was more in your head. If I am a Bishop then you're definitely a Rook neither of us are pawns to Enshishi. I guess you really do only care about me on all fours. You're something else. I'll be waiting for you. I can't wait to hear what lies you tell your fiancée about coming here. I can't wait to have that thick, long, Ecruen dick rock hard in my mouth all night again." the words rolled off her tongue so perfectly.

I hung up the phone again, I wasn't angry, she didn't call back.

I hung up and hung my head in shame from how tight my pants had gotten. I'm still flesh and blood.

I knew the day I saw her again we would have issues. I thought this was all behind us and these days have been growing insane. My lust called for me to visit Carmen. I needed relief.

I've never been in this position before. I refuse to have a woe is me perspective on cheating. Rose didn't deserve it. It was less about what was deserved, and more about the Erdun bombshell with a dripping mouth waiting for me in La Vida.

It was never about hurting the woman I'm with. I need pussy right now. New pussy, the fucked up sex you have after fights. No one would know...

My youth was calling me, begging me to take her up on her offer. I had few others memories with Carmen other than training until near death or having sex until we were unconscious. Our time together was nothing else. No arguments or fighting, either pain or pleasure.

There would be nights at parties or mornings during meetings we would disappear. She had a mighty fixation for me. I felt addicted to relieving my experiences with Carmen. We would return to the group half an hour later as if nothing had happened with the discreteness of two highly trained assassins.

Those Natalie and Halle prided themselves on being prudish, it was their upbringing. Under the veil, Carmen was down-to-earth and simple to please because she took care of herself. It was rare for her to ask for help though the times were rare, it happened. It usually involved me doing most the work and nearly dying in the process.

When Carmen was around me there was no arguing, no demanding, and no denial. She was mine. If I snapped my fingers and asked, she would deliver. All I had to do was ask and pull out my dick harder than a rock. She would suck my nut out my dick like a straw then let me hit it however I wanted. She loved sex as much as I did. She would undoubtedly understand. She always knew what I needed. Like calling up an old buddy for a pickup game, it was all sport for us.

I groan feeling tempted to sneak out to see Carmen even for a few moments. Rose was at the university for her classes. Halle had left to go shopping for her trip down to Maya. Neither would suspect anything if I snuck out. How do I consciously sleep with my enemy?

There was a light tap on my door as I paced my office thinking about taking a nap or getting my dick wet.

I let out a sigh, taking my seat at my office chair, "Come on in please."

"I- I was listening to your conversation." Ananda confesses hesitantly walking into my office, gently closing and locking the door behind her, "I don't think it's a good idea for you to talk or align with Carmen. Halle has never said anything positive about her my entire life and she's very mean and she's-

"I agree with you Ananda. Please take a seat." I extend my hand out to the two wooden chairs before my desk.

"I rather stand for a moment."

"Very well, what brings you to me Ms. Ananda?"

"I- I used to serve Colin as you know. I thank you for helping me out. I use some of my skills here but I could help you."

"I already use your help and I appreciate everything you do already. I'm not sure what else you could possibly do. You're doing amazing Ananda."

"I don't want you going back to the dark side and I know that woman would drag you right back to the man you used to be Morgan. I've been talking to Halle and Rose, they're very proud of your progress. They also ask about us... being intimate."

"We're not."

"I understand... are you happy with that sir?"

"Ananda, I would never treat you as Colin had treated you. I could never ask such a thing from you."

"I'm offering." Ananda covered her face, her cheeks flashing bright red.

"Oh...?"

"You don't find me attractive?"

"I mean, I do. I believe any man would find you beautiful but it seems wrong. You don't feel angry or traumatized by your experience."

"I did not like the man who was abusing me. It doesn't mean my body doesn't yearn for a man's touch. I want to feel useful-

"Ananda, you're already doing a better job at Rose as a maid. You make sure I eat. You study. I am already happy with you. I already believe you're useful."

"You're still a man, Morgan." Ananda stares me in the eyes with a yearning gaze, "I was aroused by your phone call. I imagine you feel the same."

I nod, unable to take my eyes away from her eyes studying me. Was she seriously offering herself to me so easily? I push my rolling chair back making enough space for a second person. Ananda extended her delicately to me. I held her hand as she stepped around to my desk noticing how her body had transformed under my care. Her hallowed frame had filled out, revealing her modest curves and petite frame.

I kissed her belly button as she pulled her sweater above her head, revealing her beautiful breasts held up by one of Halle's favorite lacy green bras. I stopped her before she could take her sweater off.

"What's wrong?"

"You're wearing Halle's underwear?"

"Why don't you check?" Ananda smirked trying to cover her embarrassment.

I work and pummel her tender butt in my hands, surprised at how she's grown in only a few months. I thumbed the sides of her yoga pants down revealing a pair of black crotch-less panties. I parted her pink pussy lips to see if she was serious, her moist lips release a sweet aroma. I turned her around on my desk, motioning for her to bend over. Ananda peeled her skin tight pants below her butt. I stopped her from pulling them down further before I had to taste her sweet scent.

She gasped as I sucked on her clitoris, licking her from her pearl and up her labia enjoying how sweet tasted. Ananda squirmed, making shy cooing noises as she held her booty open for my tongue to suck on her clitoris. Her juices began dribbling down my chin as she began holding back her screams, her shoulders rising and falling before she pulled away from me.

"What are you doing to me?" Ananda cried out jumping on my desk and covering her vagina with her hands.

Her chest raised quickly, a wicked smile on her lips as she opened and closed her legs with every breath. I grabbed her ankles, spreading her legs to return to the taste of honey and pomegranates. Ananda grabbed the back of my head with her left-hand and pinched her nipples with her right, arching her back as I bring her to another orgasm. Ananda let me go, heaving on my desk breaking down into giggles as she catches her breath.

"Sir... what are you doing to me?" Ananda sat up with a bright smile on her face.

"I'm giving you head." I rub my neck.

"What is head?" she laughs.

"You know oral sex right?"

"I didn't know women could receive oral sex. I never imagined it felt so divine. My whole soul feels lighter now. Are we going to have sex?" Ananda sat up.

I bit my lip, "I was actually enjoying my meal before you stopped me."

"I didn't stop you. I felt like a calm wave washing over my body. I thought my vagina was going to flow away." Ananda rubbed her vulva before my face.

I grabbed her hips pulling her off the desk and lifting her in the air. Ananda yelled as she sat in my hands in her own throne. Her legs wrapped around my neck as she grinded against my tongue as I held her up. She sat on my face letting me have my fun until she began clinging to my neck. When I let her back on the desk she melted like a puddle. Her breathing relaxed as she held her chest.

"Wow..." Ananda finally exhaled.

"Are you alright?" I ask unable to resist chuckling a bit.

"I see why these women go so crazy for you. You haven't even had sex with me and I would still try to kill you if you gave this to Carmen." Ananda smiled but she wasn't joking.

"You think it's the sex?"

"I think the idea of sex definitely is making me feel more possessive over you. I feel a lot more emotional right now than I usually do. I feel like I want to be connected to you. I still want sex with my deeply but I don't want you having sex without anyone else either." Ananda rubs her temples.

"Can you tell me more? I've never heard a woman be so honest about it all."

"I mean, maybe if it was us with Lady Gregor I wouldn't feel so possessive but I feel protective over you. I feel like I want to own you. Like, we exist instead of you and me now. I no longer feel a separation between us. I feel a continuum." Ananda explained as she rubbed her clit.

"I could listen to you talk all day." I confessed sitting back in my chair watching her pleasure herself before me.

Ananda blushed looking away from me, "Are you going to take a nap in your room now?"

"Are you joining me?"

"Umm... of course I am." Ananda giggled finally sitting up and bending over to kiss my forehead, "I want to make you an actual snack first."

"I earned a snack huh?" I rubbed her chin.

"Yeah, you did. You earned much more than a snack, sir." She kisses me deeply on my lips.

"Do you think we should still have sex?"

"Do you want my honest answer or the truth?" Ananda asked her romance fleeing her face as she bit her lip.

"Both."

"Well, honestly I want to have sex with you but I fear I'll end up obsessed like Rose or Halle. The way they act over you scares me. I would hate to see such a side of myself so absorbed by some boy. Especially if I'm meant to be free. The truth, I believe it's inevitable. I'm going to ask you for sex or for whatever you did to me. And I'll likely give you a ridiculously hard time over it if you refused me. The honest truth is I simply fear what I would become."

"Then let's be patient." I suggest feeling it was a sensible answer.

"To be honest sir, I rather just take the leap of faith and know for sure than wait. I can make my own decisions. I only pray you'll still care for me afterward. Consider marriage to me as well not only Halle or Rose."

"You would be one of my wives?"

"Yes... or else how I feel about you wouldn't make any sense. How I want to show you my devotion to you. I would need you to be serious about me like I am offering myself to you. Do you understand?" Ananda rubbed my crotch.

I nodded, kissing her neck down to her shoulder. She wrapped her arms around my neck allowing me to lift her back onto my desk. She pulled my manhood from my pants. She paused seeing my girth, looking at me in awe as she relaxed on my desk. I slapped the head of my dick against her labia. Ananda reached down, rubbing her clit quickly as I teased myself into her warmth. I felt as if I was filling up a bao bun, parting her lips and easing into her warmth. She cried out in pain but didn't stop me.

I felt what she said as I looked down at Ananda with her eyes closed. I took my time with her, going easy, enjoying the depth inside of her without being too rough. With every stroke I felt myself imprinting on her. She ran her arms up my flexed muscles as I began pounding inside her fiercer. Ananda smiled up at me, rubbing my chin as I let out my seed inside her as I tried to pull out, she wrapped her legs around my waist pulling me back in. I lost my mind, grabbing her hips and picking up the pace spending the next half hour emptying my life force inside of this woman.

As she watched me, smiling and giggling I felt connected so deeply to this innocent soul. Plucked up and used for whatever purpose of her oppressor. Now, she sought me for protection, for love, and to show her how things weren't meant to be without terror. Ananda was so warm and open to me.

"I'm all empty." I say.

"Are you tired now?" Ananda asks me maternally.

"Yes..."

"Are you going to bed and only to bed? No visits, no games, no reading? Go straight to bed." Ananda lets me go.

"That was incredible." I sat in my chair, throwing my head back closing my eyes as I regain my senses.

"No, no if you stay in your office you'll try to start working again as soon as you catch your breath. Get back inside me or go to bed." Ananda demands.

I poked open an eye imagining if this was the same woman I had saved from Colin. Regardless, I listened. Either Halle or Rose would be home soon. I didn't need to be explaining why I was raw dogging Ananda in my office. I heeded her words unable to get my dick erect again without feeling soreness throughout my shaft. By the time I laid down in my bed I didn't even bother taking the rest of my clothes off.

I woke up a few hours later naked. Ananda and Halle lay in my bed on either side of me, smoking and eating a homemade meatball pizza. Laughing and giggling as they watched TV. I poked an eye open but fell back asleep. For the first time in years I enjoyed my rest. I was exhausted, enough of the repression, regret and rumination. I am King... I am Ada.

CHAPTER 39

Pride & Possession

Morgan Ellys

Halle diligently applied mascara to her lashes. Her hand was still as she curled the brush with the skill, stillness and precision of a surgeon. Her lips were next unwinding the mocha matte lipstick, puckering her lips.

"Are you almost ready?" I called from the bathroom having thrown on suit and kind of combing out my hair, ready to go.

Halle furrowed her brows likely wondering why I would choose now of all times to ask to speak as she elegantly applied the expensive wax and oil. Perfection took patience. Her father's benefit gala could wait.

"You'll probably be the first at your funeral. You may even arrive before the casket."

"Usually how death works Halle."

Halle rolled her wonderfully made up eyelashes, "I'll be finished when I'm finished. Don't you want your wife-to-be looking her worth?"

I shrugged. She already knew I didn't care. Halle woke up looking too damn beautiful for her own good or my comprehension. I wouldn't complain if she showed up in sweatpants and a t-shirt, she would still look more beautiful than anyone else on Gaia.

"You know we have a limo driver waiting on us."

"I'll be ready in another half an hour okay?"

I grimaced feeling worse than when she asks me to take her shopping, "I can't understand how you started getting ready two hours ago-

"Women take time, alright bucko?"

I muttered a few curses under my breath as I began walking a mile to avoid a fight.

“What did you say?” she didn’t want to start a fight but there was too much of her father in her to ignore me.

I sighed, “Halle, please get ready. I’m going to the living room.”

“Morgan, what were you saying about me?”

“Watch your tone.” I shot back, giving her a look as though she lost her mind, “I said Natalie never took so long. It was rude, I’m sorry.”

“Well, Natalie has never looked as good as me a day in her life.”

I moved to respond but chuckled, “Why do your looks matter so much to you?”

“I like being beautiful...”

“You’re already beautiful. Shouldn’t you be building other areas of your life more? What’s beauty worth if it takes all this effort to ignore everything else when you could actually learn anything else?”

“Morgan, what’s a million dollars’ worth to you? If you put the million in land, it’s worth one hundred million. If you leave the one million as it is then it loses its value right? Are you trying to imply I am only a pretty face? I am investing in my social stock. This is an investment into my brand.”

“Quite the contrary, I think you’re a very well-rounded woman but the focus you put on your make-up appears as if all you care about is vanity. Presenting the deeper side of yourself rather than this diva would not hurt you. I believe it would help your brand to focus more on your substance and less of the superficial. There’s more to you but you refuse to show it to other people.”

Halle gritted her teeth but my tongue was fixed to match whatever she said.

“Come on, I didn’t mean to upset you.” I groan.

“You’re damn right I’m upset. You look as disappointed in me as my father whenever I’m working on my designs, calling them silly dresses. Sorry this doesn’t mean anything to you but it’s important to me.”

“I’m not remotely disappointed in you Halle. I seriously love you but I love all of you not only your looks. Look, I’m not trying to criticize your make-up, it's just taking a long time and I want to be on time. All I'm trying to say is I wish more mattered to you than fashion and makeup. It's great you like them and you made a great career for yourself in them. I'm genuinely happy with the amount of people who admire and revere you for your beauty. I'm marrying you, you're more important to me than what you wear or look like because I've seen more of your character. Who sees you and who doesn't is vapid. I think you can be more than-

"More than being shallow? Gee thanks."

"Am I lying though?"

Halle pointed to the door, "I'm trying to look good for you and all you have is criticism, get out until I'm finished please. It's going to make me take longer."

"Halle, none of what you're doing or decided to do is for me. It's for you. I respect it but at least I'm honest. I don't care about any of this money, make-up or fancy crap. I care about you and your soul. You can make up whatever bullshit makes you feel better." I kissed her on the cheek then started for the door, "You look great for whatever it's worth from me. I didn't realize you got more beautiful but seems if there's more room for beauty, maybe there's room for other things too."

Halle didn't know if I was insulting her or giving her compliment. She didn't want to see things outside of duality. Some things are not good or bad, they simply are and that's all.

"Thanks... I guess." Halle turned back to her makeup.

She picked up her blush, letting out a sigh before she set it back down looking over herself. I hoped she was wondering if she really needed more, wasn't she beautiful enough without it?

She looked over her golden skin, nice and tanned from her time under the Nakan sun. Then she glanced over her face and sighed. She pushed the blush away and buried her head in her arms. Oh God, it was the opposite of what I intended. I wanted to speak but bit my tongue already seeing the damage I caused sharing my opinion.

What did I say wrong? She couldn't be more beautiful to me, what could I do? God, why can't we be happy? Why did I have to share a damn ocean of consciousness, impressed by nothing anymore?

"He's going to have to get over it..." Halle says snatching up her blush as I leave the room.

I was already over it. Sitting in the living room reading a book, mostly rubbing my temples trying to figure out what I'll do after Halle leaves for Maya. I'll be here left in Nadia, waiting for this marriage, a marriage seemingly an indefinite amount of time away. Rose steps out of her bedroom, starting for the kitchen before she notices me.

"You two still haven't left yet?"

"This is seriously how you dress when I'm not home? Halle is here, you might want to change before she catches a fit again. She's been getting the best of you in training lately. Maybe consider my wisdom."

"Am I on the clock? I live here too. Not to mention I catch her too. A few good punches don't win a fight."

"Rose, you're in a thong. I'm sure she'll do more than give you a few good punches knowing Halle." I sigh wondering why everything I said needed to be contested by these two women.

"Morgan, I'm legit getting some juice then going back to my room." She throws up her hands.

I let out a sigh, setting down my book on mental health and depression, "Please, I don't want any drama tonight. Can you stop dressing like this period around my house?"

"You don't like what you see?" She teases turning for me to get a better look at pussy I've already been fucking, dancing against the wall giving me a show, "If you say no then I'll change for you."

"No, now go change!" I say unmoved, growling in my throat tired of having the same conversation with these people.

Rose looks at me, asking me with her eyes how I could be so rigid.

"Jeez, not even a smile?"

Morgan rubs his temples, "I'm not in the mood."

"Well, what's wrong?"

"Rose, I have no interest in talking about how I feel with you right now. Please go change. I'm already aggravated I'm running late. "

"You have three beautiful women in your life and still can't be happy?"

"Laugh it up." I leered.

"Oh God, you have the sexiest angry face. You sure you don't want a better look? Come growl at and squeeze my ass." Rose poked at my cheek, "Aw, you even have angry dimples."

I chuckled, "You're too much."

"I'm enough. See you even laughed. I thought maybe you were broken. No, you're only brooding over your life again."

"Can you go now?"

"If you played with my butt, you would feel better." Rose whispers in my ear, biting my earlobe.

"Halle is going to murder you, Rose. Isn't it worst enough she's leaving?"

"No, I hate these Nakan bitches."

"Watch your mouth." I give her butt a swift slap getting her attention.

Rose bit her lip as her booty jiggles. I was admittedly a bit mesmerized, slapping her booty again. Rose kisses my neck, beginning to twerk burying her head in my crotch working at my belt as she made her butt dance.

"You need to keep a look out. If Halle sees me it'll be a long night for you." Rose bites her lips.

"This is why I told you to go change your clothes five times already!"

"I really think you need to spank me more for being a bad girl." Rose pulls my cock out my pants, beginning to suck on my balls as she stroked my shaft. "You seem so stressed out. How could I leave you like this Morgan? You're only one tiny piece of fabric from some major stress relief. I can make you nut super quick then I'll go get my juice. I'll be back in my room before you know it."

"You already know it's not going to be quick. You need to get your juice and go!"

"I love when you get all authoritative. Let me suck your dick at least."

"No, it'll end up in sex. I've already asked you to stop at this point you're being disrespectful."

"You're joking if you think I'm going to let you stay horny only to have her or Ananda take care of it? This is my wood. It's a pride thing over the principle I got your dick hard. I should be the one who takes care of it. I need to finish what I started."

Soft moans begin escaping her lips as she moved her fingers between her legs. Fingering herself as her head bobbed on my length. There seemed to be no stopping her, so I grabbed her hips pulling her into my lap. I moved her thong aside, pushing into her wet warmth feeling her immediately tightening around me after spending a few months making her vagina custom-fit to my dick. Rose choked on her moans, covering her mouth as she rode my waist, bouncing on me like she was milking a cow. I released inside her, giving her what she wanted. Rose looked at me with hungry eyes. She wasn't sated quite yet even if I felt her cum twice on my dick.

"When did you get so rough?" she mused, wanting more especially before Halle came downstairs to reclaim me.

"Well, you're honestly pissing me off." I roll my eyes, "Can you get up and get your juice now?"

Rose hesitated looking in my eyes, "I want it even more now... Can you be a little rougher? I'll be quiet. I know you're mad at me. Go ahead and take it out on me real quick."

"I'm not giving you what you want. Get on your knees and I'll fuck your throat if you want to see how angry I am right now!" I challenge.

Rose shuddered at the idea of having me ram down her throat, "I'm sorry Morgan. I'll go change. Alright?"

She gets on her knees before me and I don't stop her. Rose wraps her lips around my head, stroking my shaft with one hand, cupping my balls with the other to prevent me from shoving myself down her throat. Rose, looked like my dick belonged in my mouth, making short work of my nut. Swallowing my load then wiping the residue in her mouth.

"Thank you, Morgan. We can talk in a second. Let me throw on some clothes."

I was silent. I didn't want to admit how much better she made me feel after two nuts. I almost forgot about having to spend the night dealing with Halle and Colin.

Rose steals a few kisses before rushing off to the kitchen to get her juice. She came back a few minutes later wearing sweatpants and a sweatshirt from her college with her hair down in their natural curls instead of straightened as she wore during the school week. She set a glass of juice down for me, curling up to the couch next to me.

"You have no idea how thankful I am for that quickie. I've had such a long day and I've been so stressed. If you didn't pipe me down I might have gone crazy. Thank you Morgan."

"Anytime."

"He says now... I told you. You could have been inside me, I've been here and you decided to change your mind."

"I didn't change my mind, I let my guard down and I'm hoping it doesn't bite me in the ass." I let out a long sigh, closing my eyes while I rubbed my temples.

"You don't seem remotely distressed. You look worse now than you did before... was I not good?" Rose kisses my neck, "We can try again."

"Look, I'm tired of using sex to solve my problems."

"What the hell is going on here?" I sat up, standing up quickly as I heard Halle's voice, "Great, you're ready lets go."

"Oh babe, fix your collar! Don't want to be in front of all those people with your collar ruffled." Rose advises curling into the fetus position.

"Um, I just saw his collar and his collar was fine. What the hell is going on with you two? Didn't I say back to normal?" Halle eyeballed us both with her arms crossing over her chest. "I'm already angry this bitch Carmen is coming with us or that Natalie and my dad are going to be there, I don't need this shit from you two fucking around behind my back!"

Rose looked like she swallowed her tongue staring at me to speak for me.

Halle cut her eyes to Rose, “Excuse me, acknowledge your employer when she’s speaking to you!”

“Do you sign my checks?”

“Oh, how clever I could never have seen that one coming. Oh, how you make me laugh. I did some investigating. Apparently he doesn’t sign your checks either but as long as the money is coming from his bank account and his enterprise, you work for me!” Halle holds up the rock on her finger that cost me the same as my house. “You want some dick? Great for you, I want some wine so get me a glass Miss Andale.”

“Halle, Rose… do we have to go through again? You’re already leaving for Maya can we put this behind us for now?” I yawn bored over their constant ego contests.

“A glass for my fiancé as well.” Halle shoos off Rose.

Rose looks at me wounded, “I’m not on the clock Morgan. I live here. I don’t want her disrespecting me in my home.”

“I swear to God I want any reason right now Rose. Morgan, you said she is a maid, right? Then why the hell is Ananda doing all her work? If she’s your housekeeper I am asking her to do her job. She makes enough money to pour a damn glass of wine or two, especially if she’s drinking it up.” I rarely saw Halle so infuriated whatever she felt could overwhelm her as if she had no control.

“Ever since we went out to dinner she’s seemed so irritable. There’s something Halle hasn’t told you and the entire world knows!” Rose urges deeply before standing up, “I’ll get the wine if you tell him about the Carmen Cruz show.”

“Thank you Rose, please get the damn wine before Halle sets herself on fire again and burns down my house.” I sit down on the couch nodding her away.

Halle covered her mouth, “I would never burn your house down on purpose.”

“I don’t think you’ll do it on purpose. I literally think you’ll get so angry you’ll ignite inside my house or spit up a fireball. You’re a fire-bender, you need more control over your emotions or else you can seriously hurt someone." I urge for Halle to sit down.

"You don't honestly think I'm hiding anything from you, do you?" Halle asks.

"You're acting weird. You were the main one advocating Natalie stay and work things out a year ago. You and Rose get along for a few days then you're at each other like a hyena and a lion-

"I'm the lion right? Lions usually win those fights."

"A lion might win one on one but not when the hyena is asking for back up."

"Lions have backup too."

"You're missing my point. You two are like oil and water. It's like you two can merge then slowly you separate and never get back together naturally. You can talk to me Halle. What's going on?"

"You haven't seen Carmen's show? Ananda said you were talking to Carmen on the phone. She didn't spill everything?"

"Carmen doesn't share secrets she hordes them for blackmail. Does she have something on you? She seemed very confident but scared. She said the Wolfe family is shutting down her show and she wanted to pledge fealty to my throne. So, you seem to know more about this than I do Halle, fill me in."

"I- might have- gotten mad at Natalie." Halle throws her hands up.

"Okay, rightfully so... did something happen between you two other than me? I don't think you should let me come between your friendships."

"Our friendship..." Halle smirks rolling her eyes, "Our peace treaty. This was a publicity stunt to keep balance in Naka while our fathers fight some financial war that apparently causing the rest of the world to suffer. Natalie hated my guts, she despised me and she treated me like- after we went to dinner that night I- well- I don't know, maybe I am keeping a secret from you."

"You've been angry. You're talking about leaving Naka and Nadia. And I don't think you're taking forever to get ready because of your makeup."

Halle took a deep breath reaching for the wine she asked for but hadn't arrived. Her eyes darted around the room avoiding my stoic stare, growing wearier by the second as she avoided telling me what seemed to be a poignant truth.

"Alright Morgan, I quit. I'll tell you just stop staring at me with your weird eyes." Halle raises her hand.

"Apologies I'm just confused. I thought we were straight-forward with one another? What the hell is going on Halle?"

"I fucked Natalie up. She- I- Look, okay look, we went out to dinner. After I dropped off Rose but then I saw Natalie posting some shit online. So, I drove off to where I thought she would be staying then I saw her car. I asked her to pull over but she wouldn't so I followed her home. And- she was so disrespectful." Halle laughs but there were tears in her eyes, "Like, her hands were all over me, she kissing on me like me and her were cool. She spoke to me like she owned me. It was like all the stories told me about how her family treated us until we got the power of Enshishi to protect us from the Wolfe Family. I snapped. I don't know what it was inside me but I fucked her up."

"So, you two got into a fight, how bad could it have been?"

"She was on national television in a total body cast and she told everyone you did it on Carmen's Show."

I felt like someone poured cold water over my head.

"Please don't be angry. I was trying to get out of Nadia-

"Get out of Nadia before the goddamn Regulators or Nakan Guard come searching for me!? Are you fucking kidding me? How could you have kept this from me?"

"I'm sorry! Don't get angry! I was mad. I- I let off on her ass. It was for you. I promise. She was going to ruin things for Nadia."

"You ruined things for Nadia. You made it seem like I'm the reason you're leaving and you're leaving to save your own ass. You don't want me to renegotiate our marriage but you don't even want to be in the same room as these people. How the hell could you not tell me?"

"I thought you knew! I thought you knew everything but- I'm sorry I can't take it back I nearly killed her. I thought I did kill her and we could blame it on a robber. I didn't think anyone would find out it was me. I especially didn't think she would lie about it on TV." Halle tried grabbing my hands but I didn't want to be touched.

"You might have ruined me. Are you kidding me Halle? I don't know how to deal with this at all..." I felt like I would faint.

"Look, I'm tired of playing side chick to Natalie or now Rose. It's not like I was lying to you. I didn't tell it's different. I was keeping it a secret. I hadn't watched the show either but... it is all over social media." Halle hid her face in her hands trying to gather her head until she heard the same sniggering I did. "You think this is funny Rose?"

"I'm sorry?" Rose says as she sets down the wine glasses.

"You were eavesdropping weren't you?"

"No, I wasn't I had to go down to the wine cellar." Rose throws up her hands, "I have nothing to do with what's going on."

"This is your fault. If you would have kept your damn mouth shut! If you weren't here I wouldn't be so pissed off! You should have cooked that night or just not have ever been here then it would have only been me and Morgan." Halle leaps out her seat grabbing Rose by the hair.

"Ouch, ouch let go!" Rose screams trying to dig her nails into Halle's hands.

I saw a reflection of myself. Halle's eyes turned a citrine yellow as she tried dragging Rose by her hair, "If you fuck my man again, I'll kill you! You're going to show me some damn respect!"

"Halle let her go!" I shout trying to rip her hair free without taking out a patch of Rose's hair.

"I told you! If you raise your voice at me again to defend here I'm going to kill this girl!" Halle screams slamming Rose's face into the coffee table.

Rose lay on the ground not moving as her nose began bleeding on the carpet.

I moved past Halle to check on her but she jumped in front of me shoving me a few steps back, "Don't you dare!" Halle glared at me enraged.

Rose clamored to her feet, falling over again on her butt holding up her hands to defend herself.

"Did you hear what I said to you Rose?"

Rose nodded, "Loud and clear..."

"What did I say?"

"You're paranoid... I know what it looks like but I never tried to stop your wedding. You did that yourself. Morgan said he would never disrespect right? You should trust him. I had never had any interest coming in between you two. He loves you..." Rose fell on her back, holding her nose.

Halle frowns, her eyes turning back to their normal hazel color, "You said that?"

"Who cares what I said? Get a wet towel. I think you broke her nose!" I finally move past Halle lifting up Rose's head and pinching her nose shut.

Halle kneels down placing a hand on my cheek, "I love you and I'll be damned if I lose you. Do you understand? I love you, Morgan and I'll fix my mess."

"Can you please get a wet towel?" I ask Halle.

"Listen to me Rose. We have the potential to rule the entire planet. Morgan and me not you, I believe in us and I won't play into your little game. You can have your fun. When I get back I'm taking my man back from you, you fucking maid." Halle stares into Rose's eyes then walks off.

We wait for her to return with the towel but she never does. I hold Rose's nose until the bleeding stops. My hand stained with her blood. Halle was leaving for sure sooner than later before she tried to murder someone else. Carmen's call made far more sense now. She didn't want to be on the other side of blade when I caught wind. Hopefully I gave her good enough direction already. Rumya told me to stay in Nadia, to rebuild my home and not to bother going to Naka at all. Instead Colin's vixens have successfully destroyed my kingdom before I could place the first brick. This was their plan all along right? To keep from restoring Nadia so these billionaires can remain in power and Nadia remains in the dark. Everyone in the world watches Carmen's show and I was another victim of it. Walking off couldn't stop her wrath. Breaking up with Natalie couldn't stop her wrath.

If my name is sullied and I'm already responsible for the near-death of Natalie Wolfe then I need to begin moving forward to the Commissioner and the Patriarch. If Nadia couldn't be restored in my lifetime then I could at least topple the power structure. If my good name will be destroyed over Natalie then I was taking all of Naka and Erdu down. It would take decades if not centuries to replace men like Colin Gregor and Ray Warren.

I'm leaving for Erdu in the morning. At least I might be able to negotiate peace with Warren. After seeing how Halle acted when upset I knew it was a matter of time before I had a head-on collision with Colin. God, please have mercy.

CHAPTER 40

Housekeeping

Morgan Ellys

An average morning awake at sunlight. I perform a backward bow, stretching my body tall and arms outstretched to fill my body with vigor and air. The first hours are spent in peace with meditation and exercise. No need to speak. Moving through a routine I've performed for nearly a decade to keep me at my pique mentally and physically.

Emotions escaped me. My mornings didn't consist of dealings with women and all the attention that seems mandatory. Halle wished to leave for Maya and end things with her father. Part of me wanted things to have ended a long time ago, to have never been involved and preserved my conscience and morality. It would have made refusing Rose easier and possibly kept my solitude. Had Nadia happened I would have woken and stayed. We would have all been better off had I never gotten involved with Natalie or Halle. Lessons learned... but none applicable to my life.

Now, this Rose stands with me after far too much baggage and damage under my belt. She only seems to want my seed. I wonder if she cares for me or if it's only Baat's will she wishes to fulfill.

I'm surrounded on all sides by enemies and false allies. The only man who holds truth is across the world in Erdu. My mentor and a man I once admired. I wanted to bring about his dream of Global Regulation.

But we only spread darkness and stifled life. A seed cannot be cultivated smothered under Gaia or under drought by the sun. Where were Baat and Anka in all this? Why have they remained silent everywhere but my bedroom? Anka absent entirely.

Even in my missions abroad... I found no real need for our presence. Despite whoever was in power those at the lowest rungs were treated the same, globally, no matter where you turned. The poorest citizens were liable to the words of their owners or a perceived morality of their clergy.

This world exists in virtual peace... despite hands of involvement. The world existed virtually liberated and peaceful. This world didn't need order or domination. No, it needed cultivation and compassion. Revisiting any land after our involvement they struggled for survival and food.

Perhaps those were the world differences between the two forces. The feminine Guardians allowed the world to be raised from a distance. They acted as Rakil intended. Merely tending to the needs and allowing things to grow and be as they might. Such was liberty, no? The masculine... constantly needed involvement, constantly needed their hands in things. To be overseeing, controlling, or needed things their way. It was a destructive force when unneeded.

Both are in truth. At times one needs to intervene and show a firm hand. But often times this never happens when needed. Instead rules and regulation are forced upon those who would have found morality all their own and vice versa. Those left free to their own devices who only wish to see this all burn or claim no connection or responsibility.

I come to understand, Ada is that balance. I am that balance. At least, I'm trying to be balanced.

So, many live in falsified peace under occupation. Willful blindness believing what's been happening in the latter realms won't happen to them. Colin and Warren won't stop. No... old dogs were lost in their ways. Men never quit easily.

How do I rest being the only one who knows what's fated if Colin and Warren stood unopposed?

And they wish for me to take up their charge, to continue their works. To marry Halle and reenlist and carry this out without issue for the death their dogs bring about. Did they know this no longer remained an option? I am no longer under their mind control. Halle was no longer Colin's pet. We were free to be as we wish or as fate intended. They've raised their own demise.

Colin is the devil. He must be stopped it's beyond Halle and Ananda. The destruction this man has caused has no end in sight. He doesn't care for growth or development. He shrouds himself in family words and history as though the Gregors are all that were and all that mattered. It's repulsive... even more so for his followers who adopt the same mentality ignorantly believing it brings prosperity. No, those who fight only for themselves always end in ruin. Either by the hands of those they destroy but particularly consumed by their own greed and mistrust.

I knew it must be done but at this moment... I'm unarmed. No army. No territory. I'm unable to do anything against Colin. I could take the man's life but millions if not billions would die for the sake of one man. To take Colin's life before the wedding outside of his twisted traditions would be the greatest mistake possible. With Halle leaving, it might be some time until I get my opportunity.

Even in my morning routine... my body has indeed slowed with the fatigue latent deep in my tendons and ligaments from the rigor mortis.

Perhaps Rose is right... all I can do at this time is rest.

Liberty can only be bought in blood or coin... Too much blood must be spilled. And there wasn't a dollar amount that could give Colin pause. There had to be a third option.

I abandoned my meditation abruptly to lie on my back. Surrounded by the darkness and absorbed by the silence. This was death in its full form. Is this truly what I fear? What so many live their lives to avoid. Living in the endless noise and bustle to escape this tranquility? They deafen their conscience and to never be left alone with their thoughts. This is why I do not close my eyes to rest? I too feared this inevitable tranquility and absence.

I can no longer cower. This feeling I know well. This feeling I hated. I rather live in light than to remain still and stunted in my voluntary suicide. I am no longer a corpse. This I must remember.

I was granted new life and always questioned why? To what end?

Absolution... Absolution stood with me opposing this continued chaos and death.

I must rest, revitalize, and reeducate myself from the Academy's teachings and propaganda. I need to... I need to figure out what I believe in. Perhaps the best I can do for Nadia is aid in protecting itself against Warren and Colin's perversions of peace and order.

I needn't fight any war.

Not until I stop fighting myself over what I believe.

Three beautiful women in my house and I had my pick. A wonderful lake I could enjoy but I only watched. I spend my life in this room. When there is so much life beyond it. So much of my own life yet lived. I left my coma two years ago. Perhaps it's time I awoke to what was before me.

I found relief in my meditation. Walking up the steps from my sanctuary feeling as though a weight was lifted from my body, feeling some of my elasticity returned as I removed the weights from my mind.

There was an unusual hustle around the house. My three vixens all around the kitchen in the same falsified peace the world faced. Ananda was behind the stove cooking up a storm, next to her a pile of food. Rose sat at the kitchen table tapping away at her laptop haven't changed her clothes since this morning's session. She progressed well over just a week. She received instruction before me. And Halle, sat with her headphones in at the kitchen island.

Ananda was the first to greet me, "Morning, Master Ellys your tea is boiling on the kettle. I've prepared quite the breakfast for you. I wasn't sure if you liked pancakes or French toast, so I made you a bit of both."

"He doesn't like food." Halle rolls her eyes.

Ananda ignored her, "Sit, sit, I'll bring you your meal." she pushes me along.

I glimpsed at Halle, those slender golden legs crossed over each other. Leading to where I will never return. She didn't even look up from her book.

I let out a sigh, sitting with Rose.

"Good Morning Mister Morgan." Rose smiles wide, stopping her typing.

"Rose, why is Ananda cooking instead of you?"

Rose looked at me confused for a moment then looked at Ananda, "First off, she wouldn't let me help. Second, she's been at this all morning since we finished our training session. She even went downtown Nadine to go grocery shopping."

I nodded. I knew the truth was Rose believed she was moving out of the maid position and into Halle's spot. It's been a few months since Halle decided she would leave. Rose mostly occupied herself with her classes, letting Ananda take up the load. I made note of it, setting up Ananda with a bank account of her own leaving money in it weekly for her efforts. I had no information if the same was done with Rose. Rumya informed me she was the one who hired Rose and handled her compensation. I couldn't imagine what would cause Rumya to do such a thing.

"Here, baby, check it out." she spins her laptop to me, "I've been working on it with Baat since you told me, you can only free Nadia with blood or coin. We meditated-

"You were meditating without me?"

Rose blushes, "Yes, it's helped me communicate with Baat better. Keep better control as well. She used to just dominate me when I was young."

I didn't want to question. Ada was in my ear. 'How long has this been going on? Ask her now!' I brushed it off.

I gazed over the laptop. "This is about container farming... why?"

"Well, food supplies are very low in Nadia. I was googling online and it says one of the base forms of civilization is being able to feed your citizens. Another is education. And security."

"Rose... this is fantastic." I had to know though, "How much of this was Baat's influence? How long has Baat been mentoring you?"

"Well most of this is my work! She said she was quite pleased with me. I asked for a bit of advice here and there, because she's like... you know, Baat." she giggles, covering her face. "Do you really like it?"

Do you still doubt her Ada?

'I didn't doubt the daughter of Enshishi either. I do not know these young girls, I know spiritual warfare. It's quite unorthodox to be using a vessel outside one's own bloodline. Outside her own region at that... though Ecru and N has had many masters in my absence. Who is this young girl?'

She showed up one day. She said my ex-Natalie hired her. I hope Natalie is happy she ruined my wedding arrangement.

'You ruined your arrangement... though this young girl's presence assisted. This is very good work.. This is the method of the first age.'

Self-sustenance and Self-determination. She wants to form a new nation.

"Baat approves?"

"If you do the work... we love you dearly, Jah'Ada."

"But do you love me?"

Rose raised her brow, "Um, of course."

"I can't stomach this." Halle mutters grabbing her book and walking outside.

"Trouble in paradise?" Rose asks taking back her laptop.

I nodded. Moving out the way as Ananda began setting the table with plates of food.

"What's wrong with, Halle?" Ananda asks confused.

I take a deep breath and sigh, "she wants to break off the wedding arrangement."

"What!? No, no she cannot. Where will I go?" Ananda covers her mouth in shock, "I must speak with her."

"Ananda, if you wish to stay, you can. I will offer you the same arrangement I offered Rose."

Ananda looked at Rose then to me, “What arrangement?” she looks suspiciously.

“Why are you looking at me like that?” Rose sucks her teeth.

“You ruined, Lady Gregor’s wedding you homewrecker! I do not wish any place within any of that! I just left being someone’s sex slave. I’m not doing it again.”

“Oh, please... before a couple weeks ago Morgan didn’t even know I existed!” Rose crosses her arms over her chest, “I had no problem sharing or playing my position. Halle had no problem last night. I don’t know what came over her.”

Ananda sighed, “I do not believe that. You two act far too close to simply be employer and employee.”

“We were destined to be!” Rose swoons, “I just needed the patience of Ada.”

I rubbed my temples, “Halle doesn’t believe I love her because of all your preaching Rose. As If I am somehow involved in your plans.”

Ananda covered her eyes, “I cannot return to Colin. I will not be another man’s plaything.”

“Morgan doesn’t fuck with his employees like that. I promise, Ananda it’s such an awesome job. We could even probably get you in university.”

“Job? You get paid?” Ananda asks curiously.

“Yaaaasss! And it’s Morgan we’re talking about. You barely have to do anything. I clean for a couple hours then just study most the time.” Rose closes her laptop and begins piling food on her plate, “I think this is the most that’s been cooked here since I started.”

“You aren’t very good at your job. Maybe I do need to help out here.” Ananda crosses her arms then looks at me, “I will stay. You need someone to take proper care of you.”

I nod. Looking down at all the delicious looking food.

“You better eat...” Ananda cuts her eyes at me, sitting next to me and beginning to put pancakes on my plate, cutting them before holding a forkful before me. “Open.”

“I’m not a child...” I mutter.

"Open." Ananda repeats staring at me with those cat-like eyes. "Now, Morgan. You need your strength."

"I can't eat before a kill..." I sigh.

"Excuse me? Killing who?" Ananda drops the fork, "Are you killing Colin so soon?"

"Well, I hope that I don't have to kill anyone. I have to speak with the Commissioner of The Regulator Regime. I can't rest or eat until he answers some of my questions. I'm going to Erdu. I have questions and he has my answers. If it comes to a fight then I fear I will have to kill him or... prepare for the worst. Being defeated and trying to defend Nadia. It's inevitable."

"You can't Morgan. Not before you've made an heir." Rose frets.

I sigh, "I can't ignore what's on my mind either."

"What about Nadia? Forget Erdu. Forget Colin. Let's focus on home." Rose stresses.

"If Colin is our enemy, fine... this we are aware of and can prepare to defend against Naka. However, if the Regulation Regime is rising against us as well then your plan means very little to the power they will bring that we don't have. I'm afraid this is reality. I can't be fearful of Warren or Colin. I must confront him head-on."

"Babe, please just listen. We must begin work in Nadia. If Regs come it's better to have the city united."

"No, you listen. If the Regs come there will be no more Nadia. I must confront this before it becomes an issue and..." I lean back placing my hands behind my neck, "I must know what Warren thinks of my actions. Ada believes it'll bring about conclusion. Allieve me of guilt or possibly gain a great ally."

Rose stared at me like I lost my mind, "So, you have no army yet you will walk into the mouth of the beast before rallying one?"

"All the men in Nadia are jailed in Erdu and Naka. If I survive with Warren and if he forgives me then I can reason with Anki to free the men." I rationalize.

"We have women and The Masks! If you train Halle and I to fight, you can train even more of us."

"If there are Wolves, Rottweilers, Pit Bulls, Hounds, and two Guardians are against us, you believe the simple women and children of Nadia can fight that army?"

"If you train them as you have trained us then maybe we'll stand a chance."

"Both you and Halle have divine chakra inside you. And you are both abnormally strong for any human. You are both two vicars of Guardians. Those would be civilians dying senselessly when peace can be negotiated."

"I just think you want daddy to pat your head and say good job." Rose rolls her eyes.

"I won't lie... Warren's opinion is the only opinion I hold of any worth in this world at this moment." I make direct eye contact with Rose.

"I am your- I guess I'm not anything to you." Rose stands, "I'll be in my room. And I'm taking food with me!" she grabs a small stack of pancakes, French toast, and a handful of beef bacon before marching out the room.

I turned to Ananda, "Any words from you?"

"You are both right. If things go awry, you can return back to Nadia but once at Nadia without being the established leader, who will rally behind you with an army chasing after you? However, if things go well, you needn't rush in reconstructing Nadia. You also gain a very powerful ally against Colin's Syndicate keeping things in place. Baat seems to favor you and Rose. She radiates Queen Mother Qatar's energy as if it's her own blood."

"Those eyes... you can see energy?" I was already blown away by her insights.

"I have studied much between being terrorized by Colin... I had access to Maurice Gregor's library, the old Patriarch. I have read all that I could. The Matriach also had an extensive library I have studied through. As well as some of her private journals where I discovered the secret, she wasn't able to figure it out but I did."

"Your eyes... those are from your studies, I thought monks had to meditate for one thousand years? I heard rumors of the old world."

"I awakened them through more than reading. Colin was furious... he couldn't rip out my eyes so instead he inflated me with these chests." her eyes began to tear but she stopped herself. "I have no interest in going to university but if you wished, I could continue my study if you got me a few more books?"

I nod. "Assist Halle with her plans as well. She is my rock right now. Use your knowledge to help her out."

"I will but I am no miracle worker, Halle seems very intent on meeting her mother." Ananda gulps.

"As a good woman should I'm not keeping her here. I am Ada. My home is open to you as long as you need it. I will return to both of you."

"I can see why these women favor you." Ananda smiles giving me a wink "You are quite the man. I feel very safe here with you."

I shrug, "I do as I can, and that's all I can do."

"You can eat, so get to that." Ananda holds up another forkful, French toast this time.

"That's delicious, Ananda." I muse over the cinnamon, butter and perfect flakiness of the croissants she used instead of bread.

"Is it delicious enough to finish your plate?"

"You're going to make me too heavy to move." I groan eating another few bites.

"Then maybe you will stay here with us for a while. Rest up as you were talking about yesterday. Those two seem pretty fed up with your method of doing things. They say you leave in the evening or morning without a word or trace."

"Those two hardly have any method of their own. If they understood what it took to be successful they would have a different tone. These things take effort and focus. I can't always talk about things before I do them because I am doing them without any possible verbal explanation until it's complete. It takes sacrifice so the populace can live in prosperity or in joy. It doesn't happen by being selfish or worrying about recovery. You must work tirelessly and dutifully because it must be done. Not for personal gain or congratulations. If Halle wishes to leave me because she believes my focus to be abnormally distant from marriage and sex then I understand. Since I was a child, I have only cared about the peace and security of Gaia. They were normal children, playing with dolls or going to school, I was in The Academy being brainwashed and trained for war. I care little for their opinion on how things get done. I plan to speak to a fellow Guardian and to face my judgment. I do not care about the whims or words of two naïve girls. This is the only purpose I was nurtured for to inherit the Regulator Regime or to inherit The Patriarch's power. I don't want to be anything like Colin so... I guess The Regime."

"You seem rather self-important." Ananda covers her mouth smirking beneath her hand.

"I'm not self-absorbed Ananda. I had to become self-aware to realize how people were trying to use me. If you don't know your worth then people treat you however they want. This has not gotten to my head it's in my heart. I asked for none of this, Ananda. I swear it upon my own life. I only wanted tranquility, I thought I would find it in death but I've come to understand not every person gets that. There are those amongst us who must know the harshness and savagery of this world in order to protect the masses from it. I am not delusional to believe I am one of those men. The choice was taken out of my hands and I spent my life being bred for the role. I tried to live alone in peace and now my house is filled with people who need me."

"There are Guardians and there is Rakil. You are telling me you are a Guardian?"

"No man is a god but I maybe might be a Guardian."

"No, no they aren't Gods... I believed that to be the most disturbing thing about Colin. He believes himself the golden son of Rakil. You all fail far in comparison to the almighty." Ananda shakes her head in disgust.

I smiled feeling a breath of fresh air speaking to this young woman, "Welcome to my home, Ananda."

She hugs me tightly. “I will begin washing dishes then do the laundry.”

“When you get a chance to relax, please do. Take time for yourself. That’s what all this is for anyway. There’s more to life than a clean home. Figure out your purpose and I’ll help you pursue it. I don’t imagine you want to spend your life living here. There’s a whole world out there.”

“Then I wouldn’t be listening to all you said. After the house is clean, I will read all I can in your library that might take some time sir.” Ananda held out a piece of bacon.

“My home is your home. I just hope you spend the time doing more than cleaning and cooking. There is more to life. If you wish to read at least start a blog doing book reviews.” I nod accepting the offering.

“Be safe, Morgan... more than Halle and I care for you. The world has been awaiting the return of Ada. Before you leave for Erdu, please rest and build your own home. You have lost Halle and the Gregors, I don’t advise losing Nadia and your life as well.”

“You will be a very good advisor to the Queen Regent.”

“Not to the King?”

“Halle is likely headed to Maya and Rose is likely going to Graham both traveling under my authority regardless of how I feel. Watch over them. Help Rose with Nadia until I return. Halle’s journey will take some time to prepare, help her as you can as well.”

“Do you need something? How are you getting to Erdu, are you going to take a plane?” Ananda asks handing me another piece of bacon.

I chuckle, “No, I plan on taking the rift.”

“The rift is real? I have only heard rumors of the abilities of the Ecruen people... Be safe Morgan with this Lord Commissioner. There aren’t many of your kind with command of the rift as you. The world can benefit from that alone against these forces of evil.”

I nod, “A life of being a Wolf taught me that. To know I am Ada... there is a whole other realm of power and ability I have yet to reach. Maybe I do need some rest. I can test out some of the things you learn.”

"The books..." Ananda quickly jots down a few titles, "These are what I need, they are lost and worth a thousand dollars each. There are copies in the Gregor Library if you knew a way in there I would appreciate it since you seem like you want to risk your life."

I look over the list, "These are also in the libraries in the Academy. I have seen the titles as a Pup after my initiation into the Wolves. Whether things go awry or well, I can sneak in and get them real quick. Knowledge is a powerful tool. You be safe as well, Ananda."

"Now, I thought you would rest up before seeing this Lord Commissioner."

"I'm only going to get the books. I'll be right back. I won't let him know I was there... I will be in and out."

Ananda stared at me for a minute with her eyes dilating then relaxing. "You're telling the truth. Finish eating first. My heart will be fine as long as you're nourished." She kisses my cheek. "Be back quickly, Master Ellys."

"Just call me Morgan."

"I- thank you, Lord Morgan." she fixes her eyes at me refusing to budge.

"Just Morgan."

"We are not equals..." she sighs, "you are my Master."

"We are all equals in the eyes of Rakil. He plays no favorites."

"He favors, Ada above all... You are someone I don't mind calling my Master." she pats my head then crosses the kitchen to begin washing dishes.

Such clever maids I found, at least they seemed motivated even if their servitude is to their own agendas. It made little sense why she would wish to be viewed as such. Liberty was ever sweeter. I didn't wish for a human servant, I wanted an employee but what was the difference in truth?

CHAPTER 41

Fragility of Life

Morgan Ellys

I faded into the vapor and reappeared into the hollowed and historic stone tunnels running beneath the Academy, all across Erdu. From the Academy in Patmos to Sah'ra, the desert on the bordering Naka and Erdu far north of the Nadian territory. I had taken a reprieve to the library after my botched training with Ray.

Why did things always have to head haywire when two people refused to move on their point? I feel as if Ray and I can live in coexistence... I know I can allow him to live his way. But I fear in my absence I couldn't stop him from pushing his way too stringently upon my people.

Perhaps after he's gotten some time to think and we can let cooler minds prevail.

Stone Tunnel was molded by the ancient Erdun and Ecrun, that was accepted fact. The men who worked on the project were all benders. Then used their abilities to push the stone, sand, rocks, and clay all through the underground, crafted the monasteries and underground cities.

I'm not sure when humanity fell apart. To believe I was raised in these hallowed halls of ancient knowledge. Returning to civilian life, even to the Regulators above, they believed us crazy for speaking of unified efforts and actions.

Steele never spoke on it. She never went far from the Regs and never planned to. We enjoyed what we did. We did it well. Both of us had our lives and careers set. I would be the Lord Commissioner and she would be the Veil of Justice. We would be husband and wife. Not sure there was an equivalent to a human wrecking ball. There surely wasn't one to a royal family of WMDs.

I dragged my hands along the halls looking around the claustrophobic space. To believe classes were held here thousands of years before us. Bustling with students like high schools. People would never believe it. So blinded by their own existence, sometimes we refuse to even believe others have lived here before us. Even better than we live ourselves.

I lit the small torches leading toward the hidden library where the Aalem studied in the 3rd Age. Back when Erdu sold knowledge, not mercenaries.

I pressed my hand to the ancient palm reading, as the mystic force scanned my handprints. The door rolled open, creaking out dust and fumes.

I coughed, covering my face as I entered.

"Welcome, Guardian." Another huff of smoke breathed out, filling my nostrils with smoke. "The Young Pup, my you have grown." Another huff of smoke filled the halls.

I gave the Drake Librarian a nod.

"You dare ignore me?"

"I'm busy... what do you want, Churakra?" I groaned.

If you wanted something protected, Dragonborn were perfect. The Drakes were lesser dragons, more interested in humans than their giant relatives that tended to eat them. Few remained outside their underground cities.

"To rattle your brain for knowledge. Why else would I bother with you, fleshling?" Churakra bellowed another waft of smoke.

"What do you want?"

"Your rift... you used that to enter the library?"

"How did you know?"

"I am Churakra, I know all there is to have ever known of these Tunnels." because he never left them.

"Even, the lower levels?"

Churaka huffed. He had grown Dragon-like since my childhood. Since the Wolves shutdown I suppose he's all that's truly left of the school. He was haggardly, and loose-skinned. His scales were platey as if he barely moved nor got sun. I suppose all he truly did was work the library and attempt to read all these books. Every Dragon had their vice and bondage. They lusted for power much differently than Wolves or Lions. They hoarded valueables, hoarded themselves, and hoarded their time. Each kept to themselves and burned all those who approached. Churaka only talks you to death until either you leave him alone. Or he gets his fill like some sick addict.

"Because, I was sparring with Warren. I'm tired."

"Yes...?" he gleams as I say tired.

"Too tired to blink, never too tired to punch."

"Well then, how rude. Perhaps, I wished to give you something."

"A Dragon, giving gifts... unheard of." I gave him my full attention, respecting his domain.

"Oh, Fleshling, I have four gifts for you, three for free, and something you must purchase."

"Churakra, you're my Dragon! What do I have to buy?"

"It's a surprise. If you answer my Question."

"Churakra... why can't you simply take coin or money, I have enough of that."

"You humans have ruined money, wealth is worthless if you're near immortal. But understanding, awareness, knowledge... those are things even if you paid for, you couldn't buy. So, my question is... out of all the Wolves who were raised, why are you the one who returned?"

"Is this a riddle?"

"If I knew the answer, I wouldn't need to exchange knowledge." He said frustrated. He hated his own ignorance more than anything. "Why!? I have been alone for a decade. No one has come. Why you...?"

"Ha, honestly I'm only here for a friend. She sent me after a book only existing in this monastery. Something to help defeat Colin Gregor and to restore Ecru."

"A friend... my, my this pup has friends now? You never had friends before. No, no, you were with me and my books. I liked you, you knew how to read quickly and quietly."

"I expected a riddle."

"I was simply lonely..." Churakra bellowed up pipes. "I feared I wouldn't see another life for eternity. The humans above don't believe in dragons. Nor the value of books."

"Technically you're not a dragon." He looked at me aghast as if I insulted his mother. "I'll let you have it dude." I chuckle raising my hands. "I came for three books... uh, "Elements" by Hi'jir of Erdu, "Cosmic Alignment" by Cyrus men Sah'ra, and..." I paused having never realized the last book existed. "History of Ada" by Jamar Juy Ghesit of Esha."

"History of Ada, one of my favorites..." the librarian chuckled, "Far too complex a book for a mere mortal!" He quickly became offended, I couldn't understand why. "To accept such truths of the Holy One, one must have a great spread of understanding of the spiritual realm."

"I'm not reading it, dude. I'm checking out for a friend."

"Don't bend my pages, these books are priceless." He exhaled a bit of smoke before flapping his wings to search for the books.

"Yeah there's only two or three of them in the world right?"

He looked at me and sighed, "it does not impress me you know how many books there are if you have not read them. You needn't speak up to sound intelligent flesh ape." Churakra left me, flapping his wings to retrieve the books. He hated having people in the aisles.

I stood around patiently waiting for him to return. It brought me back to my childhood. I thought I lived a lonely existence but to be the last of your kind amongst those who don't understand you- Ha, I guess we're none too different.

"Here, here Elements and the gift I promised you. For your eyes alone." He came back huffing and puffing.

"Out of breath already, huh?" I chuckle.

I flip over the books Elements, an ancient grimoire filled with seals, manifestation techniques, and the ancient wisdom of the first benders. Published in the year 500.

The second story he gave me... it was smaller by comparison. Spiraled as if any ole composition notebook.

"Your notebook?"

"Not mine... it took me some fiddling but I learned, Obatta Sameera was your father this is his journal he had hid here. I was cleaning when I found it. I have been waiting to give this to you for a few years. I expected your answer to be fate instead it was far more surprising, friendship. You have truly grown up, Pup." Churakra nearly looked as though he cracked a smile. "I have read it... The man was possessed by the devil. Fueled by rage, vengeance. He said the Dread Wolf spoke to him. Another gift... Foremica's journals." He hands me a bundle of books wrapped in lacquer. "Much the same... So, I see you again Onyx. I stare at you again in your eyes believing you long dead and long removed. Redeemed before me pulsating with grace yet you can never remember me and I remember you so well. So, long I thought you were simply some nosy braniac kid. To find out, one of my dear friends had sent his kindred to keep my company."

My eyes swelled with tears as he looked at the books.

"He was the reincarnation of Foremica... I was wrong about him." I swallowed.

"He was wrong of himself. Unsure of his beliefs, conflicted. Confused. Foremica was no God, he was a man. His great duty and love for his people brought him prosperity, in wealth but in a son who would fulfill his wildish dreams. Because in his heart he was not selfish, not a beast, not a devil. He was a man in a world who told him to hate himself, and he refused." Churakra nearly patted my shoulder but decided against it returning to fetch the other books.

After he returned we exchanged few words. My mind was in the mood for banter and I was drawn between my will of killing Colin and appeasing the only woman I cared for who happened to be his daughter. Rose deserved to see peace with her lifetime. I do not believe it will be soon but it can be achieved in her lifetime.

"I will visit you more. And I will bring back the books I took out!" I promised.

He brushed me off but the glint in his eyes said he appreciated being remembered.

I wished to take a final glance over my fight with Warren. So much left never said. I wish we could speak instead of fighting. But neither of us could use our words. And neither of us were wrong.

I needed to see what remained of our clash and battle. I needed to mentally prepare for Colin.

I pushed in the door to the training room. I half-expected Ray to still be here, meditating or back to his drills. His energy was present but after his display. I imagine there should be some resonance but not quite this much.

I wanted to survey the damage. There was a moment there I lost Ray and his power went up exponentially. Even if it was manageable. If I'm to fight Gregor, I need to understand the power of these Guardians when pushed.

In the heat of battle I hadn't noticed the enormity of the crevice falling deep down into the pits of earth. I saw an opening on his weak spot and sniped to it. He popped a damn earthquake on me, he knew I needed to get close. He was always an incredible strategist. But he always lacked creativity. I suppose that's where we differ. It wasn't sheer wit I made my name. I was inventive, constantly thinking, constantly trying to perfect or find new ways to master my crafts. Most of the dogs like the path Ray took sticking to drills and muscle memory.

Wolves were attuned to their natural selves and instinct. We each had our own personality and fighting style. A project funded through the Wolfe-Gregor treaty. A bit of personal reading in the library. We were a project. Everyone knew about the project but Wolfe walked away claiming it unethical. Then it was allegedly disbanded. Allegedly I don't exist. Good luck proving that one.

The Regulators once stood for something noble. The project proposed taking refugee kids and allowing them food and housing to patrol the streets, have a sense of duty and responsibility for their community and regions. Most do. Good and brave hard-working men. But as a Wolf, I tried doing volunteer work at the force to assist in the precincts. I couldn't stomach what I saw. From the streets or from my own brothers.

The way dogs lick each other's wounds were one thing. But the way they viewed criminals and citizens. Everyone was guilty and the dogs were always hungry for a fight. Before each mission they would glorify themselves in how they would take care of their perp. And the ever famous, "and if he runs..." I ignored it then.

Too young to care. Laughing along. I was the most talented. I entertained them. I had my own brutality. Played games with my perps. Knowing at any moment I could kill them. But I never did. I never had interest in it. What pride was there in killing the weak and the hapless? I had the power to take away their lives and gave them life. Many times these men shot or would beat the everlasting crap out of them. And instead of mourning the deaths of the victims or criminals, their dogs would immediately come to lick their wounds, filling them with plaintive validations, their own justifications and ensuring they would do the same. That made Nadia easier. Dogs were corrupted... good lived amongst them but the good are always naïve to how vile evil is. A man who justifies the death of another before mourning the loss is no man, and is not even human. Less than animals. And less than dirt. Warren had his own record. One I used to admire... I proved myself in assassinating key targets in the larger scale of the spectrum. Not children and women... there is no glory in slaughter.

Wolves had rituals. We had respect. We sacrificed a true life to fulfill our duty. I wonder how these men who worship Colin can return to their wives and daughters. Knowing the things they've seen and shield them from. To know they idolize the system's creator.

I knew we would never see eye-to-eye but I never knew we were capable of this. Especially not on each other. I can't half blame Warren.

I used to believe Ray to be indomitable. To be prepared and to be ready in all situations. But for him to have to resort to this in a higher state? I bested him. Not because of age. But because now, I am his better.

"I could never beat you, Ada." I heard a strained hacking from deep down inside the crevice. I hadn't even felt an energy signature.

Warren was raising from the abyss, laying on a bed of sandstone. He was barely holding together as the stone reached the mouth of the abyss and he tumbled over before me in piles of sand.

"You're... you're falling apart Ray!" I try to scoop him up only to have his physical form fall apart to sands between my fingers.

I was once again a child, clueless and mute. Running to my mentor. As my mentor fell apart to ashes before me. Down in the pile of sands. I needed to be a man but there was so much boy left in me.

Ray formed a hand touching my cheek, "I finally get it. Transcendence. We are merely Guardians. To be a Guardian is an honor... but we hold forces of Rakil himself inside us. Forces that will not be stopped whether we live or breathe. These forces must reach their end. I see Rakil..." Warren lifted his hand to me.

"Warren. I didn't kill you, did I?" I asked as a child. “Please, don't die...”

I'm a juvenile fool!

No man is greater than tomorrow...

He smiled with what remained of his face, "I would never give you the chance, boy." He winked, "I put my all into that fight. And my all was too much for me to handle. Anki has broken loose. You convinced me, boy... and I questioned Anki."

"He's left you?"

"No... we are still one. But our bond is fragile. My time left is short, I have lost all control of my body and it turns to sands. I have waited far too long to reach my potential as a Guardian. Instead I followed Colin Gregor... fighting another man's wars. Allowing those men to die in the name of- " he let out a weak exhale "I have gotten weaker in my old age... in my depression. I never had the proper genetics to contain Anki. I had to push my body to its limits in my heydays. I had many incidents in the past. But Anki and I are of like-minds and like-wills. Anki taught me to form a seal of my life energy to keep a limit to how much of his power I could use. But I have little energy left, my boy. Had I known this would have turned into what it did... I should have tightened the seal regardless. I have grown addled and foolish, in my age. I should have spoken to you as an Uncle not a mentor, not a man. But as a boy I considered my family. You've shown me my error."

"Just like that... and you're gone?"

"When a vessel grows weak, the Guardian takes over until the body decays. If the body dies then the Guardian moves on. This is what Anki has just told me. We did all we could to replace the seal but I am weak, my energy is gone. I fear if I use Anki's he will be released." Warren was little more than a pile of sands before me. The disembodied voice was all that remained of him. His energy all but depleted. If his chakra gets depleted then this man, perhaps my last ally will be no more.

"Please, Ada no... please Rakil, help me save my Uncle."

"Colin's grandfather... Mandel Gregor conquered an old Nakan Emperor. He stole his soul... Men hold domain over Gaia and Guardians over their realm. I followed Colin this slaughter and condemned myself to hell."

Anki let out a final roar, "I'm dying for Colin Gregor! I'm dying in his place father! I was fooled. I was fooled and should never have trusted him! I was warned. Now I die... in my mistakes." He ranted bewilderedly.

"I will kill him..."

"No!" he shouts at me using far more energy than he could strain as his soul fought to stay present with him within the sands. "Murashima... Midoriya. He is a brother of the Order... he is a descendant of the ascended Enshishi, Ryu. The only in existence to my knowledge."

"You're not dying on me Warren. Pull yourself together, soldier!"

"It's too late..." Warren said mournfully

"You can't die until you atone, Warren!" My vision turned royal violet, "In Rakil's name you will be redeemed!"

I jutted my hands into the sands entering a portal into the ether. The pile was bottomless, I nearly lost myself in the boundless potential of Anki waiting to claim the sands.

This was no time to be a child... I needed to be his brother.

"Focus on my energy, Warren!"

“It's too late, boy.” Ray shook his head, "My time is done boy, quit this! Let me die in peace!"

"You're not relieved of duty until your guard is over! And you are still the Vanguard of Ecru! Get off your ass. Stop feeling sorry for yourself, and get your shit together, you bastard! Focus on my damn energy!"

I sent a series of pulse waves of my life force throughout the sands. I'm hoping I can use my ki and my natural electromagnetic life energy. Feeling a cold steel cutting through my fingers as his energy began to reject me.

Another pulse-wave and a hand reached from out the sands and gripped my arm. I began pulling him from out the sands. Ray's face surfaced out of the sands as if taking on new life. Ray gasped for air as if he'd never breathed before.

He pulled his body from out of the bottomless sands, fleeting face, fighting against his decay toward rebirth. Clawing the grounds as the veins in his neck bulged. His eyes opened a reddish purple-blended tint shining radiant ultralight beams as if he's never needed the light of day.

"No, no, no..." his teeth chattered, "Not today, devil! Not, today death!" Ray clinched his teeth. Sands from across the room rushing back toward his reforming mass.

Ray's hands firmed and his body fell from my arms whole.

I fell back, my hands bloodied and raw.

Ray rose to his feet then fell apart once more into sands.

No... not for null.

I fell to my knees feeling my own life force draining.

Come back, Ray. Not now, I need you by my side in this fight. One battle together... please old man.

"Please... You can't go like this." a tear fell from my eye as the sudden fear of being completely alone took my heart. "Please, Ray. Not like this." My eyes swelled as I fought back the tears.

I clapped my hands together, having no life force of my own left. On my knees before the almighty above and the finite before me.

"Heavenly Father Rakil, I beseech you. Give me the ability and power to redeem my Uncle. He is the only family I have left. I know no man is greater than tomorrow. I beg of you. Give him enough life to be atoned and redeemed before you. Give him the same courtesy you extended to me."

I felt hands wrap around mine.

'I am with you, Ada. I am by your side.' Ada's energy filled. I felt the warmest hug I've felt in my life as new life, energy, and joy filled my body.

I took a deep breath with a smile knowing my victory was now in reach. I begin digging my hands into the sands once more. They were shallow. A mound of sands before me, he was at least back of this world.

"COME BACK, RAY!!" I utilized all my raw sadness into another shockwave sending all I could afford without killing myself into those sands. Trying resuscitate him.

Futile...

Futile...

The sands sat and Ray's energy was gone...

I don't understand this. I don't understand this new realm! These new responsibilities.

"RAKIL WHY DO YOU MOCK ME!?" I howl to the absent moon. I began sobbing, "No, it is I who mocks you. I have mocked you my entire life. It is I who am trying to defy your wish. God makes no mistakes they say. If you want him, I will follow your plan. You have given me a life of strife so I may be strong. If this is your will then I reject my past transgressions. I reject the Dread Wolf and refuse to live in defiance. I am your servant. I am your son." I finished my prayers. Bowing my head.

I stood wailing as I tried to pull myself together. My tears found no end. I sucked them up long enough to turn saluting the soul of my lost patron. Rest in peace, Raymond. You will surely be remembered as one of the greatest men in history.

"I don't think I'll ever be the same."

Ray!?

Ray's body struggled to reform. He remained on his back, looking more of a sand sculpture than the Commissioner. "What is this? I- I don't understand." He feels his face, "I-I feel formless... but I am still of this world. Is this death? Am I alive?"

"I- I'm not sure, Ray." I say in awe as his disembodied voice spoke to me. “Where are you? Are you in my head? Are you in the ether?”

"No, I am here. I have not crossed over, yet I have no body. There's so much I have yet to discover about this life. I have been so oblivious and limited. So, much even in my age I have yet to do I needn't wait for death... I see now the preciousness of life. So, quickly and unexpectedly. I am not meant to ensure honorable deaths for my men. I am to ensure them honorable lives. This is my charge as Anki. I am a Guardian.... I do not contain... I am a pathway of liberty and fulfillment. I will stand by you, Captain L. Sameera."

He stood before me at five-foot tall the best shape he could manage similar to his last. All the sands he could find only formed this much. Ananda could probably tell me all about this. Yet, she was in Nadia.

“I... Am whole at least.” He feels himself and touches his skin. Pinching the flesh between his brass-colored knuckles. “I am-

I hugged him, "I thought, I lost you, Ray.”

Ray seemed taken aback. But in truth... this is the only father I knew. He patted my back as I wept. Once again a child.

"I'm here, boy. I'm here." He holds the back of my neck. "I thank you, Morgan. Had you left me here. I would have been dead. Unredeemed and reborn corrupted. I thank you as brother and mentor."

"That was horrific... is this the fate I must place upon Colin?"

"In my last moments of consciousness, I remembered the name Murashima. The original family that held domain over Enshishi before

Mandel Gregor fought his way deep into Naka. His name is Saito. He's believed to be 200 years old... but only looks 50. He's one of the good guys. He can tell you how to beat Colin."

"So, I must find this man in Naka? What is he in the mountains or something?" I let out a groan. "They will understand this better? Maybe they could figure out-

"I believe Colin is past their assistance. I believe Colin is past absolution. This is now in your hands. I couldn't face you... You are the one to put an end to Colin. Seeing my own death and what was demanded of me at the gates of eternity. Colin would never accept the terms of life."

"I am done with war. I took my share of life and innocence from this world. Allow someone else to shed blood for atonement. I have to stop in Nadia... but I will go out in search of this Murashima for answers. I assure you."

Ray fell to a knee and it immediately collapsed into sands to the impact.

"I barely have enough life force to get by on. I will be in my quarters." Warren's body went limp and I braced him. "I believe I'll be fine, Captain.. at ease. Ha, I will at least take the dignity to walk back to my bed on my own two feet. Or what remains of them."

"Are you sure?"

"I will be fine, Morgan." he pats my cheek, "You're a good, kid. I'm proud of you, boy."

I smiled, bowing at my hip to my sensei, "I'm glad you're alive, Ray."

"Glad to be alive, I will cherish every day, boy." He holds out a hand and sand falls down into a cane before him. "We're going to do good work, boy... I believe in you. In the morning we will resume training. Something a bit less vigorous."

"Agreed. I can show you how I've been training lately. I see I have preserved better than I believed. I suppose muscle-memory does so much."

"Muscle memory..." Ray rubbed his chin. "If I could master these sands, I could rebuild my organs. Muscles that could move all their own without maneuvering my husk like a puppet. Walking feels so unnatural."

"I have an advisor for my Queen well-versed in these matters. If we arrange the release of the Nadian men stolen during the so-called riots. My Advisor can spend some time studying these matters deeply. And assist you in recovery."

Ray scoffed, "Can we not go through this again so early? I believe we both need our rest. Let's talk. In the morning." He shook his head.

"Ray, you speak of the preciousness of life but you will stand a hypocrite if you hold those men unlawfully. You are allowing your own soul to be corrupted by pride and wrath. Justice doesn't need to be cruel. It must be strict not harsh. These men have spent enough time imprisoned for the crime of existing. They must be released. For their sake and yours."

"You're going to be one hell of a politician, boy." Ray scoffed once more. He furrowed his lips. He hadn't the energy or the liability to disagree. "I concede. But I do not have the power alone to make that decision. I am sorry, Morgan." He hobbled off, gaining his stretch and control over the sands.

Few masters held domain over sand without living in the deserts. The steel Warden had turned to dust and sands. Even with the hobble, there was a new chipper and pep to his step.

I must investigate this process further, "Ray, you are the Commissioner of The Regulation Regime. How can you not have the power?"

"Your people are not my prisoners... they are prisoners of Colin's brotherhood."

"Set up a meeting. I want my men back in Nadia or I will be forced to question whether your life was worth saving. We do not want to have another argument. I'm sure of that, Ray."

He closed his eyes, "Colin always told me, the young eat the old if you let them. He told me you were a menace. And you would turn against me. That you would come and kill us all in vengeance and Ada was the greatest evil the world knew. Because of that I doubted you. Such a vengeance couldn't exist within you. But as I see you now. It is the only place it belongs. I will fight by you. I will arrange this meeting. But further more. I am Ray Bradley Warren, and I will not-

"I am Morgan Sameera, The Son of Rakil. The future of Gaia and Nadia and my Rose are my only concerns. Don't die for pride after we spent so long saving you. Arrange, your meeting. Free my men."

I tied my hands behind my back, pacing off toward the hot springs I spent so much time in as a boy. The underground channel was near the edge of the Academy Campus. I couldn't blink... but it would be nice reliving the walk.

I left Warren. Wishing his a fast recovery and reminding him once more to set his meeting.

A nice soak in the springs, food from the cafeteria, then return to my villa to rest. Hopefully it was cleaned in my absence. My last memory I tore the room to shreds before leaving to ward under Colin.

Hm... I wish I could just blink home and be back with Rose and Ananda. But my body was weary. Besides. I would get prattled to about my health. They'll be happier to know I relaxed, ate and slept. Though, they likely wouldn't believe it was my own idea, ha.

CHAPTER 42

Meager Restitution

Rose Paz Andale

I had wondered how he spent so much time in the dark basement until I found the light switch. There were three more doors leading to his exercise room... which he still hasn't let us use yet in training. And to his stash, an entire grow room with herb and veggies! Who knew he was such the botanist?

I sat in the exercise room with its own combat mat and fighting cage, roman chair, squat cage, and bench press. The highlight however was the plated window opening up to the lake! It was so beautiful. To imagine he might have been down here smoking a blunt and staring at this the whole time when I thought he was in meditation. If he was... he truly has been wasting his time in his head. Do I force him out of it or would I just be insulting him to address the issue? I would probably insult him addressing the issue. I had no idea how deep his understanding goes. Then again, he has yet to interrogate me and all I know. His new Ananda watched me like a hawk. I enjoyed being able to escape, see what he truly enjoys about this rutty ole place.

I sat cross legged in lotus position, my eyes cracked open juuuuuusst a bit to watch the fishes swim by.

Morgan has left Ananda and me in charge of the house. After informing us, Halle will be leaving in a week or so. He told me to have whoever repaired him the first time on call. I told him I am already by his side, and we will take on whatever befell him, and make them pay for ever daring. I think he liked that.

"Jah'Baat, praise and strengthen my covenant with my beloved Morgan. Be him Ada or just a mortal savoir. Bless his kind heart... allow him to see his magnificence and my love. Make his seed take home inside me. We find the strength to reign over Nadia in the name of the five, taken from the vain followers of one. Amen. Thank You."

My mother would call me a little sick fool for ever believing I would marry the man from that day. To ever have his children. I suppose the whole of Gaia believes he will be Halle's if you follow the tabloids. But she could never make him an honest man. Only allow him to continue on his path of self-indulgence into masochism or brute pleasure.

My mother always said that was the duty of a good wife. A man needs something to return to. He toils, works, and provides. When he returns he should find a home, not another battlefield. I don't think my beloved knows wars end... that battles subside and he needs rest. His upbringing fighting those monsters as if there is no end to the war and the conflict, fighting each other as if it's a sport.

He's like a General, up past dusk after his troops have long fallen to rest. Strategizing and preparing for the battles ahead. Reviewing the map, making stratagems and last minute preparations. Praying over the well-being and life of his troops. But when the war ends... Men return home to celebrate, be married, and embrace victory. My beloved, the General sits with a grimace and his beer. Awaiting the next battle. Wars end... but warring never subsides. Always another thing to prove, more people infringing upon the rights and love of others. Morgan would say we do it to ourselves. I think it's society. In truth... We are society, damn.

Ananda cooked a feast for Morgan. Morgan only picked off his plate then returned to his study or down here in his sanctum. He never has an appetite. We eat our fill. He bids us a good night and departs. Returning to his thoughts and stratagems.

The nights together ended. He's had his bed alone. If he ever reached it. We took turns attending his study in the evening, ensuring he at least had water or wine. He only wanted the water.

I suppose that's why I find myself down here. Attempting to meditate and take up my training. So, my beloved has one less worry. As his woman should.

"Jah'Anka, make my heart light. Jah'Ada give me your focus and patience." I whisper in my lotus position.

My thick legs didn't quite sit right one over the other. My back kept wobbling. This is NOT comfortable. I let myself roll to my back. Letting out a sigh, "I've never met an Ankaan monk as thick as me... knotting my legs up like pretzels." I bet it's no problem for his new Eshan maid... what's with those creepy eyes?

I closed my eyes. Breathing deeply. I'm supposed to clear my head but my mind only seemed to race in the quiet and darkness. How did Morgan find peace? How will my people? Our people...

I doubt a day in my life Nadia had ever been at peace. I was born to Obatta Sameera demonstrations and his troops keeping patrol of the city. He said he wanted defense for all. Protection over Nadia. To restore what he called "Ecru" to its former greatness. I suppose Morgan had a point... but was Sameera wrong?

Every decade Nadia was at the mercy of other nations who seemed to care nothing for Nadia. And then they finally made their feelings known... Turning their backs on us entirely as our men were all arrested into slavery, leaving us wide open for assault and fascism.

Morgan... Bryon... Sameera. I wonder if they're connected. If they truly knew each other. Bryon didn't surface for years after Sameera, and Morgan claims to not know much about his father. All three men saw the same thing the only ones brave enough to do anything. To take on the burdens, ridicules, and eventual assassinations...

My beloved needs me strong like Anki. Bold as Enshishi. Loving as Anka, and cunning as Baat. Focused and patient as Ada.

I must be his back and sides as he brings us forward. I will let no one take my beloved from this world. Long after Morgan saves Nadia, he will live, he will reign, he will be sovereign Guardian over Ecru, Nadia. And we will make the world respect us! Every Nadian walking with us.

Jah'Baat.. Maybe we don't need war. If every Nadian raises and speaks. Our voices will be heard by the father, Rakil. Else, we will be devoured by war or worst... become yet another realm of tyrants. Of backs turned only willing to give others their governance and ideology. What will war in the long-term prove? What has it done all this time, all these centuries? Only creating long, unhealing scars and fractures.

I don't believe in any peace signed and formed in blood. Peace... Peace must be loving and aspired toward. Peace must be nurtured and cultivated through mutual direction. To ask my beloved after a life of war to continue fighting? To continue slaying and wearing down his body to oblivion. It's not the way. It's not how I want Morgan remembered. Not, another Warlord. No. In Jah'Ada's merciful name, may my beloved be the first of men to claim a nation out of the love he has for his people, and the love his people have for him.

Wars fought to what end or resolve? For what purpose!? To only have to fight the same war later in a dick swinging contest of who's better or who's stronger? No, no more!

Nadia has seen enough bloodshed. Enough pain. Let me and my beloved's union be that of love and inspiration. Let us combat tyranny by raising the souls and dreams of the Nadians out of reach of their oppressors. Not by sending yet another generation of our brothers into the Lion's mouth or Bull's Gore. No more bloodshed in Nadia. In the name of my beloved, Morgan Leonticus Sameera, Ada of the 5th realm and beyond. Let Nadia, our union be a testament of Peace and Hope. Far more powerful than any army or weapon.

But- if not, let us show we have tried peace with all our enemies, in the end they deserve whatever the hell my beloved unleashes upon them.

CHAPTER 43

Closure Is What You Give Yourself

Halle Victorianna

I sat outside with my toes soaking in the lake.

I remember when Morgan first bought this place after breaking up with Nat. His eyes lit up when he saw the lake. It was a swamp back then. Murky water with about a foot of algae over the top. I refused to even go near it! But he loved the lake regardless. Eye for potential. He would swim in it every day and come out like a swamp monster. Now it was pristine and he doesn't even use it. What happened? I forced him to build an outdoor shower to avoid tracking inside the house. He built it himself then cursed when he needed to call a plumber to fix his mistakes.

He had such a wonderful smile. Now, all he shows is pain. I admit I've been stubborn and resistant to his pleas. It's always so insulting. No one speaks to me like that. They would never imagine me being half the things Morgan thinks I am. Who the hell does he think he is? Were things even repairable? He makes me seem like I'm an incompetent child!

I fell on my back and stare up at the sky.

Well, I guess they would never say it to my face. No... they stayed nice enough to get what they wanted from me. But I knew many of them had their own jokes.

I refused my studies for so long. Slept in instead of attending council meetings, early in the morning. Partied instead of training. First in line for Benefit Banquets or public appearances. But never for duty. I truly thought I could live my life out as Halle Gregor forever. Seemingly, I could have spent my whole life as such. But what it would demand of me to continue doing and I fear what more would be asked of me.

What a rude awakening. My own father only sees me as a trained whore! And Morgan- he speaks nicely and holds punches, I would hate to hear what he truly thinks of me. But unfit to rule under Rose of all people?

Now, I must call my mother and see if I can apprentice under her. She likely hates me more than either of them.

Since I was a child. All she ever sets upon me are demands and losses. She was heir of Qatar, in the southeast region of Maya. Morgan says she has the essence of my mother... fitting, I have little doubt she would try to take Morgan away from me as well. My father called her a temptress and succubus, a sea witch.

She refused to be a mother or a wife... She fled from Naka in the middle of the night. Then pops up whenever she wishes with her nose turned up to any and everything. Telling me to come to Maya. As if it would have been better. In retrospect... guess she was right. I thought I had everything I ever wanted in Naka.

I'm doing a perfectly good job of ruining my life all by myself. Maybe there's something more to learn. She ran away just as I did. She knew my father for what he was before any of us, apparently. I learned from my father and the Academy, what has it really gotten me? I've learned from Morgan and at least learned freedom and peace.

No one's ever been honest with me. No one ever says what's on their mind. And if Morgan tries to say something, it usually just pisses me off. What is wrong with me? The only person who seems to still think I'm the shit is me. No inheritance, no husband, I don't even have friends anymore after all this. If they were even friends to begin with. Probably my fault too. Who fucks their best friend's boyfriend? It's not like I even wanted to at first... but you have to be dutiful to your family. Right?

The pain growing in my stomach left me doubled over in agony. The pain in the pit of my stomach is so damn tight. I wanted to vomit but could only lay on my side. I felt like I was dying. Part of me wishes this was all over.

I wish I hadn't blown up this morning... I want to stay with Morgan and Nandi. They have both told me about my temper numerous times. But I doubt Morgan would take me back, he didn't even care I wanted to leave! He basically said 'good, deuces, peace.' then I had to listen to him fucking Rose. He wouldn't even let me move in and now... Rose is in my place. It happened so quickly. Like over a weekend I lost my boy-Karma is a bitch. Thanks mom. Thanks... me. Whooot, happy with yourself now? Left myself with nowhere to go but back to Naka to be fucked by my father whenever he beckons. Or to Maya to be screamed at by my mother for that being all I know.

Uugggh! Why am I so prideful, so damn quick to anger? I bet I get that from my parents...

I'm so tired of everyone's disapproval. Being judged for not facing my issues with *decorum*. I've been told aren't issues by the one man I trusted! I want to be better but how? What does better look like when you're raised believing you're the shit and everyone is just jealous? How much is true, how much can I trust. How fucked up am I really?

I want to love Morgan and be by his side. Who can I go to for help? I say this but... he seems so done with me. So over putting up with my shit and my 'naivete'. They discussed war plans today over pancakes and coffee, so casually like he was looking over homework. Was that what it meant to be a Queen? Not waiting to be told what to do or think, but just going after it to assist your King? To further your cause? It sounds so simple, yet it is something I've never had to do. I didn't even have to bathe myself until I came to college then I showered with Natalie or Morgan.

I walked inside after the sunset, my stomach growled and I hoped dearly everyone would be sitting down for dinner soon. Or the least some of those pancakes were in the fridge, they looked so good. I made no habit of eating leftovers but it seems like a petty habit at the moment. Much of what I felt began to feel a bit petty and selfish.

Maybe there was a chance for redemption?

I found Ananda and Rose, laughing amongst themselves when I entered. It turned to hushes and Rose rolled her eyes walking to the door of the sanctuary.

"You're not allowed down there." I mentioned.

Ananda was the one who corrected me, "Morgan said we have freerange of the house."

"We?" I asked raising a brow.

"Well, Lady Halle... he offered me a job this morning and I accepted it." Ananda half smiled. She wanted my approval. She clasped her hands together, bouncing on her toes.

I had little to offer, "I thought you might come to Maya with me?"

She all but rolled her eyes. "Well... Morgan sees more of a life for me than being a maid. He says I am to be advisor to the Queen!" She smiles despite me, "I had never imagined I would ever escape the Gregor Manor. I never imagined a life outside of servitude or suicide... now, I am to help Ada rebuild Ecru. This is so blessed." she had already made up her mind. I couldn't fault her.

"Oh... " Even my maid was more fit to be Queen than I. Wait, advisor to the Queen? Did I miss something? I felt a panic suddenly, "I- where is Morgan, I must speak with him!"

"He's already gone to Erdu..." Ananda bites her lip, "He um... he wanted to speak with Jah'Anki. He left looking as if he was ready for war or death." she looked away from me. "He left very quickly, there was no getting you or Rose when he departed. He ensured he would be back as soon as possible."

"No... he couldn't have." I covered my mouth, "I had no idea he had even left."

"I trust he will be back. He seemed rather confident in himself. I have little doubt he'll return within a few days or so. But- he assured me he would return. I believe him."

"I won't even get to say goodbye before I leave?" I frowned.

What have I done? Those would be my final words to Morgan?

"Why not wait for his return?" Ananda suggests, "He offered for you to stay the week. Wait for him to return, and you two could speak on new terms. He really does love you Queen Regent."

"He wouldn't want to see me... he didn't even say goodbye. I know what's wrong, he knows what's wrong. I've known- I need to fix it instead of asking for forgiveness. I can't do that underneath Morgan." I frowned down to my bones, "He's so casual about our relationship. He forgives me without me even asking. If I'm going to save my marriage to Morgan, I have to go to Maya first."

"I... I'm afraid to say I believe he and Rose are-

"I'm aware, I heard them having sex." I had no more tears, no more reasons left to cry. I've hurt all I could over Morgan and this crusade of his.

"They favor each other so deeply. I never imagined he could have such a connection. I'm ha- I'm-

I want my man back. Fuck that. With or without my father. With or without fate or destiny. I love him and will not lose him to anyone! I don't care if it's another heiress or even Baat herself. I'll be with Morgan again. On my name of Victoriana. It isn't about the money. I wanted my Lord Husband.

Ananda rose a brow, "He's a rather nice man, Halle." she chuckles, "Very sweet and kind. I can't believe he ripped that tree out the backyard, though. That was quite thrilling." she leans to look out of the backyard patio. "He doesn't seem opposed to your staying or taking on more than one wife. It isn't unheard of the vicar of Ada having more than one betrothed."

I sucked my teeth, "I'm Halle Victoriana Gregor..."

"How did you two meet?"

"I- I shared him with Natalie but that was very different. I won him. I was the better option, she fell out with him, all they did was fight and he wasn't happy with her."

"Were things much better with you?" she pursued reason but I already understood her end.

"I- absolutely! Of course they were! Morgan just doesn't want to be happy. More importantly, I felt firsthand what Natalie went through. Morgan wasn't happy with life so he left me because he doesn't think I can help. I guess- he doesn't want a relationship right now. I don't think Rose is going to have much better luck than me or Natalie. Hopefully you win his heart."

Ananda rolled her eyes, "That's a bold-face lie straight to my face. He is ecstatic with me or Rose. Him and I had quite the conversation this morning. He loves you Halle. Perhaps, you don't quite understand your Lord Husband?"

"Are you swooning over Morgan already?" I giggled nudging Ananda.

Ananda opened her mouth then closed it sharply. She sat down and shrugged. "Well, I- I've never met someone like him before. He's everything. He's like the men you read of in stories. To see firsthand the suffering. I don't think he knows how great he is or if he thinks he's great at all. I doubt anyone has taken the effort to let him know." Ananda was astute. She would make a good advisor when I return. "He just seems like he needs love. I don't think he knows what happiness is to even want for it"

And she only met him yesterday. Maybe I am dumb because that still makes no sense to me. I was raped by my father and I still understand happiness... Though, the realization I was raped has changed much of what I once enjoyed. I felt a dark cloud of misery from these past few days between my Father and Natalie. Him and I weren't even sharing the same reality. He understood the whole time. I was blind. But no one can convince me I didn't play my role. We only needed time. I needed clarity only Baat could give me at this point.

"I did love him! I took him to parties. We hung out all the time. I let him talk about whatever."

Ananda just snickered. “No wonder you lost him to Rose. He is all she wishes to speak about, if not Nadia. She worries deeply for him. Seeing them together is so… inspiring.”

“Excuse me, who’s side are you on?”

“Morgan’s now.” she shrugs shamelessly, “Your family has done little for me. He frees me and elevates me to advisor. I needn’t even be a maid truly with the way the house is kept. It seems we’ll be spending the next year formulating our strategy for Nadia. Little interest in parties or talking about whatever. Aaaannnd!! He’s going to find my books! I get to study the rift, and his powers, and the truth of the Guardians, and spiritual healing.” she claps her hands so excited, saying words that made no sense but Power and Guardians.

“Ananda, I really don’t need this right now.” I huff, “I just got dumped.”

“No, you needed it when you first met him… maybe even earlier than that. As I recall, he said you wished to leave. You were not dumped. You decided to leave to improve yourself. It’s like going to university.”

“You’re just as mouthy as Rose…” I fix my eyes at her.

“Perhaps that’s why we get along so well.” Ananda shrugs, “She’s a very nice person as well. You two could have made great Queens by Morgan’s side. You still could if you so wished.”

“I do want to be his Queen!” I whine, “I had him before anyone, before any of this! I saw him first. He was mine before he was even Natalie’s if we weren’t such bitches. I’m so pissed off.”

Ananda shrugged once more as if she expected everything that came out my mouth, “I will miss you dearly, Halle. Thank you for bringing me here. Thank you for saving me from your father. I will always remember this and I will not allow Morgan to forget how much he loves you.”

“Ananda… do you honestly believe me unfit to wed Morgan without Rose?”

“Do you want the truth… or- I’m just gonna say it because you need to hear it. I believe Rose and Morgan to be capable of anything they wish to achieve together. They have a common goal. His power and her plan seem hard to stop. I don't believe you ever even considered that perspective in your life for yourself and another person. I don't believe women like you ever really expect to do or have to do much of anything constructive. The Gregor wealth would save decades of time, if not centuries.

"I only imagine you would be sitting around the manor, attending social engagements and wearing the title of Queen. I see Rose, and I see a woman doing her damndest to earn it. To make up for every single year your money would buy and more with her own mind. You expect things to be handed to you and when it isn't you act like you want to quit or get angry. Like you don't care, can't be bothered or disinterested. Ready to move on and find something new. It's beneath a lady. Rose said he cried today over you, over all of this... I don't think Morgan is anything you believe him to be. I don't think he would ever show the other side of himself because you're scared of him. And scared of the truth, this is the worst he gets but you and Natalie are so much worst, and have been since children. I don't think you or Natalie took the time to know him or love him. It's best you leave him to those who care to as you learn how. And who wish to do good in this world regardless of their arrangement or wealth, to be with someone they love, than to go about aimlessly out on pride, humiliation, confusion, and pride!"

I wanted to be angry. To snap at her and scream about how wrong she was. But she wasn't... at all. Neither of us took that time or effort. We just talked about him behind his back about how weird or mean he seemed. We saw what we were raised to see and refused to see anything else. I even allowed Natalie to get into my head, repeating her exact words at times.

I watched us just tear him apart when all he wanted was love from us. We weren't women, we were harpies. He was trying to rebuild a city, and we had him taking us out everywhere but Nadia. Before he and Natalie broke up, he didn't even leave the house just like this now. What the hell have I allowed myself to do?

I wouldn't even listen to him. As if he was the one confused and didn't understand the issue in our relationship. I wouldn't even bother to listen to him...

"Morgan doesn't cry." I tried in vain but I knew for a fact it was a lie. I bit my thumb, shaking my head in dismay at the reality. "Morgan doesn't know love."

"He does. And I only wish my beloved cried over something more than spoiled rich bitches and psychopaths who have taken him for granted." Rose walked back up the steps.

Harsh reality came in like waves against the tide.

We stared at each other for sometime as she sat at the kitchen island opening her laptop.

I bowed my head, there was nothing I had to say. Nothing to say that I wouldn't have heard from Natalie. Is that what I have become? Was I quitting on Morgan?

"I'm going to be heading out soon, Ananda. Watch the house and Morgan." I had hardened beyond Rose's japes, my anger replaced with seriousness. "I'll be back. Tell Morgan I'm visiting my mother if he asks... Or, just tell him I'll be back."

My King was across the world and he may never came back. He was the head of the house. I was worrying about where I would go for tonight. She was worrying about a city. Maybe Morgan was right about me... No, they were all wrong. Everyone who ever tried to limit me or put me in a box. I can build cities too.

"Morgan, wanted me to come with you to Nadia." Ananda blurts out. "I- I'm not supposed to know you're going to Nadia. But Morgan wants me to come with you, Rose."

"How did you know I was going to Nadia?" Rose said disgruntled, "He knew..."

Ananda took a glance at me before smiling, "It looks like we are all going our separate ways on missions."

"I pray you two have nothing but success. Good luck. I have a flight to catch. I should be heading to Maya." I bowed my head, gripping my chair keys in my hand.

"Thank you for saving my life, Halle." Ananda hugged me, beginning to cry.

I held Ananda. As much as I wanted to cry, I could only notice Rose staring daggers at me. Don't worry. I'll be back to settle all we have started my sweet little flower.

CHAPTER 44

Reunion

Borre

A man standing at seven-foot-five in a white peacoat with golden lacquer. Two gilded bastard swords at his waist walked into his office. He stopped instantly gripping the hilt of one of the legendary swords.

"Morgan..." He forms a slight smile but his hand doesn't move from the hilt, instead it tightened. "Nice of you to join me. Usually people schedule appointments. You were never usual, boy."

The man's eyes scanned the room he saw nothing but the danger rattled in his very bones. He was ready to face it with a smile, accepting the challenge at hand.

"Hmm... Quite interesting. I've never had the pleasure of facing an adept Ecruean." The Lord Commissioner had a grin showing his pearly white teeth, each one the originals since his baby teeth fell out. A handsome man with charcoal skin. His salt and pepper hair was giving way to mostly salt.

"No... You slaughter innocents. You wouldn't want the challenge." the boy seethed with contained rage.

"Show yourself and tell me about challenges, Morgan."

"I didn't come to fight. I came to talk."

The Commissioner loosened his grip hearing the child in his voice. He relented lowering his guard. "Sit down boy. It's been too long... I don't want this and nor do you." he had long missed the boy. It was years since he allowed his protege to leave for Nadia. A decision that's lost the Commissioner a night's sleep ever since. Reports filled the ranks he was dead. His compatriot Colin Gregor said the boy was alive but off, took no joy in life and had a dark cloud over his head even Enshishi worried.

"I don't believe you." Morgan chuckled, "but I won't allow you to call me coward."

"You were never the type." Warren smiled letting go of his blade.

Morgan appears with a blade right to the Commissioner's throat. Pressed straight to his adam's apple, ready to move. A quick jerk of the wrist was all it took.

The Commissioner froze. "How long have you been behind me?" He knew Morgan was in the room but to have given up such position, even at his height. “You- how?”

"I've been following you since you left your car. You trained me well, Ray." Morgan only allowed his upper body to leave the void. His lower half perched for a quick escape if necessary.

The Commissioner smiles brightly pride filling his belly, "No... You learned well, boy. You were one of my favorite pupils."

"Who is my father, Ray?" Morgan cut straight to business. His second hand poised with another Fang to the Commissioner's spine, ready to split it in half to wound the giant.

"Sit down, boy." The Commissioner warned, “If you believe I'll die easily, you underestimate me.”

"Tell me, Ray."

"If you're asking me then you know. If you know, then you're aware you'll need to do more than slit my throat to kill me."

"I'm prepared.” Morgan's voice was absent love and familiarity.

The Commissioner's form fell into a pile of sand and blew away, all in an instant. Morgan braced his footing as the freight train of a right hook flew out from the sands and went to take his head off his shoulders. Morgan sidestepped, rolling off his charging mentor to spin on the balls of his feet along Warren's arm. Warren pivoted away slashing with his left hand until Morgan raised his forearm, deflecting the blow at the hilt of the sword then lunging in to strike. They danced. Exchanging and evading blows that would have killed mortal men. Even the pulled punches carried enough force to knock the pictures and move furniture without a touch. Though, Warren had barely any room or time to draw his blades with Morgan's relentless entry and aggression. Morgan kept the exact pressure necessary to keep him at bay. Never before had Warren felt himself stuck on the defensive in a fight. Not once before did he feel so close to death. Warren raised a wall of sand nullifying Morgan's next lunge. The office was barely enough to contain either of them. The wall of sand fell and Warren held the legendary meteorite great swords, Service & Honor.

Morgan swallowed, his strategy changing immediately with the 5 yard reach differential. He cracked his neck, spinning his kunai holding them each with the blade down. He nodded Warren on, one blade protecting his gut, his strong right-hand outright to prevent a direct blow to his head.

"You want to do this?" The Commissioner cocked both his swords preparing for the 'Bull's Gore' the fabled finisher move. Mythical only because there's never been a man to tell the story, each laid to waste from the smallest man to the mountains Warren trained on by slicing in half.

"If you think you scare me, you have underestimated my determination for answers." Morgan's eyes grew a deep crimson, his body radiating ethereal dark matter, his body encased in an armor of dark matter. "There's much I've learned you haven't taught me."

Warren moved with haste the two swords jutting out with his full-force. Little more than pure reflex saved Morgan's life. He took the blow head on, forced to use both Kunai to meet the scissored sword stab seeking to skewer him in two. Morgan met the strike at the head of the blades being driven back as Warren steps forward looking to fling him up then cross the blade in a scissor to slice him in half.

"You're still pretty fast, old man." Morgan raised both his fangs to redirect the piercing lunged aimed for his stomach.

"Death hasn't slowed you any either..." Ray lamented.

A single slip by either of these tempered veterans and Morgan could have been gored by the blades known to cut through mountains.

Ray's own eyes pushed into a rusty yellow color, his intent taking over. Morgan's eyes began glowing as he lets out a scream, lifting both his swords successfully knocking away the blow. He went for a counter strike forced to dodge and keep his distance. Neither man would stop until the either died or halted. Ray snorted out steam, gritting his teeth. Neither man wished to relent, neither man wished to continue.

Morgan stopped first. Sheathing his blade and bowing his head in respect for his elder. "It has taken much from me but not as much as a life within the Academy. I'm tired of the testing and flaunting. Tell me what I came here for or we will have to move this fight." He rose up.

"We have much catching up to do. We don't need to fight at all. I thought you were dead boy." Warren looked down in shame.

"We only have questions in need of answers, Ray." Morgan's voice was colder than the ice in his veins.

"You have the audacity to call me by my first name and act as though we have nothing to speak of after five years of your absence? I feared the worst. You're to wed the daughter of Colin without notifying me? I assumed you lost your wits!" He sounded more an uncle than foe. "I missed you, boy..."

"I lost my life." Morgan retorted gritting his teeth. "I died for The Regulation and I marry Halle to save her from Colin."

"Save...?"

"You didn't know the monster inside Colin?"

"Monster is subjective within present company. But as children I always thought Colin was afflicted. It's difficult being the son of Enshishi. His father was said to be the greatest man alive and he loathed his father."

"Colin believes himself to be the reincarnation of Rakil. He believes himself to be a God."

"No..."

"Yes, Ray, yes the Gregors commit democide to continue their bloodline. They kill the father to preserve the bloodline so the spirit of the Eternal Flame cannot escape them." Morgan shook his head at his mentor's ignorance, "And they rape their daughters to preserve the bloodline or prepare them for marriage. It's why the first Victoriana killed her father so brutally then her uncles." Morgan snarls with disgust. "Colin is next if this isn't fruitful."

The Commissioner bowed his head in shame, "Then your cause is noble. I apologize for my inactivity but it did not seem like my battle." he sheathed his blades walking around his desk, the first to take a seat conceding defeat.

"I don't care for such things. I am not here for noble causes only the truth. I didn't come for an apology or kind words, I came for answers!"

"Should you not? What greater cause exists in man's word but the truth we all fear?" The Commissioner pours two glasses of water and sips from his cup first. "No poison."

"You wouldn't poison me." Morgan sits across from him downing the cup in one gulp. "I'm only here for one thing. We can carry on with this reunion when I'm less busy."

"Information is a very valuable resource. Far more than gold or power, knowledge my boy is costly."

Morgan sighed, "I should have just slit your neck. I'm not here to play games."

"You look your sensei in the eyes and can't even embrace him or come to him as a student. Have I scorned you, so?"

Morgan's eyes wasted no time turning to dark blood colored hue in his rage, "You allowed me to lead the subjugation of my people. The lives of so many lost. Scorn is not the word. You used me! My entire life lost to this sinful cause! As your puppet when I believed myself your family!"

"That order was given by Colin and his private militia. Neither I nor any general gave such an order!" Warren protested, "I have a war to be concerned with here in Erdu, boy. Not stabilizing order within the other territories like the other Lord Commissioners attempted. That's what your police precincts should be for but your lands have no order. I have no concern with Ecru old or new. That was a Gregor ploy…" Warren sighed, "I know you do not seek an apology, but I do apologize. It's lost me many nights of sleep knowing what I allowed. I promised myself fifteen years ago I would let nothing befall the three you of, and I have failed each of you. You and Leslie became those abominations of Colin's desire, and Hinata… I don't know whatever happened after his father withdrew him from The Academy."

"You won't interfere with my restoration of Nadia?"

"I trust your mind for Order. The whole world benefits from an organization and militarized Nadia. Most of our operatives lose touch the fall into alcoholism and obesity. But you've maintained. Though, you look as though death still lives inside you."

"Guilt." Morgan admitted, "Guilt that is quickly being absolved from my system."

"Guilt for what, you performed your task and went on to live your life. I'm proud of you."

"But, I didn't kill Bryon Qatar." Morgan hung his head in shame. "I let him go and I murdered my brothers. For years this has troubled me. I don't know whether I'm a traitor or a savoir."

"No. You neutralized him and protected your city. I told you dealing with Qatar was your last mission. Afterward, you did what any man, even I, would do if he could for his own people. I am proud you, Morgan. The pride a man can only feel for his protege. You've grown far beyond my teachings, far beyond the Regime. You are your own man, and I'm honored to call you an equal."

For so long he believed Warren would drive his head through the wall. Snap his neck for his actions. Had him court martialed or assassinated.

But…he approves?

He not only approves but pride? And… he knew about Nadia all along.

"You were always a skilled and loving boy. I admired that about you. Such a thing is hard to maintain in our line of work. In men who share our ideology. Who have seen what we have. Reconsider joining me once you've resolved your issues. The Regulation needs your spirit boy. You could easily be my replacement within the decade. I had always dreamed of when you would take my seat as Lord Commissioner."

"I'm done with Regulation."

Warren frowned, "are you finished with me, boy?"

Morgan sighed, "I'm confused as to what to do, sir. Nadia needs me. They would never trust a Regulator. I would never trust the Regulators again. Not so long as Colin breathes this air of Anka."

"You wish to fight for Nadia... So, the rumors true. It was you who killed my Rottweilers?"

Morgan nods pouring another glass of water. "Every last one, it was like cutting through paper."

Warren's lip twitched. "Those were our best boy... And you slaughtered them. I dream of what we could accomplish together and fear being your enemy. I will not reject either course if the time comes. You are the son of Obatta Sameera. After we killed your father, you were taken. I'm sure either Marsha or Colin will confirm the truth."

Warren shook his head, covering his face fighting back tears.

Morgan heard nothing he didn't know. The admission sliced regardless. Sometimes it didn't matter if you saw it coming. Pain was pain. He knew his entire life and never said it.

"Ellys... L.S. Colin believed himself so clever. You were meant to be his heir, to be neutralized as an enemy. I murdered Sameera and he killed Saleem. What he did to Marsha Qatar... she vowed vengeance. A woman I've never known to hate anyone, she was sweet as a girl. We knew her since we were all children. I became this Guardian of Earth after Saleem fell. Colin claimed he had no idea it would happen. Marsha he imprisoned in Naka and used as his plaything, he had no respect for her, a high priestess. I never forgave him. I never forgave myself."

"He solely wanted to fulfill his bastardized prophecy. Halle sought refuge in my home. She is tired of being used for the glory of Gregors.

She's soon to leave my care." my gut strained to find sympathy but none lived inside me. "I'm going to kill him Raymond."

"Take care of Colin... I believe his time has come. No man is greater than tomorrow, boy. He cares little for the dream of Order." The Commissioner's head fell heavy in grievance. "I simply want to bring Erdu to rule under my hands. As vicar of Anki such is my duty. My people have grown wild, base, and unruly. In my youth I believed my duty to be more. Colin convinced me to compete to claim Gaia as our own. Colin preached this. This was what ended the First Age... Take care of him."

"I fear I'm not strong enough. I have been dead for two years. I refused to allow my body to recover. Colin surges with Enshishi's avarice and rage."

Warren grins, "Care to return to training? Just for one last go around. I could use a new sparring partner. It has been long since I could test my full might."

"I could?"

"In truth, I've missed you, boy! And your cause is noble. I will assist you as I can. I haven't a clue who your father is for certain, only my speculation."

"It's Obatta Sameera."

"If you knew why ask?"

"Confirmation... I wanted to see if you would keep lying to me. So, I am Ada, in truth?"

Warren smiles, "welcome to Guardianhood, my boy."

Morgan moves around the desk to embrace his mentor. In that moment he returned to the terrified child who first entered the Regulator Regime. He remembered being pulled down from the gallows as if born again. Morgan squeezed him tight. The Commissioner embraces the boy, kissing his forehead.

"I have protected you from Colin all I could in your life here. I needed you gone... to live your own. It was time for you to fend for yourself, brother. You were no longer a child. You were Ada and a man grown. A threat alone but we believed the marriage could bring about peace. But Nadia was never in our plans. This Ecru has dissolved. Colin has grown mad. I will assist you as I can."

"Thank you, Ray."

"You were as a son to me, Morgan. I have missed you. When I caught rumors of your death my heart broke. I hurt in a way I wasn't aware I could hurt. I am proud of the man you've become. Go forth and bring your land back to order."

"I will, sir."

"Now, let us train! I must see the power of Ada for myself."

"Ha, well enough, time to take out some of this anger."

The Commissioner furrowed his brow. "We won't be using practice blades. I suggest you contain your anger and learn to rely on your wits at all times."

CHAPTER 45

Self-Promotion and Greater Expectations

Rose Paz Andale

I had hoped Halle already left. There was little purpose for her presence. She offered very little. Her wealth wasn't even her own anymore. She clings to the title Gregor. But without it what was she truly?

Nanda sat across from me, "Morgan told me to come with you. He knew you were going."

"Jah'Ada... how does he know me so well?" I blushed.

He knew I would leave shortly after he to put this all in action. To at least prepare our people for the Regulators. Nanda told me she had the utmost faith he would return. Yes, but in what condition? He claimed to be wounded and half his capability so he confronts the Lord Commissioner Ray Bradley Warren? He still lives in disbelief of being Ada... you can see it in his heart and he would try to stand before Anki?

I did my best to talk him out of it.

In retrospect, I probably could have done more to assist him or to stop him from going after Anki but Baat resisted. This is how it must be she said. For some reason, my husband going across the world to Erdu alone to visit the Ankole Minotaur was not my concern, I could never understand. They say not to question the will of the Supreme Beings, it's because it just doesn't make any sense at times. Sometimes, because the results will upset you anyway, no matter how much you knew, or why.

It's so difficult at times to put your faith in the Guardians of this world. So many men like Colin exist without the excuse of being vicar of Enshishi. Girls like Halle exist who rather primp and preen themselves than be women. At least Halle could take a punch and sling an insult.

Baat spoke to me so clearly as a child. Of peace and all the things to come once Ada returned. Of how the evils of this world will be punished and purified, and how I would be his Queen.

It's hard to trust and have blind faith in these Guardians but all the same... the faith relies in the truth; the work of Guardians have resolve, the work of our opposition has none. At least in my path with the Guardians, I can see all we do in this world to help and build. But these evil forces will swallow us whole, use us for their whim and throw us away as trash. They're all pimps and all the same they're all prostitutes to their own greed and corruption. Shame women like Natalie exist. They pull good men straight to hell.

Yet, all the same so many emulate them. Rakil bless Morgan, give him safe passage home and resolve in his mission abroad. Return our King to us. It has been too soon he has returned to see him vanish from this world within the same decade.

"I plan on leaving in an hour. So, pack a weekend bag. We can stay at my home with mother and aunts. You can honestly stay here."

"No, Lord- Morgan told me I was to stay with you and advise the Queen."

"He did?" I groan, "I don't need you with me, Kitty. I'm only visiting family."

She nodded, I didn't know her to be solicitous or deceitful. Though, I didn't really know this girl at all. But here she sat with me, and there Halle stood alone. The Gregor heiress inherited all her family was worth... all the ashes and emptiness they have created in this world.

"Then get ready to go, we have a lot of work to do tonight... They'll be a lot of running around. Nadia is not what is was when I was a kid."

"You will protect me." Ananda nods.

"I will do my best." I frown, "I'm not Morgan, Ananda... but Nadia is my home and I refuse for his influence to be absent. People need to know Ada is back, and the King is returning to his throne."

"This is so enthralling! I will find clothes immediately." Ananda bowed and ran up the steps without another word.

Halle and I stood in the kitchen.

"When you first met me... you laughed at me. Do you remember those first few weeks? You said it was good I wasn't competition. How does it feel to be replaced?" I asked. "All the things you said about my beloved were lies... lies he believes and they cripple him because you refused to see his beauty. You only-

"I know... I know... and, I'm deeply sorry. There will be no forgiveness from Morgan. I plan on leaving tonight to go to Maya. This is not done. My father and Naka still stand opposed to Nadia. If you believe you have a better chance in assisting Morgan in that than I, then you are mistaken. I can be redeemed in the eyes of Morgan."

I smile, "Morgan bears no anger toward you. There's no need for redemption. No, my beloved only blames himself because of people like you. I wish the best in seeing my patron face to face, Halle. May the Mother of Grace have mercy upon you."

Halle's face contorted into a sick smile, "I am the daughter of Victory and Grace. This is not the end Rose."

"Halle... if you ever come back here again after all you and yours have done to use and hurt my King and my Lord. I will kill you myself. That's not a threat, that's a promise, princess. I will kill you."

The room was cold. We all had our pasts. If she thinks her father being a psychopath made her scary. She should see what Masks are facing these days. I didn't want to be a fighter but I could kill if I ever needed to protect Morgan.

We hold a glare for a moment before Halle concedes.

"Good luck in Nadia. I hope you do well. I will be back. So, I hope you'll prepared when I return." Was the last thing Halle said before leaving me clenching my fists. Hopefully to pack her bags and be gone from us.

Too long has there been stagnation of evil and corruption. Allowed to just sit while good souls feel as if they are emotionally insane or flawed. No more of this. Soon there will be a new age.

An age of peace, and liberty, and beauty. A world without Enshishi or the Gregors. Be safe Morgan.

CHAPTER 46

Allegiances and Ascension

Morgan Leonticus Sameera

Why does peace always seem so out of reach? A simple discussion. Negotiate. Diplomacy. A nation torn by war and strife. Citizens that just want to be left alone from their voracious governments. A dozen different voices barking and demanding "Live by my views or die." What type of way is this? This is what I fight against. Men and Women who believe their words to be law. Believing those who stand against them should be persecuted rather than tolerated or helped. Those who extend judgment upon their brothers rather than their hands.

"No more lazing about, back on your feet!" Ray barked at me.

My body was weary. We woke before the sun and trained only as Guardians could. We took to each other well, even with time apart. As old friends who merely took a weekend off instead of death and years.

But we had few hugs and words.

Instead we exchanged slashes and cuts. Sidesteps and sweat. Clashing then breaking away. Clashing then moving for the kill. Our experience superseded the danger. Each aim we made believing it to be the end of the sparring drill was met with brutality. This was the love of men. Knowing your brother will take your worst and bring you back humbler.

We engaged, I stood toe to toe against the legendary swords 'Honor & Service'. The horns of Anki. The Gore of the Steel Warden that has laid so many to rest.

Warren scissored his swords and came at me with all his force. I held my kunai to divert his blade. The steel sparking as he came with all his force and I attempted to stand my ground before the Ankole of Justice. Warren tossed me into the air listlessly as if swatting a fly. There was no way to resist but the man was one of the most powerful on Gaia.

Warren let out a primal scream, charging with his full force. I barely parried each slash and sweep. He was quick on his feet, dancing to my side and goring at me before I could react. I leapt into him, spinning over his blades and punching him square in the face. He grabbed my neck as he recoiled, his instincts superseding his pain, and flung me across the room. The only man I knew who could man handle me with such ease. Likewise for him.

I tumbled across the proving ground, catching my balance, posed like a panther ready for another pounce with fate.

"I am glad to have never been one of your targets. I had always imagined what end those men met. They hadn't a chance, had they?" Warren chuckles between panting. He raised his swords, each a quarter ton in weight. If he could keep moving as could I.

"I had a good mentor." I pick myself up. Ragged, worn, but all the more willing to keep sparring because of it. I stood against the greatest swordsmen alive and the Guardian of Erdu. How could I find pause?

I wasted little time getting back to my feet. I kicked off into Oblivion. The training room disappeared around me and I'm absorbed within cold, thick darkness. I held my breath to prevent inhaling the ether around me.

"We are taking to using the elements now?" Warren chuckled. He searched around the room.

His silhouette was clear deep red energy coursing within him, with deep violet contrast. The violet was the divine.

The substance was like trying to run in the ocean. Pushing straight against the tide and current. The ether never wanted you there. It was closed off to the majority of anything of even moderate existence. The ether constantly worked to push you out. The control took deep focus and skill. The hours of meditation paid off.

The physical strain I could bare. But every time entering the void it was as if my soul betrayed me as I fought against reality itself. The ether was just that. The border of time and space. Ripping holes in the fabric of the very universe to reach my target. This is what Colin feared. This is what the whole world feared. My return. My actualization and full understanding of my powers. Parts of me feared it as well. Colin could sneeze and burn down a city. I could rip a hole in reality, kill a senator and be right back in my office chair a moment later arguing with Halle or Rose over etiquette.

Bending the physical elements demanded a balance between user and element. A bonding process that requires years and decades spent engaged in lifestyle or immersed in the element. Warren himself was said to leave the face of the planet to train in the mountains and woods of Erdu for five years every other decade or so to master his ability. But this was all me. I had a knack for my power since I was young. Precision was my weapon. A false move. Loss of focus. There could be an unclosable tear until I regain my energy.

Or...

I could go in and never return. Energy didn't return in the Ether. I recall a few times I had to dig deep within myself and sacrifice my own life essence to return. There may be more within the Ether... but I did not quite know. I didn't need to, as Ray said, I needn't be a scholar. This wasn't a last ditch move. This was the beginning or ending of a fight if I so wished.

In mastering the Ether, I master the course of life itself.

"Show me what the heart of Nadia can do!" Ray tempts.

I pulled behind Ray. Delivering quick punches to his ribs. Strong, fierce, and repeated. He swung wildly unable to defend his inside on such short notice. I followed his punch spinning along his arm, delivering a spinning back elbow crashing into his jaw. He finally grabbed me but not before realizing my Fang poking him in the throat.

"Match." I declare.

"Very nice!" Ray grinned his throat punched against my blade, "You haven't missed a beat."

Ray's form fell away in a pile of sand the ground collapsing from under my feet. The floor around me began to implode. I looked up to Ray who only had a smirk, floating on a cloud of sands. I scrambled to run up the edge of the mouth of the pit that was ever further away as the pit sank into the abyss below. I leapt for the lip of the tremor holding onto it with one hand for dear life. Looking down upon the crater of missing earth beneath me. The abyss went to the pits of hell itself. Such was the power of Gaia's Guardian.

"Holy shit, Ray..." I curse pulling myself up as best I could with one arm and barely any physical energy left. Damn, I should have eaten. No calories left in the tank. I guess we're using life force now...

"You're not the only one with power." Ray's voice was profane. "I'm strong as well Ada!"

I let go of the cliff, the callouses on my hands bursted into blood as I let go of the cliff.

"Boy!" Ray shouts.

I felt the embrace of the gassy liquid of nothingness as my eyes peeled opened and the world turned to energy.

I reemerged before him, blocking his sloppy punch. I kick the inside of the knee as attempts to engage. I leap up turning my body bottom-up, locking his arm between my legs and rolling him to his back. I squeezed until I heard the grinding of bone against bone, the popping of air free the joints. I let him go, laying on my back utterly exhausted. He picked himself up only to his knees sharing my grief. Holding his arm in exasperation.

"We are done." I declare.

"I am grateful you're not my enemy." He shook his head, "The ether is not a toy... it simply cannot be allowed to be rampant."

"Perhaps violence doesn't need to be the way to begin with. You and Colin are little different. Both invasive and stubborn. If you two simply relented there would be no need for any of this. But no, you must live in your homogenized, self-masturbatory Utopias, no matter who suffers because of it."

"You don't speak to me?" Warren asks confused.

"I speak to you both. Anki can hear me." I mutter, "You claim not to be a part of Colin's plan, then prove it Ray. Be a man and fight for Gaia instead of for Enshishi."

"He can." Ray looms. "So, watch your words."

"Learn to take pause. To accept things won't always be your way. This is an inevitability of life. People must live their lives. It isn't some affront to you. It is life."

"Many do not realize, how to live." Warren replies.

"We are Guardians... we're fathers and brothers. A father cannot simply kill or punish their children because they do not agree with him! He must watch. Love and let the child grow. Let the child make mistakes. Children are their own mind and spirit, not an extension of the father but a reflection of the father. The world is in disarray because you refuse to let people live and turn against the basic laws. Then you ignore any wrongdoing on the part of Regulation but tout because people now work all day and night, and worship Colin. Is this what you have fought for Anki? For enslavement and false idols?"

"Who speaks, my protégé or my brother?"

I put my fingers to my forehead, "both."

"You sound just like him, boy... Just like Ada and you are right." Warren sat looking over at the crater, staring down into it as if somewhere on the bottom was absolution. "I wanted to bring the world to Order... and I shall, but perhaps it needn't be with violence not by force. But Order will reign."

I let out a sigh, "I fall upon deaf ears. As always, brother. We DO NOT need to spread our ideology. Our ideas must grow and change as we do! We must lead the people in practice, in our walk and in our works. The people will ultimately follow. As they always have, as they always will since their birth in the second age."

"They should follow us!"

"I have brothers and sisters, who do good work. If they simply follow one of us devotedly, is that not good enough for them to live all their own? If they observe us all, is that not better?"

"Perhaps that worked in the second age-

"It works in every age! Brother, we have fought wars. We have died and reincarnated countless times. But the lives we have lost for our ideological spouts... it is obscene. How can you still be so obstinate in believing your way is best? It stands in defiance of all the lives that live perfectly well without your influence! That you, not Colin, taught us were heretics and savages, not just people. If these debates bring death, are they not inherently wrong?"

Anki snorts, "I am done with this prattling."

"You won't accept your role in all this? The lives that have been used or died in your name? To what end, Anki?"

"I AM TRYING TO FIX IT!" he screams, "I am alone in this! I have enemies against me everywhere and they try to push me out of my seat as Commissioner. I AM FIGHTING BOY! But while you're out finding yourself, there are savages killing my men!"

"And I respect that. I am truly thankful! But for you to help in truth, you must accept, your way is not the only way. Maybe this does not need fixing. It simply needs its leaders to influence and push for amelioration for all, not simply who they favor. You plant a seed and nurture the flower to bloom, but even without your presence, nature will produce flowers."

Ray growls, "Stop this now! You will corrupt the boy and undo all my work! You will confuse him and cloud his sense of order and rule!"

"You would attempt to taint my vessel in my very presence? Raymond Bradley Warren? This farce of training is completed."

"Ada... you aren't listening." Anki fumes, "You never listen!"

"Colin is already dead. Things will be as they must from this point forward."

"That is not my brother, Young Ada... but your mentor remains. Be weary."

Ray let out a primal growl as if the morning of sparring never happened. He was immersed in a red aura, pouring from his pores. He quickly reached his feet and charged at me as if in a blind rage. Service and Honor in his hands with lethal intent. He moved as if he never felt tired a day in his life. As if stamina were no longer a concern in his realm.

"I will not fight you..." I sigh. I caught my second wind as well. The need to survive will do that. Sidestepping and evading his strikes. "This is not the way to solve your issues. We cannot allow ourselves to turn to anger and violence whenever we do not get our way. We are not children. We are Guardians!"

"Don't speak to me as if I am some petulant child!"

"I speak to you as my little brother, with still much growing to do."

Anki let out a bewildered battle cry striking and slicing, only meeting my Fangs as I match him blow for blow in half-willed attempts at defense.

Ray was stronger. He was faster. Yet still I didn't feel threatened. He was a fifteen foot man but moved and swung as if he were even larger. Sloppy and wild with all his force behind them.

"I suggest you back down before I confused your temper tantrum with an attack." I warn in the clinch with Anki. Our blades grinding against each other as he grunts and screams.

"All this talk of violence! All this talk of peace! And that's your response?" Anki strained through his frantic heaving and bewilderment. "All this talk and that's what you say!?"

"There's a world's difference between violence and self-defense. You allow your bruised ego and emotions to let you react any which way you please. Then justify it with your faulted reputation. It is not the way, Anki. It is not the way, Ray. We are all susceptible, this is why one cannot simply be right. We each defend only what we know and understand. Find it in yourself to come to understand that, please."

"Leave here now! I attempted to help the boy in his uphill battle! But you confuse my vessel and undo a lifetime of training and development. Go!"

I sidestep him, dragging my blade along his obliques. Evading his blows then leaping in once more with a series of wing chun punches, cloaking my hands in my ki slamming him in his gut, right beneath the hip. There was little muscle or meat to protect there. Just connective tissue and nerve bundles. I rattled off my aggression then swept him off his feet. He looked up to me as if he expected the finishing blow. To be spared his shame.

"It is not help you offer. You offer only your ideology instead of compassion or mentorship. We will gladly leave. You will be your own demise, dear brother." I turn my back leaving him panting and heaving.

"Leave before I rip through this body and pulverize you!" Anki lets out a bellowing roar filling the room. Ray's energy fluxed as the red aura began to radiate from his body "Leave before I send Pitbulls and Rottweilers to finish what-

I was atop of him, in an instant. I needn't a void or tear. I spun on my heels and leap across the room. A tiger tearing down his prey from a feint. With a hawk's grace. We fell to the ground as a feather. I stared down at him with crimson red eyes. My blade pressed deeply into his neck. My hand slid through the void bypassing all the tissue to squeeze his intensines. I stared through Ray's mortal body into his very soul, staring Anki in the eyes.

"I preach peace, but I have always been a warrior. If you ever, in this life or the next threaten Ecru. I will end your lineage in that very instant." I needn't shout. I needn't raise my voice. My message and intent were clear. I stared at him with critically crimson eyes until he relented, turning away from my gaze and nodding.

The red aura around Ray faded and my mentor was left sleeping. If he would even remember what happened I don't know.

I rose up, brushing off sands that seemingly change from nowhere. Surprisingly enough from my voided hand. Strange... but not my concern. I paced out the room a King. Silence was louder than any more words I could have found. I got my point across.

As Ada.. it is difficult to accept through the eyes of this young man. At times violence is necessary. As I consider the means and times of

which it might be... It is difficult to distinguish. Humanity is still very much carnal. I would hope after these centuries, after millennia, my father's pride and joy, his children would have grown and matured. But they live far too short, their perspectives are limited, and their will for those greater than themselves limited even more so. I hoped for centuries of growth, of love, of education. But those with the knowledge horde it for themselves, exploiting the ignorance of their brother. This is how centuries of potential progress get lost. Perhaps father hoped for too much. I reflect every so often in Oblivion, my True Kingdom. Perhaps humanity was born to tear itself apart. But that's something I refuse to accept.

How can one witness such great potential within its creation? But all those things that make it great can easily be its demise. All things come with cost. All things come with sacrifice. We teach them how to wield their double-edged sword but my brothers and sisters only teach their children to wield it for the wars fought over centuries rather than how to sheathe their sword to enjoy the decades.

I am in dismay...

This boy Morgan is in such dismay. We are aligned in this. In this we both find truth and love. In this we must unite.

He is ready for the violence I refuse. I must sit him away... For even after all this time of bloodshed. These centuries of corruption. I know peace and love are the answer.

At least... for some. There are obviously many on this planet who refuse to allow this to be. They refuse to accept their equality with the rest of their kin on this world, and must sit in seats of excellence and power. They believe their corruption and refusal of their humanity make them gods. No... Gods do not do this. It only makes you heathen. It only makes you enemies to all those alive. It's all built out of self-hatred and self-destruction. Many of these men must face for peace to be an option. But the force and will of humanity. The hope I have for my father's children will trump over any force of evil, corruption, or hatred. I refuse to see this world devolve into the hands and will of this tainted Enshishi. I will purify this Colin Gregor and purge him of his taint.

CHAPTER 47

Rise of The Queen

Rose Paz Sameera

I was sitting in the living room typing away at my strategy. When I was a girl my grandmother had me do a paper on "What makes a society?"

Education, Sustenance, Security, and... Land. When I was fifteen, my mother had me write a thesis. "How to manage a farm with limited time and space for maximal profit and sustainability."

They always pushed me so hard. I goofed off, and did my own thing. Smoked bud and kicked it with my girls Cameron and Jazz. But I was always about seeing this through.

Cam was a pro hoe. She always tried breaking down the game to me but I never intended on playing. My mother waited and prayed for Ada to return to serve him. I fear the worst for what their relationship will become... But I always knew with or without Ada I needed to be working on Nadia. I've been perfecting my thesis and research, I think I have something cheap and efficient that we can get going before Colin's next invasion.

"Yo!" The front door was pushed open, "Hey, were you gonna tell anyone you was home?" Theo had gotten huge. He was skinny as a kid but after he took on a mask he gained forty pounds! The goofy awkward kid was walking tall and proud.

He hugged me, lifting me into the air. This kid used to be like a little brother to me. Now he was little big brother.

"Put me down, put me down." I giggle patting his head. He lets me go. "What are you doing here?"

"Roselyn! What are you doing in Nadia? You didn't even text me?" Cameron walked inside. That's why. "So, where is he?"

"Hey Cam!"

"Where is your so called boyfriend?" She all but ignored my greeting.

Okay, Cameron.

Theo put his hands behind his head as Cameron stomped up to me.

"I watched the Carmen Cruz show I saw what he did. He broke into Natalie's home and threatened to kill her. She's so brave that she told her story anyway!"

Though, I shouldn't have been supporting the enemy.. I saw that interview and it was completely scripted. Such a heroine and an actress. She went on to Carmen's show showing photos of her beat to bloody hell and back. I don't doubt that she got her ass handed to her. Thank Jah'Anki for his justice, and bless Jah'Rakil for whoever laid hands on her. But Morgan is in Erdu and Halle was in Maya. There was no way either could have done such a thing to Natalie.

"I'm going to start this off by saying. I don't believe a word she says... but what did the show say?" Damn, my love for gossip!

"The dude's fucked up. Fucking psychopath and rapist." Cameron reamed.

"A rapist?" I groan, "Come on, Wolfe at least be creative."

"Natalie said he would force himself upon her every night!" Cameron continued, "I bet that sounds familiar doesn't it little miss maid?"

"Why on earth would that man need to force himself upon anything? And FYI, soul sista, love you dearly, but we've only knocked boots once. It was amazing. But it was only once and it was yesterday when we decided to get married."

Psychopath though? Would explain a hell of a lot. Ananda even said that earlier.

"You're going to need to come harder than that." Cameron shook her head unconvinced. "He's using you."

"Well... that's all really." Theo shrugged. "I mean if that doesn't bother you, I don't really know what's good with you."

"He's not as bad in person. He's strong... he can be very domineering. But Morgan is a good man.."

"He hit you?" Theo asked.

Theo had built a name for himself in the annexation. They called him Titan, he wasn't a Crimson Elite but he ran under Crimson's banner. Had a few comrades and a couple groups under him.

"He tried to kill me once. But then I knocked him out. I call it even." I smirk, "Do you guys get I've had a crush on this guy since I was a kid? You two were there."

"Yeah, man... but that dude is fucked up." Theo repeated. "He didn't come dressed as a mask."

"He was a civilian. He was still a boy, scared and unsure." I defend my beloved.

"He ripped through those guys like butter. But that's the type of dudes the Regs have, ya know? They got fucking super soldiers and shit. We fight these dudes man. But this dude is a whole new level."

"Well... he's a Wolf." I couldn't lie to my friends.

"Naw... naw those don't exist." Theo shook his head not wanting to believe it.. "Yo, Natalie said this guy is-

"Have you ever met Natalie Wolfe? I imagine she's a very polite cunt." I let out a sigh, "Look, he was a kid. He didn't know anything else. But now he does. He's Obatta Sameera's son. Bryon Qatar told us guys! My mother told me I was crazy. And my grandmother told me I will marry him. And yo, it's happening. So, stop hating. Stop listening to witches and harpies. And start planning your girl's wedding and bachelorette party! Àaaaayyyyye! Team Ada!" I stand up doing a celebratory dance. Clapping and swinging my hips to the music in my head.

They didn't share in my excitement or amusement.

"This girl was in a body cast, Rose. I don't know her. She was stitched head to toe. She said he broke everything in her body. Followed her home and broke in. She says he never fell out of love with her."

Jah'Ada she thinks this is about her? Just when Halle leaves the other one is nipping at our heels. Bitches, can't get rid of them. The competition just can't stay in their place.

"Yo, check it. We're gonna talk about this later. I need to talk to you guys about this week. We need to start getting this city ready."

"Ready for what? And we're not done with this. You can't marry this guy." Cameron gives me deuces.

"There's a war. So excuse me if I'm a bit more concerned with that than Cruz's lies."

"Rose, we saw Natalie Wolfe, she was completely injured. Bandaged from head to toe." Theo spoke up, "We're here to save you. Let's get moving."

"Morgan isn't capable of that."

"That's a lie. We saw what he can do when we were kids. You said it yourself." Cameron presses.

"What he did in Nadia was in self-defense. He was a marine, he protected... or thought he was protecting Gaia. But he was also a damn, kid. He did what adults asked. Like we all do."

"I don't..." Cameron rolled her eyes. "I don't trust him. And I'm not alone. Half the world watches the Carmen Cruz show."

"Then we'll just have to align ourselves with the other half then, huh?" I put my hands on my hips. "I just got done with this, with the maid. Do not try to come between me and Morgan. I worked very hard for this and-

"You have a maid, say word? She cute?" Theo smiled, "yo, this dude up in here macking!"

Cameron rolled her eyes, "He nearly murders Natalie Wolfe, and breaks up with Halle Gregor. What makes you think he could give a shit about you?"

"Excuse me?" I snap, "I believe I'm just as good if not better than Halle or this other puta. I've seen Halle, I look better. And I'm smarter. And funnier." And I give better head.

"Word?" Theo rubbed his chin, "When you meet Halle Gregor?"

"At his house, duh. Shit's going down in a major way. Feel it? So, I'm gonna need you guys to catch up on game. I'm Queen Rose Sameera. What's good? You're my royal committee, aye, go team. The King may not be back for a month and Colin can be here any day. So, we focusing on Natalie or we focusing on Nadia?" I clap my hands, "Go Team Nadia Reconstruction, that better?"

Theo looked at Cameron, "well, I think it's clear."

"Me too, I just can't trust him Rose. I need to stick with my own eyes." Theo shook his head.

"Yo, not at all what I was expecting." I shake my head.

Cameron snaps, "how can you say that? After all Carmen and Natalie said."

"I am telling you two. Morgan is in Erdu. There is no way he did anything to Natalie. She has to be lying. He already left for Erdu before the show even aired!" I tried to explain the truth to them.

"Yo, I don't even know those chicks. Rose is my girl, I'll take her word if she vouches, and I'll judge the rest for myself." Theo shrugged.

"I don't know this guy either." Cameron crosses her arms over her chest.

If Morgan thought I was bold and outspoken, him and Cam would have a field day.

"But you know me, Cam. And I'm telling you he's cool." I plead with praying hands.

"He's a patriarch, Rose."

"So was Gerald Knox, so is Crimson, so is Sameera and Bryon." I defend.

"You're going to compare him to the greatest men to live?"

"In a heartbeat." I put my foot down. "I'm not moving on the issue. I've looked in this man's eyes. And it's like I saw every man he ever killed and every woman he ever fucked. He didn't seem to enjoy any of it."

"He did it regardless of whether or not he enjoyed it." Theo commented.

"Who's side are you even on?" Cameron snaps. "She's trying to marry a pimp. That's the last thing Nadia needs."

"My baby boy was pimped. But he's over that shit. Feel it, he's going to be fighting Colin Gregor."

"Impossible, Natalie said that he's marrying Halle Gregor. She said herself he's just using you. That's why we're here. She said if you know the girl he's with warn her and tell her to run away because he will try to kill her too! I'm trying to look out for you!"

I let out a sigh, "and I'm telling you this girl is full of shit."

"Because he told you? She says he's one of those metas. With the powers. Carmen said he hypnotized her just by looking at her."

I quieted down, "Alright... so that's true. He did."

Theo's eyes widened, "Yo. I just got done telling Cam I didn't believe he did that part! That's the most fucked up part. He has that kind of power? He can just look at people and take away their free-will? Naw, I'm with Cam. He's been playing all you guys. You can't even know when you're thinking for yourself or when he's controlling you. I'm letting Crimson know-

I whipped my hand, spilling over my cup of water sending the stream to trip Theo.

"What the- did you just?" Theo looked at me as if he didn't believe his eyes.

"He's been teaching me how to defend myself against the enemies we'll be fighting. Those super soldiers and metas you were talking about. Morgan and I can teach you two, we can teach all those who are going to be apart of our kingsguard and queensguard."

"We'll fight the Hounds." Theo picked himself back up, playing it off smooth.

"We need to protect our own citizens from the criminals living here before we worry about Hounds. Morgan's in The Academy in Erdu to discuss peace with the Commissioner." I sat back down deciding to try a different approach.

"The Commissioner? That dude is King Dog!" Theo shook his head, "I don't know how to feel."

"How do you expect us to gain political power or defend against an army without strong allies?" This is gonna drive me crazy. Time to nip this in the bud. "Ya two wanna know what? I don't care! I'm marrying him regardless. My mother and grandmother approves and I adore him. So I'm doing it." I throw up my hands, "You're telling me there aren't bigger issues in Nadia than where Morgan's dick goes? He'll probably fuck his maid and he'll be fucking Cam too. I know.. But we're past that point. I'm Queen, now. We have a city together. That means far more to me. Besides none of that stops me from enjoying him because I get it first and I get it best."

Theo rubbed his peach fuzz and furrowed his lips. I expected him to look for Cam for advice on how to make up his mind. He just shook his head.

I hugged him. "You two are my friends. You will meet Morgan and be able to judge for yourself. But right now. We need to talk about getting started!"

"I'm a Squad leader... I could talk to a few others and start some patrols and scouting." Theo groaned, too cool to be hugged.

"I need dudes you can rely on. Not just anyone. This is need to know. Morgan isn't the type to keep his business in the streets. We'll let him and Halle handle this Carmen and Colin shit. We'll focus on Nadia."

Cameron was quiet.

It wasn't often I stood so stringently on something.

"A few years ago we were angry kids, running around at night in masks and lying to our parents about where we were. Now, this is my council to take back our city from poverty and pestilence. For so long I ached over the future of our city. Now, we have an honest chance to be more than nothing. To set a new course for our city."

Theo stood and raised his fist, "Hell yeah! I'm all fired up! This is our Prime Minister! I'm all for it!"

Cameron stood from the couch, "I guess it's inevitable. You can't do anything without me." She sighs flipping her braids out her face. "I'll need to stick by your side and make sure you don't get hurt."

"Oh here we go." I laugh rolling my eyes and hugging my childhood friends. "We're going to do something incredible here."

Each of us paused with the sudden vibration in the air.

Ananda came running downstairs, "Morgan's here! I can feel his energy!" she cheers then stops dead when she notices Theo and Cameron. "Oh, guests. I'll fix something to-" her instincts fought against her excitement. "Morgan!" she shouted running out the front door.

"She's gorgeous..." Theo's jaw dropped. His eyes followed Ananda out the door.

"Hmph... he's a pimp." Cameron rolled her eyes.

"He's my husband to be. Stop hating, girl." I stand and go after Ananda. Now, that she said it there was a powerful aura around. It didn't feel like the Morgan I had been living with, the energy was stronger than anything I ever felt. This permeated through the walls and filled the room. It was bright and lifting. "Holy fuck... he's been working out."

I began to chase after Ananda feeling like I was being magnetized. Ananda was already hugging and dancing toe-to-toe with Morgan. Holding his neck with tears swelling her eyes.

"I didn't think you would be back for so long! Rose tried to kill me. I'm so happy to see you!" she was overjoyed tears falling down her face.

"Ha, calm down Ananda." He brushes her hair away from her face and kissed her forehead. "I have your books for you." Ananda's eyes lit up and she hugged him even tighter. "Ha, Ananda, calm down a second or else I can't get them from my satchel."

I watched on a bit taken aback as they hugged so tightly. She said she would be my replacement soon. Morgan wouldn't allow it.

"Rose..." he let her go and smiled as he saw me. "Come over here, what are you waiting for?"

"An invitation." I run up to him and he lifts me in the air, spinning me around. I threw my legs up in his arms as he held my big ass up as if I was weightless. "I missed you, I didn't think you were coming back so soon."

"I will always come back for you, baby." as far as cheesy lines went, he won a medal. But it didn't stop me from kissing him and squeezing his neck.

He carried me inside, a bit off even.

"Yo..." Theo was standing as we approached. Cameron was cowering behind him. "What's good, bro?"

Morgan's energy shifted immediately, returning to the dark and volatile darkness from the house as he hid his energy. He let me down. Eying and sizing up Theo. They looked the same size, but Morgan's muscle density gave him 30lbs on Theo at least. Morgan stared at Theo walking up to him, and looking up to my little big brother. Morgan simply walked past Theo as if he wasn't there and stepped before Cameron. My stomach sunk as Theo's face twisted from the disrespect. Why did they have to start something?

"Hey bro! Stay away from-

Morgan's head turned quickly and Theo flinched.

"Ha, Theo please don't get hurt trying to be tough. Morgan isn't the playful type." I warned. Morgan looked unamused and exhausted.

Theo's bravery failed him as he looked at Cameron for confirmation, his guard began to fall. Theo let out a sigh and shook his head, giving up on the fight.

"Damn, you're a cold-blooded man. I know what you mean now Rose... every man you ever killed, in your eyes." Theo said with apprehension only raising his guard once more.

Morgan's raised a brow and turned to me.

I only shrugged knowing I couldn't tell Theo any better.

He looked back at Theo. Theo closed his eyes and ran into Morgan full charge.

"That won't work on me." Morgan seemed irritated.

Morgan evaded Theo effortlessly. His eyes glanced at me every other punch. He lets out a sigh, and steps into Theo, shoulder tackling him

and tripping his feet from under him. A move he taught me and Halle. He called it basic defense but the timing and speed were inhuman.

"Stay down, upstart." Morgan was already breathing ragged but he wouldn't back down from a fight. "I already fought The Lord Commissioner. Don't die for no reason."

"My name is Titan!" Theo shouts getting back to his feet and running at Morgan once more.

I tugged Morgan away, grabbing his arm and stopping Theo in his tracks. "We were talking, baby." I join Morgan's side, rubbing his neck and pulling him from Cameron who stood frozen. "You're scaring my guests, babe. Please, sit down... this is a diplomatic issue."

Morgan nods letting his eyes leave Theo and follows me to the lazy-boy.

Ananda joined Morgan's side, staring at Cameron and Theo, sitting on the arm of the couch holding the ancient tomes. I was drawn between both sides as my friends sat on the couch across from my love and our maid. I stood not wanting to choose sides.

"So, babe this is Cameron Harambee and Theo Knight. Friends, this is Morgan Sameera and Ananda..."

"I have no family name. But, I will be a Sameera as well." Ananda declares. "Morgan calls me Bhavan."

"Great..." she got his name before I did just by saying it.

"Welcome to my home, we are all the Nadian Reconstruction committee. If there are any objections or concerns then let's state them now."

Theo glared at Morgan still angry and ready for a fight. Morgan was unconcerned. He glanced over the two then back to me.

"She's from the conference?" he looked at Cameron grinning.

"You remember her but you didn't remember me?" I snapped at him.

"She was the clown. All that damn make-up. I could never forget how angry you looked. Almost identical without the make-up now."

I snickered and Cameron's mouth opened.

"Yes. I do have an issue. I will not serve for for a misogynist! Or a murderer."

"A misogynist? You're kidding right? On what basis?" Morgan groaned.

"Natalie said you were. She said you were a murderer. A rapist. And a psychopath and it is more than evident!"

"Yes. Yes. My sitting in this chair is so oppressive and menacing. Fine then, hurry off I won't have a coward in my midst. If sitting is so scary you will need to hide when things come to roost." Morgan began to stand to excuse himself.

"You walked in here and attacked Theo!" Cameron accused.

"Your friend attacked Lord Sameera first!" Ananda says immediately to his defense. Surprising everyone with her fierceness.

"He tried to use those eyes on me." Cameron covered her eyes.

Morgan laughed, "I did no such thing, child. It's not an attempt, it's one and done. I don't use my eyes unless I'm forced to or in a bind. I fight with daggers for a reason, Junior. You came running at me and got put on your ass. You're letting your cowardice and your woman make your decisions for you. A very unhealthy and redundant combination."

"See that's sexist! You're a misogynist!" Cameron declares.

Morgan just laughs, "you're a coward because you are a coward. If you believe your vagina makes you as such, then you are the sexist, no? There have been outstanding woman who have fought by my side and who have tried to take my life. You're a coward. Listening to the Queen of Cunts for your decisions? How the hell do you even know, Natalie?"

"Babe, she was on the Carmen Cruz show. She said you broke into her house last night and attacked her...Tried to kill her." I crossed my arms over my chest. "Can you explain that, please?"

He could be anywhere in a split second. From what he showed me and what little I knew, he could easily have done it. But- it just doesn't seem like Morgan.

"If I wanted her dead, she wouldn't have been on that show and no one would have found out. I have absolutely no idea what you're talking about." He says with confidence. "I have been in Erdu until a few moments ago. I slept in my old villa in The Academy. I even ate a few real meals. Now, I have business in Nadia most the morning and afternoon. I had no time to accost Natalie. You're likely looking for Halle. She's at the lake house if you care to interrogate her."

"Halle has gone to Maya." I said concerned with a new theory.

"Hmm... maybe I should have put Karma in a coma." He mutters, rubbing his own neck until Ananda relieves him.

Halle really did that to Natalie? How, when? My stomach churned. I would need to train a bit more.

"Ask Halle if she knows anything. I had greater issues to attend to." Morgan rolled his eyes. Setting a hand on Ananda's hip. She leaned down for him. "take your books to your room here. And run me a bath. I have a few wounds I must clean from my fight."

"You're hurt?" Ananda whined.

"I fought with The Guardian of Earth. Yes, I took some damage." He bowed his head reavealing a few bruises and cuts along his shoulders, "things went awry in Erdu. There was a falling out between Ada and Anki. I lost Ray to the ethereal for a moment. I saved him. I'm not sure what remains. His body is gone but his consciousness remains. He can materialize but.. he's crossed over to the other side. I need you to figure out what's going on, Ananda."

"He broke his seal?" Ananda covered her mouth."Did you see Anki? Why were you two pushing so hard? You could have gotten killed! Morgan you-

"He was nothing more than sands until I pulled him out the ether. At least what I could hold on to. He reassembled himself, but I believe I lost my mentor. Focus."

"Anki shouldn't be sands... he's the rock. It's called Forced Ascension. When the Vicar loses its life force or physical body under immense pressure. The Guardian begins to take over completely. The Vicar remains until its life force eventually gives out completely. But if he's only consciousness and instead of stone there was sand, I'm afraid Anki might not be Anki." Ananda rattled off.

"What the hell are they talking about?" Cameron asked. "Guardian? Is the commissioner dead or not."

"Death is a very confusing notion past the laymen idea. The physical form peeling away isn't quite death. The soul and mind remain. If both are developed a soul can remain or be reused for centuries. If the mind was strong then they can find a way to stay anchored. But the physical form literally being gone... hmm. I guess you can call it a sort of death. I always assumed the two forces shared a body. It seems the Guardians hold occupation in the vicar's soul then rather than the body. This is curious."

"What?" Theo definitely didn't understand.

"This is why I'm not concerned with you upstarts." Morgan sighs. "Please, Ananda. See what you can find. I have other journals you can look through for details. I need to view them first. From my father and an ancient relative apparently."

"Yes, Lord Sameera." She kisses his forehead and runs upstairs.

"What work have you all gotten done?" Morgan asked returning his attention to us. "Defenses. Food. This garden project of yours?"

"I have been typing it out a bit more, but we haven't gotten started." I frowned, "I only got to Nadia today as well."

He nodded, "we can begin work together. First, I need to attend to my wounds."

"We're not done here!" Theo snaps.

"If you wish to be humiliated boy. We can go through this whether I am injured or not. I suggest allegiance. Behooves everyone involved."

"Truth. Sounds good." I clap sitting in Morgan's lap. "See, there are much larger concerns. And a lot of work to get done. Let's focus on Nadia. All of us."

Morgan nodded, "Sounds good. Baby."

"I have my eyes on you, Morgan." Theo stands, "Let's go Cam. We gotta get the team together while they play house."

"Theo don't be so-

"Naw. I'm not trying to hear it. I'm doing this for Nadia, my home. Not for your dude. I wish you the best Rose. Don't get hurt with this guy. You see what he did to his ex. And he killed The Lord Dog. You're messing with some weird forces. He said it himself. Don't get lost in this dude, man." Theo leads the way out the door.

Cameron glanced back and smiled, "You may not be that bad. But we're watching you, Sameera." she was beginning to see what I see in him. I knew she would come around.

Morgan nodded, having lost interest after Ananda went upstairs. He reclined the seat and let out a sigh of relief.

"Just the two of us." He smiles wrapping his arms around me. "I missed you, Rose."

"You too Morgan." I laid in his arms across the sofa, enjoying the softness of our throne. "You're back so soon. I expected you gone for a month."

"I thought I would be back by noon. I didn't intend on staying so long but I had to rest. I needed answers. It was all Colin... Nadia, the domination, it was all Colin. Even the death of my parents."

"What are you gonna do?"

He was quiet, "I've already done quite a bit. I need to speak with Takio Murashima . I visited Vincent Cree."

"What did you do to Don Cree?" I asked wondering what he could possibly have to say to the leader of the Mafia's drug cartel in Nadia.

"I enforced my will." He said plainly. "I took the land upon the mouth of the Tigress. And the lake. And two of the warehouses for my whim."

"For how much?"

"I walked into his compound and told him who I was and I would kill him in front of all his men if he resisted. He fell to his knees and begged for mercy."

"Theo tried to fight you. You wouldn't have hurt him would you?"

"I could have knocked him out clean multiple times in his wildness. He is strong. But he doesn't know what he's doing."

"I told them we could train his most trusted."

Morgan nodded, "good, it's all coming together, Rose." He smiled bright closing his eyes.

"Your wounds?"

“A few cuts and gashes. I'm walking and on my feet. I'll heal. Some bandages and a massage, I'll be fine.”

“I can massage you.” I kiss his cheek, “Ananda can cook.”

“She'll like that. Did you bring my stash as I thought you would?”

“Not all of it...” I muttered, but damn how did he know? “There is some green. And some of your blades. I thought maybe I would need the protection.”

He smiled, “I'm proud of you.”

“You should be. I'm pretty awesome.”

“I'm definitely becoming aware.” he pinches my side, tickling me.

“Stop!” I whine, as he continues regardless. I squirm and wrestle him in his arms. “Stop!” I hit his chest and he lets me go, holding his chest tight and holding up a hand. “Take off your shirt.”

“I have it under control.”

“Show me, Morgan.”

He sighs lifting his shirt to a open cut going across his chest, and another down at his hip. This was nothing to him? Or was that simply his machismo? It scabbed over poorly. Still dripping puss and fleshy. How could he be moving at all with this type of injury? How did he even heal so quickly if he only left a couple days ago?

“Go upstairs and take care of them now. I don't even want to hear about how you got these... he's supposed to be an ally.”

“He got the worst of it.” He said smugly.

I didn't share his pride, “Morgan...”

“We were sparring for the upcoming battle with Colin. We're both men, we didn't use practice swords.”

“You could have died!”

“He almost did.”

“Why are men so stupid!?”

He had no response only a smirk.

“In retrospect.. practice swords would have been a lot more practical.” he scratches his neck. “I'm sorry, baby.”

“In retrospect... go upstairs, now!” I snap getting off of him.

He sat up grumbling below his breath.

"What was that!?" I shout.

"Nothing Rose, I'm going..."

"Good! And stop fucking training with real swords, dammit! No fucking more!"

"Alright, alright." he puts up his hands, "give me a kiss before I go."

"Hmph... you don't deserve one." I shake my head.

He wrapped his arms around my hips, and kissed my cheek. "I'm sorry for being so stupid. My penis got in the way of better judgment."

My inner child swooned with joy. But I was pissed! "Don't let it happen again Morgan."

"Alright, Rose. Alright. One kiss."

I turned into him and wrapped my arms around his neck, leaning on my toes to kiss him as deeply as I could. Enjoying every second of my husband to be. My King and Savior.

"I love you, Rose Andale-Sameera."

"Rosalyn Paz Andale-Sameera." I correct him. "I love you too, Morgan."

He leaves me to take his bath and likely have Ananda wash his back and tend to his wounds. I admittedly nearly lost my head, seeing the wounds. But he handled it so casually. I was almost afraid to ask him what his worst was. Even more so to imagine what awaited when he fought Colin. He took on a Guardian and was back in my arms. Nothing on this planet will stand against us.

CHAPTER 48

Bonding of Gods and Men

Morgan Ellys

"What was your code, Captain?"

"To walk right in the eyes of Rakil. To do well by myself and others. To ward others from the taint of evil. And to conquer all demons that come before me."

We meditated underneath a crashing waterfall. Breathing deeply. Being soaked by Baat's grace. Even when you're gone... you're with me, Rose.

"So. Do you understand why I forgive you for Nadia?"

"To an extent. Those men were beyond saving. That's what Ada told me."

"So, you've built your connection. Interesting. So young."

"What do you mean?"

"Do you know how many children Colin killed trying to find you?"

"I don't... I assumed we were the first." My chest tightened. "This was to find me?"

"Global security he called it... super soldiers that could be anyone. Small units capable of infiltrating any organization, governmental body, or to just murder and take the fall. He wanted suicide soldiers. Men he beat beyond any sense of consciousness of self. With full devotion to Enshishi... I chose you as my student. I refused to allow Colin to have you. I got this for my trouble." He pointed to the eye that had been missing all my life. The scar tissue still unhealed. "I apologize. I wish I had the strength you did to resist Colin. Colin told me a false narrative. He told me of the Gregors and their glory. He knew I was viable to be Anki before I did... he used me. That was a mistake I never made again. After Maurice's death. I worked my ass off to become Commissioner. I needed a force to keep Colin at bay."

"How could a man be so strong? I have noted multiple times I could have killed Colin if I so wanted."

"Yet you haven't?"

"He was one of us." I was ashamed, his duty and fraternity blinded me from what was demanded and righteous.

"So, were those 50 men. Yet they hadn't any of the blood Colin held."

"I do not wish for Colin to die. He's just a pathetic old man who has nothing but his family's name and a short history. He clings to it so dearly. He will die with it naturally."

"You will leave him alive to refuse him his wife?" The Commissioner chuckled. "You truly are cold-blooded."

"I haven't noted a Gregor that lived past 66. A book that Qatar gave me. The only one beyond that was Victoriana who lived for 120 years."

"I am not the one you wish to speak to. Those men and names are before my years."

Ray was in his early 50s. Though still fit enough to continue operative work, so he did. Seems his name of Commissioner is almost obligatory. An honor for the best men amongst them and even he fell to Colin's deceit.

"What is this issue you're avoiding with the Regulators? What am I missing here?"

"Hmm... Colin and I grew up together as boys. He was always off. Eager. Zealous. And charismatic. Honestly, he was the reason I even became a Regulator. Back then it was only an idea of his grandfathers. A militia of men of like-minds keeping order across Gaia. We were just boys. The capital of Erdu and Naka were much closer when Mendel Gregor was Patriarch. There was no Ada. Enshishi had told us for centuries he was God. My nature was to have my own mind... I operated with the only truth I knew but as the Gregor family grew so rapidly it was difficult to disagree with them, the evidence seemed to be writing itself. It seemed factual without evidence. They had the wealth, the power, and taught us weakness and poverty were a sin.

"Many of us in Erdu helped to bring about Order in the North. Our people lost our ways. But what we left in our wake under Mendel wasn't what I believed we were fighting for. I was a Captain then. I had to make a choice... to either leave the Regulators or to push forth and gain more control to direct it where I wanted. I fought wars... I murdered men. I did what I needed to do to secure land and territory for those who wished to have honor, order, and were willing to stand on their own feet. But the Gregors only wanted land and wealth for themselves, in retrospect. Many of my own have turned against me. There stands a divide between us. One that has grown between Colin and I in this rivalry we have. I resist him. But Colin doesn't fight like Mendel nor Maurice. They were both lions true. Colin is his own beast. A snake... beneath even Enshishi attempting to bring all Guardians down to his level. He will use any trick or method to reach his end. What's worst is he believes he is God! He corrupted the Regulation Regime. Many of my men fight for nothing more than destruction and homage to Enshishi. It is false glory and brutish, yet they cling to it with such pride. I- I believed much of this hopeless. I feared Colin ever getting his hands on you again. Once I learned the truth... the Gregors weren't the first family to hold the might of Enshishi. He chose them. Because only they wished to satisfy his hunger."

"So... Colin is beyond saving?_

"Colin is beyond reach and voice of the father Rakil. He makes up his own law and ethics depending on his needs and moods. He creates trouble just for laughs. He is diluted in his thinking beyond rationale, my boy. This man believes himself a god. He believes he is a god and his will is God's will. And he has the family history and power to back up his delusion. Enshishi is the Guardian of Fire, Of Power and Perseverance. He will not quit until he kills you. Until he destroys everything you know and love and turns the world against you. It has been like this before the first age. When there was just the moon and the stars. And Guardians walked the earth unbounded to mortal bodies. Enshishi rose and slain us... it repeats because this is simply his nature. He is evil. And he will never do right." Anki offered but his voice lacked the same force it did in my youth.

"Victoriana did not sit on the throne herself. She had a King... an advisor but a King. I saw very little input from the Queens. Perhaps it was the union."

"Gregors don't fare well with the daughters of Baat. Unless they leave them wounded or scorned. They only view women as whores and nuisances. They have no respect for the daughters of Rakil!"

I nod. "So. He must die?"

"You understand, Captain?"

"My name is Morgan Leonticus Sameera. I will do what is necessary for Nadia."

Warren stands looking down upon me and extending his massive hands. I place my hand in his and he helps me to my feet.

"You have grown so much boy. Rest. We will resume your training in the morning. You must learn how to call upon Ada."

"Am I not Ada?"

"No man is a God, boy. You know this. We carry them within us. We are the creations and images of Rakil. But we are not Rakil. Some of us grow to have more power than others. But never more power than the world needs. Those who do are Enshishi's followers. Brother to none. Enemy of all." Anki patted my back.

"I thank you..."

"History always repeats itself unless it stands corrected. And no man is greater than tomorrow. That is the law that binds all."

"So this fall is inevitable?"

"Ada stood to Enshishi. But too late... Adas have stood to Enshishi sooner and brought about great peace. The inevitable follows action. But one cannot be afraid to act. The action needn't always be aggressive.

I have come to understand my older brother as a being of peace. Deeply and truly. But with power so great... it was Ada who created Tartarus, the death that stretches to the first Mouth of Naka. His power is so great Enshishi has forced us to fear it. But he embraces all. Enshishi refuses all, needing to sit above them all killing and raping his own siblings. This is what I have learned, Young Ada. Assist Ada and be blessed eternally. Embrace Enshishi and you are always wanting. My decision is easy in this age. I am no longer ignorant nor naïve to this world... I understand my duty by your side in this war. Brother."

"Warren?"

"Anki... I speak to you Young King."

"Ha... please don't call me that."

"It is what you are." Anki said confused, “I wish to honor you.”

"Ha... seriously. Just doesn't sound the same coming out your mouth. Morgan is fine, Anki.My ex-fiancee she- ha nevermind." I brush it off.

Warren's lip furrowed. "What perversions taint your mind?" He tried to remain serious but ended up laughing along with me.

"The beautiful women inevitably in my future." I chuckle rubbing my neck.

I had almost thought I might escape them yet. But fate. They have seen me before I have seen myself. They will see me beyond myself. Rose and Halle.

"Can man truly have more than one love at once?"

Warren returned back to me, "I can't say I ever quite imagined you being such the philanderer. You were such a peculiar kid. I assumed your only loves would be your duty and your business."

"So, yes?”

"If you wish to take what I said as you please. Then we can play this game all day. But if you want answers-

"If a man can love both his duty and his business. He can devote his time to two important but conflicting goals."

"Duty and Business are highly encompassing. It leaves little time for extra."

He had obviously never been deeply in love with a woman.

"Perhaps that's your problem. Why work more than one needs to live? How much does one need? We are not Colin. Wealth is for naught. All the time I spent under Colin and in La Vida. For those who obtain it, wonderful as long as it's given back to the community."

"Yet, you speak of polygamy?"

"Ray, there are those who will never in their lives make more than they currently earn in their entire lifetime, and have destroyed themselves and their entire perspective of reality worshipping what they will never have." I shook my head, he believed me naïve. "To your point. I speak of allowing two women who truly love me. To love me. And to be with two women who I truly love. These women have sacrificed their very well beings to pursue me. Do I turn my back on them to leave them with those scars alone? I did not just ask for these women, Ray. They were my duty.They both found me and refused to leave me."

"I never married again after my first wife." Ray shrugged. "Never quite understood women. Never quite cared too. I pay for sex."

"Excuse me?"

"At a certain point, you must accept reality. If a woman is going to be your duty. Then your business becomes consumed by your duty. Instead of your duty fueling your business. Women require too much. Sit upon our lives and expect to be fed, clothed, and sheltered with nothing to contribute but a warm cunt. There are women who offer a warm cunt and leave to fend for herself the next morning. But no matter what. You're paying for sex."

"Women like providers."

"We should only provide to those who deserve it. Who offer something. Who have worth, virtue, and value. Not to vapid mouths or empty brains. The women of this generation have grown empty in Enshishi's graces and power. Seduced by evil."

"Jah'Rakil, Raymond spoken like a virgin." I crack up laughing.

"Excuse me!?"

"Ha, hey calm down, big guy. I just..." I couldn't contain my laughter. "Come on, man. You can't seriously think that's all there is to it do you?

There will always be advocates of Enshishi but you have two nieces. Rose is nothing like this. There are women who abide by the teachings of Baat, of you, of Anka." I stretched out, "I agree with everything you said, simply not the scope. Women are impressionable. We must protect them against evil and corruption."

"You're engaged to Halle Gregor. Even I know the vapidity of that one." Anki speaks up.

"Ya'know, smarts aren't everything." I fall back on the branch. Finding myself suddenly missing my ladies. "There's something special about a woman's love. A man's love is so rigid. It's loyalty and respect. Our love is so conditional. But women connect with you on this emotional level. Something you're not supposed to feel. Something I didn't even know was there before I met Natalie..."

"Haha, you're sounding pretty gay, boy. You like these girls because they give you warm fuzzy feelings in your belly. Ha, that's pathetic, soldier." He had a booming laughter I didn't hear very often.

"I love them because they make me feel like I'm worth more than just a soldier or weapon of war. With them I was a King before I even decided to raise Nadia. I was a King before I even knew I had a crown to claim. They have my back and worry for me in ways I ignore out of masochistic pleasure... Ha, it's silly but- I'm not sure what I would have done without them. A brother may save you from death. But this two women saved my life."

Ray smiled. "People make love seem so dreadful. The commitment to a women to seem as some awful endless torment. But I suppose if you care for them deeper than flesh. I could see how it could be worth the commitment. That's what Ada taught anyway. But few women interest me. I am a King in my own right. I have multitudes to care for and whose lives must find some honorable end by my judgement. An endless war to maintain order within Erdu. And mastery of myself and convening with Anki. I have no time for women."

"I think those exact words got me Halle. No lie. She looooved it."

We both shared a laugh. Anki, Ray. Ada, Morgan. It mattered little. We are one. It feels good to be with another person who understands this.

The girls cannot attest to that. I doubt they fully understand the capability that rested in their souls. That their rivalry was far beyond their control and conscious. It was a fight to be one when their flesh seemed so different.

'Baat fights with herself over who will rule Maya and who will watch you.' Ada informs me.

Watch me? Hmm.... Rose obviously. She'll likely take Halle if she reaches standard. Or this Ananda.

'Was she also divine?'

No... but she's incredibly bright. Those eyes. They're the Crescent Awakening.

'She's a witch?'

She's well-read.

'There is little difference in whatever gnostic veil one wishes to use. It is all frivolous in the eyes of Rakil if it is not his word.' Ada scoffs.

Hmm... such egoism sounds a bit like Colin. Maybe retain judgment considering who your vicar once was?

'We are all created in the image of the Father. But they my friend, are all creations of us and Gaia. This world is what we are. This is the burden of Ada. This is how the four were created.'

Did they ever tell ya the one about the stones and glasshouses?

'You are treading some ethically tumultuous waters...'

We are talking about Baat.

'You take this all in stride. She has admitted to corruption. I am the authority. She is meddling in matters beyond her control. Even if you wish to love these women, they must decide for themselves. With their own minds. And you must decide out of love.'

You never struck me as the love type. I was growing bored with civilian life. It feels good to have purpose again.

"Boy. You've drifted." Warren calls out to me.

"Apologies I was speaking with Ada."

"Such a young age... Rakil has truly trusted you with a lot. So it is so... your generation will be the ones who will undo all this. The Age of Titans and Tyrants are at its end. Here stands Order and Liberty. Jah'Ada." Ray pats my back. "I only wish my 20s were so exciting. Living dreams and raising nations all your own. I was still fighting other men's wars." He grimaced. "I will assist you as I can, Morgan. For 20 year-old Raymond Warren and for your father, Sameera."

"I will find atonement in my father's stay. The city he loves will be rebuilt and his soul will find peace."

"You must kill Colin."

"I'm weary Enshishi will attempt to claim my soul. If I break Colin's then what becomes of Enshishi?"

"I cannot say, because I do not know. I am not well-versed in these matters. I listen to Anki and I serve Erdu. I never needed to become a scholar. But a man who believes himself God is a danger to all those alive. A man such as Colin holding this delusion will remain ruinous until his fall. Ada has ignored Enshishi before and the world burned, The Mountains of Jir and Tartarus were created from their bout. You are surgical and calculated. I trust this won't be an issue for you."

"I don't think Colin will make it that easy."

Ray stared up to the sun, "The evils of this world will fight until their very last breath. They do this because they know they are already defeated. An enemy that knows their defeat is neigh will fight voraciously and haphazardly, they have no reason to care about others or fallout. They simply want their death not to be in vain. Evil conquers good because the meek will take this fight and mistake it for power. But it is fear, it is cowardice, it is dangerous. You must end this with Colin."

I nod, "If Colin comes to Nadia. I will kill him. But I have much I need to do before then."

"You believe he is worth redeeming?" Ray asked.

"I am not the type to just go looking for a fight. If I can ward against Colin and protect Nadia, I will be happy. The city has already lost so much. I will not put myself out of commission again to fight Colin, to leave what little territory I do have open to ruin. I will establish Nadia first, and anyone who wishes to oppose me will meet their end."

"Spoken like a true King."

Ray and our finished our meditation. There was little more to say and less to see. I got what I needed and earned myself back my greatest teacher and ally. We were united.

Ray told me the Brothers of the Order of the Sun Lotus were to be meeting within the month. Since I was not yet ordained a member I would be refused entry. My presence would only cause suspicion and contempt. They would attempt to use diplomacy to reason with Colin. Ray hoped with the united force of the world's affluence standing against Colin he would be forced to bend. He would report back to me and let me know our course of action.

Diplomacy wins the day. Rose will be proud. But in my stomach I was doubtful. If Colin would refuse the terms of life at the Gates of Eternity then what respect would be have for the mortal men of Gaia?

CHAPTER 49

No Man is Greater Than Tomorrow

Morgan Leonticus Sameera

Halle moved on to Maya to be with her Lady Mother. I remained with Rose and Ananda in Nadia as her ladies built raised garden beds and a few of my men helped them in building aquaponic units to distribute. We needed food to last our people throughout the winter. I was obstinate about assisting all of Nadia. A cruel reality is that not all of us wish to be saved. There are many advocates of Colin even to their own demise. It mattered little what we did or said to them. They were taken with Enshishi and his allure of boundless riches and powers that these people rather die for than live amongst their brothers. They were enemies in my mind. Ananda agreed having the same difficulty even finding those amongst Colin to disagree with his animosity. Rose remained hopeful those people would all change sides once they saw our works. It's easy to jump ships once you realize the other isn't sinking. I had no interest in these people joining my boat. I had what I needed here in Nadia, as I've waited so long for it.

Ray had been in contact with me. Murashima informed me of all I needed to know. Without killing Colin it was futile. Hinata was meditating in Tartarus. Ray arranged a meeting of the Order of the Sun Lotus to sit and treat with the other leaders in Naka and Erdu.

The way of the world made little sense to me. I had all the power I needed within myself to kill Colin and erase his taint and all those Gregors who profited off slavery and genocide created. But to do so would take Ada from this world and leave me Enshishi. I would wed Halle and move on to sit atop the Gregor wealth. I have created this as my plan B. To kill Colin and work toward purifying Enshishi's taint to rebirth as Dragon or Phoenix. But, I would need to remove myself from the world. Take Enshishi to the deepest jungle thicks I could find and battle with him in my subconscious. I've told no one of this plan.

As far as Rose is concerned we're doing it. Colin is at bay. Halle is safe. This is all that concerns me. Rose and Ananda were by my side, safe in the Qatar manor. I was here overseeing the growth of my 'kingdom' from a porch. Everyone looking at me sideways but needed the work. I offered an opportunity to be fed and protected if they joined my family. Most who took it weren't much able-bodied, but they certainly were appreciated. Orphaned children, and single mothers came to us all together. Homeless men and young boys seeking purpose and refuge. We had camps and tents popping up more every night.

Rose believed we were doing all we needed. I didn't share her optimism or comfort. If I had something I wanted destroyed I would await opportunity. The mistake we make is thinking our enemies will eventually just forget we exist. Our issues would fade away or mistakes just disappear. But no... no... unless we confront these things they just wait until we're weakest and seize upon us.

Colin wasn't patient. He wouldn't bide his time until I was weak. But Colin wasn't aware he was prey. Until recently I wasn't aware I was the hunter. But if I cannot kill Colin what the hell can I do? I await the call of these men in Naka to return my call.

I was seated upon the stoop overlooking the block as everyone built and trained. We didn't have a force to withstand an army. Though, we could easily eat through the next year with all we've gotten done.

"Hey, babe. Can we talk?" Rose walked out the house and sat with me. "I have great news for you!"

I looked up to her, "what's up babe?"

She sat with me and laced her fingers with mine. "we're really making progress, huh?"

I kept quiet, "You all will be good on food..." I gave up on the ideological war between us, we spoke from completely different experiences and perspectives.

"We all? Where are you going?" She caught me immediately, "You just got back, Morgan. You can't run a nation like this."

"Naka... then Zilaypenah where I will remain until I purify Enshishi."

"You cannot go!" Rose looks up to me. "What happened to peace, Morgan?"

"Reality. Any day Colin and his men can come." I sat up taking my arm back, "There's an ally in Naka, one from my childhood who has been training. There's an Order of men with elitist asshole syndrome making decisions about the nation. I'm going to apply my skills and deal with this situation."

Rose let out a sigh, "You can't go Morgan, I need you here in Nadia."

"Rose, these are your people and you're capable of-

"I'm pregnant. You have to stay and raise your child!" she crosses her hands over in her lap, letting out a deep exhale. Rose bit her thumb cursing to herself, "surprise..." she waves her hands and they fall again.

"You're pregnant?" I tried to ask as calmly as I could in my shock.

A baby? Baat got what she wanted...

Rose smiles up to me and holds my hands. "Yes, love. We're having a baby!" She gestures for us to go inside.

I took pause unable to move immediately. I had a child coming into this world. A madman to the East. And this was my army? There were children about here as well. Little girls and boys helping their mothers. When I first came they were but babies. I had to ensure they grew to be old fat men and women.

"Baby, let's talk." Rose urges me.

"There's nothing to discuss... killing Colin isn't an option." I sighed.

I had no interest in words, women always wanted to speak. I need a course of action. Halle told me I couldn't just kill my problems. Ada says Colin believes he has me. We are ethereal brothers. Should we not be fighting? But this man is the devil. I need to protect my citizens and my son... but even then I'm willing to kill Colin to ensure their future. Rose believes in peace. I am Ada, I should believe in peace. But with a child. Killing my enemy as soon as possible seemed my most reasonable response. She would bear some repulsion to how simply the feeling comes to wipe a man off Gaia as if he never existed.

"Morgan..." Rose pats my back, "sweetie?"

"What do I do, Rose? Do I wait for the end? Sit here and play King?"

"You're not playing King. You are King."

"Not yet..." I stand walking down the stairs crossing my arms behind my back. It helped me think better.

I scanned the block for improvements. We needed defenses. We needed a strong perimeter around the city block.

Rose would be upset. She wanted to sit down and talk, have a discussion about all this. But I wasn't interested in the talk or softness. A leader had to be willing to die for his people. I wish we waited until this issue subsided. Now, we're caught in a trap we created for ourselves. The only thoughts clouding my mind are Colin trying to take Rose from me. I wouldn't be effective like this just cowering and waiting. I needed to know his neck was broken to sleep at night.

"Young Ada!" Takio Murashima joined my side, "You seem distracted? What is bothering you?"

"My girlfriend is pregnant. My wedding with Halle hasn't dissolved fully. And Colin-

"Colin will be dealt with. Focusing on home will allow you to grow here. You will be thankful a decade from now. You stayed. Adas have died for being so quick to run into fights. The real revolution is at home not the battlefield. Colin wants war."

"I wouldn't play into war. I would find myself on his window sill and at his throat." I grunted almost insulted by the accusation I would lead these people to death.

"If that is the way we will maintain order. With assassinations and sneaking. There will be no order. We must have a strong home base." he countered destroying my response. "You go after Colin and the beast within is released, what will you do? You fall or even leave Enshishi an ounce of strength he will come here and he will destroy everything you love."

"You are here to ensure that Takio. How will my opposition respect me if I allow another to fight my battles?"

"You are allowing your men to defend their King and his Kingdom. This is what Leaders must do!" he stresses.

"I am not a leader. I am a Messiah... that's for null if I do not save the people from Colin."

"Perhaps you are here to save your people from the test of time. You told me yourself. You were done with war. Do not let your boredom lead you to your death." He smiles patting my shoulder. "When you're my age, you will be glad you chose to raise your territory and your family. If you want a war, fight it with culture and finance." Freedom can only be bought in blood or coin... "We are attempting to move past the death and bloodshed, no?"

"Even to the evil and criminals?" I asked unsure even where I stood anymore. "I used to be so sure of all this. Those without an insignia were evil, those with the insignia were good. Those with money were desirable, those without are not. Now, having realized how much was for null... I simply don't know what I think anymore."

"What good will be brought from you being the one to kill Colin versus Hinata or Warren?"

"Warren isn't in fighting condition. Last we met he almost crossed over. He lost his physical form. He was just sands."

"Sounds though he ascended. He is a pure element now. He will be stronger than ever! His body will no longer limit him. You can rely on your men!" Takio squeezes my shoulders, "You must have faith in something other than yourself, especially with your faith being so shaken."

"This just doesn't feel right." I shook my head, "I went through all this, to sit on the sideline and watch the battle? This seems wrong." I rubbed my chin pondering another option.

"For the life of your child. Do you believe your child will not need both his parents? Not need your guidance and love rather than your memory before he is even born? Is this not the world we wish to create, a world men will no longer be torn from their families too young to even know there's more to life than conflict and death?" Takio Murashima took my hand. "Reconsider where our time and energy must be spent. You are a King. You must do more than war. Up until this point your child will only long for the man you were, not what you're attempting to be."

He had wisdom on multiple topics. I trusted his word. I trusted his perspective... but if this enemy is so fearsome. If he is a Guardian and I am the strongest allegedly, then should I not be the one who fights him? Instead I am urged to allow diplomacy to reign supreme. To allow another, even if once my mate, to take up my war under my banner.

"Babe?" Rose came up on my side. "Mr. Murashima." She bowed. "Can we talk, please, Morgan?"

"Rose, not now."

"This isn't Rose. We need to speak Ada." her crystalline eyes pierced through me. "Now."

Takio Murashima took a step back and went to his knees. "This is truly beyond me." He bowed. "It is an honor to be in your divine presences."

"Rise up, Takio..." I sigh rubbing my temples.

"Stay down." Baat snaps at me slapping my arm, "You are a King now, he honors you! You are his God, he praises you. You will always feel this way if you don't change your perspective! These people follow you, yet you are following and taking their lead and counsel. They want yours!" She pokes me in the chest.

I stare Baat in her crystal green eyes with my blood red crimsons. "If you want to be my counsel, stop using my beloved to speak to me. Meet me, speak true Baat Qatar."

"Come to Maya... we will speak then." she rolls her eyes, "this is yet another honor you refuse to see beauty in. This is my granddaughter and our devotee! You know her, she isn't some daft girl. She's brilliant and discerning. She gives her life in service to you and your name, and you are the father of her child!"

"You're stripping her of her free-will. I can't abide by that. I can't... it's like a fog in my mind. It's like I'm on repeat." the hairs on my neck stood.

"Your human conscious is limiting your Guardian ability. Rose would make a better container than you right now." Baat sighs. "Come inside, we will speak further and I'll try to find you a way to Maya. We haven't much time and we must speak."

"I can use the Void."

"I believe you honestly believe that to be the extent of your abilities because it's all your enemy taught you." She said out of disappointment. "What have they done to you my beloved? You do not know right from wrong? Our world needs a leader. For years to come. Enshishi will be an issue until the end of times and the 15th age. But here we all are in the 7th age and Enshishi is still alive. You are the one who controls the flames, can move the mountains, part the seas, and command the winds. But you think all you can do is hop portal to portal. You are eternally and internally stronger than Colin Gregor. Do not allow your soul to be lost trying to kill Enshishi. Taking back Ecru will halt Enshishi for centuries to come. Stay here."

"Perhaps I'm not the leader you believed me to be. I'm not sure I can do that." I sighed.

She smacked me. Glaring at me. "Why do men have to be so stubborn!?"

"Why must women be so idealistic?"

"You're a violent brute!"

"You're a naïve child! Women do not live in reality!"

"Men are stuck in the past!"

"We're stuck in what works and don't put our faith in the untested." I correct her. "I have seen with my own eyes my great need to intervene and take out Colin Gregor. Yet, a whole life he remains out of reach. I'm killing him. Right now." I turn my back ready to blink. Rose wraps her arms around my waist. "You're attempting to spare Colin after you yourself called him the devil?"

"I'm trying to save your soul! I don't give a fuck about Colin! Stay home, baby!" Her eyes swell with tears beginning to cry uncontrollably. "You will be torn from the world for another 1000 years and this poor boy will live his entirety as his own enemy. For the sake of Morgan Sameera and the people of Gaia. Allow the Murashimas to handle Colin! Allow fire to fight fire. Do your works here, baby. Don't worry about Enshishi. He is all that is evil in this world. All that is wrong. You are a redeemed soul, Morgan. Do not sacrifice that playing into his trap. There is no winning when dealing with Enshishi. He is corrupt, clever, and is never afraid to use brute force or trickery especially when he doesn't have to, in order to win."

"I understand, now..." I grit my teeth. "I am to be a woman."

Rose's hand smacks me so hard my lip bled, "How hard is it not to right now? To restrain yourself from giving into your pure vice and anger? That is the strength and force of will that will guide us to the 8th Age and beyond! Not Enshishi. Enshishi only hopes to destroy this world. He can only understand the physical and the wealth. But he doesn't know the intrinsic beauty and simplicity that you have taught me, Ada. However, if you give into the very same vice and anger you're withholding yourself against he will devour your soul without a drop of blood on either side, he will simply take it. Please... reconsider."

I had no more words or options. I was pressed against the wall.

"It will take some time before I am fine with this decision. And I will be ready to kill Colin if the opportunity arises. But if you two advise me to stay, it would be foolish and prideful to refuse your counsel." I stood and walked back inside the house, not wanting to be around anyone.

Rose followed regardless. She kept pace behind me. She didn't speak or prattle.

I sat on the couch staring down at my feet. She sat by me and rested her head on my shoulder.

I held her head, "this feeling... whether it's only with $50 in my pocket or trying lead an entire city. This feeling, it always comes back. The cycle never ends."

"You're a hustler baby. You're intelligent. And you're patient. I'm here for you." Rose kisses my cheek. Rubbing my stomach as she nuzzles my neck, "Baby, I'm glad you're not gone."

"Colin Gregor will get his... part of me knew his life wasn't mine to take. Even as a kid, I knew a man who would potentially be my responsibility or affect me. But try as he might. I never let Colin get to me. Once you put it like that... I had to maintain my mental edge." I gave her a wink, "you could see by the way his men look at him. By how his people act. I needn't do anything to Colin. If I allow him to live long enough his empire will crumble upon his head. He wishes to die before his failures can be realized. I cannot allow for this to happen. He will live to be 70. He will live to see the Gregor Family die and all the land they've stolen reclaimed. He will live to see the world rebuke him and realize all the lies. And he will stand powerless because the world has chosen their King. Though many do not know me. And will reject my name. They will do my works and walk beside me whether they know it or not. We all wish to live. And to be happy. Joy can't be monopolized."

"Jah'Ada, bless."

"I'm thankful for you, Rose."

"I love you, Morgan."

"I love you."

"I told you the booty would be here once you came around." She smiled. "We're all alone. If you're not gonna fight. Wanna go upstairs and take out some aggression."

I grin, "I get to marry you?"

She straddles my lap, and kisses my forehead. "Aren't you lucky?"

"I'm blessed." I lift her up in my arms.

"I don't mean to make you feel like a coward or weak, Morgan. But there are people here we can rely on and we must. No man is an island. You're still strong beyond belief in my eyes. But it isn't just your raw power. You are strong inside and out. No one is above you."

CHAPTER 50

Smile of a Stoic

Morgan Leonticus Sameera

I'm not aware of the will of Rakil. He's supposed to guide me by signs. Perhaps I've been blind? He's supposed to be my patron above all yet-

Perhaps less time spent in refusal of fate will better serve for a future? One for all. No longer my ruminations. No longer seeking validity or guidance for existence. Perhaps, he trusts me... as if anyway. My development, my goals and wishes- he sees past the fears I have of myself and the harshest evils in this world.

He is Father. I can accept and respect this. If the force that can grant me infinite purpose in this world, can also grant me the joy I have in my hands.

To know I may still act upon the side of good, righteousness, glory, and joy. To know my soul is still my own, not yet lost. The rest of my person- lost in time, molded by experience, or in my own self-proclamations of identity. I can choose to shrug off such burdensome robes, and become a light for those around me.

Baat, dear mother. I thank you for bestowing your daughters upon me, to show a greater life worthy of living and worthy of leading. But this is not going to be easy. Having been aligned with our enemy for so long-

There is no assistance that will come for Nadia. No one waiting for the recovery or rise of a new Ecru. They've replaced us, and wish the lot slaves. But Rakil, dear father, you have shown me the err of my ways, and with it the delusions of our enemy.

Our enemy replaces human decency, companionship, and family with terror, greed, and diversion. I felt orphaned for so long but when I wanted to open my arms, in the least the possibility of love. I was drowned. I was drowned in Baat's grace with women who refused anything but to be along my side. Did I fail to reciprocate?

My mind in the past. My heart nonexistent. They were young ladies. Even the spoiled ones, wanted my attention and affection. I refused. This is the truth. To listen and trust them. To let go when we're both hurt, and to stand along them when we were weak. No, I stood in the rain... and if anyone wanted to be with me, they needed to endure the storm. Instead, I should have stepped inside, I had a nice home, good allies. But all I knew was alone, and the sickness of standing in storms.

I- wish my discovery of purpose was enough, but there remains so much to be done. Within me and in the world. In truth, my ambitions will take decades, and after my death even then citizens must be responsible to defend, and build their own lives. But with the threat of savages wishing to destroy the legacy of Ada, and enslave my people- Even in Colin's death he will have a cabinet of men meant to keep his will alive.

How can people believe their death is a sacrifice for greater when after thousands of years of war, death, pillage and rape there's been no net gain. Not for humanity, not the people... only the God-kings. Humanity is falling for their own lies. How many work their entire lives, sacrificing love and their family for the sake of this bounty, this happiness, this- this gift of Enshishi. Enhshishi, who has failed us all including himself! This endless lust for Enshishi's blessings, but all fire does is burn all those who draw too near!

Enshishi was meant to be our Guardian. Our protector against all who wish to harm Rakil's creation and his children. Instead, he has become the demise of all things, all people in this world. Where he is, is evil, ego, individualism, ignorance, greed, lust, pride... he must be purified.

Rose will likely wish me home, there is probably dinner ready turning cold. I could have checked in, but haven't a clue where to find her within all this. We should have made plans, I miss her. I want to be in my woman's arms. Instead, here I am in Exigo, waiting for joy in my bird's nest from nearly a decade ago, eating beans two years past their expiration date thinking of how to end Colin's reign. She would smack the can from my hands, yell at me for eating them, then start making her goat stew. Ahh... if I was home, we could make love all night.

Duty calls.

I have half an hour until I meet Takio, Rose and Ananda will have to wait. I could at least call for her to start the stew, maybe ask for a back rub when I get home.

I let out a sigh.

Guess I'll have to settle for stew another time. For now, I must focus on Mark's keeper.

I hopped down the fire escape in a few leaps, reaching the ground-level. I broke into a light jog. I felt fine physically, aside from some bruises and scars. But my life energy was bankrupt after today. I have enough left for a blink or two before I puke blood or go incapacitated. For the most point, Takio seemed as though he only wanted to speak. I didn't fear him- not from the fist-fighting perspective. He gave off an aura of honor. He also had a ferocious energy about him, something deep in the bones and veins. A familiar energy- not Enshishi, not Colin but the same incorrigible fire.

Takio sat outside the gym, he greeted me with a large smile and open arms. "You have arrived, I assumed you would be asleep with your wife! I thank you for coming so late." Takio smiled as I approached the gym. Having slowed to walking because I was spent. "It's an honor, Lord Ada."

"Please, Morgan Sameera." I bow before the master and my elder. "I'm gracious for the invitation."

"Hmm clinging to mortality I see." Takio smiled, "or haven't fully accepted your place on the pantheon?"

"I believe such need for titles add to our issue." I rub my neck, "I suppose the latter. I don't wish to be another god-king holding domain over his people. I wish to lead."

"It's the lack of respect for such titles in my opinion, if we refer to the corruption and false worship." Takio smiled patting my shoulder. "Either in those who wear them, or in those without them. We have lost many traditions. Respect is one of them."

"I'm glad you would have me. You are quite wise." I chuckled finally hearing someone sensible.

"I might as well all the study and meditating over these decades." Takio gave me a wink, "My family has prepared for your return for sometime. Centuries perhaps. My father has been most patient and anxious to meet you."

"I'm honored truly." I smile, giving Takio a polite nod of assurance. "I- I have found few allies who truly understand what's at stake."

"To be expected. There are few alive to know of the Guardians. Let along Enshishi and Ada. Our battle is human ignorance and arrogance."

"I battle Colin and his followers."

"Noble indeed. I suppose you came for a tour of the city, no?"

I nod.

He hindu squats to his feet using only his toes and properly functionality to stand tall. Takio seemed a formidable man. Standing a few inches under six foot with nearly two hundred pounds. But wore a pair of thick silver framed glasses, and walked with his hands crossed behind his back as a scholar.

"So, where do I begin in Nadia? To save the city."

"The hearts and souls of the people."

"What does that even mean?" I rub my neck with robust confusion.

"Means sentimental victories. My brother informs me you were in class with my nephew, Hinata."

"Hmm... Yes, yes we were. That was nearly a decade ago. You're Hinata's- Murashima." Damn, even back then the father pushed his soldiers into my life. "How has Hinata been?"

"I imagine unwell, it's a very disturbed world we have developed. Hinata has been in Tartarus training under our grandfather, Saito. He is- well if I may trust you with this information. He is training to purify the spirit of the Guardian of Fire. To bring back Ryu."

"He- Hinata will be able to contain Enshishi after his death?"

"In theory, yes... It's our hope you are interested in this endeavor."

"As long as I nor Colin am the Guardian of Fire. I'm fine with that." I wiped a tear from my eyes. "I was fearful I was born to sell my soul. I- I hoped the father wasn't so cruel."

"You were born to guide the newest version of the human will, my King. I suppose we are all unsure of what this entails or will require."

"I- I'm so thankful for this news, we can move forward as best we can toward making the most important fields of preparing Nadia, now! Rose will be so happy."

Takio smiles, "May I act as your advisor, King Sameera? This has been an honor I awaited since childhood. Though, I believed I would be postponed such a pleasure with your absence and the original King's unfortunate end."

"I thank you for your honesty. Your assistance and guidance are welcomed brother." I embrace Takio Murashima.

Tonight I was expecting to have to watch over my back with a potential enemy. Instead, I found an ally. I wonder how many more people are awaiting to stand up, not solely for my cause but for their own lives and works. There is a greater tide of humanity awaiting us.

Hinata was probably one of the few students in our lives who could compete with me. The name Murashima had no value to me. Nor did Enshishi or Ada in those days of youth. Saito Murashima however, Son Saito rather was rumored to be a 200 year-old hermit living in the mountains of Western Ontar in Tartarus, Naka. The expanse of land nearly 5,000 miles formed after the first fight with Ada and Enshishi. The opposing land in Esha is nonexistent. The land in Tartarus was dead down to the molecules. All but some animals who adapted to the brimstone and hellfire, and volcanoes were in the land. The old man was expected to be a rumor, old tale, or dead. Yet, his son little over 50 was before me. Was Saito Murashima the soulless man who lost Enshishi to the Gregors? It'll explain both his age, and ability to train Hinata.

"Can I join their training?"

"Perhaps after. They're rather far along. I nor my brother could nor would withstand. I mean no disrespect in saying, it's best you leave them to it. Tartarus is nearly 130 degree on its coldest day. Our father is training him in the ancient way. When this resolves, my father would delight in teaching you. Last we spoke Hinata was meditating near the Mouths of Vulcanus, nearly 200 degrees. He trains to be a Guardian." Takio smiled. "Shall we walk?"

"After you, good sir." I bowed my head allowing him to step before me. "I'm glad we have an alternative to me. In truth, I've grown tired of the bloodshed and death. I felt as if my hands were bounded."

I could at least report good news back to Rose on the matter of possession. Enshishi was beginning to fade to the background of my mind. Perhaps finally Nadia and its reconstruction, growth, and liberation can be my first, and last focuses for this world.

Our conversation ended on a kind note. Mutuality was stronger than friendship. Being glued together with commonalities is not the same as building common cause and future.

There were young men, in truth none too far from my age. They looked to me as if they saw a ghost.

"It's you..." One kid looks up with a mask in his hands. "you're him."

I smile politely, "Morgan Sameera. There will be peace in Nadia."

"Fuck yeah!!" The men chorus. "Fuck the racists, fuck the fascists!" Chants filled up around us.

"These are the young boys left fighting for Justice in Nadia. Many of their fathers taken or killed. We've done our best in training them, but a sensei is not a father."

"No, but teaching a man to use his own hands allows him to find his own purpose. The war is in our hands now."

"Fuck yeah!" The men chorus once more.

"All we need is Mark back and the strongest guys ever will be on our team!"

"Damn right." They chorus.

We stepped out of the warehouse gym into the harbor air. Breathing deeply and exhaling the salt air. The warehouses were virtually empty.

The men were dressed in their costumes, and Masks. They saluted upon departing leaving to patrol the streets for corruption.

Once they were gone. Takio and I walked along the street as he pointed out the details of the city. The municipal corporation... Court, where nothing got done of production or worth. The following buildings were of use. The chambers of commerce, the farmer's co-op, the ancient monastery replaced with a Gregor office building, and the closed foundry.

We ended the tour at the edge of Graham and Nadia.

"Further is Graham, formerly Grand Ba'ath where Baat was born to Ada. Formerly Ecru... We've lost much territory to finance, war and time."

"All lost can be regained." I pat Takio's shoulder.

Takio smiled, "I will report to you soon, and we will begin rebuilding Nadia."

"I must see the Queen. I thank you for all you've done today Takio."

"I've done nothing but assist you in advancing the ideas of growth and love."

"Two things I felt were for null, for sometime."

"Then I thank your wife." Takio winks, "hopefully you'll find some joy, within all this.It’s important to focus on solutions rather than complaints or destruction."

"You know what... I think I have." I smile on. "Do you know where Lady Qatar once lived?"

Takio smiled, "violet-blue home in Graham. One of the largest with an orchard leading straight to the door. Five miles from here. So, your wife is-

"Baat... Yes." I wanted to smile but my better judgment told me not to. "Baat sent one of her children into my life, Enshishi sent many of his own attempting to influence and deter me."

"Blessings, brother. I am so gracious for your visit today."

"They'll be more. Thanks for the description. I think I'll try to find a good view to blink over."

"I could give you a ride?" Takio chuckles, "I'm parked only a couple blocks away."

I thank him graciously. I couldn't blink unless I could visualize the location. Not to mention I was exhausted down to my marrow. I've made difficult close calls. But after giving so much of my own life force to save Ray. My abilities began to show me more and more, my only limitations were my ignorance and conscious of this supple world beyond my sight.

"So, how does it feel being back in Nadia? I moved here to Mido's dismay. He wishes to see the family as it was when my father was a boy."

"Do you not?" I asked not truly ignoring his question. Having little to offer in way of an organic response.

Takio smirked,"That was two whole centuries ago. The world is so vastly different. I have purpose here, as I would there. Mido, doesn't like being looked down upon and hates the Gregors. So, he works quite hard to improve our family's station."

"Who is Mido? And who is looking down upon your family?"

Takio sat behind the wheel of his station wagon. As he adjusted his mirror, he seemed to have noticed the severity in his eyes and let out a pained sigh. "Ada, I'm happy to discuss this with you. Our family was once the Keeper of the Eternal Fire, The protectors of Naka, and the Guardian Ryu. Today, the children of Kisaka all wish to go to La Vida or be Gregors. It makes Mido sick, I suppose it's why I moved to the city here in Exigo, away from that turmoil. To not see it, to not have to deal with my Brother's anger."

"Why not help him rebuild? It's your family's honor and duty."

"Legalities of demons, their blasted Sun Order or whatever it's name is these days. I moved, my friend because my people have only lost their power. But the Nadians were robbed of everything! I have two brothers, Mido is the eldest and angriest. And two nephews, both working very hard alongside their fathers. Someone must assist those who have fallen in our absence. Not simply hope to rise as phoenixes. The Dragon is also an incomplete form, there has only been one Dragon in history-

"Victorianna. Gregor..." I sigh.

"Um no... Victorianna was another Lion, perhaps a Dragon... she never truly showed herself. Gregors rarely change. Before all, before either the Lion or Dragon, before the Guardians took to humans, before humans were on Gaia. The Guardians were energy, were animals. The first human Phoenix was Hiro Muriega Murashima, he lost his bending to Onyx Men Sah'ra in the rise of Ecru. He liberated both their souls from the taint of darkness. Two truer brothers never existed. It was Hiro's insurmountable fight against Luno who was within Onyx, and Onyx's mourning and regret that led to the resurrection of Hiro. Then once more the Phoenix and Hawk were of this world."

"Sounds as though, Ada and the Phoenix are opposites."

"Rakiham, the Phoenix, is the pure fire, pure light. He is the Sun. Nadir the Panther is rooted in the moon, the bright light before Rakil birthed the sun. The perception is opposition, such is our current state. But in truth- the Guardians are all brothers and sisters. All the Guardians. All of us as humans. As children of Rakil. This what we in Kisaka and the Ecruen knew to be fact. To be the true story of the sun and moon. While the rest represent Gaia, the oceans, and the air we breathe. Those two are the light keeping us all alive and protected."

"I've never heard much about this side of the story. The Gregor corruption is so deep, even I'm not aware of myself. I didn't wish to be Luno... instead I wished to die."

"No, no, boy. Most have not heard any of this history. It's strange, for us in Kisaka it's readily available. In our books, in our libraries, or elders screaming on the streets of the old days before our kids cared for wealth, materialism, and voluntary dishonor. If you leave Kisaka there's nothing outdoors or about, just lies, ignorance and apathy to hear truth." Takio stopped at the light although it was green. His head fell into his hands. "I see why my brother is so frustrated, it isn't simply the Dragon's hunger within him. I- I just can't give into the anger, it's a temptation."

"Anger is a temptation?"

"Yes, all emotions are on the stage of tempestuous. If unjust or indirect, they're solely reactionary, ego-filled swings in one's energy and mood. Selfishness. Joy, however, that's eternal. Sadly, so are vengeance and melancholy. He looked over at me. Your sadness is palpable, I wish I could fend for you. But wouldn't know where to start." Takio parked in front of my lake house. "Here we are, Lord Ada and Lady Qatar's home." It was a beautifully painted home with purple walls and a golden trim.

"Thank you, Takio. This was incredibly beneficial. Please contact your brother for me. We need to discuss this Enshishi issue. He must know how the spirit can be purified instead of destroyed. I- if anger truly is a temptation worthy of corrupting my soul, there must be a better way to defeat Colin."

"This was all an honor! On the subject of Midoriya, he was fervent in contacting you some years ago, but- you were indisposed. He sent messages to your properties."

"Yeah... I was dead." I rub my neck, "I'm back now. My mind is clearing, so, please let me know however I can assist your family."

"Will do, and likewise! My family is in Naka. I suppose Rakil has put me here for you, so... you know where to find me when I can be of use to you or the Queen."

"Takio, can you contain the eternal fire?" I ask out of curiosity rather than practicality.

"Oh, no! No!" Takio raises his hands, nearly having a heart attack, "This is what you meant." he rubbed his chin, "I'll contact Midoriya once I return home. His son is in Tartarus. Both will be happy to hear you are well. Hinata was quite worried as a child for you. It's turned him more toward duty, he left for Tartarus willingly, the boy knew the stories since he was a lad. I'll update you with their response." I shake Takio's hand. He smiles brightly as a tear falls down his cheek. "I'm so glad you are well, Morgan. Enjoy the rest of your weekend."

"Greatly, appreciated. The world will turn to the light once more." I wave, climbing out of the station wagon and stretching out. Feeling rejuvenated to some degree. Enough energy to enjoy my love and return to bed.

Takio pulls off the curb and I turn my home. So, this is where my mysterious maid springs from when asks for day to herself and two thousand dollars. She paints my home? There's so much this girl has kept secret from me, and I have given her my heart. Fate she'll call it. Fated and destined love. Cheers to the future I suppose. Time for rest.

CHAPTER 51

Perfect Weekend

Morgan Leonticus Sameera

I held a blunt between my lips, looking over the balcony. I took in a deep breath of fresh air wishing I hadn't broken my old rod.

The fishing is good this time of year. Everyone in our small town contributes to keep the lake well maintained so the fish can breed harmoniously. I used to sit out by the lake every Saturday when I first moved in. Sitting peacefully with my toes in the sandy grass, smoking from my pipe and watching the sunrise, I loved it. When I moved out life was so simple without any women in my home. I had my home to myself, my thoughts and to my peace. Now, there is endless drama and prattling.

Since Halle left for Maya I've been told repeatedly to take some time for myself. I can't first but I've always wanted to get into gardening. Hell, I can grab another fishing rod while I get the lumber. I have plenty of tools already. Build a couple garden boxes, plant some veggies and fruit, and maybe grab a fruit tree. Would be great to drink a few cases of beer, catch some fish to grill over an open flame.

I get to do it alone...

Wow, that was fun to say.

"I get to do it alone." I chuckle.

It's its own luxury. Some time to enjoy my solitude.

Oh, I can finally use my record player and listen to my vinyl collection. And I can eat those venison sausages and steaks in the deep freezer. While I wait for them to thaw I can teleport to Erdu and go for a dope hike. Spend the rest of my time listening to good jazz music, throwing back a few beers and grilling the catch of the day or just eating some venison flank steak.

My stomach rumbles thinking about my day.

Hopefully Rose or Ananda already made some lunch. Yeah, one of them is cooking something absolutely delicious. I can smell the savory scent of burgers or something beefy cooking up in the kitchen. I love not having to tell them what to do. They simply go about their business and do their job.

Since they have lunch cooking up I could probably rush out and be back in time to get some progress on my garden boxes. I'll have the store measure up and cut the slabs then I can probably get one finished, eat some grub while I enjoy another marijuana cigar then do the rest once I have a good meal in me.

"Hey Morgan, are you hungry?" Rose says without turning.

The way this girl walks around my house was shocking to me. A pair of knee-high socks with shorts barely covering her butt, the outfit seemed backwards to me. I wore a pair of blue jeans with sandals so maybe I'm the square. I won't complain she looked amazing, letting me squeeze her butt as she reaches for my blunt.

"You're already done cooking? I was hoping to get some work done before I ate but I can eat first."

"I mean it's no big deal, I guess I can bring it up to your office." She says a bit disappointed.

"No, I'm actually going to build a garden box. I'm going to blink over to the store and buy some wood and a new fishing rod."

"You fish?" Rose was engrossed.

"When I get an opportunity, it's very peaceful. I broke my old rod catching a fat bass."

"Can I join you?"

"Uh... you fish?" I rub my neck already feeling my perfect day coming to an end.

"I've always wanted to learn! I never knew someone who actually goes out to fish."

"I'm really not much of a teacher... I guess I can grab you a rod too while I'm at. You can find your own spot to fish and I'll fish at mine."

"Wow, you can buy me one? And maybe one for Ananda but I doubt she's going to stop reading anytime soon."

"I'm rich, girl. I've been meaning to buy a few rods but I've been busy since I moved in. I broke my first rod the first month I was here. Been so busy this past year, I don't honestly remember the last time I had a chance to enjoy myself."

"You've only lived here for a year? It must be much better than renting. I don't think I've ever cooked a fish straight out of water."

"I can prepare the fish, you or Ananda can cook it. In another year we'll have some fresh produce to go along with it."

"Another year with me around, I didn't know you were planning so far ahead." Rose kisses my cheek.

"I'll be here in a year and I'll still need your services. You're welcome to finish out your doctorate here if needed."

"I love working for you."

"I suppose because other jobs have stricter dress codes."

"I thought you would like my outfit. I was wearing it for you. I didn't know you would be out gardening." Rose bit her lip and cheeks flushed red.

"I was advised to take some time to enjoy myself."

"You finally listened to me something I said! Not to mention you taking my garden box idea!" Rose cheers.

"Ha, I am good at taking advice Rose."

"Yeah, but you have a lot of people involved in your life Morgan. I guess you can take that as you want. As long as you keep it out there I don't care."

"What do you mean?"

"Well, I rather you kept the other women out our love life. They seriously bring drama. I rather you view our home as your safe haven instead of a mental asylum."

"I wasn't expecting that response."

"Ha, you thought I would say I want you all to myself?" Rose kisses my neck.

"You seem to enjoy sharing more than most people I know."

"I can see why you'll think that. I'm enjoying my youth but it doesn't mean I'm trying to experiment forever."

"Well you seemed dressed to get my attention."

"Oh shut up, I was hoping this would get you out of your bat cave."

"I'll humor you, what is the bat cave?"

"Or your fortress of solitude, whatever you want to call the place where you go to be miserable."

"Where would you suggest I spend my time, Rose?"

"You should be inside me." Rose lifts herself up swinging in the air by my neck.

"Ha, I rather get started on my box."

"Do you think I only like you for sex, Morgan?"

"It seems to be all you're concerned with honestly." I shrug.

"I was told that's all men wanted, honestly." She replies.

"Well, I am a Guardian right? Makes sense I want more from a relationship than sex. I'm down to fish with the two of you."

"Great, I am too!" Rose pats my cheek then moves to leave me, "Come down when you're ready to eat."

"What did you cook? It smells amazing." I call out, poking my head out the door to catch her before she left.

"You think it smells good? I thought you never ate because you didn't like my cooking." Rose giggled closer to the door than I expected.

"Well, Ananda definitely has a craft all her own in the kitchen but I love your cooking as well. Tell, me what did you make?"

"It's a family recipe, some tomato soup with cheesesteak sandwiches. You had some steak in the freezer I decided to make for lunch."

"I really wanted steak today. It's like you read my mind. It's the deer meat?"

"Oh it was deer? No wonder it smelled so different. Where did you get deer meat?"

"How do you think a man gets deer meat? I hunted some deer. Had a butcher separate it for me, there's no beef in my fridge."

"You're telling I've been eating deer meat this entire time?"

"If you've been eating the meat in the freezer then yes it's been bear, deer, boar, duck, bison or goat. I had some gator in there but I have no idea what happened to it."

"Next you'll say you had a partridge in a pear tree."

"No, but I did get some quail and its eggs."

"When did you go hunting?"

"Usually when I want to kill someone I go hunting instead. Keep me from getting arrested. If I would allow myself to even be restrained."

The way she was looking at me was a mix of horror and intrigue. She began brushing against me as she found her words. It wasn't often Rose was speechless but it was priceless. Rose reached for my crotch causing me to jerk away laughing as I lightly stiff arm her away.

"Ha, I'm going to head out to the store now. Keep my venison warm I won't be too long."

"Dammit Morgan, you're such a tease. There's no way you had all those meats..." Rose began chuckling.

"No, I did. I just didn't want you trying to jump my bones again. You've been eating hunting meat since you've been here. Unless you went shopping for something else, you've been eating my kills." I smirked feeling a bit devious for not telling her sooner. "How'd you like it?

"I don't think I can ever go back. I thought it was like Wagyu Kobe Beef or like organic... I can never go back to normal meat again. I guess your dick was an extension. I could never go back to normal dick again, so get ready because I have 8 years until I get my doctorate."

"Rose, why is it every time I'm around you all you can talk about is sex?" I smack my face.

"You're sexy... as fuck bro. Like have you looked in a mirror? You're hot, ripped, chocolate and your dick is the size of my forearm."

"If you keep fucking around you'll end up pregnant."

"Maybe that's all my evil master plan, Morgan." Rose sneers.

The room filled with laughter until my laughter became uneasy thinking of all the unprotected sex I've had finishing inside this girl.

"We're going to get you a doctor's appointment as soon as possible. You and Ananda both, we can't keep having sex."

"You don't want children?"

"I do but... I want to at least be married to the mother of my kids not getting married because of the kid."

"What if you could have the baby and carry on with your life?"

"Why would someone want that?"

Rose shrugs, "I would rather you stay and raise our son but you're a busy man. I won't ask for any money but-

"Rose what the hell are you talking about? This is like the fifth or seventh time you brought up having my baby. What's up?"

"I want to have your children..." Rose rolls her eyes turning her back to me, "You're not going to stop me."

"Whatever you say crazy lady, I'll be back. Maybe, we should take a serious break from sex."

"No, Morgan. It's fine. You think I'm on the pill, remember?" Rose smirks.

"I think you're on the pill?"

"I'm joking with you." Rose laughs, "I'm going to go eat your deer meat. I'll keep your sandwich in the oven."

I felt like I was missing something obvious but I wasn't going to ruin my day over it. Having some kids around the house would brighten this place up. Ha, having a kid with Ananda and Rose would be a treat as well. I could imagine a son with me and Rose's boisterous personality and knack for leadership. I could see having a daughter with Ananda who would be a little lady, always reading a book or solving the world's issues. Or vice versa, the idea didn't sound too bad.

Could I bring children into a world controlled by Colin? Natalie and Halle never seemed to like the idea of kids. I imagined children with them would like have Ananda or Rose raising them anyway.

Probably time to start watching where I put my dick before I end up with kids from each of these women. Or make them honest women. Start a small family and do our own thing without worrying about nations, politics or finances.

Was marriage such a bad thing? To Halle I probably wouldn't mind all in all if she calmed down but she was a burning flame. Carmen or Natalie... hmm... not after all they've done maybe in my previous life when I was mentally weaker and in desperate need of approval. Now, the idea of a life with Ananda and Rose by my side seemed peaceful, simple and my reality.

After finishing off the last of my blunt I blinked over to the nearest hardware depot, browsing around the lumber as if I had been there all along. I found a stranded cart in the aisle and began pushing up the hallway. Picking out a couple 16ft oak planks to slice down into 4ft slabs, about two sets for two separate boxes probably all I could finish before it got too late for fishing. Speaking of fish... I blinked over to the nearby outdoors section to grab a couple rods then flashbacked to the lumber cutter. I strolled around the giant planks of wood kicking at my ankle and the fishing rods slapping me in the face.

Grabbing some soil, need some seeds, probably could use a watering can... what $12 for a watering can? Absolutely not, I'll stop by a dollar store and grab one. Let me get out of here before they get me with this overpriced crap. If I wanted to wait I could have ordered something straight from a manufacturer to bypass these middle man stores making hundreds of millions off convenience.

"Sir, your total is $111 would that be cash or card? Feel to tap with your cellphone as well!" the cheery cashier greets me and dismisses me all at once.

"That will be... crap I forgot my wallet on my balcony."

"Oh, that's fine sir. I can set your items aside and hold them until we close tonight at 11pm." He quickly offers a solution.

"No, it's cool."

"You don't want them?" he sounded concerned as if his very job depended on this single sale.

"I'll be right back, hold on." I tear open a hole in space-time, hopping through as I walk back to my house.

I can't believe I forgot my wallet. Maybe that's my fault for smoking before shopping. Glad I didn't end up spending more money.

I reach out of the fabric of reality to grab my wallet off my bed then march my way back to the store.

"Here's cash bro, sorry about the wait." I nonchalantly hand over cash.

"Oh god, how did you do that! You were here then gone now you're here... how did you do that so quickly? I didn't even finish my sentence!" the cashier fell over himself holding out his hands.

"Come on man... I'm just trying to get in and get out." I yawn.

"I- I'm sorry sir you just like- that's um... $111 please."

"Here's cash bud." I offer over $120 waiting patiently for my change.

"Okay... will that be all sir?"

"Yea sure... hey can I bring the cart back before you close tonight?"

"Umm...."

"I'll bring it right back hold on." I sigh flashing back to my room with my shopping cart, unloading everything on my floor then using twice again to drop off the cart and get back to my room without using any energy.

When I was a kid using the void would drain my energy. As I got older it became second nature and I barely felt the energy expenditure. I also invested years of training to develop a nearly bottomless chakra pool. I wouldn't recommend my training pathway to anyone else but it worked for me at least.

There was a knock on my door as I changed into my swim trunks then cautious footsteps entering my room.

"Hey... is there a tropical storm or something outside? I keep feeling a huge wind." Ananda's eyes transfixed on me widening as she saw all my supplies, "Are you making a mud bath?"

"I am going to build some gardens and do some fishing do you want to join in?" I offer grabbing the bags of soil.

"Do I have to...?" Ananda asks curiously watching me as I headed to my balcony, "Are you going to throw them down won't they burst?"

"Not quite what I was expecting." I say before leaping off my balcony to the ground below, setting down the bags of soil then leaping back onto my balcony railing.

"Okay... I was not aware that was humanly possible. What was that 20ft?"

"Pretty high I guess."

"You can jump higher?"

"I can fly under the right conditions." I snicker.

"Can you teach me how to fly?"

"If you want to learn then you have to fish with me or garden with me."

"I don't want to do either of those things." Ananda groans sitting on my bed.

"I don't want to teach you how to fly."

"I'm a good student."

"I'm a good fisherman."

"I rather garden..." Ananda says grabbing the seeds.

I pick up the lumber and hold out my arm for her. Ananda hesitantly inches closer to me likely weary I would jump of the balcony with her. Instead, we hover off of the ground floating to the balcony and down to the ground gently.

"How do you do that?"

"An old Eshan man taught me." I reply picking a good spot to start building.

"Do you remember where he lives? Do we go to him?" Ananda begins her game of twenty-one questions usually turning into fifty questions, if I feel like entertaining her curiosity.

"He died."

"How did he die? Was it quick? Was he sick?"

"I was contracted to kill him. He wanted to past down his technique before he died. When I found him he assumed his time was up. I trained under him then at the end. We dueled. I won. It was a pretty long fight but-

I noticed Ananda beginning to shake when she heard me beginning to tell my story.

"It was quick, painless and I buried him."

"Did he have family...?"

"To my knowledge, he was a hermit living alone in the forests of Erdu."

"Do you enjoy killing people?"

"No?"

"Are you good at it?"

"Very."

"How did you learn how to kill someone?"

"I was kidnapped at a young age, forced to fight for the Regulator Regime-

"I mean but like why you? Why take some kid into the military and how does he end up flying and jumping over buildings?"

"I don't know Ananda." I say grabbing a couple nails.

"Am I annoying you?"

"No, I just don't want to scare you."

"You don't scare me... you intrigue me."

"Why?"

"I couldn't imagine you being a fighter. You don't seem like the type of man who likes conflict. You're too permissive and laidback. It seems weird someone would go through the lengths to remove you so far from your nature to become a killer."

"They weren't considering my nature when they were training me." I let out a sigh.

"What were they considering?"

"Creating a human weapon capable of stopping an army alone or destabilize a government."

"Have you ever destabilized a government?"

"I typically found a way to end my missions as bloodless and orderly as possible. I usually found a way to chop off the head of the snake or to broker a peace deal. I never tried to leave someone's home worse than I left it."

"Clever... have you ever built a government?"

"Technically, I've mostly been building governments instead of destroying them... Hey, can you come hold these two pieces of wood together right here?" I motion Ananda over.

I take a 6 inch nail from my mouth using my thumb to shove the nail straight through the 4x4 slabs. Moving to the opposite side and repeating the process. Within half a minute of maneuvering we finished the first box. We finished the second a bit quicker once she understood the process, an extremely quick learner.

"You just nail wood together with your fingertips..." Ananda shivered.

"I did."

"I would hate to be your enemy. I can't realize how gentle you have been with me."

"I would never hit you Ananda!" I say almost offended.

"Oh, I might when we... you know." She blushes.

"Have sex?"

"Yes... that... if you could do that to a nail then you've been very careful with me." She remarks admiring my craftsmanship. "Have you considered where you would put them?"

"Sorta but nothing definite, I'm guessing you have a suggestion?" I counter her question with a question.

Ananda's eyes constrict as she scans my backyard then her eyes widen for a brief moment before returning to her scanning. She gets up and starts skipping away motioning for me to follow her. I lift up the two boxes in a slow speed chase to the side of the house. Ananda claps finding a spot where the sun was hitting perfectly.

As I laid down the boxes she shooed me off as she began adjusting them in place. I blinked back to grab the soil then flashed back to drop them off.

"I didn't have any time to finish." Ananda complains pointing to the box, "Then you move it."

"Can't we leave it where it's at? I'm planning on starting the garden here then I'm going to move the boxes to a new location. Start a new garden elsewhere until I have a nice forest growing around my house."

"So you only have to build two boxes?" Ananda rubs her chin nodding along to my logic.

We finish setting up the boxes and pour in the soil. Each of us took on a box in order to make the work quicker. I rake out the bottom of my box getting rid of the grass underneath before spreading my soil. Ananda ran inside to grab newspapers to lie across the bottom of her box before pouring her soil down in small plots where she planted her seeds. I pluck out a dozen seeds from varying packs. The strongest will grow roots down into the bottom. Ananda leans against me admiring her work.

"Are you going to finish spreading your soil?" I rub my neck at her minimalist design.

"After I see which seeds germinate I'm going to plant more. I'm hoping to slowly fill up the plot with plants. So after a couple years maybe you'll truly have a forest."

"You have a very brilliant mind Ananda."

Ananda blushes, covering her face and walking away from me.

"What did I say?"

"You said you'll teach me how to fly. So, if I'm so brilliant help me to command my element."

"What is your element?"

"Well, I've been able to study air-bending but I've never been allowed to practice bending. I feel like I would be good at it. Anytime I was caught, I punished harshly I would like to be strong enough to stop anyone from ever punishing me again."

"Have you ever created a breeze before?"

"Not on purpose but sometimes it feels like when I'm scared there's a storm outside and when I'm happy, like really happy to the point of laughing out loud there's like a gentle breeze."

"It means you have a deep chakra pool like me but you probably have no connection or control over it. First you need to have chakra potent enough to feel. Maybe people lose this when they are children so as they grow their potential pool gets shallow. I first want you to focus on feeling your own life force energy. Do not close your eyes try staring at your belly button and breathe deeply. Focus on feeling the energy in the pit of your stomach."

Ananda pulls off her shirt, placing her hands on her waist staring down at her waistline barely holding her eyes open. Her eyes fixated on her bellybutton, constricting tightly as her face began to turn red.

"Nothing is happening."

"Are you overthinking?"

"Yes... I am thinking about the energy and focusing on what it will look like in my hands."

"Have you done this before, you made it seem like you were a novice."

"No... I haven't tried it before this is my first time but-

"How are you going to know what something looks like if you've never seen it before? How could you hold any expectation at all? You need to practice clearing your mind and simply focusing on your own energy. Do not try to see it or feel it, you are the energy."

Ananda let out a deep sigh, relaxing her shoulders standing still and holding her pose.

"You may not get it your first day but if you practice for five minutes at a time build up to ten then work on it for an hour. You want to work be able to hold a ball of your energy for a full 24hrs while fasting. When you learn to control the ball of energy then the process of flying is basically shrouding the magnetic wave between your body and the air molecules with your energy. As you master the process of shielding then you can propel your body upward. When you master hovering and levitating then you can start getting enough lift when you shroud your body to fly and pray there's a strong enough wind to keep you up."

"How long does it normally take people to learn?"

"Normally people never learn this technique at all. It took me a week to learn but this was a very intense week with brutal training. I basically meditated for seven days straight on my energy without ceasing."

"A week... so maybe I can build this up and learn it in a month or a season?"

"Or you could learn it even faster than I did. You have natural affinity and a pretty great thought process. You could probably find a way to use your air bending to propel yourself without fully shrouding yourself. You can use the air's natural energy instead of your own."

"Hmm... I have a good idea for that. I'm going to practice for a while okay? You can leave me." Ananda waves me off not breaking her pose.

Her look of determination showed me she was tired of being pushed around, mirco-managed and doubted. I left her to her training and expected to find her studying more about this for rest of the evening once she was exhausted. Her ambition was rare. It was a drive to be stronger. Something resonating deep inside my soul but today is about me relaxing.

I walked around my property enjoying the beautiful view as it neared to the evening. I set myself up by the lake with my rods, a case of beers and a couple blunts to enjoy the next couple hours of patience. I leaned against a tree sipping on a Yuengling once my rod starting biting, nearly dropping my beer to hold on with both my hands.

"Hey, I'm ready." Rose cheers finally joining me after the first forty minutes of my fishing.

"Grab my waist, help me pull this in it's a big one."

"Can't you just force it out the water?" Rose asks running to my side helping me ground myself.

"If I pull too hard it can break the line but... hold my rod real quick." I suggest.

"What? Why?"

"New fishing techniques, hold my rod real quick, hold it tight and don't let go."

Rose reluctantly grabs my fishing rod, immediately dropping to her butt as the pull of the fish tried dragging her in the water.

I dove into the lake, swimming vigorously to follow the line a few yards from the shore seeing the giant bass that broke my old rod. It jerked and pulled at the piece of deer meat on the end of my lure, greedily fighting to eat the deer meat on the end of the hook piercing its nostrils. I jutted out my hand before it could break its attention from its meal gripping him under the neck by its gills. I suddenly felt my body lifting out of the water into the air in a bubble. Rose began rolling me back to shore dropping me on the lakeside as the bass tried flapping and jumping out of my grip. I held on grabbing a knife from my waist to slice straight through its belly.

"It's still living!"

"Usually how death works..." I mutter beginning to gut it, removing its bloodline, membranes and feces chute running along its spine. "It just needs to be brushed out for the bones and cleaned."

"You didn't even hesitate to kill it."

"If you see an opening and don't take it, the opening may never appear again." I let out a sigh a bit annoyed by her prattling.

"Can we pray over it?"

"Feel free."

Rose kneeled in front of my, holding the fish underneath my hands and bowing her head, "Father Rakil and Mother Gaia, thank you for this fish and its sacrifice for our nourishment. Thank you for giving us one of your children for our sustenance. Amen."

I smiled feeling a bit better about the act myself after her prayer. It presented a new outlook to the experience. A bright light at the end of the horror of murder, at the end we all must return to God. Even for our meals, we must bow our heads in reverence to God.

"Amen... I think I prefer your method. How about this time I hold the rod and you grab the fish at the end of the lure."

"Well, I was actually aiming my ability at you. It's to restrict people who are stronger than me. I'm not sure I focus enough to grab a fish's energy."

"Ananda is training her chakra control and connection. You have a very deep connection to your element. You very personality seems to be like water. I suggest you dip your toes in the water, do your breathing exercises and feel the vibrations in the water. Focus your ability on the source of the movement rather than the energy. If you're facing off against any enemy it'll be a good ability to have available instead of being overwhelmed. Perhaps a stronger bubble for a stronger enemy but if you could create a 1000 bubbles to restrain an army then-

"Then we can protect Nadia?"

"At least momentarily, we would need a plan after the bubbles pop. Want to give it a try?"

"It's not like you'll let me say no. You train 24/7 so might as well get my training in so you don't wake me up out my sleep to do pushups tomorrow morning." Rose stretches out.

We worked together well. As I got a pull on the line, Rose grabbed the catch using a bubble casted around the lure. At first her bubbles were around 3ft in diameter because she couldn't read the energy signature. As we smoked a bit more, enjoying ourselves, relaxing, and vibrating at the water's frequency she began catching fish all her own following the vibrations and movement of the fish. At the end of the day we only kept around ten fish of the ones we caught. We released those who seemed pregnant or too small back into the water to keep the ecosystem at balance.

Ananda eventually joined us once she smelled the fish crackling in tin foil on an open flame. It wasn't long before we were all eating by the lake. The girls grabbed some plates and wine for themselves. I ate with my hands from the tin foil enjoying our hard work for the day. We ended up in my room lying over my room filled with weed smoke, listening to albums until I fell asleep enjoying the rest. Hopefully nothing interrupts our peace. I enjoyed myself with these beautiful women lying in my arms as they watched some movies on my TV. Turning off my music as soon as I began snoring, I didn't mind jazz wasn't for everyone.

CHAPTER 52

Queen Sameera

Rose Paz Andale-Sameera

I lay on Morgan's chest wondering where his other woman was at. I mean. I didn't care. I was the lucky sole recipient of his love and attention. But why me and not one of these rich hoes, right?

"Let me up for a sec. I have to use the bathroom." He lets out a long yawn waking up.

He holds my waist letting out a long yawn as his chest rises and falls back down. He turns to his side holding me in one arm like I wasn't carrying all this butt. And got up in a fluid movement.

I followed after him. The bed felt so empty without him.

"Sup?" He groggily greets as I enter the bathroom.

"Just thinking about being the other woman."

He sighs, "Rose-

"I'm not complaining. Believe me I'm happy to be on the side. I get to actually make you happy." I grin taking his dick in my hands and helping him piss straight.

He relaxes, closing his eyes and I stroke him until he's finished.

"I can't believe I fit you inside me..." I lick my lips and my legs shudder as he stiffens.

"I can't believe you give it back so well." He smiles with a sense of pride I've never seen. He knew the dick was good, that's dangerous. But made me even more attracted. This man isn't lonely, he was bored.

"I love it..." I blush. "But I just like seeing the relief. After you cum and you can just lay with me. Nothing else matters to you."

"I'm just happy to be with you. It gives me peace of mind."

"Don't say that like we have something," I laugh. "I'm just the maid you happen to be fucking. Like you don't have other mistresses."

He shook his head. "The situation with Nat and Halle got out of hand but all the same. You're the one I'm with right now." He sighs not wanting to deal with my badgering.

"Morgan don't talk like that. We don't have a thing. You're not with me." I tease him.

"You are my mistress."

"Just me?" I ask suspiciously, "not some blonde with big titties?"

"I love your titties just fine, babe." He pulls me in.

"I don't have any titties." I giggle as he kisses my neck and my cheek. "I just have all this ass." Right on cue he gives my butt a smack.

"I waited my whole life to be with a woman with an ass like yours. Thank Rakil, girl, I'm so thankful for you."

I just beamed as he held me. Kissing me and nuzzling my neck.

"Let's go to our bed..." I groan wanting him inside me once before day broke and he left our bed.

Our... I wonder if he'll get mad. "Come on, babe, let's go to our bed." I repeated.

He just nodded smacking me on the butt once more before letting me take his hand and lead him back to bed. I felt his eyes on me the whole while. My butt jiggled and bounced as he reached but never quite touched it. Teasing me more than I teased him.

"I've never had someone so in love with my butt, before." I marveled.

"Never had someone with a butt to love this much." He lifts me onto the bed.

My legs had a habit of spreading for Morgan whenever he so much as glanced at me. So as soon as I hit the bed I was spread eagle for him waiting with total loss of control as his tongue touched my pussy.

"Only you eat my pussy this good." I bit my lip looking down on him as he slurps and licks.

I leaned my head back. How well I suck his dick and I still don't think I compare. There's something about the man I adore touching me that made me weak. But when his warm tongue makes love to my clit I lose all sense.

I wanted to cum... It'll be three hard orgasms before he thinks of putting his dick in me. Suddenly, I felt I needed a side hoe for him to put his dick in while I recovered. I see why the situation got out of hand. Dick like this will make you fall in love. You couldn't just give this up. But it was far more than one could handle and still have insides.

"Baby... can I blow you. I can't take it." I held him back as he got on top of me.

"You'll be fine."

"Morgan... My pussy hurts so fucking much." Yet I felt his dick easing against me and I loosened right up for him. Proved me wrong. "Morgan..." I moan meekly as more of his length slides inside me. I wrap my legs around his waist and my arms around his neck. We kiss. Our tongues dance and he eases deeper inside of me.

"Better?"

"Perfect, baby. Perfect." I kissed his cheek, rubbing his back and kissing him where I could.

I would never say it aloud... unless he was tearing my guts up like earlier. But, I feel like this dick was made for my pussy. He just eases inside me like he has a goddamn door swipe.

But now? Round of applause. My pussy is exhausted and he's taking his sweet ole time. Easing deeper inside me. Kissing my neck and keeping his hands all over me. Taking me past my limits.

"I'm about to cum..." I cling to him, "did you hear me baby, I'm about to cum?"

He nods pulling me closer and digging deeper. I grinned. I couldn't imagine the smile plastered on my face as I felt the total release of my senses.

"Don't stop baby, get your nut." I plead holding my legs up for him.

He grabs a handful of my ass and slammed his hips into me. I let my legs go so I could squeeze him close to me.

I lost my head as our love making turned to skin slapping and fucking.

"I'm cumming..." He grunted releasing his nut inside me.

He bit his lip, his seed shot inside me, mixing with my juices. He curled up, laying on top of me as he caught his breath.

We laid entwined in each other's arms and bounded at the mound.

"Morgan?" I heard soft snores above me as he drifted back to sleep. His cock still squeezed tight in my pussy. I had no complaints using my legs to ease him in and out. Getting off once more before wrapping my arms around him and drifted off to sleep.

CHAPTER 53

The Order of The Sun Lotus

Borre

As the new Royal Family organized their people and convinced their King to relax, and recover from the years of war, hardship, and stress. Thousands of miles away in an Underground Bunker in the middle of the Erdu desert. The most illustrious men on Gaia were gathered around making their plans for the coming year. Deciding what business will flow, and who will need to compromise their plots. It's where the elite came to put their cards on the table to prevent conflict. At least once it may have been. In the days hundreds of years ago, these meetings were held in Town Hall or the Governance Chambers. The mayors, governors, and senators were given open access to listen however not to discuss what the tide of humanity was facing. In these days of power, the conversation began and ended at this table to Colin Gregor's whim.

The grand meeting hall hosted a round table. The Brothers of the Order stood around the table. At the helm was their senior brother, Lord Commissioner Ray Warren, reciting the Laws That Bind.

"We as brothers are committed to the security and order of this nation. We as brothers work as a unit in the interest of our nations. We as brothers are the beacon of light, shining clear across Gaia to the amelioration of Gaia. May our fraternity reign supreme. No man is greater than tomorrow."

"In the name of Enshishi." Colin finished all smiles, "What? No one is going to honor their God? It is a part of the pledge!"

Ray Warren looked on the table. Across from him was Midoriya Murashima, dressed in a beige suit. The Middle-aged samurai and business tycoon sat with his arms crossed defiantly.

Midoriya let out an obstinate sigh, the eldest brother and current leader of his family. "My brother, silence is a virtue."

Colin laughed, "Silence is weakness."

"Order!" Ray barked looking over the group.

Next to Colin sat Mordin Wolfe. He was an elderly and sagging old man, whose body gave way long before his age caught up. Portly and shrewd. He tapped the table lightly, waiting his turn to speak. Absorbing all around him before opening his mouth. He was the head of the Wolfe Family, the Holy Father. Dressed in a simple black suit, his beard scented with oils, and a small round hat atop his head.

The fourth brother came from Esha, in the southeast. A brown-skinned boy wearing a tunic, his eyes hanging low. "There's quite the tension. Is there something we must discuss?" He was a young man, new and uninterested in order. But the allure of the power of the Sun Lotus attracted many men through the ages. "Ha, seems like you lost yourself a bit Ray." The last time he had been in the Commissioner's presence was fifteen years ago the Eshan was no older than five or four, hiding behind his Grandfather's leg.

Colin's eyes perked up looking over his old friend, "you've lost some weight." He rubbed his chin. He looked around the table looking the fifth brother in the eyes. "And you Powell?"

Desmond Powell, inhaled a mouth of air shifting in his seat. Then needed another to sit up straight. He was winded as he leaned into the table. "I am honored to be here as representative for Don Knox in this transitory phase leading toward a greater union between the Order and the Family." He inhaled once more, taking a handkerchief from the bottom of his XXXL Tuxedo pocket. "I pledge my life and soul to Enshishi."

Colin smiled with joy and assurance, leaning back and kicking his feet on the table. "Murashima and Warren are having some pride issues it seems, you Mordin?" Colin stared Mordin right in the eyes, turning his gaze to his longtime rival. "Do you have something to say?"

"Have some respect... take your feet off the table." Mordin muttered.

The Wolfe Family had become a world contender. Their presence added an essential balance of wealth and military power to the Order. Though, face to face the old man was of little match outside a match of wits. Outside of the peace treaty, he cared little for any of these paltry meetings. Likewise for Midoriya. The sanctity of Naka is all that concerned them and their people. The strings pulled themselves through rapport and reputation.

Colin scoffed, "Ha, I'll put my feet any damn where I please." Colin leaned back further, stretching out his thirteen-foot frame looking at the five-foot- six man. "Or do we have words, Mordin?"

Mordin looked away, tapping that desk. He wondered why he came to these meetings. The Order had once been disbanded for this same carelessness and bravado. A man of his stature being held hostage every four months by a Gregor.

"Do we have business to discuss?" Mordin let out a defeated sigh. "Or is this a continuation of your narcissism?"

"We will discuss business when you pledge your allegiance to my family, as your God." Gregor smiled with pleasure. "If not... I may have to do a God's duty and smite you."

Desmond Powell chuckled a sloppy and greedy laugh, "Is it so hard, to bow before your God, Mordin?"

Mordin looked Desmond Powell in the face, "I'm sorry, who are you?" The Multi-trillionaire lifted his long nose, more of a beak. "You're sitting in a true brother's seat. Your presence is an insult."

Desmond Powell looked aghast, "I- I-I-

"You're here in the place of Gerald. A greater man than you could hope to be." Mordin had never been a supporter of the Knox Family or what they've done in Erdu. But Gerald Knox had a resounding presence upon history. One incontestable even to a rival such as Wolfe.

"A dead man." Desmond smiles with a hapless shrug.

Mordin's anger couldn't be hidden, "Insolence! How dare you!?"

Colin groaned, "Gerald is dead. Well dead. It's over." He concludes.

"Spoken proudly from a man who killed his father." Midoriya shook his head, "there is no honor remaining in this order." he let out a sigh. "I sit here out of duty to my family. Two of us out of murder of their own leaders and family. There is no honor, here. Ray, we must disband this unholy union."

Colin's face twisted and he sat up, "Do we have words, runt?"

Midoriya smiled, "I have no words for you, young lady. But if you wished to fight I am ready when you are, Gregor. False-idol."

Colin's mouth lit up with orange flames, glaring at Midoriya who only smiled.

Midoriya continued, "I have spoken to my older brother, Takio. It seems the True King has returned. A boy whose father you had killed. And a war you attempted to start but brushed under the rug. We heard no words of this. No more lies of The Lion upon the throne of God-hood. I was growing sick to my stomach with my people digesting such lies. Ignorant to their own heritage. Now, it seems the truth of your inferiority has come to light." Midoriya spit, a proud Murashima.

"You want a fight, Murashima? Want another Gregor to rip your soul out your body?" Gregor chuckled reminding the man half his size of his place. "Ha, come on then I was hoping this would get exciting." Colin enjoyed the hilarity. A single threat sent most these men running. "Come on then, come on then now, ha fight me! I've been waiting for one of you to get the sack to challenge me. And Once I kill you, I'm burning down Kisaka and Edo, I'm taking your wife and daughters as my own, and I'll have your men hung for treason."

Midoriya only laughs, "A grey-haired child sits amongst us. A grey-haired child leaves the world cowering in fear. If you wish to end your life, please continue. I have been waiting for you to break the treaty since I took my seat here years ago. Watching, waiting, marking your every weakness, marking your every quirk."

Mordin swallowed looking to Midoriya was admiration and concern. Mordin was impressed with the astounding cool confidence of the man nearly his age, threatening to discipline Colin. No, threatening to kill Colin.

"It's nice to have a fan." Colin yawned.

"I am your reckoning, Gregor." Midoriya smiled brightly, "The True King walks amongst us and he learns from my brother of your tyranny and destruction."

Midoriya was the shrewdest of his brothers. Takio was a loving and gentle soul, the incredible fighting prowess seemingly wasted upon a teacher. Their youngest brother, Bacho was more business minded. Working as Midoriya's advisor.

Midoriya the was last student to the immortal Saito Murashima, aside from his son Hinata. Leaving the mountains out of disgust of his people's submission and within his lifetime reestablishing his family as a central power in Naka. The moment Midoriya learned the truth at ten years of age he was set upon reclaiming his family's name. His own son currently training and meditating under Saito for just that.

Colin's smile was gone, "did you hear him threaten me, Ray?"

The whole table turned to Ray wondering his allegiance.

Ray bowed his head, "I have trained and spoken with the True King... Enshishi is a false-god." Ray confirmed, "Morgan Leonticus Sameera is the True King, Ada and has my allegiance."

Colin's heart sunk, he stared at a table of enemies. His last friend and ally refused to make eye contact out of shame and disgust for ever having association. His lip twitched, a rumbling and gurgling bubbling in his solar plexus. Colin felt a new emotion, one he loved more than anything but had never embraced. Fear swelled inside his gut crippling his movements and muting his tongue.

Colin became defensive, something new to him, "He lies... Enshishi-

"Enshishi is a being engraved in destruction. And your family is too weak and undisciplined to control his power. You give into it and believe yourselves all powerful. You choke the life and beauty out this world and can exist with a smile on your face." Midoriya's eyes never left Colin, his side eye on Powell. "But I needn't kill you. You are an old man. With a creature far too strong lurking inside you. I give you a few years before Enshishi grows tired of your prattling and foolishness and consumes your very soul and body. Once Enshishi realizes how weak his vessel who has put all his faith into, you will both disappear from this world."

"Shut your damn mouth, boy." Gregor warned in a low growl. His eyes glinting an citrine hue.

"And your family name will disappear in history like all the families you destroyed for your false wealth and power." Midoriya continued unafraid. "All the cultures, people, and history your people have destroyed..."

"Shut your fucking mouth!" Gregor growled.

"You dishonorable. Weak. Petulant. Corrupt-

"Shut your mouth!" Colin erupts like a volcano, flames spurting from his mouth.

Warren raised his hands, a wall of sand rose nullifying the attack.

Colin took one final look at Ray. "Traitor!" He exhaled a round of fireballs, leaping from his seat.

Midoriya summoned a blade of electricity from his hands. Slicing through the flames. He had a wicked smile on his face as if his body was coming alive for the first time.

Ray's body gave way to dripping sands as his energy rose to the air.

"You attacked a brother during a meeting, Colin... that is grounds for permanent expulsion." Mordin said with shock. He never believed Colin would be fool enough to put himself out there so crudely. "You... Colin is expelled from the Order! You are expelled!" Mordin felt such glee finally rid of his nemesis.

If only they could remove him from the table.

Colin's lip furled, growling as he looks around the room. All he had to rely on was the walrus of a man who could barely manage his seat without losing breath.

"What is this?" Desmond demanded answers. "I thought we were all friends here!?"

"This is Colin's resignation from the order." Midoriya smiled, "hail the true king, Morgan Sameera."

"I stand with my pupil." Ray's disembodied voice echoed.

Gregors knew no surrender.

Colin took a large inhale and released a smokescreen to fill the room. He used the veil to loop around the perimeter of the room. He wouldn't let himself surrender but he wasn't fool enough to be killed. He search for an exit in the underground bunker.

The sizzling of lightening cut through the air as Midoriya came upon Colin. Cutting right through the air. Colin turned raising a flaming hand, the Claws of Enshishi, as he let out a primal scream, rushing at Midoriya.

Colin’s skin began peeling away leaving chips of lava dripping out the holes as his flesh began peeling. The Aura of the beast began rushing out of his pores immersing himself in the citrine and purple eminence.

The lightning and molten flames clashed, engaging and disengaging. Radiating with energy and light. Every meeting of their auras sent shockwaves through the room.

One man fought for the restoration of his family. The other for survival and greed.

Colin’s flaming hand jutted forward grabbing Midoriya by the shoulders and threw the grown man, clear halfway across the room.

Colin rushes in after Midoriya. Midoriya rolls on his feet as if unaffected. The lightning blade growing larger with his concentrated rage. Larger and turning a pale white from its original yellow hue. Heating up to the sun itself.

Midoriya closed his eyes, taking a deep breath.

Colin's hands turned to molten magma, dripping upon the ground as he faced off with Midoriya. Burning holes dripping straight through the steel and earth beneath.

"I'm going to rip your head off your shoulders." Colin grins, "little man. I'll kill you like my forefather killed your weak grandfather!" Colin roars through the voice of Enshishi.

Midoriya only smiled. In a flash the old man was gone. His blade sliced through Colin Gregor like butter before Colin could even reach top speed.

Colin's legs continued running until they eventually fell to the floor, walking in circles before tripping over its own lifeless legs. Colin's torso was on the ground. Staring up to the ceiling. His eyes blinking open and close, fighting to stay awake. Gripping the ground. Gasping for air. He couldn't believe it. In a single movement he was sliced painlessly in half.

Colin's eyes met Midoriya in his last moments of consciousness, "This isn't over you fucking runt." He cursed. "I'll fucking haunt you. I'll kill your family from beyond the grave you tiny cunt."

"This was over the moment I was born in this world." Midoriya drove his blade right below Colin's ribcage. He twisted it, emitting the incapacitating lightning wave through what remained of the Patriarch.

Colin's form was charred and paralyzed.

"If there are cowards amongst us, leave now. Get us some water and contact Ada... he was right. This fight isn't over." Midoriya bowed his head. "I have destroyed the hereditary seal. Soon, Enshishi will regain conscious and claim the body."

Midoriya knew they had only moments before Colin's body dissolved away, leaving them with the Beast itself, Enshishi.

Desmond Powell shook his head, "you... you killed him!"

"You have plenty of time to suck your lover's cock while we wait." Midoriya challenged, "you are expelled as well." Midoriya walked back to his seat ignoring Powell. Catching his breath and taking out his phone.

Ray's physical form returned looking on to his old friend. He wished there was more he could say. But this was the inevitable end of Colin Gregor. After all he had done, being cleaved in two seemed like mercy from Midoriya.

"Enshishi himself?" Ray sighed. "I almost hoped his soul could be redeemed."

Midoriya laughed, "He was an asshole! King of Assholes." He spit. "Get Ada on the phone. We need him here immediately! Hinata!"

From the dark shadows of the ceiling a young man dropped down behind Colin's seat. Taking the twenty foot drop from the ceiling effortlessly. He was the spitting image of Midoriya. With natural spiked hair sailing back. His almond eyes looked around the room.

"Hold on, who says your family inherits Enshishi's power." Mordin stood up. He was unnerved with the boy's sudden presence. He wished to inquire but the fate of the Patriarch showed there was little time for questions.

"Do you care to fight me, old man?" Hinata asked politely.

"No, but I have a daughter who will be of age. She is a smart girl. She will be a reliable heir as well."

"Enshishi would eat her soul alive." Midoriya laughed off. "Hinata has trained his entire life."

"Why your child and not mine?" Mordin raises his voice. "Ray this isn't how the order works!"

Ray's eyes almost fell from his skull, "you would be out your wits if you believe I would entrust the fate of the realm or the power of a Guardian into an untested, child who hurt my pupil without remorse. Sit down, Mordin. I didn't see you stand to fight, you have no claim here."

"Why can't I be Enshishi?" The kid laughed. The whole room turned. He raised his hands in defense, "hey, hey relax it was only a joke. My body's already occupied. I don't think I will be coming back to one of these meetings a bit too lively for me." The kid stood dusting himself off. "Deuces, Migos." He threw up a peace sign.

"Nor will I! We fall into civil unrest and infighting? Are we animals?" Mordin stands riled up. "And you refuse my daughter because of her rapist? We need a force to defend us against this Ada as well!"

"We needn't worry about Morgan." Warren assured.

"He had his way with my daughter and young Halle Gregor now my daughter is in the hospital fighting for her life!"

“Morgan has been in Erdu with me. I’ve heard of the same incident, he was not responsible.”

“Why would she lie to me?” Mordin asked.

Midoriya let out a sigh, "Your daughter is weak. You are weak. Your blood is weak. Ada is the True King." Midoriya threw his hands up. "So, leave now. We cannot wait for your daughter to leave the hospital and get better. You are in no condition to absorb the energy you would be ripped apart. So, here we stand out of options with time ticking. Leave weak Wolfe. Leave and plot your revenge."

Mordin stood to his feet, "you have become brutes. This is the man you are entrusting your future too?"

"No man is greater than tomorrow. Midoriya and I have heirs. We will move on, grow too weary of battle and our bodies will one day lay to rest. No man is greater than tomorrow, Mordin. I entrust the future to the children. The strongest of this generation not those we hand-pick. We have two men time tested and proven to be leaders. That is rare, Mordin. I do not make this decision with my heart or bias. I make this based off the fact we have a Wolf and a Bushido in our hands with power in themselves that could match either of ours."

Midoriya bowed his head. "Killing Colin was easy and a pleasure. But taming Enshishi is far out my hands. I believe only the true king or Hinata can because I know I am not strong enough."

Mordin nodded, "this all sounds of superstition to me." With that he parts tucking his hands behind his back and walking off toward the double doors leading out of the bunker following the young man, hoping to have a few words with the boy of seeming like-mind.

Desmond Powell struggled to his feet, "I will not stand for this, murder and atrocity!"

"If he can stand at all," Midoriya let out a sigh. "Hurry along then piggy. We must prepare for battle."

Desmond Powell moved with an impressive swiftness getting out of the room as Colin's body began to twitch and move. Desmond let out a shout running off out of the bunker.

"Here it comes..." Ray let out a sigh remembering the horror.

"You bastards!!!" Colin shouts clawing and flailing for life as his stomach begins imploding into lava. "What's happening to me!?" His voice immediately turns to horror as the immense pain Ray was quite familiar with came over the Patriarch.

Ray turns his head, but in his new form even removing his eyes didn't stop him from seeing.

Midoriya, "We need backup Ray!"

"There is no phone service down here. We are on our own." Hinata cursed taking a deep breath.

Ray lifted his hands commanding sands to rush from the sleeve of his lacquered jacket. Grinding the floor to dust and covering Colin. Buying them time as the lava eats through the sands growing infinitely as they came from the deep immortal flames of War. He finally manages to contain Colin when the sands cease to grow. Using his energy and focus to contain Enshishi. Buying them time as they attempt to devise a plan.

There was only so much the sand could do, melting away and being boiled into glass encasing Colin's body in a ball of magma. The magma began to grow, taking on legs nearly two stories long. Two massive arms slammed out of the magma. Gripping down into the ground and pulling out the enormous head of the beast.

Enshishi stood at full height, scraping the ceiling of the bunker. Furious, heaving, and ravenous.

Hinata stood in front of both Ray and Midoriya. He tossed off his stealth shirt, it would have only burned to Enshishi's touch. The young man walked before Enshishi unafraid.

"I am Murashima Hinata, of the clan Pyre, blood of the Dragon and Phoenix. I will tame you and if I cannot, I will destroy you." Hinata grinned.

Enshishi kneeled down, still towering over Hinata.

"I'm going to destroy everything and everyone you ever held dear, boy."

"Good luck, I was raised in the volcanoes. You can have them!"

Hinata sent two hands back, turning them into lightning blades containing his energy into the two Katanas as he surged toward Enshishi. Enshishi had trouble dealing with Hinata's speed, and before he could defend himself the samurai found both his swords into Enshishi's flesh.

"Was that meant to hurt!" Enshishi roared, grabbing Hinata and ripping him from his body, tossing the body to the ground listlessly.

A column of sand, jutted from the ground slamming into Enshishi's chest. Serving only to knock the beast back a few steps. The hulking monster slapped the pillar away taking into a sprint, moving at a speed considerable to Hinata's, swiping Midoriya clear across the room. He looked around for Warren wanting to rip the traitor in half. He only found another pillar slamming into his jaw, reeling him.

For a brief moment the Lord Commissioner appeared, grounding his feet into the ground, drawing back his hands. He took a deep breath then a murderous barrage of obelisks into Enshishi, his form fading away as he pelts Enshishi.

If the beast felt pain, he refused to show weakness. Each obelisk found their mark, upon his face, his chest, his limbs, and even his genitals. The Lion of flames didn't falter, his pain only added to his fury.

"I am God! I am God! I am Lord Enshishi, strongest being on Gaia, strongest in the ether. I claim this world in my name! I will war will Rakil! I will ascend to the heavens and snap Rakil's neck!" he taunts and screams.

The men looked up their end. Exchanging looks and understanding, they would die containing this beast. They accepted their fates. Charging back into battle.

CHAPTER 54

Wrath and Redemption

Ananda Sameera

I choked on my tongue. My brain sizzled. The room was hazy. I was choking on thin air, my body convulsing as my consciousness flicked in and out like a flashing light. Was I dying?

I tried to close my eyes, but every each time I tried to find some solace in the darkness. I could only see Colin's body burning alive, my own body burned and sweated heavily. He was burning alive, in excruciating pain, my skin was ablaze. I'm dying...

I wanted to rip my eyes out my skull. I wanted to rip a hole in my thought so I could breathe. But my body did nothing. I have no control.

The door to the guestroom slammed open and Morgan looked around frantically. When he saw, it took Rose to block him off from going into a rage. He shoved Rose aside to kneel by my side.

I looked up to him longing.

A strong hand clutched my forehead, and for a moment the image of Colin faded. I never imagined concern would fit so easily on this man's face. But it was genuine.

"How...? How did you stop it?" I held his hands, tears swelled my eyes, "Don't move your hand, don't... I don't want to see it again, I don't want to see it."

"See what, Ananda?" he asked softly, stroking my hair. "You were having a seizure?"

"I- I don't know. I heard Enshishi cursing. Then... I fell. I fell and there was so much pain, Morgan. I was burning alive. I couldn't move. I couldn't breathe." I squeezed his hand, crying and reaching for him. He lifted me, carrying me to my bed.

Rose sat on the edge of the bed, not looking at Morgan. "Are you okay? You looked as if you were possessed."

"I- I may be." I grimaced, "I've made deals with dark forces to get away from Colin. To sabotage him when i could. When I awakened my eyes, he knew I had been sneaking into the library. That's when he got crueler, using me as his toy."

"For reading?" Rose looked confuse.

"For plotting to kill him... for trying to negotiate freedom for my family. For being too attractive in his sight. Whatever my crime was, I was punished every day and hour of my life for it."

Morgan said nothing, the concern was gone and replaced with something far more familiar. The cold focus and detachment.

"You never know what it is... he is a lunatic Morgan. He would praise me, then strike me right after. He was a monster. I don't know what he did to me..."

Morgan said nothing. His eyes fell into a crimson as his hand moved from my forehead down to my heart. He cringed as his hand moved to my stomach.

"What did you see...?" he forced himself to ask.

"Colin... his body was burning alive. He was melting apart, suffocating, and cursing, cursing, cursing."

"Baby?" Rose felt the energy change as well.

Morgan shook his head, "You're a chakra container of Enshishi's energy... it's from the rape, it's pure hatred and anger. Sex leaves energy behind... I can't let him live for this Rose. I have to find him and kill him."

Rose frowned, the one thing she's been trying to prevent and avoid was coming to fruition. She wanted peace so badly. I felt terrible I was the cause of this argument.

"Morgan, don't kill Colin for me. Rose won't-

"Hey... you can go. You can do what you must Morgan. I never want to see Nanda like this again, or anyone. I- I can take care of Nadia. If Colin is gone, I can take care of Nadia." she put on a brave face but it didn't last long before she buried her face into her hands. "Just handle your duty, Morgan. I can't believe I stopped you for so long and Ananda got hurt."

Morgan nodded his head. He kissed Rose's forehead, "I love you. I will return to you, make a nice dinner, you two." he tried to reassure her but she only pulled away.

Rose stood up to leave, not saying a word as she walked out the room. Not wanting to cry in front of him. It would be an awful sight to witness before facing his destiny. Though, never saying goodbye was a pain all its own.

"Yosh..." Morgan exhaled.

"I will make you anything you want, Morgan. Anything."

"Oxtails, mac n cheese, rice n beans, chicken, collards, and strawberry soda." It was a simple enough request, "Make whatever you can for dessert."

I wiped my eyes, hugging the man who continuously took away my pain.

"If I don't come back- advise the Queen. Make sure Nadia grows into her wildest dreams."

CHAPTER 55

King Sameera

Morgan Leonticus Sameera

There were several power forces clustered together. Miles... Cites... Districts... there. Where is that? My hand in Ananda's stomach gaining my vision through her gut. She squeezed my arm. Enshishi's energy outshined all others around it for a clear region. His energy was like nuclear hot flash on the ethereal plane.

"I've found him..." I smiled then looked down to Ananda. She rubs my chin and kisses me softly. "Take care of yourself... don't die on me, Ananda."

"Then move quickly. I'm not sure I can take another episode like that."

"Rose is here beside you, Ananda."

I blinked. Trusting fate.

I stepped out the void into what seemed to once be a meeting room. Immediate survey. The table was split open and overturned. The walls were scorched to hell. Craters lined the walls and floors. Seems diplomacy only goes but so far. I stepped into what was unraveling into a one-sided fight.

A lion's head mounted upon its muscled three story bipedal frame. Enormous paws one engulfed in electricity the other in molten flames. He looked down upon us with a wide grin. Under his foot there was a young man. Resisting all he could to scream for dear life to give the creature pleasure. His skin seemed resistant to the flame. He needed a spot.

"Father!" Hinata was under Enshishi's foot. He was once in the Academy with me. The only who could seem to keep up. We were children then.

"Our King has arrived." A man in a beige tuxedo greeted me. "Lord Ada, I am Murashima Hiro Midoriya it is a pleasure for you to finally join us." He didn't seem all too thankful.

"Morgan!" Ray's voice was in shock, he formed "how did you find us?"

"My maid told me she felt a disturbance, she was having a seizure. My wife gave me permission to leave." I stepped closer.

Though danger was imminent and before me. I felt no danger within me. I felt no fear. I stood before the creature and he stared down upon me.

"You..." Enshishi hissed, "you have finally arrived?"

"The True King is Here..." Hinata said in a labored breath. He looked ragged, as though he fought as hard as he could to little or no avail. "God bless, Jah'Ada!" He screamed from beneath Enshishi's enormous feet being crushed into the ground.

I looked down at my palm. I felt an energy radiating from my fist. The anger I've been refusing to wear on my sleeves.

"Yosh..." I kicked off my back foot, pulling back my hand. The Matriarch told me I was stronger. Eternally stronger than Enshishi. I felt as if my hand was moving through a torrential tide. I used my strength to force my palm through the ether sending a shock-wave toppling Enshishi over.

The young man wasted no time getting to his feet and joining the line of scrimmage. Ray and the old man, Midoriya stood beside us.

"I'm glad you're here, boy." Warren confirmed.

"Rose sure isn't. Want to bring me up to speed here?" I ask as Enshishi shakes himself off, rising to his feet.

"We were meeting with the order. It devolved into bullying and heckling. Then a duel. Midoriya slayed Colin and disbanded The Order of the Sun Lotus. Hinata found here. You've arrived after we held off Enshishi the best he could."

"So, you're the King, now?" Hinata joined my side. "He's strong as I could imagine. Me and my father are just getting started."

I extended a hand, and Hinata squeezed me tight in a hug. Childhood compatriots reunited.

"I've been through hell... now that you're here, It's time to make a quick return trip." he smiled.

"Don't let me interrupt. This is your party, brother." I smiled, "I would like to ensure our odds if you don't mind."

"Hell yeah, I'm going all out!" Hinata sparked up squeezing me tight as I loaned him some of my strength, letting my energy radiate around my body for him to absorb.

"Get back, kids!" Midoriya stuck his thumb into his mouth breathing in deeply and his body filled with air and blood. His skinny frame instantly bulged with lean muscle. He looked as if he lost two decades. Once again 30. "I will end this."

Before us stood a behemoth engulfed in flame.

Enshishi's laughs gutturally hurled out flames. He spotted our new formation and instantly began suppressant fire.

I leaped to my left, holding up my arm lacking any of my usual armor. I sadly am not flame retardant. I roll over on my shoulders and leap to my feet. I looked on to better see the creature.

I looked him in his citrine orange eyes burning like the sun. I reached for my kunai looking for any weak point. But found no weak points and no daggers. Enshishi was a mass of muscles, a flaming molten mane protecting his backside, far too thick and hot to hope to reach through to his neck. There was little I could do without another few shockwaves. But those exhausted far too much of my own life force. It would be easier with an element to command over. Instead, I only commanded the ether.

Midoriya took a strong pose. He took point and we took his side.

Midoriya faced off with the behemoth. He punched and palmed sending forces of energy through Enshishi who seemed to absorb with bliss. Each blow releasing electricity and extreme brute power with each blow. Midoriya's blows did however leave Enshishi staggered and stunned trying to force his way through the force waves. They rattle every liquid in your body. Leaving you off balance, unstable and disoriented. The fluids in his ears swishing about forcing him off his feet. The fluid in his stomach making him wretch and curdle. His bloodstream struggled to deliver oxygen to his organs. He could resist the power all he wished but the damage was being done on a microscopic level.

In a single swipe Enshishi sliced through Midoriya's insides sending him flying through the wall, knocking the air of him deflating the old man. Midoriya laid trying regain consciousness in time to push his guts back into his body as they began to spill out.

"Father!" Hinata yelled going to his side. "Stay awake Baba, we'll handle this."

"Fucking bastard!" Midoriya cursed fading in and out fast.

Enshishi coughed up blood, and walked about woozy and unfocused forward to end the father and son while they were distracted.

"I am your King..." I whisper into his ear appearing behind him. I leap down from his massive shoulder. My energy focused around my hand in an ethereal blade slicing through his muscled chest cavity. Violently and long overdue. But as my hand entered his chest my nail began melting as he was mending his wound instead of carving deeper into his chest. I won't win this on a physical level. I thought I had found a weak spot. To rip out his very heart. Even his skin was molten... how? Was he only appearing in this form? Only manifesting before us when he was in truth only energy after losing his human form.

Enshishi's eyes bulged. Enshishi spun, shaking me off. I was lost in mid-air, preparing myself to impact with the ground. He had other plans. He pulled back his paw, using all his might smashing me into the ground. My knees buckled immediately under the raw power. Had I even the chance to stand. He slammed atop me once more, burying my body down into the steel beneath the floor. The paw engulfed into electricity fell upon me. The voltage frying my nervous system.

Something that big, shouldn't be able to move that fast. But who am I talk. I have the ether. Come on body, we're not dead yet. Get it together! I need my strength right now.

"I am King!" Enshishi roars raising both his hands over his head. He brought them down with all his might hitting the wall of sands created by Ray. A gust of sand wept under me pulling me from the fight.

"Thanks Ray."

Enshishi began rushing for me on all fours huffing and grinning. A second gust of sands wept under his front arms bringing him to the ground, collapsing as a chakra laced net formed through the sands.

I was lucky. There wasn't a single weak spot in sight. Enshishi was a ball of energy and muscle enforced with rage and chakra. He fought against the sands, wrestling and slashing. Roaring and was pushing against them with such zeal and vigor as if he already knew he was free.

"Is that all you can do, Ray?" I asked. "We need something harder."

Ray smiled, closing his fist and the sands turned as concrete solidifying around Enshishi.

"Hinata! Free attack. Hold him Ray!" I called, my mouth the only thing that could work in my state.

"I love you, Father." Hinata bows his head.

"I couldn't be prouder of you, go kill that bastard." Midoriya patted Hinata's cheek letting his son return to the fight as he sloppily, painfully seared his own skin closed. Unwilling to die by Enshishi's hand.

Hinata's arm enveloped in blue electricity. He moved faster than light tearing through the room only leaving a blur of fading light. When we were kids he had to use his top speed for impact, he called it the blue arrow. Now, he moved beyond the speed of light ripping through the chakra net of sandstone and straight through Enshishi.

As he exited his father used his remaining power, bringing both his fist down in a chakra infused axe handle. Smashing down into Enshishi's mass.

The hit shook the floor. The steel I-beams gave away completely underneath splitting apart underneath Enshishi.

Hinata and Midoriya stood across the fray, regaining their composure. Midoriya fell to a knee panting and exhausted, shaking his head trying to will forward. Hinata stared on with my frustration as Enshishi recovered quickly back into fighting shape.

What did we have to do? We've hit him with our hardest. There was no going hand-to-hand. Midoriya was ripped open. My nervous system was fried.

I couldn't move but I'm not invalid. Alright Ada... I need you.

My eyes peeled wide open, the room drenched in crimson as I looked once more for a weak spot. This time beyond this realm.

The room faded away from me. My spirit climbed out of my body walking slowly past the void of death into the ether. Rakil guided my steps as I blindly stepped beyond the void into the ether. I got to get a closer look at the Chakra. From a distance it seemed as though his energy was one flowing flame. But there was a mortal inside Enshishi's form. Colin's body floating in two halves within the flame.

"Morgan? Morgan?" Ray shouted shaking my body, but it was unresponsive.

My mortal eyes began to bleed as I stared through Enshishi's body. I fought hard remembering all those years on the table. Bordering that treacherous line of death as I began pushing my soul's limit outside its body.

Colin's body frail as if sucked out of any source of life a human could have. But his heart was still beating. The body was dead but his heart was still beating. Colin is dead none of his own energy remained. Yet energy was flowing through him. The two halves of his corpse floating beneath the mounds of muscle and violent chakra.

"Nothing you can do can stop me!" Enshishi roars. "Nothing..." he took pause as if something was amiss. "Where is Ada... where is he?"

I reclaimed my physical form, cloaking it within the void to bring it within reach. Commanding it to my soul's point with all the focus I could muster. I had little time left before I went blind for good. In a foul swoop, my soul repositioned in the void behind Colin. I slingshot myself forward, going straight through Enshishi's stomach. He didn't feel a thing. The room reappeared only coated in red now from my own blood flooding from my eyes.

I held Colin's heart in my hands. It was beating artificially with dark magic and possession. A golden seal inscribed across the aorta. Walking from behind Enshishi studying the dark magic. Joining Midoriya and Hinata.

"Give that back!" Enshishi demands in horror at my act.

"Come get it." I smile tossing the heart up and down in my hand. The giant mound of smooth muscle twice the size of my fist. "Was this your Trump card? Keep Colin alive long enough to kill us all? Keep healing yourself until we ran ourselves into the dirt? Very clever."

"Morgan what did you do?" Hinata asked in awe as Enshishi dropped to his knees clutching his stomach and chest.

Enshishi let out groans of pain. His energy flickered temperamentally as he tried to make up for the loss of Colin's life, dying all over again.

"I figured his body worked like Ray's sands. He still needs a mortal anchor to keep from crossing over into the spirit world. He was using part of his energy to fight, but the majority was to keep Colin's body reanimated on life support. You're baseless Enshishi. And arrogant. You thought that would be enough." I let out a sigh.

"That's my King!" Hinata cheered. He looked on with a grin and a fixated power. His arm closed itself in electricity. The muscles in his neck bulged. Hinata let out a roar rushing Enshishi head on.

Enshishi spit out balls of fire and electricity. But Hinata seemed to be moving faster than my own eyes could follow. Especially now. His energy blurring in and out of time and space until his whole body was a manifestation of blue electricity, darting like an arrow through the air.

Enshishi raised his arms only for the arrow to pierce straight through his chest. Enshishi howled, Hinata ripping a hole right through the chest cavity, exiting out his back. Hinata rolled to his feet turning over to see Enshishi flailing. Enshishi looked down as if he wasn't aware he could hurt. As if pain and mortality was quickly becoming a new concept to him. To imagine all the centuries he's used such a foul trick.

He fell to his knees in pain for the first time in his thousands of years of existence in this world.

Without a mortal form he was relying on his own life and energy. With the mortal alive he was running off an infinite loop of death and resurrection with Colin's body taking all the damage. A lifeless punching bag as we fought the mass of energy acting out against us.

I gave Colin rest free from Enshishi's torment. The games Guardians play yet only the vicar suffers. It seems even these creatures beyond mortality were cowards when it came to death.

I helped Midoriya to his feet. I left the heart with him as he began leaving the bunker. His fight was over. He played his part and played it well. His age returned, if not a few years older.

I had one more trick up my sleeve. Even without the infinite loop. Enshishi would be fearsome. I had to begin fighting this battle at a higher level.

I blinked before Enshishi in his weakened state. My vision failed me, but it was unnecessary, I rationed the time between my vision and my sight, Rose would never forgive me if I went blind. He peeked up, a grin crossed his lips, taking the bait immediately. He raises both his hands ready to clap me into a pancake.

"Ray!" I called before flashing back to my original position, glad my eyes weren't connected to my instant transmission.

Enshishi's eyes widened as three steel pillars jutted from the ground piercing through his arms and gut. He released a gasp of pain. The immensity of the pain left him paralyzed, even if only for a few moments. Enshishi's face lost his grin and he struggled to even register moving as the massive weight of his body only served to impale him further.

"Release me!" Enshishi shouted out of irritation rather than pain. His form already beginning to burn through the steel. This would take all day. Even without Colin's heart, he was still pouring energy through Colin's body to keep himself in limbo. He attempted to defy death. The blasphemy that stood before me. I would not stand for such utter disrespect!

"Hinata give me another blue arrow... we're going to retrieve Colin's body, separate them."

"Yosh!" Hinata cheered giving a thumb's up, "let's kick some ass, King!"

He got into a three point stance ready for takeoff. He kicked off his feet. I blinked inside of the beast's physical form. Enshishi roared and screamed, bounded by Ray's melting steel pillars. Trying his best to free himself. We had only one chance once he was free or he would kill us all.

Hinata tore a hole straight through Enshishi's pelvis tossing Colin's legs across the room. Hinata breathed heavily the toll being to take on his body. Even as kids Hinata would give all he could with a smile.

I carried Colin's torso looking down at the pathetic old man who was shriveled to nearly nothing after Enshishi sapped his energy. His skin clung to his bones. His face sunk into his skull. I hadn't seen Colin in months since learning under him. And this is the last image of my former father-in-law. He deserved death... but no man deserves this fate. I'm so glad Halle can't see what's left of her father.

He was skinny and frail. He looked as if he decayed for fifty years, nothing but the bones poking beneath his skin.

Enshishi's screams of terror and horror were endless. Echoing through the bunker as his energy began to fade from the physical realm without a mortal anchor to pour his energy through. His own pain too much for him to fixate upon. He would either fight or flee back to the heavenlies to be punished by Rakil.

"This isn't over!" Enshishi screamed. "I will have my day, Ada!"

Hinata took to a knee, letting out agonizing screams. His body began to swell. He looked to me filled with terror. He bloated with Enshishi's energy as Enshishi's physical form faded entirely. I suspected it worked exactly like Warren's sand, I never imagined this ending. Hinata's body stood all its own electricity radiating off of his body and striking from all over. He became a lightning rod as he began fighting to keep his very soul.

"Leave me! I will deal with this!" Hinata shouted. Thunder clapped in the room, lightening snapping off the ground. Fireballs fell from the ceiling. As Enshishi's power rushed into him. Hinata tried expending as much as possible to maintain a balance as it all came so quickly.

I was preparing to move until a curtain of sand hung over my head, as the fireballs fell. I could barely see the turmoil. A wave of sand swept me off my feet as Ray rushed me out of the bunker.

"You fought well, brother." Ray's voice consoled me carrying me out of the bunker.

I was rushed off, dodging and bounding on the sled of sand being brought to the door. Even in the hall leading up from the underground were laced with the energy. The bunker was expansive. But we were elevating, Ray rushing me to the surface. Two metal beams appeared from the ground as lightning struck around me. The metal beams tore through the bunker doors before me and I was thrown out rolling over to my back. Happy to be alive. I can't wait to fuck Rose after all this violence.

I was last to my feet. Ray was on his knees panting, "The world moves so easily to my whim. But it's so easy to lose myself without a physical form." Ray stood leaning against the wall falling in and out of sands into the desert as he regains his breath. "We've defeated Enshishi..." his disembodied voice said with pride.

"I was expecting a greater challenge." I rubbed my neck, "You all could have handled that alone."

"How did you know about Colin's heart?" Midoriya asked slapping my back. "Because I sure as hell had no idea that was possible. I doubt my ancestors did either."

"I saw it." I pointed to my bloodied eyes. The vessels in my eyes popped. I was lucky I didn't have a stroke. Rose would not be pleased. "My vision... I used my vision to see beyond the physical, the energy flow was inconsistent. I began to lose my vision when I magnified Colin's body in the mass of all of Enshishi's. It was as if Colin was physically there, but being protected in the eternal flames around him. Enshishi was more of a spiritual armor around a corpse than a physical being himself. You were trying to kill the undead. He was wasting your energy until you all killed yourselves."

"That is why we needed you! We would have been fighting Enshishi for hours without you. Without you figuring out his strategy we were dead." He showed me his sloppily seared stomach. He would still need massive surgery but he was alive to care for his children. "You are our King. Your presence was felt and greatly appreciated."

Ray patted my back. "I followed your leadership, Captain. Even I took pause in figuring out how to stop Enshishi. I walked into that battle believing we had already lost. I had no means to contact you."

"Thank you, Ray having my back all these years."

The electric storm and Hinata's screams didn't stop. I heard them both deep inside my conscience. No one else seemed to notice but I couldn't ignore the deafening cries.

"I have to go back in, Anki..." I smile up to Ray with red eyes, blood falling like tears as I was pushing my poor mortal body to its limit. "It is my duty."

"It's dangerous." Midoriya warned. "We could still lose you to Enshishi. It might just be a trap, Morgan. Hinata is strong. He can endure. This is what he was trained for, to receive the spirit of Enshishi and purify the soul of the beast!"

"Hinata was running off fumes after that last Blue Arrow. I can't let him be consumed. If it's a trap, I'll gladly be a fool. I have to at least know he's well."

Ray nodded his head, "I will cover you the best I can."

I smile patting Ray on the shoulder, "You were always a good mentor but this is my battle for now on." I blinked leaving him on the outside.

Hinata's body was glowing orange, bloated to nearly three times his form as if he was about to explode.

"Morgan, go!" Hinata and Colin screamed in unison, "You must go!"

"Stay calm, I'm here for you!" we had been such good friends. Even beyond death my father-in-law wished me well. Perhaps Colin could have been redeemed with more time. Now, we'll never know.

"You can't touch me... it's a trap!" Hinata screamed, "He won't submit! The spirit is still undefeated!"

I nodded walking up to him as lightning struck around me. Cracking off the ground. Snapping behind and in front of me. A thin veil of sand was dripping over my head letting me know Anki's presence was with me.

I put my hand upon Hinata's head. I was pulled inside of him by the vacuum. It took all my strength to resist the immediate pull without severing my ties to Gaia. I gripped down hard into the infinite chakra. I had Enshishi right where I wanted him as he tried to bring me to fight in the spiritual realm.

"At last I will conquer you Vicar of Ada!" Enshishi roared gleefully.

"In the name of The Father, Rakil I rebuke this dark spirit! Father, give this man your strength to conquer the soul of your fallen son. Let this man do your works, purified and right within the name of Rakil! Reborn from the destruction! This is a new servant father. I will command and sit upon the helm of your Kingdom!" Ada's voice joined my own. "Father! Subside this storm! Subside this man's suffering. Enshishi false Lord of fire, submit to Rakil!"

I fell from the sky into a realm beyond the void. Everything lit ablaze in a conflagration of exploding magma. I rolled on the ground as my pajamas were burned to dust straight off of my skin.

My only relief was from shielding myself with my ethereal energy, still I sweated profusely. The high risen sun above me weakened my shield. I had only felt Enshishi prowling his energy far off in the distance stretched long as if he was on all fours. In mere seconds he rushed over miles to pounce upon me encased in a meteoric flaming cone bouldering me into the ground.

The last time I felt such pain I was in the basement of a skyscraper loaded with C4 before it collapsed on me. So much pain. So many close calls. My reflexes no longer existed and my powers activated all their own.

I had retracted my shield moments before the blow, sacrificing the protection to be able to absorb all his raw primal energy and chakra as Enshishi pummeled me into the ground. With each strike, each bolt of electricity, with each meteor right-hand I took, I stored his energy. I exploded my shield delivering all his damage back and 20x more from the ground zero impact. I followed up by pointing my palm upward unleashing a powerful ray of energy gripping my wrist to focus the ray and the keep my hand from flying off.

Enshishi had leapt in the air to avoid my attack narrowly avoiding being erased from existence. I closed my palm, quickly gathering my bearings to raise my hands to the sky dropping a massive pulse of gravity bringing Enshishi straight back to the ground fighting the increased gravity. I blinked atop of his skull quickly performing my signature, “Single Touch of Pure Painful Death” reaching through the ether and void into Enshishi skull. I scoured through, embracing the flames and licking of molten energy pulling Hinata from his brain.

I had never felt so much power rushing through me. The pulling subsided. Perhaps Enshishi still attempted but my will to resist him came easier. Pulling Hinata from the eternal flames within. Enshishi’s screams resonated of his own power within him as he willed himself to fight. I was unsure, panicked and gasping. His understanding defeated by reality. His flames burned me until my arms bled. But I cared little of the sheer pain as long as Hinata was well.

"NO! I WILL HAVE THIS BODY!" Enshishi's disembodied voice cried, as his brain began tearing out from its stem, pushing me away, peeling away from me. "GET OFF OF ME!"

I refused to let him go. Not until Enshishi had subsided and my wife, Ananda and my entire continent could live in safety.

"Damn, you Ada! You bastard. You coward! You woman! Damn, you Ada!" The taint screamed.

Enshishi's screaming stopped abruptly. The energy faded. And his body fell limp.

I flashbacked to my position as Enshishi wailed and cried in horrific pain. Dropping the massive lump of grey-matter onto the ground. I sliced through the enormous brain releasing Hinata on the ground. He had grown but he looked no different than when we first met. There was no longer anything to fear, no longer a need to hide in the darkness.

“How could you have beaten me? How?” Enshishi coughed and gasped barely intelligibly as he fell to his back in agony.

“I’ll set us both free Enshishi, my old friend.” I console solemnly ending Colin Gregor’s legacy.

I held out my hand finally closing my eyes from its excruciating pain and releasing my erasure wave. Another unstoppable wave of nether energy onto Enshishi to end his suffering. Wiping him from existence.

"Ada..." Hinata looked up drained and exhausted.

"Stay with me, brother." I pleaded. "Stay with me Hinata Murashima."

"I'm not giving up, bro. I'm not done!" Hinata cried grabbing my arm and squeezing me.

All traces of the taint were gone. The whole of Tartarus stood silenced aside from the two of us panting.

I stood with his exhausted body in my arms. Blinking out from our hell and falling to my knees before Warren and the other living Murashima. A portly man stood and a shrewd older man who reminded me of Natalie.

"What is wrong? Is all well?" The older man asked. He seemed disturbed. "Who are you?"

"I am Morgan Leonticus Sameera, the True King of Gaia. And you?" I looked up from my knees.

He rolled his eyes, "I am Jonah Mordin Wolfe. The father of the woman you nearly killed. Some King."

I chuckled, "Well, this is most certainly news to me."

I sat on the sands in the middle of nowhere. Even finding this place came with deep difficulty. Had the men here not been so strong I wouldn’t have found their energy signature. Soon I’ll be in bed with Rose.

“You’re taking me lightly?" Mordin kept going back in forth in his mind.

"You are dismissed Wolfe. We have nothing left to speak about." Like father, like daughter.

Mordin nodded, "Be weary of Wolves, Young Man."

"I am the only Wolf Agent here I'm concerned with or fear." I only laughed.

His disbelief seemed petulant. I felt an exhaustion I hadn't felt since Nadia. My body yearned for a rest only death could bring. The rift took it all out of me. Yet, I stood, alive and well.

I joined the Murashimas congratulating their favorite son. I leaned against Midoriya who readily helped me, leaning on his shoulder.

"You two fought so well. I'm proud of you." Ray said with a smile. Outside of battle he had a tranquil aura. "It was an honor to fight by you."

"The day couldn't be won without you, Raymond." Midoriya cheered.

"Ha, I'm just an old man. I distracted him while those two did the real work. You two are the leaders of this new generation. We are but relics." Ray chuckled, "If I could fight as you two in your age-

"Thank god you didn't." I chuckled, "At my age you weren't a good guy, yet."

Ray smiled hugging me, "I love you, Morgan." He squeezed me tight, "I lost my brother today, and today I gained three true new ones. To fight with you all was an honor. I am proud to call you both brother."

"Ha... So, now that, that's over... Do you think you can give us a lift, Morgan?" Hinata asked, "It took quite some time getting here."

The others all perked up, in agreement.

"Only if you're going to Nadia... after this I'm taking a shower and chilling with my beloved. Might have a nice celebration tonight." I looked to the rotund man and to Mordin, "you two are invited to the festivities."

"I would take a ride and perhaps a plate of food." Desmond rose his hand shamelessly. "I came with Colin... for what good that was worth."

Mordin sighed, "I too came with Colin through the secret tunnels, I will take those back to Naka. I have much to think on." He gave a polite nod walking back inside the bunker with his arms crossed behind his back.

"He's going to be a problem." Hinata sighed.

"He was already a problem, now he's going to make a point of it." I corrected.

"Alright everyone. One quick blink. Hold on tight to me. I'm not responsible if your insides get torn out from the Void."

"What? Maybe I will walk..." the fat man waved it off. "I have much to think about as well."

"It was a joke fatty. We'll be enemies tomorrow. Today, we celebrate a new life for us all." I extend my hand.

He grabbed my hand. The others placed their hands on my shoulders. It would take a lot of energy to transport this many. But we will be fine. I had enough left to get back to Rose's energy signature.

Colin Gregor was gone... wiped off the earth and the soul of Enshishi cleansed.

It's a new day, yes it is.

CHAPTER 56

Dividends

Rose Paz Andale-Sameera

There was a large commotion suddenly erupting downstairs. I sat by Ananda's side wiping the sweat off her brow. She slept off and on, bed ridden. She claimed to have no energy and her face reflected the same, sunken and soft. She breathed hard but she was alive and that's all I cared for.
She opened her eyes from her sleep with a bright smile. "Rose, he's back! I can feel his energy!" Ananda squeezed my hand, smiling wide for the first time all night. "We haven't started cooking!!" She struggled to move. Even more with me holding her down.
"Ha, relax you've been asleep. I think he'll understand." I try urging her back into bed.
"I think he'll be hungry." Ananda pouts still weak and drowsy. "I feel fine now. Let me up, I have to go to the store! We haven't even went shopping!"
"Ananda... Just rest, you're acting like him." I couldn't help but giggle. "He's quite understanding he'll forgive us for not cooking."
"From Ms. Walk To Nadia?" We both laughed. "I truly feel better Rose." Ananda smiles, anxiously looking at the door. "Colin's gone... Truly he is. Enshishi is gone. I can feel it. He did it." She lifted her stomach the

veins and arteries were dilated properly. Her belly turning back to its caramel color.

Her temperature went down. She was still looking sick but miracles usually didn't happen instantly. I relented letting her get out of bed. As if his return was all she needed to keep living. I felt the same. As his energy grew stronger it felt as if I could finally breathe again.

She hugged me, "Thank you, Rose."

"Of course Ananda." I pat her leg.

She leaned on me as we walked downstairs to find my living room filled with strange men. And in the midst stood my beloved, being cheered and hugged for his valiant job well done.

My eyes swelled. I allowed myself to believe he wouldn't return and he proved me wrong. He was so full of surprises, this one was the greatest.

"Morgan..." my breath was distilled from excitement as I pushed past the group feeling around. "My love, you're home."

I was so excited I hardly noticed his eyes bandaged all around. The bandages stained red and wet. But, he's alive. His eyes were closed, scabbed over shut. He bowed his head and nodded. Their laughter and congratulations stopped and I was left to him in the shamed silence. He was alive... And here. And blind.

"Baby, What happened?" I asked rubbing his face. Running my fingers down his chin lifting up his head. "How did this..." I removed my hand to find his blood on my fingertips.

"We won." He said holding my hand to his face. "your hands are so cold. It's quite refreshing after coming from hell and back." He smiled. He kisses my knuckles and falls to a knee. "Believe it or not, I've never formally asked a woman this. Rose Paz Andale, will you marry me?"

His men gasped. Their shock concerned me little.

"We are already married, by souls. Now, tell me what happened to your eyes!" I was past that point. My name is Rose Paz Andale-Sameera, he must not have known yet... Well, I'm glad he's finally caught up to speed. "I must call my mother. She can heal you. Is this permanent?"

"My Queen..." A middle-aged man standing next to Mr. Takio walked up to me.

His beige suit was of such fine quality. Perhaps once. It was burned to little strands of fabric. Torn in half only cutting below his chest. The rest was burned and mangled. The wound on his stomach crudely burned shut.

"Rakil..." I covered my mouth stepping back from them. "God no."

All this from Colin?

He went to a knee, bowing his head and shoulders. "We could not have won the day without your husband. It is an honor to stand before you Madam."

'That is Ryu's son... And the boy by Morgan. It's Ryu himself!' Baat snaps in my ear. 'stand straight. Lean forward. No, you're slouching. Up tall girl!'

I was too dull to process her words. Too overloaded with what I saw. I'm not sure what I expected when I allowed him to fight the devil. None of them seemed fazed but the damage was before us. My husband's eyes were bleeding out his head. His men were charred and burned. One bloated and haggardly, though from feast rather than fighting. And the last was dripping sand from his face all over my mother's carpet!

"Are you blind?" I repeated my question. "Is this permanent, has the bleeding stopped?"

"I... I don't know. I think I'm fine. But the bleeding wasn't slowing." I realized the 'bandages' were makeshift of his shirt. "I... needed to do it Rose."

"DO WHAT!? Just for Colin, Morgan? I thought you all would have this fight! Morgan... You're blind."

"My Queen, if I may interject." Takio's brother rises off his knee. "Midoriya Murashima, my son Hinata."

"Yo!" His son finger salutes. "Thanks for letting Morgan come out Rose-Sama."

"You may not, sit yourself somewhere I'm talking to my husband." I snap back, not trying to hear a word they had to say until Morgan said it himself. "Morgan-

"Madam... I'm trying to explain. If i may?" Midoriya continues, frustrated yet respectful.

'Be respectful girl!'

I roll my eyes, "Go ahead. I need to sit anyway." I feel my way to the arm of the couch, blinded by confusion and anger.

"This wasn't the work of Colin, I killed Colin in a duel but after- From the stories, when a Guardian escapes and materializes on this plane, it's a danger to all. It manifests into its anamorphic archetype. Each Guardian has a purified incarnation, a base form, and corrupted self. We live in the 7th age, to suspect numerous Guardians are corrupted. We did not fight Colin. We fought the actual Enshishi and we nearly had died." He bowed at his hip. And rose only slightly. "I had overestimated myself and let revenge and rage consume me. Even in my youth I could have never been prepared, and as an old man with wisdom and experience. I still could never have figured out how to defeat Enshishi as your husband did."

I gripped Morgan's shoulder, resisting the urge to smile. One of us had to be weary. He couldn't keep throwing himself into the fray like this at the loss of himself. I know he believes he has to, but he must save himself. Especially now.

He looked up to me and patted my hand. He kissed my knuckles.

"I'm here, we won the day. This is all about to end." he smiled, disarming me for a moment.

"To my understanding you have a child, thank god he is safe and his father has returned. May he grown strong. Colin was conquered quite easily, but we needed Ada to ever stand a chance against Enshishi. It was Enshishi who we fought. It was Enshishi we conquered. It was Enshishi we purified." Midoriya clutched his fist. "We have won the day, yes my Lord. Now, Hinata must endure for 7-21 days until Enshishi is purified."

"Honesty is valued." I looked at Morgan, "but my question is the same. What happened and is this permanent?"

"Rose... we've only returned when you came downstairs." Morgan sighs.

"If I may, Miss... um your name? True name." The sand giant walks up to me and kneels, still only managing down to my eye level.

"Andale-Sameera..." I corrected him with sharp eyes. "Do you understand?"

"Um-" the giant took pause then looked to Morgan for confirmation. Morgan grinned. The "Lord" Commissioner let out a grunt and shook his head. "We haven't quite discussed marriage, boy. I still had hopes for you and my selections."

The fuck did that mean?

"We'll work out the details, Ray. But this is the woman I love." Morgan smiles, sitting in his lazy boy. He was breathing ragged. "Ahh... Never thought sitting would be so welcome. Everyone please at ease." He lowers his lids setting the down as he let off his guard completely. "Ha, I thought we were dead for sure. After he knocked me unconscious I thought I was done for." Morgan chuckles rocking back and forth. "I never knew Guardians were real!"

That was just how he was... He had to put his all into everything. At least he was alive, right? Maybe even I keep telling myself that, it'll be enough to still my heart. He seemed so calm despite having driven himself to the pits of hell to return for our safety. Baby... Out of all these men why do you look the worst? They should of took the the fall for you.

'Men die for the Queen. The King fights for the kingdom. He fought. He is alive. Save the rest. Join him. You focus on him because he's the only one your heart is with. All these men are suffering greatly from this battle.'

Hmm... I wonder, to what extent can Baat hear my thoughts? I have never truly questioned until I began meditating. I had never even felt the barrier until last night watching over Ananda. Baat was right there. She's not inside me... It's more as if she's over my shoulder. Looking after me. But... Still- me. Like if I fell back she would push me right back to my feet. Ha, I guess I mean that literally and metaphorically. I had three other Guardians to consult with about it. I'm happy my decisions and actions were my own after all.

"Madam, your-" he took a deep breath exhaling like a bull, breathing like a stuffed pig. I can't do this." He stands up. "Holding this form is hard enough without tolerating this foolish summer love." He snorted.

"You must be Ray Warren." I roll my eyes.

His lip twitched similar to Morgan's, "I am the Lord General Commissioner Ray Bradley Warren, thank you. That young man is Captain Morgan Sameera, yes. But I am not quite sure who you are." He fixated his eyes on me from the ceiling.

"I told you who I am Borre." I cut my eyes at him. "I am Rose Paz Andale-Sameera." I stared him right into his eyes.

He matches my gaze the same cold detached look from Morgan. "You've told me who you think you are." He let out a sigh. "I see you have your hands full, Captain. Call me when you recover and we'll set up for a debrief with the rest of the brothers. I will find my leave shortly."

"Sounds fine, don't go too far. The Gregor Estate should be calling us soon after they get word of Colin. I hope you aren't stalling to report what happened." Morgan nodded.

"You fine with that?" Midoriya asked Hinata.

"Yeah, I'm cool with it. I feel good after whatever Morgan did. I've never seen that much power before. We'll head home. There's much to do in Naka as well." Hinata stretched. "Where's the grub? I'm starving."

"I told you we should have started cooking!" Ananda pouts.

The walrus I deduced to be Desmond Powell by his girth and Knox Family crest. "I'm afraid I will not be joining. I will not be joining this new order. The family seems as if it'll be taking a different direction after all. The Family could perhaps consider an allegiance..." He backed up from the furniture his eyes darting for an exit.

Is Desmond Powell in my house? That fat greedy walrus was huffing and puffing.

"You were not invited, nor spoken to. Now, leave before I get your blubber all over this fine young lady's furniture. You got back home. Now go on with your plotting before I send you to join your master in hell!" Midoriya was quick to anger, setting off like fuse.

"Do you know who you're speaking to?" Desmond Powell buddles up to Midoriya, stabbing Midoriya in the chest with his sausage fingers. "Should I? I thought you were Colin's yuppie. You do something but eat?" Takio's brother was having a roasting session. "Your lover is dead, I bet he loved to snuggle up to your rolls. Now, he's gone, so must you be if you wish to live." his hand began to glow blue as the energy particles sizzled into a ball of lightning.

"Take it outside!" I bark at them.

"I will not take this lightly. Nor will I forget, a Powell's memory is better than an elephant's!" Powell began to back up in fear. Tripping over himself as he looked for the door overwhelmed by what he witnessed.

"If you had stayed for the fighting instead of waddling back to the surface. Perhaps you would know who you're speaking to. This is not the Order of the Sun Lotus. We are the King's Guard." Hinata was stretching for the chase. He smiled giving a thumbs up then pointing it down, "I'll burn down whatever army you put before me, in a glorious blaze!"

Midoriya Murashima. The Warden of Ryu.

The Commissioner. The Guardian Borre.

Hinata Murashima. The Guardian of Fire... maybe he's evil, maybe less evil than Colin.

Morgan Sameera. Ada...

Each man stood beside their King waiting for the command to rip Powell to shreds. The bull, the lion, the dragon, and my love the Panther. The desire in each of their eyes. I suppose they had enough energy to play chase the pig. Their energy together was so overwhelming and securing.

I squeezed Morgan's shoulder firmer as my heart began beating realizing I was a member just as well. Ready to rip his head off if he so much as threatened my love or my city.

Morgan simply looked on to Powell, "I have already gotten what I needed from the family. Ensure my land is available and Hinata won't be visiting you in your bedroom. If the family wishes to appeal for operations, so be it. Honor your King, assist my Kingdom, and stay out my way."

"Well put, Young King." The Commissioner nodded, dead glared at Desmond Powell, "Let Vincent know I'll be waiting to speak to him."
"I- I well... Gentlemen I didn't mean to seem so hasty." Desmond put on smooth as peanut butter smile. “Ha, if we're protecting the true king then maybe, I can reconsidering staying for a plate or two. Will there be pork tonight?”
"I would never put you and haste in a sentence again." Midoriya spit.
Morgan came back with a hard three. That'll be hard to match if this is going to stay mutually interested. All I had were Theo and Cameron. He aligns himself with Ryu and Anki so easily... should I be proud or worried? We’re three Guardians but I didn’t trust either of them for the life of me. It was good they were going back home. I wish I could believe in a unified front as Guardians but I didn’t believe either would last long.

The Guardian of Fire had Natalie, Carmen and Halle who I doubted would respond to Colin’s death with silence. I have never met Natalie or Carmen but if they were worse than Halle I believed even for his safety and sanity Hinata was best left returning home. Halle alone worried me with how she dealt with Natalie. What terrified me more was Natalie getting back up after the beating. I didn’t want any of this fire drama in my house or my continent. No good would come with having the battle for Enshishi ground zero at Nadia. Let them destroy their own continent fighting over their Guardian. It was like housing a nuclear warhead ready to explode.

Worst was what I feared from The Regulator Regime if Morgan didn’t return to Erdu. This Warren guy is going to die any day now. I see it all through his energy and fluctuations in his form. He seemed like he was barely holding himself together. As strong as his spirit might be he was doomed. I hate to say it. If I can’t find a way to spar this old man’s life then Nadia might be doomed along with him. Once word gets out about Colin’s death there would be a response. Without the Commissioner living to tell his side of the story then we might be held responsible for the death of both The Patriarch and The Commissioner.

"I- I bid you gentlemen adieu, you will not have to worry about me, I'm sure." Powell raised his hands, "Good tidings to the happy couple. I know many good caterers and, and I will send you many gifts for your wedding. Adieu!" Desmond hurried out the door with surprising speed. He didn't even look back. Beelined across the yard and headed up the block.

Morgan reclined back and I fell into his lap. He seems calm. He trusts these men regardless of their affiliations. I hope he realises that's what friendship is regardless of how close they may be to us. He didn't come together for these men. These men came together to fight for him. Should I be angry... Why do I feel so angry?

Maybe because I'm lying to myself, we knew nothing of what these men were planning. They nearly destabilized the entire world. I'm pissed because they dragged Morgan into their mess, to keep saving their lives because they can't use diplomacy?

I tried to keep him from killing his own fiancée's father. For these old men to fight this battle alone? I- I-I- believe in peace but I've never been naïve. This was an affront to peace. I was an obstruction of Morgan's justice. There were other options and for so long I believed none available. We joined to fight the true enemy only to allow more in our living room.

I have to think about this alone. I have to honestly take a moment and just breathe before I try killing them all out of blind rage. No, Morgan couldn't know I had anything to do with their deaths. I know someone who could help me. I knew someone who could match any member in his King's Guard without as much as a whisper.

"Rose, we can talk about this later." Morgan pats my hand as if he read my mind. "Let's just be happy for now."

"Thank you, I'm glad you're home. I'll... I need to take a bath." Everyone but Morgan dies... hmm... everyone but Morgan dies but Hinata needed to die first.

"May I join you?" He asks sitting up with me in his arms.

"Of course you idiot..." I blushed nearly losing my head. I hope he has some energy left. "There's space enough in our home for all you men to rest up and recover before heading your asses back home. Ananda will order dinner so none of you poison it. Me and the King are going to talk." And make the bathroom steamy.

"Me and my son will be staying for sometime. To ensure Nadia reaches its necessary point. My younger brother is watching over Lusaka, Kisaka, and Edo. I'm happy to have acquired them in your name. My daughter has returned as well. We will gladly leave your home but I own many businesses in Nadia." Midoriya bowed. "Where may we lay our heads?"

No... no he dies first.

"Mr. Midoriya, you are sliced in half and your son looks like he seen a ghost. If you think that's bad one of the vicars of Enshishi is training under the High Priestess Marsha Qatar. Two others are here in Nadia at this very moment."

"One was also a Wolf... Codename Karma." Morgan adds.

"We can protect ourselves."

"My two goods says no you can't" I poke Midoriya in the chest sending a wave through his bloodstream so microscopic it'll take him a week to feel. "You have less than a week to leave Nadia or they will find you."

Midoriya opened his mouth but closed it. He shook his head letting out a slight yawn. He held out his hand excusing himself as he began a fit of coughing beginning to walk away from us.

"I'll assist you! And get dinner started. Oh there are so many people here!" Ananda says overwhelmed, blushing and getting flustered. "I- I never expected Morgan to have guests!"

Morgan groaned, "Bhavan that's what you think of me?" He slaps his forehead.

Ananda giggles, "Yes... What was I supposed to think?"

His head falls to the side, holding his forehead. "I have to admit..."

"See!" Ananda claps. She was in new spirits freed from the darkness and fear. "Follow me gentlemen! I'll lead you to the guest rooms!"

"This place is huge..." Hinata notes looking around. On another glance he was black and blue bruised around his back, and arms. He carried himself with the same determination as Morgan. A brave face despite his immense pain. "And a real bed after all this time... I may not wake up for a day or two." He grins clapping his hands together. "Hell yeah! I'm fired up, this is going to be great!"

He tried so hard to push himself forward. To keep motivated. It made him look like a fool if he couldn't even beat Enshishi by himself. They all had their guard down. Everyone but Morgan, who even blind, was staring dead at me as if he felt my murderous intent.

"I pray you all realize how serious it is you leave Nadia. Head up, we'll all get some rest." Morgan gives Hinata a pound as he passes by. Then turns his attention to his mentor and protector. "Are you staying Raymond?"

Ray looked around and sighed, "I'm afraid sleep won't do me much good in this condition. I'm going to find a place to meditate on the grounds. Call for me when you need me. I'm going to convene with this spirit keeping my feet planted. I'm proud of you, boy. I suppose now, you're a King? There is no one more deserving. Call for me when the food is ready. I may not have a body but I'm sure Borre has an appetite."

I wave and The Commissioner's lips jerk back in hidden anger. He gives a curt salute then excuses himself to leave.

"Ew, why doesn't he like me?" I suck my teeth, "Is he always this much of a dick?"

"He wishes for me to marry an advocate of Anki. He's always had his niece in mind for me, Mackenzie Warren or Colonel Steele, the famous General's daughter." Morgan yawns, "Nevermind them, I haven't known those women in years. Nor was I the man I am. I rather have you, he'll have to respect our union regardless of his preference. I have chosen you, Rose."

We were left alone. His hands began feeling all over me. Running across my breasts, down my stomach and between my legs. His soldier stood at attention at least answering my hopes.

"Hurry up, get in the bathroom..." I bite my lip tugging him along. "I need you to take care of somethings Mr. Smooth."

He slapped my butt softly, "I'll need you to hold my hand until my

eyes heal."
"Baby... I'll hold your hand until you die." I suppose I take the new title for corny love lines.
The fear in my heart subsided. I'm not sure I'll get over him losing his sight... I still wondered how.
"How did this happen, Morgan, truly?" I laced my fingers with his. I began to walk but he hesitated every few steps. "I won't let you fall baby."
"I feel a fool... I don't want to bump into anything." he didn't want to admit but reluctant.
"Haha, I will make sure you don't crash, baby." I giggle, "Don't think I'm not still wondering. You all didn't answer me earlier, don't avoid my question now."
"Gritty details or-
"Give me the juicy deitz!" I do my best maniacal Carmen Cruz impression. "Get it? It's Carmen babe."
"Uhhh... What?" He laughed. He's never seen the show obviously... Awkward laughter for one. "Well, enough. I'll tell you... Well once we stop moving I'll tell you." He puts his hand up on the wall. "can we go to my place? I won't need you as much there."
"I like this. Maybe you'll stay your ass home, now." I bump him with my hips, he laughs. "Now, story time." I help him take his first step up the stairs.
His lip furrowed as I treated him as an invalid. He didn't say it but took his arm back and grabbed the railing. He marched up the steps, taking another phantom step and nearly tripping over himself. I don't think he realized I had to protect him while he was blinded. He couldn't see how his comrades scrutinized and lied to his face. I don't think they were manipulative. I thought they were all opportunists.
"Dammit, nearly lost my neck." He held his chest. "I had no idea what I was stepping in. I would have at least gotten dressed if I thought I had time. Instead... I lost my eyes and nearly lost my head."
I rub his back, "If I have to deal with this without screaming and crying then you can too. Ya know, ya can wrap your arms around my waist and

follow me down the hallway, baby."

"Oh, I can gladly take you up on that." He kisses my neck, squeezing me tight as we waddled down the hall, pressed to each other. "Where are you taking me?"

"Trust me... You'll love it." I kick the bathroom door open with my feet. I turn in his arms, rubbing his chin and kissing him.

He grabs handfuls of my butt, keeping me close to him. Ananda beat us there, sitting on the edge of the tub as the water ran.

"Don't mind me." She whispers waving away my attention.

Nor did I care about her seeing us, as much as I cared about Morgan knowing how happy she was he's back.

I kissed him down his neck, removing his dirty, singed and blood-stained pajamas. I kissed down his scarred throat, wounded chest, down his stomach, tugging at the drawstring of his sweatpants. He was harder than a diamond as I pressed my face to his bulge. Kissing the imprint of his cock.

"We've stopped, now tell me where am I? I hear... water."

"Do you ever stop thinking?" I roll my eyes.

He combed his fingers through my hair as I let his cock fall out his pants. I licked the head of his cock, down to his balls. He was steaming hot as I handled him.

"Alrighty, baby." He tried to begin his story stopping to moan as he entered my mouth. "Enshishi seemed unbeatable. Every attack we made, he recovered instantly or brushed off as if being swatted by toddlers. It seemed off, impossible. He was either- damn Rose what are you doing?"

"Keep telling the story and you'll find out baby." I pull him out for a second, weaning him back in my mouth. I caught glimpses of Ananda watching, biting her finger. "I love this story."

I would kill for this man but not her... poor thing had already been through so much. I wonder if she was even ready for sex.

He nodded catching his breath, "I felt like he was bluffing or hiding something. I once fought Colin before.... oh... I knew his heart was bad. I knew he had an ability called the Phoenix Resurrection. It was only a shot in the dark, so I used my true sight. I noticed a strange chakra currents in his solar plexus. I focused my eyes... Then I felt- felt god damn, Rose." I gripped his tight butt as his sweatpants fell to the floor, his hips slowly stirring. "My eyes couldn't see alone, but I knew there was more. I think I unlocked the God's Eye. Everything was different I didn't see red. I wasn't desperate. I felt fearless... I felt like I let off my shackles and felt unlimited power. So, I prayed as you advised. I called upon Ada, it was like a door, and then I pushed through. I felt the strain physically but my body was astral projecting. I could walk outside my flesh, it was as if i was walking through the ether on Gaia. That's when I saw Colin's decayed dead body floating in Enshishi's energy. As much as I hated him, I couldn't let any being suffer such a fate. I preserved the body in the ether until I negotiate peace with Pierce Hawke of the Gregor Family."

The mood was gone but the thrill was alive. My clothes were next to come off as Morgan didn't wish to stop. My jeans were peeled off of me. He stretched my shirt pulling it over my head. He licked his fingers then began rubbing my clitoris. I lifted my leg on the edge of the tub. I felt a tongue and warm mouth replace his hands, too small to be his own. Ananda began to kill our beef for real. Seemed she enjoyed the story herself.

"Colin's body was broken, he was gone... He resembled human tree bark. Petrified from the life Enshishi was sucking from the body."

I moved to my back, grabbing a handful of Bhavan's hair as she licked me from booty to pussy as I've never had before. Morgan stroked his magnificent cocoa dick over top of us his precum dripping like nectar. He probably couldn't see us but he could hear our soft moans. Ananda moved to him, slobbing on head of his cock as her saliva and his juices dripped on the floor, then returning to my pussy as if that's where she rather had been. I didn't mind one bit.

"Good little maid." My back arched. I grabbed my Lover's cock, stroking him short and hard.

"I knew that was our parameter. Enshishi was attempting to defy death by using Colin as a soul anchor and conduit. First I took out Colin's heart. It was inscribed with curse markings. Then I-

"Oh, Morgan." Ananda moans leaving me once more as I stroke him and she slurps down his shaft. She wanted to show her gratitude.

"That was checkmate. Once I knew his trick... The fear had left me. At that point I had entered the ether moving far past the void and blinking. Hinata and I took out Colin's body. I used my soul as a slingshot then sent my life force through the ether like a bullet. He charged his aura until his whole essence was an electric blue arrow. Together we tore through Enshishi releasing him from his existence on this planet.

"Yes, yes, then what baby tell me!?" I screamed as Ananda rubbed my clit as quickly as she could, her tongue working my labia.

"Enshishi cursed and screamed, damning us as he died. After the whole place turned to a Maelstrom of lightening and molten flames falling from the sky through the entire bunker. We escaped, leaving Hinata. Hinata nearly lost his life containing Enshishi until I returned and called upon Ada to banish the demon once and for all."

Ananda lifted her head with my juices all over her mouth. She sat down against the hot tub breathing heavily. She motioned for Morgan as she eased him halfway down her throat before she gagged. He retracted but she grabbed him, not letting him get too far away. She looked on dreamily. "It's much bigger than Colin's." Ananda lusted over his cock, being face fucked against the hot tub. Her eyes rolled to the back of her head as his nut dripped down her lips. I wasn't even mad, she was made for pleasure.

"Damn, Ananda..." He cursed. He hated using her but couldn't pull his dick out, as he did his nut dripped down her chin and neck. She looked up with her bright smile. "Damn." He moaned pushing back her mouth as she accepted him. She was ecstatic.

"Colin's dead, Nanda." I rubbed the sweat off her forehead and licked the cum off her chin. "You don't have to do this anymore." I kissed her cheek.

She motioned me closer before kissing me, his nut filled my mouth as her tongue swam in my mouth. She saved it for me. Dribbling down our throats as we kissed each other, the head of his cock between our love. I felt Ananda's energy, so lively, joyful, and passionate.

"If you may excuse us Bhavan, I wish to have my wife now." He rubbed her chin. Helping her to her feet.

“I know you’re worried about me but I can tell the difference between a friend and predator. I like you Morgan. You can protect me when I’m not making my own decisions, respectfully My King.” Ananda bowed her head.

She frowned looking into him, she opened her mouth wide. He took her one last time until his cock was dripping wet. Her smile returning as she's helped to her feet.

"He's all yours Rose. I don't think I can have sex quite yet but that was amazing." She blushed, "I told you, I wanted you to be Queen."

"Yes, you did and I believe you now." Maybe I was talking with my thoroughly satisfied pussy as far as I was concerned this is how you show loyalty to your Queen if you're gonna be fucking my husband.

Morgan slap her little butt and she giggled. She seemed like such and innocent girl until she got his cock in her mouth. She only wanted to be on our team.

"Let's make more babies." I led Morgan to sit in the steaming hot waters. I didn't even need to ease. I slammed my ass on his dick. Sitting in his lap until his back shots bent me over the tub. I squeezed his cock tight pushing all my weight against him. He gripped my hips holding me right there.

Ananda claps her mouth, "that looks so good..." She bit her lip, "I-I-have to start cooking, ooo Rose, wow."

"Don't wow me all I'm doing is getting my ass handed to me." I grunted. He pulled my hair back, my head jerked to the ceiling and a tear rolled down my eyes. "Ada... Ada... Don't stop." The Guardian in me moaned softly as he leaned over to kiss me and okay with my natural c cup breasts. My toes curled up, Baat and I both hit the wall, as my juices ran down his girth and length. It was as if we turned to each other and asked 'did you hear that?' I moved my head back to kiss him. Our tongues danced, he squeezed my nipples. His stroke slowed as the water moved with us in gentle waves. Ananda had ran off before she ended up reneging.

"Are you going to cum for me baby?"

"I just wish I could see your face..." He relented, he sat back, breathing heavily.

"Is it selfish to ask you to keep laying it down though?" I rose out of the waters so his seed wouldn't be lost.

He chuckled, pulling me on top of him. I loved his obsession with my butt. I rode him slow and easy, looking behind me to watch him kneading and molding it. If he thought his sense of sight was preventing his nut, he surprised us both as he began gushing inside me. Digging his nails in my booty. I tightened as my body reacted to his semen, milking him dry. I'm not sure if you can retroactively make twins but dammit I wanted to try. I want to have all his kids.

Tears swell in my eyes, "Ooo, ooo baby right there. Yes, Morgan it's yours." I bite down in his neck, wrapping my legs and arms around him.

"I love you, I love you."

"I cherish you, I adore you, you're my Queen."

Baat and I once more were agasp. My legs shook, I felt weak. He was different. This wasn't the angry, confused, lost man I met a few months ago.

"I love you." I laid in his arms. Rubbing his chin and his chest. "What's next?"

"Building the city, training up ourselves and our Guard, finding allies, and whatever the fallout is from Colin's death."

"What about Carmen and Natalie?"

He shrugged, "could it really be all that bad? I imagine they'll be after Hinata for now but once they leave. We'll be dealing with hell."

"Half the world watches her show, Morgan."

"Then we only speak to the other half." My feelings exactly.

He sank down in the hot water and tilted his head back. "Your place totally kicks ass, I should get one of these installed. Put it in the basement for after training."

"Why don't you stay here?"

"Bad memories... This is the house Bryon was in before he- you are related to Bryon Qatar?"

"Bryon Qatar was my uncle. Bryon Saleem was my grandfather. I am Violet Qatar's daughter, Granddaughter to the High Priestess, Marsha Qatar."

Morgan grew quiet I thought from distrust, "I didn't kill him Rose. Honest, I didn't touch anyone. I- I couldn't." I thought I had finally lost his allegiance instead he spoke from guilt.

"I know baby. Bryon told us all about it. He told me about you and how you nearly killed Colin Gregor when you were only 17. He's safe and living how he always wanted. He's done much for us. The Brotherhood has lost leadership and many of the men were arrested. But an army is there if we can access it and the Masks-

"I don't want to work with vigilantes. I want order, it's the only way to build. Not a bunch of pissed off unruly kids." He groaned, "The city can't be saved as a whole, some simply want to do whatever they want to do!"

"They want leadership, real leadership. And we all want to see the city better. Morgan we need to work with all of Nadia, The Mafia, The Masks, The Brotherhood, and even these corrupt politicians."

"They're best staying out my way for now. Nadia will need an actual code of law before there can be any allegiances."

"I was a mask..."

"Hmmph... I remember you mentioning that before," He was quiet, "Not now... I'm not going to tarnish my victory in another losing battle of perspectives with you."

"Because you know you're wrong?"

"Because you're far too naïve." He smirked.

Just when I thought things were perfect, reality set back in.

"Baby... you really need to respect my opinion."

"I understand Rose. I- I don't fault them. They're angry, they're scared, and they don't trust. I'm not saying you're naïve because of your age or as if you're a fool. I am saying those people who mention are already at war with each other doing anything to beat the other. This is exactly why they're going to be a threat. A city needs peace, order, and law to prosper it's mandatory. Especially after all these years of disarray and corruption, we need some direction. If Titan wishes to join us. I will accept all the help I get. In Rakil's name, Rose. Anyone who wishes to stand beside me in improving this world has a seat at my table. However, they need to obey my laws and abide by social order to rebuild the city. Anyone else outside of this-" he shook his head, "I am The Guardian of Nadia not because of my compassion, it's because I get things done and I protect my own. Anyone who doesn't see themselves within my vision is an enemy."

"Well baby, what is your vision?" I kissed his cheek, then his nose. Liking the way it sounded sans the whole fascist rhetoric.

"I want every man and family to be provided for from their own city and work. No more pencil pushing, work. No jobs, work. That's why I love your plan. We will build, we will work for ourselves and our city. Nadia will be a family, a community. The bazaar will be back as it once was. The homeless will be given homes and work. Our focus will not be for wealth or corruption but for the amelioration of all. I don't care about war, or wealth, or even needing to have a throne to be King. I will provide, protect, and please my own. The Mafia, the Masks, the corrupt Regime. I will stand for none of it for the honest, hardworking Nadians."

"Hmm... I like TV, Morgan. That sounds incredibly rustic."

"Ha, we'll discuss details as time moves forward." He brushed my hair out my face, and kissed my forehead. "We'll figure it out."

I held his hand to my cheek, laying on his chest and squeezing him.

"Rose, baby, why are you crying?" He lifted my chin with such alarm.

"I'm so happy you're here. I'm so happy you're real. Flaws and all. I love you." I squeezed him as tightly as I could.

He had no response. He kissed my forehead once more and ran his hands up my back. Laying in each other's energy as we enjoyed the hot tub.

www.ingramcontent.com/pod-product-compliance
Lightning Source LLC
Chambersburg PA
CBHW051732020826
48982CB00014BA/438

9781736142509